MIRAGE

The Twelfth Transforming

Stargate

The Eagle and the Raven

Child of the Morning

MIRAGE

PAULINE GEDGE

HarperCollins*Publishers*

This book was originally published in Canada in 1990 by Viking Penguin under the title *Scroll of Saqqara*. It is here reprinted by arrangement.

Map by Jonathan Gladstone/j.b. geographics

Library of Congress Cataloging-in-Publication Data

Gedge, Pauline, 1945–
  Mirage / by Pauline Gedge.—1st U.S. ed.
    p. cm.
  ISBN 0-06-016541-3
  1. Egypt—History—To 332 B.C.—Fiction. I. Title.
PR9199.3.G415M57   1990
813'.54—dc20   90-55569

For Bella, with love and deep appreciation

ACKNOWLEDGEMENTS

The verses at the beginning of each chapter are taken variously from Margaret Murray's *Egyptian Religious Poetry* (Connecticut: Greenwood Press, 1980) and *Life Under the Pharaohs* by Leonard Cottrell (London: Pan Books, 1955).

MIRAGE

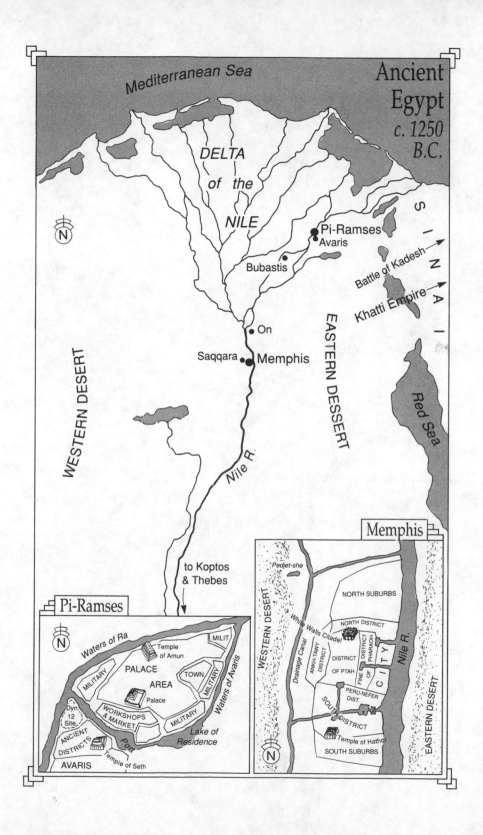

Khaemwaset's Immediate Family

Khaemwaset: Prince. Fourth son (third surviving son) of the pharaoh Ramses the Second, sem-priest of Ptah, priest of On, magician and doctor. Thirty-seven years old.

Nubnofret: Princess. Khaemwaset's wife. Thirty-five years old.

Hori: Prince. Khaemwaset's second son. Priest of Ptah. Nineteen years old.

Sheritra: Princess. Khaemwaset's daughter. Fifteen years old. Her name means "Little Sun."

Khaemwaset's Larger Family

Ramses the Second: Pharaoh of Upper and Lower Egypt. Khaemwaset's father. Sixty-four years old.

Astnofert: Ramses' Royal Wife and Queen. Khaemwaset is her second son. Fifty-nine years old.

Ramses: Crown Prince and Heir Apparent. Astnofert's first son and Khaemwaset's older brother. Forty-three years old.

Si-Montu: Prince. Khaemwaset's older brother. Forty-two years old. Disqualified as prince in line for the throne because he married Ben-Anath, daughter of a Syrian ship's captain. Head of his father's vineyard at Memphis.

Merenptah: Another of Astnofert's sons. Khaemwaset's younger brother. Thirty-one years old.

Bint-Anath: Queen together with her mother Astnofert. Khaemwaset's younger sister. Thirty-six years old.

Meryet-Amun: Daughter of Ramses the Second's first wife, Nefertari. A lesser Queen. Twenty-five years old.

Friends

Sisenet: A noble of Koptos, living in Memphis. Forty-five years old.

Tbubui: A noblewoman of Koptos. Thirty-five years old.

Harmin: Her son. Eighteen years old.

Servants

Amek: Captain of Khaemwaset's bodyguard.

Ib: Khaemwaset's steward.

Kasa: Khaemwaset's body servant.

Penbuy: Khaemwaset's scribe.

Ptah-Seankh: Penbuy's son and his successor as Khaemwaset's scribe.

Sunero: Khaemwaset's agent at Ninsu in the Fayum.

Wennufer: High Priest at Abydos and Khaemwaset's friend.

Antef: Hori's male servant and confidant.

Wernuro: Nubnofret's female servant.

Bakmut: Sheritra's female servant and companion.

Ashahebsed: Ramses the Second's cupbearer and old friend.

Amunmose: Chief Keeper of the Door of Ramses the Second's Harem in Memphis.

Chapter 1

*'Hail all ye gods of the Temple of the Soul,
who weigh heaven and earth in the scales,
who give funerary offerings.'*

The cool air was a welcome shock. Khaemwaset stepped gingerly into the tomb, aware as always that his was the first foot to be placed in the grey sand of the floor since the mourners, themselves long dead, had backed up the stairs before the sweepers and turned in relief to the blazing sun and a hot desert wind many centuries before. In this case, Khaemwaset mused as he carefully trod the narrow passage, the sealing was done over fifteen hentis ago. A thousand years. I am the first living being to breathe this air in a thousand years. "Ib!" he called sharply, "Bring the torches. What are you dreaming about up there?" His steward spoke a soft apology. There was a flurry of small stones which bumped sharply against Khaemwaset's bare and dusty ankles, and Ib slithered to stand respectfully beside him while slaves moved past with obvious reluctance, carrying the smoking flames.

"Are you all right, Father?" Hori's light tenor voice echoed against the dim walls. "Will we need to shore anything up?"

Khaemwaset cast a swift glance around and shouted back a denial. His initial enthusiasm was quickly turning to a familiar disappointment. His were not, after all, the first feet to tread the sacred floor of this ancient prince's resting place. As he came out of the short passage and straightened he saw, in the wavering torchlight, the clear and heartbreaking evidences of robbery. Boxes that had contained the dead man's earthly possessions were strewn about, empty. The jars that had held precious oils and wines of the best vintage of the day were missing, their only vestiges a few pieces of brittle sealing wax and one broken stopper. Furniture lay tumbled almost at Khaemwaset's feet — a stool of plain design, a carved wooden chair whose legs were strangled ducks, their sightless eyes and flaccid necks holding up a curved seat and a backrest where Hu, the Tongue of Ptah, knelt and smiled, two low dining tables from which the delicate inlay had been stripped, and a bed that had been shoved against one plastered wall in two jagged halves. Only the six shawabtis, motionless and sinister, remained untouched in their niches around the walls. As tall as men, fashioned of black-painted wood, they still waited for the spell that would bring them to life to serve their masters in the next world. All the work had been simple, clean and pleasing in line, elegant yet strong. Khaemwaset thought of his own house, stuffed with the glittering, ornate crudeness he so despised but his wife admired as the latest fashion in furniture, and sighed.

"Penbuy," he said to his scribe, now hovering discreetly at his elbow, palette and pencase in hand, "You may begin to record what is on the walls. Please be as accurate as possible and remember not to fill in any missing hieroglyphs with your own guesses. Where is the slave with the mirrors?" It is always like driving recalcitrant cattle, he thought as he turned to study the massive granite sarcophagus whose lid was askew. The slaves fear the tombs, and even my servants, though they dare not grumble, load themselves with amulets and mutter prayers from the time the seals are broken until the moment when the placatory food offering is left. Well, they need not worry today, his thoughts ran on as he bent to read the inscriptions on the coffin while a slave held a torch. Each third of this day is lucky, for them at any rate. A lucky day for me would be the finding of an untouched tomb crammed with scrolls. He smiled to himself and rose. "Ib, bring down the carpenters and have the furniture repaired and set in the correct places. Have the jars of fresh oil and perfume brought in also. There is nothing of interest here, so we should be on our way home by sunset." His steward bowed, waiting for the prince to precede him along the suffocating passage and back up the short flight of stairs. Khaemwaset emerged, blinking, beside the pile of rubble his diggers had thrown up in their efforts to uncover the tomb door, and waited for his eyes to adjust to the blinding whiteness of the noonday sun. The sky was a dazzling blue, meeting the pure yellow of an undisturbed and endless desert on his left which shimmered as he gazed.

To his right the plain of Saqqara held the naked pillars, crumbled walls and tumbled masonry of a city of the dead, ruined far back in the depths of time and now possessed of a lonely and solemn beauty, the fine-worked stones all a pale beige, their sharp edges and long, running lines reminding Khaemwaset of some strange inorganic desert growth, as stark and comfortless as the sand itself. The stubbed, terraced pyramid of Pharaoh Unas dominated the desolation. Khaemwaset had inspected it some years before. He would have liked to restore it, to smooth its stepped sides into one pleasing whole, to dress its symmetrical face with white limestone, but the project would have taken too much time, too many slaves and conscripted peasant farmers, and a great deal of gold spent to provide bread, beer and vegetables to the workers. Still, even eroded as it was, it had a mighty presence. Khaemwaset, during his minute investigation of the Great Pharaoh's monument, had been unable to find any name carved upon its surfaces, so he had provided Unas with renewed power and life by the hands of his own master craftsmen and had, of course, added the inscription "His Majesty has ordered it to be proclaimed that the chief of the masters of the artists, the Setem-priest Khaemwaset, has inscribed the name of the King of Upper and Lower Egypt, Unas, since it was not found on the face of the pyramid, because the Setem-priest Prince Khaemwaset much loved to restore the monuments of the kings of Upper and Lower Egypt." His Majesty, Khaemwaset reflected as he began to sweat in the heat and his canopy bearer came hurrying to shade him, had not objected to his fourth son's odd obsession, provided full credit was given to himself, Ramses the Second, User-Ma'at-Ra, Setep-en-Ra, in the matter of permissions and gracious credit to himself, the One Who Caused All to Be. Gratefully Khaemwaset felt the shadow of the canopy settle around him, and together he and his servant walked to the red tents and carpets where the bodyguards were rising to reverence him and his chair was being set in the shade. Beer and a fresh salad were waiting. He collapsed under the tasselled eaves of his tent, took a long drink of the dark, satisfying beer, and watched his son Hori disappear into the dark hole in the ground from which he himself had just come. Presently Hori reappeared and began to supervise the line of servants already carrying tools in their brown arms and clay jars on their shoulders.

Khaemwaset knew without looking that the eyes of his clustered entourage were also on Hori. He was without a doubt the most beautiful member of the family. He was tall and very straight, with an easy, graceful walk and an upright carriage that somehow managed to avoid being either arrogant or aloof. His large, black-lashed eyes were of a translucent quality, so that enthusiasm, humour, or any other strong emotion made them glitter. Delicate brown skin was stretched over high cheekbones, and under those compelling eyes were often violet hollows of seeming vulnerability. Hori's face in repose was youthful, contemplative, but when he smiled it broke into deep grooves of sheer pleasure, lifting him from his nineteen years and making his age suddenly indefinable. His hands were large and capable but also artlessly attractive. He loved mechanical things, and as a child had driven his tutors and nurses to distraction with his questions and his unfortunate habit of taking apart whatever contrivance was to hand. Khaemwaset knew how lucky he was that Hori had also taken to the study of ancient tombs and monuments and, to a lesser degree, the deciphering of inscriptions in stone or in the precious scrolls his father collected. He was the perfect assistant, eager to learn, able to organize, always willing to relieve Khaemwaset himself of many of the burdens on their explorations.

But it was not these things that caused the eyes of everyone in his presence to dwell on the young man. Hori was blissfully unaware that he exuded a strong sexual magnetism to which no one was immune. Khaemwaset had observed its effects time and again with a wry, quiet appreciation tinged with regret. Poor Sheritra, he thought for the thousandth time as he finished the beer and inhaled the intoxicating, wet coolness of the salad. Oh my poor, ungainly little daughter, always trailing about in your brother's shadow, always overlooked. How can you love him so much, so unreservedly, without jealousy or pain? The answer, also familiar, came immediately. Because the gods have set in you a pure and generous heart, as they have given Hori the unselfconsciousness that saves him from the excessive self-love of meaner men who are perhaps as beautiful.

The servants were coming out of the tomb mouth for another load. Hori once more plunged into darkness. Overhead, two hawks hung without movement in the scentless, fiery air. Khaemwaset began to doze.

Several hours later he woke on the pallet in his tent, rose to stand while his body servant Kasa poured water over him and patted him dry, and went out to see the results of his servants' labours. The mound of earth, sand and rubble beside the tomb entrance had shrunk, and men were still at work shovelling the remainder into place. Hori was squatting in the shade of a rock with Antef, his servant and friend, talking desultorily, their voices clear but unintelligible. Ib and Kasa were consulting together over the scroll that contained the lists of gifts to be placed around the dead prince, and Penbuy, seeing his master push the tent flap aside, came hurrying, a sheaf of papyrus under his arm. More beer and a plate of honey cakes appeared, but Khaemwaset gestured them aside.

"Go and tell Ib that I am ready to make the food offering for the ka of this prince as soon as I have taken a last look inside," he said. With Penbuy pacing respectfully at his sandalled heels, he made his way back to the now small entrance under a softly bronzing sky. Red light was beginning to send streamers across the sand and the desert was rose-pink beside him, couching deepening shadows.

At his coming the workmen drew back and bowed. Khaemwaset ignored them. "You come also, for any last moment comments I may wish to make," he said over his shoulder to his scribe, and he squeezed through the half-closed door and padded along the passage.

The last light of the sun followed him, casting long tongues of coloured flame of a quality so dense that Khaemwaset felt he might pick them up and caress them. They did not, however, penetrate to the coffin itself, deep in the cramped little room, and Penbuy came to a halt where his palette would still be illuminated. Khaemwaset crossed the almost palpable line that divided the fingers of sunset from the eternal gloom of stillness and stood looking about. The slaves had done their work well. The stool, the chair and tables and bed had regained their pristine form and been returned to the position they had occupied for generations. New jars neatly lined the walls. The shawabtis had been washed. The floor had been cleared of the litter the unknown thieves had left, and had been swept.

Khaemwaset nodded and moved to the coffin, inserting one finger into the gap left by the twisted lid. He fancied that the air striking it was colder than that in the rest of the tomb, and withdrew his finger hastily, his rings scraping on the hard granite.

Are you watching me? he thought. Are your ancient eyes vainly trying to pierce the thick darkness above you, to find me? He ran his hand slowly over the thin film of dust that had collected through the eons, sifting invisibly and softly from the ceiling to lie thus, undisturbed until now. None of his servants would wash a coffin, and this time he had forgotten to do so himself. What will it be like, his thoughts ran on, to be dried, shrivelled skin, to be bandaged bones lying immobile in the dark, watched by the sightless eyes of my own shawabtis, listening to nothing, seeing nothing?

For a long time Khaemwaset stood, trying to absorb the atmosphere of mingled pathos and otherness, the unattainability of a past that always taunted and whispered to him of simpler, grander ages, while the last rays of sunlight went from red to a sullen scarlet and began to thin. He did not really know what it was that he sought in his wanderings among the mute debris of the past. Perhaps it was the meaning of the breath in his body, the beating of his heart, a meaning that might transcend the revelations of the gods, though he loved and revered them. Certainly it was a need to slake the thirst without a name that had possessed him from his childhood and that, when he was younger, had brought tears conjured from some mysterious source within him that spoke of loneliness and displacement. But of course I am not lonely, I am not unhappy, he told himself while Penbuy coughed politely but warningly behind him and the tomb's shadows began to snake towards him with the message to be gone. I love my family, my Pharaoh, my beautiful and blessed Egypt. I am rich, successful, fulfilled in life. It is not that . . . it never has been that . . . He turned abruptly before a wave of depression could overwhelm him.

"Very well, Penbuy. Let the tomb be sealed," he said sharply. "I do not like the smell of this air, do you?" Penbuy shook his head and scuttled up the passage, with Khaemwaset following more slowly. The whole undertaking had left a sour taste in his mouth, a feeling of futility. It is all dead knowledge that I acquire from the scrolls and tomb paintings, he thought as he emerged, walked past the bowing slaves, and heard the crunch of their shovels in the earth once more. Old prayers, old spells, forgotten details to round out my history of Egypt's nobility, but nothing that might give me the secret of life, the power over everything. Where is the Scroll of Thoth? What dark, dusty niche hides that treasure?

The sun had gone. In the mild, velvety sky a few stars had begun to prick and the chatter and laughter of his entourage quickened under the sudden flourish of fresh torches. Khaemwaset all at once wished to leave. Signalling to Ib he strode into his tent. An oil lamp now flickered by the cot, casting a friendly yellow glow, and he could smell fresh perfume. Ib padded forward and bowed. "Tell Hori to robe now," Khaemwaset said, "and bring me my sem-priest's garb. The acolytes can charge the censers and be ready. Are the food offerings blessed?"

"Yes," Ib replied. "Prince Hori has been performing the prayers. Does your Highness wish to wash again before dressing?" Khaemwaset shook his head, suddenly weary.

"No. Send an acolyte and I will do the ritual cleansing. That will be enough."

He waited in silence. Kasa appeared, the voluminous black-and-yellow striped sem-priest's garb held reverently across his outstretched arms, and stood with eyes downcast as an acolyte presented the Prince with a silver ewer full of scented water and helped him to undress. Khaemwaset solemnly began the ritual washing, murmuring the appropriate prayers to which the boy responded, and the sweet-acrid wisps of incense smoke began to curl between the tent flaps.

At last Khaemwaset was ready. The acolyte bowed, picked up the ewer and withdrew, and Khaemwaset held out his arms while Kasa slipped the long robe over his head. Both men went outside. There Hori waited in his role as a priest of Ptah, holding the long censer cup from which grey plumes floated, and the food offerings for the ka of the prince whose tomb they had politely disturbed lay upon golden dishes.

The little procession formed and moved with stately grace to the now invisible tomb entrance. The slaves were on their faces. Khaemwaset stepped forward, taking the censer from his son, and began the prayers for the preservation of the dead and the enjoining of the ka not to punish those who had today dared to look upon a sacred resting place. It was now fully dark. Khaemwaset watched his own beringed, long fingers glitter in the torchlight as they dignified the time-honoured words with gestures of respect and appeasement. He had performed the same ceremony a hundred times over, and not once had the dead expressed offence at his probings. Indeed, he believed that his careful restorations and food offerings had resulted in blessing upon himself and those he cared for from the kas of princely beings long dead and quite forgotten.

The ceremony was soon over. The closing words fell flat in the warm darkness. At last Khaemwaset knelt beside Hori to be disrobed, and rose while Kasa wound his white kilt around his still well-muscled waist and laid his favourite lapis-and-jasper pectoral across his chest. His eyes were gritty with fatigue. "Are you coming home?" he asked Hori when Kasa had left to summon the litter bearers.

Hori shook his head. "Not unless you want me to help Penbuy file our finds today, Father," he replied. "The night is so sweet that Antef and I are going fishing."

"Take a bodyguard," Khaemwaset admonished automatically, and Hori smiled and turned away.

It was a long walk to the city of Memphis from the high plateau of Saqqara, down through the stately palm groves and across the drainage canal, now little more than a smooth ribbon of darker darkness that momentarily reflected the lights of the Prince's escort. Khaemwaset, swaying in his cushioned litter with its tasselled curtains turned back so that he might look out upon the soft night, reflected, as he so often did, on the peculiar character of this, his favourite city. Memphis was one of the oldest places of continuous habitation in Egypt, and the holiest. Here the god Ptah, creator of the universe, had been worshipped for two thousand years. Here a long succession of kings had spent their sacrosanct lives, so that an aura of grace and dignity imbued every street.

The ancient core of the city could still be seen, the White Wall of Menes that had once enclosed the entire population but was now merely a tiny oasis of calm where rich and poor from all over the country came to stare and comment.

Sightseeing was a national pastime, the thing to do if one could afford it. Khaemwaset smiled a little sardonically to himself as his bearers entered the palm plantations and the sky was blotted out by a forest of stiff, feathery fronds that rustled pleasingly in the dimness. History had become fashionable—not the history over which he himself pored with such single-minded determination, but the stories of the conquests and personalities, miracles and tragedies of the kings of old. Guides thronged the market-places of Memphis, eager to fleece country noblemen and wealthy merchants alike in exchange for titillating stories of a spurious past lit up with juicy, if highly doubtful, palace scandals of one hundred, one thousand years ago. Men took up chunks of stone and hacked their names and often their comments into the White Wall, the outer court of the temple of Ptah, even the gates of the temples of the kings in the old Ankh-tawy district.

Khaemwaset had begun to employ burly Hurrians to patrol the monuments of the city. He had ordered offenders to be lightly beaten if caught, and his father, the august Ramses, had not objected. Probably because he does not care over-much, Khaemwaset surmised as the palms became fewer and the black night sky once more soared above him. He is too busy raising his own monoliths to posterity, and expropriating the work of his ancestors to his own glory where it is most convenient.

Dear Father, Khaemwaset thought with an inward chuckle. Ruthless, arrogant and deceitful, yet full of lordly generosity when it suits you. You have been more than generous with me. I wonder how many complaints you have received from the noble foreign defacers of our marvels? Three-quarters of the populace of Memphis are foreigners enamoured of our strong economy and our supreme hierarchy. I wish you did not love them quite so much. He felt the bare feet of his bearers move on to something hard, and presently the night began to lighten with the orange glow of the city. They were behind the quietness of the Ankh-tawy district, where the temples hulked in a shrouded gloom relieved only occasionally by the tiny dot of a torch held for a priest going to or from his nightly duties. Beyond the rearing, dusky pylons and soaring pillars was the district of Ptah, dominated by the god's mighty House, and beyond that was the Fine District of Pharaoh, with its two canals running to the Nile, its palace, often neglected, often rebuilt by successive pharaohs from time immemorial, and at present resplendently restored and added to by Ramses. Its tumultuous docks and warehouses were interspersed with the hovels of the very poor.

The White Wall citadel was to Khaemwaset's right, and he caught a glimpse of its tall, now grey presence before the bearers emerged from its shadows into the district North-of-the-Walls, where he and many other nobles had their estates. This was a full city away from the noise and stench of the South district where the foreigners—Canaanites, Hurrians, Keftiu, Khatti and other barbarians—worshipped at the shrines of Baal and Astarte and conducted their loud and rude businesses with Egypt.

Khaemwaset often visited the foreign noblemen on their own estates that mirrored the gracious, peaceful enclaves of the North-of-the-Walls. His father entrusted him with much of the affairs of the government, particularly here in Memphis where Khaemwaset had elected to live. In his capacity as the most revered physician in the country he was often consulted by the Semites, but he did not like them. To him they were polluted streams invading the limpid, clean flow of his country's society, carrying the corruption of strange gods to diminish the reverence due to Egypt's faithful and powerful deities, the poison of exotic cultures, debased morals, cheap business dealings. Baal and Astarte were fashionable at Court, and Semitic names abounded, even in pure Egyptian homes of every strata. Intermarriage was common. Pharaoh's dearest and most trusted friend was a Semite, a silent, spare man named Ashahebsed. Khaemwaset, a courtier born and bred, was well used to disguising his true feelings and did so with ease. He had had many dealings with this man, who now preferred to be known as Ramses-Ashahebsed, and had done no more than mildly insult him by refusing to use the prenomen "Ramses" except on written documents.

The temple of Neith was dropping slowly behind him and his bearers slowed, obviously tired. The torchlight was brighter now, for the inhabitants of North-of-the-Walls could afford to employ light-carriers to patrol the streets. Khaemwaset rearranged his cushions, listening to the challenges of the night-watch and his foot soldiers' response. Occasionally his herald, Ramose, would call a warning and Khaemwaset would watch the passersby go down in the dusty street to touch their foreheads to the earth until his litter had gone. But the people were few. They were at home, eating or preparing for evening visiting with friends, and the night life of the city had not yet begun.

Presently Khaemwaset heard the voice of his own porter and his gate creaked open. Bodyguards saluted from their stations outside the high mud-brick wall as he went through, and the gate clanged shut behind him. "Put me down here," he called. "I will walk now." Obediently, the litter was lowered and he alighted, beckoning to Ramose and his soldiers. He set off along the path that skirted the rear garden and intersected other paths—one into the shrubbery and towards the fish pools, now invisible but for dark smudges to the left, one to the kitchens, granaries and workhuts of his servants, and one to the small but pleasantly appointed house where Khaemwaset's concubines lived. There were not many of them, and he did not often visit their domain or summon any of them to his couch. His wife Nubnofret ran their lives as she ran her family household, with rigid efficiency, and Khaemwaset left it all alone.

The path now ran under the shadow of his house wall and round the corner to the front, pausing to detour under the white entrance pillars with their bright red and blue painted birds that trailed palm fronds and river weed from their sharp bills. It ran on across Khaemwaset's carefully nurtured lawns and between the sycamore trees to the white watersteps and the calm, swiftly flowing river. At the junction Khaemwaset paused, sniffing the air, his eyes turning towards the Nile. It was the end of Akhet. The river was still full, a rolling brown and blue torrent of fecundity, but it had returned to its banks after the annual flood and the peasants had begun to fling seeds onto the saturated ground. The feathery palms that lined the drainage canals, the acacia thorns and sycamores, all glistened with the sheen of new, pale-green leaves, and in Khaemwaset's gardens the vivid clusters of flowers had begun to bloom with an abandon that assaulted the eyes and filled the nostrils with delight. Khaemwaset could not see them but their scent was all around him.

He watched the early light of the new moon glint fretfully on the river, now silver slivers, now darkness, as the night breeze stirred the choked growth on the banks and lifted the tree branches. The watersteps were a deserted invitation, and he envied Hori who must surely even now be reclining in the bottom of his skiff, Antef beside him, their fishing lines tied to the boat while they watched the stars and gossiped. His fountain tinkled like music in the darkness, and the monkeys sighed and snuffled in their favourite spot under the stone basin, which still held the warmth of the day's heat. "I would like to drift on the river tonight," Khaemwaset remarked to his patient retinue, "But I suppose I must see what has been going on in my absence." Privately he thought that an hour on the river would not do him any good. He was inexplicably tired. His lungs hurt from inhaling the old air and dust of the tomb, and his hips ached. A massage and a good sleep on his own couch would help. "Ramose," he said to his herald. "Tell my wife that I have returned and I am in my own quarters. If Penbuy's litter has come back, I will look over any letters from the Delta that may have been delivered in my absence. Tell Ib I want food immediately, and Kasa can wait until I have finished with Penbuy before giving me a massage. Amek?" The captain of his bodyguard approached and bowed. "I will not be going out tonight. You can stand these soldiers down." Without waiting for a reply, he walked in under his pretty pillars.

His reception hall, where guests were greeted and entertained, was spacious and cool, the floor tiled in plain black and white, the walls plastered and painted with scenes of himself and his family fowling in the marshes, fishing, or relaxing in the garden under their sunshades. The colours he had insisted be used when the house was built were the traditional whites, blacks, yellows, blues and reds of antiquity, and the few pieces of furniture set about for his guests were equally simple in design, made from Lebanon cedar inlaid with gold, ivory and lapis.

He had managed to override his wife's protestations here. She had not wanted to give their guests the impression that the mighty Prince and sem-priest Khaemwaset, son of Pharaoh and virtual unofficial ruler of Egypt, had poor taste, but after a violent argument she had for once been defeated.

"I am a royal son of Egypt," Khaemwaset had finally and uncharacteristically shouted at her, "and Egypt led the world in all matters of fashion, government and diplomacy for uncounted hentis! My servants are pure Egyptian, and my family is guarded by Egyptian troops, not foreign mercenaries! My home is an Egyptian sanctuary, not a Semitic brothel!"

"Your home is an Egyptian mausoleum," Nubnofret had responded coolly, unperturbed by her husband's startling loss of temper, "and I do not like being known as the wife of Khaemwaset the Mummy. The impression we give to foreign dignitaries is quaint and perhaps even insulting." She had shrugged her robe higher on her broad shoulders, and one hand had gone to the massive gold and yellow enamelled flowers at her throat.

"And I do not like my wife to be seen flaunting the polyglot sewer that Egypt has become!" Khaemwaset had flared back. "Look at you, Nubnofret! You are a Princess of the purest noble blood, yet you mince about in so many frills and flounces that you look like one of the poppies everyone is rushing to grow in their gardens, just because they come from Syria. And that colour! Purple! An abomination!"

"You," Nubnofret had said pointedly, "are an ancient, croaking toad. I will wear what I like. *Someone* must keep up appearances. And before you say that we are royal and above such petty considerations, let me remind you that it is I who must entertain the wives of the Khatti, the Syrians, the Lybians, while you do business with their husbands. Egypt is an international power, not a provincial backwater. These wives leave my house knowing that you are a force to be reckoned with."

"They know that already," Khaemwaset had snapped back, his temper receding. "They cannot function without my breath upon their backs."

"And you cannot function without my superb organization." As usual, Nubnofret had had the last word. She had sailed out of the room, her ample hips swaying regally, her magnificent breasts high, and Khaemwaset had listened to the swish of her many-pleated robe and the click of her gold sandals with frustrated amusement. She was formidable, loving, and the most stubborn woman he had ever known, he mused as he quickly left the gloom of the reception hall behind and took the right-hand passage to his quarters. She had mutely acquiesced in the matter of the hall but had had her revenge with the rest of the house, so that sometimes Khaemwaset felt as though he lived in a trader's shop. Treasures, knick-knacks and strange, useless things from all over the world littered the rooms, tastefully arranged of course, for Nubnofret had been raised in the best of households herself, but claustrophobic to her husband, who dreamed of the quiet internal spaces and the jewelled emptinesses of the past.

Only his private office escaped her. It was full of his own messiness, though the adjoining library of scrolls was kept scrupulously tidy by Penbuy. Here Khaemwaset could escape and be at peace.

He strode beyond the closed doors to his sleeping apartments, where a drowsy servant squatted on his little stool, and went on to enter the office. Here, several lamps of finest honey alabaster glowed golden. His chair waited, drawn out from the desk, and he was about to sit down with an audible sigh of release when Ib knocked, followed him in, and bowed. He set a tray on the desk, lifting the linen cloth to expose steaming stuffed goose, fried inet-fish, fresh cucumbers and a flagon of wine sealed by Khaemwaset's own vintner from his vineyard outside Memphis. Khaemwaset waved him out and fell to with relish. He had almost completed the meal when Penbuy was announced. With a sinking heart, Khaemwaset watched the scribe place several scrolls on the desk. "Do not tell me," he groaned. "The marriage negotiations have broken down again."

Penbuy managed to nod in the middle of his bow. Quickly he went to the floor, crossed his legs and laid his palette across his knees. "I am afraid so, Prince. Shall I read you the scrolls while you finish your meal?" Khaemwaset thrust one at him by way of an answer and went back to the pile of warm shat cakes.

"Begin," he ordered.

Penbuy unrolled it. "From the Mighty Bull of Ma'at, Son of Set, User-Ma'at-Ra, Setep-en-Ra Ramses, greetings to his favoured son Khaemwaset. Your presence in the palace at Pi-Ramses is required as soon as possible. The matter of the Khatti tribute, including the dispatch of the Khatti bride for the Mighty Bull, needs your immediate attention following a letter from our envoy, Huy, even now at the court of Hattusil. Speed north on wings of Shu." Penbuy looked up. "It is sealed with the royal seal," he added, letting the scroll roll up with a slight rustle. He laid it aside and took up his pen. "Do you wish to reply, Prince?"

Khaemwaset dabbled his fingers in the water bowl and sat back, folding his arms. The war between the Khatti and Egypt had been over for twenty-eight years and the official treaty had been signed twelve years ago. The final battle, fought at Kadesh, had nearly meant the end of Egypt as an independent nation. It had been a series of small but mounting disasters of misinformed spies, misplaced military divisions and inept commanders, but Ramses still insisted on portraying it on all his monuments and flagrantly on all his temples as a brilliant success for Egypt and a crushing blow for the Khatti. In fact, the Khatti had brilliantly ambushed the full might of the Egyptian army and had almost effected a rout. The battle had been a stalemate. Neither side had gained an inch.

When tempers had cooled fourteen years later, the Great Treaty was signed and sealed and exhibited in Karnak. Still, Ramses persisted in regarding Kadesh as an Egyptian victory and a Khatti rout, and the treaty as an act of desperate submission on Muwattalis's part.

Now Muwattalis's son Hattusil was offering one of his daughters to Ramses to cement friendly relations between the two great powers, but haughty Ramses, ever unwilling to admit anything even close to weakness on the part of a ruler who was also a god, saw the gesture as one of appeasement and submission. The Khatti had recently suffered a disastrous drought. They were weakened. They were afraid that Egypt would take advantage of their temporary situation and begin to despoil their countryside. Therefore they were more than eager to tie Ramses to the treaty with a diplomatic marriage.

Worse, Khaemwaset pondered as he began to compose a reply to his father in his head, Hattusil, in his rush to hold out his arms to his kingly brother, had promised Ramses an amazingly large dowry of gold, silver, many ores, horses without limit, cattle, goats and sheep by the tens of thousands. Indeed, it had seemed to Khaemwaset and a sniggering Egyptian court that Hattusil was prepared to move the whole of Khatti into Egypt with his beautiful daughter. Ramses had approved. This was a tribute for the father's defeat at Kadesh.

"Prince?" Penbuy said softly.

Khaemwaset came to himself and apologized. "Forgive me, Penbuy. You may begin. The usual greeting, for I can't be bothered to list all my father's titles correctly. Then, 'In the matter of my gracious Lord's summons, I shall be in Pi-Ramses with all speed to aid in the expedition of Your Majesty's intended nuptials. If Your Majesty would leave the official exchanges of mutual trust and the dowry negotiations to me, your unworthy son, and not continue to heat the gruel with your own holy but undoubtedly contentious opinions, a passable soup might soon be served. My love and reverence go to you, Son of Set, with this scroll.' " Khaemwaset sat back. "Give it to Ramose to hand to a messenger. Preferably a slow and inept one." Penbuy smiled frostily, his pen still scratching the papyrus. "Really, Prince, do you think it necessary to be quite so . . . so . . ."

"Forthright?" Khaemwaset finished for him. "You are not paid to criticize the tone of my letters, impudent one, only to write them and get the spelling correct. Now let me seal it."

Penbuy rose, bowed stiffly, and placed the scroll on the desk.

Khaemwaset had just lifted his ring from the wax seal when the door opened without announcement and Nubnofret swept into the room. Instantly Penbuy bowed himself out. Nubnofret ignored him, coming to her husband and placing a noncommital kiss on his cheek. Wernuro, her body servant, remained meekly in the background with head bowed. Nubnofret, Khaemwaset thought for the hundredth time as he hid a smile and rose, knew how to keep the members of her staff firmly in their places.

"I see that you have eaten," his wife remarked. She was dressed in one of the loose, informal robes she liked to wear in the evenings when there were no guests, the voluminously folded scarlet linen draped around her lush curves and tied to one side with a gold-tasselled girdle. A heavy red jasper-and-gold ankh hung from her right earlobe and bumped gently against her exquisitely painted face as she looked up at Khaemwaset. She had shed her wig, and her reddish-brown, chin-length hair formed a perfect frame for her wide, orange-hennaed mouth and green-dusted eyelids.

She was thirty-five years old, still ripely beautiful in spite of the fine lines Khaemwaset knew were fanning across her temples under the black kohl and the slight grooves to either side of those inviting lips. But her voluptuousness was something she would have dismissed had she been aware of it. Brisk, efficient and full of common sense, Nubnofret sailed through the reefs and shoals of household accounts, training of servants, entertaining for her husband and rearing her children with the consummate ease of the woman addicted to duty. She was intensely loyal to Khaemwaset, and for that he was grateful. He knew that, in spite of her need to keep him safely moving in the family dance she had choreographed, in spite of her sharp tongue, she loved him dearly. They had been married for twenty-one years, securely and comfortably.

"Did you have good fortune today, Khaemwaset?"

He shook his head, knowing that she asked out of politeness, not interest. She regarded his hobby as a demeaning pastime for a blood prince. "Not at all," he replied, touching the place where she had kissed him and finding it damp with the freshly applied henna. "The tomb was ancient but damaged both by water and the depredations of robbers. It was impossible to tell how long ago both disasters occurred. Penbuy examined a couple of scrolls and has doubtless filed them in the library by now, but my store of knowledge remains the same."

"I am sorry," she replied with genuine regret, her gaze dropping to the scrolls under Khaemwaset's hand. "Is there a message from the Delta? Trouble in marital paradise?" They grinned at each other. "Perhaps we should move to Pi-Ramses until Pharaoh's plans are consummated. You have almost worn out our barge with your to-ing and fro-ing."

Khaemwaset was suddenly full of tenderness for her. He had not missed the faintly discernable note of longing in her voice. "You would like that, wouldn't you?" he said gently. "Why don't you take Hori and Sheritra north for a month or two? My father does not need my attendance all the time, Nubnofret. The affairs of Egypt are at the moment purely routine, apart from the marriage negotiations, and I am free to continue a few of the projects I have begun at Saqqara." He indicated his chair and she sank into it and began to pick over the remains of the food. He recognized the expression of stubbornness on her face. "My architects and I are working on new plans for the burial ground of the Apis bulls," he went on, "and I have two restorations in progress, one on Osiris Sahura's pyramid and the other at the sun temple of Neuser-Ra. I . . ."

She held up a hand containing a piece of now cold goose, waved it at him and popped it into her mouth. "I have long since ceased to feel affronted by your insistence on putting dead stones before your living family," she said coolly. "If you will not go to Pi-Ramses, then we will stay here with you. You know you would be very lonely if we left you to the care of servants."

It was true. Khaemwaset moved to perch on the edge of his desk. He folded his arms. "Then have the servants pack a few things, and come with me tomorrow. Father needs another diplomat to undo the trouble he has undoubtedly caused. He will also undoubtedly ask me to examine and prescribe for him, and anyone else he fancies might need my services. Besides, I would like to visit Mother."

Nubnofret chewed thoughtfully. "Very well," she said at last. "Hori will want to come too, but Sheritra will not wish to mingle at court. What are we going to do about her, Khaemwaset?"

"She is just shy," he answered her. "She will grow out of it. We must give her time and treat her gently."

"Gently!" Nubnofret snorted. "She is already indulged too much, by Hori as well as by you. Even now she waits to say goodnight to you but I have told her she must not count on your coming tonight." She licked her fingers then snapped them. Wernuro immediately came to life, glided to the desk, dipped the linen that had covered the food into the finger bowl, and began to carefully mop her mistress's greasy hand.

"Why not?"

"Because a message has come from Pharaoh's harem here. One of the concubines is sick and requests your attention." She left the chair and approached the door. "Goodnight, my husband."

"Goodnight Nubnofret. Sleep well." At a sharp word from her the door swung open, the door slave bowed her out with Wernuro three paces behind her, and Khaemwaset was alone.

Unwillingly he left the office and walked through into his library. Coming up to a large chest he reached to his belt, extracted a key and unlocked it. A pleasant smell of dried herbs wafted into the room as he lifted the lid. He carried a small box back into the office and called for Kasa and Penbuy. "Ramose," he reminded the Chief Herald who had appeared at his summons, "send my apologies to Amek if he has retired to his barracks, but I need two bodyguards immediately. I must go into the city."

An hour later he was being bowed deferentially into Pharaoh's Memphis harem. It was large but well appointed, with airy suites of rooms for the many women Ramses had taken a fancy to and had acquired, and had as often forgotten. They lived for the most part indolent lives, waited on hand and foot and with nothing to do but gossip, quarrel, care for their superb bodies and compare notes on their distant master, but a few of them conducted their own businesses in Memphis and the outlying farmland. They were allowed outside the harem if properly escorted and could administer their own estates or small industries. Some oversaw the weaving of flax into linen, some owned vineyards or farms and a few carried on a flourishing trade in foreign exotica by caravan and sea.

Khaemwaset had no interest in any of them apart from their illnesses. He had written a work on the diseases particular to women that had become something of a handbook for other physicians, but women as vehicles of pleasure left him largely unmoved. The passions of the past and the mind were much more heady to him.

He greeted the Keeper of the Harem Door more brusquely than he had intended and the man immediately went to the floor, his forehead pressed to Khaemwaset's sandalled feet in the age-old gesture of supreme submission as he apologized profusely for inconveniencing the great Prince. Khaemwaset impatiently waved him to his feet.

"Pharaoh would not want an apprentice examining one of his women," he said as they walked along a passage off which, at regular intervals, dainty wooden doors of intricate design were firmly closed. "Who is my patient?" The Keeper stopped outside the last door and Khaemwaset came to a halt, Penbuy and Kasa behind him. Amek's two soldiers had separated, one to watch each end of the long hallway.

"She is a young Hurrian dancer. The Mighty Bull saw her perform a year ago and invited her to take up residence here. She is a quiet little thing, very beautiful, and has been teaching the other women some of her steps." He did not knock, but pushed open the door and stood back respectfully. "It keeps them amused and it also gives them some exercise. Most of them are very lazy."

Khaemwaset dismissed him and walked into the room. It was cosy without being restricting, with a good couch, a few chairs and a scattering of cushions, a shrine, now closed, several tiring boxes no doubt holding a dancer's gaudy clothing, and a door that obviously led out into the communal gardens. A slave was sitting on a stool by the couch, telling a story in some foreign tongue—Hurrian, Khaemwaset surmised—in a high, sing-song monotone, and the little patient was listening raptly beneath her linen sheets, her black eyes reflecting the light of the oil lamp beside her.

At Khaemwaset's approach she spoke a sharp word to the girl and struggled to rise, but Khaemwaset waved her down.

"Formality is not necessary in the sick room unless petitions to the gods are involved," he said kindly as the slave retired to a corner and Penbuy and Kasa took up their stations. "Now what is the matter?"

The girl stared at him for a long moment as though she had not understood, and Khaemwaset wondered how fluent her Egyptian was, but then, with a sidelong glance at his companions, she pulled back the sheets. Her delicate little body was covered in an angry red rash from neck to exquisitely turned ankles. After an intent look, Khaemwaset relaxed both in relief and disappointment—relief that he would not have to spend much time in the harem at this hour and disappointment because the case was not in the least unusual or interesting. With a nod he summoned the Keeper of the Door. "Have any of the other women exhibited this rash?"

The man shook his head. "No, Highness."

So the problem was not communicable. "What about her diet? Does she eat the same food as the others?"

"Many of the women have their food prepared separately, as they like it," the Keeper replied readily. "This girl eats from the harem kitchens and I assure you, Prince, that the meals are the finest and freshest quality." Khaemwaset indicated to Penbuy that the taking of notes was not necessary. "Of course it is," he said more sharply than he had intended, suddenly not willing to ease the man's anxiety with tact. "The rash is simply treated. Make a balm of equal parts of Cyperus-of-the-Meadow, onion meal, incense and wild date juice. Have the slave smear it all over her twice a day, and the itching and redness should be gone in a week. Send for me if not." He was about to turn away when he felt a hand tug at his kilt. He looked down. "Do I not need a spell also, great Prince?" the dancer's heavily-accented, light voice inquired. "Will you not make magic over me?"

Khaemwaset met those alert black eyes with a smile, and taking her supple fingers in his, he sank onto the couch. "No, my dear, it is not necessary," he assured her. "The evidence of demon-induced illness is lacking. You have perhaps taken too much sun, or been swimming in dirty water, or you may have even brushed against a plant that your body does not like. Don't worry. The recipe I gave your Keeper was found many years ago among the proven remedies in the temple of Osiris at Abydos and cannot fail."

For answer she suddenly pressed his hand to her mouth, and the shock of the touch took him unaware. He withdrew hastily and stood. "See that she is anointed at once so that she can sleep," was his last command before retiring into the passage, and he hurried out the doors, across the gardens, and onto his litter, his mind full of the need for his delayed massage and then a deep sleep.

With Penbuy and the soldiers dismissed and himself at last behind the closed and guarded doors of his own inner chamber, he allowed Kasa to remove his shoulder-length black wig, unscrew the turquoise earrings he favoured and rid his arms and hands of rings and bracelets. The kilt was unwrapped and laid aside. With a gusty sigh of weariness and pleasure, Khaemwaset lowered himself onto his couch, face down among the soft pillows, and felt the warm scented olive oil drip from Kasa's dish onto his back. He closed his eyes. For a long time he gave himself up to the contentment of Kasa's strong hands kneading away the muscle knots of the day's tensions and sliding firmly over his buttocks and legs. Then Kasa said, "Your pardon, Prince, but you neither look nor feel well. Your skin has the consistency of goat's cheese tonight. The underlying muscles are becoming flabby and unsightly. May I prescribe for you?"

With mouth buried in cushions, Khaemwaset chuckled. "The physician should take some of his own advice?" he said. "Prescribe if you wish, my friend, and then I will tell you if I have the time or the inclination to obey. I am, as you know, thirty-seven years old. Nubnofret also nags me about my aging body but truly, as long as it serves to carry me through my duties and does not interfere with my pleasures, I prefer not to inconvenience it." Kasa's stiff fingers suddenly dug into his muscles and Khaemwaset could feel the man's disapproval.

"Scrambling in and out of old tombs and climbing pyramids requires a level of fitness in a man that your Highness is fast losing," he objected sententiously. "I who love you beg you to order Amek to give you regular wrestling bouts, archery practice and swimming time. Your Highness knows that he is neglecting a fine constitution."

Khaemwaset was about to formulate a brisk reply when his mind all at once filled with a vision of his little dancer patient.

He had not consciously evaluated her body, only her complaint, but now he remembered her flat, taut belly, the smooth delineation of muscles under the skin of her thighs, the economical swell of hips over which no fat was laid. The picture made him feel old and melancholy, and vaguely empty. I'm tired, he told himself. "Thank you, Kasa," he managed. "Put the oil away. Remove the paint from my face and hands and bring the night lamp. And please tell Ib that I am not to be disturbed by any sounds of packing tomorrow." He submitted to his body servant's quiet, expert ministrations until at last he saw the door close and he was alone with the friendly flicker of the tiny flame imprisoned in its alabaster jar, and the room's thick, slow-moving shadows.

Pushing the pillows to the floor he reached for the ebony headrest—Shu holding up the sky—and set it under his neck. He again closed his eyes and began to drift, still in the grip of the curious sadness that had come with the memory of his father's tiny concubine and her perfect body. Why is it troubling me? he wondered dimly. What was it about that girl, seen for such a brief moment, that has tapped a well of such reflection in me tonight?

Then he knew, and was wide awake. Of course. She had somehow reminded him of the first woman he had ever had, a girl actually, no more than thirteen years old, with long, quick legs and the beginnings of firm breasts that had been at the time all dusky nipples that had hardened intriguingly under his questing tongue. He could taste her now as though he had possessed her not an hour ago. She had been one of the many little slaves employed in various easy ways by Pharaoh's more august servants. Khaemwaset, himself barely fifteen, had walked into the palace's reception hall to dine with some three hundred of his father's guests. He remembered the pungent odour of the melting, perfumed head cones, the waft of massive bunches of lotus flowers everywhere, the din of laughter that overpowered the musician's polite ripples.

The girl had approached and bowed, slipping a wreath of cornflowers over his head, standing on tiptoe to do it, and Khaemwaset had felt her naked breasts brush his chest, her warm, scentless breath envelop his face, before she retired and bowed again. Later, slightly drunk and flushed with the heat of the night and good food and his father's especial attention, he had seen her flitting among the guests with golden party favours on a tray. He had walked up to her, taken the tray, handed it to a passing boy and ushered her impatiently into the garden.

The night had been very close and very black, like her eyes, like the triangle of coarse hair his fumbling fingers had been desperate to explore under her flimsy kilt linen. They had copulated behind a bush, just out of sound of a Shardana soldier standing guard, then she had giggled, re-tied her clothes and sprinted away.

They had not exchanged a single word, Khaemwaset remembered, gazing into the silent shadows of his ceiling and groaning softly as the memory unfolded. Doubtless she had known who he was, but he had neither known nor cared about her. Sensation had been his goal that night, and now his brain played back to him the movement of her muscles under his hands, his mouth, the slightly tart taste of her tongue against his, her black, black eyes becoming heavy-lidded with passion and staring into his before he gave himself over to his own lust.

He had forgotten her until now. Other girls were taken—in the evenings by the river, in the heat of drugged summer afternoons behind the granaries, in his own rooms on impulse—then at sixteen he had married Nubnofret and four years later been appointed sem-priest of Ptah at Memphis. His life's work began, and the urgent messages of his senses became fewer and weaker as stronger passions superceded them. Sadness for what is gone, yes I understand that, he thought, as once more he composed himself for sleep. But the emptiness? The loss? Why? The only hole I truly thirst to fill is the one that waits for the Scroll of Thoth, and if the gods will it, that I will find and the power that goes with it. Poor little Hurrian dancer. How many times has my father woken desire in that exquisite body of yours? Do you hunger for him day after day, or do you whirl away the fire? He slipped into unconsciousness, and the memories did not follow.

Chapter 2

'How beloved is he, our victorious ruler!
How great is our King among the gods!
How fortunate is he, the commanding Lord!'

He woke late the following morning. Ib, true to his orders, had
kept the fuss and bustle of the impending journey away from his
door so that he was able to eat his habitual light breakfast of
fruit, bread and beer and wander to the bath house undisturbed.
Already, resentment was filling him as he stepped off the stone
pedestal and held out his arms so that Kasa could dry him. He
did not want to go north, did not want to tread daintily and warily through the eggshell maze of negotiation, did not really want
to see his father, but he told himself sternly that his mother at
least would greet him effusively, and he would make time to
visit Ramses' splendid libraries.

Back in his quarters he sat so that his cosmetician, under
Kasa's wary eye, could paint the soles of his feet and the palms
of his hands with henna, and while the orange paint dried he listened to Penbuy give him the messages for the day. There were
few. A letter had come from his cattle steward in the Delta to tell
him that twenty calves had been born and recorded. The scroll
that made his mouth water, though, was of a massive bulk that
Penbuy laid reverently on the table by his couch. "The plans for
the burial place of succeeding Apis bulls are finished and await
your approval, Prince," he said, smiling at Khaemwaset's obvious delight, but Khaemwaset, after running a hand over the
warm papyrus, regretfully left it unread. It would be a treat to
look forward to when he came home.

The henna was dry, and the cosmetician began to slide the
black kohl around Khaemwaset's eyes while his jeweller opened
the box containing his necklaces. Khaemwaset picked up a copper mirror and surveyed the man's handiwork critically, his eyes
straying to the contours of his own face. What he saw reassured
him. I may be a trifle flabby, he thought, and having slept on it I
will take Kasa's advice, but I am still a handsome man. He ran a

reflective forefinger along the line of his tight jaw and the cosmetician exclaimed in annoyance. My nose resembles my father's. It is thin and straight. Nubnofret still remarks on my nose.
My mouth is perhaps a trifle uncompromising but full, thanks to
my mother. Good, clear eyes. Yes, I could still attract any woman
at court . . .

Amused and perplexed, he set down the mirror with a snap.
Such odd thoughts, he smiled to himself. Khaemwaset, mighty
prince of Egypt, the boy in you is clamouring for attention today.
You have not heard his voice in a long time. Then he forgot his
juvenile self as his jeweller approached, and he selected electrum
bracelets, a pectoral of precious silver and blue faience work and
several gold rings. The man was slipping the last of the rings
onto his fingers when Ramose, his herald, called sonorously
from the door, "The Princess Sheritra." Khaemwaset turned with
a smile as his daughter hurried across the floor.

"I missed you last night, Father," Sheritra said as she gave him
a quick, ungainly hug and, blushing, put her hands behind her
back. "Mother said you probably wouldn't be able to say goodnight to me but I waited up for a while anyway. How is the concubine?"

Khaemwaset returned her embrace, hiding the mild stab of
dismay he often felt when he had not seen her recently. She was
all gawky bones and graceless lines, his fifteen-year-old treasure.
Her legs were too long for her small frame and she often inadvertently tripped over her own feet. The servants had laughed en-
dearingly at her unconscious antics when she was small but, out
of affection for her, they laughed no more. Her fleshless hip
bones jutted painfully sharply against the form-fitting linen
sheaths she stubbornly wore, even though Nubnofret had time
and again tried to persuade her to don more fashionable and certainly more flattering pleats and flounces. It was as though,
knowing her many physical deficiencies, she had decided out of
sheer pride not to try to compete in the world of feminine vani-
ties, because to do so would cheapen who she was.

Nubnofret was continually telling her to stand up straight, for
her shoulders curved over a chest almost as flat as the stomach
below it, and she did try to walk with more height and grace to
deflect her mother's often waspish aim, but it did no good. Her
face was a pleasing oval, with an expressive, generous mouth

and large, lustrous eyes, but the Ramessid nose had run riot and dominated her features.

A more impudent, outgoing girl might have turned such handicaps into triumphs, but Sheritra was shy, sensitive and withdrawn. Those who knew her well—her father, Hori, her servant and companion Bakmut, the other members of the household staff and a few lifelong family friends—loved her for her intelligence and generosity, her kindness and gentleness. But oh Amun! Khaemwaset thought as he submerged the dismay and kissed her forehead under the wealth of waving brown hair, she blushes at everything, my sweet misfit. Where is the prince who will take her?

"I don't know how the girl is today," he answered, "but as I have not heard from the Keeper of the Door I must presume she is better. Have you decided to come with me to visit your grandfather and investigate the markets of Pi-Ramses?"

Sheritra shook her head once, a sharp denial. "I don't think so, Father. Bakmut and I will enjoy having the house to ourselves. I will sleep very late and have all my favourite scrolls from the library read to me while I eat, and I shall swim and poke about in the flower beds with the gardeners." She was speaking too quickly, looking away. Khaemwaset took her chin and turned her head, meeting her anxious brown eyes.

"It would do no harm to spend a few hours at court," he said softly. "If you faced those whom you fear your shyness would begin to fade, darling one. Soon your mother will begin to do more than just talk about a betrothal for you, and you should at least know what the young bloods look like before names are laid before you."

She pulled away from his warm fingers. "It is not necessary," she replied steadily. "You know you will have to pay a larger than usual dowry to be rid of me, Prince, and it is a matter of complete indifference to me whether I marry or not. No one is going to love me, therefore I do not care in whose bed I ultimately lie."

Her painful honesty was distressing to hear. "Hori is coming," Khaemwaset pressed, still wanting to persuade her, unwilling to sail away and leave this wound behind. She grinned.

"Of course he is! The women will ogle him but he won't notice. The young men will whisper about him behind his back, but he will be oblivious. He and Antef will scour the markets for new and marvellous foreign inventions to pick apart, and after chatting with Grandfather who dotes on him he will disappear into the House of Life as you will disappear into the House of Books, and will only emerge to buy me a very expensive gift." Her eyes were sparkling, but behind their gleam Khaemwaset saw the disappointment in herself that he read there so often. He kissed her again.

"I am sorry, Little Sun," he apologized. "I do not want to push you into anything that causes you discomfort."

She grimaced. "Mother does enough pushing for both of you. Have a lovely time in Pharaoh's magic city, Father. I believe that Hori is already on board *Amun-is-Lord* so you had better hurry." She straightened and left the room and Khaemwaset, his heart aching, opened his shrine to Thoth, charged the censer himself and began his morning prayers.

His flotilla cast off from the watersteps an hour after noon. *Amun-is-Lord* carried Khaemwaset, Nubnofret and Hori, while ahead went their bodyguards and behind, the household servants. A suite of rooms was always available to Khaemwaset in the palace House of Ramses Great in Victories, and of course a full complement of palace slaves, but he preferred to be waited on by his own staff.

The day was hot and clear. Khaemwaset stood on the deck, leaning over the rail, and regretfully watched the palm groves with their backdrop of yellow sand and the sharp silhouettes of the Saqqara pyramids slide out of sight. Nubnofret was already settled under an awning that had been attached to the small cabin amidships, reclining on a mountain of cushions with a cup of water in one hand and a fan in the other. Hori stood beside his father, elbow resting against Khaemwaset's own, his hands loosely clasped. "Memphis is a fine sight, is it not?" he said. "Sometimes I wish that Grandfather had not moved the capital of the country north. I can see the strategic advantage in a seat of government close to our eastern border and located on a river that empties into the Great Green for good trade, but Memphis has the dignity and beauty of the rulers of old."

Khaemwaset's eyes remained on the riverbank as the green confusion of spring glided by. Beyond the fecund, brilliant life of the bank with its choked river growth, its darting, piping birds, its busy insects and occasionally its sleepy, grinning crocodiles, was a wealth of rich black soil in which the fellahin were struggling, knee-deep, to strew the fresh seed. Drainage canals were full of still water that reflected the intense blue of the sky and were dappled in the shade of the tall palms lining the cuttings. The villages, once the city was out of sight, were the drowsy mud and whitewashed figments of a pleasant dream, shimmering sometimes in the afternoon heat, usually deserted but for two or three donkeys standing idly flicking flies with their tails, and the odd small child running after a flock of white geese or squatting naked in the dirt.

"I would hate to see the Nile choked from the Delta to Memphis with the ships and boats of merchants and diplomats," he answered Hori, "and Memphis itself would become increasingly filthy, noisy and sprawling, as imperial Thebes used to be in the days of the last Thothmesids. No, Hori. Let Memphis be a city of peace to fuel my vision." The two men smiled at one another.

For the rest of the afternoon they drifted happily with the strong current of late spring, passing Ra's home, the city of On where Khaemwaset also sometimes served as a priest, and then turning into the Nile's eastern stream.

Just beyond On, the river ceased to be one mighty force and began to meander in three large ribbons and two or three lesser tributaries towards the Great Green. The western stream bordered the desert. At its northernmost point it fed the most famous vineyards in Egypt, where the coveted Good Wine of the Western River was fermented. Khaemwaset's storerooms held a large supply of it, and while his compatriots were often seduced into tasting exotic wines that came at great cost from places like Keftiu or Alashia, he remained faithful to the dark red bounty of the Delta.

Through its centre flowed the great river, past that most ancient of capitals, Buto, now nothing more than a temple and a small town, and thence to Tjeb-nuter and out into the Great Green. Khaemwaset and his boats ran north-east, into the Waters of Ra that would take them to their destination.

They tied up for the night by the Sweet Water Canal that had been cut due east to join the Bitter Lakes. Already the dry tang of the desert was merely an occasional puff of evening breeze overwhelmed by the richer, heavier odours of the Delta farmland. Papyrus thickets jostled and whispered, their dark green stems and beige feathers losing colour steadily as Ra dropped to the western horizon. The delicious aroma of orchard blossoms came wafting, although the orchards themselves were not yet in sight. Verdant growth, both cultivated and wild, tangled everywhere.

All the next day they drifted through the Delta's amazing variety of plant and bird life, stopping to eat Hori's freshly caught inet-fish at noon and then lazily sliding on while Ra turned from white to gold to pink and red. By the time night fell once more, the Waters of Ra had become the Waters of Avaris, they had passed the temple of the cat goddess Bast at Bubastis and the river was beginning to be crowded.

They did not sleep as well that night. Craft continually passed them, and challenges rang out regularly across the quiet Nile. Khaemwaset spent an uneasy few hours in vivid and decidedly unpleasant dreams before waking at yet another screamed question and brusque answer. His head ached mildly. Calling Kasa softly so as not to wake Nubnofret, he was washed and dressed and gave the order to resume their journey before the sun was an hour into the sky.

Just before noon, the city of Pi-Ramses straggled into view on their right—first the ungainly hovels of the very poor who now inhabited the site of the original town of Avaris and who seemed to cluster around the brown pylons and steep walls of the temple of Set, and then a heap of rubble Khaemwaset knew was the remains of a Twelfth Dynasty town. Hori and Nubnofret were watching a donkey caravan labouring beside the river. Beasts, merchants and drivers alike were dusty, and sand clung to the bright blankets covering the loads. Goods from Sinai, Khaemwaset surmised, perhaps even gold from my father's mines, on its way to effect more beautifying in Pi-Ramses.

He turned back to the ruins, now swiftly passing by, and the great canal his father had dug to surround the city was there, already congested with craft of every shape and size, their captains swearing and jockeying for place. Khaemwaset signalled a little regretfully to his wife and son and they retired behind the anonymity of the cabin curtains. There was a pause, and Khaemwaset knew that his captain was running up the imperial colours of blue and white. After a moment the din outside began to diminish and their boat began to move. The commoners were giving way to Pharaoh's great son, and Khaemwaset sailed up the Waters of Avaris in a space of reverence. Nubnofret tutted.

"They become more vituperous and violent every time we make this trip," she remarked. "Ramses should have the junction patrolled by the Medjay, who could organize the traffic. Hori, raise the curtain a little now. I want to see what is going on."

Hori obeyed, and Khaemwaset gave a secret smile. Nubnofret always wanted to know what was going on.

His captain shouted, this time a crisp order to the rowers, and *Amun-is-Lord* began its slow tack to the right. Soon the ruins and the temple of Set drifted out of sight to be replaced by straggling thick trees sheltering city dwellers seeking shade and conversation. On the left there was no vegetation, only a haphazard, cacophonous and unlovely confusion of workshops, warehouses, granaries and storage facilities teeming with noon life. Behind them, Khaemwaset knew, were the faience glazing works for which Pi-Ramses was famous, and continuous with the canal was more of the town, this time a quieter sequence of modest, white-painted merchants' homes and the little estates of minor noblemen engulfed in gardens and orchards. The apple trees were in full bloom, the scent enveloping the party in a heady, almost palpable mist, and pale petals rocked on the glittering surface of the water and lay in white mats against the banks.

The canal had widened into a vast pool and their craft was negotiating through a port jammed with vessels of every size and description being loaded and unloaded, while sailors gathered on the quays to gamble and small boys called to one another or dove into the churning water for the trinkets the idle would throw.

But soon the mêlée began to fade. *Amun-is-Lord* slowed as it approached the lake of the Residence, Pharaoh's private domain, and the soldiers guarding its entrance challenged Khaemwaset's men. Then they were through the narrow space left by the vigilant, armed boats and were floating past the southern wall that solidly protected Ramses' privacy and on, under the shade of more vibrant orchards, to the gleaming, slick marble watersteps against which Pharaoh's barge, aglitter with gold and electrum, rocked. Three other craft were tied to the white-and-blue poles. Khaemwaset's captain let out a string of commands, and

Amun-is-Lord bumped discreetly into its place.

Nubnofret let out a sigh of relief. The noise of the city was a subdued background hum, and only the lyrical songs of birds disturbed the sacred peace. "I hope there are litters waiting for us," she remarked, rising with her customary fluid grace, gathering her linens about her and bending out of the cabin. Hori and Khaemwaset followed. Already the two other boats were tethered and Khaemwaset's guards had spread out on the watersteps and were standing at attention. At the top of the steps a small delegation waited, and as the family walked along the ramp that had been run out, the members went to the ground in prostration. Seti, Vizier of the South, a man of elegance and dignity, bowed low, the crisply pleated ends of his calf-length white kilt brushing the hot stone. "Welcome once again to the House of Ramses Great in Victories, Highness," he smiled. He was carrying his gold papyrus-topped Staff of Office. Gold bracelets tinkled on his wrists as he rose, and his carefully manicured, strong hands were alive with the glint of gold and carnelian. Khaemwaset met his steady brown eyes and smiled back. "It is good to see you again, Seti," he replied, while Hori and Nubnofret were receiving renewed homage from the Vizier's entourage of scribes, heralds and runners, and behind them all the ramp was withdrawn. "I trust all is well with the King of Kings?"

Seti inclined his black-ringleted head. "Your father is well, and eager to see you. Your suite has been swept and refurbished, Prince, and I am sure that you are tired after your journey." He gestured, and with a flurry of activity three litters moved forward. "Pharaoh has set aside tomorrow morning for discussions with you in regard to the marriage contract, and he does not require you to be present this evening at dinner, although you are of course free to eat with him if you choose. If you do not choose, and if you are not too fatigued, he begs you to evaluate the tax estimates for the coming year that have just come in, and the percentages to be distributed to Amun and Set."

Khaemwaset nodded, secretly irritated. His father had placed the bulk of the government in his hands. Why did he not simply let him get on with it and not keep trying to subtly nudge him toward certain emphases like a child being trained to acquire self-discipline? Khaemwaset signalled, his litter was lowered, and he swung himself into the silken cushions. "Very well," he said as his bearers lifted him. "Send me Suty, Paser the High Priest of Amun, and Piay an hour after dinner. Do not bother with a scribe. I will use Penbuy. Greet my father and tell him I will dine alone tonight." Curtly he gave a command to Ib, waiting quietly with the rest of his servants. "The noon meal as soon as possible and prepare it yourself," he said. "Then I will rest." Seti and the rest of the crowd stepped away. The guards ringed the three litters, and Ramose walked ahead and began to call the warning, "The Great Prince Khaemwaset of Memphis approaches. Down on your faces!"

Khaemwaset sat back, trying to quell his annoyance at his father's manipulations, his selfish desire to be back in his office in Memphis, his impatience with everything that separated him from his slowly growing academic preoccupations. I am turning into an irascible old man, he told himself, hearing the sounds of marching feet and the sudden harsh bark of a commander from beyond the north wall of the precinct, where the huge military barracks and training ground ran down to the Lake of the Residence. There was a time when the demands of the palace and temple were important to me, when I gladly put my duty to my father before all else, but now they are irksome and I wish only to be allowed to labour over my legacy to Egypt, my crypt for the holy Apis bulls and my larger duty of restoration, without interference from that wily old man. Why? He moved restlessly, seeing but not seeing the idle groups of white-clad courtiers in their transparent linens go down before his progress like wind-shaken boughs of blossom, dappled in shade from the clustering trees before Pharaoh's mighty House. There was no answer to his private question, and it only served to intensify his nervous mood. The words "getting old" revolved sardonically in his mind.

They had come to a halt. Nubnofret was peering in at him. "Khaemwaset, are you asleep already?" she asked, and he blinked into her handsome, exquisitely painted face, aware all at once of the cleavage between her heavy, yellow-draped breasts as she bent towards him. Grunting, he stepped out of the litter, Nubnofret beside him, Hori behind, and they began to ascend the wide steps that took them almost at once into the cool, pleasing gloom cast by the palm-headed columns, soaring to be lost high above.

Ramses' palace, as complex and bewildering as a city in itself, had been built by his father Seti the First, and enlarged by the son into its present state of breathtaking opulence. Its façade, under the awesome pillars, was of turquoise tiles close-set with lapis to form a gleaming network of dark and light blue. Its floors and walls were glazed tiles set with intricate designs of the Delta's myriad plant and animal life, or were dazzling white plaster splashed with bright colours. The doors, requiring two men to open and close them, sent a lingering aroma of expensive Lebanon cedar throughout the hundreds of rooms, and were chased and inlaid with electrum and silver or plated with beaten gold.

Flowers were everywhere—strewn underfoot, clustered around the walls, garlanding pillars and people alike in an eternal spring. A man could become lost in its gleaming vastness for days, and Ramses was careful to provide slaves whose job was simply to guide and direct visitors and guests through the endless halls. Its libraries—the House of Life, where maps, official weights and measures, sky charts and dream keys were stored, and where all scientific work was done, and the House of Books, holding all archives—were famous throughout the world and always thronged with scholars of every nationality. Its feasts, its musicians and dancers, were equally notorious for the sheer exotic abundance of the food, the expertise of the music makers, and the beauty and grace of the dancers.

At its heart sat Ramses King of Kings, Son of Amun, Son of Set, wealthy beyond the dreams of most of his subjects, omnipotent and aloof, the Living God of the only country in the world that really mattered. Khaemwaset, striding behind the echoing voice of Ramose still calling his warning, was impelled once again into a grudging admiration for the House. He knew his way around it very well, having been raised here, and no longer regarded it as the magical miracle he had when a child, for he knew the pyramiding weight of minute organization that kept its flowers fresh, its food abundant and its servants always on hand, but its concept never failed to win his wonder.

Ramose had at last halted before two looming silver doors flanked by seated gods almost as high as the cross-beam. Amun with his feathers gazed serenely back along the polished corridor, while on the left a granite Set glowered down on the party, his long, wolfish nose aggressively raised. Khaemwaset gestured and the doors swung inward onto a wide, pillar-forested floor of turquoise pieces that cast a soft blue glow over the interior. The family walked into it and the doors were reverently closed.

Nubnofret moved at once. "I shall freshen myself and then pay my respects to the Empress and the Chief Royal Wife," she told Khaemwaset. "You will know where I am if you need me. I do hope they have not scented my water with that strong attar they used last time. I cannot stand the smell and I did tell them, but doubtless they have forgotten . . ." She planted a kiss on Khaemwaset's neck, still talking, and disappeared into her own rooms with her retinue. Kasa and Ib, already present, waited.

"What will you do?" Khaemwaset asked Hori. The young man smiled, his face breaking into the creases that quickened the hearts of every woman in the court, and his translucent kohl-rimmed eyes narrowed.

"I shall go to the stables and look over the horses," he answered his father, "and then Antef and I will see who we can find to share a few cups of wine with. Can I go to dinner with Grandfather tonight?"

"Of course. Just make sure that if you get drunk there are at least two of my soldiers to escort you back to your apartments. I will see you later, Hori."

He watched for a moment as his son swung back through the hall, his strong brown legs and white kilt tinged with the steady glow of the turquoise floor, then turned to Ib. "Is the food ready?" The man nodded. "Then let us go within and I will eat briefly before I sleep." His doors were flung wide and he passed into the place that had been his second home for more years than he cared to remember.

First there was a small and functional room given over to business and working receptions. It had once been a place of entertainment when he was much younger and definitely more frivolous, but now it exuded the stern atmosphere of labour and was scrupulously tidy. Beyond it were his sleeping quarters with a huge, lion-footed couch, golden censers standing before the shrine of Amun, an ivory-topped table and ebony-inlaid chairs. The aroma of steaming food mingled pleasantly with an undercurrent of fresh beeswax.

Khaemwaset liked the room but for the fact that voices echoed faintly, so that he felt he might be sleeping in a temple. But the whole of Pi-Ramses is a temple, he thought as he sank to the floor on a cushion and Ib drew a tiny table close to him. A temple to my father's godhead, a burst of sustained praise for his military exploits, his infallibility. The bread was still warm from Pharaoh's mighty kitchens. "It has all been tasted," Ib commented. Khaemwaset set to with a will. Later he lowered himself onto the yielding mattress of his couch, pulled the smooth sheet to his chin and fell asleep without reflection.

Four hours later, freshly washed and clad in the long robe of a vizier, he was welcoming the kingdom's Chief Treasurer, the High Priest of Amun and the chief of all temple scribes, and listening patiently to their monotonous figures regarding the apportionment of taxes to the gods, both foreign and indigenous. Before long the officials were wrangling over which temples deserved the greater subsidies, and with an inward sigh and a surreptitious glance at the waterclock Khaemwaset settled down to arbitrate their demands as tactfully as he could. The task was important, for the slighting of a foreign god could result in a diplomatic incident, and he did his best to give it his full attention, but he was relieved when at last his decisions were accepted and he was able to send the men away after a few moments of general conversation and wine sipping.

Walking through into his sleeping quarters he took a few grains of incense, lit the charcoal in the tall censer stand and sprinkled the myrrh onto the glowing blackness. Immediately a harsh, sweetish-grey smoke began to plume upwards. Khaemwaset opened the doors of the shrine, prostrated himself before Amun's benign smile and, lying on the cool tiles, he began to pray.

At first his words were part of the formal evening litany spoken each night far away in Thebes, where Amun towered in the heart of the temple of Karnak and ruled that city as he had done for centuries, but before long the solemn lilt of ritual gave way to a few stumbling personal pleas, and then silence. Khaemwaset lay with eyes screwed shut, aware of the solid resistance of the floor at his knees, his thighs, his elbows, breathing in a minute film of dust and the smell of beeswax.

Amun, something is wrong with me, he half thought, half prayed. I do not know what it is, indeed, the stirrings of discontent and something else, something alien and alarming, are so faint in the deep recesses of my ka that I wonder if I am not mistaken. Is it the beginning of disease? Do I need a purge, a week of fasting, an elixir? Is it a lack of proper exercise? He remained very still while he probed himself. A reluctant distaste for his father, the palace, the showy arrogance of Pi-Ramses, the paper-shuffling important ministers, began to spread like the fiery rash on the little dancer's body, and he let it grow. I am the greatest magician and physician in Egypt, he thought again bitterly, yet I am held in awe only because I in turn hold the reins of government in these hands, these hands that dig, that search, that would willingly relinquish the dry, dumb details of administration if they could hold just once the Scroll of Thoth, the key to all power and all life. Sometimes I think that I would even relinquish my ka itself for the opportunity to possess the two spells the Scroll is said to contain. One spell gives the power of bodily resurrection to the one who legitimately speaks it, and the other gives him the ability to understand the language of everything living under the sun. I command all people in the kingdom save my father, but I do not command the birds, the animals . . . or the dead. I am aging, my ways are becoming increasingly set, and I am afraid. I am running out of time while somewhere far down in the earth or entombed in rock or lying on the breast of a magician who was mightier than I are the words that would make me the most powerful man Egypt has ever known.

He groaned and sat up, crossing his legs, his eyes on Amun's gold sandals. Once the quest was like a game, a young man's ideal, full of excitement and pregnant with strong possibility. I played with it happily while I was learning medicine, beginning a family, working with my father, sure that I was the most favoured man in the world and the Scroll would fall into my lap as a gift from the admiring gods. Then I began my great labour of restoration and exploration and the game became the underlying cause of everything I did, a dark, constant pulse of waning hope and mounting frustration that gradually ceased to be a game. For seventeen years I have searched. I have grown mighty in knowledge but I have not found it.

His back had begun to ache, and he scrambled to his feet and stretched, reaching down to close the shrine. Thoth, god of the wisdom I worship, he thought angrily, why do you deny me this thing? I am the only man worthy of possessing it, yet you hide it from me as though I were an ignorant peasant who would do it harm.

The room seemed cold to him. Walking to the waterclock he watched the slow drip and realized that the hour was late. Nevertheless he was restless. Snatching up a woollen cloak he went out, and, ordering the guards on his door to follow, he took the long walk through the quiet palace to the House of Books. The librarian was dozing just inside the huge double doors. He woke, and seeing who it was, made his obeisance and allowed Khaemwaset to pass.

For a further two hours Khaemwaset wandered the rows of neatly catalogued scrolls, pulling out one here, one there, exchanging brief words with the few scholars who preferred study to sleep. But the touch of old papyrus did not reassure him tonight as it usually did, and the contents seemed to him as dry and lifeless as the atmosphere in the library.

He left abruptly, intending to try and rest, for he knew tomorrow would be full, but at the door to his apartments he paused. He could hear Hori's voice coming with a crack of yellow light further down the hallway, and Antef answering. On impulse, Khaemwaset turned left and approached his wife's rooms. The guard at her door saluted and knocked for him, and presently Wernuro appeared, bleary-eyed and tousled, and bowed. "Is your mistress still awake?" Khaemwaset asked tersely.

"Why no, Highness," the woman answered, suppressing a yawn. "The Princess retired over an hour ago."

Again Khaemwaset hesitated, then he pushed into Nubnofret's reception room. One lamp burned on a table in the corner but it was sufficient to show him the welter of cushions, cosmetic boxes, wilting flowers and discarded wine cups that told him she had spent a pleasant evening with friends and had, for once, uncharacteristically, allowed the no doubt exhausted servants to leave the mess until morning. "Thank you, Wernuro," he said. "Go to sleep out here. I will wake you when I leave."

Wernuro acknowledged him, but he was already picking his way to the farther door. The servant had left it ajar. Beyond, in the larger room, Nubnofret lay mounded in sheets on her couch. Khaemwaset could see the slow rise and fall of her breathing. The air was sweet with the tang of the clustered apple blossoms someone had set in a vase on the table beside her. It acted on him strangely as he moved softly to the couch and perched on the edge, conjuring every spring journey he had made to Pharaoh's city and, mingled with that, a cascade of ancient emotions long dormant, belonging to his boyhood and youth when he had been resident in the palace. "Nubnofret," he whispered. "Are you awake?"

His answer was a mutter. Nubnofret turned over, and as she did so the sheet slipped to her waist. Her sleeping robe was very thin, and Khaemwaset's gaze became rivetted on the large, now flaccid breasts beneath with their dark aureoles and permanently raised nipples. Her warmth and the odour of her body rose to him as he sat there, shivering slightly and drawing the cloak more tightly around his shoulders. Her hair, now fingered through with grey streaks, lay in a welter upon her pillows, and in repose her face was smooth and calm.

Khaemwaset thought of the early days of their marriage when they had made love often, sometimes more in an effort to get to know each other than in passion, but it had been good. Neither of us could be called spontaneous people, he mused, but sometimes a joyfulness overtook us and we sought each other out like children rushing to play. Does she remember, I wonder, and does she wish that we were once more as close, or does she relish her many duties and look back on those days as part of a youth now thankfully gone? She knows that I rarely bother my concubines. Does she ever lie on her couch at home and long for my body? We still make love, but formally, the scratching of an occasional itch. Oh Nubnofret, ripe and stern, where has the time gone? His impulse had evaporated. As he rose she stirred and mumbled something and he turned back, but she was still asleep. He sent Wernuro back to her corner and returned to his own quarters.

In the morning he had himself dressed, jewelled and painted with care, and taking Amek, Ramose and Ib he went to visit his mother. Astnofert still retained the title of Empress bestowed on her when Ramses' favourite for twenty years, the glorious Nefertari, had died. Nefertari had been Ramses' full sister, and thus Khaemwaset's aunt, but Astnofert was a half-sister. At fifty-nine years old she no longer stood beside her husband as a reigning queen for she was bedridden. Ramses had also married his daughter by her, Khaemwaset's younger sister Bint-Anath, who had been Chief Royal Wife for the last ten years, and who at thirty-six bore an uncanny resemblance to the dead Nefertari. Another queen, Meryet-amun, daughter of Nefertari, shared her father's bed, but all Ramses' affection went to Bint-Anath. Khaemwaset hated her Semitic name but liked her, for she was alert and intelligent as well as being ridiculously beautiful. He did not meet her often, and they did not correspond, but their few encounters were always affectionate.

Khaemwaset watched for her as he and his retinue, with Ramose calling the warning, walked sedately through the palace to the women's quarters where Astnofert lay in solitary splendour. Though he caught a glimpse of Meryet-amun, her haughty profile gliding by surrounded by guards and twittering female courtiers, his sister was not evident. At the entrance to the women's quarters he left Amek and Ramose and went on with Ib.

His mother's suite was not far into the harem. It opened out beyond the customary sheltering doors of the long passage into four rooms of magnificent size and luxurious appointment. The fourth room, smaller and more intimate than the others, led straight onto a covered walk and then the harem gardens. Astnofert liked to be carried to a couch there during the day so that she could lie and watch the movement of the wind in the trees and the activity of the women who filled the grass with their pastimes, gossiped away their sometimes tedious days and held their often drunken parties in the timeless heat of summer nights.

It was here that Khaemwaset found her, a grey-haired, thin lady propped up on pillows, her yellowing, unpainted face turned to the bright flow of sunlight beside her. In a corner of the room a harpist was rippling out a plaintive melody, and at Khaemwaset's approach a servant began to gather up the cones and spools of the sennet game she had been playing with the Empress. Astnofert's head came round in greeting, and in spite of her physical debility the gesture was still full of the grace and regality that had made her a famous beauty in the days of her youth. She smiled with difficulty, and Khaemwaset bent to kiss first her withered hand and then her lips.

"So, Khaemwaset," she said, the words hard and precise as she laboured to form them correctly. "I hear you have been summoned to drag Ramses out of yet another marital thorn bush. He does seem to enjoy the prickles, doesn't he?"

Another servant had quietly placed a chair for the prince and he sank into it, leaning forward and inspecting his mother's features intently. He did not miss the tremor of her fingers as she spoke, or the increased filminess of her eyes.

"I think he flings himself into trouble for the fun of the diplomatic game afterwards, Mother," he replied, chuckling. "How are you? Is there any more pain?"

"No, but you might have a word with my physician about the poppy mash you prescribed for it." With a slow wave of her hand she dismissed the servant, who retired carrying the sennet board, and she turned back to her son. "The nasty concoction is not dulling the twinges as it used to and I'm afraid he has perhaps lost the recipe you gave him."

Khaemwaset considered lying to her but then he changed his mind. She was dying a slow death and she knew it. "The recipe is not at fault, and neither is your physician," he answered her steadily. "When the poppy is taken day after day it begins to lose its efficacy, or rather, the body becomes habituated to it and needs more of it to perform the same task." She was nodding, her rheumy but sharp eyes fixed on his. "Much that comes from Syria is an abomination to me, Empress, as you know, but the poppy is a great blessing. If you were suffering a temporary complaint or were under the power of a curse that I was in the process of lifting I would refuse to let you take any more . . ." Here he hesitated, but those greying eyes, the whites brown with disease, did not flinch so he continued. ". . . but you are dying, dear Mother. I will order the physician to give you as much poppy as you want."

"Thank you," she said, her mouth quirking in a half-smile. "You and I have always been honest with one another, my dear. So now that my health has been discussed and disposed of, tell me why you are looking so haggard."

He stared at her, unsure. Outside there was a sudden burst of shrill feminine laughter as a group of young concubines sauntered past, leading three freshly washed spider monkeys that were vainly trying to sit down and groom themselves, and as Khaemwaset took a breath to answer Astnofert a pair of bluebirds dashed, trilling, into the room, circled, and flashed away into the trees in streaks of irridescent colour. Without warning he was shaken by a violent pang of longing to be one with them, to be soaring free and heedlessly into the vast, hot sky, away from this room in which death crept, invisible, towards the woman who had given him life. "I really do not know," he said at last. "The family is fine . . ."

"Yes. Nubnofret entertained me for a while last night."

". . . and my estates prosper. Father expects no more from me than he has always done . . ."

She laughed, a dry wrenching sound that was nevertheless full of humour. "Which of course means that he expects everything!"

"Even so!" Khaemwaset summoned a grin, then sobered. "But . . ." He was unable to finish, and in the end she attempted a shrug.

"Immerse yourself in finding a husband for little Sheritra," she advised him. "You need a new project, and there is one right under your nose."

He did not rise to the bait. He and his mother agreed on everything but the handling of his daughter, and here she sided most emphatically with Nubnofret. "I *have* a new project, waiting for me at home on the Saqqara plain," he said ruefully, "if I am ever able to get to it. Have you seen Father recently?"

She did not pursue the matter of Sheritra. "He comes to visit me once a week," she replied. "And we chat of inconsequential things. He tells me that the stela erected at the quarries of Silsileh, the one showing you and me, Bint-Anath and himself and Ramses as heir, has been finished. I wish that I could attend its dedication."

You can be sure that my dear brother Ramses will attend, Khaemwaset wanted to say sourly, but he did not. Of the few pleasures left to his mother, the contemplation of one of her sons instead of Nefertari's on the future throne of Egypt was the greatest. "Is my brother Merenptah at court?" he enquired.

"No, I do not think so. He is travelling in the south, keeping his eye on some of his building projects. He will probably call on you as he passes Memphis on his way home."

"I suppose so."

There was little left to say. Khaemwaset, after a few more moments of idle conversation, got up, kissed her, and took his leave. Her hand was cold and leathery as he pressed it briefly between his own, and he was all at once eager to feel hot sun on his skin, to raise his face to the sky and close his eyes against Ra's blinding glory.

Leaving the harem he took a shortcut to the family's private garden. It was empty. Noon was approaching and the shadows under the sycamores were thin and short. The surface of the blue-tiled fish-pond was glassily still and water splashed monotonously into the fountains' basins. Khaemwaset held his fingers under the glittering flow and found it silky and warm. He was aware of the sun's fire slowly burning through the crisp striped linen of his headgear and it was very good. He had the curious and illogical conviction that he had been reprieved, that like a prisoner spared from execution or a very young child sent out to play his senses were wide open to every sweet assault of his surroundings. Yet he felt grubby, tainted after breathing in his mother's slightly offensive, dry breath, and he could still sense her icy touch. Bending he plunged both hands under the fountain's cascade and then leaned forward until the water lapped almost to his shoulders. I love her, he thought. It is not that. I do not want to die in the knowledge that all dreams are shown to be illusion. Though he stood there for a long time, watching his hands through the distortion of the moving water, he could not feel clean again.

He ate a light midday meal with Hori and Nubnofret. Hori, after sleeping late, was on his way to the House of Life with Antef and would then take a litter into the markets of the city, and Nubnofret had been invited by Royal Wife Meryet-Amun to join her for an afternoon spent sailing up some of the smaller tributaries of the Nile. Khaemwaset listened to their plans with half an ear, his mind already on the coming meeting with his father. He ate sparingly, had Kasa change his linen and set out with his escort for Pharaoh's private office.

The closer he came to the heart of power in the palace, the more crowded the halls and waiting rooms became. Often he had to slow while Ramose's voice was raised a notch and minor officials and nobles, slaves, servants and foreigners, went to the floor in reverence. But eventually he stood outside the oasis of quiet that was Ramses' place of business behind the vast throne room where he sat to receive the adulation of citizen and ambassador alike.

Khaemwaset waited while the Chief Herald announced him. He was ushered in immediately, and as he walked towards the huge, untidy desk behind which his father was already rising he took note of those present. There was Tehuti-Emheb the Royal Scribe, a man of few words but a powerful and silent personality who knew more of his master's mind and the true state of Egypt's health than anyone. He was already kneeling in prostration, his palette on the dark-blue, gold-shot lapis tiles beside him. The Khatti ambassador, Urhi-Teshub, his curling black beard and conical red hat faming an impressive face, was bowing slightly in the white ray of sunlight falling from the clerestory window high above. Ashahebsed was smiling frostily as he also laid himself full-length on the floor.

With a mute gesture Khaemwaset bade them all stand. He came up to Ramses, went down to kiss the jewelled feet and the long fingers airily extended, then rose and embraced his father. The servants who had been motionless around the walls sprang to life and for a moment the men by the desk were surrounded by a flurry of quiet activity. Wine was opened, tasted by Ashahebsed, and poured. Linen napkins appeared in a pristine pile on the edge of the desk. Scented water, pink and warm for the rinsing of the fingers, was laid discreetly, well out of the way of the scrolls piled before Pharaoh, and beside it several plates of various delicacies wafted the aroma of cardamom and cinnamon to Khaemwaset's nostrils. The servants withdrew backwards, bent double. Ramses ignored them.

"Khaemwaset, you do not look well," he commented in his laconic, cultivated voice. "The physician is always loath to prescribe for himself, is that not so? Take some wine and sharpen your wits, Prince. I am glad to see you."

Was there reproach in that mellifluous tone? Khaemwaset looked affectionately into the clear, bright eyes ringed in thick kohl. Pharaoh was wearing long jasper-and-gold earrings that swung against his thin neck and almost touched his gold-hung shoulders. The cobra and the vulture of supreme kingship reared over his forehead on the golden band that kept his red linen helmet in place, and his fastidiously hooked nose and delicately thin lips gave Khaemwaset a renewed impression of his father as the mighty hawk god, Horus. He was exquisitely groomed, from his hennaed and ringed hands to his well-clipped toes, and

Khaemwaset, watching him seat himself, arrange his flowing linens and place his hands on the desk, admired and was amused by every calculated move.

Ramses was vain, manipulative and still, at the age of sixty-four, undeniably magnetic. "Though you did not dine with me last night," Pharaoh went on, folding his fingers together one by one, "I know that you were able to complete the small task I requested. Sutekh will get his due again this year. I will command an offering to him in your name, so that he will gaze only upon your deed and not the seditious thought that surely filled your heart as you sealed the subsidy order."

Now Khaemwaset laughed, and at the sound the officials dutifully laughed also, politely and briefly. "I will dine with you tonight, Mighty Bull," he promised, sinking into the chair Ramses was indicating, "and as for Mighty Set, well, he has no cause to vent his anger on me. Do we not communicate in the making of my spells?"

Ramses inclined his head. The cobra's crystal eyes glittered as he did so. "Indeed. And now to work."

Urhi-Teshub stirred behind Khaemwaset, cleared his throat and came forward. Tehuti-Emheb rattled his pens.

"What is the trouble with the latest negotiations, Father?" Khaemwaset asked.

Ramses rolled his eyes to heaven, fixed the unfortunate Khatti ambassador with a cold stare and waved at his scribe. Khaemwaset turned.

"Hattusil, king of the Khatti, is now requesting that the princess's dowry be delivered with rather than before her arrival," Tehuti-Emheb said. "He has been having much pain and soreness in his feet, and consequently the gathering of the dowry is slow. The drought in his land has further interfered with his good intentions."

"Good intentions," Ramses broke in with cool sarcasm. "First he promises me the greatest dowry ever paid in his eagerness to ally himself to the most powerful House in the world. Then months go by, and I see nothing. Then I receive a letter from Queen Pudukhepa, not from Hattusil himself mind you, telling me without a shred of apology that part of the palace was burned down" — here he sniffed delicately — "and therefore the first payment is delayed."

"Majesty," Urhi-Teshub protested, "I myself was present when the fire broke out. The destruction was terrible! My queen was much tried, seeing my king was away performing ceremonies for the gods, but she did not fail to write to you. Egypt was not forgotten!" His accent was guttural, his expression pained.

"Perhaps not," Ramses retorted, "but the fire was a most convenient opportunity to change the terms of the agreement. Now my dear Khatti brother whines of sore feet, as though he himself must sally forth from his citadel and personally chase every goat, every horse. Are there no viziers in his land? No competent stewards? Or must his wife take command of everything?"

The Khatti ambassador was obviously well used to such stinging diatribes. He waited calmly, his hands tucked into his brocade gown, until Ramses had finished. Then he said, "Does Your Majesty perhaps doubt the honesty of his brother? Is he casting aspersions on the king who has kept the Treaty of Kadesh that his illustrious father made before him, in spite of pressures from the Babylonian King Kadashman-Enlil to make a new treaty with him?"

"Kadashman-Enlil is a slippery little weasel," Ramses mutered, "in spite of our renewed diplomatic relations. And I happen to know, Urhi-Teshub, that your king is in fact squabbling with the Babylonian." He bit into a honey-and-almond cake, chewed thoughtfully, then dabbled his fingers elegantly in the water bowl. "Why should I trust Hattusil?" he asked grumpily. "He refused my request to revise the treaty and give me more of Syria, and then I heard that he himself is claiming the very portion I wanted."

"It was Khatti's portion in the first place, Divine One," the ambassador responded firmly. "According to the more ancient treaty between the Khatti and your father, the Osiris One Seti, in very clear terms . . ."

Khaemwaset sighed inwardly. Urhi-Teshub had made a tactical error in mentioning Seti. Ramses' father was a sore point with him. Seti had been a man of taste and vision. His monuments and his greatest work, the temple of Osiris at Abydos, displayed artistry of such fineness and beauty that one caught one's breath at the sight of it. But worse, Seti had succeeded in his wars where Ramses, in spite of his protestations to the contrary, had failed rather ignominiously. Khaemwaset listened to the two men wrangling back and forth, and thoughtfully sipped his wine. When he was ready he broke in, careful to interrupt the ambassador, not his father.

"I do not see the point of all this," he said firmly. "We are here to bring the marriage negotiations to a successful close, and with all respect, Urhi-Teshub, if you wish to discuss the matter of the validity of old treaties you might arrange another time." The ambassador bowed and smiled, obviously relieved. Khaemwaset turned his attention to Ramses who was pettishly, though gracefully, playing with his wine cup. "Our own ambassador Huy is in Hattusas," he reminded him. "Send a message to the effect that we are willing to receive the dowry at the same time as the princess, providing Huy personally makes sure all gifts are present at the time of departure. Hattusil cannot be blamed for fires and illness, only for tardiness."

"He boasted too long and too loud," Ramses remarked. "I suggest that we request a five percent increase in the amount paid, to compensate us for all these delays. After all, tribute is definitely due to us." He cast a wily, sidelong glance at Khaemwaset. "I am not sure that the princess is worth the strain these negotiations are placing upon my royal heart. I might just decide to break them off and marry another Babylonian instead."

"Hattusil himself might do the same if we put unnecessary pressure on him," Khaemwaset objected. "We are talking about a dowry, Father, not tribute as you well know. Give the Khatti king the benefit of the doubt, but make it clear that he is expected to fulfil his bargain completely. You do not wish to appear greedy and grasping, do you?"

"I want what is due to me," Ramses said emphatically. He sat back, his stooped shoulders curved over the weight of gold and silver on his chest and his braceleted arms loose along the carved lions' spines of the chair. "Oh very well. Tehuti-Emheb, write the damned letter to Huy and one to Hattusil expressing my displeasure at the delay and my suspicion that he is simply too poor to make good his boast, but tell him that I will magnanimously wait for the fruition of these extremely trying negotiations."

"His Majesty spoke in haste," Khaemwaset said deliberately to the scribe. "Leave out His Majesty's suspicion." The man nodded and bent over his palette. Ramses chuckled. "This meeting is over," he pronounced. "Out, all of you. Khaemwaset, you stay." The ambassador bowed and, together with the scribe, backed down the long hall and out the doors. Ramses did not wait for them to disappear. He got up and beckoned Khaemwaset. "Call your steward for your medicine bag,' he ordered. "Ashahebsed, do it for him. Come into the inner room, Khaemwaset, and examine me. My chest pains me sometimes when I breathe, and I have breathlessness occasionally. I need a potion for fatigue also." He did not wait for his son's acknowledgement, but strode away. Khaemwaset followed. His father's condition was not reversible, but he had never dared to tell Ramses so, even though he knew that Pharaoh would blithely ignore his words. He was convinced that he would indeed live forever.

Chapter 3

'Praise to Thoth . . .
the Moon beautiful in his rising . . .
he who sifts evidence,
who makes the evil deed rise up against the doer,
who judges all men.'

By the time Khaemwaset had examined his father, found no change in his condition and prescribed an innocuous elixir for his fatigue, the afternoon was far advanced. He was tired himself, more from the strain of the negotiations than from any physical activity. His horoscope, which he as a magician cast for himself and the rest of the family at the beginning of each month, warned him that the last third of this day would be portentous, either extremely lucky or dismally unlucky, depending on his own actions. The ambivalence of the prediction annoyed him, and he thought of it again as he made his way back to his apartments to sleep until dinnertime. He often enjoyed Pharaoh's great feasts. Guests from all over the world were invariably present and included fellow scholars, magicians and physicians with whom he could talk and argue. But today the horoscope's odd pronouncement would lurk behind any congenial contact he might make.

The family's private suite was empty. Khaemwaset did not bother to summon Kasa to undress him. He stripped off his clothes, took a long drink of water from the large jar always standing full in the airy hallway and collapsed onto his couch with relief.

An hour after sunset he, Nubnofret and Hori were announced and walked together with their train into Ramses' largest reception hall. At the striking of the Chief Herald's staff upon the floor all conversation had ceased until Khaemwaset's titles were called, but as he and the others proceeded into the room the din began again, and Khaemwaset felt as though he were wading in noise.

Hundreds of people stood in brightly clad groups, or milled

about, wine in their hands, talking and laughing, their voices fusing to echo off the many papyrus pillars and the silver stardusted ceiling in mighty waves of sound.

A slave girl, naked but for a blue-and-white ribbon about her waist, came up to them bowing, and placed garlands of pink lotus and blue cornflowers over their heads. Another offered scented wax cones to be tied on their wigs. Khaemwaset bent good-humouredly, feeling the soft hands of the girl fumble with the ribbon, his eyes already scanning the crowd.

Bint-Anath was approaching, her many-pleated, floor-length sheath floating scarlet around her, her slim shoulders visible under a billowing white flounced cloak, and the long black ringlets of her wig already glistening with melted wax. The slave girl walked away and Khaemwaset bowed to Egypt's Chief Wife. "Greetings, brother," Bint-Anath said cheerfully. "I would stay and talk to you but it is really Nubnofret with whom I want to gossip. I have not seen her in a very long time. Do excuse me." She was like a goddess, like Hathor herself, moving lightly in the circle of reverence the guests had provided, her pair of massive Shardana guards towering beside her and her exquisitely gowned and painted retinue behind.

"You are more beautiful every time I see you, Bint-Anath," Khaemwaset said gravely. "Of course I excuse you. Write me a letter instead."

She gave him a dazzling smile and turned to Nubnofret. Her female attendants were no longer chattering among themselves. Their glances flickered furtively over Hori, away, then back to the young man's matchless face and brown, well-muscled body. He grinned at them engagingly and Khaemwaset, catching Antef's eye, winked at him.

One girl, bolder than the rest, came up and, after bowing to Khaemwaset, addressed Hori directly. "It may be that having been in Pi-Ramses only two days, you lack a dinner partner, Prince," she suggested. "I am Nefert-khay, daughter of Pharaoh's architect, May. I would be pleased to entertain you while you eat and perhaps sing for you afterwards."

Khaemwaset, amused, noted Hori's preliminary quick assessment turn to slow interest as he took in Nefert-khay's high breasts and supple waist under the yellow sheath, her dusky kohled eyes and moist mouth. Hori inclined his head.

"As May's daughter you must also enjoy the privilege of dining in the first row next to the dais," he said, "so lead me there, Nefert-khay, and we will be ready for the food as soon as Pharaoh is announced. I'm hungry."

They wandered away, threading easily through the crowd, and Khaemwaset watched them go. Antef had tactfully vanished, but Khaemwaset knew that though Hori might dine cheerfully with the girl, get drunk with her, kiss and compliment her and perhaps even essay more urgent caresses in the privacy of the sprawling gardens, he would end his evening lounging by the river or in his suite with Antef.

Khaemwaset knew that his son was not attracted to men, though rarely a man might be sexually drawn to him. He liked and appreciated the young women who flocked around him, but his emotions, and therefore his body, remained unengaged. For Hori, the one could not operate without the other.

Khaemwaset spared a moment of pity for May's forward little daughter, then went to seek out his own small table on the dais where already the members of Ramses' immediate family were gathering. Lowering himself to the cushions provided, he exchanged a few polite, cool words with his brother, the Crown Prince Ramses, already deep into his cups, and with Second Wife and Queen Meryet-Amun, before the Chief Herald's staff hit the floor with three resounding booms and the hundreds of voices trailed away. "Exalter of Thebes, Son of Set, Son of Amun, Son of Temu, Son of Ptah-Tenen, Vivifier of the Two Lands, Mighty of Twofold Strength, Valiant Warrior, Smiter of the Vile Asiatics . . ." The Herald's voice droned, and here Khaemwaset smiled a trifle grimly. ". . . Lord of Festivals, King of Kings, Bull of Princes . . ." Khaemwaset ceased to listen. Every forehead in the hall was resting on the floor and his own was buried in the cushions he had been sitting on a moment before.

The Herald at last fell silent. Khaemwaset heard the crisp slap of his father's sandals on the dais by his ear, followed by the lighter tread of his sister. Bint-Anath settled herself beside him with a wriggle and a sigh, Ramses bade the crowd rise, and Khaemwaset resumed his cushions and pulled the low table towards him.

Pharaoh leaned past his daughter-wife, resplendent in his

blue-and-white striped helmet surmounted by the golden cobra and vulture, his sharp eyes heavily kohled, his eyelids lustrously green. Rings glittered on each of his fingers, and ankhs and Eyes of Horus tinkled on his concave chest. "I drank some of the potion you prescribed for me, Khaemwaset," he said. "It was disgusting and I don't think it has done me any good, unless it is responsible for my vast appetite tonight." At the foot of the dais the symbols of his divine royalty—the crook, flail and scimitar—were being set in their holders by their Keeper, and a contingent of Shardana guards was lining up between the dais and the crowd. At a signal from Ashahebsed, standing discreetly behind the royal table, food-laden servants began to pour from the shadows and a mouth-watering aroma stole through the mingled odours of scented wax, flowers and perfume. Ashahebsed began to serve Ramses.

"You expect miracles from all those around you, including me," Khaemwaset answered warmly. "Give the medicine a chance, Father. You might try going to bed earlier, too."

Ashahebsed was tasting the food. Ramses watched impatiently. "I am just as busy in bed as out of it," he said wickedly. "My women are killing me, Khaemwaset. So many of them, and they all demand satisfaction! What am I to do?"

"Stop acquiring so many," Bint-Anath broke in, laughing. "Listen more closely to Suty when he tries to tell you how much gold your harems are draining from the royal treasury every day. Then you might be deterred from further purchases and contracts."

"Hmm," was all the reply. Ramses began to eat steadily, though with a delicate grace.

Khaemwaset's table servant had filled his plate also, and he ate and drank with appreciation for the excellence of his father's cooks. He saw Nubnofret close to the dais, sitting with a few of her female friends among the nobility, and not far from her he spotted Hori and Nefert-khay. She had both hands resting on his bare shoulder and was nuzzling his ear as he ate. With a pang, Khaemwaset thought of his Sheritra. What was she doing at this moment? Saying her prayers, walking in the torch-lit garden with Bakmut's undemanding company? Perhaps she was sitting in her room, knees drawn up to chin, wondering what *he* was doing and castigating herself for the shyness that prevented her from plunging into life. He would have liked to have seen her here, eyes aglow with wine and excitement, her fingers drawn to some young noble's shoulder and her mouth pressed against some adoring ear. Pharaoh was directing another comment in his direction. His brother Ramses was slumped over his food and humming tunelessly to himself. Khaemwaset gave himself over to the pleasures of the evening.

Several hours later, full of stuffed goose, cucumber salad and various pastries, slightly inebriated, Khaemwaset found himself near the north doors of the hall talking to his friend Wennufer, High Priest of Osiris at Abydos. The noise had not abated. If anything, the crowd had become more raucous as the wine jugs emptied and the entertainment had begun. Shouts and snatches of song erupted here and there as guests expressed their approval of the fire-eaters, the jugglers and acrobats, the sinuously naked dancers whose hair brushed the floor and whose golden finger-cymbals clicked out a taunting invitation together with their sweat-slicked hips.

Khaemwaset and Wennufer had retired to a relatively quiet place where they could both talk undisturbed and enjoy the night wind wafting through the open double doors from the dark garden beyond. Pharaoh had left some time before. There was no sign of Hori, and Nubnofret had come to Khaemwaset earlier to let him know that she would be spending the greater part of the rest of the night in Bint-Anath's suite. He had kissed her absently and turned his attention back to Wennufer's argument with regard to the proper origins of the heb-sed festival, and both men were soon oblivious to the uproar around them.

Khaemwaset was engaged in making a strong point, his face thrust close to Wennufer's and his wine cup extended so that the nearest slave could fill it, when he felt a touch on his arm. He ignored it, dimly presuming that someone had jostled him, but it was repeated. Irritated, he turned.

An old man stood before him, coughing with an attempt at the polite control Khaemwaset had come to recognize in those with chronic lung conditions. He was slightly bent, and the hand that had importuned Khaemwaset was already returning to clutch an amulet of Thoth that hung on his wrinkled chest. He wore no other ornament. His shaved head was bare, as were his yellowed feet. He might have been ugly with his seamed jowls and unhealthily puffy features, but for his eyes. They were alert and fixed Khaemwaset with a steady gaze. The man wore an old fashioned thigh-high winding kilt over which his belly sagged, and tucked into its belt was a scroll.

Khaemwaset met his glance with an impatience that quickly turned to bewilderment. Those eyes seemed familiar. A fellow priest? he thought, from On or Memphis? Then why so poorly dressed? He could pass for a peasant. One of my back-room servants, those on whom I rely but rarely see? Then what is he doing in Pi-Ramses, and how, for that matter, did he obtain leave to enter here? If he is a servant, often seen but not consciously acknowledged, I had better have a word with Nubnofret about retiring him. The poor man looks as though he already has one foot in the Judgement Hall. He repressed an urge to embrace the stranger that was followed by a sudden cold shudder of what felt like repulsion. Wennufer, seeing his friend's abstraction, had fallen silent and was sipping his wine and staring into the dishevelled crowd, ignoring the petitioner altogether—for Khaemwaset was sure the man was a petitioner of some kind. For medicine, I expect, he thought.

Khaemwaset began to grow sober under the stranger's level stare, yet he could not look away, and gradually he saw something in those depths, a lurking terror quickly masked. At last the man spoke. "Prince Khaemwaset?"

The question was a formality, Khaemwaset knew. This man was perfectly aware of his identity. He managed to nod. "I cannot examine or treat you at this time," he got out, surprised to hear himself whispering. "Petition my Herald for an appointment."

"I do not want to be treated, prince," the stranger answered. "I am dying and I have little time left. I come to ask a favour of you."

Favour? Khaemwaset saw that the full lips were trembling. "Then ask," he urged.

"It is a very serious matter," the man went on. "I beg you not to take it lightly. The fate of my ka hangs in the balance."

So it was an affair of magic. Khaemwaset relaxed. The old man wanted a spell of some kind, either chanted for him or written down to take away, but even at the thought the man was shaking his head.

"No, Prince," he said huskily. "It is this." He looked down, the torchlight sliding over his bald scalp, and fumbled at his waist, withdrawing the scroll. Carefully he held it out and Khaemwaset, his interest piqued, took it, turning it over in his practised hands.

It was obviously very old. The papyrus had a brittle fragility that made his fingers suddenly gentle. It was quite thin, perhaps not more than three revolutions, yet its weight was curiously great.

Around them the feast swirled. The musicians kept up a loud harmony of harp, lute and drums, whose rhythms shook through the tiled floor. The revellers shrieked and danced. But around the two men, standing half in the shadows sweeping through the doors, there hung an aura of timelessness.

"What is it?" Khaemwaset asked.

The old man coughed again. "It is a thing of danger, Prince," he said. "Danger to my ka, danger to you. You are a lover of wisdom, a great and well respected man, devotee of Thoth, god of all wisdom and knowledge. I beg you to perform a task that I in my arrogance and stupidity am not allowed to accomplish." His eyes had gone very dark, and Khaemwaset could see a pleading in them that was almost painful. "I am running out of time," the man urged. "Destroy the scroll on my behalf, and in the next world I will prostrate myself before mighty Thoth a thousand thousand times for a thousand thousand years on your behalf. Please, Khaemwaset! Burn it! Burn it for both our sakes! I can say no more."

Khaemwaset looked from the agonized face to the wound scroll in his hands, and when he glanced up again the man had gone. Annoyed yet oddly feverish, he hunted through the people with his eyes but caught no glimpse of a naked, freckled skull, a bowed chest. He became conscious of Wennufer at his elbow. "Khaemwaset, what are you doing?" the priest asked testily. "You are too drunk to go on discussing, perhaps?" But Khaemwaset muttered a quick apology and walked away, out the doors, past the surprised salute of the guards and onto the dew-soft darkness of the lawn.

The uproar behind him slowly receded until he was pacing the dim greyness of the path that doubled back along the north wall of the palace to a place where he could reach his quarters quickly. As he went he held the scroll gingerly, afraid that it might crumble if he tightened his grip.

Such nonsense, he thought. An old man is dying and wishes for a few moments of recognition before he goes. He plays a silly game with me, knowing that I, even with holy blood in my veins, am the most approachable of my family. The scroll is probably no more than the names of his servants and what they are paid. A joke? Hori's joke? No. Wennufer, perhaps? Of course not. Is it some kind of a test my father has prepared for me? He considered that possibility for a few moments, his gaze on the indistinct path blurring beneath his feet. Ramses did test the loyalty of his subordinates at unexpected times and in odd ways. He had done so periodically every since the top echelon of the army had been dismissed following the debacle of Kadesh. Khaemwaset, however, had never been the object of such a trial. Neither had any other members of the family.

But would we know? he wondered as he turned the corner into the full glare of a dozen torches lining the approach to the eastern door. What if we have been repeatedly tested and repeatedly passed without ever being aware of such a calculated thing? But if a test for me tonight, what kind? What for? Am I to burn the scroll without reading it and thus prove that my higher loyalty is to my king over my love of learning? Supposing that I read it and then disposed of it. No one would know that I had unrolled it first. He glanced swiftly behind him but the gardens lay in a perfumed darkness, the shrubs uneven smudges against the bulk of the wall, the trees black-armed and impenetrable. No, he thought, feeling foolish. Father would not have me followed and watched. I am being ridiculous. Then . . . what?

He was coming up to the first torches and his steps slowed, then stopped. He was directly under a torch. If he had raised a hand he would have been able to touch the leaping orange flames that danced and guttered in the night air. Taking the scroll in his fingertips he held it up to the light with a confused idea that he might be able to read it without unrolling it, but of course it remained opaque, only paling a little in the torch glow. He held it higher. This is insane, he told himself. The whole episode smacks of madness. He could feel the heat of the torch on his face, his quivering hand. The papyrus began imperceptibly to blacken and he could sense it pull inward and curl. It is very old, he thought. There is a small chance that it is indeed a thing of value. Hastily he pulled it away from the fire and looked it over. One corner was singed, and even as he held it a tiny portion broke away and drifted to the ground. Very lucky or horribly unlucky, depending on my actions tonight, he told himself, thinking of his horoscope. But which action, burning or saving, will bring fortune? For he was all at once certain that this was the moment of which the horoscope spoke, and there would be grave consequences either way.

For a long time he stood irresolute, remembering the old man, his begging eyes, his urgent words. He wanted to get rid of this burden thus placed upon him, yet at the same time he was assuring himself that his judgment was impaired by wine and the lateness of the hour, that he was stretching a meaningless encounter into something portentous and fateful. Groaning quietly, he tucked the scroll into his voluminously pleated waist and walked slowly out of the circle of torchlight, through the succeeding band of deep shadow, and on to the palace entrance, where two guards sprang to attention and made an obeisance. He wished them a good night, and was soon being admitted into the family's suite. Ib and Kasa came hurrying to meet him.

"Where have you been, Highness?" Ib asked, impatience and relief written all over his face. "One minute you were talking with the High Priest and the next you had vanished. Amek rushed away immediately to find you and presumably he is still looking. You make our tasks difficult."

"I am not a prisoner of my servants, Ib," Khaemwaset retorted testily. "I came through the garden and entered by the east gate. I expect my bodyguard to be aware of my movements at all times." And that is not entirely fair, he thought as he saw Ib flush, but he was suddenly so exhausted that he could hardly stand. "Kasa, bring hot water and wash the henna from my hands and feet," he ordered, "and please hurry. I want to go to bed. Am I alone here?" Kasa bowed shortly and went out, and Ib answered.

"Her Highness is not back, and neither is Prince Hori. Nor is any of their staff."

I am gently and suitably rebuked, Khaemwaset thought with an inward smile. He placed a placatory hand on Ib's shoulder. "Thank you," he said. "You may retire, Ib." The man bowed his departure and Khaemwaset strode through into his bedroom.

Fresh flowers had been placed in vases in the four corners. Two lamps burned, one in a tall golden holder in the middle of the floor and a smaller one by the couch, whose sheets had been turned down invitingly. The room murmured of quiet, undisturbed rest. Khaemwaset sank into his chair with a sigh and felt for the scroll. It was not there. He checked his belt, felt among his linens, looked about on the floor, but there was no sign of it. Kasa knocked and entered, a boy bearing a basin of steaming water behind him, and Khaemwaset rose.

"Did either of you see a scroll lying on the floor by the door or in the hall?" he asked. The lad, eyes downcast, shook his head and, hurriedly setting the bowl on its waiting stand, he backed out. Kasa also shook his head.

"No, Highness," he answered.

"Well go and look," Khaemwaset snapped, his fatigue evaporating. "Look carefully."

A few moments later his bodyservant was back. "There is no sign of any scroll."

Khaemwaset pushed his feet back into the sandals he had so recently removed. "Come with me," he said, and rushed out into the hall, his eyes searching the floor as he went. Indeed, there was nothing. He left the suite, Kasa behind him, and retraced his steps with infinite care, but Pharaoh's gleaming and now empty passages lay unsullied under the dim light of torches nearly spent.

Khaemwaset went out onto the path. The same two guards were leaning sleepily on their spears. Both scrambled to attention. "Do either of you remember seeing a scroll in my belt as I passed you earlier?" he asked them peremptorily. They both denied it. "But would you have noticed?" he pressed them. "Are you sure?"

The taller of the pair spoke up. "We are trained to be observant, Prince," he said. "No one enters the palace with anything suspicious on their person. We would not, of course, suspect you, but our eyes travel everyone automatically and I can assure you that you stepped through our salute without any scroll." It was true, Khaemwaset thought angrily. The Shardana were quick of eye and would stop anyone they even suspected of harbouring a weapon.

Nodding his thanks, he reached down a torch from the lintel and, bent almost double, scoured every inch of his short journey from the garden to the passage doors. There was nothing. Kneeling, he scanned the stone for the tiny charred piece of papyrus that had broken loose under the torch, but it was nowhere to be found. Swearing under his breath he investigated the grass to either side of the path, parting it carefully while Kasa watched in obvious bewilderment, but came up empty.

In the end he strode back to his suite. His heart was racing.

"Rouse Ramose," he told Kasa. "Bring him without delay." Kasa opened his mouth to protest, but closed it again and slipped away.

Khaemwaset began to pace. It is not possible, he thought. I passed no one. I thrust it into my belt, took five paces to the door, and came here directly. Not possible. A dread began to steal over him but he fought it down. Danger, the old man had said. To me. To you. Have I failed? Or have I passed some mysterious test? He put a hand to his chest and felt the frantic action of his heart. Sweat had broken out along his spine. He could feel it begin to trickle into his kilt.

When Ramose, sleepy and slightly dishevelled, bowed before him, he almost ran to the man. "I have lost a valuable scroll," he said. "It is somewhere in the palace or perhaps in the gardens. I will give three pieces of gold to anyone who finds it and brings it directly to me. Spread the word, Herald, begin now, to anyone still wandering the palace." All sleep had left Ramose's eyes. He bowed his understanding and hurried out, straightening his linens as he went. He had scarcely closed the door when it opened again and Nubnofret came into the room. An odour of stale wine and crushed lotus blooms preceded her.

"Whatever is going on, Khaemwaset?" she queried. "I almost bumped into Ramose as he was rushing out of the suite. Are you ill?" She came closer and peered at him, then exclaimed, "You certainly look ill! Oh my dear, you are white. Sit down." He allowed her to push him into his chair. He felt her cool hand steal over his forehead. "Khaemwaset, you have a fever," she pronounced. "You really hate Pi-Ramses, don't you, and the city hates you, for its demons always make you mildly sick. I will call for a priest. You need a spell that will drive them forth."

Khaemwaset caught her arm. Fevers were indeed a matter for magic, being caused by the possession of demons, but he knew that he had brought this illness upon himself and no evil power inhabited his body. Or does it? he wondered suddenly, confusedly. Was my decision to keep the scroll the wrong one, giving it the power to quietly transform itself and enter me? Am I now harbouring something evil, something destructive? Nubnofret was waiting, her arm still resting in his grip, her expression questioning. He shuddered, then began to shiver uncontrollably.

"Khaemwaset, you are frightening me." Nubnofret's voice came to him from far away. "Please let me go." He came to himself and mumbled a stiff-lipped apology, withdrawing his hand. His wife kneaded her arm. "Kasa!" she shouted. "Put him to bed. Look at him!" Kasa came running, and with a glance at Nubnofret, helped Khaemwaset out of the chair and onto the couch.

"But no priest," Khaemwaset muttered. He lay on the couch, still trembling, and drew up his knees. "I am sorry, Nubnofret. Go to bed and don't worry. All I need is a good sleep. I have lost a valuable scroll, that is all." Nubnofret visibly relaxed. "In that case I quite understand," she said scornfully. "Other men might suffer so at the loss of a child but you, my dear brother, sweat and quiver over bits of papyrus."

"I know," he answered, clenching his teeth against the shivering. "I am a fool. Goodnight, Nubnofret."

"Goodnight, Prince." She sailed out of the room without another word. "Is there anything you require, Highness?" Kasa asked uncertainly.

Khaemwaset lifted his cheek from the pillow and peered up at the anxious face of his servant. The effort was almost too much. A great heaviness was on him now, so that his eyelids drooped and closed of their own accord. "No," he managed in a whisper. "Do not wake me early, Kasa." The man bowed and left quietly, at least, Khaemwaset thought that he did. If Ptah had decreed the end of the world at that moment, Khaemwaset would not have been able to force his eyes open. He heard the pause for Kasa's bow, the light sound of his footsteps across the floor, the polite click as the door closed, but those things came to him from far away, from the other side of the city, from another world. He fell into sleep like a man who loses his footing and goes sliding down the edge of a dark pit, and immediately he began to dream.

It was noon, a summer noon of intense, merciless heat that stung his nostrils and rendered him almost blind. He was walking, head downcast, along a road of white dust that reflected up at him the sun's cruel bite. Just ahead of him a woman strode. He could see no more of her than her naked ankles, powdered with little puffs of the fine sand her progress stirred, and the rhythmic revealing and concealing of her strong brown calves as the scarlet linen she wore flowed with her stride.

For a while, in spite of his growing exhaustion and the sweat that continually ran into his eyes, he was content to watch the slow, almost relentless way her muscles flexed and loosened and her toes gripped, splayed, then flung back tiny showers of dust, but soon a need to see the rest of her took hold. He tried to lift his head, and found that he could not. Straining, he contracted the muscles of his neck, pushing, compelling, but his gaze remained fixed on the road gliding ponderously beneath that graceful tread.

He began to wish that she would stop. He was gasping from the heat and began to stumble with fatigue. He called out, but his words were nothing more than tiny wisps of burning air on his lips. Stop! he thought desperately, please stop! But her pace did not vary. In spite of the sense of hypnotic compulsion growing around him, he attempted to veer into the grass he dimly knew lay to either side of the track, there where trees cast a shade for which he would have died, but his legs kept marching, marching, drawn into the woman's oblivious confidence.

Khaemwaset finally woke with the first hesitant light of dawn and the early chorus of birds. His room was shrouded, calm. His night lamp had long since gone out, and he smelled the faint, stale odour of the used-up wick mingled with the rank smell of his own body. He was trembling with the aftermath of his nightmare and his sheets were sticky. Fever dream, he thought, as he struggled to sit up. Nothing more. He reached for his night table, the frame of his couch, the delineations of his face, in an unconscious need to reassure himself that he was now awake, in a world of substance and sanity. As he did so he realized that his penis was engorged and fully erect, and he was overflowing with a kind of sexual excitement he had not felt in years.

He lay quietly, stilling his breath and his mind, then he called softly for Kasa and ordered his morning bath and food. Already the palace was stirring around him, but distantly. His suite was always relatively silent.

Kasa was tying Khaemwaset's sandals when Ramose was admitted. Khaemwaset bade him speak, his heart suddenly tripping, but the Herald had no news. "My assistants report that no one approached has seen or heard of the scroll, Highness," he admitted. "But we will keep spreading your request and the promise of a reward. I am sorry."

"It is not your fault, Ramose." Khaemwaset stood and waved him out, sending for Amek at the same time. While he waited for his bodyguard he could not resist a rapid search of his floor, his reception room, the entrance hall of his suite, but he came up empty. Amek appeared and saluted. "Get out my litter," Khaemwaset ordered. "This morning I want to go in person to the House of Ra and say my prayers with the other priests." He did not know what he wanted to say, or why he felt such a strong urge to stand in the temple and breathe the incense, the aura of power and peace, but he knew he would regret any change of mind.

He spent his remaining few days in Pi-Ramses in discussions with the Viziers of the North and South, several foreign ambassadors, temple administrators and his father. He visited his mother once more, took an afternoon stroll, suitably guarded, through the colorful markets of the city in search of the perfect gift for Sheritra, and went hunting in the marshes with the Khatti ambassador, whose feathers turned out to be less ruffled than the hapless ducks he brought down with the throwing stick.

Nubnofret had, as always, forgotten her ire. Khaemwaset saw little of her and Hori until the day when they embarked for Memphis and home. He himself seemed fully recovered from the strange fit that had overtaken him on the night he lost the scroll. To his chagrin, it had not been recovered. He did not think that it would. Deeply hidden was the growing conviction that spirits had been abroad, that for some reason of their own they had for a moment dissolved the barrier between the living and themselves, and he had been the point at which the wall wavered. The old man was either a great magician in communication with unseen powers, which Khaemwaset doubted, or he was a spirit himself and his scroll a thing of smoke and air that had faded into nothing with the approach of dawn.

The warnings of his horoscope, the vivid memory of the edge of the scroll curling and blackening under the torch, the old man's urgent plea, were thrust to the back of Khaemwaset's mind. He would go home, look at the plans for the Apis burials, begin digging again at Saqqara, and recover his strong sense of self. Only the dream truly continued to haunt him. He forgot none of its details, and for a long time a woman's bare feet in the dust could give him an inadvertant pang of fatigue and lust.

He and the rest of the family sailed home laden with purchases for the house and gifts for Sheritra and friends in Memphis. The river had shrunk even further in the time they had been away, and now was flowing with a turgid slowness. The return journey took longer in spite of a steady breeze from the north because the current was against the craft and the oars had to be used.

Khaemwaset, impatient as always to see the calm forest of palms set against their backdrop of pyramids and desert that heralded his city, sat under a canopy on the deck of *Amun-is-Lord*, his thoughts already on his next project. Nubnofret dozed, lay in the seclusion of the cabin with nourishing creams on her face to help ease her skin's transition back to the dry desert air, or played board games with Wernuro. Hori and Antef strewed the sun-baked planks with the puzzles and toys they had picked up in the markets for dissection. Surely, Khaemwaset thought, as the oars splashed and the canopy slapped in the wind, we are the most blessed, harmonious and fortunate family in Egypt.

Chapter 4

'Death calls every one to him,
they come to him with quaking heart,
and are terrified through fear of him.'

They docked at the watersteps of Khaemwaset's estate shortly after breakfast, the servants scattering immediately to their duties. Sheritra, hearing the confusion, came running to greet them, and there were hugs and reassurances before they retired to the garden. Already the boats were being unloaded, and Khaemwaset knew that later they would be dragged from the water and inspected for repairs. He sank onto the grass in the shade of his sycamores, Sheritra beside him, with a gust of pure pleasure. His fountain still tinkled crystal into its stone basin. His monkeys watched the arrival with lofty boredom and went back to lolling beside the path. His comfortable old house still welcomed him with sun-drenched walls and orderly flowers. He heard the bustle of brisk activity begin inside. In a while Ib would ask him if he wanted the noon meal in the garden or in the cool of his small dining room, and Penbuy, freshly washed, would be waiting for him in his office. He watched his daughter exclaim over her gifts, her plain face flushed with excitement, and for once Nubnofret did not keep up a steady barrage of admonition and advice as the girl hunched over the bright jewels and cascading linens and knick-knacks in her lap.

Presently Ib could be seen, approaching with his dignified, unhurried walk from the back of the house. Penbuy was with him, and even at this distance Khaemwaset sensed that the man was barely containing some violent emotion. Nubnofret, usually indifferent to such things, also looked up, and Hori scrambled to his feet.

"Highness, will the family be eating here or in the dining room?" Ib asked. Khaemwaset did not answer, indeed, he barely heard the question. All his attention was fixed on his scribe. Penbuy was trembling, his eyes glowing.

"Speak!" Khaemwaset said. Penbuy needed no further invitation.

"Highness, a new tomb has been found on the Saqqara plain!" he blurted. "The workmen had begun to clear the site of Osiris Neuser-Ra's sun temple in preparation for your orders on its restoration, and behold! a rock of large size emerged. It took the Overseer three days to remove it and lo! beneath it was a flight of steps."

Khaemwaset, in spite of his quickening pulse, smiled at Penbuy's uncharacteristic loss of aplomb. "Have the steps been cleared?" he snapped.

"Yes. And at their foot . . ." He paused for effect and Hori exclaimed, "Well get on with it, Penbuy! You already have our attention. We are your captives!"

"At their foot is a sealed door!" Penbuy finished triumphantly.

"It is too much to hope that the seals are original," Hori observed, but with a question in his voice. He looked at Khaemwaset, who rose.

"What do you think?" he asked his scribe. Penbuy shrugged, already settling back into his customary controlled decorum.

"The seals appear to be originals," he answered, "but we have encountered clever fakes before, Prince. The thrill of the moment engulfed me. I am sorry. Your Overseer of Works is of the opinion that we have indeed found an untouched tomb."

Nubnofret sighed ostentatiously. "You had better pack up the Prince's meal and give it to the servants who will accompany him, Ib," she said, and Khaemwaset shot her a grateful, humorous glance.

"I'm sorry, dear sister," he apologized. "I must at least inspect this find today. Ib, have the litters brought round. Hori, will you come?" The young man nodded.

"But I beg you, no break-ins today please, Father! I have not even had time to be washed!"

"That depends on what we find." Khaemwaset was already preoccupied, his words spoken absently. A new tomb, new inscriptions, new knowledge, new scrolls, new scrolls . . . Do not expect anything, he told himself sternly. He chances for something fresh are slim. My horoscope for the last third of this day is very bad. So, for that matter, is the rest of my family's, so I doubt if this find will yield anything worthwhile. All at once he was seized with a desire to tell Penbuy, "Have the earth and sand shovelled back over the entrance. My most pressing project is the work for Osiris Neuser-Ra and he shall have his restoration," but his curiosity and mounting excitement won out. Neuser-Ra could wait. He had been waiting for hundreds of hentis and would surely be patient for another day or two. Amek was approaching, the litter-bearers with their folded burdens behind.

"Is there any urgent business on my desk?" Khaemwaset asked. Penbuy shook his head. "Good. I will make this up to you somehow, Sheritra," he went on, turning to her, but she grinned up at him and held the gossamer blue linen he had given her to her face. "I am used to it," she laughed. "Enjoy yourself, Father. Find something wonderful."

Something wonderful. Suddenly Khaemwaset was filled with boyish anticipation. Gesturing to Hori and kissing Nubnofret's cool cheek, he got onto his litter and was soon swaying towards the temple of Neith and the Ankh-tawy district. His stomach growled its hunger, and the linens he had donned on the boat that morning were limp and itchy with sweat, but he did not care. The hunt was on once more.

By the time he alighted from his litter with the churned plain of Saqqara baking in the afternoon sun all around him, he was thirsty as well. His servants were hurrying behind, some pitching the small tent he always used, some lighting a cooking fire, and the long-suffering Ib was already directing the laying of Khaemwaset's camp table for his belated noon meal. Hori came scrambling through the sand to join his father.

"Phew!" he said. "No matter what time of the year it is, Saqqara is always sweltering! Please control your lust for an hour, Father, and take pity on me! I simply must eat, but I also want to stand with you when you examine the seals. I suppose that is the entrance, there." He pointed across the hot expanse of waste to where Osiris Neuser-Ra's ruined temple lay. Beside it, just outside the jagged, truncated outer wall, was a gigantic boulder and an untidy heap of dark sand and gravel. Khaemwaset reluctantly turned back towards the tent and the table, now shaded by a flapping canopy and laden with food, where Ib stood behind his chair, arms folded.

Khaemwaset and Hori set to with relish, talking easily as they ate and drank, but presently the conversation died away. Hori fell into an abstracted mood. Chin in hand and eyes downcast, he traced the folds in the tablecloth with a knife. Khaemwaset's mood of elation gradually faded to be replaced by a growing uneasiness. He sat back, eyes drawn to the temporarily deserted hole in the desert floor, and it seemed to him to be both beckoning and warning. Mentally shaking himself he turned away, draining the last of his beer and rinsing his fingers, but soon his gaze returned to that ominous gash in the sunny reality of the desert and in spite of himself he imagined it as a portal to the underworld, out of which a cold wind blew.

He had sometimes been superstitiously anxious at tomb openings. The dead did not like to be disturbed. But he always made sure that proper offerings for the kas of the deceased were laid beside the coffins, broken belongings mended, and endowments reactivated, and he had seen earth replaced over the resting places with a feeling of satisfaction, knowing the gratitude of the Osiris ones.

This was different. Fear seeped towards him, sliding invisibly over the shimmering yellow sand like the demonic serpent Epap himself, and once more he was tempted to order the tomb covered over. Instead he rose, tapped Hori on the shoulder and left the pleasant shade of the canopy.

With Hori beside him and Ib and Penbuy behind he soon reached the steps. They were hot under his sandals, though in places the stone was still thickly dark and stained with the damp of centuries. There were five of them. Khaemwaset halted before a small, square rock door, smooth and once plastered white. On its left, rotting brown rope was intricately knotted around metal hooks embedded deep in both door and surrounding stone.

Encrusted over the massive knot was a dry and crumbling ball of mud and wax. Khaemwaset bent closer, aware of Hori's light breath on his neck. The young man whistled. "The jackal and nine captives!" he exclaimed. "Father, if the tomb had been desecrated and re-sealed the imprint would be a crude imitation of the sign of the House of the Dead, or even simply a chunk of mud. And look at the rope. So ancient that a touch would crumble it away!"

Khaemwaset nodded, his gaze intently travelling the door. There was no sign of a forced entry, although the plaster had flaked away in several areas and was a noxious brown in others.

Of course an untouched door did not mean an unrobbed tomb. Thieves had always been ingenious in their efforts to reach the treasures that were buried with the nobility. Suddenly Khaemwaset found himself hoping that the interior was *not* intact, that more dishonest, foolhardy men than he had drawn the sting of wrath within, had leached the old spells that protected whoever lay waiting in the darkness beyond this mysterious door.

"Prince, I am afraid," Ib said. "I do not like this place. We have never seen a seal unbroken before. We should not be guilty of the first sin."

Khaemwaset replied, still studying the rough surface before him. "We are not thieves and desecrators," he said. "I have never yet committed sacrilege against the dead whom I study. You know that we will re-seal the door, leave many offerings for the ka, pay priests to pray for the owner. We always do." Now he swung to face his steward. Ib's eyes were shadowed, his expression grim. "I have never seen you like this before, Ib. What is the matter?" It was not just Ib, Khaemwaset saw. Penbuy was clutching his palette to his naked chest and chewing his lip.

"This time is not like the others, Highness," Ib blurted. "Last night, in the boat on the way home, I dreamed that I was drinking warm beer. It is a terrible omen. Suffering is going to come upon us." Khaemwaset wanted to snap at him not to be a fool, but such a dream was indeed a thing to be taken seriously. Ib's words had unleashed the fear in him again and he tried not to let it show on his face.

"Forgive me, Prince," Penbuy broke in, "but I also have doubts about this tomb. Today, when I wanted to perform my morning devotions to Thoth, my patron, the incense would not light. I replaced it with fresh grains, thinking that the old ones might be tainted, but nothing I did caused it to heat. Then I was overtaken by a fit of shivering and I could not move for some time." He came forward, his expression strained. "Pass over this tomb, I beg you! There will be others!"

Khaemwaset's mood of unease intensified. "Hori?" he said.

Hori smiled. "I slept well and said my prayers in peace," he answered. "I do not mean to belittle these omens, my friends, but the day is only half over and they could have nothing to do with this tomb at all. Will you turn from a find such as this?" he pressed his father. "Don't tell me that you also have received warnings!"

Khaemwaset's mind filled slowly with a vision of the old man, the scroll in his trembling fingers, the torch fire blackening . . . crisping . . . Not warnings, he thought. But a premonition, a tremor of apprehension in my ka. "No," he said slowly, "and of course I will not refuse this gift of the gods. I am an honest man. I do good in Egypt. I will offer the ka of the inhabitant here many precious things in exchange for what we may glean." He straightened and touched the rope, feeling tiny pieces of it fall into his fingers like fine grit. "Ib, call my master mason and have this door chiselled out." He pulled hard on the rope and it parted. The seal cracked in two with a tiny sound and fell into the dust at his feet. He stepped back, startled. Ib was bowing silently and retreating up the steps and Hori had his nose to the hot stone, examining the crack between the door and rock. Khaemwaset and Penbuy sat together on a step and waited for the mason and his apprentices.

"It is unusual to find a door and not just a hole plugged with rubble," Penbuy remarked, but Khaemwaset did not answer. He was now fighting his own sense of dread.

When the mason and his assistants arrived, the others retired under their canopies. From where he was sitting, half bemused by the mid-afternoon heat, Khaemwaset could see the dark line made by the chisels grow into the outline of a door. In another hour the mason came and knelt before him, his slick, naked chest and legs and blunt hands filmed in white dust.

"Highness, the door is ready to be forced," he said. "Do you wish me to open it?" Khaemwaset nodded. The man went away, and soon the grind of crowbars on stone could be heard.

Hori came and squatted before his father. Silently they watched the huge square inch outwards, revealing a widening gulf of blackness. Presently Hori stirred.

"Here it comes," he said quietly, and Khaemwaset tensed.

A thin plume of air began to pour from the aperture and billow upward into the limpid sky. It was very faintly grey. Khaemwaset, watching the horizon shake through it, fancied that its odour reached him, dank, unbearably stale, with an almost indiscernible hint of the charnel-house. The smell was familiar to him, having assaulted his nostrils on numerous similar occasions, but he thought that this time the steady stream had a particularly virulent edge.

"Look!" Hori said, pointing. "It seems to be spiralling!" Indeed, as the gush reached its zenith it was forming odd shapes. Khaemwaset thought he might have made pictures of them if they had not dissipated so quickly. Then the moment was over. The column of foetid air blew away and he got out of his chair, Hori at his heels.

"Be careful of traps, Father," he reminded Khaemwaset, who nodded brusquely. Sometimes the tombs held cunningly concealed shafts that dropped straight into bedrock, or false doors to lure the unwary into dark pits.

Khaemwaset came to the stair, hesitated, took a deep breath, and plunged down and through the crack the masons had managed to force. Servants with lit torches hurried behind, and Khaemwaset paused just inside the short passage to allow them time to illuminate the interior. They were obviously reluctant to do so. But then, he thought in the few seconds while they fanned out, they always are. So am I, this time. The orange flames wavered, sending streamers of shadow racing for the corners. Penbuy rattled his palette as he extracted a pen. Hori was panting lightly. Khaemwaset took his son's arm without realizing that he did so, and together they moved into the tomb.

Although the ancient air was gone, the smell of damp and decay was very strong. Penbuy began to cough, and Hori wrinkled his nose. Khaemwaset ignored it. The ante-room, though very small, was exquisitely decorated and scrupulously tidy. It was also undisturbed. With a thrill of sheer excitement Khaemwaset saw the tiring boxes neatly stacked, the furniture in place and without so much as a scratch, the sturdy clay jars with their precious contents of oil, wine and perfume still sealed. Six stern-faced shawabtis stood motionless in their niches, waiting for the summons of their master to work in the fields or at the loom, and around them the walls gleamed with life. Vivid scenes were laid upon the white plaster.

Walking slowly, Khaemwaset marvelled at the delicacy and vibrancy the dead artists had achieved. Here the dead man and his wife sat at meal, pink lotus blooms in one hand and wine cups in the other, leaning towards each other and smiling. A young man, obviously a son, in short white kilt and with many necklaces entwined over his red chest, was offering a piece of fruit to the baboon perched at his feet. Baboons were depicted everywhere—gambolling in the painted garden where the little family reclined at their ease by the fish-pond, running behind the man as he held his spear and chased a lion across the desert, sitting with tails curled around their furry hips as the three humans had their skiff poled through a riotous green marsh in search of ducks. There was even a baboon sprawled asleep at the foot of the couch where a bilious sun was sending its early rays to wake the two who slept. Interspersed with the friezes and unfolding delights of the family's earthly existence were black hieroglyphs exhorting the gods to welcome their worshippers into paradise, to grant them every blessing and reward in the next life, and to watch over their tomb. Hori, who had been talking to Penbuy as the Scribe began the work of copying what inscriptions he could, came over to Khaemwaset. "Have you noticed something strange about all these pictures?" he remarked.

Khaemwaset glanced at him. "The baboons?"

Hori shook his head. "No, not the baboons, although they are indeed extraordinary. The man who lies in the other chamber must have been a great devotee of Thoth. No, I mean the water. Look closely."

Khaemwaset did so, and was soon intrigued. Wherever the man, his wife and their son appeared, their feet were in water. Sometimes it rippled in little white wavelets. Sometimes it flowed over several different kinds of fish, and once it was contained in bowls around the figures' ankles, but whatever they were doing they did in water. "These people must have loved the Nile passionately to have decorated their tomb with so much of its blessing," Khaemwaset whispered, the sibilance rushing in a small echo around the room. "And there is something else, Hori. This man was, I think, a physician like myself. Look." He pointed to where several surgical instruments were shown beside a long panel of hieroglyphs. "The script is a prescription for the unconquerable AAA scourge, and beside it is a catalogue of spells for the subduing of disease demons."

Together they wandered around the walls while Penbuy followed more slowly, his pen busy. Then Khaemwaset paused with a cry of satisfaction. In a tall recess, just before the gaping door that led to the burial chamber, stood two statues. The woman was tall and graceful, her eyes smiling out into Khaemwaset's own under her short, old-fashioned granite wig and blue-painted headband. One arm was at her side. The other embraced the waist of her husband, a lean, also smiling man with a square face and mild expression, dressed only in a short kilt and sandals. One leg was outstretched in a stride, and in one hand he held a stone scroll. As in the rest of the tomb, the artistic work was of a fineness Khaemwaset had rarely seen. The eyes of the statues glowed darkly. The jewels around the woman's neck were picked out in blue and red and the tassels of her sheath glinted with gold paint.

Khaemwaset bent to the plinth. "So," he said after a moment. "We have found a princess, and presumably a prince, although I cannot read his name. The stone is scored through where it should be."

Hori's fingers stroked the gash. "This is not the work of vandals," he said presently. "I think the plinth was damaged when it was being set up in here, and the workmen did not have time to repair it." He stood straight. "Still, his name will be on his coffin."

"I agree," Khaemwaset affirmed. "She has a haunting name, the princess. Ahura. Very unusual. Now, Hori, can we date this find?"

Hori laughed. The sound slammed against the walls and the shadows seemed to convulse at its force. One of the servants cried out in fear and Khaemwaset, his momentary absorption forgotten, wanted to clap a hand over his son's mouth. "Why are you asking me?" Hori chuckled. "I can merely assist you, O wise one. I think the dating will be almost impossible. The furniture is severe and simple, perhaps belonging to the age of the Great Pyramids, but the decorations resemble closely the beautifying that was done during the reign of my great-grandfather Seti. The coffins may give us more clues."

Khaemwaset did not want to go into the other room and neither did the servants. They were clustered silently close together. Penbuy was lost in his work. "The statue of the prince has a scroll in its hand," Khaemwaset said to Hori. "At least it looks like the symbol of pharaonic authority. That is very odd and might even be considered blasphemous, seeing that only kings may be represented with the sign of temporal power."

But Hori merely nodded and gestured to the servants to proceed into the burial room. They hung back, their eyes wide, their faces pale under the flaring lights they carried. Khaemwaset, picking his way towards them, wondered if his expression held the same nervous tension. "It's all right," he said to them kindly. "Am I not the greatest magician in Egypt? Is my power not mightier than the powers of the dead? Give me a torch." He swept one out of a shaking hand and, with a conscious stiffening of his will, strode through into the other room.

He almost dropped the torch, and had to stifle a cry. Directly before him, huge, as the flame revealed it, was Thoth himself, in his ibis beak curved towards Khaemwaset, his wise bird's eyes twinkling. In his right hand he held a pen and in his left rested a scribe's palette. The whole life-size statue glowed with the warmth of animation, and as Khaemwaset's pulse slowed he realized that it was plated over in solid gold. "Thoth," he whispered, and stepping towards the god he knelt and prostrated himself, kissing the shining feet. Behind him an awed Hori was also performing his obeisance and the servants were standing in the doorway exclaiming, their fear temporarily gone.

Khaemwaset rose shakily, and it was then that he saw the coffin lids. They were leaning against the plain whitewashed wall to either side of the god, two slabs of solid, palely polished quartzite, and Khaemwaset stared at them stupidly. "But it is not possible!" he blurted. "No robber has been here. Why did the prince choose to lie uncovered?"

"Perhaps he is not here at all." Hori's voice fell flat in the tiny space. With one accord, father and son turned round, and in the turning Khaemwaset felt a rush of the dread that had begun to stalk him ever since he had first seen his workmen's pile of damp sand and ominous gap beside it. His palms became slick and he gripped the torch more tightly. "No," he whispered. "He is here. They are both here."

The coffins lay side by side on stone bases. Torchlight was playing on them, and the shadows within gathered densely. Hori's happy mood had fled. Soberly he edged closer to his father. Once more Khaemwaset had to will himself to move. What is the matter with me? he thought angrily. I have gazed on the dead a hundred times and more. I am a sem-priest after all, and a physician. No, it is the malevolent magic I feel in here that is turning my blood so chill. Why in the name of Amun are these coffins open?

The first bandaged corpse lay with right arm at its side and left bent across its breast. A woman. The Princess Ahura. Khaemwaset stared down at her for a long time. Beneath the dusty windings, now brown from the embalming salts that had sucked the moisture from her body, he could see the shapes of many amulets, and he counted them off in his mind. Some would be placed on the skin itself, but he recognized the Buckle of the Girdle of Isis that protected the dead wearer from any abomination, and also on the neck the Amulet of the Tet, the spine of Osiris that gave the corpse the power to be reconstituted in body and spirit in the next world. Just below these familiar swells lay an enormous Amulet of the Collar, a plate of gold and turquoise that covered the withered breast and sparked tauntingly at Khaemwaset. He shuddered. The Amulet of the Collar gave the wearer the power to free himself from the funeral swathings that held him captive. "It's beautiful," Hori breathed beside him. Grim-lipped, Khaemwaset nodded.

Gingerly he passed to the second coffin, some of his fear evaporating under the mysteries they had found. The prince lay with both arms at his side in the male position. He was as simply bound as his wife. His Amulet of the Collar matched hers, gold and turquoise, and at first Khaemwaset did not see the thing by his right hand. Then he bent closer with an exclamation of surprise.

"Hori! There's a scroll in here," he said. Leaning over the edge of the sarcophagus he touched it gently. It resisted his fingers and was quite dry. He pushed at it a little harder and the hand itself quivered.

"It is not actually in the prince's fist," Hori observed. "He was well bandaged."

"No," Khaemwaset answered. "I do believe that the scroll has been sewn to him. See how the hand moves when I tug on it." They straightened and stared at each other.

"A dilemma," Hori said softly. "To take scrolls from a tomb to copy and then return is one thing, but are you willing to cut it off his hand, Father? We have never lifted anything from a coffin before, only from boxes in ante-rooms."

"I know," Khaemwaset snapped testily. Already the familiar lust was rising in him and he glanced back to the roll of papyrus and the hand that curled around it. "If the coffins had been decorated and inscribed with the proper spells we might have found some explanation, but they are completely bare. Not even the Eyes for the corpses to see out into the room. What could be so important that the prince ordered the thing actually sewn onto him?"

"This is a serious matter." Penbuy had come up behind them and was peering into the coffin, his palette under his arm. "The inscriptions tell me nothing, not about baboons, not about the water depicted everywhere, and where, Highness, is the young prince, the son? Did he die elsewhere and was therefore buried elsewhere?" He paused, and when there was no reply he went on. "I humbly submit my doubts to you, Prince. Close up this place and leave the dead in peace. Do not take the scroll. I do not like the air in here."

Khaemwaset knew his scribe was not speaking of the musty smell. He did not like the air either, but under his dislike, his disquiet, was the pulse of his eagerness. A precious scroll, so precious that the prince had made sure that it was buried with him. A large mystery in the midst of many small ones. He had found many scrolls in his digging, usually left by robbers because they had no value to any but a scholar. They were the favourite stories or poems of those who had enjoyed them in life and intended to go on enjoying them at the feet of Osiris. Sometimes they were proud lessons mastered in youth and lovingly preserved. Sometimes they were boasts—lists of the valuables some noble had amassed, the gifts he had given to some Pharaoh at the celebration of the New Year, or the number of slaves he had brought back from military campaigns.

But this . . . Khaemwaset stroked the scroll thoughtfully. This belonged to the realm of the urgent, the sacred, the vitally important to the prince whose brittle bones and withered skin clutched at it so possessively. I deserve at least a look at it, Khaemwaset thought, with a flash of mutiny against his innate virtue. I honour the dead with my restorations. Let this dead man for once honour me in my search for knowledge.

"Osiris Neuser-Ra's temple awaits your expert hand," Penbuy put in hopefully. "You surely do not wish to anger him, Highness."

Khaemwaset ignored his scribe's clumsy plea. "Hori, give me

a knife," he ordered.

There was an outbreak of whispering from the servants pressed together by the doorway. Hori pulled a short copper blade from his kilt belt and passed it to his father. Khaemwaset bent. For a moment he hesitated, his eyes on the prince's face, aware of his own amulets—the Eye of Horus for happiness and vigour that swung from his chest and the Amulet of Isis's Buckle that lay between his shoulder-blades to protect him from demonic attacks from behind. Then, holding his breath, he reached into the coffin and, taking the scroll carefully, pulled it taut so that he could see the stitches attaching it to the hand. The copper blade was very sharp. One by one Khaemwaset slit the threads, marvelling that they were so strong. The hand jerked stiffly. Penbuy had backed away, but Hori was watching his father's actions intently.

Khaemwaset gave a sigh of satisfaction and drew up his prize. It was not very thick. He handed it to Penbuy. "Roll it gently in linen," he said, "and carry it home yourself, Penbuy. Do not give it to one of your assistants. Put it on my desk in the office and tell whoever is guarding the door today not to let anyone near it. I will read it, you can copy it, and then I will replace it." Unless it is very valuable, his mind ran on silently. Then I will keep it, put it in my own library, or perhaps even donate it to the House of Books at Pi-Ramses. This prince has no need of it now.

"I do not approve," Penbuy said forthrightly, holding the scroll with distaste, and Khaemwaset rounded on him.

"Your approval or disapproval is as nothing to me!" he said coldly. "You are my servant, nothing more. Remember that, Penbuy, or you may lose your position in my household!" Penbuy whitened, bowed and left the room without another word. Hori looked solemn.

"You were somewhat hard on him, weren't you, Father?" he protested. Khaemwaset glared at him.

"That is not your business, Hori," was all he said.

It was a shock to emerge into the red drenching of sunset. Khaemwaset and Hori stood at the head of the stairs, breathing the pure desert air in grateful gulps. The evening breeze had sprung up, warm and reassuring, stirring their filthy kilts and drying the cold sweat from their bodies. Hori spoke for both of them when he said, "How fine life is! I am not ready to lie in my tomb yet, Father, in the dark and cold. Egypt is too winsomely lovely!"

"No one is every ready," Khaemwaset answered slowly. He felt light-headed, dislocated, as though an age instead of a mere afternoon had gone by while he was in the tomb. "Let us finish whatever food and beer is left, Hori, while the tents are being struck, and then we will go home and make our peace with your mother and Sheritra." They walked away from the gathering gloom of the hole behind them. "Ib!" Khaemwaset called to his waiting servant. "Leave the organizing here to the under-steward. Go home and tell Amek I want two soldiers to guard this site. I will remain until they come."

Hori looked at him curiously. "Two soldiers, Father?" he said as they reached the table and sank into the chairs beside it. "You usually don't bother with soldiers at all, only a couple of workmen."

"But this tomb is untouched," Khaemwaset pointed out. "We did not examine the chests and boxes. Who knows what wealth they contain? We will leave them alone, but if word of our find gets out we may have all kinds of rabble trying to force a way in and steal. Better to stand Amek's men with spears and knives at the entrance.

But it was not robbers that he feared. No, not at all. He drank the beer that had been placed before him, watched the shadows of night begin to creep across the desert and wished that Amek's men would hurry.

Full night had fallen by the time he and Hori alighted from their litters and walked into the house. Khaemwaset did so with a vast relief. The chatter and pattering feet of his servants, the aroma of the evening meal, the gentle flicker of the lamps being lit, all served to restore to him a sense of security and normality. Hori went off to his quarters, and Khaemwaset was just entering his private dining room where Nubnofret was already seated when Sheritra and Bakmut came in. The servant retired to the wall and waited to serve her mistress. Sheritra gave her father a hug. "You are back in time to tell me a story tonight," she said. "You will, won't you? How grubby you are!"

Khaemwaset good-humouredly returned her embrace, kissed Nubnofret and, going to his low table, called for water to wash his hands. "I have not had time to change my clothes," he apologized to his wife. "I did not want to hold you up while I did so."

She did not appear to be annoyed. "I have had plenty to do while you were gone," was all she said on the subject. "Did you find anything interesting, Khaemwaset?"

At that moment Hori entered, Khaemwaset signalled for the meal to be served and a general conversation began. The family's musicians, a harpist, lute player and drummer, accompanied the desultory to and fro of the talk. Nubnofret had not really wanted an answer to her question, and Khaemwaset was relieved when she did not pursue the matter. He was afraid that Hori might prattle of the thing his father had done, but Hori and Sheritra, their tables touching, were engaged in some private discussion of their own.

Khaemwaset, though hungry, found that he could not eat. As night deepened and a sweet wind blew through the windows whose flax mats were still raised, his thoughts revolved around the scroll, surely even now resting on his desk, waiting for him. With an effort he tried to concentrate on Nubnofret's words.

"Your brother Si-Montu came today while you were out," she was saying, her ample arms across her table, beringed hands clasped around a wine cup. "He was disappointed to find you gone. I gave him beer and honey cakes and then he left."

Khaemwaset suppressed a sigh. He knew that she did not approve of Si-Montu, considering him loud and rude, but her true criticism was that he had married beneath him. "What did he want?" he asked mildly. "I hope you made him welcome, Nubnofret."

There was a small silence. Nubnofret removed her rings, considered them, and replaced them with deliberation. Hori signalled for more bread.

"I am not ill-mannered, Khaemwaset," she rebuked him. "Your brother wanted an afternoon with you, drinking in the garden. That was all."

Khaemwaset felt a rare rebellion flare in him. "He may have married the daughter of a Syrian ship's captain and thus disqualified himself as a prince in line for the throne," he said evenly, "but he is a good and honest man and I love him. I would have enjoyed his company."

"I like Uncle Si-Montu," Sheritra's light voice broke in with uncharacteristic defiance. She was looking directly at her mother, her colour high, her hands working in her linens. "He always brings me something strange when he comes, and he talks to me as though I had some intelligence. Ben-Anath is beautiful, and shy like me. I think the story of their meeting and falling in love and marrying against Grandfather's wishes is wonderful."

"Well if you expect to meet someone and have him fall in love with you, my girl, you will have to take yourself in hand!" Nubnofret retorted, cruelly but rightly interpreting the longing in her daughter's tone. "Men are not attracted to plain women, no matter how clever they are."

Sheritra's flush deepened. Her hand stole into Hori's and she looked down. Khaemwaset gestured, and the servants began to clear away the debris of the meal.

"Send Bakmut to me when you retire," he said to his daughter, "and I will come and talk. Why don't you and Hori take a walk around the garden?"

"Thank you, Father," she replied, and rising, her hand still clutching Hori's, she turned to Nubnofret. "I apologize for displeasing you yet again, Mother," she said stiffly. "If you wish I will eat dinner alone in my rooms tomorrow so that I may not interfere with your digestion." She and Hori were gone before Nubnofret could make a comment.

Khaemwaset smiled inwardly in spite of his sympathy. Sheritra had a streak of stubborness in her, and had managed the last word. Nevertheless, he reprimanded Nubnofret. "If you cannot accept Sheritra as she is," he said coldly, "I will consider sending her to our estate at Ninsu for a while. You hurt her more than she will admit. In the Fayum she will be near Pharaoh's harem, which doubtless contains women with more sympathy than her own mother. Sunero is a good agent. His family would be happy to keep Sheritra for a while."

Nubnofret's shoulders slumped. "I am sorry, my brother," she said. "There is something about her that raises my ire no matter how I try to conceal it. I want her to be beautiful, to be sought-after . . ." She slapped her palms against the table and stood, drawing her floating yellow linens around her. "I may not like Si-Montu for his uncouth ways but I agree with my daughter. His romance with Ben-Anath set my heart fluttering as well. Why am I never able to admit my agreement?" She hesitated, and Khaemwaset had the feeling that she wished to kneel and put her arms about him, but she only smiled faintly, clicked her fingers at a servant girl who had dropped some scraps, and sailed out of the room.

Khaemwaset sat on briefly, unaware for a time that the musicians had stopped playing and were waiting to be dismissed. I will not examine the scroll until I have visited Sheritra, he thought. I do not want to begin what will surely be a painstaking investigation, only to be interrupted. Perhaps a turn around the fountain would be in order, and then a quick glance at the messages from the Delta. There is no point in bathing now. He got up, and his harpist coughed quietly. Startled, Khaemwaset let them go, then walked through into his public reception room on his way to the garden. But somehow, instead, his feet took him to the side door, the passage that ran behind the main rooms to the sleeping quarters, and from there to his own rooms.

The scroll lay alone on the polished sheen of the desk, a safe distance from the alabaster lamp that customarily illuminated Khaemwaset's night work. Penbuy was thorough and careful. At a word, the guard on the door closed it, and Khaemwaset was alone with his find.

Folding his arms he approached the desk, paused, began to pace around it, his eyes never leaving the delicate thing in its shroud of fresh white linen. Would it unroll easily, or break as he tried to flatten it? His fingers itched, yet a reluctance was on him, a shrinking from whatever the moment when he sat and touched it might bring. The night was quiet. An occasional burst of laughter floated to him very faintly from his neighbour's garden where, he presumed, they were entertaining guests. A brief impurity in the oil of the larger lamp in its stand by the far corner made the flame spit and crackle before settling to a steady cone once more. If I wait any longer I will still be here at dawn, Khaemwaset told himself irritably. Sit, you fool! But for a few seconds more he hovered, fighting the fear of disappointment if the scroll should prove mundane, fighting the fear of something else, something unnameable. Then he pulled out his chair and removed Penbuy's protecting linen.

He was struck again by the scroll's pristine appearance. No mark of age or dust was on it. It had obviously been handled with exemplary care, both by the prince himself and by his embalmers. Khaemwaset touched it with the same reverence.

Slowly he eased it open. It moved resiliently, with no sign of a tendency to crack. Indeed, Khaemwaset came to the end of it unexpectedly, let it go, and watched it roll up again with bated breath lest his mistake should cost him the contents. But it simply rustled on the desk then lay still.

So short! Khaemwaset thought, and the writing still so black. He pulled the lamp closer. I need Penbuy and his palette to take down my reading as I go. I will use him tomorrow. Tonight I just want to read it over.

He began to unroll it once more, both hands under the jet black characters, and was soon mystified. The hieroglyphs were like nothing he had ever seen before. They seemed to be the primitive forerunners of the present formal Egyptian script, but so ancient that their vague familiarity was a deception. The wording was in two halves, and when he had perused the first half he returned to the beginning, first getting up to go into his library and bring back a palette, pen and ink. Painstakingly he copied each character, and underneath he placed a possible meaning. The work was laborious and his concentration sharpened until he was unaware of his surroundings, the frown on his face, even the presence of his body. Not for a long time had he been so challenged, and excitement flowed through him like fine wine.

Someone knocked on the door. He did not hear. The knock came again and he shouted "Go away!" without lifting his head. Bakmut opened and bowed.

"Many apologies, Prince," she said, "but the Princess is now on her couch and begs you to come and say goodnight."

Surprised, Khaemwaset looked at the waterclock beside his chair. It showed him that two hours had gone by since he had begun work.

"I cannot come immediately, Bakmut," he replied. "In half an hour I will be there. Tell Sheritra to wait."

Bakmut bowed again and withdrew. The door clicked shut, but Khaemwaset did not notice. His head was down.

Soon he had several sentences roughed out, even though their meaning still eluded him. A hieroglyphic symbol could represent the syllable of a word or a complete word in itself, or a whole concept encapsulated in the one sign, and the signs themselves, though superficially recognizable, were ambiguous. He played with combinations, covering the papyrus on his palette with his own thin sure script, but when he had exhausted all the possibilities he still had no idea what he was seeing.

He began to whisper the words, pointing with the end of the pen as he went, thinking that they might as well have been ancient Assyrian for all the sense they made. But they did have a familiar cadence that puzzled him. He started again, this time half chanting. There was definitely a rhythm inherent in the sentences. He had done all he could on the first half of the scroll, where there was a break before the fine black lettering began again.

Falling silent, it occurred to him suddenly that the rhythm was familiar because the words were the building blocks of a spell, and as every magician knew, spells had a particular flow to them, when chanted, that poetry did not have. I have been singing a spell of some kind, he thought, sitting back with a shudder of apprehension. That was stupid of me, to voice and thus give power to something that I do not understand. I have no idea what just came out of my mouth.

He waited a moment while he came fully to himself, his gaze travelling the quiet room. The small lamp on his desk was guttering, its oil almost gone. The larger one still sent a steady flame upward, but it would not for long if the wick was not trimmed. The deep, restful silence of night had thickened throughout the house and Khaemwaset once again consulted the waterclock and was shocked. In three hours it would be dawn.

Hurriedly wrapping the scroll in the clean linen he rushed out, making his way quickly to Sheritra's suite. The door was ajar and a lamp still burned within, casting a pale light into the passage. Khaemwaset eased the door fully open. Bakmut had fallen asleep waiting for him on a cushion just inside the threshold. Stepping over her he crept to the further room. Sheritra lay curled in a bundle of disordered sheets, breathing lightly. The scroll she had been reading while she waited for him had fallen to the floor. Khaemwaset stood over her, ashamed. This is the second time lately that I have let you down, my Little Sun, he thought sadly. For all my talk, I am little better than your mother. I am so sorry.

He made his way back to the office. The scroll still lay where he had left it, an innocuous beige cylinder amid the turmoil of his attempts at translation. Nothing in the room had changed. Well, whatever the spell I inadvertently chanted, it has had no effect on me or my surroundings, he told himself with relief. It is probably nothing more than a recipe for the relief of constipation, sewn to the hand of a man who suffered that malady all his life and feared that he might go on suffering it in the world to come if he did not have his precious panacea with him.

Khaemwaset smiled to himself, but the unspoken joke did not touch the sense of depression and guilt lying like a weight around his heart. I am the greatest historian in Egypt, he thought, sobering. If I cannot translate this scroll, no one can. It is no use showing it to any of my colleagues, though I may try, for their knowledge is not as wide as mine. Besides . . . He picked up the scroll and moved through into the library, carrying the lamp with him. Besides, they would want to know where I got it. Penbuy was right. I am a thief, albeit a well-intentioned one. Let him copy it swiftly and then I will sew it back on the prince's fingers. I will leave the work on the second half of it until the copy is complete. I am too tired and too frustrated to attempt it now. And too afraid? his mind mocked as he closed the lid of the chest where he had laid the scroll. You were lucky, chanting a spell you did not understand. The second half might bring a demon, or a death in the family, if you are so stupid again.

He desperately needed sleep, but he had one chore to perform before he could fall onto his couch and take refuge in unconsciousness. The spell he had sung haunted him with its unknown consequences, and he knew he must protect himself from any damage he might have done. Locking the library door behind him, he opened the chest where he kept his medicines. It was full of carefully labelled boxes and jars. He withdrew a box, and out of it he took a dry scarab beetle. The dark scarabs were useful for certain common maladies and he had dozens of them stored, but for his purpose tonight he needed the glittering, irridescent golden scarab that lay on his palm refracting the light.

Taking a knife, he gently removed its head and pried off its wings, putting the body in a small copper urn. Clumsily, for usually he had an assistant present to do such things, he lit a piece of charcoal in the portable grate, covered the dried corpse with a little water from the jug that was always kept filled by Ib, and, while it came to the boil, he unlocked another chest and drew forth a small sealed jar, breaking the hard red wax with reluctance. The oil of the apnent serpent was fearsomely expensive and hard to acquire.

Getting down an alabaster cup he laid in it the wings and head, and murmuring the proper incantations, covered them with the oil. The water was now boiling. For a few moments he watched the almost weightless body of the insect bob and churn, then he lifted it out with a pair of tongs, his mouth forming the continuation of the spell, and laid it in a bath of olive oil. Carefully he tipped the water over the charcoal, which hissed and steamed. In the morning he would complete the spell that would drive away any sorcery or evil incantation by combining the two oils with their contents and drinking the resulting mixture. He would have done so at once, so immediate was his anxiety, but the segments of the scarab had to steep for the required number of hours before being ingested, in order to provide the proper guard.

Khaemwaset was by now so fatigued that he re-locked the chests and at last the library door in a haze, and was almost staggering as he made his way through into his sleeping quarters. They were in darkness. He knew that the night slave lay just outside the door, on a straw palette in the passage, but he did not bother to rouse him. Feeling his way, Khaemwaset reached the couch, pulled off his kilt, kicked off his sandals and collapsed under the sheets that smelled faintly of the lotus water in which they were rinsed. He was asleep immediately.

In the morning, after his ablutions, prayers and a breakfast eaten in the blessed privacy of his own quarters, he made his way to the library. Taking new charcoal he once more lit a small fire and, continuing by memory the spell he had begun the night before, he poured the scarab's body in its bath of oil into the cup that held the head and wings. He no longer felt hounded or afraid. Setting the cup above the charcoal, he waited for the oils to boil. He knew that in order for the spell to achieve its maximum protection he must abstain from sexual intercourse for seven days. The practice of magic often required such strictures, and many of his fellows found them irksome, but a week without sex meant little to Khaemwaset.

The oils were now boiling, sending the slightly bitter aroma of the apnent serpent into the air. Taking the tongs, he removed the cup and placed it on a ledge to cool a little, leaving the charcoal to burn itself out. The concoction had to be drunk very hot and he kept a close watch on it to make sure it did not lose its heat too far.

Then, after chanting aloud the last of the spell, he took the cup and rapidly drank, feeling the now heavy body of the scarab slide on the oil down his throat. I have undone my foolishness of last night, he thought with a light heart as he went back into the office and began to gather up the pile of papyrus sheets on which he had worked. Penbuy can file these scribblings with his copy of the scroll but I will not give up my attempt to translate it. No ancient writings have beaten me yet and this one will be no exception. "Penbuy!" he called, knowing his scribe would by now be waiting outside the door to conduct the day's business. "You can come in. What letters have arrived from the Delta?"

When he had finished dictating the necessary replies, Khaemwaset remembered that he must make his peace with his daughter and went in search of her. He found her in the small antechamber that led to the rear entrance to the house, watching the house snake drinking the milk that was always placed ready for it. She greeted him with a smile.

"I think he is grateful," she commented. "When he is finished he pauses and looks about, if someone is near. If not he merely slithers away. I know, because I sometimes hide to observe him."

Khaemwaset kissed her smooth forehead. "I must apologize for last night, Sheritra," he said contritely. "I became absorbed in some work and forgot all about you. I am not the most reliable of fathers, am I?"

"I forgive you," she said with a teasing solemnity, shaking a finger at him, "but to make up for it you will have to read to me tonight for twice as long. Oh Father," she went on. "I am not a child anymore, to fly into a rage or cry myself to sleep if I am sometimes overlooked. I understand perfectly."

But you do cry yourself to sleep sometimes, he thought, looking at her as her attention returned to the snake, still motionless with its muzzle in the white froth. Bakmut told me so during one of her reports to me on your progress. You cry at your own inadequacy, in anger at yourself. I understand you perfectly also. "I am planning a little escape today," he said. "I intend to steal away for a few hours and return just in time to swallow the first course of dinner. Will you join me?"

She grinned conspiratorially at him. "Mother will expect me to play her my lute lesson," she answered. "If I am not to be found she will have several choice things to say to me tomorrow." She pursed her lips. "Well, I am used to that. I would love to come with you, Father."

"Good. Meet me after the noon sleep, at the rear of the garden."

She nodded and squatted, for the snake had now raised its head and was lazily regarding her with its black, unblinking stare. Khaemwaset left them.

He and Sheritra got onto their litters at the garden gate a little after the noon sleep and, accompanied by Amek and four soldiers, set off for the site of the tomb. As they swayed through the northern districts of the city they talked of inconsequential things, happy to be in each other's company. Guiltily they smiled and laughed, and Khaemwaset thought how Sheritra looked almost pretty with her tinkling carnelian bracelets hugging the brown of her gesticulating arms and the black braids of her wig stirring against her graceful neck as she spoke.

Before long they were being dappled in the grey shade of the date palms whose tiny green fruit was just beginning to appear, and then Saqqara opened out before them above the short hill that gave the ruins such a lofty isolation.

As they came up to the tomb and alighted, Hori saw them and waved. Khaemwaset ordered the litter-bearers into the shade of the canopies and he and his children descended the steps and entered the welcome gloom of the first chamber. Penbuy, his duties in the office concluded, was already at work copying inscriptions. Khaemwaset's artists had set up their easels and were reproducing the beautiful paintings that covered almost every inch of the walls. Others were seated on the sandy floor, open chests beside them, laboriously making lists of the contents. At the door three men, with copper mirrors angled to catch the sunlight and direct it within, were standing patiently.

Sheritra drew in her breath. "But this is lovely!" she exclaimed. "Such detail! Grandfather should come and see!"

"It would only remind him of the crudity of his own artists," Hori rightly pointed out. "You will send him copies of the work being done, won't you, Father?"

"I always do." Khaemwaset took Sheritra's elbow. "Would you like to see the dead, my dearest?"

Sheritra was not squeamish. She nodded eagerly and, with her father on one side and Hori on the other, bent her head under the low lintel of the farther doorway.

Inside the light was softer, more diffused. The two sarcophagi bulked dimly, and Thoth was a dusky, authoritarian presence. The three approached the bodies. Sheritra said nothing. She merely leaned over each one and studied it.

"She is the Princess Ahura," Khaemwaset told her. "We do not know the Prince's name. Their son is not here, obviously. Perhaps when all the work is done we will know better."

"Poor things," Sheritra said softly. "Undoubtedly it is a wonderful thing, to sit under the sacred sycamore tree with the blessed dead in Osiris's kingdom, but, Father, I am more than glad that soon we will get on our litters and go home to Mother's superlative feast."

"Sheritra, you are such a greedy little thing!" Hori teased her. She replied lightly, and Khaemwaset listened to their banter without paying much attention to the words. His own glance had passed very carefully over the corpses. Nothing had changed. Even the ends of the threads that had bound the scroll to the prince's hand were curled as he remembered them yesterday. He was aware of a relief pooling through him like warm water, and was at a loss to explain it. He felt happy, boyish, full of fun.

"How long before the work is completed and the tomb can be re-sealed?" he asked Hori.

The young man considered. "It is hard to say," he replied. "It depends on the artists, of course. No repairs are necessary, so all should be ready for the offerings very soon."

"I think we should put the lids on the coffins," Khaemwaset said slowly. "It is not right for these two to lie open to the dust like this, and besides, if in the future thieves do get in, the lids will discourage them from pillaging the bodies for precious amulets."

Hori looked at him curiously, and Khaemwaset wondered if something strange was showing on his face or betraying itself in his voice.

"Very well," Hori agreed. "We take a risk, seeing that we do not know why they were not put in place originally, but our intentions are pure and will doubtless absolve us from any retribution from the dead."

Khaemwaset's bright mood began to fade. "We will leave you to your labour," he said to his son. "Remind Amek's men that the guard is to be maintained until the tomb is finally closed, will you, Hori? And make sure the fellahin get plenty of beer and vegetables. Their jobs are the hardest." He moved back towards the stronger light of the antechamber and the blessed, living white light of the direct sun shafting down the steps. "Sheritra," he called over his shoulder, "It is still too early to go home. Would you like a jaunt through the city? We can see what new baubles are on display in the markets."

"I suppose we might as well sin fully," she called back, and together they walked to the litters.

Instead of turning north to skirt the temples of the kings in the Ankh-tawy district, Khaemwaset ordered the bearers to veer south, cutting across the edge of the southern suburbs where most of the common foreigners lived and crossing the canal that was fed by the Nile and linked the temples of Hathor in the south and Ptah in the north. Khaemwaset had not bothered to include Ramose in his entourage, and it was sturdy Amek who called the warning to the increasingly thick crowds to give way and pay homage to the son of Pharaoh.

Soon the noise and stir of the Peru-nefer district began to assault their senses, and the narrow streets of riverside Memphis intersected around them, lined with two- and three-storey mud houses and shops and fronted by canopied stalls behind which the keepers shouted their wares. In spite of the crush of people, the braying of donkeys and the shrieks of naked children rolling in the dust and litter, Amek managed to keep a space of reverence around his royal charges.

Sheritra saw something that caught her eye and Khaemwaset ordered the litters halted. He watched her as she scrambled onto the street, her linens displaced and her sandals forgotten in the bottom of her litter. Sheritra rushed across to a stall piled with vases and oddly carved boxes that surely came from Alashia, judging by the weird sea creatures illustrated on them.

But once there her shyness took over and she hung back, arms folded, eyes on the display. Khaemwaset gestured to Amek, who went to her and discreetly asked what she was interested in, and, while she whispered and Amek haggled, Khaemwaset looked through the milling bodies to the river, glimpsed briefly and then lost again as the people moved.

He was enjoying himself. Nubnofret would be aghast if she knew that her daughter was standing in a public place amid the dust and offal, engaged in a purchase of insulting cheapness while beside her three men were reeling, drunk, onto the street from the inviting coolness of a beer-house.

Soon Sheritra came up to him, arms wrapped about an ugly, biliously green pot, a wide smile on her face. "It is a disgusting thing," she said breathlessly, "but I like it and I will make Bakmut fill it with blooms. Where are we going now?"

Khaemwaset ordered the litters turned homeward on the river road with a sense of regret. The afternoon had been worth the sharp words Nubnofret would rain on their heads. The road that followed the bank of the water was much wider than the city streets, and they were able to sway along side by side. The crowds were still plentiful but moved in a constant fashion, and their progress was faster.

They had crossed the bridge over the canal that led from the river to the watersteps of Ptah's temple when Khaemwaset, idly watching the weaving citizens ahead, suddenly stiffened and sat straight. A woman was striding away from him, her naked feet kicking up little puffs of dust. She was tall and supple-spined, moving with a confident, loose swing of her hips that caused those around her to step out of the way. Khaemwaset could not see her face. She held her head, with its cap of gleaming black hair, very high, and was not glancing to right or left. Her arms swung unselfconsciously, brushing her white-clad thighs, and on both wrists she was wearing twisted silver bracelets that resembled snakes.

"Look at that woman!" Sheritra called across to him, pointing. "That one, there! What presence she has, doesn't she, Father? Her walk is almost arrogant, in spite of the fact that she is wearing a very old-fashioned sheath and no sandals."

"Yes, I see her," Khaemwaset called back, hands clenched in his lap, neck craning to keep her in view. Her sheath was indeed old-fashioned. It followed the contours of her lithe body in white curves, beginning at her shoulder blades, clinging to the small of her back and ending at those flexing ankles. Khaemwaset's eyes travelled its length, noting how her firm buttocks under the gleaming linen were clenching and loosening, clenching and loosening . . . She had cut a slit up one side of the tight garb in order to stride out, and he watched her long brown leg appear, straighten lazily, then disappear, only to fill his vision once more.

"Is that a wig, do you think, or is it her own hair?" Sheritra was saying. "In either case, no one wears their locks like that any more. Mother would not approve of *her*!"

No, she would not, Khaemwaset thought, his throat tight. There is a controlled ferocity about that walk that would antagonize Nubnofret immediately. "Move faster!" he shouted at his bearers. "I want to catch up to that person. Amek, run ahead and stop her!" Why are they not all staring at her? he wondered. He watched Amek struggle through the crowd as the pace of his bearers quickened, but with a sinking in his stomach he knew that his captain would not catch up with her. Even as he became aware of his own nails digging into his palms and released the frenetic grip on himself, she was swallowed up and was gone. Amek came back. "I am sorry, Prince," he said. "For all her grace, she ate up the ground."

So Amek had noticed also. Khaemwaset shrugged. "Do not worry," he replied, "It was just a passing fancy, and we must be getting home." Sheritra's eyes were on him in speculation. He glanced down at the white marks on his palms then looked across at her. "I have been more curious than circumspect," he said, and she smiled.

"One may appreciate beauty without any blame," she comforted him. "I too saw that she was lovely."

For once the self-deprecation in his daughter's voice merely annoyed Khaemwaset. He grunted, barked a loud order and twitched the curtains of his litter closed, riding to his front gate and the challenge of his gatekeeper in his mud hut with eyes closed and a growing sense of loss.

Chapter 5

'Oh Man, who givest way to thy passions, what
is thy condition?
He cries out, his voice reaches to heaven.
O Moon, accuse him of his crimes.'

As he and Sheritra moved stealthily through the house, Khaemwaset could hear the servants chattering as they lit the lamps in the garden. "We are both filthy, and reek of the bazaar," Sheritra whispered. "Do we appear like this but on time, or do we wash and be late?"

"We wash," Khaemwaset answered firmly. "Tardiness is not as high on your mother's list of crimes as dirtiness. Be quick though, Sheritra."

They parted. In Khaemwaset's quarters Kasa was waiting, his arms full of towels, clean linen and appropriate jewellery laid out on the couch. "The Princess is furious," he said in answer to Khaemwaset's brusque query. "She wanted to know where you had gone. The Princess Sheritra did not play her lute today." Khaemwaset was already on his way to the bath house with Kasa padding behind. "I know," he said. "These little escapes of mine are scarcely worth it, Kasa. Nubnofret's wrath is a terrible thing when roused. Wash me quickly."

Before long he was stepping from the increasing gloom of the house into the warm evening glow of the garden. Sheritra was already there, sitting with her knees drawn up under a plain blue gown, her encircling arms hung with several lapis bracelets and a lapis circlet resting on her brow. Her face was unpainted. She was talking to Hori who was lounging in the grass beside her, his hair damp from his own bath. Khaemwaset approached them through the soft twilight, taking the chair behind which a servant was bowing. He had time to do no more than greet his son before Nubnofret appeared from between the pillars, a servant bearing a tray of delicacies behind her. Khaemwaset took a clove of garlic steeped in honey, aware of Nubnofret's frozen face as she sank gracefully into the chair beside him.

Sheritra was giving Hori a spirited account of their day. "And we saw the most extraordinary woman!" Sheritra said. "Wasn't she, Father? Sort of arrogant but easy, if you know what I mean." Nubnofret turned quizzical and rather too sharp eyes on her husband, and Khaemwaset found himself suddenly unwilling to discuss the creature who had paced ahead of him, tall and supple and magnetic, and had left a tiny bleeding scratch in his mind, like the swipe of a cat's claw. "She was indeed unusual," he agreed. "Nubnofret, how much longer is dinner going to be?"

"Not more than a few minutes," his wife replied, obviously annoyed, "though I am surprised that having come home late you wish to rush to your food."

For a little while longer the family shared their news in the rapidly darkening garden, while the lights in the house began to cast pale beams over the velvet flowers and the crystal movement of the fountain became a grey cascade. The fish in the ornamental pond at the farther end rose to the surface and made little eddies as they snapped at the mosquitoes that swarmed over them, and the monkeys shambled close to the group and squatted, their eyes on the tray and their furry hands outstretched.

Finally Nubnofret relented. Nodding at Ib as the household's Senior Steward, she rose, and the others followed suit.

I wonder what that woman is doing tonight. The thought came to Khaemwaset without warning as he mounted the few wide steps between his pillars and turned towards the wonderful mix of aromas blowing from the dining room where the musicians were already playing. Has she a husband, and are they walking together in their garden, enjoying the night breeze? Does she live with her parents, perhaps, a person of inscrutable aloofness, scorning men, even now alone in her apartments while her family entertains some eager suitor who will never have the privilege of touching her? No, his thoughts ran on as he took his place in the pile of cushions. She is not a girl. Many suitors have come and gone but she is not interested. She is a commoner who knows that her worth is greater than all of them, and she waits for a prince.

Nubnofret was settling herself beside him, and for a moment Khaemwaset felt the lash of her tongue. "I am used to being deserted by you on any occasion you might find boring or not necessary for good governmental relations," she hissed, "but I will not have you subverting my authority with Sheritra or encouraging her to shirk her duties in this house! I will not have you teaching her that self-indulgence is acceptable."

Looking into her fiery eyes, he wanted to explain that he had been trying to apologize to Sheritra for letting her down the night before, but he could not make the effort. Not at the moment. "I am really sorry, Nubnofret," he said quietly, "and you are right. I will not argue with you." She blinked and sat back, her expression softening. She had obviously expected a sharp retort from him. He kissed her softly on the cheek and suddenly she took his face in both her hands and pressed her full mouth against his.

"You drive me to distraction," she said throatily, "but I love you all the same." She tasted of sweet honeyed wine, and her tongue had flicked his own.

In spite of his intention to devote the rest of the evening to his family, Khaemwaset found his thoughts circling the mysterious woman while his mouth spoke of inconsequential things. He saw her heels rise, her calves tighten as she walked. He saw her white sheath rub against her outer thigh. It is ridiculous, he told himself. Egypt is full of beautiful women of every nationality. I see them every time I leave home, enter a temple, move through the palace at Pi-Ramses. Why this woman? He had no answer, and in the end dismissed her from his mind with the energy of years of self-discipline. He had his cup refilled for the fourth time, noticing that for once Nubnofret was matching him, and did his best to join his children's light-hearted conversation but the wine was better, rich and cool, and in the end he fell silent and let it lead him where it would.

Later, as he slid rapidly towards sleep, he was aware that he had had more wine than was good for him. Drunkenness was a pleasant pastime. Everyone indulged themselves, but Khaemwaset knew that he was becoming too old, at thirty-seven, to function well the following day if he had imbibed too freely the night before. Nubnofret will have a sore head tomorrow too, he thought, mildly annoyed with himself as his eyes closed and he pulled the sheets up over his shoulders. I drank from guilt and she from irritation, I suppose. One should only drink from joy. That was his last coherent thought.

He dreamed, and in the dream he was sitting on the grass in a

Delta orchard, under the full weight of a noon sun, but there was no discomfort, only a feeling of tremendous well-being. Good, he thought in his dream, closing his eyes and lifting his face. This is an omen of great pleasure to come. The trees around him were heavy with ripe fruit, and now and then he could hear the soft thud of an apple detaching itself and falling to the ground. For a while he remained thus, in a bath of contentment, not wondering, for this was a dream, why the scent of blossom was so strong at harvest time.

Then another awareness began. His penis was stirring, swelling under his plain linen kilt, becoming fully hard. Another good omen, his dream self thought happily, opening its eyes. My possessions will multiply. Through the glare of sunlight he thought he caught a flicker of movement in the shade where the trees stood dusty and motionless. White linen, the suspicion of a brown leg with foot pointed, a hand sliding around a trunk, the fingers long and graceful, caressing the bark. I am as hard as that wood, he whispered, and full of sap. Full of sap . . . He was dizzy with pleasure and the tension of his erection, his eyes on those fingers stroking, pressing, exploring . . . He woke with his knees drawn up, both hands around his penis. He was oozing sweat. His sheets lay in a crumpled pile on the floor.

Groggily, with an unpleasant lurching in his head, he staggered up. Damn the wine, he thought, grabbing a handful of linen and winding it around his waist. He groped his way to the door and stepped out into the passage. He had no idea what time it was, but it felt very late. The house was silent. Stumbling a little, he made his way to Nubnofret's suite and let himself in over the snoring body of her guard. Wernuro was also fast asleep, limbs akimbo on her mat by the door. Khaemwaset went around her and straight through into his wife's bedroom.

She too was snoring gently, her sleeping gown open to the waist, sheets bunched around her knees. This is not Nubnofret, he thought dimly as he bent over her. Not my fastidious wife. This is Nubnofret my drunken wife. The words increased the sexual urgency that had impelled him there. He eased clumsily onto the couch beside her, pushing the thin linen away, and his lips closed over her nipple. It hardened immediately and she moaned, pushing against his mouth. He felt her legs untangle, her thighs part.

"Khaemwaset?" she murmured.

"Yes," he whispered back. "Are you awake? Am I welcome, Nubnofret?"

For answer she took his hand and placed it between her legs, her head coming up to receive his kiss. Her body smelt of the heavy perfume she liked and her flesh was hot and yielding. He made love to her in the daze of his dream and his need, hearing her cry out her own climax moments before his own exploded. He collapsed onto her, trembling and wet, but she went on crying. "Nubnofret?" he grunted, puzzled and disoriented, and she pushed him roughly away.

"That's Sheritra," she said tersely, and slid out from under him, reaching for her gown at the same time. Dazedly he fumbled to tie the sheet once more around his waist, and they hurried into the passage.

Wernuro and the guard were now awake, Wernuro struggling sleepily to light a lamp. Nubnofret brushed past them. Khaemwaset's eyes were on the tumble of russet hair down her back, the swift padding of her naked feet under the floating white gown. Naked feet, he thought, suddenly confused. Naked feet. Sunlight. Apple orchard. My dream. Like a blow he knew then that the woman who had been lurking behind the laden tree in his dream was the same one that he and Sheritra had pursued that afternoon, and he had just rendered the protecting spell of the morning null and void by making love to Nubnofret. How did it happen? he asked himself, aghast. To me of all people! Such loss of control is inexcusable. I am unguarded, we are all defenceless.

Nubnofret was turning into Sheritra's quarters just as Bakmut was coming out. The servant bowed. "What is wrong?" Nubnofret asked sharply. "A nightmare, I think," the girl answered. "I am on my way to fetch a little wine for the Princess, to calm her. She is fully awake now."

Khaemwaset did not wait. Stepping past the two women, he strode to Sheritra's couch. his daughter was sitting up, arms about her knees in a characteristic gesture, her face pale. When she saw him she held out her arms and he sank onto the couch while she buried her face in his shoulder.

"What is it, Little Sun?" he asked soothingly. "It's all right now. I'm here."

"I don't really know," Sheritra replied, a quaver in her voice though she was trying to keep it steady. "I never have bad dreams, Father, you know that, but tonight, just now . . ." She shuddered and lifted her head. "It was something terrible, fearsome, not a person or an animal but a feeling, like something growing behind me, without eyes or ears but aware of me as prey, something malevolent to devour me."

Nubnofret had seated herself and taken Sheritra's hand. "Bakmut will be here in a moment with the wine," she said reassuringly, "and you will drink and sleep again. It was only a dream, my dear. See, your father and I are here and your things are all around you, safely and sanely. Hear that owl, hunting? You are at home in your own bed, and all is well." She was stroking the pallid hand as she spoke, smiling at both of them. Khaemwaset was overcome with tenderness for her. He put his free arm around her shoulders.

"I'm sorry to have disturbed you," Sheritra said. "I did wrong today, Mother, and this may very well be the punishment of my conscience."

For once Nubnofret did not take advantage of the statement. "I do not think so," she said. "Here is Bakmut. Drink the wine, and we will stay with you until you fall asleep again."

Sheritra's plain features relaxed. Taking the cup, she drank deeply, then burrowed down into her pillow. "Tell me a story, Father," she asked drowsily, and, with an amused glance at his wife, he began to do so, but he had only recited a few sentences when Sheritra's breathing became regular and her eyes ceased to flutter under the pale lids. He and Nubnofret crept out and Bakmut closed the door behind them.

"We used to do this when the children were very small," Nubnofret said to Khaemwaset as they walked back down the passage. "Although Sheritra was so frightened, I felt almost young again." She smiled at him wistfully out of a welter of disordered hair.

"You feel old, Nubnofret?" he asked, startled. "But you never . . ."

"I never give any indication of my years?" she finished for him. "That does not mean that I do not feel them, Khaemwaset. I am not altogether the coldly efficient mistress of a royal household, you know." Khaemwaset looked for accusation in her face, but there was none. She was staring up at him hesitantly, like a young girl longing for a kiss but too afraid to make the first move, love in her still sleep-swollen eyes. He took her in his arms. "Will you stay with me tonight?" she begged. "I have not felt the warmth of your body beside me for so long." Again he looked for recrimination and found none.

"I would like that also," he agreed, and thought to himself, The incantation is destroyed. What harm can it do? Yet as he lay on his side under her sheets and felt her fit her body around his, he saw again the woman on the street, and all at once the dark house around and over him seemed full of the foreboding of Sheritra's nightmare. He fell asleep with a prayer on his lips.

In the morning he had a lingering headache and a huge fatigue. He and the rest of the family, subdued and quiet, gathered briefly in the coolness of the reception hall before scattering to the day's duties.

"I am going to look over the long-neglected plans for the Apis burials, and then I am going to spend some time in the temple of Ptah," Khaemwaset told them. Nubnofret's answer was a pair of raised eyebrows. She kissed him on the neck and drifted away. Khaemwaset noticed with amusement that Sheritra was following her dutifully.

"I will spend the day at the tomb," Hori announced, "but this evening I have been invited to a party in the foreigners' quarters. I shall see you at dinner, Father."

Khaemwaset's eyes followed his easy swing and perfectly muscled legs, then he turned away with a sigh. What it was, to be young and handsome, rich and sought-after. He was sure that Hori's horoscope, day after day, showed every third as full of luck, while his own was becoming increasingly ambiguous.

Back in his office, Penbuy placed a load of official correspondence on the desk and went to the floor in readiness for dictation. Khaemwaset, with a regretful glance at the shaft of brilliant late spring sunlight splattering the floor from the clerestory windows high above, opened the first with a mutinous jerk. After I have made a special offering to Ptah and begged him for his beneficent protection for this house I will take a jaunt on the river, he promised himself. I will think of nothing but the wind on my skin and the birds in the thickets.

Once the correspondence had been taken care of he summoned his architect, and together they spent a couple of hours over the plans for the Apis bulls. The architect's work had been very satisfactory, and Khaemwaset gave orders for the excavations to begin before he retired to his quarters for a light lunch, a careful wash, and a change of clothes. Then with Amek and Ib he got onto his barge and was rowed the short distance to the canal down which Ptah's sacred boat was floated from his temple during times of festivity.

Leaving the barge at this point, Khaemwaset walked beside the canal, under Ptah's sacred sycamores, to the god's watersteps and from there along the hot granite paving between the two massive pylons and into the outer court, his small train of servants following behind.

The court was comfortably crowded with worshippers. Incense rose above the pillars of the inner court in a barely visible cloud, and the murmur of the singers and the rattle of their systrums could be heard. Khaemwaset removed his sandals and handed them to Ib. He had brought his favourite turquoise necklace with its Eye of Horus counterpoise as an offering to the god whom he served full-time for three months of every year. Holding it to his naked chest he walked towards the inner court, careful not to nudge the common people who were standing praying, eyes closed and arms extended. Amek and Ib had retired to the wall where there was shade.

Khaemwaset stepped through to the inner court. Here there were only priests and musicians. The worship of Ptah went on all day, from the time the sanctuary was opened at dawn and the god fed and clothed to sunset, when the small, dark secrecy of his home was closed and locked. For a moment Khaemwaset paused, caught up in the ritual of song and the praise of the dancer's bodies, before he found a space and began his prostrations.

Both inner and outer court were unroofed, and the sun beat down upon Khaemwaset as he rose and yet again laid himself face down on the sandy floor. He prayed the words of tradition first, extolling the smiling god who had created all things, and then stood and begged Ptah to remember that he, Khaemwaset, was an honest and faithful servant who needed the eye of the god turned upon his household because of his own foolishness. He prayed long and earnestly, but reassurance did not come. Instead, he gradually began to feel that he had made a mistake, that though the god would accept his gift, Khaemwaset should be praying elsewhere. It is Thoth whom you serve in the pursuits closest to your heart, the thought came. It is Thoth whom you have wronged with your greed for knowledge and more knowledge, for the power only the gods may possess. Are you afraid to bare your soul in this way before Thoth instead of Ptah? For Thoth is more understanding but less forgiving. His servants are the only ones who know the ecstasy and the terror of his wisdom.

In the end Khaemwaset capitulated. Approaching the closed sanctuary he ceremoniously passed his gift to the priest on duty there and began to thread his way back to the massive open doors that led to the outer court through the swaying, chanting dancers. He was about to pass through the gloom of shade the door cast when he saw her.

She had been standing behind a group of petitioners and was in the act of turning away towards the pylons. Khaemwaset caught a brief glimpse of her face—confident, withdrawn, straight nose, wide black-kohled eyes under a fringe of gleaming hair—before her back was towards him and she was striding away with that indolent yet purposeful tread. She was wearing a yellow sheath, still of a body-hugging, old-fashioned cut that accentuated every curve, but over it billowed a transparent white ankle-length cloak rimmed in gold.

Khaemwaset watched it float behind her sandalled feet, then he sprang after her. The crowd had thickened, and it seemed to him that everyone milling in the flaming hot air had all at once moved to place themselves between himself and his quarry with a malicious purpose. "Out of my way!" He jostled and pushed, heedless now of who prayed and who simply stood in wonder at Ptah's mighty edifice. "Get out of my way!" An indignant murmur went up, and the temple guards who always stood at intervals around the walls began to move forward. "Don't you see her?" Khaemwaset shouted to Ib and Amek who were hurrying towards the disturbance. "You, Amek, you saw her yesterday. Run after her! Run!"

The guards had recognized him and had halted, irresolute. Khaemwaset plunged between the pylons and out onto the wide courtyard before the watersteps. He looked up and down. But there was no sign of her. He ran to the edge of the courtyard and peered along the south side of the wall, but the expanse was empty. The north side was also deserted. The canal rippled quietly, blue and serene in the afternoon furnace. Trees lined it, and with a rage he seldom felt, Khaemwaset knew that his quarry, oblivious to the stir she had created, had simply walked in under the trees for their shade on her way to . . . Where? Where? Ib and Amek came up to him, panting and bewildered, and Khaemwaset grimly held on to his temper, knowing that none of it was their fault.

"Did you see her?" he asked Amek. Amek eyed him as though he had gone mad.

"Yes, Highness," he said, "but it was not possible for us to catch up with her. You were closer than we were."

"All right." Khaemwaset closed his eyes and winced. "All right. I want you to go home and turn out all the soldiers you can spare. Put them in civilian clothing. Describe this woman to them. Tell them to search Memphis, but discreetly. No one in the family is to know anything about it, do you understand?" They nodded, still confused, but he did not care. No matter what, he was determined to stand face to face with the creature who had invaded his dreams. It is as though someone has slipped a philtre into my wine, he told himself, or conjured a spell of compulsion on me without my knowledge. I feel drugged with her, each sighting immediately translated into a thirst for more, like poppy juice to those in pain. Is some fellow magician trying his strength on me for a joke?

His servants were still staring at him indecisively and he turned away from them, half running beside the canal, eyes searching the welcoming deep shadows under the forest of trees and trimmed grass to his right, but knowing, knowing, that she was not there. His barge still rocked peacefully where the canal met the Nile. His captain was squatting beside the ramp, talking with the steersman, and both men rose and bowed as he came up to them.

Barely acknowledging their reverence he hurried onto the deck. "Take me home!" he commanded. "Quickly!" They sprang to do his bidding.

During the short ride to his watersteps he sat tensely in the small, airless cabin, trying to control the fever of impatience that gripped him. He had forgotten his plan to spend the rest of the afternoon on the river. All he wanted to do was pass the time in the best way possible until his servants began to come to him with news.

Once off the barge, he went straight to his office. Penbuy was there with one of his junior scribes, making fair copies of the rough work they were doing in the tomb, and Khaemwaset asked them to occupy themselves elsewhere. Penbuy shot him a curious glance but of course obeyed, and the door closed discreetly behind them. Khaemwaset began to pace. There were a dozen tasks he could address and he knew that there was the healing of distraction in them, but for once he lacked the power to do what was best. I have no doubt that eventually I will find her, he thought, arms folded as he wandered the large, quiet room. If necessary I will employ the Memphis police. And I also have no doubt that when I do, she will turn out to be a disappointment. Dreams that become reality always do. She will be either very simple, an unlettered commoner without intelligence, uncouth and loud-mouthed, or a spoiled bitch from some minor nobleman's household, a woman with social pretensions, strident and tasteless.

He paced until he grew tired, then he left the office and went out into the garden, lying on a flax mat with a cushion under his head in the shade and trying to doze. His gardener could be heard somewhere near the watersteps at the front of the house, talking to his apprentice as he tended the shrubs that lined the path. The monkeys, not far from him, snuffled and gibbered half-heartedly in the dragging stillness before sunset that never seemed to end. Birds dipped into the fountain and out again, refreshed, shaking their wings and piping deliriously.

After a while Khaemwaset heard someone approaching and sat up, every nerve instantly alert, but it was only Sheritra. She flung herself down beside him, her skin beaded with water, her long hair darkly roped over her shoulders. Bakmut had followed her and was standing some distance away. "Mother gave me as many chores as she could think of this morning," Sheritra said, her hands busy squeezing the water out of her hair, "but in the end she had to let me go, so I went for a swim. Spring is definitely over, isn't it, Father? The days are beginning to be uncomfortable and the crops everywhere are above the ground. What are you doing out here?"

Khaemwaset propped himself on one elbow and watched the water drain in clear rivulets past her neck and into her tiny cleavage. He had not intended to, but he said, "I saw the woman again. In the temple of Ptah."

Sheritra did not need to ask which woman. Her deft fingers went on sliding down the slick coils of hair. "Did you speak to her?"

"No." Khaemwaset began to pluck idly at the grass. "She was leaving the outer court when I noticed her. I had Amek and Ib with me but none of us could catch up to her. I have sent them to search, and I am waiting for word."

Sheritra called and Bakmut came forward, offering a comb. The girl took it, Bakmut retired just out of earshot, and Sheritra began to pull it through the thick tresses. Already wisps had dried and were curling and blowing about her face. Keeping her eyes fixed on the bathing birds, she said, "Why are you so determined to find her?"

Khaemwaset thought he felt a soft movement against the back of his hand, and looked down. There was nothing, but, unbidden, the memory of the little dancer with the skin complaint came back to him, the sudden shock of her mouth against his skin in gratitude. "I do not know," he confessed, "and that is the truth, Sheritra. I only know that I must look into her eyes and hear her voice before I can be at peace again."

Sheritra nodded sagely and fell to scooping up the rapidly drying droplets of water along her leg. "I hope you are disappointed," she said unexpectedly. Khaemwaset saw a blush bloom up her neck and give a reddish hue to her brown cheeks. "Why?" he enquired, though he knew, and marvelled at her perception. "Because if you are not disappointed, if she is anything at all like your image of her, your interest in her will grow." Khaemwaset was puzzled by the urgency in her tone.

"But even if it did," he objected, "what would be the harm? Many men have concubines and very happy families. What threat do you see, Little Sun?"

She did not respond in a girlish way to his attempt to cajole her with the meaning of her name, or his deliberate teasing emphasis. All at once she swung to face him directly and, though the blush was now fiery, she met his eyes. "You are not an emotional man, dear Father," she said. "You are always calm, always fair, always kind. I cannot imagine you in love with anyone other than Mother, though I can see you adding to your concubines on rare occasions." Now she dropped her gaze. "But only for a little variety, you understand, not to be disloyal in your heart to Mother. This woman . . ." She swallowed and forced herself to continue. "This woman already fills your thoughts. I can tell. I do not like it."

He was tempted to laugh at her description of him, her assessment of the situation. All girls saw their fathers as benevolent gods around whom their households revolved in the rightness of Ma'at, as beings of purity and awesome wisdom. There was a little of that attitude in Sheritra's view of him. But her fear was of something else, something a mature woman might sense, the threat of an overwhelming sandstorm that might scour away the fairness, the kindness, and release the lurking abandon she suspected lay beneath. Well, is there such a recklessness hidden within me, he wondered while he smiled at her gently, unknown even to myself? He had no answer, and did not know what "being in love" was like.

"She is a mystery, that's all," he replied after a moment. "Like scrolls in tombs or inscriptions waiting to be deciphered. When I have deciphered her and found her to be a disappointment, as so many of the ancient inscriptions are, I will be at peace. So you see, Sheritra, there is nothing to fret about."

She grinned at him, her solemn mood gone. "I had not looked at it in that way before," she said. "Good. In that case, have your adventure, Father, and tell me how it progresses. I must confess to being just a little intrigued myself." Picking up the comb, she gathered her towel around her and rose. "A new snake has taken to slithering in the back door," she went on, "and I am trying to make it welcome. Our usual resident is coiled up in a cool corner of the reception hall but I must lure the other from whatever garden rock he is sheltering under. A lot of house snakes bring good luck, don't they?"

He agreed and watched her amble away across the garden, her thin legs like a crane's, her shoulders hunched. Bakmut followed, and the garden was empty once more.

Khaemwaset got up, plunged his head under the fountain's steady coldness and took a turn around the house, greeting the servants he met, but he was not able either to take his belated excursion on the river or go into his quarters. Returning to his spot on the grass he sat numbly, his head eventually buzzing with the need for sleep, feeling jaded with self-disgust.

At last, as the sun westered and the light in the garden began to soften, Ib came to him. The man was grubby and tired. he bowed perfunctorily, his mouth rimmed in grey dust, his nostrils edged in sand that clung to his sweat. Khaemwaset bade him sit, and Ib sank thankfully to the grass. "You had better not let Nubnofret see you in that state," Khaemwaset said. "What news do you have?"

Ib shook his head, and Khaemwaset's heart sank. "Very little, Prince," the Steward admitted. "Thirty of us have been combing the streets and public places of the city all afternoon. Many people have seen this woman, but of those that have seen her, none has spoken with her." He eased off his wilted kilt and used it to rub his face. "And no one has any idea where she lives."

Khaemwaset pondered for a moment. "Thank you, Ib," he said at last. "Take whatever time you need to wash yourself, then organize the thirty into groups of five each. Write a watch for them of four hours each, rotating, and tomorrow they can begin again. One of them will eventually hear or see something." He felt Ib's disapproval and sent him into the house, but he himself sat on. I have wasted almost a whole day, he thought dismally. I have sat here like one of the insane, and what other response from Ib did I expect? Yes, Prince, we have found her, she is waiting for you in the reception hall? Khaemwaset hauled himself to his feet and stalked after Ib. The Steward was nowhere to be seen and Khaemwaset summoned Kasa, spent a delicious half hour standing in the bath house while his servant scrubbed him down and doused him with lotus water, then, freshly dressed, he went in search of his wife.

He found her in her quarters with her cosmetician, having her makeup renewed after the sleep. She was obviously pleased and not a little surprised to see him being admitted, and she swung round on her stool. Kohl glistened around her magnificent eyes. The lids had been swept with green paint and her lips freshly hennaed. She was wearing a loose cloak, open down the front and bunched loosely on her knees, and he was struck as he had not been in years by her luscious curves. "This is an odd time for you to be seeking me out!" she exclaimed, smiling. "Is something wrong, Khaemwaset?" He went to perch on the edge of her disordered couch. "Nothing at all," he said. "Are you busy now, Nubnofret? Would you like to take a turn in the barge before dinner, just as far as Peru-nefer, and sit on the deck? We could watch the sun set and play a little sennet?"

"I really shouldn't," she said hesitantly. "Mice have got into one of the granaries in the rear courtyard and spoiled the grain, and we will be short of bread. Our farm steward is coming shortly to take my order for more grain from the big granary, and I must supervise the laying of gazelles' dung to repulse the mice." She was making her excuses with regret, Khaemwaset saw.

"What do we have a kitchen steward for?" he objected. "Let him oversee the matter. You have trained them all well, Nubnofret. Let go for once."

She thought. Then, "You are right," she agreed. "Give me a little time to dress, my dear, and I will join you at the water-steps."

He did not really want to go on the river with her. He wanted to find an isolated, private spot and stand there, kneel there, lie there, until the moment when Ib came to him to say that the woman had been run to ground. But he knew the dangerous irrationality of that urge and fought it off determinedly. The river would be beautiful as Ra descended into the mouth of Nut, and it would make Nubnofret happy. The thought of making Nubnofret happy brought to him an engulfing guilt and he smiled, nodded and left her apartment quickly.

In the weeks that followed, Khaemwaset went through the motions of his duty with grim and iron determination, while his servants scoured the streets of Memphis. Khaemwaset forced himself to inspect the as yet barely begun excavations in the desert for the Apis mortuaries, and see to the dredging of several canals on his agricultural estate. No news of Pharaoh's labyrinthine marriage negotiations with the Khatti came from the Delta, and Khaemwaset was relieved. The last thing he wanted was to answer a summons to attend his father in Pi-Ramses when all his inward attention was fixed on the reports of his soldiers each evening.

His sleep was troubled. He dreamed of high winds that whipped the surface of the desert into a howling maelstrom of sand, of the Nile in a flood that spilled over Egypt and kept on pooling, lapping, eating inexorably mile after mile, of the cooking fires in his own kitchens that spread and grew until they towered, hungry and angry, over the whole city, lighting it with an ominous orange glow.

When the time came for the casting of his and the family's horoscopes for the coming month, he performed the task fearfully, with more than his usual meticulous attention to every detail. The prognosis for himself was very bad. According to this, he thought as he wrote the results at his desk, I should take to my couch and not stir until the month of Hathor is over. I do not see death here, or physical accident, merely bad luck. Merely. He chuckled without a trace of humour. Nubnofret's signs for the month were much as they always were—no more than slight tremors in an even flow that seldom changed—and Hori's, always so strongly fortunate, showed a mild dip in the number of days. Sheritra's horoscope was almost as bad as Khaemwaset's own.

When he had finished the work, which had taken him a whole day, he pushed it hastily into a drawer and sat back with a kind of despair. I can send Sheritra to Sunero's house at Ninsu if she would go, he thought. Nubnofret and I did discuss the possibility. But would that be pushing her into the place where her luck will be worse, or will keeping her at home precipitate the disasters that I see? There are no answers. We have lived through illness, dynastic deaths, royal intrigues, he thought again as he rose and left his office. All showed beforehand as unlucky days. The only surprises were the occurrences themselves. We will weather this month as we weather everything. But he knew, as he wandered down the passage and out into the fading daylight, that his confidence was spurious. Something alien was in the air, and he acknowledged it with great mistrust.

He was curiously reluctant to visit the tomb at Saqqara. Penbuy and his other scribes and artists were still at work there, and Hori spent several hours overseeing their efforts every day, but Khaemwaset stayed away. He wanted it closed and sealed. He wanted to give the scroll that he had cut so avidly from the bandaged fingers of the corpse to Penbuy to be copied so that the original might be returned, but so great was his distaste for it that he let it lie where the scribe had locked it away. Eventually, he

knew, he must either continue the work of deciphering the enigmatic thing or put it back where it had come from, but he did not
need to decide anything just yet. Daily, Hori laid before him the
intricate, riotous scenes and hieroglyphs faithfully reproduced
from the tomb's plastered walls, eager to discuss them with his
father, but Khaemwaset found excuses to simply disregard them.
"They are beautiful but not particularly informative," he told his
son. "We can go over them once the tomb is closed but at the
moment my attention is taken up with the Apis bulls." It was a
lie, and Hori knew it. Looking at his son perched on the edge of
the desk, sandalled foot swinging, he had been going to say,
"Leave me alone, Hori," for Ib had come to him not an hour before with yet another shake of the head, but he restrained himself. "Just get Penbuy to file it away and I will find a few idle
moments within the next day or so to go over it." Hori, shooting
him a keen glance, slid off the desk and went away.

Khaemwaset sat on blindly, staring into nothing. When did all
this begin? he was thinking, but he was not even sure what "this"
was. Slowly, he mentally girded himself for another family dinner, another evening in the cool of the garden or listening to
Nubnofret's not unpleasant observations, then blessed unconsciousness followed by yet another long, hot series of hours that
he must fill or go mad. An obsession. Yes, it was nearly that.
Then let the moment of meeting come, let it shatter me with furious disappointment, and then, O please Thoth, please Ptah,
please Hathor, goddess of beauty, let my life return to its former
sane state!

One week into the month of Hathor, Khaemwaset began to
give up hope of tracing the woman. Reluctantly, he called in his
soldiers. To his relief, he found that the moment of his admission
of failure brought with it the first intimations of peace, and his
mind began to calm. He returned to his studies, his few select patients, and his duties with the beginnings of an honest interest.
His horoscope still made him anxious but he decided that he had
been in such a restless condition that he had not done the casting
properly.

On the third day of the second week of Hathor he set out to
confer with Si-Montu regarding the promised grape harvest in
the royal vineyards his brother oversaw on the outskirts of
Memphis. Pharaoh had sent a request for figures on the expected

yield and Si-Montu had in turn sent a message to Khaemwaset, worried about the appearance of blight on some of the vines but more than happy to have an excuse to while away a hot afternoon drinking beer and talking about nothing in particular. Khaemwaset had welcomed the invitation and had set off in his barge with Kasa, Amek and two bodyguards to have himself rowed beyond the northern limits of the city to where his father's vines luxuriated, tended like spoiled children behind their high, sheltering walls.

Khaemwaset sat on the deck under the small awning, enjoying the morning breeze that would turn in a very few hours to the scorching breath of a Ra growing in power and intensity towards high summer. The riverbank as he travelled north and away from Memphis's industry and markets was carefully cultivated. One noble's estate followed another, one set of clean white watersteps with tethered barges and skiffs giving way to lawn, shrubs, trees, a wall, and then another tier of water-lapped steps. The river road ran behind these private enclosures, encircled the North-of-the-Walls suburb, and returned to meander beside the Nile just before it crossed the northernmost canal. Ramses' vineyards, surrounding Si-Montu's inviting home, grew beyond the canal and were fed by irrigation canals bridged by the road.

Khaemwaset watched the last well-groomed estate drift by, a tangle of river growth follow, and the road appear again, choked as ever with laden donkeys, barefooted peasants and litters borne by dusty slaves. He did not mind the return of their babble. Today he felt peaceful and optimistic. The wet-scented air cooled the sweat from his brow under the black-and-white striped linen helmet he wore. The Nile was a glittering blue, slapping gently and rhythmically against his craft. His captain called the beat to the rowers, his sing-song voice seeming to blend with the noise from the bank, the shrieking of the birds that dipped over Khaemwaset's head in search of flung food and the pad-pad of Kasa's tread as he came from the cabin to proffer cool, mint-flavoured water and dried dates. Amek stood in the prow, his eyes, as ever, slowly circling the bank, the other craft slicing the water, the fellahin, working the shadufs that poured wet life onto the fields of the farther bank.

Khaemwaset had just thanked Kasa and was raising the gold cup to his mouth when his gaze caught a flash of brilliant scarlet among the dun confusion of animals and bodies on the road. His hand froze. His mouth went dry. Then a rage such as he had never known filled him, galvanizing his limbs and flooding his lungs. She was threading her way through the crowd with the easy grace he had come to know so well, had seen so tantalizingly often in his cursed imagination, a white ribbon encircling her forehead and fluttering down her straight back, the sun glinting on the simple circle of silver around her throat and playing against the silver bracelets rubbing loosely from wrist to forearm. As he came to his feet and stared, that horrendous anger pulsing through him, he saw her raise one languid hand to brush a strand of wind-teased black hair away from her cheek. Her palm was hennaed bright orange. You bitch, he thought, trembling, the weeks of misery and restless compulsion churning in his mind, Ib's face each frustrating evening, Sheritra's silences, Hori's disappointment, even his servants' exhaustion, known but not seen, all jumbled together to form this towering urge to violence. Bitch, bitch, oh bitch! "Captain!" he shouted. "Steer for the bank immediately! Amek!" The cup had fallen from his grasp and he was vaguely aware of Kasa bending to retrieve it as Amek strode across the deck. "As soon as the boat hits the bank I want you to stop that woman." He pointed, and Amek's eyes followed his shaking arm. The man nodded. She was coming towards them along the road, in the direction of the city, and they had ample time to cut her off. This time, Khaemwaset thought fiercely, teeth clenched, this time you will not escape me. "When you have stopped her, ask her her price."

Amek's black eyebrows rose. "Her price, Prince?"

"Yes, her price. I want a night with her. I want to know how much she charges."

The captain of his bodyguard bowed and without further ado kicked of his sandals, went to the side, and prepared to jump onto the muddy bank the moment the barge struck. Khaemwaset stepped back under the awning, scarcely aware of what he had said. The shaking was abating but the anger was still there, a steady coal heating his blood and making his fingers curl into fists.

The barge bumped the bank, and even before it ceased to quiver Amek was over the side, knee deep in mud and splashed to the chin. The woman was almost level with him, unknowing, unseeing. Hurry, Khaemwaset thought. Tensely, he watched his man pull his tough soldier's legs from the mire one after the other, grasp the straggling river growth, and haul himself up, staggering then sprinting onto the road. Now, Khaemwaset's chaotic mind called. Now, Amek! Amek ruthlessly pushed the crowd aside, and a second before the woman would have passed, spread his feet apart, drew his short sword, and brought her to a halt.

She stopped slowly, one knee flexed under the tight sheath that was the hue of some exotic bird, her hands still loose, and Khaemwaset, his anger becoming swamped in anxiety, found time to admire her seemingly unshakeable aplomb. He saw Amek speak, his sword held against his mud-spattered leg, and expected the woman to glance towards the barge when the request was made, but she did not so much as move that proud head. Her lips parted. She spoke briefly and made as if to step aside, but Amek once more barred her way, speaking quickly. This time her chin came up and her mouth moved rapidly, forcefully. Amek leaned forward. So did she. They glared at one another. Then, abruptly, Amek sheathed his sword and the woman eased into the flow of travellers, passing Khaemwaset and the barge, passing out of sight with an infuriating serenity. Khaemwaset found that he could not swallow. Indeed, he could hardly breathe.

The barge captain had run out a ramp and Khaemwaset, hands still curled tightly in upon themselves, watched Amek come striding up it, across the deck and in under the shade of the awning. He bowed. Khaemwaset fought for air, for his voice, and found both.

"Well?" he croaked.

Amek grimaced. Drying mud was beginning to flake from his legs and he wiped at a streak of it on his cheek. "I made the request," he said. "I put the question with great tact, Highness."

"Of course you did!" Khaemwaset snapped impatiently. "I know you, Amek. What did she say?"

The man looked uncomfortable and his eyes slid away from Khaemwaset's. "She said, 'Tell this presumptuous man, your master, that I am a noblewoman and no mean person. I am not for sale.'"

Khaemwaset's mouth suddenly filled with saliva. "You pressed her. I saw it!"

"Yes, Prince, I pressed her." Amek shook his head. "She simply repeated, 'I am a noblewoman and no mean person. Tell that to your rude and arrogant master.'"

Rude and arrogant. Khaemwaset heard a string of curses go reeling through his head. "Did you at least try to find out where she lives?"

Amek nodded. "I told her that my master is a very rich and powerful man who has been seeking her for a long time. I thought that she would be complimented and thus soften her stance. But my words made no difference at all, in fact she smiled rather coldly into my face. 'Gold cannot buy me and power cannot frighten me,' she said. I did not want to exceed my instructions and arrest her, Highness. I had to let her pass."

Khaemwaset's fist came up and caught Amek on the side of the jaw. Amek, unprepared, went down and lay for a moment, stunned. Then his head lolled and he fingered his mouth. Arrest her! Khaemwaset's mind was yelling. Arrest her, beat her, you should have dragged her on board and thrown her at my feet! Then all at once reality collapsed upon him and he knelt, aghast at what he had done. "Amek!" he said urgently, helping his guard to his feet. "I am sorry. I did not mean to strike you. . . . By Amun I did not . . ."

Amek managed a weak smile. "I have seen her face," he said. "I do not blame my prince for striking me. She is very beautiful. I am the one who must apologize. I have failed my prince."

Yes, you have seen her face, Khaemwaset thought, sick to the heart. You have felt her breath on you, you have noted the flicker of her eyelids, the rise of her breast as she drew breath to answer you with such scorn. I want to hit you again. "No," he said shortly. "No, you have not." And with that he swung abruptly on his heel and disappeared into the cabin, pulling the curtains closed savagely behind him.

He had not given the barge captain further instructions. He sat in the blue-tinged dimness of the cabin with his knees drawn up, eyes jammed shut, rocking to and fro in humiliation and the anger that had become directed now at himself. I have never struck a member of my staff before, he thought in agony. I have reprimanded, I have shouted. I have come close to losing my temper on many occasions, but never, never have I hit out. And at Amek! A man of silent loyalty, great efficiency, a man who has shielded and protected me for many years. He bit his lip, feeling the barge slip off the mud of the bank with a slight jerk, hearing the captain shout an order. It will do no good to apologize again, Khaemwaset's thoughts ran on. The harm has been done. I can never take back that moment of sheer insane fury. And at what? He leaned back against the cabin's cedar-fragrant wall and opened his eyes. A woman. A woman who got away from me. Amek did his duty then refused to break a law of Ma'at by compelling her into my presence.

He heard Kasa's hesitant knock on the outer wall and pulled himself together. "Come!" The man opened the curtain, entered and bowed. "In the absence of any command to the contrary, the captain is proceeding to my lord Si-Montu's watersteps, Highness," he said. "Do you desire anything?"

Khaemwaset suppressed an urge to burst into hysterical laughter. I desire that infuriating mirage of a woman. I desire to wipe out the last hour. I desire the balm of soul I used to take entirely for granted. "Bring me water," he said, "and the dates." He had been about to order the barge to return home but suddenly the idea of pouring everything into the ears of his favourite brother was irresistible. He drank the water Kasa brought, nibbled on a few dates and brooded.

Ben-Anath greeted her brother-in-law with her usual affectionate embrace and installed him in the garden under the shade of a giant spreading sycamore. After assigning him a servant and apologizing for having to leave him temporarily unentertained, she bowed and went back into the house. Khaemwaset was relieved. Ben-Anath was an easy woman to be with, but in his present state of mind he did not think he could make an effort at polite family conversation. He asked the servant for beer and when it came he forced himself to sip it carefully. He wanted to gulp it down and ask for more. He wanted to get drunk on this hot, completely frustrating afternoon. But the need to talk to Si-Montu was greater.

Presently his brother came striding across the grass. He had obviously been at work in the vineyards and had taken a moment to wash and change his kilt, but other than the strip of white linen around his thick waist he was naked. His brown body was chunky and formidable, not from drawing the bow, wrestling, or chariot-driving, but from sweating beside his labourers; his presence gave Khaemwaset great comfort. Rising, he kissed Si-Montu's damp, bearded cheek. Si-Montu waved him back to the cushions strewn on the reed mat and sank down beside him. "What?" he expostulated. "Drinking beer in the middle of the finest vineyard in Egypt? The grapes will wither and die from chagrin, Khaemwaset. How are you? Bring a jar of the five-year vintage!" he shouted at the servant, then he fixed Khaemwaset with a bright, altogether too piercing eye. Si-Montu might look like a peasant and roar like a sailor, Khaemwaset reflected, but he is neither. He is a royally educated prince of the land, and too many people forget it.

"Si-Montu, if I start drinking wine today I will not stop," he confessed, "and as to how I am, let us deal with Pharaoh's business first and then I want to talk to you."

Si-Montu nodded equably. Khaemwaset had always been grateful for his brother's ready acceptance, his reluctance to pry. "Very well," Si-Montu smiled. "Father's request can be dealt with very quickly. The grape harvest will be enormous this year if I can control the beginnings of the blight. The fruit is coming nicely, very tiny but huge bunches. However, the leaves and some of the vines themselves are turning black. You can take a look, physician, and perhaps prescribe something I might try. Ah!" He waved at the servant who had appeared with a tray, a dusty sealed jar, and two alabaster cups. The man held the jar so that Si-Montu could inspect the seal, then broke it and poured the wine. Khaemwaset watched the rich, dark liquid, suddenly suffused with sunlight, stream into the cups. Si-Montu held up an admonitory finger. "One cup now, then you will inspect the vines and send Father the bill for your services, then another cup, or the whole jar if you choose." He grinned, and Khaemwaset, in spite of himself, smiled back. "If you wish I will have the wine removed after you have drunk two cups." He handed Khaemwaset the wine and raised his own cup. "To Egypt! Long may she rule the only areas of the world that really matter!"

Khaemwaset drank to the toast. The wine slipped down his throat, tart-sweet and cool. a great vintage indeed. Before long it began to spread its aristocratic warmth through his veins, and for the first time that day he relaxed, talking with his brother of their families, their enemies, foreign affairs—of which Si-Montu knew little and cared less—and their various agricultural hold-ings.

Si-Montu finally rose, and together they went carefully through the vineyard. Khaemwaset noticed, with wry humour, that his brother had not bothered to order them a canopy. They stood together in the stunning heat, fingering leaves and dis-cussing the problem. Khaemwaset made some suggestions. Si-Montu concurred. No one knew more about the care and cultivation of grapes than he, but still, Khaemwaset was able to help.

Then they ambled back to the garden and the second cup of wine. "So," Si-Montu invited as soon as they were settled. "You look as though you have just fought your way back from the Underworld and slain the Great Serpent to do it. What's wrong?"

Khaemwaset told him everything. Once open the wound flowed copiously, and the sun had begun to set before he at last fell silent. Si-Montu had watched him the whole time, not com-menting, grunting now and then, and when Khaemwaset's voice ceased he drained his cup and refilled for both of them, then fell to tugging absently at his beard.

Ben-Anath appeared and raised her shoulders. Si Montu held up two fingers at her and she smiled, nodded and faded back into the still thin but lengthening shadow cast by the house. Khaemwaset envied the pair of them their perfect communica-tion.

"When I fell in love with Ben-Anath," Si-Montu offered, "the whole court tried to persuade me that I had gone mad. Father talked at me by the hour. Mother threw every luscious woman she could cajole or threaten at my feet. I was finally barred from the succession. But did I care?" He laughed. "Not a bit. Not for a moment. All my energies went into wooing my woman." Khaemwaset smiled inwardly. Si-Montu's energy was consider-able and, concentrated on one thing, it was well-nigh irresistible. "She was only the daughter of a Syrian ship's captain, but gods she was haughty! Then she was worried that I would resent her because my decision to marry her had stripped me of almost ev-ery royal privilege. But I have never regretted that decision." He fixed his brother with a suddenly sober glare. "Do you love Nubnofret like that?"

"You know that I do not," Khaemwaset answered truthfully. "I love her as far as I am capable of loving . . ."

"As far as you see love," Si-Montu broke in, "which is only as far as you deem it safe. And who is to say which of us is happier or wiser? Look at it sensibly, Khaemwaset. You have a loving wife and good family. You are feverishly desperate, probably for the first time in your life, to sleep with a woman you keep seeing on the streets. Well what of it?" Khaemwaset held his cup to be refilled and Si-Montu hesitated. Khaemwaset nodded curtly. Si-Montu sighed and filled it to the brim. Then he went on speaking. "Many men have suffered through the same affliction. It is called lust, my bookish brother. Lust. that is all. You agonize over it as though it represents the destruction of everything, including yourself, but of course it does not. You have two choices." He wiped a few droplets of the blood red liquid from his moustache, his blunt, calloused fingers moving thoughtfully. "You can either keep searching for her—and you know, don't you, that you will eventually find her?—and then keep offering a variety of good things to her until you find the key to unlock her virtue, at which time you take your fill of her. Or you can push her away each time she sneaks into your vitals and in six months you will be wondering what all the fuss was about." He cocked an eye at Khaemwaset. "Of course, you might also be wondering what you missed, but that, dear brother, is not in your nature."

It was not at one time in my nature, Khaemwaset thought, but I am changing. I do not like it and perhaps I cannot make you understand it, Si-Montu, but I don't think that I can control it any longer. "What would you do?" he asked aloud.

"I would tell Ben-Anath," Si-Montu answered promptly, "and she would say, 'Scurvy son of a dessicated pharaoh, if I am not woman enough for you go and take your fill of the street. When you come crawling back to admit to me that there is no woman like me in the world, you can sleep in the kitchens among the little female slaves who by then you will be accustomed to calling your equals.' But then," Si-Montu finished simply, "I still desire no other woman the way I desire my wife. Do you want my advice?" Khaemwaset nodded mutely. "Stop chasing this phantom, start giving Nubnofret her due as a beauty and a most accommodating wife, and close that tomb."

Khaemwaset blinked. Even through the gentle wine fumes

floating pleasingly in his brain he was conscious of shock. Si-Montu was staring at him steadily. "The tomb? I have told you my anxieties over it but it has nothing to do with my present dilemma."

"No?" Si-Montu said. "I am not so sure. You treat the dead very arrogantly in your polite but nonetheless ruthless quest for knowledge, Khaemwaset. You fancy yourself safe because you restore, you make offerings, but did it never occur to you that the dead might merely wish to be left alone, or that what you take is not in fact equal to what you imagine that you give? I am not easy about this latest endeavour of yours. Close it."

Khaemwaset felt dread clutch at his heart. Si-Montu, with his usual facility for unconsciously striking the nail on the head, had voiced Khaemwaset's own fears with a lucidity he himself had lacked. "I do not believe in any connection," he replied, forming the words carefully because he was getting drunk, and because they were a lie.

Si-Montu shrugged. "You are probably right," he agreed indifferently. "Now it is time for dinner. You will stay, of course? I have no boring guests tonight, unlike the many dinners at your house I am forced to yawn through!"

They got up and walked in the dusk towards the house. Khaemwaset felt a great deal better, but there was a seed of mutiny in him. Si-Montu had no right to accuse him of a kind of rape—Si-Montu, who knew nothing of history or the preciousness of rare things, and who had never held a priestly office. He, Khaemwaset, did not rape. As for the woman . . . He entered his brother's dining room to Ben-Anath's smile and took his place before the little table prepared for him. As for the woman, he would find her, even as his brother had said. Lust or not, she conjured in him a feeling he had never known before and he was determined to explore it. He had no intention of telling Nubnofret. She would not understand. And the gods? He succumbed at last to the inviting effects of the wine. If the gods had wished to punish him or indicate that his studies were insulting to them, they would have let him know a long time ago. For was he not their friend? He lifted his cup for more wine and fell upon the first course of the excellent dinner Ben-Anath's cooks had provided. A harpist began to play. Khaemwaset was enjoying the evening, enjoying himself fully, for the first time in months.

He woke late the following morning in Si-Montu's guest room with little memory of the night before. The servant his brother sent to see to his bathing and dressing and to bring him food told him that a message had gone to his wife during dinner and his own men had been cared for.

Khaemwaset sought out Ben-Anath, thanked her for her hospitality, gathered his staff, and cast off for home. Si-Montu was already out in the vineyards. I cannot remember the last time I drank so freely, Khaemwaset thought as he sat leaning against the outer wall of the barge's cabin, but the wine Si-Montu produced was indeed fine. I have no headache, only a feeling of lightness and a slight loss of balance.

But then he did remember. He had drunk too much, though not nearly as much as he had last night, at his father's feast in the palace when the old man with the scroll had accosted him. That was a curious affair. His thoughts ran on as the oars of his rowers dipped and pulled against the current, lifting dribbles of glittering river water into the bright sunlight. I lost the scroll. A pity. I feel guilty about such carelessness. Well, the matter is over, closed. I must not drink to excess again.

All the time he was thinking his eyes were on the bank, and they remained there until the river road veered sharply west and the nobles' estates began. But today no flutter of scarlet linen increased his heartbeat and Amek stood stolidly in his customary position at the prow. Khaemwaset did not know whether he longed to see her or was afraid that she might indeed magically appear and cause him once again to lose all civilized volition. But his watersteps hove into view, one of Amek's guards on duty by the mooring pole, and Khaemwaset had been spared another encounter.

Disembarking, he went immediately to find his wife. Nubnofret was in her quarters dictating a letter to one of her friends at court. She looked up and smiled as Khaemwaset was admitted.

"Was it good to get drunk, dear brother?" she asked. "You look well rested."

"Yes it was," Khaemwaset admitted, acknowledging the inclined head of Nubnofret's scribe with a nod. "I did not intend to stay away, Nubnofret. I apologize if I have inconvenienced the household."

"You have not." She rose and came to him, running a sharp but gentle nail down his cheek and kissing him on his naked chest. Her mouth was soft, and Khaemwaset sensed no reproach in her attitude or in her warm gaze. By now the story of his astonishing loss of control in striking Amek would be spreading among the servants, who loved to gossip, but to Nubnofret's credit did not dare carry family business to the staff of other households. He wondered for the first time whether Nubnofret permitted Wernuro to whisper such gossip to her, and was conscious of despair. I cannot expect my exploits to remain a secret from the rest of the family, he thought while he smiled back at his wife. Oh how wearing, how mind-consuming is deceit!

"Nothing of note has come from the Delta, or so Penbuy tells me," Nubnofret was saying, "and there were no unexpected guests. Please don't forget, though, that May will be staying here within the week on his way back from the Assuan quarries. Excuse me now, Khaemwaset. I must finish my dictation. I have a lot to do today." Her lustrous black eyes told him that she would hurry through her chores and be at his disposal as soon as possible. He had in fact forgotten about his father's Chief Architect, and his heart sank. At one time he would have welcomed such a distinguished and cultivated guest, but now he wanted them all, his father, his brothers, his governmental contacts, to disappear so that he could be alone and concentrate on . . . He turned abruptly. "Let me know when you are free," he replied. "We might take a swim later."

Escaping to his office, he saw that Hori had placed yesterday's work in a neat pile on the desk. Khaemwaset went to it briskly. Enough nonsense, he thought. The sooner I study these the sooner the tomb can be closed. I have wasted too much time and effort that should have been directed towards the work of my own architects. But before he sat he summoned Ib. "Revive the search parties," he ordered. "I don't care what it takes, but I want that woman."

Chapter 6

'Come, songs and music are before thee.
Set behind thee all thy cares;
think only upon gladness until the day cometh whereon
thou shalt go down
to the land that loveth silence.'

The month of Hathor slid away and Khoiak began. May proved to be an entertaining guest, as usual, and left gifts for them all before gliding away in his gilded, flower-bedecked barge. Khaemwaset cast the horoscopes for the new month and found no changes from the month before. This time, however, he was oddly detached from the task and viewed the outcome with something close to indifference. What would be would be. Egyptians were on the whole a cheerful and optimistic people, he knew, but they did not disregard the power of destiny's fingers sometimes astir in their lives, and Khaemwaset, as time went on, felt himself more and more in the grip of fate's implacable hand. There was almost a perverse comfort in the awareness. He saw his patients and performed his other duties, receiving the continually negative reports of Ib and Amek with equanimity. Tomorrow, next month, next year, it did not matter. He knew she would come and he waited for her.

Khoiak's days grew increasingly hotter and the crops stood high but still green in the little fields. Hori was spending most of his time, now, in the coolness of the tomb, its mysteries fretting him, and Sheritra swam, read and withdrew into her own world. Worship went on in the house, sometimes in the temples where the family prostrated together before Ptah or Ra or Neith. Khaemwaset knew that before long he would be summoned to the palace again, for ambassador Huy must surely be on the point of returning to Egypt, but he put his father's annoying, amusing negotiations out of his mind. Summer was coming, a time of stultifying heat, endless hours when reality always seemed to acquire different dimensions and the eternity of burning air and white light seemed to fuse mortal Egypt with the immortal paradise of Osiris.

One day, Khaemwaset had just finished a period of dictation with Penbuy, some notes he had been making on the reign of Osiris Thothmes the First, when Ib entered the office and bowed. The noon meal was over and the hour for the afternoon rest was fast approaching. Khaemwaset glanced at his steward, sensing a further duty to be performed, and was annoyed. He wanted to lie on his couch under the soft swish of the fans and doze. "Well?" he snapped. Penbuy was gathering up his pens, ink and scrolls, his own eyes heavy with the need for sleep at this warm hour. On Khaemwaset's signal he left the room.

"Your pardon, Prince," Ib said, "but there is a young man here who requests a moment of your time. His mother needs medical attention."

"What young man?" Khaemwaset asked testily. "The city is full of good physicians. Did you tell him that I only treat the nobility or cases that might be of particular interest to me?"

"I did," Ib rejoined. "He says that his mother is indeed a noblewoman, and no mean person. He would be grateful for your personal consultation, and his uncle will pay you well for your trouble."

Khaemwaset started, then recovered. "I am not interested in more gold," he grumbled. "I already have plenty. What is wrong with this woman?"

"Apparently she somehow drove a large wooden splinter into her foot. The splinter has been removed but the foot is festering."

"Then I do not need to go myself. I can prescribe at once." He was relieved. "Send in the boy."

Ib retired, and Khaemwaset waited. Presently a shadow fell across the open doorway. Khaemwaset looked up. A young man about Hori's age was bowing profoundly from the waist, arms outstretched. Khaemwaset noted immediately that his hands were finely tapered and well cared for, the palms hennaed, the nails clipped, the skin soft. He was shod in good leather sandals with gold thongs and his kilt linen was certainly of the tenth or eleventh grade of transparency. He rose and stood tall, his gaze meeting Khaemwaset's, neither subservient nor proud, but merely expectant. He wore his own hair, Khaemwaset noted. It

fell black and completely straight to his square shoulders. A
thick band of gold encircled his neck and one large ankh, symbol
of life, hung from it on his slim but beautifully muscled chest. In
comparison to his hair, his eyes seemed grey. They followed
Khaemwaset's assessment closely, but with detachment. There
was something almost familiar about him, in his straight stance
perhaps, or the way his mouth curved naturally upward at the
corners. Khaemwaset decided that he was the most perfect
specimen of young manhood apart from Hori that he had ever
seen.

"What is your name?" he asked.

The youth inclined his head. The black hair swung forward,
gleaming dully. "I am Harmin," he answered, his voice as steady
and cool as his eyes.

"My steward told me of your mother's complaint,"
Khaemwaset said. "He also told me that your family is a noble
one. I thought I knew, at least by sight, every noble family in
Egypt, but I have never seen you or heard of your name before.
Why is that?"

The young man smiled. It was a winning, affable smile to
which Khaemwaset was hard put not to respond. "My family's
modest estates are at Koptos, just north of blessed Thebes," he
said. "We are of an ancient lineage, tracing our line from the
days of Prince Sekenenra, and though we are members of the
minor nobility and have never held high offices, we are nevertheless proud of our blood. It is pure. No foreign flow has com-
mingled with it. During the days of revived trade with Punt, after
the great Queen Hatshepsut rediscovered that land, my ancestor
was steward of her caravans along the route from Koptos to the
Eastern Sea."

Khaemwaset blinked. Few historians, let alone ordinary
Egyptian citizens, knew anything of the fabled queen who was
said to have ruled as a king and had built a mortuary temple of
unsurpassed beauty on the west bank of Thebes. Those who had
studied the site were inclined to ascribe it to the warrior pharaoh
Thothmes the Third, but Khaemwaset had always disagreed. His
interest was piqued. Nevertheless, he said, "I should have heard
of you if you have lived in Memphis for any length of time."

Harmin's smile broadened. "My mother, my uncle and I took
up residence here about two months ago. There is little to do in

Koptos anymore, Highness, and we have a good steward to care for our small farm there."

Khaemwaset was still not satisfied, but to pry further would have breached good manners. He was, however, convinced of the young man's noble breeding. "I do not need to see your mother," he objected kindly. "I will prescribe for her though."

Harmin took one swift step forward. "Forgive me, Prince, but we have applied the per-baibait-bird with honey and that drew out the splinter, and then we dressed the wound with a poultice of human excrement crushed in sweet beer yeast, sefet oil and honey, but the infection increases."

"So you have consulted another physician?"

Harmin looked surprised. "Why no. My mother is well versed herself in remedies, but this time she is no longer able to treat herself. She would be more than honoured if you would examine her foot."

Perhaps I had better, Khaemwaset thought reluctantly. The poultice applied was a common one for open wounds but he put no faith in it himself. It often seemed to make the problem worse. Sighing inwardly he dismissed the youth. "I will come," he said. "Please wait in the outer hall."

Harmin did not thank him. He did not even look satisfied. He bowed again, turned on his heel and disappeared, his sandals shushing softly on the tiled floor, his stride slow and easy.

Khaemwaset went into his library, unlocked the box where he kept his medicaments and drew out a leather satchel containing dressings and other things he often needed for his patients. His head buzzed with the demand to be laid on a pillow and his eyes were scratchy. Quickly he re-locked the box and followed Harmin.

Ib was sitting on his stool in the passage. He rose. "Shall I come with you, Prince?" he asked.

"No," Khaemwaset answered. "I do not need you for this one, Ib. But I will take Amek."

There was no sign of Harmin in the hallway. Khaemwaset found him waiting just within the shade cast by the row of coloured-splashed pillars at the front entrance to the house. He was standing motionless, arms loose at his sides, head slightly inclined towards the sound that was floating over the rows of thick shrubbery that helped to separate the paved pathway from the rear gardens.

Khaemwaset halted in shock. The voice of Sheritra, high and pure, was filling the hot air. She seldom sang, and when she did it was almost always children's verses, but today the words of an ancient love song pierced Khaemwaset to the heart. "Your love, I desire it, like butter and honey. You belong to me, like best ointment on the limbs of nobles, like finest linen on the limbs of the gods, like incense before the Lord of All . . ."

Harmin half turned towards Khaemwaset. "That is a beautiful voice," he commented.

"Yes it is," Khaemwaset responded shortly. Sheritra would have been embarrassed and ashamed if she had known of her audience. He jerked his head at Harmin and began to walk towards the river. "From which direction did you come?" he asked. "Where is your house?"

"Beyond the northern suburbs," Harmin replied, now at Khaemwaset's side. "I took a skiff across the river and then walked, Highness. It was a fine morning."

Nothing more was said. Khaemwaset invited the young man aboard his barge, Amek and a soldier following, and the captain gave the order to cast off. At this time of the day the Nile traffic was sparse. Those who could were taking the afternoon rest and the watersteps of the nobles were deserted. He had presumed for some reason that his patient would live in one of them, although he knew the majority of their inhabitants personally. But Harmin gave no sign that they should veer towards the bank.

The river road appeared, almost empty of travellers. Those compelled to be on it were quiet in the heat, and the barge drifted beside it like a mote of dust falling along a sunbeam. The river's surface was glassy and almost still.

They passed the bridged canal near where Khaemwaset had seen that damnable flash of scarlet, but the scuffed road was now empty. There were a few respectable homes, modest but neat, fronting the west side of the road and surrounded by fields of tall grain, then there was nothing but crops, drooping in the heat, and the water poured rhythmically into the thin, hacked irrigation canals that fed them as the fellahin lowered the shaduf buckets on their long wooden arms into the Nile and hauled on the ropes to raise them to the level of the canals that criss-crossed the fields.

Khaemwaset thought of his daughter and the secret, painful

places of her soul. If anyone deserves to be loved it is she, he thought sadly. She must have been alone in the garden, for even Bakmut is not allowed to hear her sing.

Just then Harmin stirred and pointed. "Prince, please tell your captain to begin to tack towards the bank," he said. "Those watersteps, there." He was indicating the east bank, not the west, where there was little human habitation and the vegetation clung to a miserably small strip of land before the desert took over. Khaemwaset had never paid it much attention. But indeed a set of very small watersteps led up from the river into a grove of palm trees, and Khaemwaset glimpsed a smudge of white wall far beyond. He shouted a command and the barge began its ponderous sweep.

The house was indeed isolated. Between it and the mud sprawl of homes where the managers of the fields lived and worked for their aristocratic masters there must have been half a mile in each direction. Palms straggled along the bank, it was true, and one could easily miss their sudden cluster if one was not looking for it.

The watersteps had one mooring pole from which white paint was peeling. The barge nudged it, a sailor jumped out to secure the trailing ropes and Khaemwaset rose. Signalling to Amek, he invited Harmin to precede them, and without another word Harmin led them up the steps and along a dirt path that meandered happily through the dappling shade of the trees whose tall, smooth trunks smelled sweet and whose stiff fronds whispered high overhead.

The house was nestled in a small clearing. Khaemwaset noted at once that it had been fashioned of mud bricks, and seemed to lean into its environment with perfect harmony. The white-painted plaster with which it had been surfaced was missing in places. Five or six workmen were busy with fresh plaster and whitewash. Harmin apologized. "The house had been vacant and uncared for before we moved in," he explained. "Mud is a good substance for the construction of a house, but it needs constant maintenance."

I know of no nobles who would dare to live in a mud home like a peasant, Khaemwaset thought, intrigued. Not nowadays. If any of my friends or family had bought this property they would have torn down the construction immediately and ordered cedar from Lebanon, sandstone and granite from Assuan, gold from Nubia, to build something they considered suitable. There is a mystery here.

But he liked what he saw as they approached the entrance. He knew how cool mud bricks kept a house, and sure enough a slight draught of refreshing air came funnelling out to greet him from the small reception hall.

Harmin turned and bowed. "Welcome, Great Prince," he said. He clapped his hands and a servant appeared, barefoot and clad only in a loincloth. "Would you like some wine or beer and perhaps a shat cake before you see my mother?"

Khaemwaset was quickly surveying the hall—the square, doorless opening to the passage beyond, the large, plain tiling under his feet. He was aware, as though a healing balm was stealing over him, that a comfortable silence reigned. The constant dull rumble of life that burgeoned on the west bank could not be heard. No neighbours disturbed this blessed peace with music or laughter. Even the low, light voice of the palms did not seem to penetrate. He felt himself loosening, all tension leaving his stomach, his shoulders.

Harmin had not missed Khaemwaset's appraisal. He gestured around the room. "As you can see, we follow the old ways," he told him, "and we do not apologize to anyone for doing so, Prince."

It was as though he had read Khaemwaset's mind. The walls were white but painted carefully with Nile scenes, desert animals and representations of the gods. Each scene was divided from the others by a painted date palm running from floor to blue-tinged ceiling. Cushions were piled in the corners. Three chairs of aromatic cedar, spindle-legged and delicate, ribbed in gold, stood about, and one long, low table of the same design on which stood a plain alabaster unguent jar for the anointing of guests and a clay vase that held thickly bunched late spring blooms. Two incense stands, stern in their rising simplicity, had been placed to either side of the inner doorway, and in niches beside them Amun and Thoth resided, the gold of their bodies gleaming dully in the pleasing, cool dimness.

Here there was no fussiness, nothing overly ornate, nothing imported. Even the air, carrying faintly the mixed odour of lotus flowers and myrrh, seemed completely Egyptian. Khaemwaset drew it into his nostrils with a deep breath. "No thank you, Harmin," he smiled. "I will see your mother first. Amek, come with me as far as her chamber. Set your guard at this door."

He saw Harmin's glance flick over Amek's bulk before the young man turned to the rear. Khaemwaset followed, his satchel in hand. I could live in this place forever, he thought as the feeling of well-being in him expanded. What work I could do! What dreams I could dream! But it might be dangerous. Oh yes, it might. I would gradually discard my duties to my father, to my Egypt, and sink into the past like a flower cast upon the bosom of the Nile. What kind of people are these?

The passage was narrow, dark and utterly plain. But at the farther end the brilliance of the afternoon cut the darkness in shafts like knives, and Khaemwaset could see a small rectangle of lawn, a few flowerbeds in a busy array of colours and a pond choked with waxy white and pink lotus over which bees hovered. Harmin turned abruptly to his left, stood aside and bowed. "Mother, the Prince Khaemwaset," he said. "Highness, this is my mother Tbubui."

Khaemwaset entered the room with the usual words of reassurance ready on his lips. She had injured her foot. She would not be able to rise and reverence him, as the little dancer had tried to do. Strange, he thought, strange that she should come to mind just now. He was about to speak, to tell this woman not to try and move, when he heard Amek draw a quick breath behind him. It was a tiny sound, come and gone in a second, but Khaemwaset simultaneously halted. He felt the blood leave his face. The white walls of the pleasant room wavered and he fought to keep his control. He was aware of Amek's comforting presence at his rear, Harmin's grey eyes on him with what was surely bewilderment, his own fingers gripping the satchel as though he would die if he dropped it, then he recovered and managed to move forward.

"Greetings, Tbubui," he said, and marvelled that he could sound so sane.

The woman was sitting in a large chair beside a couch draped in glistening sheets, her leg propped up on cushions above a stool. Both bare, languid arms were draped loosely over the wooden rests, and heavy silver rings winked at him from her slender fingers. She was smiling at him above a jumble of white linen—sheet or cloak he did not know which—her hennaed mouth curving, her black, kohled eyes regarding him steadily. Black, black, he thought dazedly, and her hair black as night, black as soot against those exquisite collar-bones, black as the anger she conjured in me the last time I saw her on the Memphis river road, striding scarlet through the crowd. I have found her. No wonder my servants could not, with her living on the east bank!

But no. He moved towards her cautiously, as though at a sharp movement her image might shiver and disappear. I did not find her. Fate found her for me and cast me on her shore like a drowning sailor vomited onto a stretch of sand. Does she recognize me? Amek? Surely Amek! He saw her level gaze transferred to the Captain of his Bodyguard then back to him. The smile widened, and Khaemwaset was suddenly terrified to hear the sound of her voice.

"Greetings, Prince, and welcome to my home," she said. "I am honoured indeed that you should choose to come and examine me in person, and I apologize for any inconvenience I may be causing you." The voice was cultured, well-modulated, a voice accustomed to giving orders, greeting guests and entertaining visitors. Khaemwaset wondered what it would sound like throaty with passion. Setting down his satchel and bending over her foot, he clenched his jaw and forced himself to reply. She had a very faint accent. So did her son, now he came to think about it, but it was not any of the accents of foreigners he knew.

"I am not inconvenienced," he said. "Harmin told me of your efforts to cure yourself, and I could then do no more than come and assist you." He began to unwrap the bandages around the foot, willing his hands not to tremble. In a moment I shall touch her flesh, he thought. Control yourself, physician! This is a patient! His lungs were full of her perfume, a light but musky hint of myrrh blended with something he could not identify. He kept his gaze on the unwinding.

At last the bandage fell to the floor and Khaemwaset forced himself not to hesitate. Gently he pressed the swollen, purple flesh around a mound that did not in fact appear to be infected but that certainly, though dry, had not closed. Her skin was cool, almost cold. "There is no infection here," he announced, looking up at her from his squatting position. "You have no burning in the groin?"

"None. Harmin was perhaps overzealous in his efforts to persuade you to come, Highness. I am sorry. But the wound will not in fact close."

She pushed her hair behind her small ears with both hands, and Khaemwaset saw that she was wearing a pair of heavy silver-and-turquoise earrings fashioned into the shape of two ankhs and hung with tiny scarabs. The sight of the scarabs reminded him of the trouble he had gone to in order to avert the spell of the nonsensical scroll, and the night he had spent in Nubnofret's bed, negating his protection without a second thought.

"How long has it been like this?" he asked. She shrugged, and the linen slipped down her breasts, revealing the tantalizing shadow of a cleavage.

"For about two weeks. I soak the foot twice a day and have it poulticed in a mixture of milk, honey and ground incense to dry it up, but as you can see . . ." She gestured along her leg, and Khaemwaset felt the tips of her fingers brush his helmet. ". . . my treatment is not efficacious."

That state of the flesh puzzled Khaemwaset. Its colour suggested tissue that no longer lived. "I think I must take needle and thread and sew this," he said at last, rising. "It will hurt, Tbubui, but I can give you an infusion of poppy to help quell the pain."

"Very well," she said almost indifferently. "It is my own fault, of course. I go barefoot too much."

Bare heels, Khaemwaset thought again. Nubnofret walking ahead of me in the passage on the night Sheritra had her bad dream. You, Tbubui, barefoot in your white, old-fashioned sheath, taunting . . . Surely you recognized Amek!

He had brought with him everything he needed. He asked for fire, and when it was brought in a tiny burner he prepared the poppy infusion. Tbubui watched him in silence as he worked in the odd, enveloping stillness of this extraordinary house.

When it was ready he handed it to her and she drank it obediently. He waited for it to take effect, and selected needle and thread.

Harmin had long since gone, and Amek had taken his position by the doorway. Khaemwaset sensed his resentment though he did not move. This was the woman for whom his master had struck him.

Khaemwaset forced himself to concentrate on the task in hand. Carefully and neatly he sewed the gash closed. Tbubui neither flinched nor groaned. One he looked up from his artistry to find her eyes on him, not dazed from the poppy but alert and full of something he thought he read as humour, but of course it could not be. He continued, in the end wrapping fresh linen about her foot and instructing her to go on applying the poultice. "I will return in a few days to inspect it, and then we will see," he said. She nodded, quite composed. "I have a great resistance to pain," she replied, "and also, unfortunately, to the poppy. Now, Prince. Will you take wine with me?" He nodded and she clapped her hands sharply once. A servant glided into the room, and while she was ordering a chair brought forward and jar of wine opened, Khaemwaset for the first time looked about her chamber.

It was small and cool, the walls unadorned. One table supporting a lamp stood by the couch, which in contrast to the rest of the surroundings was high and lavishly gilded. It was piled with pillows and a-tumble with sheets. Khaemwaset looked away, a dozen questions beginning to reel through his head. Is your husband here? What are you doing in Memphis? Did you know that it was I who sent Amek after you? And did you in turn send Harmin after me? Why? The wine and the chair arrived. He sank into it gratefully and picked up his cup, wondering how he might bring up these things, but she forestalled him.

"I have a confession to make to you, Prince," she said. "I recognized your bodyguard the moment he stepped into the room, and then of course I knew who it was who had sent me such an impudent invitation through his mouth." Khaemwaset flushed and forced himself to meet her now mocking smile. Impudent. He felt like a chastised child.

"I refused it, naturally," she went on, sobering, "and although I was momentarily complimented, I thought no more about it. Then I injured myself. You are the best physician in Egypt . . ." She shrugged as though admitting an embarrassing foolishness. "I remembered the incident only when your man walked into my room. I am sorry for my rudeness."

Khaemwaset immediately protested. "Your rudeness! It is I who must apologize to you. I have never before done such an impulsive thing but, you see, I had caught glimpses of you in the market, in the temple of Ptah. I set up a search but could not find you. My intentions . . ."

She raised a hand, palm out. "The intentions of a son of Pharaoh and the mightiest prince of the land are above reproach," she finished for him. "I have heard that you are not only a student of history, Highness, but an admirer of the ancient moral codes. If the guard had identified you I should have turned aside to greet you. I too am a wistful dweller in Egypt's past and I would have been delighted to talk with you on certain matters. As it is, I can only thank you for your forbearance today."

She was gracious, slightly shamed, her undeniable magnetism subdued by a pretty anxiety to be forgiven and understood. Khaemwaset wanted to stroke the hands that had fallen and were clasped in her lap, to soothe and reassure her.

"I would like to make up for my insensitivity," he said. "I invite you to dine with my family in two weeks' time. Please say you will come. Bring Harmin, and of course your husband." Her eyes narrowed in a smile though her mouth remained still.

"I am a widow," she explained, and Khaemwaset fought an urge to swallow. "My husband died some years ago. Harmin and I live with my brother, Sisenet. He went into the city earlier but should be back by now. Would your Highness care to meet him?" Khaemwaset nodded. Tbubui looked towards the door. "Harmin, find your uncle," she asked, and Khaemwaset realized that the beautiful young man had at some time noiselessly re-entered the room and was standing just inside, arms folded and feet apart in the stance of a guardian. Khaemwaset wondered a little uncomfortably how long he had been there and what he had heard.

Harmin slipped away at once. Khaemwaset sipped his wine, enjoying the excellent vintage. He commented on it to Tbubui and she smiled.

"Your Highness has a discriminating palate," she observed. "It is Good Wine of the Western River, year five."

"Of my father's reign?"

She hesitated. "Indeed."

That made the wine twenty-eight years old. It must have cost Tbubui or her brother a small fortune in gold, unless they had had it stored somewhere since Ramses' fifth year. That was the more likely explanation. Good Wine was still the best and most popular among the nobles, even, he supposed, in faraway Koptos. He savoured it carefully.

Before long Harmin returned. With him was a short, spare man, thin of face and with his sister's grace of movement. Unlike his nephew, Sisenet's head had been shaved and he wore a simple wig trailing one white ribbon.

Khaemwaset, sitting waiting for the man's reverence, had the distinct impression that they had met before somewhere. It was not that he and Tbubui shared the same shape to their dark eyes or the same pleasing quirk to their mouths. Khaemwaset, watching Sisenet approach with body bent and arms outstretched in the traditional gesture of submission and respect, thought that the feeling of recognition came from some entirely different occasion, then dismissed it. He bade the man straighten, and met his cautious gaze. His whole mien, though welcoming, projected a mildly suspicious reserve that Khaemwaset believed he must carry with him at all times. Khaemwaset spoke first, as was customary given his higher rank.

"I am pleased to meet you, Sisenet. I admire your house very much, and envy you its singular calm. Please sit."

The man sank into a cross-legged position facing him and Tbubui. He smiled slowly. "Thank you, Highness. We prefer our privacy to the excitement of the city, though we sometimes take the skiff across the river. May I ask how my sister's injury is progressing?"

They talked for a while until Khaemwaset had finished the wine, then he rose to leave. Sisenet immediately came to his feet. "I shall expect all of you at dinner in two weeks," Khaemwaset repeated, "but before then I shall return and check on your wound, Tbubui. Thank you for your hospitality." Harmin showed him out, walking beside him through the now dusky palms to the watersteps and bidding him an affable good night.

He was shocked to see how much time had gone by since he had climbed this same stair. The sun had already set behind Memphis and was limning the pyramids that crowded the high plain of Saqqara in blade-sharp relief. The Nile's surface had lost depth and now reflected a dark blue, almost black sky. Dinner would already be under way at home. "Have the sailors light the torches," he ordered Amek, and stood leaning against the deck rails as the barge cleared the watersteps and headed for the western bank. He was all at once very tired, in mind as well as body. He felt as though he had run a dozen miles under a hot sun in the cloying sand of the desert, or had spent the afternoon reading a long and particularly difficult scroll.

I have found her, he told himself, but he was too fatigued to conjure the triumph that should have accompanied the thought. She is no disappointment. She is not loud-mouthed and common, or arrogant and cold, but an intelligent and polite noblewoman. In some ways she reminds me of Sheritra. The sound of his daughter's voice came back to him, plaintive and appealing, but now it seemed to embody a curious wildness, as though, while she sang gently, Sheritra had been gyrating and writhing in a courtesan's dance. Khaemwaset leaned more heavily against the gilded handrail and wanted to go to sleep.

He strode into his dining room full of apologies, but Nubnofret waved him to his table with an imperious gesture. The three of them had finished two courses and were beginning the third, while Khaemwaset's harpist played. His wife put down the fish she had been raising to her mouth and swirled her fingers in the waterbowl.

"Don't be silly, dearest," she expostulated. "Ib told me that you had been called out to see a patient. You look terribly tired. Sit down and eat." Suddenly he was ravenous. Swiftly he pulled his table against his knees, pushed aside the wreath of blooms waiting for him to wear and signalled for food.

"Well?" Nubnofret prompted as he began to pull his salad apart. "Was the case interesting?"

"They seldom are anymore, are they Father?" Hori broke in. "I think you have examined every disease and variety of accident possible in Egypt."

"That's true," Khaemwaset admitted. "No, Nubnofret, the case was not interesting, a wounded foot, but the people were." He concentrated on the food, chewing it and manipulating his bowl so that he had an excuse not to look at her. "The man, his sister and her son have recently moved here from Koptos of all places. They are obviously of noble birth; in fact they trace their line beyond the time of Osiris Hatshepsut. The sister has an interest in history and I have invited them to dine with us in a couple of weeks." All at once he realized that Tbubui had chatted to him and her brother without the slightest indication of the pain she must have been in following the surgery. She had smiled, even laughed, her foot motionless on the stool and swathed in fresh linen. She either felt little, as she had told him, or she was able to hide it extremely well, knowing that good manners dictated the full entertainment of a guest of his lineage. You fool, he told himself, contrite. You should have taken your leave immediately, not stayed to slurp wine, however fine, and make polite conversation. It was up to you to walk away, not them to dismiss you.

"To dine?" Nubnofret echoed him. "That is not like you, Khaemwaset. They must have made an impression indeed, to be accorded such an honour."

He now trusted himself to look up. "They did."

"In that case, give me three days' warning. Sheritra, sit straight! Your back is as hunched as a monkey's."

The girl obeyed automatically. Her eyes were on her father, and Khaemwaset felt their keenness before she dropped her gaze to her plate once more.

Hori began a conversation to do with the plans for his tomb. He had begun to design it early as every Egyptian should. Nubnofret, after a time, changed the subject to the renovation of the kitchens. Khaemwaset joined in easily and the meal ended cheerfully. Nubnofret excused herself. Hori went to seek Antef. Sheritra, who had said little, stirred on her cushions but made no move to leave. The servants removed her table and Khaemwaset's and he, seeing her abstract mood, signalled that the harpist should continue to play.

"Have you had a happy day?" he asked her.

"Certainly, Father," she replied. "I have been particularly lazy though. Bakmut went into the city to run some errands for me and I fell asleep in the garden, then I had a swim. Who was your patient today?"

Khaemwaset inwardly cursed her question. Fleetingly he began to compose a lie, then discarded it. "I think you can guess," he answered quietly.

She uncrossed her legs and rearranged her linens, then fell to playing with her gold earring, twisting it round and round, her head on one side. "Really?" she said. "How extraordinary! The woman you seek is placed at your feet like an unexpected gift."

Her choice of words made Khaemwaset uncomfortable, guilty.

"It was indeed a strange occurrence," he responded awkwardly.

"And were you disappointed?" She could not disguise the hope in her voice.

"Not at all," Khaemwaset said grimly. "She is lovely, gracious and well-bred."

"And coming to dinner." Sheritra let go the earring. "Is that wise?" Then when he did not reply she burst out, "Oh Father, I wish you wouldn't! I really wish you wouldn't!"

It would do no good, Khaemwaset knew, to pretend that he did not know what she meant, and to do so would be insulting. Her homely face was flushed, her eyes unnaturally bright with concern. "I do not think you have anything to fear," he said deliberately, kindly. "I do not deny to you, Sheritra, that I am almost irresistibly drawn to her, but between a wish and its fulfillment are many decisions, many choices. I have already done the right thing in the eyes of the gods and within the confines of Ma'at. I shall doubtless do so this time." He did not realize for a moment that he was lying on both counts.

"Is she married?" Sheritra asked a little more calmly, though her colour remained high.

"She is a widow." Khaemwaset found it very difficult to hold her gaze. "You know that I could offer her a contract of marriage if I wished, my dearest, and put her in separate quarters on the estate with her son, but I don't think she is the kind of woman who would resign herself to the position of Second Wife. Whatever happens, your mother's well-being is my first concern."

"So you feel that strongly about her?"

He was immediately irritated. "I have seen her four times and only talked with her once! How do I know?"

She looked away, her hands now restless. "I have upset you, Father," she said. "I am sorry."

He was silent. Presently she got up clumsily, shook back her hair and walked out with as much dignity as she could muster. The music of the harp continued to trill and flutter through the lamplit room.

He gave Nubnofret her three days' notice and was standing above the watersteps with Ib and Amek in plenty of time to greet his guests when they arrived. He wondered if they would disembark hesitantly, climb the stair with the reluctance of the momentarily overawed, but their small craft hove into sight, was challenged by his river guard, tied up, and they emerged and walked towards him without a trace of self-consciousness. Sisenet was simply clad in a plain kilt and leather sandals, but several strands of gold hung with ankhs and miniature crouching baboons lay on his chest, and gold bracelets hugged both his arms. He was carefully painted and wore a gold-and-malachite scarab ring on the index finger of each hand. Harmin was similarly dressed. A gold circlet passed around his high forehead and held down his gleaming black hair just about his ears, and from it a single gold ankh rested against his brow, giving startling emphasis to his kohled grey eyes.

But Khaemwaset's gaze was drawn to Tbubui. She too was in white. He had wondered if for this occasion she might adopt more fashionable dress—flounces and hundreds of tiny pleats, intricate borders and fussy jewellery—and was irrationally relieved when he saw the tight linen sheath that gripped her lithe body from ankles to breasts. She, like Harmin, wore a circlet, but hers was wide silver, though the ankh on her forehead was as plain. A silver necklace with a red jasper pendant descending into her cleavage and a loose girdle of silver net with a red tassle swinging between her hidden knees were the only acknowledgement of formality. Khaemwaset was glad to see the white sandals on her feet. She followed his gaze and laughed. Her perfect, somewhat feline teeth shone against her hennaed mouth and brown skin.

"Yes, Prince, I have learned my lesson," she smiled. "Though I am sure that once I am fully healed I will forget it. I cannot abide too restrictive a mode of dress." Khaemwaset had a mental picture of her wriggling out of the tight, slitted sheath, bending over to lift it past her feet so that her breasts swung free, turning towards him naked, one knee flexed as it had been while she talked to Amek on the dusty river road.

"I see the bandages are gone," he commented. "Are you still in pain?"

She shook her head and they began to move along the paved path, around the house towards the garden. "The sole is a little tender, but that is all," she replied. "You do fine work, Highness. And that reminds me." She signalled, and the servant who had accompanied them came forward and handed Khaemwaset a jar. "Good Wine of the Western River, year one," Tbubui said. "My payment for your time and trouble."

Khaemwaset thanked her, careful not to be effusive, and passed the jar to Ib. By then the group had left the path and were walking on soft grass towards the family. Nubnofret stood waiting, Hori and Sheritra behind her. The visitors at once bowed to them. Nubnofret bade them rise, and Khaemwaset made the introductions and indicated chairs. Hori at once engaged Harmin in conversation, the pair of them sinking to the reed mat and the cushions face to face, arms curling about their knees. Sheritra, as was her custom, sought refuge behind Khaemwaset's chair. He had expected Nubnofret to begin to chatter to Tbubui while wine and delicacies were being offered by an attentive Ib and his underlings, and indeed he saw his wife lean towards the woman, but Sisenet forestalled her even as she took a breath.

"Highness, perhaps the Prince has told you that my sister and I moved here only two months ago," he began, "and since then we have had a great deal of trouble finding suitable staff. We left many of our servants in Koptos to maintain the estate there and we have tried to replace them, but Memphis servants seem sloppy and deceitful. Have you any advice?"

Khaemwaset saw Nubnofret's green-shaded, large eyes light up. She swung from Tbubui to Sisenet. "You are right," she said, waving Ib away. Nubnofret always kept a clear head when guests were present. "Untrained, the common people here do have a tendency to laziness and lying. I can give you the address of a couple who recruit and partially train servants, and who will be answerable for their behaviour until they have been fully integrated into your household routines. They do not operate cheaply, of course, but then . . . ."

Khaemwaset felt a hand on his arm, at once withdrawn, but the touch had been cool. "Some of our new servants simply left us," Tbubui remarked to him as he inclined in her direction. "I think the silence overwhelmed them, despite the good wages we offered. Slaves might be a better proposition."

He watched her take a slow, long swallow of wine, her throat working, her hair falling back, and was aware that Sheritra's eyes were fixed on him from slightly behind his chair.

"I do not approve of slaves serving the household directly," he said, "though I did buy a few for the kitchens and stables. Loyalty appears to go hand in hand with dignity."

"An old-fashioned but agreeable philosophy," Tbubui smiled. "Pharaoh does not agree with you, though. The population of slaves allowed to multiply, foreigners serving Egyptians and other foreign noblemen, is frighteningly extensive."

"Why frightening?" Khaemwaset asked, intrigued. He noted that Sheritra had hitched a little closer so that she might hear better.

"Because one day the slaves might realize that they outnumber the free and might take steps to wrench that freedom from us," Tbubui said simply. Her expression was serious, sober, a student of human nature discussing that nature with another student. Her gaze was direct.

"Such a wish would be foolish," Khaemwaset objected. Privately he was thinking, one does not talk to women in this way. Women run households and handle their businesses, practical things, but they do not play with theories. He could not imagine this kind of talk with Nubnofret. But with Sheritra . . . A hand appeared beside him, slid a spicy pastry from the plate on the table, and retired. So she had relaxed enough to be nibbling. That was good, a surprising sign. "Our army is powerful, swift, and well armed," he went on. "No uprising of slaves, no matter how strong, could withstand my father's soldiers."

"The army itself contains thousands of foreign mercenaries." Startled, Khaemwaset looked around. The voice was Sheritra's. "Imagine, Father, if they decided that their loyalties lay with blood ties, not with Grandfather's gold!"

"You are right, Sheritra," Tbubui replied, nodding at the girl, "and surely your father will agree with us. Egypt needs purifying."

He did agree, and had been arguing for the sake of arguing, but now he found himself left out of the conversation. Sheritra, her shyness forgotten for some reason known only to herself, was answering their guest without a trace of diffidence, and Tbubui was replying with all her attention. Most people did not take the trouble to draw Sheritra out. After the exchange of obligatory pleasantries they would turn their minds and faces to the gorgeous Hori and the rest of the family, and Sheritra would retire into the shadows, eating nothing, drinking little and escaping as soon after dinner as she was permitted.

But Tbubui had somehow drawn out the girl, put her at ease without ostentatiously trying, a ploy that had failed many times when well-meaning guests tried it. Khaemwaset realized that he had been deep in his own thoughts. He came to himself in time to hear Tbubui say, "But Princess, think of the expense such a policy would entail! What pharaoh could afford it? Even Ramses the Lord of All could not!"

Khaemwaset blinked. Sheritra was now at Tbubui's feet, wiping crumbs from her mouth, her colour high not with embarrassment but with enjoyment, even though Tbubui was actually disagreeing with her, something Sheritra all too often took personally. "Why not?" his daughter objected heatedly. "Let him put a tax on each one first! The gods know, Tbubui, that there are plenty of dirt-poor Egyptian fellahin who would welcome a chance . . ." Khaemwaset let his glance wander. Harmin was now talking to Nubnofret. He was on his feet, one hand on his slanted, trim hip, head bent over her while gesturing with the wine cup held in his other hand. She was looking up at him attentively, absorbed, perhaps even admiringly. Sisenet was sitting in silence, his eyes on the fountain, his expression closed.

Reluctantly Khaemwaset acknowledged that he must leave Tbubui's presence and be a proper host to her retiring brother. He turned in time to see her cross one long leg over the other. The slitted sheath fell back, exposing a breathtaking length of dusky thigh. Though the woman's attention never left a gesticulating Sheritra, Khaemwaset somehow knew that the movement had been for his benefit, and Tbubui was fully aware of his glance.

Dinner was a happy, noisy affair. At Khaemwaset's request, Nubnofret had demanded the presence of all musicians in the Prince's pay, and his young dancers and singers as well. Normally, Khaemwaset liked to dine in relative quiet, particularly if his guests were present on official pharaonic business and would want to talk seriously after the sixth course, but this time he had wanted entertainment. Spring flowers were everywhere, heady in their ripeness, and incense filled the air with a bluish haze. The dancers wove about the little tables, finger-cymbals clicking, weighted hair swinging, and the singers' harmony filled the ears of the company.

Khaemwaset had been careful to place Sheritra close to himself and the doors so that she could both be protected and beat a silent retreat when she wanted to. But he found her place taken by Tbubui, a laughing, animated, altogether bewitching Tbubui who joked, fingered her injured foot with mock alarm and kept up a stream of entirely fascinating conversation that included Nubnofret as well as himself. Hori and Sisenet had their heads together over the wine and were discussing something in private, inaudible voices.

Harmin sat beside Sheritra and she did not seem to mind. Once in a while he would touch her — on the shoulder, on the arm — and once Khaemwaset happened to see him putting a white lotus bloom behind her ear, smiling in answer to her chuckle. What is happening to us all tonight? he wondered delightedly. It is as though a spirit of good-humoured recklessness has invaded the house, so that surprising but good things might overtake us at any moment.

The party did not break up until the dawn. Even when good manners demanded that the guests be allowed to go, the family gathered on the watersteps in the grey, fleetingly cold un-light, as if to drain the last drops of their company. Looking around at their palely lit faces, Khaemwaset was surprised to see Sheritra's still among them, and startled by the expression of half-hungry eagerness all of them carried. No one was drunk, but all, though exhausted, were still exhilarated. The torches that had burned all night on the visitors' barge in preparation for their departure were extinguished. Tbubui, Sisenet and Harmin made their reverences, went aboard, and the family watched the craft angle out of sight on an oily, waveless river. Nubnofret sighed.

"It is going to be a hot day," she said. "Well, Khaemwaset, they were excellent company and I should like to invite them again, even though their accent is provincial and their taste in everything is quaint, to say the least."

A return invitation from his wife for no reason other than a desire to see her guests again was high praise. Khaemwaset felt absurdly complimented. But he did not agree with her that their accent was a provincial one. He had travelled Egypt on official business far more often than she, and knew that if he had heard it before he would have placed it.

"They are interesting people," Sheritra put in, and added rather grudgingly, "I think they really liked me and were not talking to me just to be polite." No one dared to comment for fear she might misconstrue what was said and her evening would be spoiled.

"Sisenet is widely read," Hori said. "It is a pity that you did not have more time to spend with him, Father. I was telling him about the tomb, about our problems interpreting the wall scenes, and he offered to try and help. Do you mind?"

Khaemwaset considered. He felt a little guilty that he had had so few words with the man, but he had sensed that Sisenet was a person of few words anyway and was self-sufficient in his silences. "I only mind if he is no more than a thrill-seeking amateur," he replied, "but you would have guessed that, and put him off. I suppose he may have something to add to our speculations."

Nubnofret gave a prodigious yawn. "What a charming young man Harmin is!" she said, blinking like an owl in the strengthening light. Khaemwaset, tired though he was, could almost see the machinations begin behind those huge, shadowed eyes. Oh do not say anything just yet, he begged her silently. I saw Sheritra's response to him too, but a chance word now will earn her scorn and that will be that. However, Nubnofret did not go on. She yawned again, bid them good morning and walked away. Sheritra met her father's gaze.

"They were all charming," she said deliberately. "As a matter of fact, I liked them."

Khaemwaset put an arm around her thin shoulders, suddenly loving her with a fierce protectiveness. "Let's get some sleep," was all he replied, and together, still linked, they turned towards the house.

Chapter 7

'I am unto thee like a garden,
which I have planted with flowers
and all manner of sweet-smelling herbs.'

Over the next few days Khaemwaset cast about for some excuse to visit Tbubui again. Her foot had healed well, and he knew he would not meet any of them at the social and religious functions he attended in Memphis as Pharaoh's representative. Nobility they might be, but their blood was not sufficiently blue to allow them to hold any major offices; besides, they did not seem drawn to court life or the maze of governmental administration. There were many such families in Egypt, living quietly on their holdings, paying their taxes and sending the obligatory gift to the Living Horus on New Year's Day, immersed in the simple life of the villages and the mundane concerns of their people.

But they are not usually so erudite, Khaemwaset thought on more than one occasion as he returned unwillingly to his routine. The soil of the land to which they relate so closely clings to their feet. Why are these three so different? What has brought them from the backwater of Koptos to Memphis? If they were bored, then why not go directly to Pi-Ramses? If Tbubui is ambitious for Harmin, that would have been the logical choice, for she is bold and learned and would have no difficulty getting herself noticed. I will ask her if she would like me to bring the youth to my father's attention, perhaps get him a minor post at court where he can show his skills and advance on his own. All he needs is that first connection. But it was too soon, he realized. He did not want to appear patronizing. Nor did he want Tbubui to think that he was merely ingratiating himself with her. Which, he reflected ruefully, would probably be the truth.

It was Hori who solved his dilemma. He approached his father a week into the month of Tibi, waiting until Khaemwaset had dealt with the daily correspondence before ambling into the office and perching on the edge of the desk in his customary fashion.

"There was a letter from your grandmother today," Khaemwaset told him. "She writes cheerfully but her scribe took it upon himself to add a note to the bottom of the scroll. Her health is failing rapidly."

Hori frowned. "I am sorry to hear it. Will you be going north then?"

"No, not yet. She is well cared for, and I do not think the situation is critical." Khaemwaset regarded the prospect of more weeks in the Delta with the horror of a trapped hare. He wanted nothing more at the moment than to cultivate Sisenet and his sister without interruption. The thought came tangled with shame, but he consoled himself by imagining that the scribe would have asked for his presence more explicitly if his mother's condition had been dangerous.

Hori sighed. "So many people speak of her with awe," he said quietly. "She must have embodied everything that was good and beautiful in her day. Aging is so sad, isn't it Father?"

Khaemwaset ran his eye over the perfectly muscled thigh resting on the polished wood of the desk, the flat, taut stomach, the straight shoulders and upright spine before him. Hori was smiling at him faintly, his translucent eyes ringed in their long black lashes, those appealing crinkles around the sensuous curve of his mouth.

"It is only sad if the years behind have been wasted," he commented drily, "and I doubt very much if Astnofert regards her life as a waste. And speaking of waste, Hori, you are well into your nineteenth year and will soon be twenty. You are a fully royal prince. Don't you think it is time you started casting about for a wife?"

The smile left Hori's face. His dark, feathery eyebrows shot up in surprise. "But I have been looking, Father!" he protested. "The young women bore me and the older ones are unattractive. What am I supposed to do?"

"Let your mother and me find you a noblewoman, and then form your own harem. I'm serious, Hori. Marriage is a duty for a prince."

Hori snorted. "Yes I know. But I look at you and Mother, how comfortable you are together, how your few concubines languish away because you so seldom bother with them, and I keep hoping that I might also find someone who would share my life, not just run a household. In that respect you have set a bad example, Father!"

Khaemwaset forced a smile. Guilt threatened him and he beat it back. "Nubnofret and I are perhaps not as close as you seem to think," he said quietly.

"You were at one time," Hori broke in loudly. "And look at Uncle Si-Montu and Ben-Anath! That is what I want, Father, and I will wait another ten years if necessary in order to have it!"

"Very well." Khaemwaset did not feel like arguing. "I can see that I am to support you for the rest of your life." Hori grinned engagingly and slipped from the desk. "Why did you come to see me?"

"Oh yes." Hori flung himself with artless grace into the empty chair on the other side of the desk. "I received a message from Sisenet assuring me that his offer of help at the tomb was not polite fiction, and wanting to know when his presence might be welcome on the site. I wanted to ask you about it again, just to make sure it is all right."

"Send a reply and invite him tomorrow, mid-morning," Khaemwaset said quickly. "I will join you both. Even if he has nothing much to say, we can give him a meal."

"Very well. I'm looking forward to it. I think I might invite them all. Tbubui herself seems to be a woman of great education." His eyes slid away from Khaemwaset's. "Have you prepared our horoscopes for Tibi?"

Khaemwaset looked at him curiously. "No," he said slowly. "For some reason I am loath to do it this month. Last month's and the month's before were so catastrophic for me, and to a lesser extent for you, yet the time has passed without great incident. I am beginning to wonder if I am making some fundamental mistake in my method."

"I would not exactly say that the time has passed without great incident," Hori mused, already heading for the door. Then he turned and stood still, hands behind his back. "Father . . ."

"Yes?"

After a moment Hori shook his head. "Oh nothing. I shall ask Mother if it is all right to bring them back here for the noon meal tomorrow. Or they might even invite us."

"They might." But Khaemwaset spoke to an empty doorway. Hori had gone.

Khaemwaset had not visited the tomb site for several weeks, but it had not changed much. He stood under the shade of his canopy at the top of the stairs, piles of dry rubble to right and left, Penbuy behind him and the guests coming towards them over the shifting plain of Saqqara. Watching Tbubui's sandals sink and rise, spewing sand as she walked, he wondered fleetingly if the heat and grit were causing her pain, and why in any case Sisenet had not ordered litters for them. Then his thoughts were caught away in the rhythmic swing of her hips under the white sheath, the darting of her kohled eyes as she took in the site.

The three came up and bowed, and the waiting canopy-bearers rushed to cover them as Khaemwaset had instructed. Tbubui's pupils widened under the shade. Khaemwaset, bemused, saw the rims of black enlarge. The whites were almost blue in their purity.

Hori came hurrying from the dim entrance, a welcome on his lips as the one who had proffered the invitation. Khaemwaset noticed an agitation about him, but he seemed happy enough.

After a few moments of idle chatter, Khaemwaset ushered them down the steps and into the constant coolness of the short passage. With a nod he gave Hori permission to take charge of Sisenet, but Tbubui also wandered away.

Khaemwaset followed her with his eyes, all at once oblivious of his surroundings, all his being intent on the sweet, alluring curves of her, the rise and fall of her heels, the clean sweep of her throat and neck as she looked up to study the bright paintwork.

When she came to the two statues she halted, and stood for a long time staring, then she leaned forward and caressed them, her light fingers moving gently over every groove. "We love life so passionately, we Egyptians," she said. "We want to hold onto every hot desert wind, every heavy odour from our garden flowers, every touch from those we adore. In building our tombs and preserving our bodies so that the gods may resurrect us, we spend gold like water, tossed down our summer-parched throats. We write spells, we perform rituals. And yet who can say what death means? Who has returned from that dark place? Do you think one day someone might, Prince? Or perhaps already has, without our knowledge?" She stepped towards him. "They say that the fabled Scroll of Thoth has the power to raise the dead," she went on, watching him intently. "Will it ever be found do you think?"

"I do not know," Khaemwaset answered awkwardly. "If it exists it will be protected by Thoth's powerful spells."

She came closer. "Every magician dreams of finding it," she said softly, "if indeed it lies hidden somewhere. But few could control it if they did. Do you desire it, Great Prince, like the others? Do you hope that you might stumble across it each time you open a tomb?"

Was there something mocking in her tone? Many nobles regarded the magicians' search for the Scroll as a naive joke, and if she did too he would be bitterly disappointed. It seemed from her expression that she was privately amused by something. "Yes, I desire it," he answered straightforwardly. "Now would you like to go into the burial chamber?" She nodded, still smiling.

Hori and Sisenet were already there, their low voices drifting, disembodied, past the torchlight. Placing an authoritative hand on her arm, Khaemwaset accompanied Tbubui and they walked into the room where the two coffins lay. Once more he watched her as she released herself from his grip and went forward, leaning into the unknown man's sarcophagus.

"There are cut threads attached to this man's hand," she commented at last, standing away. "Something has been stolen from him." She looked squarely at Khaemwaset. He nodded.

"You are correct," he replied. "The body had a scroll sewn onto it, which I took. I have treated it with great care, as I do all my finds, and when it has been copied it will be returned to this coffin. I am hoping it will add to the sum of our knowledge of the ancients."

She made as if to say something, then obviously thought better of it. Hori and Sisenet were engaged in knocking on the walls. "Here! It is here," Hori said, and the other man put his ear to the plaster.

"Strike once more," he requested. Hori complied, then Sisenet straightened. "It sounds as though there is another chamber beyond," he observed. "Have you considered the possibility that this wall is false?"

Khaemwaset tensed as Hori nodded. "Yes I have," he said hesitantly, "but to explore it would mean tearing apart these decorative scenes. Now that would be true vandalism." He glanced at his father. "In any case, the decision to do so is not mine to make. My father must take the risk."

Under no circumstances, Khaemwaset thought, is that wall coming down. I do not know why I fear this tomb but I do. Something in my ka shrinks from it. "We can discuss it later," he said briskly. "Sisenet, my son tells me that you are an informed historian yourself. I would be happy to hear your explanation for all the water depicted in this tomb. The inscriptions are few and we are puzzled."

Sisenet smiled faintly, looking at his sister, then at Khaemwaset. He shrugged, with an artless, aristocratic grace, his black eyebrows lifting. "I can only hazard a guess," he said. "Either this family adored spending their leisure in fishing, fowling and boating and wished to preserve their delight and prowess with line and throwing stick, or . . ." — he cleared his throat — ". . . or water represented some terrible cataclysm to them, a curse fulfilled, perhaps, and they felt compelled to chronicle it in the paintings of their daily lives." He shook his head. "I am not much help, I'm afraid. Nor do I know why the coffin lids were left standing against the wall."

"There is no way to tell," Hori said heavily, and Khaemwaset pulled himself together. He had been watching Sisenet as the man was speaking, that odd feeling of familiarity tugging at him once more. In this setting it was stronger, as though Sisenet naturally blended with these ancient surroundings, his self-sufficiency somehow one with the heavy stillness no sound or activity could dissipate, his air of slightly arrogant authority a part of the cold dignity of the dead. The small puzzle annoyed Khaemwaset until, as Sisenet glanced at him without expression, he was suddenly reminded of the statue of Thoth overshadowing the dim chamber. Of course, he thought with relief. The level, unblinking stare of the god, his air of secret wisdom and implacable judgment, was mirrored in Sisenet's unshakeable calm. He smiled.

"The hour grows late, and Nubnofret will be waiting to serve us lunch," he said. "Be our guests, I beg, and let us leave this mustiness."

They accepted his invitation. Outside, the canopied litters were waiting under a blistering sun and the bearers dozed, their backs against the relative coolness of the enormous rock that had blocked the entrance to the tomb. Hori immediately invited Sisenet to share his litter, forcing Khaemwaset reluctantly to offer his to Tbubui and Harmin, who had stood in the middle of the larger tomb chamber the whole time without uttering a single word. Khaemwaset would have preferred to ride into Memphis with Tbubui's long, thinly clad leg resting against his own. He himself commandeered Ib's litter. "Why did you not bring litters?" he asked Tbubui as she slid onto the cushions beside her son, and in the act of propping herself on one elbow she smiled up at him.

"We prefer to walk when we can," she replied, her kohled eyes half-shut against the brilliant light. "Walking is a constant pleasure and delight, Prince. The heat here is as nothing to the heat at Koptos and besides, Koptos is barren. We walk, we smell the river, we enjoy the movement of the shade. Our skiff is moored at the Peru-nefer docks."

"You walked all this way?" Khaemwaset said unbelievingly, and she nodded. "I will send a servant to order your skiff to our watersteps," he offered, and stepping back, signalled to the bearers.

He spent the time on the journey back to his house reliving his moments beside Tbubui in the tomb and pondering Sisenet's words regarding the water. Either explanation would be satisfactory, he reflected, unseeing eyes fixed on the closed and lightsuffused curtains of the conveyance. But I prefer the latter. That tomb is not a peaceful resting place. Something awful sleeps there, and I can well believe it is a family's doom.

It was then that he remembered Sisenet's comment about the coffin lids and he leaned forward, frowning. How had the man known that they were standing against the wall when Hori and I first penetrated the inner room? Hori must have told him. All the same, Khaemwaset thought again as the litter swayed and lurched into the noise of the city, I will ask.

Lunch was a cheerful affair, taken outside under a large awning. After he had eaten, Khaemwaset sat hugging his obsession to himself like some invisible cloak, pretending to drowse while his slitted eyes followed Tbubui's every move. To his chagrin, she had few words for him. She was dividing her attention between Nubnofret and Hori, who lay sprawled in the grass at her feet, speaking rapidly and seriously to the one, laughing fetchingly with the other, and Khaemwaset, vaguely annoyed, thought that he had never seen Hori so animated and entertained.

Sisenet was sitting a little apart, both hands around his wine cup, watching the monkeys caper and gibber by the pool. He seemed content enough, with the self-sufficient coolness Khaemwaset was beginning to recognize as uniquely his. Khaemwaset had talked to him while the food was being served and had managed to ask him how he had known about the coffin lids. He had looked bewildered for a moment and then said, "I don't remember, Prince. Hori must have told me last time we dined. He and I talked at great length about the tomb." Khaemwaset was satisfied. They had chatted for a few more minutes but Sisenet had seemed disinclined to carry a conversation and had retired to the wine, leaving his host to give Tbubui his undivided, though clandestine, attention.

Shcritra had run out to greet the guests without a trace of the bashfulness that was her curse. She had answered all questions freely, eaten whole-heartedly, and was now perched on a pile of cushions under one of the sycamores with Harmin, both of them drowned in the tree's deep shade. Khaemwaset took a moment to appreciate the young man's classical good looks, his glossy, straight black hair, his long, ringed fingers, before thinking, very well, very well. It would surprise me, for surely Harmin, once known, could have his pick of any Memphis beauty, but perhaps he is as rare a bird as Hori and will understand my daughter's hidden qualities. I must investigate this family's lineage. He turned his hidden gaze back to Tbubui. Presently he rose. "Tbubui," he said, "I believe that you are interested in medicine."

She glanced up at him lazily, obviously somnolent with the heat. "Yes, Prince, I am. I suppose Harmin told you."

"Would you like to inspect my remedies?"

For answer she rose. Nubnofret glanced their way but Khaemwaset, reading her absent expression, knew that she did not mind. He started for the house.

"Do you treat your own staff?" he asked Tbubui as they passed into the welcome gloom of the hall and made their way to Khaemwaset's office. "Or have you your own physician in residence?"

"I prefer to treat them myself," she answered behind him, and Khaemwaset could have sworn that he felt her warm breath between his naked shoulder-blades. "That way I am learning all the time. They do not seem to mind my mistakes!"

She stood looking about the orderly room, now filled with the deep, drugged stillness of the later afternoon. Khaemwaset unlocked the library and beckoned her within, closing the door behind her. Without pause he opened the chest that contained his herbs and philtres, not marvelling at how he was breaking his own usually rigid rule regarding whose hands disturbed them, and Tbubui became immediately brisk and curious.

She examined them carefully and questioned him fully on their cost and use, the seductive, magnetic woman gone, replaced by one whose intelligence and concentration inflamed him in a new way.

He forced himself to answer her rationally, to make his voice obey him, but he was trembling as her heavily ringed hands caressed his pots and jars, and her hair fell forward as she bent over the chests.

Handing the collection back to him her fingers brushed his, her inadvertent touch cool although beads of sweat had collected in the hollow of her throat and the skin between her breasts glistened with moisture.

At last he locked his medicines away, then stood, intending to usher her out. He found her with her head thrown back and her eyes closed, one hand working the back of her neck. "It is so quiet in here," she murmured. "Almost as quiet as my home. This room has an atmosphere that banishes the outside world as though it did not exist."

Khaemwaset's control deserted him. Sliding his own hand behind her neck he forced her back until the wall stopped them, then he leaned into her and brought his mouth down on her own. A stab of pleasure such as he had never known lanced his abdomen and he groaned, preternaturally aware of the soft underside of her lips as his tongue flicked over them, the cold resistance of her teeth before they parted. Her breath was in his mouth. Then it was over. He withdrew shakily, his own breath coming hard, and she lifted a hand to her face, brushing against his penis lightly, briefly, as she did so.

"What ails you, Prince?" she said in a low voice, her eyes all at once heavy-lidded, her nostrils flaring. "Why this?"

You ail me, he wanted to blurt. I sicken from you like a love-hungry youth. Your mouth is not enough, Tbubui. I must have all of you, my tongue in the valleys I can imagine so painfully but not yet see, my hands gauging the texture, the temperature of your skin, my body ceasing to obey my mind and for once knowing only its driving need. For once . . . He did not apologize.

"I sought you for a long time," he said huskily. "My servants grew exhausted. I was robbed of sleep, my food was as the sand, dry and tasteless. That kiss was compensation for it all."

"And was it compensation enough, Prince?" she asked, her smile gently mocking. "Or will you demand a full recompense? It will not be easy. No, it will not. For I am of noble birth and no mean person."

Immediately an urge to violence mingled with his lust. He wanted to bruise her lips with his teeth, knead her breasts until she cried out. For one blinding moment he hated her constant poise. The words of desire died on his tongue, and with a curt gesture he ushered her from the room.

The guests left at sunset, though Nubnofret had invited them to stay for the evening meal. "We have another commitment, unfortunately," Sisenet explained, "but we thank you for your boundless kindness. Remember to send me word about that wall in the tomb," he added, turning to Hori. "I am very interested. Indeed the whole day has been intriguing. I have enjoyed myself enormously, standing alive in the presence of the dead."

They took their leave, and began to file up the shadowed ramp at the foot of the watersteps. Their skiff waited motionless on the red-splashed, smooth mirror the Nile had become at that hour.

All at once Tbubui stumbled. With a cry she slipped towards the unguarded edge of the ramp, arms flung out to catch a non-existent rail, and Khaemwaset jumped forward, but before he could reach her Harmin had pulled her back.

"Are you all right?" Khaemwaset called, hurrying up to her. She nodded, trembling in every limb, her face chalk white. Harmin, an arm across her shoulders, turned her and she walked unsteadily into the skiff. Sisenet followed without speaking a word, and the tiny boat cast off and glided away. Khaemwaset returned to his family.

"She is not harmed," he replied to Nubnofret's silently raised eyebrows.

"Her reaction to the prospect of a tumble in the mud was rather extreme," Nubnofret commented, and Hori shook his head.

"Not really," he said. "Her husband drowned, and ever since she has been mortally afraid of water. Apparently he fell from a raft during a boating party at Koptos. He had had too much wine, and the Nile was in full flood. His body was recovered miles downstream four days later."

"How do you know?" Khaemwaset asked sharply, with resentment.

"She told me," Hori answered simply, "because I asked her."

Sheritra shuddered. "How dreadful!" she exclaimed. "Poor Tbubui!"

Khaemwaset gently took her wrist. "So you are going into the city with Harmin tomorrow," he said. The young man had taken him aside earlier and had coolly requested his permission. Khaemwaset had gladly given it. "You must of course take Amek and a soldier with you," he insisted to Sheritra, "and be home in time for dinner."

"Of course I will!" she replied impatiently. "Do not fuss so, Father. Now I will change my linens before we eat." She disengaged herself, shouting for Bakmut, and went into the house. Hori had already wandered off, Antef appearing from the rear garden to meet him. Khaemwaset and Nubnofret looked at each other.

"She is going to fall hard," Khaemwaset said slowly. "I don't know what that young man has said to her, but already she has changed."

"I see it too," Nubnofret agreed. "But I am full of fear for her, my husband. What can he possibly see in her? He is new to Memphis. She is the first girl he has met here. He will discard her when his social life becomes more varied. Sheritra is too sensitive to handle such a crushing rejection."

"As usual, you give her no credit," Khaemwaset responded angrily, feeling as though his wife had attacked Tbubui herself.

"Why is it not possible for Harmin to appreciate all the qualities in Sheritra that are not visible? And why do you immediately presume that he is merely dallying and will desert her? Let us at least give both of them the compliment of optimism."

"You always were blind to everyone's faults but mine!" Nubnofret snapped back bitterly, and turning on her heel she stalked away across the darkening lawn, her linen floating wraithlike behind her in the gloom.

By the time they sat down together for the final meal of the day, her anger had lessened to a stiff formality. Khaemwaset deliberately set himself to making her smile, and in the end succeeded. They drank their last cups of wine sitting side by side on the watersteps that still held the warmth of day, knee to knee, watching the barely perceptible flow of the quiet water. In the end, Nubnofret put her head on his shoulder.

For a while he let it rest there, inhaling the aroma of her tumultous hair, loosely holding her hand, but then a mild desire woke in him. "Come," he whispered, and rising he led her in under the tangled shrubbery beside the steps and made love to her.

But as he did so a distaste for his wife began to rise under his sexual urgency, a repugnance for her large, soft breasts, the spread of her ample, pliant hips, the wideness of her generous mouth now parted in pleasure. There was nothing hard, spare, driving about Nubnofret, and by the time Khaemwaset rolled from her and felt the dry grasses and twigs dig into his back, he knew that he would rather have been making love with Tbubui.

Sheritra tried not to break into a run as she saw Harmin smile a greeting from his vantage point in the bow of his barge. For a fleeting moment her defences came up and she wished with all her heart to be safely in her room talking with Bakmut, far away from this sudden complication, this enormous risk. But soon the shrinking was replaced by a feeling of happy recklessness new to her. Forcing her shoulders back she walked towards him with all the grace she could muster, Amek and his soldier behind. Harmin bowed as she negotiated the ramp and she bid him a good morning, thus giving him the freedom to speak.

"Good morning, Princess," he answered her gravely, signalling for the ramp to be drawn inboard. Amek and the other man took up their stations at either end of the craft, and Harmin drew Sheritra towards the cabin.

His family's barge was not as large nor as sumptuous as Khaemwaset's, but it was hung with pennants cut from a cloth of gold on which black Eyes of Horus had been painted. The curtains, tied back, were also cloth of gold, tasselled in silver. Sheritra took the upholstered stool Harmin indicated, watching him covertly as he arranged cushions for himself on the floor, then turned to offer her fresh water and slivers of cold beef marinated in garlic and wine.

He was dressed as simply as his barge, with a plain white kilt hugging his long thighs and stern leather sandals on his feet, but his belt was set with turquoise, as were his thick silver braclets and the lightly linked pectoral lying against his brown chest. The amulet counterpoise nestled between his flexing shoulder-blades was a row of tiny gold baboons, symbols of Thoth, protecting the wearer from certain spells designed to pierce the victim from behind.

"I have seen the Nile reflecting exactly the colours of your turquoise," Sheritra remarked hesitantly, a shyness on her with the ritual of accepting food and drink. "Those are very old, are they not? So often now the stones available are inferior. They are all blue, not the ancient greenish-blue Father finds so attractive."

Harmin went into a crouch on the cushions and grinned up at her, his kohled eyes glittering. "You are right. They have been in my family for many hentis and they are supremely valuable. They will be passed down to my oldest son."

Sheritra felt her cheeks grow hot. "I thought we were going to walk today," she put in hurriedly, "although drifting on the Nile is a great pleasure." She took a gulp of water and the fire in her face began to ebb.

"We will indeed walk, and perhaps by the end of the day you will beg to be returned to the barge," Harmin teased her. "But I decided to save you the dust and heat of the river road into Memphis. Also, if we find the bazaars overcrowded or boring we can be back on board in a matter of minutes. Look! We are already passing the canal to the old palace of Thothmes the First. I suppose you have been within it many times when your grandfather is in residence at Memphis."

"Why yes, I have," Sheritra began, and before she realized it, she was chatting about Ramses and his court, her father's political contacts, life as a princess. "It is not as wonderful as you might think," she said ruefully. "My daily routine and my education were far more rigidly controlled than that of a daughter of the nobility, and now that I have finished being tortured and you might think I am free, I face the prospect of being eventually betrothed to some hereditary erpa-ha to preserve Ramses' family dynasty. I don't mind the idea of being married, of course, but I do mind the certainty that my future husband will not love me. How could he? I look more like a peasant's daughter than a princess!"

Her voice had gradually risen and she had become more and more agitated without realizing it, until Harmin put out a protesting hand and, coming to herself, she understood what she had said. Her hands flew to her face.

"Oh Harmin!" she cried out. "I am so sorry. I have no idea why I am talking to you like this."

"I know why," he said calmly. "There is something about me that made you trust me from the first, isn't there, Little Sun?"

"Only my father calls me that," she said faintly.

"Do you mind if I do?"

She shook her head mutely.

"Good. For I feel that I have known you since my own schooldays. I am easy with you, and you with me. I am your friend, Sheritra, and I could wish to be nowhere else today than here beside you with the sun beating on the water and the crowds kicking up sand on the bank."

She was silent, her gaze ostensibly on the things he described while her thoughts played with his words. So far the only man she trusted was her father, and that was because he had earned her respect. The male faces who had appeared and as quickly disappeared from her life had earned nothing but her self-conscious scorn for their vapidity, their refusal to recognize her intelligence, their not-quite-hidden contempt for her homeliness. She knew that she was perilously close to such strength of feeling for Harmin that her whole life would be engulfed, and she herself changed. She already respected him for his frankness, the genuine way he had casually dismissed her exterior as of no account and had touched those chords in her that had so far vibrated only for Khaemwaset.

But friend. What did he mean by friend? Was his interest truly one of sharing minds? Well, it is all you can really hope for, she told herself sadly. But his next words caused her heart to pound.

"Your skin has the translucence of a pearl," he whispered, and she turned abruptly to find his black eyes fixed on her. "Your eyes are full of life, Princess, full of vitality when you allow your ka to shine through. Please hide no more."

I capitulate, she thought, panic-stricken. My judgment is even now deserting me. But oh Harmin! For Hathor's sake stand steady on the rope! I am giving birth to the self I have fiercely protected all my life, and it is still half-blind and helpless under your strange gaze.

"Thank you, Harmin," she replied steadily, and suddenly flashed him a bright grin. "I will hide no more from you. I care nothing about the rest of Egypt." He laughed and began to wolf down the cold beef, spearing it on a tiny silver-hafted dagger, occasionally holding bites to her mouth, and she, all at once ravenous, could not eat quickly enough.

They tied up at the southern docks on the outskirts of the foreign quarter, and instead of walking back through Peru-nefer to the central city, Harmin turned her south. Sheritra felt a tremor of concern. She had never plunged into this teeming life before, let alone on foot, and she was glad of Amek and his man's comforting bulk ahead and behind. But Harmin, tactfully guiding her with a touch on her elbow now and then and an encouraging smile, did not allow her to be jostled, and soon her fear evaporated.

As they ambled the donkey-choked, noisy streets she began to blossom under the cloak of anonymity and was soon exclaiming over the cascade of various nationalities flowing around her. Hurrians, Canaanites, Syrians, Semites, Dwellers of the Great Green exploded a bewildering myriad of languages in her ears. The bazaar stalls groaned under cloth of every grade and richness, gaudy jewellery, miniatures of the gods of every nation in every type of wood and stone and household items by the hundreds.

She and Harmin wandered through it all, fingering, laughing, bargaining for fun, until Sheritra suddenly became aware that the human traffic had thinned and the street they were on could now be seen, a short stretch of dazzling whiteness ending in a mud wall and an open gate.

"What is that?" she asked curiously. Harmin brushed a smear of dust from her temple.

"It is a shrine to the Canaanite goddess Astarte. Would you like to go in?"

Sheritra stared. "Is it permitted?"

Harmin smiled. "Of course. This is a shrine, not a temple. We may watch the worshippers without having to pray ourselves. I believe Astarte has a mighty temple in Pi-Ramses with many priests and priestesses, but here she has a small staff and the shrine's routine is fairly simple." As he was explaining to her, Harmin was ushering her forward. Together they entered through the open gate, finding themselves in an intimate outer court, unpaved and divided from the even tinier inner court by a waist-high mud wall.

Both courts were crowded with people praying or chanting, but as Sheritra approached the heart of the shrine the cheerful bustle died away. In the respectful space surrounding the statue of the goddess a lone priestess was dancing, finger-cymbals clicking, hair ornaments jangling. She was naked and moved sinuously with eyes closed, thighs flexed, spine arched. Just beyond her was Astarte. Curious, Sheritra looked her over, both attracted and repelled by the full, upthrust breasts, the flaunting curve of the stone belly, the strong spread of the immodest legs that seemed to invite any who dared to stand within them. Sheritra glanced at Harmin, expecting his gaze to be on the dancer, but he was watching her. "Astarte gives the pleasure of orgiastic sex," he told her. "But she is also the goddess of all forms of pure love."

"One would never know it to look at her!" Sheritra responded tartly. "She reminds me of the whores infesting the Peru-nefer district. Our own Hathor is also goddess of love, but with more politeness and somehow more humanity."

"I agree," Harmin answered. "Astarte really has no place in Egypt. She serves cruder, more barbaric races, which is why her shrines cluster in the foreigners' quarters of the cities. Still, she is probably older than Hathor."

"Grandfather has much sympathy for the foreign gods," Sheritra told him as they left the sacred premises. "Because he has red hair and it runs in our family and we come from the nome of the god Set, Ramses has made him his chief protector. He is Egyptian, of course, but Grandfather also worships his Canaanite counterpart, Baal, and regularly goes into the foreigners' temples. To me it is wrong."

"To me also," Harmin agreed quietly. "I share your views and those of your father, that Egypt is slowly being debased by the free introduction of so many strangers, both gods and men. Soon Set himself will be confused with Baal, Hathor with Astarte. Then let Egypt beware, for her fall will be near."

Impulsively Sheritra stepped forward and kissed him on the cheek. Behind her Amek coughed discreetly. "Thank you for one of the most lovely days I have ever had," she said fervently.

By the time Harmin emerged from the beer-shop with a flagon and four cups, Sheritra had found a small patch of tired grass under the shadow of a wall. Amek and the soldier bowed their thanks and drank quickly, standing up, but Harmin joined Sheritra where she had flung herself down, and for a long while they sipped and talked. The beer was strong and very dark, unlike the paler brew that appeared on her father's table each day, and her head was soon swimming, but the sensation was most agreeable.

Eventually Harmin returned the flagon and cups, helped her to her feet, and they made their way back to the barge and the drowsy sailors. The sun was lipping the horizon, seeping orange-yellow through the dust motes hanging in the air, tinging Sheritra's skin with a golden hue and becoming netted in her hair. She ascended the ramp, almost staggering to the cabin, and sank onto the pile of cushions with a gusty sigh. Her legs ached pleasantly and she was beginning to be hungry. Soon Harmin joined her and the craft slipped away from its mooring and turned to the north. Sheritra sighed again. I feel almost beautiful, she thought happily. I feel carefree and frivolous and full of laughter. She turned to Harmin, who was beating the dust off his kilt and staring ruefully at his filthy feet. "This has been wonderful!" she said.

He agreed, half laughing, she knew, at her uncharacteristic enthusiasm, but she did not take offence. "Today we did things of my choosing," he said. "Tomorrow I must attend to various duties at home, but the day after you may decide where we go."

Her eyes widened. "You want to spend yet another day with me?"

"Don't be foolish, Princess," he admonished her, and she heard a mild disapproval in his voice. "If I did not want to see you again I would not have suggested it. Is there to be a return to the suspicious Sheritra of old?"

She felt chastened but not insulted. "No, Harmin," she said meekly. "I do not believe that you are dissembling with me. Very well." She folded her hands primly and stared thoughtfully at the sunset-drenched water lapping by. "I know!" she said finally. "We will take Father's barge and Amek and Bakmut and float south past the city to the first secluded stretch of river, and we will spend the day swimming and catching frogs, and then we will eat sitting on the bank and then we will hunt duck in the marshes! Yes?"

He glance down at his smudged kilt. "Alas no," he said sadly. "I cannot swim, Highness. Like my mother, I am afraid of water. I do not mind being on it, but no power on earth can coerce me into it." His face came up and Sheritra saw it entirely sombre. "I would enjoy watching you swim, though, and the frogs and ducks, well, I can manage that."

She reached out and stroked the warm, stick-straight hair. "I am sorry," she whispered. "Then I will plan something else, a surprise, and you will not know where we are going until I come for you. Agreed?"

He nodded, seeming still in the grip of some cold thought, but then he smiled. "I have a confession to make to you, Sheritra," Harmin said quietly. "I hope it will not offend you."

Sheritra met the steady dark eyes regarding her own. She had forgotten her self-consciousness, forgotten to remember that the face he was scrutinizing so closely was mildly repugnant to most men and therefore a thing of shame. "You will not know until you try me," she answered and then blushed, aware of the unintended provocativeness of the words, but he either ignored or genuinely did not notice their baser meaning. With a small gesture he took her hand, running his thumb gently over her open palm.

"When I came to beg your father to treat my mother, as I was leaving and was waiting for him, I heard you singing."

Sheritra gave a low exclamation and tried to pull her fingers from his grasp, but he restrained her.

"No, do not recoil," he went on. "I had never heard such a glorious sound. I had intended to go down to the watersteps but I lingered, unable to move. Such sweetness filled me, Sheritra! I stood there until your father found me, wondering if the beauty of the singer's face matched her tones."

"Well now you know that they do not," Sheritra said curtly. But in spite of her cutting words she searched his expression with a hidden desperation, looking for a flicker of insincerity, the well-known, tiny falter of deceit. She did not find it. Harmin's eyebrows descended in a frown.

"Why do you do yourself so much injustice?" he asked, "And how do you know what I regard as beautiful? I will have you know, foolish girl, that I had imagined this singer as a woman of fire and spirit. That, to me, is beauty, and you have both, do you not, under that diffident exterior?"

She looked at him wonderingly. Oh yes! she thought, yes. Fire and spirit I have, Harmin, but I am a long way from betraying myself to you, for I have too much . . .

"You have too much pride to show yourself to anyone but your family, don't you?" Harmin smiled. "You fear that you will be repulsed, and your gifts belittled. Will you sing that song again for me now?"

"You ask a great deal of me!"

"I know exactly what I am asking of you," he insisted. "Courage. Now will you sing?"

For answer she sat straighter and willed herself not to blush. Her first notes were hesitant, and her voice cracked once, but soon her confidence began to flow and the ancient, sensuous words carried clear and sure across the river. " 'Your love, I desire it, like butter and honey. You belong to me, like best ointment on the limbs of the nobles, like finest linen . . .' " She sang only the woman's part of the song, omitting the lover's response, and she was startled when Harmin broke in softly, " 'My companionship will be for all the days, satisfying even for old age. I shall be with you every day, that I may give you my love always.' "

Both fell silent, then Harmin left the stool, lowered himself onto the cushion beside her and, taking her face in both his warm hands, he kissed her gently on the mouth. Her first impulse was to panic. She wanted to struggle, pull away, but his lips were so unthreatening, tasting of dust and beer, and their pressure did not increase, so that in the end the tension went out of her and she put both hands on his smooth shoulders and kissed him back. When they drew apart she saw his eyes somnolent with desire. "Little Sun," he murmured. "I am greatly looking forward to the day after tomorrow. My horoscope told me that my luck would be phenomenally high this month and lo! here I am beside you."

Sheritra smiled shakily, afraid that he might kiss her again, but she was coming to recognize his almost uncanny intuition regarding her needs. He scrambled to his feet, regaining the stool, and began regaling her with stories of his life in Koptos. Once at her watersteps, he thanked her with formal grace for her company, placed her in Amek's care and disappeared into the cabin, twitching the curtains closed behind him. Sheritra had time to be bathed and to don her most feminine gown before sweeping in to dinner with her chin held high.

Chapter 8

'I am strong as Thoth,
I am as mighty as Atum,
I walk with my legs,
I speak with my mouth in order to seek out my foe.
He has been given to me and he shall not be
taken from me.'

Hori had slept unusually late that same morning. He had planned to rise with Ra and join Antef on the river for some fishing before going to the tomb site. His body servant had dutifully roused him an hour before the dawn, but before the man was out of the room, Hori had dropped into a bottomless pit of unconsciousness again, emerging four hours later disgruntled and out of sorts.

He took his time eating in bed, calling for the harpist to soothe his agitation while he forced bread, butter and fresh fruit into his mouth, and by the time he stood on the raised stone of the bathing house having scented water trickled over his body, he felt almost himself again. Almost. If his father had cast the horoscopes he would have been able to consult his and thus plan a day that had undeniably begun badly, but as it was, all he could do was take some sensible precautions. I will not do my archery practice today, he thought as the servant wrapped a kilt about his waist and held his jewels for selection. Better to stay away from sharp instruments. Neither will I go out in the chariot with Antef later. I will dictate some letters, look over the latest work from the tomb and then while away the rest of the afternoon talking to Sheritra in the garden. He pointed absently at a silver-and-carnelian pectoral and a couple of plain silver bracelets chased with scarabs, and the man pushed them over his unco-operative hands. I wish I could remember what I dreamt, his thoughts ran on. Then it could be interpreted and perhaps the day salvaged. Ah well. I have neglected my prayers of late. Antef, if he has forgiven me, can open my shrine and prostrate himself beside me before I do anything else. But upon his enquiry his body servant told him that Antef had gone into the city on several errands that demanded his personal attention, and would not be back for hours.

Hori immediately gave up the idea of praying. He sat beside his couch and for a time dictated letters to various friends in the Delta, his ailing grandmother, and his fellow priests of Ptah who were doing their active service for the god in the great temple at Pi-Ramses. He then riffled through the ongoing work of the artists labouring to copy the scenes in the tomb, but the thought of the tomb made him irritable. What is the matter with me? he thought for the hundredth time. I will find Father and ask him about Sisenet's theory, see if he wants to knock down that wall. But Khaemwaset was closeted with a patient and Ib advised Hori not to wait for him. The undercurrent of restless frustration that had been simmering under the young man's usually sunny calm became a flood of annoyance, and he ordered out a skiff and oars. Refusing an armed escort he ran down the watersteps, flung himself into the graceful little craft and began to pull himself down river.

The day was very hot. Summer was advancing with the inexorable tread all feared, and Hori, bent over the oars and cursing under his breath, was soon bathed in sweat that ran into his eyes and rendered his hands slippery on the wood. The river was drying up slowly. Already its level had dropped appreciably from the previous month, and the water had begun to acquire the thick, oily texture of its lowest ebb. It flowed reluctantly in the direction Hori was going, but he strained every muscle he could, trying to work away his mood.

When he stopped briefly to mop his face and tie back the hair that was sticking to his cheeks, he was surprised to see that he had almost rowed himself past the northern suburbs. What now? he wondered. Shall I turn back? But he decided to go just a little farther, and set to again, though his shoulders ached and his legs protested. Father won't like me to be out without a soldier, or Antef at least, he said to himself. It is rather foolish. I should at least have the royal colours flying somewhere on the skiff, so that these damned fellahin crowding the river do not shout and swear at me as I get in their way. If I pull for the eastern bank the traffic will be lighter.

He veered in that direction, rowing grimly, and had just decided to turn around, go home and order a heket of beer to drink in the garden when he glanced automatically behind him and saw Tbubui emerge from the very small cabin of a skiff little bigger than his own and step onto the land. Immediately his foul mood began to lift. Here was someone who could take him out of himself. Quickly he manoeuvered his craft towards the bank, shipping the oars and calling out, "Tbubui! It is I, Hori, son of Khaemwaset! Is this where you live?"

At his shout she paused and turned, seemingly not at all startled to be addressed in such a way. Hori's skiff nudged her narrow watersteps and he scrambled to stand beside her. She was wearing a short, loose, one-shouldered sheath that left one breast bare, a fashion not favoured for many years, but after a surreptitious glance Hori realized that the unclothed breast was hidden by a waist-length white gauzy cape. She was unshod. Gold anklets tinkled as she stepped back, smiling a greeting. "Why, it is young Hori!" she exclaimed. "What are you doing rowing in this heat? Come into the house and I will have a servant wash you. You are in a lather!"

He grinned, feeling foolish and irrationally annoyed that she had called him "young." He saw himself at a complete disadvantage. "Thank you," he answered, "but I can just as easily turn my skiff around and go home. I row often to strengthen my arms for the bow and my legs for the chariot."

She ran an appraising eye over his sweat-drenched thighs and calves. "The exercise is obviously most efficacious," she commented drily. "Do come and keep me company for an hour or two. My brother is away today and Harmin is rambling the city with Sheritra."

Why so he is. I had forgotten, Hori thought. So I will be alone with her. Somehow I don't think that father would approve, but the prospect of a wash and some refreshments on this abominable day is most attractive. Besides, she will be entertaining. He bowed his acceptance and they mounted the steps together and started along the cool, palm-lined path to the white house that had so captivated Khaemwaset. I must stink, Hori thought as he tried to follow her light conversation through his embarrassment, and here she is floating beside me, her linens so pristine, her perfume like a cloud surrounding her. Myrrh I think, and something else, something . . .

"Welcome to my home," she said, and stood back to do him a

formal reverence as he went in. The coolness rushed to meet him and immediately his spirits began to rise.

A servant came padding on smooth, silent feet, and Tbubui bade Hori go with him. "He is Harmin's body servant," she explained. "He will attend you in his room, and find you a kilt while your own is being washed. When you are ready he will escort you to the garden." She left him without waiting for his thanks, and he followed the servant, looking curiously around the bare, whitewashed walls of hall and passage.

He was not as addicted to peace and quiet as his father, nor did he dismiss every new fashion in furnishing and domestic decoration, but the starkness of this house appealed to the solitary in him. He unconsciously breathed more deeply as he turned in through a plain cedar door and found himself facing a large couch marked at one end by a headrest of creamy ivory, a cedar bedside table inlaid with ivory on which stood a fat alabaster lamp, a jewel box, a wooden wine cup and, flung between them, an ostrich fan with a silver handle. An empty brazier huddled in one corner, and three plain tiring chests were lined up against one wall. A closed shrine stood on a pedestal beside the incense holder.

The room was thus crowded, but Hori received the impression of great space and stillness. He could detect nothing of Harmin's personality in this place. Silently the servant opened a tiring box, selected a freshly starched kilt and a leather belt, laid them on the couch and came to Hori. He removed the sweat-stained garment, slipped off his leather sandals, lifted his jewels from him, then beckoned. Hori gave a nod and followed. To the bath house I suppose, Hori thought, secretly amused at the man's efficient muteness.

Some time later he emerged, refreshed, and walked across the small square of lawn to where his hostess was waiting, leaning back in a chair, swathed in a voluminous white linen cloak. Hori was disappointed. He had vaguely hoped that she might be still in the short sheath but without the pleated cape. The garment she now wore was tied at the neck with a white ribbon and fell to the grass in undisciplined profusion, a startling contrast to the raven blackness of her hair and the bronze of her face and hands.

The garden itself was remarkable in that, after the lawn and the miniature pond and a few flower beds, it was given over to the haphazard forest of tall palms. Tbubui sat beneath one of them, protected by its spindly shadow. Hori felt that if he shouted his voice might echo among the pillared trunks. Tbubui waved him over.

"That's better," she observed. "You share Harmin's build. His kilt looks well on you. I hope it is comfortable while your own is being laundered." She patted the empty chair beside her. "Sit next to me, or on the mat if you prefer." Her manner seemed slightly patronizing to Hori, and as he took the chair he thought, I am not your son. Neither am I a child. Don't treat me like one! She reached to the camp table between them. "Wine or beer?" she inquired. Hori watched the cloak slide open to reveal a length of shapely brown arm adorned with one very wide, heavy silver bracelet gripping her wrist. Her palm was hennaed a brilliant orange. Hori, indeed all the nobility, hennaed his palms and the soles of his feet in either red or orange, but on this woman the practice struck him suddenly as barbaric, exotic.

"Beer, thank you, Tbubui," he said. "I worked up a terrible thirst on the river!"

She poured for him, handed him the cup, then wriggled into the chair, drawing her knees up sideways. The movement was lithe and girlish without being coy. How old are you? Hori wondered to himself as he drained the cup and held it out to be refilled. Sometimes you seem merely a child and at other times your beauty is ageless.

"You have a wonderful family, Prince," Tbubui was saying. "The daunting formality of a blood prince's home is tempered perfectly by the warmth and humour of its members. We have been honoured by your family's attention."

"My father is less a prince of the blood than an historian and physician," Hori answered, "and he was delighted to discover similar interests in you and your brother."

"Do you share them yourself?" she queried. "I know that you share his historical projects, but do you assist him with his medical cases?"

"No. I do not really care about that," Hori told her, somehow embarrassed to meet her eyes. His gaze travelled the S-curve of her buttocks, thighs and knees under the softly heaping linen cloak. "I do enjoy Father's work of restoration, for I have journeyed with him all over Egypt, and I must confess I am excited over each tomb opened, but I do not regard the work as obsessively as he does. Often he will put it before his obligations to Pharaoh." Immediately he felt disloyal, and held up a hand. "I did not mean that," he corrected himself quickly. "Pharaoh orders and my father obeys, of course. I mean that though he obeys he sometimes does so reluctantly, particularly if he is in the middle of some crucial piece of ancient translation or about to actually penetrate a tomb." You had better be quiet, he told himself desperately. You are digging this hole deeper and deeper. But Tbubui was smiling across at him. A bead of purple wine hung trembling on her lower lip, and as he raised his eyes to hers he saw her tongue come out and slowly lick her mouth. Her own eyes did not leave his face.

"And the tomb he has most recently penetrated," she prodded him encouragingly. "Is he obsessed about it also?"

Hori spread his arms, the beer slopping perilously. "He was very excited about it at first," he said, "but later he made many excuses not to come to the site. He would not even look at the work the artists were doing for him, copying scenes. I sometimes wonder if he has some secret fear about the place. I have been doing all the organizing." He grimaced, deprecatingly. "This wall, the one your brother and I tapped," he went on. "I am very curious about it, but I do not want to bring up the subject with Father for fear he will refuse to let me make a hole in it."

"Then why ask him?" Tbubui said, and when Hori's eyebrows shot up she waved a dismissive hand at her words. "No no, Prince! I am not inciting you to disobey your father. But it seems to me that the project may be swallowing more time and effort than he is really willing to give, that he is stretching himself too thinly among his duties, and that is why you find it difficult to lure him to the site as often as you would wish. Think about it. If you went ahead and opened up the sealed chamber you obviously believe is there, you would be saving him the trouble of an annoying decision and the bother of overseeing the work." She shifted, slowly extending her legs and letting them find the grass below. The cloak did not follow. Spellbound, Hori found himself staring at an expanse of golden skin that gleamed with an almost glossy patina. And was there not the suspicion of a dark triangle where her loins vanished under the bunched cloak? "As you said," she went on kindly, "you are the one doing all the work this time, yet he is the one making all the decisions. Who knows? He might be proud of a son who can take the initiative occasionally, particularly if he trusts your judgment."

"Oh he trusts my judgment," Hori answered thoughtfully, wrenching his attention back to her face. "I will think about what you have said, Tbubui. I would certainly be very disappointed if I sought his permission to open that chamber only to have it withheld."

"Then do not ask him. And if he is angry, tell him that I, Tbubui, corrupted the pure obedience a son owes his father and his wrath must fall on me!" She spoke lightly and then laughed, and he laughed also, all at once happy to be in this garden, in the heat of a dazzling afternoon, sitting beside a woman whose wit and strange beauty attracted him in a way no one had ever done before.

He remembered his boredom with the perfect, painted beauties of his grandfather's court, the many times he had been on the verge of falling in love only to be deflected by the discovery of a coarseness, an inappropriate sense of humour, a lack of instinctive judgment or a previously hidden ignorance on the part of the young woman who had initially caught his attention. But here, he thought deliberately, is a combination of intelligence, fine breeding, beauty and selflessness.

The silence that had fallen between them was not awkward. Tbubui had relaxed, head thrown back, eyes momentarily closed, and Hori sipped the last of his beer and gave himself over to the contentment.

Presently Tbubui said, "You are quite the most handsome young man I have ever seen. I knew of your reputation as the greatest male beauty in Egypt long before I met you, Hori, and it is pleasant for me to be able to concur with the general opinion."

Hori snorted. "I know of it too," he replied, "but I hardly ever think about it. Such a foolish, useless thing to be recognized for! No man or woman can take credit for his or her appearance. What intelligence can produce an aristocratic nose or a pair of alluring eyes? Foolishness!"

"Nevertheless, a magnetic physical appearance can be very useful in obtaining what one wants," Tbubui objected quietly. "And the manipulation of it is not necessarily evil. You, of course, being of royal blood, do not need to put your beauty to any use. To you it is an annoyance. It can bring you nothing you do not already have."

Except your respect, Hori thought suddenly, your response. I would like to make more than a passing impression on you.

She glanced at him sideways and asked, "Have you no betrothed, Hori? No young woman with whom you are planning a life? Surely at your age, as a prince of Egypt, you are obliged to marry."

Hori sighed. "You sound like my father!" he joked. "Khaemwaset worries regularly about my single state. He threatens to find me a proper young Egyptian daughter of the ancient nobility and force a betrothal if I do not hurry up and find one myself. But I must confess," he finished, leaning over the table, "that such a thing is usually far from my mind. When I sign a marriage contract I want it to be with a woman I whole-heartedly love. I want what my parents have."

"Ah." The sound was noncommital. "What your parents have. And what do they have, my young idealist?"

Was she mocking him? He could not tell. Thoughtfully he scrutinized the wide eyes now warmly submitting to his gaze, the thin nose, the sensuous outline of her smiling mouth. "They have mutual respect, closeness, and a firm and unshakeable love."

Her smile slowly faded and she stared at him. "I do not think so," she whispered, "for your mother's voluptuous womanhood languishes for want of recognition, and your father is still a child."

"You are impudent, Tbubui," he said coldly, and for the first time they faced one another as equals. Finally she nodded.

"Yes Prince, I am impudent. But I do not apologize for telling the truth."

"What truth?" he flashed back. "You have known us for so short a time. You presume too much!"

The corner of her mouth twitched. "I presume upon good manners, that is all. If I have offended you I am sorry, and I must say, Prince, that your defence of your mother and father is very pleasing to me."

"I am glad to hear it," he responded stiffly, already turning over her words in his mind and realizing that the moment of her honesty had somehow begun a relationship between them, had transcended the polite to-ing and fro-ing of acquaintance that had to precede the easy unselfconsciousness of friendship.

She stood, pulled open the cloak, then folded it about her again and resumed her seat. The artless gesture was so natural that it had not roused him, but he wanted to stroke her hand, ruffle her hair, pull teasingly at the massive silver earring swinging against her neck.

"I should like to visit you again," he said. "You are a fascinating woman, Tbubui, and I like your company."

"And I yours," she answered. "Come whenever you like, Hori. I enjoy your conversation, but I also have relished feasting my eyes on such matchless male delights! You have done me a favour."

He let out a guffaw of genuine amusement and was saved from a response by a movement in the trees to his left, from the direction of the river. Harmin appeared, striding along the path under the palms whose shade had already thickened as the sun dipped closer to the horizon. The face he turned first to the house and then to them was pale and closed, but on recognizing Khaemwaset's son he immediately set a formal smile on his lips and came up to them, kissing his mother on her proffered cheek and bowing to Hori.

"Greetings, Harmin," Hori said politely. "Has my sister had a pleasant day?"

"I have done my best to make it so," the young man replied sharply.

"It has been a pleasant day, then, for all of us," Tbubui interposed. "The Prince was rowing past our watersteps just as I was disembarking, Harmin, so I invited him to enliven my afternoon. But I suppose it is time to consider dinner."

"Before then I must rest," Harmin said a little petulantly. "Although the day was full and very sweet, I missed the hour on my couch, and I must confess I can barely do without it, no matter how seductive the blandishments of other pursuits." He gave them another wan smile and went into the house. Hori had the impression that his somewhat fretful words were merely the surface wisps of smoke from a smouldering inner fire. He wondered how Sheritra, obviously the blandishment today, had fared, and as he watched his twin in physical magnetism disappear he decided quite suddenly that he did not like Harmin very much. The thought alarmed him.

He rose and stretched. "I must go," he said, tempering his

abrupt words with a smile. "I have enjoyed being here more than I can say, Tbubui, but now if my linen is ready I should row myself back." She acquiesced by leaving the chair, and together they followed Harmin into the house.

Evening was already seeping through the bare rooms, and as yet no lamps had been lit. Hori, standing in the hall entrance surrounded by painted scenes from which all colour seemed to have been sucked, and staring uncomfortably at the dim statues of Amun and Thoth, whose curved ibis beak and small beaded eyes were all at once predatory, was aware of two things. He wanted to put his hands on Tbubui, but beside his desire was a wave of sinister loneliness that was stirring to wakefulness with the impending night. He almost shrieked at the approach of a servant carrying lamps, then laughed at himself.

Tbubui returned, his kilt over one arm, and thanking her he went into the passage and quickly exchanged Harmin's for his own. A sullen yellow light was trickling from the crack under the door of Harmin's bedchamber, and somewhere in the house, someone was picking out a plaintive, sad little melody on a lute. Hori shuddered.

Hurrying back to the hall he took his leave of Tbubui, left greetings for Sisenet who still had not come home, and walked as fast as he could through the gathering gloom under the palms to the blessed flow of the river. He was amazed to see Ra still just about the horizon, a glorious, fierce splash of red and orange, with the ruins and pyramids of Saqqara black before him. Hori clambered into the skiff, dropped his oars into the fiery water and set off for home.

By the time he got there it was quite dark, and the torch that normally illuminated the watersteps had not yet been lit. Cursing, he stumbled up the steps, but once on the path to the house his normal good humour came back. A mouth-watering aroma of roasting beef and strong onion-and-garlic soup wafted to his nostrils from the kitchens to the rear of the servants' courtyard, and cheerful light spilled out onto the grass from the pillared terrace, through the open door of the dining hall. A servant approaching carrying two blazing torches. He paused and bowed. "A good evening, Prince," he murmured before hurrying on, and Hori returned his greeting, mentally discarding the unease Tbubui's house had created in him.

He entered his home and made his way to Sheritra's suite. The guard at her door admitted him without demur and he walked into a blaze of lamplight. Sheritra sat at her cosmetic table, a place, Hori knew, that she seldom bothered to occupy. She was dressed in a white, gold-shot sheath of many flounces that shimmered as she breathed. Gold thongs held her sandals to her feet, twined like snakes about her arms and encircled the waist-length braids of her wig. She is sitting straight, Hori thought as he came up to her. She turned with a smile, and Hori successfully hid his astonishment, for her face had been painted a fashionable yellow. Gold dust clung to her eyelids, and black kohl rimmed them flatteringly. Her mouth had been hennaed a rich red. "You look breath-taking," he said. "Do we have official guests tonight?" He flung himself onto her couch, arms behind his head, his favourite spot during the hours they would while away together, and she gave a shriek.

"Hori! My sheets! You are filthy and sweaty!"

He ignored her indignation. "Well? Guests?"

Those lips, familiar yet foreign in their new adornment, curved upwards. "No. I just felt like taking a few pains with my appearance tonight." A hint of defensiveness crept into her tone. "What of it?"

"Nothing," he assured her hastily. "I like it very much. But why, Sheritra?" Even her father did not have the freedom with her to ask such a question, but Hori knew that her heart was open to him. He was her elder brother, her friend and protector against whom walls were not necessary.

She picked up a copper mirror and stared into it intently. "My eyes are not too bad with plenty of kohl to bring them forward, are they, Hori? And my lips? Coloured, are they more acceptable?"

"Sheritra . . ."

The mirror hit the table with a slap. She swung round. "Because I had a wonderful day in the foreigners' quarter with Harmin. He made me feel beautiful, Hori. No one else has been able to make me feel that way. Tonight I want to look the way I feel."

There was a new confidence to her, Hori noted. Not the old arrogance of defiance but a new awareness of herself as a woman that was not waiting to be challenged.

"Then he must have made you feel like the goddess Hathor herself," Hori observed slowly. "And how did you make him feel, Sheritra?"

The suspicion of a blush spread under her yellow face-paint. "How do I know?" she flared. "You would have to ask him!"

"You must at least have some idea!"

For answer she rose and glided over to perch on the edge of the couch beside him. "Actually I believe that he is very fond of me indeed," she admitted. "Oh Hori! He kissed me! What do you think of him?"

"Harmin?" Hori teased her, in order to buy himself some time.

"Who else!" Sheritra snorted. "Really, Hori!"

I do not like him, Hori thought. And I am afraid for you, little one. Yet I realize that my assessment may be tinged with guilt, because of my sudden lust for his mother. What would Harmin think of me if he knew? Hori shifted uneasily on the couch. "Well?" Sheritra pressed.

"I think he is a most extraordinary man if he can win your trust and your heart, dearest," he answered as truthfully as he was able. "But do be careful. You do not yet know him very well."

"I know that his eyes do not slide away from mine when he compliments me," she said, "or when he tells me exactly what I am thinking and fearing. I am so safe with him, Hori, so at peace. I can be myself and he understands."

O Amun, Hori thought. It is much worse than I imagined. "I am happy for you, Sheritra," he said gently. "Please keep sharing it with me. I do love you very much."

She kissed him swiftly, in a gush of unfamiliar perfume. "I share everything with you anyway," she said. "Dear Hori! What do you think of Harmin's mother? Father seems quite taken with her."

Hori sat up and clasped his knees. His muscles were beginning to stiffen with the day's violent exercise and he massaged his calves absently. "I had forgotten that you were with him when he first saw her," he mused. "She is beautiful, of course, in an odd way . . ."

Sheritra glanced at him keenly. "So she has caught your interest too, has she?" she said. "I like her, for she treats me as an equal, not a shy fool. But if I were you or Father . . ." She hesitated.

"What?"

"She is that rare kind of woman who can inspire obsession in a man, but there is something else about her, some mystery, a thing not quite nice. If I were you or Father I would be on my guard." She spoke simply and seriously, and Hori stared at her. I do not know about Father, he thought miserably, but for me it is already too late. I want to be with her, watch her. He got off the couch.

"I suppose I had better have myself cleaned up before dinner," he said. "Don't react to any comments on your appearance tonight, Sheritra. Behave as though such dress is quite usual. Mother's approval will be insulting. Father will notice but say nothing. Unless, of course, you want to explain your feelings to them both. I suggest you wait a while for that. I will see you at dinner." He left the cosy, warm room and made his way to his own quarters. As well as being sore and tired he was suddenly, unaccountably, depressed.

That night he lay on his couch, headrest in place to ease his protesting spine, and watched the flickering of the night lamp cast mobile shadows on his blue-painted, star-spangled ceiling. He relived his time with Tbubui, bringing to mind her brown body, her slow smiles, with a mental and physical unrest that disturbed and puzzled him. There is nothing of the coquette in Tbubui, he thought uneasily, yet she exudes a flaunting sexuality in everything she says and does.

His mind veered to what she had said about the tomb. She is right, he decided, glad to push the afternoon behind a saner matter for deliberation. Father has lost interest in the project. The least he could have done was admit as much to me and allow me to continue with it on my own. Tomorrow I will order the destruction of the wall. I am very eager to see what is beyond, and perhaps Father will find his enthusiasm rekindled if I find something of note.

He saw his father briefly in the morning and, feeling slightly guilty, he almost blurted out his plans. But Khaemwaset seemed withdrawn, and in the end Hori ordered out his litter and was carried to Saqqara without sharing the confidence. Guilt continued to trouble him as he sat cross-legged behind the sheltering curtains, but he remembered Tbubui's words and managed to suppress it. The day was one of relentless heat and blinding light,

Tibi careening towards Makhir, and he thought with longing of the cool dimness of the tomb.

The Overseer of Works came to meet him as he alighted before the tent that now had a settled, mildly dishevelled air of permanence. Hori paused to drink the water held out to him before walking with the man to the chipped steps leading down. At the foot, the artists and workmen clustered, talking idly and waiting for the orders of the day. They bowed as Hori descended and he returned their reverence with an absent smile. "Let us get out of the sun," he said.

Inside, the tomb was much as he had first seen it; indeed, with the floor continually swept it looked fresher. Hori drew in a deep breath of the now sweet, damp air, and his spirits rose. This had become his second home. It was he who had laboured here in a fruitful peace, establishing respect among the workmen, commanding a fleck of paint here, a fragment of new stone there, to make this resting place fitting for its inhabitants once again. His father's reluctance to share the sheets of papyrus placed on his desk every day had disappointed Hori, but as he slowly surveyed the painted walls, the uneven floor and shrouded grave goods, he acknowledged Khaemwaset's other responsibilities and tried to be mollified.

Signalling to the expectant Overseer and the Chief Artist, he walked through into the coffin room. "That wall," he indicated. "Have the scenes and inscriptions now been copied fully?"

"Yes, Highness," The Chief Artist replied promptly. "The work was completed three days ago. Indeed, the task of copying the whole tomb will be finished in another three days."

"Thank you. Overseer, is it possible to remove a section of the wall by cutting out small blocks and then replacing them later? How much damage to the painting would there be?"

The man hitched at his thick kilt. "If you are mistaken, Highness, and there is no room beyond, and the wall is solid rock covered in plaster, we cannot pierce it, of course. We would bore a series of holes, insert wet wooden wedges and split the rock as closely as possible to the neatness of blocks. But the stone will crack where the seams are weak. I cannot guarantee neatness."

"Even if there is a room beyond, and the wall is nothing but wood and plaster," the Chief Artist interposed, "the fine paintings will be destroyed. Certainly, Highness, in that case, it could be taken apart neatly, but the plaster will inevitably flake, taking the scenes with it in tiny pieces."

"Could they be reproduced from the copies already made?" Hori asked.

The man nodded unwillingly. "Yes they could, and in the most authentic way, but Highness, they would not be the originals no matter how cleverly done. Who knows what prayers and spells were lovingly chanted over this great work?"

Who indeed, Hori thought. But there is nothing loving about the atmosphere of this place, no matter how at home I feel in it. The prayers and spells are more likely to have been curses and evil incantations. What should I do? His servants fell silent and stood quietly waiting while he stared at the floor, brow furrowed. He was tempted to ask himself what Khaemwaset would do, but his father had always been too supernaturally involved with this particular unveiling and besides, had he not abrogated his right to make the decisions here? Much as I love him, Hori thought, I have been the beast of burden in this case and I deserve the reward of the responsibility for this decision. Eventually his head came up.

"Bore one hole," he said to the Overseer. "There, where the sky converges with the palm tree. If the wall is rock, the hole will not be too difficult to fill and paint over again. If not . . ." He turned on his heel. "Bring me word when it is done."

He thought his Chief Artist might protest but the man said nothing, and Hori made his way out into the sunshine. It smote him like a blow, and with it came a vivid memory of Tbubui wrapped in the gossamer folds of the linen cloak, the hot breeze stirring her black hair as yesterday she lifted the wine cup to her mouth and smiled at him over its rim.

Hori trudged through the sand to his tent and flung himself into the chair under the awning's shade. Eyes narrowed against the glare, he squinted into the nothingness of rolling sand and a hectic blue sky and wondered how he might suggest to his father that an older woman of minor noble blood from a backwater like Koptos would make a suitable Chief Wife for one of Egypt's foremost princes.

In about an hour the Overseer was bowing before him, blinking owlishly through the fine grey powder clinging to his face.

"The hole is bored, Highness," he said in answer to Hori's sharp query. "Part of it is through wood. I must surmise that we are dealing with a hidden door that has been plastered over."

Hori rose. "Take your men and sound it carefully. We do not want to tear out more than is necessary. When you have measured and marked, use fine saws. Open the door for me." He repressed the urge to run into the tomb, to see the telltale hole for himself, and besides, his men, skilled and well trained, would do the work as efficiently without him. The Overseer bowed shortly and Hori called for food. He wished Antef were here, but Antef had requested a few days to visit his family in the Delta. Hori missed him. *What if Father decides to visit the site today?* Hori thought suddenly with a stab of anxiety. *What shall I tell him?* Guilt over the tomb mingled with guilt over his feelings for Tbubui, but he mentally shrugged, thanked the man who was setting a meal before him, and began to eat.

He went inside the tent after his lunch, lay on the camp cot and slept. His steward woke him two hours later as he had requested, and once more he sat under the awning, slaking his thirst with beer while a servant gently washed from him the sweat of his dreams. Out on the plain, a desert dog was panting in the thin shadow of a small, half-buried rock, and in the fiery bronze afternoon sky a hawk wheeled lazily, its cry echoing spasmodically through the stultifying air. *We must break through today,* Hori thought anxiously. *What is taking them so long?* He watched the cool droplets of water on his bare thighs evaporate.

In another hour the Overseer was once more toiling to him through the burning sand. Something about his gait warned Hori, and he came to his feet, his heart pounding. The man bowed clumsily. Hori beckoned him in under the shade.

"Well?" he prompted urgently.

The man was breathing hard. "There is a room beyond," he blurted. "Very dark, Highness, and smelling very bad. Water began to trickle over the lintel into the coffin chamber long before my men had completed the cutting of the door. They are very uneasy. As soon as their duty was done they left."

"Left?" Hori repeated. "They ran away?"

The Overseer stiffened. "The servants of the illustrious Khaemwaset do not run away," he replied. "They were so apprehensive, Highness, that I told them to go home and return tomorrow morning."

Hori said nothing. The Overseers of every department of works were competent leaders who knew their underlings, and interfering with their methods of control was always foolish. "Very well," Hori said after a while. "Are torches lit? I will take a look."

The Overseer hesitated. "Highness, it might be wise to summon a priest," he said. "Someone to burn incense and petition the gods to protect you and the inhabitants of the tomb, to . . ." He faltered.

"To what?" Hori asked, interested.

"To forgive you."

"Do not be pompous," Hori retorted. "It does not suit a man streaked in sweat and dirt and looking like a woman whose face is caked in meal of alabaster and natron for the good of her skin." Seeing his servant's acute embarrassment he relented. "Do not fear," he said. "Father and you and I have been doing this work together for many years. And am I not a sem-priest of mighty Ptah myself? Come. I want to see this mystery."

The air in the tomb had changed again. Hori smelled it as soon as he left the cramped entrance passage and emerged into the first chamber. The rank odour of old, stagnant water pervaded his nostrils and he fancied that he could feel it, slimy against his skin. The Overseer shuddered. Hori moved quickly to the coffin room where two torchbearers were huddled together, their backs against a wall. They were nervously facing a black, jagged aperture, low and narrow, at whose raised foot the light reflected slickly. Small streams of other darkness were trickling over this lintel and spreading out haphazardly toward the coffin plinths. The odour now was disgusting, yet it tantalized Hori with a memory as swiftly there as gone. He had of course smelled rotten water before, though never in circumstances like this. Now his mind blended it with something else, something wonderful, then snatched it away. Hori picked his way to the hole, gestured impatiently for a torch and, when it was placed in his hand, peered forward with arm outstretched.

The room was very small and appeared to be unfinished. The walls were plain rock into which man-sized but empty niches had been crudely hacked, probably for shawabtis that were never installed, Hori surmised. Ribbons of wet mildew snaked every-where. The floor was a sheet of black, rank water that only dully gave back the flaring torchlight and lapped with a slow, easy menace against Hori's feet. In the centre, islanded by that shal-low, mysterious sea, were two lidless coffins. Hori drew in his breath. Craning, holding the torch as far out as he could, he tried to divine the contents but was shown only leaping shadows. With a grunt he ducked his head and stepped gingerly into the water. The Overseer gave a low exclamation behind him, which he ignored. The movement stirred the dark expanse and it circled out from him and kissed the farther wall with a soft sucking sound. Hori's flesh crawled.

Slowly he waded towards the coffins. The water deepened but not much. He felt it just over his ankles and he cringed from the slippery texture of the long-submerged rocky floor beneath him. Nevertheless he kept going, almost unconsciously reciting a litany to Ptah under his breath, and in a moment he was peering into the coffins. They were nothing more than great troughs of roughly hollowed stone, and both were empty. Looking carefully into their pitted depths Hori decided that they had once been oc-cupied. There were traces of blackened embalming salts mingled with body fluids that over time always discoloured the stone.

Carefully, deliberately, he quartered the chamber, his feet questing. Not for anything in the world would he have placed his hands down into that murk. But his toes did not stub against the things he sought. "There are no lids," he said aloud, his voice falling flat and muffled.

Then he gave a startled shout. The torch had shown him a small arch let into the base of the right-hand wall, just big enough for a man to crawl into. Leaning down he inserted his free hand. He felt cold, dry, sandy rock canting upwards at a gradual rate. Everything in him shrank from what he knew he must do. Damn you, Antef, he thought, annoyed. Why did you have to go away just now? You would have been fearless here. You would have helped me. "Overseer!" he called. "Come here!"

There was a moment of whispering. Hori did not turn round. He waited, feeling all at once alone and very vulnerable, the sheer aloofness of the place sending prickles along his spine. I wish I had summoned the courage to tell Father after all, he thought. I wish he were here, standing beside me, taking charge with the aura of authority and security that reassures us all, servant and family alike. Nothing terrible ever happens around him.

After a while he heard the Overseer splash into the water and then felt a touch on his shoulder. The man was trembling but obedient. "What do you think of this?" Hori demanded. The man examined the aperture, then straightened.

"It looks like a crawlspace of some kind," he replied. "It is not a natural fissure in the rock."

"I did not think so either," Hori agreed. "Hold the torch down, as low as you can. I am going to see where it leads."

He did not wait for objections. Thrusting the flame at the Overseer he lay on his stomach, arms and head in the hole. His kilt quickly soaked up the foetid water and his muscles contracted with cold revulsion. Grimly he pushed himself forward. His shoulders caught. He wriggled them free. "The air is cleaner in here!" he called, "and I am sure I feel it stirring from somewhere above." If the Overseer replied, Hori did not hear him. Ahead was thick blackness. He squirmed on, up a gently rising grade, keeping his head low, his elbows and knees soon grazed on the gritty rock. Panic threatened to immobilize him but he repressed it forcibly, thinking of the men who waited behind him, bravely controlling their own fears.

It seemed to Hori that he crawled on for an age, that surely the sun must have set by now, that he had only the illusion of movement and he was really making motions that were taking him nowhere. But suddenly the top of his head met something hard and sharp and he recoiled with an oath, turned on his side, and explored with his fingers. The way was blocked by a large stone, but even as he worked at it, it shifted. Bracing himself against the walls of the crude tunnel he pushed. The rock quivered. With all his might, Hori heaved, feeling that his strength was diminished because of the total darkness, knowing it was not true. The rock ground, squealed a mild protest, then all at once gave, letting in a great shaft of blinding light. Hori recoiled. His eyes gushed tears. Blinking, he forced himself forward and in another few minutes his head was free and he was gazing painfully out upon a slope that ambled to a palm grove. The city danced in the haze beyond it. An angle of beige stone obscured his vision to the right, and pulling his hands loose he grasped it and heaved himself free.

As he did so, his knee scraped over something lying just within the lip of darkness he had left, and he cried out in shock, jackknifing to find what it was. His fingers scrabbled inside the tunnel and withdrew a single earring, now glistening dark red with the blood that was pouring from his knee. Wiping the jewellery on his kilt, his face still contorted with pain, he examined it.

A large piece of mottled blue-green turquoise shaped like a teardrop was set within a heavy lacery of purple gold. It was dull and encrusted with sand, but Hori knew it was very ancient. Turquoise like this was no longer worn and had become very expensive. He knew that Egyptian artisans now had the secret of the production of purple gold. The goldsmiths of the kingdom of Mitanni, long since absorbed into other empires, had made it and traded it to Egyptian nobility for centuries until the Egyptians themselves had learned to fire it. Modern purple gold was a more even blend that gave the precious substance a mere purple sheen. The thing Hori was turning over in his filthy hand had the distinct purple tracery of an ancient Mitanni craftsman.

Excitedly he gripped it and began to hobble down the slope. He knew where he was. The tunnel had ended in a discreet angle of part of the outer wall, now derelict, that had once surrounded the magnificent complex of Pharaoh Unas's pyramid and funerary buildings. To any idle eye the rock blocking it would have looked no more than a small untidiness.

As he limped under the hot sun, Hori was conscious of a deep disappointment. No wonder the seals on the main entrance had been intact. The rock at the exit had been far too loose. Thieves must have found it and worked their way into the tomb through the tunnel. Anything of value in the newly opened chamber would of course now be gone, and the miscreants had dropped the earring as they hurriedly escaped.

Then what of the bodies? his thoughts ran on under the insistent throbbing of his knee. Robbers often tore corpses apart in their hunt for valuable amulets and would leave the dismembered remains strewn about the chamber, or jumbled in the coffins themselves. Had the two bodies simply dissolved in the water, so that he had been wading in diluted embalming fluid? He shuddered.

He had now stumbled his way around the sprawling ruins of Unas's resting place and had turned towards the familiar chaos of his excavation. Two of his servants squatted under the awning of his tent, and the Overseer's departing workmen had left a pile of jumbled tools at the foot of the debris beside the descending steps. The whole scene seemed melancholy under Ra's pitiless late-afternoon cruelty.

When he was close enough, Hori hailed the servants. Startled, their heads came up, then one of them disappeared behind the tent. A moment later the litter and its bearers came struggling over the sand. Gratefully Hori sank onto it and was carried the last few yards to the tent. He inspected his knee. The gash was to the bone and jagged, and he marvelled that such a small thing could inflict so much damage. But perhaps it had been wedged beside a sharp stone, he thought. I will need this stitched closed. Father will be pleased. He grimaced.

The litter stopped. "Go into the tomb and tell the men to come out," he ordered his steward. "Tell them I am here." He allowed the other man to help him into his chair but forbade him to wash the wound. The few minutes he had spent unprotected under the sun had made him slightly dizzy and he gulped a jar of beer and watched the Overseer and torchbearers disgorge, puzzled and uncertain, from the tomb mouth. "That tunnel leads up and out into Osiris Unas's ruins," he explained to the incredulous Overseer. "If you explore the outer rim of the walls you will find it, and the stone I pushed away to get out. Replace the stone. Post the guards on this entrance, and go home."

The man nodded. "You are injured, Highness."

Hori managed a grin. "It was an adventurous few minutes. I will see you tomorrow." He did not wait until the men had dispersed. Still clutching the earring, he pulled himself out of the chair and back onto the litter, and gave the command to take him home. It was time to talk to Khaemwaset.

Chapter 9

'How pleasant is mine hour!
Might an hour only become for me eternity,
when I sleep with thee.
Thou didst lift up mine heart . . .
when it was night.'

He wished that the ride could have been longer. He dreaded telling his father what he had done, and now that the deed was accomplished he was less sure that Tbubui had been correct in her advice. Nursing his knee, he sat brooding with the curtains closed oblivious to the hum of the city around him and fighting the sense that his maturity was slipping away until he was a little boy again.

His hope to enter the house unobserved proved vain. As he eased himself from the litter at the rear entrance, Sheritra came out, a cup of milk in her hand, and exclaimed, "Hori! Whatever have you been doing? You are filthy and scratched from head to toe and you smell awful!" She came closer. "And how did you hurt your knee?"

For answer he uncurled his fingers. The earring lay glowing complacently on his palm. "I opened the secret chamber in the tomb," he admitted ruefully. "And I found a tunnel. This was lying in it and it ripped my knee. Now I must confess to Father. Where is he?"

"In Mother's rooms, playing sennet." She traced the wound with one gentle finger. "He will be furious with you, Hori, you know that, don't you?" Then her gaze became fixed on the jewel. Lifting it, she turned it over thoughtfully. "Ancient turquoise," she commented. "This might mollify him a little if you are lucky. It reminds me of the turquoise Harmin was wearing yesterday. He had a fortune in ancient stone on his wrists and around his neck."

Those in love bring up the name of the beloved at every opportunity, Hori reflected wryly. Aloud he said, "What is a member of an impoverished noble family doing with a fortune in turquoise?"

"They are not impoverished, only modestly wealthy," she rebuked him quickly. "And besides, Harmin told me that the stones are heirlooms to be handed down to his son." She passed him the earring. "You had better find Father. I don't suppose you noticed the new house snake sunning himself as you came in?"

Hori shook his head and left her, making his way along the passage towards his mother's rooms. His leg was now stiffening and he forced it to bend, the pain in his body and the discomfort in his conscience rendering him entirely miserable. He did not even have Antef to put the day into a better perspective.

Khaemwaset and Nubnofret were sitting on low stools just inside the steps that led down to the cloistered terrace and the side garden beyond. Their heads were together, bent over the sennet board, and as Hori went towards them he could hear the rattle of the sticks and his mother's low laugh. Wernuro rose from her corner and bowed to him, and he smiled at her, coming up to his parents and halting self-consciously. You are a man, he told himself sternly. You made an adult decision. Now stand by it, you fool. His father was making a move, hand stroking his chin as he pondered the board, and it was Nubnofret who looked up, the breeze from the garden momentarily fluttering her scarlet linen. Her smile of welcome faded. "Hori!" she said. "What happened to you? Wernuro, bring a chair quickly."

Khaemwaset gave him one glance. "And wine also," he added. "Was there an accident at the tomb?"

The young man sank back into the chair Wernuro had placed respectfully behind him, noting at the same time the lack of surprise in his father's voice and attitude. It was almost as though Khaemwaset was waiting for something untoward. "Father, did you do the Tibi horoscopes by any chance?" he suddenly asked. Khaemwaset shook his head. "For Mekhir then? Mekhir is almost upon us." Again Khaemwaset shook his head. He was waiting for an explanation, and again Hori had the impression that his father had steeled himself for bad news. There was an air of strain about the alert, handsome features, a tension in Khaemwaset's thickset, muscular body. For the first time, in spite of the trouble Hori felt he was embroiled in, he found himself looking at his father objectively, as another adult male, divorced from the hazy cocoon of fatherhood, authority and long familiarity that had always blunted Hori's perception.

Khaemwaset is a man in torment, Hori thought in surprise. How good-looking he is, with his intelligent eyes and wide shoulders! What is happening in the secret life of his ka? With these astonishing and somehow reassuring thoughts Hori's confidence came surging back. My father is a man just like myself, the revelation came. No more, and no less.

"Well I suppose we can do without our horoscopes for another month," he said slowly. "It does not really matter. And in answer to your question, Father, there was no accident at the tomb. I opened a door in the false wall today."

A dead silence fell. Wernuro's small movements as she poured wine for Hori went almost unnoticed. Hori raised the silver cup, drank and replaced it. Khaemwaset was staring at him intently, obviously angry but also, it seemed to Hori, afraid. Nubnofret had turned towards the terrace and was gazing out at the trees, now stirring against a softly reddening sky. This was none of her business.

At last Khaemwaset spoke, his voice unnaturally steady. "I do not recall giving you permission to do such a thing, my son." His eyes remained fixed on Hori's face. Hori found himself entirely calm.

"I did not ask it," he replied. "I took the responsibility for the decision upon myself."

"Why?"

Tbubui's reasoning unwound through Hori's mind, and all at once her arguments seemed spurious, selfish. I have been lying to myself, he thought, still in that same brilliant calm. I will tell him the truth.

"Because I wanted to," he said. "You have shown little interest in the tomb and its findings, indeed, often you seem afraid of it. It has consumed the greater part of my time for the last three months. I chose to knock out the wall at my own convenience instead of waiting for you to do the deed at yours."

Khaemwaset blinked. His hand strayed to the sennet board and he picked up a gold cone, his thumb exploring its smooth surfaces absently. "The paintings?" he said. "Are they destroyed?" The anger was still there, Hori saw, simmering under this man's rigid control.

"Yes," he replied brusquely. "The wall is in fact mostly rock, with a wood-and-plaster door set approximately in the middle of it. Opening the door meant reducing the scenes to flakes of plaster. I intend to have it rebuilt and the scenes repainted later."

There was another awkward silence. It was as though Khaemwaset longed to ask the inevitable question but dared not do so. At length he carefully replaced the cone on the House of Spitting, spread his hennaed hands palms up, and found the courage. "What was beyond the door, Hori?"

Hori sipped the wine and found himself hungry. "There is a small chamber containing two coffins, both empty. The coffins had no lids. They either never existed or they have vanished. The floor of the room is ankle-deep in stagnant water. There are niches in the walls where the shawabtis ought to be standing, but they too are empty."

Khaemwaset nodded, his eyes still on his hands. "No inscriptions? No paintwork?"

"None. But I believe that the coffins were once occupied. Thieves broke in and rifled the contents, and probably tore apart the corpses. They entered through a narrow tunnel that links the chamber with the desert. I injured my knee crawling through it and dragging myself over this." He held out the earring. His father took it slowly and examined it, and Nubnofret came to life.

"How lovely it is, Khaemwaset!" she exclaimed. "Clean it and it would beautify any aristocratic neck!"

"I will clean it," he said with difficulty, "but it will be replaced in the tomb."

"No," Hori spoke up. "*I* will clean it and put it back." Khaemwaset shot him a dark glance but, to Hori's amazement, he passed back the gem and rose.

"Come and I will dress your wound," he said. "Nubnofret, we will finish the game later." His tone brooked no argument. Meekly Hori stood and followed him.

Khaemwaset cleaned, stitched and bound the knee without a word. But as he was closing his herb chest he said, "You know that I am violently angry with you, don't you, Hori?"

Hori wanted nothing more, now, than to go to sleep. "Yes I do," he answered. "But I also know that you are afraid. Why?"

His father stood motionless for a moment, then he sighed and slumped onto one of the large scroll containers. "Something has changed between us," he said. "Indeed the whole fabric of this family is changing and I do not know whether it is for good or ill. The scroll you saw me take—I read part of it aloud, trying to translate it. And since then there has been Tbubui and this tomb. Sometimes I feel as if we have set out along a path from which we cannot turn back."

That is not all, Hori thought, regarding his father's shadowed features. What the rest is, I have no idea. "So you have not seriously considered the answers to the mystery of the water, the baboons, the scroll itself?" he asked.

Khaemwaset straightened. "Of course I have!" he replied sharply. "But I am not sure I want to know the answers."

"Why? Shall we consider them now, together? Four bodies, Father, two of them hidden away behind a false wall. A tomb undesecrated, a secret but ravaged chamber, surely this is the challenge of a lifetime!"

"You should not presume that the inner chamber was robbed," Khaemwaset said carefully. "I will come with you tomorrow and see it, but it sounds as though the place was either never finished or deliberately left crudely cut and unpainted." He got up and offered an arm to his son. "Many times I have wished that we had left the accursed place alone. Let me help you to your couch."

Hori gratefully leaned on him. In a rush of affection, the young man was tempted to blurt out his visit to Tbubui, his growing preoccupation with her, but the touch of his father's flesh somehow forbade it. There will be time enough, he thought painfully, drowsily. That is a fight I must be healthy to win. I wish he had offered me poppy, but perhaps the withholding of it is his way of punishing me for my arrogance today. As soon as possible I will go to Sisenet's house and tell Tbubui what I have done.

Along the passages the servants were lighting the torches, and in his suite the lamps already glowed. Khaemwaset lowered him onto his couch, told him he might eat there later and bade him rest. Before his father had left the room, Hori was asleep.

He did not wake for dinner. A servant brought food, which after a time cooled and congealed, but Hori slumbered on. He came to himself once, sensing the lateness of the hour by the air of deep calm that suffused the house. His night lamp had gone out and his body servant lay snoring quietly beyond the bedchamber door. His knee throbbed in a relentless rhythm but he knew it was not the pain that had woken him. He had been dreaming something unsettling, something verging on nightmare, but he could not now remember what it was. Struggling up he poured himself water and drank thirstily, then lay down again and stared into the darkness.

When next he formed a conscious thought, his breakfast was being placed by his feet and the doors to his private shrine were being opened. Today will be difficult, he thought, picking at the food. Father will still be in a bad humour and my wound will be at its worst. Well, at least Antef comes home soon. But the thought of his servant and best friend returning did not give him the stab of excitement it should have. Antef would wait for Hori to suggest a hunting expedition, a fishing afternoon, a jaunt to the markets or a boating party with other friends. They had always been close. Antef had never crossed the ephemeral and sometimes complicated line of deference that must forever separate him from his royal companion. Still, theirs was a warm and companionable relationship. The gossip mongers of Memphis had at one time gleefully spread the rumour that Antef was in fact Khaemwaset's son by a concubine or, better still, a servant girl, but the story soon died. The Prince was too upright a man not to acknowledge his offspring, and Memphis was full of juicier topics of conversation.

In Antef, Hori had found his equal in matters of opinion, taste and physical pursuits, and Antef could keep a royal secret as well as any well trained servant. All the same, Hori thought as he lit the incense before Ptah and hurried through his morning prayers, I do not know if I wish to divulge to him my interest in Tbubui. A woman can destroy a friendship, indeed, Tbubui is already affecting my feelings for Antef. I do not want to go hunting or roaming in the markets with him. I do not want to spend my leisure time in the garden drinking beer and teasing each other about the last wrestling bout we had. When I was younger we traded lies concerning our sexual prowess but I cannot betray Tbubui like that. If I confide in him will he understand that I want to spend most of my time with her? Guiltily, he wrenched his mind back to the smiling golden god with his gleaming blue lapis cap whom he served, and finished his obeisances with proper attention. Then he ordered out his litter, allowed his body servant to paint his face and limped out of the house.

Two hours later he stood with Khaemwaset amid the rubble left when the false wall was torn down, staring at the two newly-exposed coffins. Torches had been fixed to the rock on either side of the untidy hole and they sent an unsteady red light into the chamber which did nothing to dispel its sinister atmosphere. After a while Hori retired to the camp stool his servant had brought, his now stiff leg flung out before him, and watched his father pick up a lamp and splash his way to the coffins. Khaemwaset grimaced as Hori had done at the distasteful odour and feel of the pool. After a careful examination of the sarcophagi he waded back to his son.

"You are right," he said briskly. "They were occupied at one time. But if the bodies were dismembered by thieves in search for valuables and flung into the water, there would be some trace of them. The linen windings and mummified flesh would have dissolved but not the bones. Are you sure nothing lies under the water?"

"Nothing," Hori replied firmly. "I hated to do it but I slid my feet over every inch of the floor. It is slimy rock, no more. Father, is it possible that the princess Ahura and her husband were first buried there, in the small chamber, and later, when the tomb was inspected and found to be seeping water, the sempriests had new coffins made for them out here?"

"It is possible," Khaemwaset agreed. "But then why is the first burial room so poorly executed? Did these people have three chambers instead of the customary two, one for goods and one for bodies, and if so why? For a child, perhaps, or children? But if that is so, if the tomb was opened later by other members of the family, why the subterfuge of a false wall? What had to be hidden, Hori? There is nothing in that room. Thieves look for valuables, small things, and may destroy but ultimately leave behind anything not easily portable. Yet beneath the water there is no trace of splintered furniture, shrine pieces, statutes, anything. And if the chamber was prepared for other members of the family, surely it would have been as lavishly decorated as the rest of the tomb." He pushed his feet back into his sandals and Kasa knelt to lace them. "Only one child, a son, is depicted on these walls," he went on. "I confess I am completely puzzled. I do not think that we shall ever unravel the answers."

"Well what of the scroll?" Hori suggested. "Can you not look at it again, Father? And perhaps this time it will be clearer to you? It may contain some hint for us."

"It may," Khaemwaset said doubtfully, hesitantly. "And I know that if we repair and re-seal this place without exploring all avenues of speculation you will always be dissatisfied."

"Will you not also wonder about it from time to time?" Hori asked diffidently, noting his father's unease. Khaemwaset was glancing slowly around, one hand tightly gripping the Eye of Horus pectoral resting on his broad chest. He shook his head emphatically.

"I think I have hated this place from the moment Penbuy came to us with news of its discovery," he said in a low voice. "I still do not know why. Have the workmen begin to rebuild this wall, Hori. There is nothing more to be gained by leaving it down. I am going home. I cannot bear the stench of this water, and it has fouled my kilt."

Hori watched him rub at a grey splatter as he moved quickly towards the glow of sunlight filtering along the passage. Then he was gone. The Overseer of Works and Khaemwaset's Master Mason stood politely with eyes downcast, waiting for instructions. Hori left the stool. "You had better begin the reconstruction," he told them. "I cannot be here today but you have my authority to make any decisions necessary regarding the wall. I shall be back tomorrow morning."

I hope Father can bring himself to examine the scroll again, he thought as he negotiated the steps with his servant's discreet assistance and collapsed, with a curse at his swollen knee, onto his litter. I hardly considered it as a factor when I was chewing on the tough problems of the water and the baboons and now the walled-off room, but I am now beginning to believe that it holds the key to this aggravating excavation. Nothing else does, and the inscriptions and scenes Penbuy's assistants have so painstakingly transcribed are pretty but useless. "To the watersteps," he commanded with a thrill of pleasure. The earring lay wrapped under the little cushions. He intended to visit Tbubui, with it and his adventures yesterday as the excuse. Had she not, after all, begged him to let her know what transpired? She would commiserate with him over his knee. She would ply him with good wine, make him comfortable, her sympathy would shine from those huge black eyes. Now that his father's somewhat cursory examination of the find was over without so much as one sharp word, the rest of the day stretched ahead full of latent possibilities. Hori closed his eyes and smiled.

Although he would have preferred to walk, he was carried from the skiff along the winding path under the tall palms. The house was as he remembered it, low and freshly whitewashed, rambling and silent. He felt he had left it years ago. The front garden was deserted and for the first time Hori wondered if his appearance might be inconvenient, but as he alighted and told his bearers to wait for him under the trees by the riverbank, a servant came out, bowed and stood stoically. He was entirely black, a pure Nubian, Hori conjectured, with powerful shoulders and a blunt face. He reminded the young man of the shawabtis in the tomb, black ebony with gold collars, each deaf and dumb until the moment when their master would call them to perform their duties in the next world. "Tell the lady Tbubui that Prince Hori is here and wishes to speak with her," he ordered. The man bowed again, still with head lowered, indicated that Hori should precede him into the entrance hall, then vanished. Hori sank onto a chair. In spite of his rapid heartbeat, his anticipation, the almost stultifying peace of the house began to settle over him.

He did not have long to wait. Tbubui herself came gliding towards him, reverencing him several times as she did so, a welcoming smile lighting her features. She was barefoot, as usual, one golden anklet tinkling as she moved, her wrists imprisoned by two thick, plain gold bracelets. Beneath the thin white body-hugging linen of her sheath her brown skin could be glimpsed, and this time Hori made no attempt to wrench his gaze from the clean curves of her hips and thighs, the slight quiver of her breasts. Her hair had been imprisoned in a dozen braids, exposing the noble length of aristocratic neck and her pure, uncluttered chin. Green eye-paint gave her eyes a lustrous sheen, and her mouth was hennaed orange.

"Highness!" she exclaimed as she came up to him. "Your knee! Whatever have you been doing?"

She might be talking to a child, Hori thought a little mutinously. That is how she sees me. As a child to be condescended to and indulged. He realized that she had not waited for him to speak first as she should have done and he pushed himself to his feet.

"Greetings, Tbubui," he said coolly. "I took your advice and opened the false wall in the tomb yesterday. Today I come to tell you what transpired."

Her smile widened. "Wonderful! But you look drawn, Prince. Are you in pain? Would you like wine? I do not suggest the garden today. It is too hot. Let us retire to my suite where there is a comfortable chair and some cushions."

Hori's rebellious moment melted away. He followed her awkwardly into the rear passage and turned right, away from Harmin's quarters. Presently she entered a room and held the door for him. A female servant rose from the corner and bowed.

"Your Highness should take the chair by the couch," Tbubui said. "I can testify to its comfort for I spent much time in it when my foot was injured. You!" She addressed the servant, "Bring a footstool and cushions and a jar of wine." The girl inclined her head and hurried away. Are all the servants here forbidden to open their mouths? Hori wondered, taking the chair. I have not heard one of them speak.

The footstool was brought and piled with cushions. The quiet girl lifted his leg with the lightest of touches and settled it on the softness, then went away, came back with wine, poured and was dismissed. Tbubui sat on the edge of the couch. Out of the corner of his eye Hori noticed a tiring chest with lid flung back and a scarlet sheath spilling over its side. A vanity table covered in neatly aligned pots and jars stood next to the chest, and on the floor, as though flung there, was a scarlet ostrich fan.

"It is so wonderfully cool in here," he said slowly, picking up the silver wine cup. "To you, Tbubui. Life, Prosperity and Happiness!"

"Thank you, Prince," she smiled. "An old wish and a very welcome one. Now please tell me what happened to you yesterday. And what did Khaemwaset say when you told him what you had done?"

The couch behind her was neatly made, the shine of the linen subdued by the half-light. An ivory headrest stood beneath it. She was looking at him expectantly, leaning forward, her mouth slightly parted, her small teeth glimpsed within. It would be so easy to sully that perfectly made couch, Hori thought. One lunge and I would have her on her back, out of breath, disarmed by surprise. Would she cry out? I do not think so. Gasp? Perhaps. In

either case I could have my lips against hers before she could recover her aplomb. The savagery and vividness of the scene that
had burst into his mind horrified him and he forced a deep
breath. "Father was very angry," he said with an effort, "but he
concealed it well. Today he inspected what I had done but made
no comment."

She nodded, and he went on describing the events of the previous day—his tension, his feelings of trepidation and excitement. She listened attentively but, when Hori began to talk of the
tunnel, he sensed an increasing agitation, though she did not stir.
She seemed all eyes, intent and alert. "But how mysterious!" she
interrupted him. "Did you explore this place?"

"Yes," he said triumphantly. "I did. And I found this." he extracted the earring from the pouch at his belt and handed it to her.
"That is what tore my knee, but it was worthwhile, do you not
think so? Such lovely old turquoise and such fine goldwork to
hold it." It lay on her hennaed palm like a drop of limpid Nile
water, blue and green, and Hori, eagerly searching her face for
approval, saw a most peculiar expression flit across it. Greed,
satisfaction, anger, he could not decide which. "Put it on," he offered, and she smiled very slowly.

"Will I not enrage the ka of the lady who once owned it?" she
asked with a trace of mockery, and Hori smiled back.

"That lady's ka must know that I intend to put it back in the
tomb unharmed," he stated, "and besides, how could she be offended to see her precious thing adorning so much beauty?"

For answer she pushed a braid behind her ear and screwed the
earring into her lobe. It swung gracefully to and fro beside the
long sweep of her neck and did indeed look as though it had
been made for her. "Hori, fetch me a mirror," she asked, then she
laughed. "I was forgetting about your poor knee. I will get it myself." Sliding off the couch she swayed to her vanity table, and to
Hori there was something dreamlike about her motion, something private, as though for a moment she believed herself alone.

Grasping the copper mirror lying face down on the table she
held it up like a votive candle in both hands, chin raised, eyes
half closed, back arched, tilting her glossy head this way and that
and murmuring gently. Hori could not catch what she was saying. Then she returned the mirror with a snap and came back to
him. "I wonder what happened to its mate?" she said. "Perhaps

thieves made off with it, as you have surmised. A pity." She regained the couch, this time sliding back on it languidly. One foot remained on the floor, the white sheath parting at the slit to reveal the long brown strength of thigh and calf. "Would I be permitted to wear it for a little while?" she asked, and at her tone of pretty submission Hori's heart once more began to thud. He nodded, not trusting his voice.

Her movements had stirred the air and her perfume was suddenly in his nostrils, the myrrh of sex and worship and that other fragrance, elusive and tantalizing. She was stroking the earring with the fingers of one elegant hennaed hand. "You have told me of your escapade yesterday and of Khaemwaset's response," she went on. "But Highness, you have not yet spoken of any conclusions to be drawn from the new discovery. Does the small chamber shed any light on the rest of the tomb or its inhabitants?"

"Not really," Hori admitted. "Having seen the tomb, Tbubui, you and your brother know as much about it as we do. A shameful admission! Father and I are supposed to be the historians."

"But so is Sisenet," Tbubui added. "He and I have often discussed the nature of the water, the baboons, the lids, to no avail. Tell me," she went on, her fingers still absently fondling the earring. "What happened to the scroll Khaemwaset cut from the dead hand? You do not mention it at all."

"Father still has it in safekeeping," Hori answered. "He does not look at it any more. He tried to decipher it, you know, and was defeated. Strange that you should mention it, Tbubui, for it came into my mind quite forcibly today that it may well hold the key to all the irritating mysteries of the place. I intend to ask Father if I may inspect it." She cast him a smile of indulgent sweetness as if to say, If the greatest historian in Egypt cannot decipher it, how can you? and Hori was mortified. "Of course such an inspection on my part will be all but futile," he hastened to say, "but who knows? I may thus prompt him to attempt another translation. My workmen are even now re-sealing the second burial chamber and soon the whole tomb will be closed. Time is short."

Her hand left her ear and drifted down to rest on her thigh. Hori's gaze went with it. "I would very much like to see it also," she said with a charming diffidence, all superiority gone. "But my interest would seem entirely frivolous to your august father.

However, my brother has some skills in the matter of the translation of ancient scripts. He might possibly be able to help."

Now it was Hori's turn to feel a secret scorn. "Your pardon, Tbubui, but your brother is surely no more than a clever amateur," he replied loftily. "The scroll is fragile and irreplaceable, and unskilled hands might damage it."

"Oh, I think there is no fear of that," she countered softly, her eyes huge in the dim light of the chamber. "Sisenet is used to handling valuable scrolls. He has deciphered all the records left by Osiris Hatshepsut's caravan overseers who were, as you may remember, our ancestors."

"No, I did not know that," Hori answered. "Then if you like I will ask my father's permission on your brother's behalf, to try to read the scroll. Will he be interested in it?"

"Oh yes," Tbubui said slowly, emphatically. "He will be very interested indeed. More wine, Prince?"

When he nodded, she rose from the couch in one fluid movement, took up the jar and bent to pour for him. It seemed to Hori that she came closer than was entirely necessary. He inhaled the gush of perfume and warmth rising from her cleavage, and seeing her braids fall forward he gently pushed them back. Her shoulder was inches from his mouth, satin-smooth and gleaming. Unable to resist any longer, he learned forward, closed his eyes and pressed his lips to her flesh. It was cool and tasted of lotus water. Still with eyes tightly shut he moved his tongue towards her neck and down, seeking the delicious hollow of her collarbone then up, up and over her chin. At last her mouth was there, slightly parted, her lips soft and yielding. She had not stirred. Thrusting his tongue between them he kissed her ardently, trying to salve the wound of lust, his hands going blindly to cup her breasts that were fuller, heavier than he had first supposed. But when he broke away, dazed and breathing hard, he found the wound throbbing more fiercely than before.

"Well, young Prince," she murmured. "That was flattering."

"Flattering?" he burst out. "I am besotted with you, Tbubui! I cannot eat or sleep for desiring you. Now I know why the gorgeous little girls of my grandfather's court left me lonely and wanting something I did not recognize until now. I was aloof, self-sufficient. I was asleep!" His voice was coarse and ragged, his expression strained. "Let me woo you, persuade you that I am more than a youth. You could do worse than be betrothed into the most powerful family in Egypt!"

Her eyebrows rose. "But my dear Hori, you do not really know me at all. How can I be anything but a body blending with a fantasy to you? Explore my character and you may find yourself disappointed." She stroked his hair with a gentle, maternal touch. "This is infatuation. Nothing more."

He struck her hand away then snatched it up and kissed it fervently, licking the tips of her fingers. "I have never been a young man with a light heart," he groaned. "This is not infatuation, Tbubui. It will last."

She made no move to withdraw her hand. "You would be the laughing-stock of every noble in Egypt," she warned him. "My blood may be aristocratic, but it is not the blood of full grandeur required of a prince's wife. I am too old for you."

He laid her fingers between both his palms and managed a wan smile.

"And how old are you?"

There was a pause. Then she chuckled. "The gods have given me thirty-five years."

"I don't care!"

"But I do. I cannot bind a man so young." She pulled from his grasp and he at last sat back. His head was drumming and he felt a little sick. Suddenly he became aware of the pain in his knee.

"Do you feel nothing for me, then?" he asked.

"Whatever would your father say?" she countered. "Hori, you are an attractive man and I am not immune to your magnetism. No one in Egypt is immune. But I must regard you as a dear young friend. You may visit me whenever you wish, providing you keep your feelings a secret from your family and other friends. Is it agreed?"

"Agreed," he whispered. His poise had deserted him long ago, replaced by the need to prove himself as a man that her perhaps unconsciously patronizing attitude made worse. "But you did not answer my question."

"Yes, Prince," she said pointedly. "I did. Now would you like something to eat? A fresh dressing for your wound?"

No dressing can heal my wound, he wanted to shout. Everything in him demanded that the conversation be continued, that she be forced to admit a desire for him equal to his own, but a new wisdom advised a temporary retreat. Frontal attack would not work. Tbubui must be won with stealth, with a patience barbed in small thorns of aggression.

"Thank you, no," he replied briskly. "I must go home. I have business waiting. Your hospitality was boundless as usual, Tbubui." He did his best to keep the sarcasm out of his voice. She rose, unscrewed the earring and handed it back to him with obvious reluctance.

"We in this family revere ancient turquoise," she said. "This piece is of incomparable delicacy and beauty, and I shall perhaps try to have it copied. I appreciate being allowed to wear it, Prince." Hori wrapped it and returned it to the pouch. Clumsily he pushed himself out of the chair, and without another word she followed him into the passage.

The afternoon was far advanced, a blazing furnace of heat and light that shocked him after the coolness of her bedchamber. He took his leave with some of his accustomed dignity and she smiled wryly into his eyes, bidding him to come back at his earliest convenience. His litter was waiting. Grunting, he reclined on the cushions, gave his command and twitched the curtains closed.

Some moments later, something made him lift the heavy covering and glance back at the house. Tbubui was standing in the shadow of the entrance, gazing expressionlessly after him, and she was not alone. Her brother stood beside her, one arm across her shoulders, his sombre face as blank as hers. Quickly Hori withdrew and let the curtain fall, but the vision of those two frozen and somehow ominous sentinels stayed with him, clouding the otherwise burning day.

Khaemwaset's mood was still uncertain when the rest of the family gathered to dine just after sunset. Accustomed to a father of even temper, Sheritra prattled on about Harmin during the first two courses and was shocked into silence when Khaemwaset told her sharply to be quiet. For once Nubnofret defended her, saying, "Really Khaemwaset, there is no need to be rude!" But he did not answer, lifting food to his mouth that he hardly tasted and not hearing at all the pleasant music filling the hall. He was aware of Hori's unusual withdrawal, his monosyllabic answers to his mother's casual questions, and made a mental note to inspect his son's knee the following day, but forgot the thought as soon as it was complete. When he had returned from the tomb to his office, Penbuy had read him a scroll from Wennufer, his priestly friend, setting out the retort to an amicable argument the two had been engaged in, now, for months, regarding the true burial place of the head of Osiris, and Khaemwaset had found himself profoundly bored with the whole question. Huy, Mayor of Memphis, had sent a note inviting him to dine and he had told Penbuy to decline on his behalf. Si-Montu had written in his own hieratic scrawl to let his brother know that the grapes were recovering from their blight and filling apace. The mention of disease had made him think of the message from his mother's scribe, but he thrust the guilt of his inaction regarding her failing health to the back of his mind. He would dictate a cheerful letter to her soon. From the Delta had come the reports of the men detailed to measure the steadily shrinking level of the Nile, and his scribe's voice, monotonously reeling off the list of figures, had given Khaemwaset a sudden lancing pain in the gut that he did not even bother to treat.

Lust for Tbubui inflamed him. He could not have cast the vivid visions of her body, her laugh, her gestures, from his mind if he had wanted to. Every call upon his time and attention infuriated him, and Hori's abrupt revelation yesterday was a distraction of enormous proportions.

As soon as the evening meal was over, Khaemwaset rose and left the hall, striding out into a far corner of the garden where he stood rigid, watching the rising of a pale, waning moon. He had made a supreme effort earlier in going to his wife's suite and entertaining her once more at sennet, and it had been almost too much for him to bear.

He had not wanted to go to the tomb that morning. The tomb was one catastrophe in an ocean of irritations. He had wanted to stay where he was, in the event that Tbubui might call on him for some reason. In a few days he intended to visit her, with a herbal recipe as the excuse. He knew that in fact he needed no excuse. She was a widow and he a prince, entitled to as many wives and concubines as he wished, but in his heart he felt besmirched, made guilty by this passion. Its power had already swept him away so that his work, his family, his position meant nothing anymore. He had already determined that nothing should stand between him and the object of his desire. Coldly, he was beginning to plan his campaign of acquisition.

Sighing, he let the sensuous beauty of the night—the scented, fitful breeze that fluttered probing fingers against his naked skin, the soft black sky with its mat of stars—insinuate itself into that place already turbulent with obsession. His thoughts turned to the turquoise earring Hori had revealed with a mixture of pride and shame, but immediately he saw it resting against a tall brown neck, entangled in black hair that smelled of warmth and myrrh. It would suit her so well. "Ah Thoth," he groaned quietly, arms coming up to cradle his pain, "if you love me then help me. Help me!" The god's symbol now stood small and hard-rimmed above the house, its light an indifferent, alien thing.

Khaemwaset sank to the grass with his back against a tree. For a long time he watched the cheerful glow of lamps within move from room to room and eventually be extinguished. Beyond the garden wall, where the servants' compound lay with its granaries and the huge kitchen, came the intermittent sounds of laughter and the rattle of dice and click of knucklebones, but soon these faded into the deepening lateness of the hour.

A lamp appeared, hovering just beyond the shrubbery, and Kasa's voice called, "Prince, are you out here?"

"Yes," Khaemwaset called back without rising. "I am too restless to retire, Kasa. Leave my couch turned down and water in the ante-room so that I may wash before bed. Then you may go to your own quarters."

"Wash yourself, Highness?" Kasa's indignation was clear though Khaemwaset could not see him. "Really, I . . ."

"Sleep well, Kasa," Khaemwaset broke in firmly, and the lamp made an agitated sweep and disappeared beyond the invisible pillars. In truth, Khaemwaset's eyes burned and his head felt thick with weariness, but beneath the physical symptoms he was preternaturally alert.

When the last lamp had been put out in the house he got up, intending to take a turn around his estate and perhaps watch the river for a while, but instead he found himself descending the watersteps, untethering the small skiff, clambering into it and running out the oars. This is madness, his sane self protested, aghast, but his driven, dreaming self established a rowing stroke, took note of the shrouded, deserted banks and the empty stretch of moon-glittering river, and matched Tbubui's name to each pull.

The northern suburbs glided by, sunk in silence. Once Khaemwaset passed a large lamp-bedecked raft crowded with revellers, but their noise soon grew faint. He pulled for the eastern bank, scarcely conscious of his aching thighs and shoulders. I should not be doing this, he told himself peacefully. If anyone sees me they will think that the great Prince has taken leave of his senses. Perhaps I have. Perhaps I am in the grip of strong magic, perhaps I am even at home on my couch floating in the illusion of purpose, movement, under a spell of Thoth's moon. Well then, let the spell continue. Let it bind me tighter, let the night dissolve time and reality so that I may stand unseen before her house as a young man in love, without cumberances. Water dribbled silver from the oars and the surface of the river rippled away to be quietly lost in the shadows of the bank.

Her diminutive watersteps were easy to miss, crowded as they were by choking river growth, but Khaemwaset manoeuvred the skiff unerringly to bump against them. He disembarked, made his boat fast and stepped up onto the path. His feet made no sound on the sandy ground strewn with brittle fallen palm leaves. The trees themselves marched away into duskiness on either side like the pillars of a temple, and their spreading height made a canopy. Khaemwaset felt even more strongly that he was walking a dream. One more bend in the track and the house would be before him, its white walls dimmed to a mysterious grey, its tiny windows blind. He padded on.

All at once a flicker of movement to his left caught his eye, and some of the weight of unreality slipped from him. He stopped. Someone was stalking him. I should have at least brought Amek with me, he thought, senses suddenly alert. I am a fool. He waited tensely for another flutter between the trunks. It came, and then Tbubui was walking towards him, threading her way barefoot, the delineations of her face and body blurred in the half darkness. Her hair was loose and tousled, a black cloud framing scrubbed features, and with an inward wrench Khaemwaset saw that she was naked but for a flimsy sleeping kilt tied about her hips. She came up to him and halted without the least surprise.

"Prince Khaemwaset," she said. "I should have guessed it was you. The air is full of your presence tonight."

She had not asked what he was doing there. Unadorned by any jewellery, her face fresh and unpainted, she looked about sixteen. I am a young man in love, Khaemwaset thought happily. Oh Tbubui! "The thought of you makes me commit outrageous acts," he replied. "I had planned to circle your house like a lovesick youth and then go home. Forgive my eccentric behaviour."

"It is no more eccentric than mine," she countered with a slight smile. "I like to wander under the palms at night if I cannot sleep. And sleep often eludes me of late."

"Why is that?" he asked quickly, his throat constricting. She raised dusky eyes to his.

"I am not sure," she whispered, "but I know that I am lonely, Prince. Rest does not come easily to the discontented." She clasped her hands together under her chin in an artless, youthful gesture. "My brother is not a communicative man though he loves me, and Harmin . . ." She shrugged. "Harmin is a young man carving out his own concerns."

She began to wander away, not in the direction of the house but farther in under the trees. Khaemwaset kept pace with her. He took her hand and it was a natural, simple thing to do. Her fingers curled around his. She came to a halt in dense shadow and he pulled her to face him, fumbling for her other hand.

"I love you also," he said urgently. "I think I have loved you from the first moment I glimpsed you walking in the dust along the river road. I have never been in love before, Tbubui, not with my body, mind and ka all crying out." He released her hands and took her by the shoulders, touching her neck, the curve of her ears, brushing across her eyes in a kind of ecstasy. "I want to make love to you now," he hissed. "Here, under the palms."

"I long to lie in your arms," she returned in a low voice. "I have wondered what it would be like so many times, and then when I looked into your eyes and saw my desire mirrored there . . ." She rubbed her cheek against his questing fingers. "But I do not give myself lightly, Khaemwaset, as some women might. I live sternly as the ancients did, and abhor the moral corruption of this age."

Khaemwaset sank to the sand, pulling her with him. Her words had merely skimmed his mind, and all he clung to was the admission from her own lips that she longed to lie in his arms. Forcing her gently onto her back he buried his face between her breasts, his hands kneading her thighs. Feeling the soft kiss of linen there he loosened it and raised his head. She lay naked under him, concave belly lightly lifting and falling, the simplicity of her stark hip bones an agony of pleasure in themselves.

He began to draw his tongue over the skin between them but she took his head in both hands and forced it up, her mouth seeking his. This time the kiss was hers, the moans of delight were hers, and she thrust against him with an urgency that rendered him momentarily weak. He broke away and straddled her, victory awe and passion a tumult within him, but she suddenly wriggled from his grip and rolled away, lying face down on the earth and panting. Khaemwaset put out a hand but she cringed away, then she sat up, pulling her knees to her chin.

"I cannot," she muttered. "Forgive me, Prince."

He wanted to shake her in his frustration. He wanted to fling her once more onto her back and hold her down, push himself inside her and release the dammed-up flood of pain that was now a constant burden, but he did not. He stroked her hair with one long, tender caress, then withdrew his hand. "I have a beautiful house on my estate," he said steadily. "It is large and airy and full of precious things. Its garden is complete with a fish-pond and a fountain. I have not entered it for a long time. My very few concubines live there." He smiled wryly, but he did not think that she could see his expression for the depth of the shadows. "I have seldom bothered them over the years. Nubnofret was enough for me, but now . . ." He paused but she did not look up. Her forehead was resting on her knees. "Now I want you with me," he went on. "Move into that house, Tbubui. Come as a privileged member of my household. Your every need will be met, yours and your son's and your brother's. Let me take care of you."

Slowly her head came up and turned towards him. Khaemwaset could see the cold glimmer of her eyes. "Princesses may count themselves fortunate to end up in the harems of kings," she said distantly, "but I will be no man's concubine, languishing the long hours away in waiting for a man whose infatuation fades under the onslaught of fresh beauty, and who in the end does not summon her at all. She remains his property, though, and may not claim her freedom.''

"Tbubui, it is I, Khaemwaset, who makes you this offer!" he expostulated, amazed. "I am not by nature a profligate man. I would honour you with my body to the end of my life!"

"You were not a profligate man," she objected, and now her voice seemed disembodied and deadly cold, "but forces have been wakened in you that will not be quelled, O prince. With me or without me, your long-suffering Nubnofret cannot satisfy you any longer, whether you know it yet or not."

"You woke those forces!" Khaemwaset cried out. "You changed me! It is you towards whom they are directed, and you who will always control them. I love you!"

"Yes, you do," she agreed, still in that flat, remote tone. "But I am sorry, Prince. I cannot accept your offer. And I cannot give you my body whenever you desire it as a common whore would do. Such a thing would destroy me."

Khaemwaset became aware that he was grinding his lips between his teeth and his hands were clenched into fists. With conscious deliberation he uncurled his fingers, relaxed his jaw and lay back with eyes closed. For a long time a silence fell. Neither of them moved. The palm grove around them was utterly without sound.

Then Khaemwaset rose, getting to his feet without haste. Hands on his hips he stared down at her. "Get up, Tbubui," he commanded. She did so, brushing her buttocks, knees and elbows like a child who has been told not to muddy a new kilt, then she stood before him with downcast eyes. "Your words were strong," he said, "but they confirm in me the knowledge of your good breeding and sound morals. Such women are rare. I love you more, not less, for your position, my dear sister." It was the first time he had called her a lover's name and she made a small, throaty whimper. "Under the law I am permitted to take another wife," he went on boldly, though his other self, the cautious, sober self who wanted only to be returned to its placid old existence, listened in horror. "Until now I have not wished to do so, but I will have you, Tbubui, do not doubt it, and if it must be through marriage, then I gladly offer it." Taking her chin he forced her to look at him. Her expression was blank, even sullen, her eyes veiled. "I will have a marriage contract drawn up between us and you will live in my house, in a suite I shall build for you. Are you agreeable?" Her eyelashes fluttered as though she were coming out of a deep trance.

"Dear Khaemwaset, dear Prince," she said softly. "I love you, but never think that I refused to give myself to you in the hope that you might be pressured into marrying me. The marriage of a blood prince is a serious matter. Let us both take some time to consider it well."

He held her urgently. "But you will consider it?"

"Oh yes," she smiled. "Indeed I will."

All at once he wanted nothing more than to be at home, on his couch where he could think. "Come and visit us tomorrow afternoon," he begged. "Spend some time with Nubnofret. She already thinks a great deal of you and enjoys your company. Life as a princess has much to recommend it, Tbubui."

"I am sure it has," she responded gravely.

He pulled her close and kissed her, this time with an almost violent ferocity, then he pushed her away, turned on his heel and set off briskly for the watersteps. He did not look back. She had not met his kiss with equal fervor but he had the distinct impression that its savagery had excited her. If I am to offer her a contract, if she is to marry into the royal family, I must institute a thorough investigation of her roots, he thought, his eyes on the soft ground gliding by beneath him. Her blood must be pure, her lineage untouched by treason or any other offence against Egypt. Penbuy can do it. He can also draw up the contract, but quietly. The thought of his brother Si-Montu, who had cheerfully married a commoner, and a foreign one at that, came into his mind, and he wondered whether his need to research Tbubui came from some small warning part of him that existed solely for his preservation. I am being foolish, he told himself happily, dazedly. My desire is now within my grasp. It will be difficult to tell the family but, after all, I will be doing nothing more than that which is my right. Father might even approve. He has always been amused at my sober tastes in everything. He felt lightheaded and slightly drunk, and indeed he stumbled twice before he got to the watersteps and his skiff, still tied to the peeling paint of her post. He was sure that he had left it a dozen hentis ago.

Suddenly he had the overpowering impression that he was being watched. Halting, he peered about, trying to pierce the thick gloom under the trees. "Tbubui, is that you?" he called, but there was not even a breeze to whisper an answer. Khaemwaset stood very still, breathing shallowly. He was more certain than ever, though he could see nothing, that an unseen presence lurked close by with speculative eyes on him. If he had been in less of an internal turmoil he would have left the path and searched angrily, but as it was he hurried down the steps and into the rocking craft. The night was no longer a magic spell of romance and timelessness. It was a shroud hiding the ephemeral, nameless things that preyed upon human beings in envy. He could not pull away from the watersteps quickly enough.

Chapter 10

*'Set not sorrow in thy heart,
for the years are not many.'*

Dawn was only three hours away when Khaemwaset fell onto his couch without bothering to use the water Kasa had dutifully left for him. His night lamp was low and guttering. He blew it out, thinking that he would doubtless sleep very late the next morning, but to his surprise he woke refreshed at his usual time, unaware of having dreamed and feeling full of vigour.

After he had been bathed and dressed and had opened the shrine in his quarters to say his morning prayers, he went over the events of the night. Perhaps they were a dream I had, he told himself. They seem so unreal in the full light of early morning. But he was humming as he talked to himself, for he knew the difference between vision and reality.

When he had finished his morning prayers and was capping the incense, Hori was announced. Khaemwaset handed the long incense holder to Ib and turned to greet his son. But the warmth in his heart that he wished to spread over everyone he met today was dampened as he watched the young man approach. Hori was limping, of course, but it was his face that gave Khaemwaset pause. He was pale, even haggard, with black smudges under his eyes and a stoop to his ordinarily straight spine. Concerned, Khaemwaset's eyes flew to the knee, fearing infection, but the gash had closed well and the stitches were all visible. "Hori, what ails you?" he asked.

Hori looked surprised and then shrugged. "Do I look that ill?" he said with an attempted grin. "My knee hurts, Father, but I don't suppose you will want to remove the stitches until the last moment because of where the injury is. May I sit down?"

"Of course."

"I did not sleep well," Hori went on, lowering himself into the chair by Khaemwaset's couch. "I cannot remember what I dreamed but it was terrible, dark and full of foreboding and menace, and I woke feeling sick. It is wearing off now."

Khaemwaset sat on the couch and observed him carefully. "You need three or four days of strict fasting," he said. "Let your body cleanse itself and your ka become quieter."

"You are probably right," Hori agreed. "I wish you had cast the horoscopes, Father. Phamenoth will soon be upon us and I do not like going blind through the days not knowing my unlucky hours. I find it impossible to make correct decisions." He was not speaking directly into his father's face. His gaze roved the room and his hands were woven tightly together.

"Something else is troubling you," Khaemwaset insisted. "I will cast the horoscopes for Phamenoth, I promise, but will you not talk to me, Hori? Let me help you."

Now Hori's glance came to rest on his father and he smiled. "There is nothing wrong, believe me, Prince. I will take your advice and fast. I think that Antef and I have been imbibing too freely, eating too recklessly and falling into bed too often with the dawn."

Khaemwaset, remembering his moment of unease on Tbubui's path the previous night, shivered a little. "Antef is due to return today."

"Yes." Hori pulled himself straighter. He had not yet been painted and Khaemwaset was relieved to see that already some colour was flushing his cheeks and his eyes were regaining their translucent glitter. "Father, have you taken another look at the scroll yet?"

Khaemwaset did not need to ask which scroll. For the past three months there had only been one scroll, throbbing on the edge of his consciousness like a tooth beginning to rot. "No I have not," he answered. "Why do you ask?"

Hori's eyes once more left his and were fastened on the far wall. "Because yesterday I paid a visit to Tbubui. I had hoped to see Sisenet but he was not at home. He is an erudite man and I thought I might discuss the tomb with him again."

A formless anxiety blended with jealousy shook Khaemwaset. "You spent time with Tbubui?" he asked sharply. "You went there without telling me? You were alone with her?"

Hori blinked. "Yes. We think that it would help to have the scroll deciphered. She offered her brother's assistance. She told me that he has had some success in translating ancient writings and, with your permission, I would like to invite him here to inspect it."

"She is coming here this afternoon to visit Nubnofret," Khaemwaset said with a curious reluctance. "I will speak to her about it then. I suppose that Sisenet can do the scroll no harm." But will it do him harm? came the irrational thought.

"Coming today?" Hori exclaimed. "How do you know? She said nothing of it to me yesterday."

Something is definitely straining Hori, Khaemwaset thought. I wonder what it is. "Your mother keeps expressing a wish to see her again and so I sent a message to her house in the evening," Khaemwaset explained. "She did not reply, therefore she is coming." I have never lied to my son before, he thought gloomily, but I have the feeling that it will not be the last time. Is he, in his deliberate silence, lying to me by omission?

"Oh," was all Hori said. "In that case I will not go out today. The scroll interests me greatly." He struggled out of the chair, suddenly kissed his father in an uncharacteristic, swift gesture and hobbled out of the room.

Tbubui arrived just after the noon sleep, when the greatest heat of the day still permeated the house. Khaemwaset had told a delighted Nubnofret that she was coming specifically to spend an hour or two in gossip; therefore it was Wernuro, Nubnofret's female servant and companion, who waited at the watersteps to greet and escort her.

Nubnofret had just risen when her guest was announced and was sitting at her cosmetic table, mirror in hand, naked but for a piece of thin linen tied loosely about her waist. Her cosmetician was touching up her kohl but at her word he immediately withdrew. Nubnofret swept to embrace her guest.

"Tbubui, how lovely that you decided to come and see me," she exclaimed, enveloping the other woman in perfumed musk. "I knew that we would become friends. It is important to have friends, is it not, when one is married to a man who in turn is married to his many duties? Come. Sit down. Forgive my unmade couch, but I have only been out of it a short while." She sighed. "The heat is becoming unbearable and it does make my eyelids swell so. I must say that you look very fresh!"

Tbubui had not taken the chair. She had settled herself cross-legged on the couch, pillows at her back. Nubnofret noted that today she had abandoned the very old-fashioned tight sheaths she usually wore and was dressed in a charming ankle-length white gown gathered into an embroidered yellow yoke high on her neck. The garment was sleeveless and looked very cool. A band of gold gripped her upper arm and long gold droplets swung from her ears. Though she was finely painted, her hair was wound on top of her head and completely unadorned. She wriggled into her position and smiled brightly at Nubnofret.

"I like the heat," she said. "I sleep well in it, Highness, though I am not silly enough to walk out under the sun at this time of year. Would your Highness like to join me on the couch?" Nubnofret collapsed onto it with a sigh and lay on her side, propping her head with its tumble of curls on one hand.

"Wernuro will bring drinks and pastries shortly," she said. "I decided that we should stay indoors. My bedchamber is a little cooler than the furnace of the garden. There is not even a wind to funnel down the wind-catcher. Tell me, Tbubui, are you becoming acquainted with any of our Memphis nobles? How do you like life here?"

Tbubui laughed. It was a spontaneous, free sound, but Nubnofret thought that it revealed too much the feral quality of her small teeth. "We receive numerous invitations from the inhabitants of the northern suburb," she said. "I am sure that they are curious about us in a kindly way. But we accept few of them. We like our life to be quiet and well ordered. Memphis is beautiful and exciting, but it is usually enough to know that the pleasures it offers are set out like food on a plate for us to taste when we wish."

"Do you not find life dull, then?" Nubnofret asked. "Running your household cannot take up too much of your time."

"No it does not," Tbubui agreed. "But I am at present dictating a history of Egypt's relations with the rest of the world during the time of Osiris Hatshepsut, she who gave my ancestor the caravan route from Koptos to the Eastern Sea, and when I am not doing that I am walking the city. I like to walk."

I am not sure what to make of you, Nubnofret thought with a twinge of envy. Your responsibilities are few, unlike mine. You are free to do exactly as you please. Your roots are deep in Koptos. Then why are you here?

"That is an odd occupation for a woman," she said, more tartly than she had intended. "Writing history, I mean. As for the walking, I can see what it does for your body. You are tightly made, Tbubui!"

"Highness, you should not underestimate your own beauty," Tbubui protested, and Nubnofret realized that the woman had correctly interpreted the mild bitterness behind her own words. "Men do not always like a woman's body to be thin and muscled. Your breasts surely embody the essence of womanhood, being full and so large-nippled. Your hips swell with a most pleasing roundness, and the slight pouch of your belly speaks to a man of fecundity and sensuality. You were made for love."

Nubnofret was taken aback by Tbubui's directness and made even more uncomfortable by the minute brush of the woman's hand on her calf, but the touch was reassuring, a gesture of sympathy. "I wish Khaemwaset agreed with you," she laughed. "I do not think that he even sees me anymore. To him I am the organizer of his household, the mother of his children and the hostess to his many official guests." She made a small grimace. "My time is over-full with those duties, so that often even I feel sexless. But that is the way of life, is it not, Tbubui? Romance is for one's first youth, not for the hard glare of a long marriage."

"It does not have to be that way," the other woman responded gently. "Does Khaemwaset seek his concubines sometimes?"

Nubnofret privately considered the question. Was it a breach of good manners or the natural query of one adult woman to another? She decided, watching her guest's open, warm expression, that it was the latter. She shook her head and pushed her hair, sticky with heat, away from her forehead. "He never goes near them. I myself have not seen them for a long time. They come and go freely from their house, see their relatives, take journeys with permission and sometimes come to help entertain dignitaries. They are lovely women but not, of course, the kind one can befriend. No, Tbubui. If Khaemwaset needs a body he comes to me."

"I know that he loves you a great deal," Tbubui said. "He may appear to take you for granted but he values you highly."

"That may be," Nubnofret sighed again, "but his love is for a companion, a friend. It is not the delight one takes in a lover.

Still, I do not complain. I am happy." For the first time the words she used in her inward self so often suddenly sounded hollow. Am I indeed happy? she wondered. Am I? "And you," she countered. "Your husband has been dead for a long time. Are you not lonely?"

"Yes, I am," Tbubui answered frankly. "But I would rather remain a widow than marry just to alleviate my loneliness. I do not need another's wealth and I have dear Sisenet to care for me. I need love, Highness, but not at any price. The terms must be mine."

Nubnofret found herself liking Tbubui very much. "We know many great men all over Egypt," she said. "Would you like to meet some of them? I am a good matchmaker, my dear!" They both dissolved into howls of laughter. Nubnofret sat up and wiped her eyes on her waist linen, and at that moment Wernuro came in, bowed, and proceeded to set out water, wine and beer, and dishes of pastries and sweetmeats.

"Thank you for your offer, Highness," Tbubui gasped, "but I think I prefer to bore myself than have others bore me. I will have wine," she continued in answer to Nubnofret's silent invitation. Wernuro withdrew quietly.

"But what of Harmin?" Nubnofret pressed. With her highly developed sense of precedence on the social scale and the importance of one's place in it, she could not imagine a family with noble blood that did not want to advance. "Does he not desire a post at court or at least a priestly appointment?"

"I do not think so," Tbubui replied, sipping her wine. "He will of course inherit my personal estate, small though it is, and he already has the disposition of his father's wealth. He likes to be comfortable but he is not much inclined to rub shoulders with the powerful and mighty."

Nubnofret was pleased. Sheritra's obvious interest in the young man had caused her mother some anxiety, lest he should be merely attempting to get closer to the seat of power in Egypt. "I do hope he and Sheritra are enjoying their day," she said cautiously. "They have gone up river, I believe, to observe the wild life of the marshes and, if they are lucky, glimpse a crocodile. I do not envy them the heat."

Tbubui held her wine cup in both brown hands. "I have been meaning to speak to you about the Princess," she began hesitantly, "I understand that she is very shy and suspicious of people."

"Yes she is," Nubnofret said. Her thirst had been great and half her wine was already gone. A pleasant inner warmth was making her langorous. "Sheritra has no confidence in herself at all. She is intelligent and of course a great prize for any aspiring young nobleman, but she will look at none of them. I was greatly surprised when she accepted you so readily."

"She senses perhaps that I enjoy her company." Tbubui uncrossed her legs, stretched them out and leaned further into the pillows. "I have a favour to ask you, Princess."

What a pity, Nubnofret thought lazily. I am always happy to do favours for my old friends, or women of my own standing, but this woman is not yet either. And I had begun to like her. She waited.

"Allow Sheritra to come and stay at my house for a while. I often feel the lack of feminine company, living as I do with two men, and she and I could have much to say to each other. I think I can help her with her appearance and her confidence and she can make me laugh."

Laugh? Nubnofret thought. Sheritra able to make someone laugh? I suppose the invitation is not so foolish. Khaemwaset was talking some time ago about sending Sheritra to the Fayum to stay with Sunero's family if I did not stop nagging the girl. Well, she needs nagging. The familiar feeling of mild exasperation Sheritra could always conjure began to itch at Nubnofret. "But Tbubui, what of the blossoming relationship between my daughter and your son?" she objected. "It is not acceptable to put them under the same roof."

"It is my roof, Highness," Tbubui reminded her, "and my ethical standards are high. The Princess would of course have her servants with her, and such guards as Khaemwaset saw fit to include in her entourage. We are a somewhat staid household," she finished, smiling. "We need livening." Nubnofret capitulated with wine-induced speed. Life without Sheritra for a month or two would be so peaceful, and perhaps she and Khaemwaset might find a new closeness without the barb of her daughter's personality to come between them.

"She is not just any princess," she reminded the other woman. "The blood of the gods flows in her veins and as such she must be treated with reverence and guarded well at all times. But . . ." She smiled. "We will ask her when she returns home and then consult my husband for a final word on the matter. Gods! This heat! Would you like to bathe?"

Tbubui nodded and thanked her hostess. Nubnofret summoned her sweating servants, and the two women were soon standing naked side by side on the bathing slabs, drenched in cool lotus water, wine still in hand and chattering gaily about the latest treatment for softening the hair.

When Sheritra arrived home at sunset, flushed and animated from her day, she found them still deep in conversation, now reclining on reed mats by the pool. The heat was over for the day and lawn, flower beds and her mother and guest were all saturated in a copper glow from the last of the sun. Both women looked up with a smile as she came to them across the dry grass, and Nubnofret patted the mat by her ample hip.

"Have you had a good day?" she asked, and Sheritra, sinking beside her under the deepening shade of the blue-and-white striped awning, noted the two empty wine jars lying between them and her mother's pleasant slurred speech. She was taken aback, for she seldom saw Nubnofret the worse for wine, but she was also secretly amused. The folds of her mother's face, already, at age thirty-five, freezing into a permanently preoccupied, stern expression, had softened, and her lustrous eyes were full of a contented laziness.

"I have indeed," Sheritra answered, returning Tbubui's half-obeisance with a nod. "Harmin and I found a little bay on the west bank about five miles upstream from the city where a neglected old canal emptied into the Nile. It was quite choked up with growth and nests and wildlife and we poked about in it for ages. But we didn't see a crocodile. We ate in the barge's cabin because of the heat. Harmin has gone home." She turned to Tbubui. "I do apologize, Tbubui. If I had known you were here I could have invited him to join you and you could have left together."

"It does not matter, Princess," Tbubui replied. "Your mother and I have spent a delightful afternoon free of all male company and I am sure that Harmin's presence would have spoiled it!"

Sheritra regarded the two of them curiously. They seemed to exude an essence of indolent femininity, an aura of purely

womanly shared confidences, that made her slightly uncomfortable. She did not have any close friends of her own sex. She had
always scorned the frivolous conversations of the daughters of
her father's acquaintances, silly giggling girls who thought and
talked of nothing but fashion, cosmetics, what hairstyles were
currently in vogue in the Delta and which young men had the
most attractive bodies. She felt, looking from her mother's somnolent, bemused face to Tbubui's sensuously sprawling limbs,
that all those subjects had been thoroughly covered by them today. Nubnofret confirmed her suspicion.

"We have done nothing all day but sip wine and talk about
completely inconsequential things," she explained. "It has done
me good."

"I have enjoyed it also," Tbubui put in. "I have no female
company and I do not talk to my servants." She glanced at
Nubnofret as though something else was expected, and
Nubnofret grunted.

"Tbubui has kindly invited you to stay at her home for a
while," she said. "I think that the change might be good for you,
Sheritra, if you want to go. What do you think?"

Sheritra studied her mother's face and analyzed her tone.
Sometimes a similar question held the expected answer within it
and the girl knew that she was not really being given a choice.
But this time she could hear no unstated coercion, nor could her
over-sensitivity detect an eagerness to have her out of the way.
Nubnofret was smiling at her with kohl-smudged eyes slitted
against the sun. Time with Harmin, Sheritra thought. Hour after
hour in his company, talking, drinking him in with my eyes, perhaps kissing him, perhaps . . . But it was not entirely proper, not
quite the accepted thing. She pondered, frowning unconsciously,
and her mother added, "Of course Bakmut would go with you,
and a scribe and your body servant. Your father would provide
suitable guards." And someone to report to him on my every
move, Sheritra added ruefully. But that is how it should be.
"What does Father say?" she asked.

"I have not spoken to him about it," Nubnofret confessed. "I
decided to see how you felt first. Well?"

"Do come, Princess!" Tbubui urged. "I would be so honoured
by your company and would have someone to talk to. Harmin
will also be overjoyed, I'm sure." She cast a sidelong glance at

Nubnofret that plainly said "Have I gone too far?" But Nubnofret was working lotus oil into her fingers and merely nodded.

"I daresay he would," she responded drily. "But I do not object to that, providing he is never alone with my daughter." She looked up suddenly. "You do not have to go, Sheritra."

But you want me to, Sheritra thought angrily. I can see that you do. If I decided to spite you I would simply decline the invitation, but you know, don't you Mother, that I cannot pass up this chance to be with Harmin. "On the contrary," she said, "I would love to go. Thank you, Tbubui."

The woman smiled warmly. "Good! I shall have a room prepared for you, in fact I shall give you my bedchamber as it is the largest in the house. We have several empty rooms." Sheritra did not protest. As a princess it was her right to occupy the best accommodation. "When would you like to come?" Tbubui pressed.

Sheritra regarded her mother levelly. "Tomorrow," she said.

Tbubui sat up. "Good!" she repeated.

At that moment Khaemwaset and Hori stepped out of the terrace's shade and came towards them, Hori limping awkwardly. Tbubui rose and reverenced them with a grace that sent a pang of envy through Sheritra. A month ago I would not have cared, she told herself, or even if I did it would not have been such a violent caring. I would have sneered at her, but now I want that unselfconscious assurance for Harmin's sake. She herself scrambled up for her father's kiss. Hori gave her a twisted grin and sank into one of the chairs the servants were rushing to provide.

"So," Khaemwaset began, his eyes on Tbubui after a cursory but warm greeting to his wife, "we males come to interrupt an obvious idyll. You all look satisfied with yourselves. Have you settled the affairs of Egypt between you?"

It is not like Father to be condescending, Sheritra thought. He seems very uneasy. And why is Hori staring so sourly at the ground? Well, I will not let either of them spoil my day. Her mother was talking of Tbubui's invitation and Sheritra listened as she and Khaemwaset tossed her decision about between them. Her father was not exactly objecting. It seemed to the girl that under the prescribed, formal objections was an eagerness to see her go that was equal to her mother's. Puzzled and a little hurt, she tried to catch his eye, seeking reassurance, but could not.

Tbubui was watching, her gaze, also narrowed against the sun, moving slowly from one to the other. She made no move to interrupt and Sheritra thought that her stillness had a smug quality about it. Finally her father turned to her.

"I shall miss you, Little Sun," he said merrily. "But of course your mother and I will visit you often until you are ready to come home again."

Mother will not, Sheritra thought mutinously, and you, dear Father . . . All at once an idea flashed into her mind and she exhaled quietly. Could it be? Khaemwaset was now jovial, animated. Sheritra turned her attention unobtrusively back to Tbubui. She was smiling to herself and fanning a hand across the blades of grass, to and fro. Sheritra again inspected her father's sparkling eyes and wide gestures, her heart sinking. So that was it. If I am actually in Tbubui's house I give Father an excuse to visit there whenever he wishes. And I am suddenly convinced that he will wish to visit a very great deal.

Sheritra did not know why the conviction of Khaemwaset's interest in the other woman was causing her anxiety. Perhaps such a change would be good for him, be rejuvenating for a while. But the girl, remembering the odd and awkward conversation she had had with him not so long ago, was sure it was not so. She herself liked and admired Tbubui, but then, she was not a man. Tbubui was dangerous to men, her instincts told her.

Surreptitiously, from under lowered lashes, she scrutinized her brother. Hori's shining dark head was down, his eyes fixed unseeingly on his bruised knee. Oh Hathor no, Sheritra thought with something approaching horror. Not both of them! Does Tbubui know?

She and Khaemwaset were discussing the scroll. "I have decided to let Sisenet inspect it," Khaemwaset was saying reluctantly. "But he will have to do so here. I am responsible for its safety before the gods and the ka of the man who owned it. I am truly at the point, Tbubui, where I would welcome any assistance in its deciphering." Tbubui answered immediately, intelligently, and Sheritra looked at her mother.

Nubnofret had withdrawn from the conversation. She lay full-length on her side, eyes closed, and something about the stiffness of her pose told Sheritra that her mother's afternoon was not ending as delightfully as it had begun.

Without warning Sheritra felt hot and weak. Emotional undercurrents swirled around her—her mother's formless apprehension, Hori's sulkiness, her father's uncharacteristic animation—and in the centre of it Tbubui, who a short time ago had been all lazy, sultry woman and who now was all serious, earnest student of history. Does she know? Sheritra asked herself again. If she does suspect, then surely she would not be extending an invitation to me! Or would she? She came to her feet and the conversation broke off.

"Father, give me leave to go into the house," she said. "I have spent a full day in the sun and I am very tired. I want to be bathed before dinner." She knew that her words were stilted, that she was standing slouched and ill at ease, that she was once more the family embarrassment, but she could not help it. Surprised, Khaemwaset nodded.

"Of course," he said.

Sheritra forced herself to turn to Tbubui. "I will arrive at your home tomorrow afternoon," she said.

"Until then, Princess," was the polite reply.

Sheritra left them, hurrying around the pond and the gurgling fountain and past the flower beds in an agony of self-consciousness, feeling as though they were all staring at her back. She reached the entrance and rushed inside with great relief. Perhaps I should not go, she thought dismally, unaware of the guards' salute as she passed them in the passage. Perhaps Tbubui is using me as an excuse for Father to visit her without suspicion. And perhaps you are an overly sensitive idiot, another voice mocked her, with too much imagination for your own good. Be selfish, Sheritra. Put yourself next to Harmin and do not worry about the rest.

Just before the door to her own quarters she looked up and her reflection met her, a stooped, pinched, homely girl to whom even the smoothly beaten copper of the floor-to-ceiling relief could not give the illusion of beauty. I cannot change myself, she thought in a dismay that bordered on panic. Only he has the power to change me and I am determined to be given that chance. For once I will not care about any of them. She turned away from the daunting copper image and entered her rooms.

The evening meal that day seemed interminable. Her mother, obviously suffering a headache, had done her best to entertain two of Pharaoh's Heralds who had arrived unexpectedly on their way south into Nubia. Later, Sheritra sought out Hori. He was sitting morosely just inside the main entrance of the house, his foot propped up on a stool, gazing into the stultifying hot darkness that seemed to take its breathless heat from the orange torches now illuminating the forecourt and the paved path to the watersteps. He glanced up as she folded her linens under her and sank by his feet at the top of the entrance stair. The smile he gave her was his usual winsome grin, but she was not deceived.

"You are unhappy, aren't you, Hori?" she said without preamble. "I do not think it is the pain of your knee, either."

He stirred, swore softly, then chuckled. "Your perception is always disconcerting," he replied. "No, it is not my knee. Father will remove the stitches tomorrow."

She waited for him to go on but he did not. Fleetingly, she wondered if she ought to keep silent, but she was afraid of the distances that were opening in the family, the imperceptible rifts between her parents, between her father and herself, between her father and Hori. She felt a desperate need to remain close to this beautiful brother whom she loved so much, for without him, she realized, she would have no one. In spite of her passion for Harmin she did not yet trust him completely. "You are in love with Tbubui, aren't you?" she murmured. For a while she feared that he was not going to answer her, or worse, that he would lie, but in the end he slumped forward and his cheek brushed her hair.

"Yes," he admitted, and his voice cracked on that one word.

"Does she know?"

He sighed. "Yes. I told her everything when I went to see her yesterday. She suggested that I could visit her whenever I wanted but that we could be nothing more than friends."

Her heart went out to him. He sounded confused and hopeless. "Do you accept that?"

He straightened. "Of course not!" he snapped. "I will find some means of winning her. I am after all one of the most sought-after single men in Egypt and certainly the handsomest. She cannot resist me if I flaunt my body in front of her often enough."

Sheritra was appalled at the cynical tone. "But Hori, you have never . . . your strength has been . . . ."

"Well perhaps I have simply not cared enough until now to

turn my good looks into the weapon they are," he grated. "She has no man. If someone else held her affections she would have told me. No, Sheritra. She eats at my vitals and one day, one day, I will eat at hers."

She was shocked both at the crudity of his language and the coarseness of his voice. Desperately she sought the brother whose cheerful, constant unselfishness had made him beloved among so many. "Have you spoken to Father about it?" she asked.

"No. When she surrenders I will approach him, but until then it is none of his business."

So Hori, wrapped in his own agony, was oblivious to Khaemwaset's. It was just as well. The implications of the situation came into Sheritra's mind in all their potential horror. Quite apart from the strife that would ensue between her two favourite men, there was the future. If Hori won her he would of course build another wing onto the house and she would be under Khaemwaset's gaze at every hour. But surely that was better than having her here as Khaemwaset's Second Wife, with all the authority that position entailed. Tbubui at dinner, Tbubui commandeering the barge, Tbubui and Khaemwaset on his couch while Nubnofret lay alone . . . And Tbubui and me, Sheritra thought, shrinking. Tbubui and Hori. Oh gods. Let me be wrong about Father. Let Hori's infatuation end as suddenly as it began.

Hori once more bent close to her until she could smell the sour wine on his breath. "You are going to stay with her tomorrow," he whispered. "She likes you, Sheritra. Talk to her about me. Make her think. Will you do that for me?"

She jerked away. "I will try, Hori," she cried out, "but all is not as it seems. Oh why did she have to come into our lives! I am afraid!"

He did not answer, did not try to comfort her, and she got up and left him, walking through the murmurous house towards her own apartments where her servants were packing her belongings. Her mind told her to order the things returned to their tiring boxes but her heart yearned for Harmin. He had kissed her again today, both of them lying in the long grasses at the river's edge, hidden from the eyes of servants and soldiers on the barge. The sun had been a dreaming, sultry presence making her pliant, liquid with desire, and Harmin's black hair had fallen across her neck, his tongue cool against the convolutions of her ear. I can do nothing, she thought as she entered her ante-room to Bakmut's somewhat harried bow. I cannot stem the disquieting tide of powerful change sweeping over this family. I am no longer apart from it, for it is tumbling and buffeting me also. Each one of us must look to himself.

She left the watersteps late the following morning with Bakmut, all her personal servants and four guards, selected by Amek and approved by her father. Nubnofret had bid her a casual goodbye, embracing her briefly and assuring her that she must come home as soon as she wished. But Khaemwaset had drawn her aside and thrust a piece of papyrus into her hands. "Your horoscope for Phamenoth," he had said brusquely. "I cast them all last night. Little Sun, I do not like it. Read it for yourself as soon as possible and remember that I am only as far away as the mouth of one of your guards. I will come and see you within the week." Suddenly she clung to him as though she had been banished to the Delta for some heinous crime, missing him already. Yet under the burst of homesickness was the cold core of her determination, and besides, she had not missed the undertone of eagerness in his voice. Kissing him on his cheek she turned and walked onto the barge. Hori had not appeared at all. She waved to her parents once and disappeared into the cabin.

It took the rowers less than an hour to pull the barge to Tbubui's watersteps, even though the prevailing north wind of summer had begun to blow and the river was so low that very little current remained to carry them along. Sheritra sat in the cabin, a silent Bakmut at her feet, the horoscope still unread in her hand. She felt tense, dislocated, as though instead of going to stay with a new friend for a few weeks she was setting out across the Great Green, her destination unknown. Exacerbating the impression was the knowledge that both her parents, for dissimilar reasons, were glad to see her go, and Hori too wanted her away from home to help him pursue his own ends. It was irrational, Sheritra knew, but she felt that he had betrayed her.

In spite of the light familiar voices of her servants gathered under the awning on the deck, in spite of Amek's stolid, reliable soldiers into whose hands she would have placed her life without a second thought, she felt defenceless and very alone. I should move to Pi-Ramses, she thought painfully. Grandfather would give me a suite in the palace. Aunt Bint-Anath would care for me. I hate Memphis now. That daunting awareness made her realize fully for the first time how far behind she had left the fragile, shy girl she had been such a short time ago. I am still fragile, she thought grimly, oh so very fragile, but not quite in the same way. There was an innocence about me then that I can recognize only now, but should I mourn or rejoice at the change? I cannot say.

Harmin was waiting for her, standing on the bottom riser of the watersteps and gazing upstream when she emerged from the cabin at the captain's warning shout. Sheritra could see his brooding face lighten with a smile as he spotted her, and he bowed several times as her scribe handed her reverentially onto the stone beside him. At her word, the rest of her train began to stream along the sandy path towards the house, but the guards and Bakmut remained with her.

"Harmin," she said, and he was free to speak.

"Welcome to my home, Highness," he responded gravely. "I cannot tell you how delighted I am that you decided to accept my mother's invitation. I am your humble slave and I promise to gratify any desire you may express while you are here."

She met his eyes, aware as never before of the strong, regular beats of her heart, the raw constriction in her belly as she looked at him.

"I have a litter here for you," he went on. "The path is not long but the heat is great."

"Thank you, I have brought my own," she replied. "But I don't really need it today, Harmin. I prefer to walk. What a lovely shade the palms cast! Shall we go? I am eager to see this house for myself. Father and Hori have described it as unique. Bakmut, give me my whisk." She started forward and Harmin fell in with her step. The flies of summer were growing thicker every day, a scourge of black, salt-seeking creatures that settled with a maddening persistence around the eyes and mouth and on any sweat-slicked skin. To Sheritra they seemed more aggressive and numerous here under the palms than at home. She applied the black horsehair whisk to her naked flesh with an absent-minded precision as Harmin spoke of the fecundity of the trees, the coming date harvest and the report of his steward on the progress of his crops in Koptos.

"My father took very little interest in his holdings," he explained, "and relied on the steward to handle the fellahin, but I liked to walk beside the canals at home and watch the grain and the vegetables spring up fresh and green."

"You speak as though you miss it," Sheritra observed, and he agreed.

"Sometimes I do," he said softly, "but I do not miss Koptos itself. My early memories of the town are not very happy ones. See Highness!" He pointed. "Our house!"

Sheritra's first impression of the building was not like Khaemwaset's or Hori's. In spite of the fresh plaster and whitewash, in spite of the lone gardener toiling in the small garden, the estate had a forlorn, neglected air. The walls seemed bleached rather than unstained, the lawn a struggle to hold back the palms rather than a pleasant clearing, the quiet privacy an atmosphere of dereliction.

But that impression soon faded. She greeted a bowing Tbubui and Sisenet and entered the plain hall with curiosity. "I can see how my father was delighted with your home," she told them after glancing about. "It might have been built and furnished a hundred hentis ago!" Then fearing that she had offended them she added hastily, "Such taste and simplicity is wonderful, Tbubui. One cannot think or pray when one is surrounded by ornate clutter." She could hear her servants somewhere beyond the transverse passage at the rear of the hall, and the clatter of boxes. Her soldiers ignored the family, vanishing into the house with the authority of the Prince behind them, and her scribe followed, palette in hand. There was no sign of the household's own staff.

"Come, Highness," Tbubui said as Sisenet bowed again and excused himself. "This is the way to the room I have prepared for you. Please command your servants to order the routine of the house as though it were your own. Ours will not interfere." Meekly Sheritra stepped after Tbubui's yellow-swathed back, feeling Harmin behind her. "The passage at this end leads directly into the garden," Tbubui was saying. "There is a door but it is only closed when the khamsin blows, to keep the desert sand out of the house. My brother, Harmin and I will be sleeping at the other end. I am sorry that there is no room for your servants to stay in the building itself but there is ample room for them at the rear, in the compound."

"Bakmut always sleeps on my floor," Sheritra said, and turned in at the door Tbubui was now standing beside. The room was not large but, like the rest of the house, it seemed so. Sheritra swiftly took in the couch, table, chair, stool and cosmetic table and nodded to Bakmut. "Have my things brought in."

"I have removed my own tiring chests," Tbubui told her, "but of course if your Highness needs them they are at your disposal."

Sheritra smiled and touched her briefly. "Thank you, Tbubui. You have gone to great trouble to make me comfortable." The woman and her son understood the dismissal. As the door closed behind them Sheritra sank onto the couch with a sigh. She would have liked more light, for the room was very dim, but more light would have meant more heat and the sweet coolness was very welcome. "I will not need the fans here," she remarked to Bakmut. "See that my own linen is put on the couch, and send the scribe to me as soon as the soldiers have worked out a schedule. Do you think we will eat before long, Bakmut? I am very hungry."

"I can ask, Highness," the girl said, and went out. Sheritra sat on, listening to the silence, her eyes on the two high patches of square white light on the farther wall cast by the windows that had been cut just under the ceiling. The thought that Harmin was somewhere close by gave her a thrill of excitement. I am going to enjoy this to the fullest, she told herself, her earlier misgivings forgotten for now.

She ate a simple and exquisitely prepared meal in the hall, sitting cross-legged on cushions before a low cedar-and-gilt table, waited on by her own steward who tasted each dish before serving her. Khaemwaset had his own tasters but they were seldom seen. The food at home was pronounced safe before it arrived in the dining hall and the courtesy here, performed in her presence, a reminder to all of her exalted station, titillated her. Many nobles had tasters, particularly those closest to Pharaoh, who had reason to fear the ambition of underlings, but it was obvious that Sisenet did not bother with one. He, his sister and his nephew ate with a delicate relish, talking to each other and Sheritra with easy grace, so that soon she felt entirely at home.

When the meal ended, all disappeared to sleep away the worst heat of the afternoon and Sheritra, freshly washed, slipped between her own sheets in Tbubui's bedchamber contentedly.

Bakmut had placed her sleeping mat against the wall behind the door, but on Sheritra's dismissal she continued to hover beside the couch, obviously troubled.

"What is it, Bakmut?" Sheritra asked.

The girl clasped her hands together, eyes downcast. "Forgive me, Highness," she said, "but I do not like this place."

Sheritra sat up. "What do you mean?"

Bakmut bit her lip. "I am not entirely sure," she replied hesitantly, "but the servants of the house, they do not speak."

"You mean that they do not speak to you? They are rude?"

Bakmut shook her head. "No, Highness. I mean that they do not speak at all. They are not deaf, for they respond when spoken to, and I do not think that they are dumb, for I saw one of them lick her mouth, but they simply never say a word."

"Perhaps their mistress has trained them that way," Sheritra offered. "Each household is different, you know that, Bakmut, and the demeanour of servants varies depending on their employers' way of life." Surprised and apprehensive, she found that she was fighting to keep a stridency out of her voice, wanting to reprimand Bakmut for attempting to coalesce her own vague fears. "This family has a need for more silence than we do," she went on, "and probably the servants have been commanded not to speak unless their instructions are not clear. It is nothing. Put it out of your mind."

Bakmut still hesitated. "But the silence is not nice, Highness. It weighs on me."

"You are simply not used to it," Sheritra said with finality, lying down again and easing the ivory headrest more comfortably against her neck. She bit back an impulse to tell the girl to keep reporting her feelings and impressions, and closed her eyes. Bakmut's feet could be heard padding to the sleeping mat by the door and her little sighs as she composed herself brought a sense of security to Sheritra. My guard is outside in the passage, she thought. My staff have flooded the house. Harmin is within the sound of my cries, and I have embarked upon one small adventure solely for myself. What is this unease that borders on fear? I do not like the silence either. It is not calm, not a contented aura through which we might all move. It is like an invisible veil of obscure purpose that isolates us, cutting us off from events outside its power. Still with eyes shut, she smiled at her fanciful diagnosis. And I believed our house to be quiet! she thought. You are still a timid child, Sheritra. Grow up! She sensed the implacable force of the early afternoon's heat searing the thick mud walls that cocooned her. Bakmut groaned briefly in her dreams. The sheets slid silkily against Sheritra's smooth skin and she slept.

Chapter 11

*'From the evil-doer the quay slips away.
He is carried away by his flooded land.'*

Khaemwaset sat behind his desk, his head swimming in the close airlessness of his office, and stared down at the papers littered between his hands. It was the beginning of Phamenoth. Sheritra had been gone for three days and Khaemwaset missed her, surprised at the definitely hollow place she had left. He had not realized how much he had taken for granted the moments when he would turn a corner and find her bending with milk for the house snakes, or glance up from his meal to where she would be folded, one knee up, her linens askew, frowning over her food while the ebb and flow of family conversation swirled apparently unheeded around her. The garden, wilting and struggling under an intensifying sun, seemed forlorn without her presence. He had grown so used to Nubnofret's sharp reprimands and his own automatic rebuffs in defence of his daughter that he had been scarcely aware of them, yet now when he, his wife and Hori settled in the dining hall to while away the evening hours, he cast about for what was wrong and discovered the absence of one familiar habit.

Hori was unusually preoccupied and uncommunicative. Perhaps he missed her also. He was gone from sunrise to dinner time and no longer sought out his father with an eager account of his days. Khaemwaset presumed that he was still overseeing the work on the tomb and roaming the city in his spare time with Antef, and it worried him to see Antef on several occasions wandering moodily along the paths of the estate by himself. Khaemwaset had removed the stitches in Hori's knee and the boy no longer limped. The wound had healed well but would leave an untidy scar. Khaemwaset wanted to ask his son what he had done with the earring, and what was the cause of his distress, but found he could not. A wall, still insubstantial but strengthening, had appeared between them. Hori had withdrawn and Khaemwaset found himself unwilling to pierce that almost sullen shell. He had his own agonies.

Two days after Sheritra's departure he had summoned Penbuy and, wrapped in an atmosphere of complete unreality, had ordered his Chief Scribe to draw up a marriage contract between himself and Tbubui. Penbuy, with his impeccable manners and the restraint of good breeding, had given his master the briefest of stares, blanched a little under his deep olive skin and sunk cross-legged to the floor, arranging his palette in the pose hallowed by generations of scribes. "What title is the lady to receive?" he asked primly, pen poised.

"She will of course immediately become a princess when she signs the document," Khaemwaset said, hardly recognizing his own voice, "but her official position here will be that of Second Wife. Emphasize in the contract that Nubnofret remains Chief Wife and Superior Princess." Penbuy wrote.

"Are you aware of her assets, Prince?" he asked at length. "Do you wish a clause giving you the right to control any or all of them?"

"No." Khaemwaset was finding the exchange more difficult than he could have imagined. Guilt and dread were making him testy, but he had now lived with the two negative emotions so long that he was able to ignore them. The feeling of brittle illusion surrounding what he was doing was very strong. "I know nothing of her assets save that she has some property of her own. Her late husband's estate went to Harmin. I have no desire to meddle in her commercial affairs."

"Very good." Penbuy's head went down again. "And what of her son?" he queried. "Is he to share in your bequest to Hori and your daughter in the event of your death?"

"No." Khaemwaset's answer was curt and he was sure he saw a relieved loosening in his scribe's stance. "Harmin does not need anything from me. Nor is he to receive any princely title unless he marries Sheritra. He must not know that, Penbuy."

"Naturally," Penbuy purred, writing industriously. "But what of any offspring from this marriage, Prince?"

Khaemwaset's gut churned. "If Tbubui gives me children, they must share equally in my wealth with Hori and Sheritra. You will include the usual clauses, Penbuy. I am to provide for

Tbubui, treat her with respect and kindness and perform such accepted duties as a husband is obligated to do. And before you ask, her brother will not be mentioned in this contract at all. He is incidental to this negotiation."

Penbuy laid his pen carefully on the palette and for the first time looked up at his master. "Prince, you do remember that as a member of the royal family your choice of wives is subject to Pharaoh's approval," he reminded Khaemwaset with pursed mouth and expressionless gaze. "If the lady's blood proves to be too common and you pursue this course, you run the risk of being removed from the list of blood princes in line for the throne."

It was Penbuy's duty to say those things, but Khaemwaset was angry nonetheless. I do not care, he thought savagely. I will have her in the face of any opposition, my father's included. "Merenptah would be delighted to see my name removed from that list," he said, forcing a chuckle. "As to the lady's blood-line, I want you to go to Koptos and research her claims. Add a last clause to the contract to the effect that she may sign it but it only becomes valid subject to confirmation of her noble status. That releases me from any legal pressures in the event that she has lied to me or my father refuses me the marriage." But it means nothing, he had thought privately. All of this, it means nothing. It is only a way in which I may lure her here, under my hands and eyes, forever.

Penbuy smiled faintly. "Koptos," he said with resignation. "Koptos in the summer."

Khaemwaset rose. "A disagreeable assignment, I know," he acknowledged, "but I trust no one else to perform the task as thoroughly as you, old friend. Have the document ready to sign tomorrow, and, Penbuy . . ." The scribe looked at him questioningly. There was a small pause while Khaemwaset, outwardly in control, fought to form the next words. "Nubnofret knows nothing of this. Nor do Hori or Sheritra. Keep your counsel. You will leave for Koptos tomorrow afternoon."

Penbuy had nodded, risen and bowed himself out, leaving Khaemwaset feeling strangely dirty. I do not care what my servant thinks of my deeds, he told himself firmly, for what is he but a tool, an instrument for my use? Yet Penbuy had been his advisor for many years and Khaemwaset had had to choke back the desire to ask the man for his opinion. He had not wanted to hear it.

Now he sat bowed by the heat, the completed papyrus before him covered in Penbuy's neat, faultless script. He had read it and sealed it, and it waited now for Tbubui's approval.

Beside it lay another scroll, the sight of which filled Khaemwaset with distaste and reminded him of the night of panic that had sent him hurrying to a spell of protection he himself had so soon negated. I cannot look at it now, he thought, his fingers tapping anxiously over the notes he had made then. Penbuy has gone to Koptos, and while he is away I must talk to Nubnofret. But what is the point of upsetting her before Penbuy returns with the results of his investigation? another voice objected. The last clause releases you if necessary, so take the document to Tbubui, obtain her seal, see what Penbuy discovers and then talk to Nubnofret. There is no hurry. Work on this mysterious piece of history you have been avoiding. Call in Sisenet, then scour your mind of it and put it behind you. Once Nubnofret has accepted the situation with Tbubui the future will be richer, lusher, more satisfying than you ever dreamed possible. Lay this scroll to rest first. Overcome your cowardice and begin now.

With a dragging reluctance he rolled up the contract, pushed it to one side and set the ancient writing and his notes in its place. Calling the servant who stood stolidly in the corner he asked for beer, recognized his own delaying tactic, and with a grimace began to work. Tomorrow I will visit Sheritra, give Tbubui the contract to study and invite Sisenet to assist me, he decided. It is time to return to reality. But the briskness of his decision did nothing to lift the cloud of insubstantiality that dogged him. He felt as though months ago he had somehow become detached from himself, that his being, his time, had been bifurcated and his other self, more heavy with blood and life, with sanity and substance, was even now living out his correct reality, while this shadowy self had been nudged onto a pathway that might or might not bring him back in the end to a reunion with that other self. The thought gave him a moment of sick dizziness, but it passed, and he bent with an unconscious moan to the riddle of the dead man's treasure.

He spent the following morning impatiently listening to his steward's report on the progress of his crops and the health of his animals. In two months the harvest would begin, and all prayed that the reaping might be accomplished without disease or blight developing on the grain. Khaemwaset's cattle were fat and healthy, his fields fully mature, tall and green.

After curtly thanking his managers, he read a message from the palace. His mother was very ill and her Chief Steward had taken it upon himself to inquire of Khaemwaset whether he could make the journey to the Delta to treat her. The polite, subtle request threw him into a fever. She knows she is dying, he thought furiously. She knows that I can do nothing more for her. It is her staff, her stupid cow-like retainers, who still believe that I can somehow magic her back to health. She has her husband to comfort her, and whatever faults great Pharaoh has, he loves her and does not neglect to visit her. Surely in dying she wants her husband, not a son she rarely sees, by her side? Tersely he dictated a letter to the steward telling him that he would come to Pi-Ramses at his earliest convenience, which would not be for some time, and that Pharaoh's physicians were as competent and reliable as he.

There was also a brief communication from Amunmose, Chief of Pharaoh's Harem in Memphis, complaining that the physician appointed by Khaemwaset himself to see to the medical needs of the women was incompetent and had been dismissed. Could the Mighty Prince suggest a replacement? Now now, Khaemwaset thought with nagging irritation. Tomorrow. I will see to it tomorrow.

On his way to Nubnofret's quarters he came upon Antef. The young man was scantily clad in nothing but a loincloth. A quiver of arrows was slung over his shoulder and his bow hung negligently from one slender hand. Khaemwaset brushed past him, then halted and turned.

"You go to archery practice, Antef?" Antef nodded. He looked unhappy and tired. "Will Hori join you?"

"No, Highness," Antef replied. "I have not seen the Prince today. He slept late and then hurried out." His eyes would not meet Khaemwaset's and Khaemwaset felt a wave of sympathy that answered the deep sadness in the pleasant boy.

"You have not seen much of my son lately, have you?" he said gently. Miserably Antef shook his head. "Can you tell me what ails him, Antef? Without betraying his confidence, of course."

"I would tell you if I knew, Highness," Antef blurted, "but

Hori no longer confides in me. It is as though I have displeased him in some way, but by Set I cannot imagine how!"

"Neither can I," Khaemwaset said gently. "I am sorry, Antef. Please do not lose patience with him."

"I do not intend to, Highness." Antef smiled wanly. "I think he will talk to me eventually."

Khaemwaset nodded and passed on. He did not want to dwell on Hori's mysterious change of face, preferring to believe that his son's good sense would reassert itself without interference.

When Khaemwaset was announced, Nubnofret was standing in the middle of the bedchamber, hands on her hips, amid a welter of gowns and cloaks. Wernuro and two body servants were sorting through the brilliant piles of beaded gilded linens and a harried-looking scribe sat at his mistress's feet, pen working furiously. "Put that one aside," Nubnofret was saying. "It can be altered for Sheritra. And those two have worn patches on them. They had better be cut up. Such a pity," she smiled, turning for Khaemwaset's dutiful kiss. "They were my favourites. I am ordering new clothes, dear brother. The linen woven from last year's flax is particularly fine and I have requisitioned a good portion of it."

"So you will be busy all day?" Khaemwaset asked hopefully. She made a rueful grimace.

"Yes. The gown-maker is coming. Why do you want to know?"

"I am going to visit Sheritra," he said carefully, "and at the same time I will invite Sisenet to come and peruse the scroll. I thought you might like to see your daughter and spend some time with Tbubui."

In spite of the enforced steadiness of his voice she looked at him curiously. "Sheritra has only been gone for three days," she pointed out. "And you can just as easily send a herald to Sisenet. You have neglected patients, Khaemwaset, and although Penbuy is loyal to you and does not complain, I am aware of the official correspondence piling up on your desk. Such irresponsibility is not like you."

I am not answerable to you, he thought, annoyed. Sometimes you affect the tone of a mother with me and I hate it. "Such things are not your concern, Nubnofret," he rebuked her, with what he hoped was kindness. "Run the household and leave my business to me. I have been very tired of late and I see nothing wrong with an afternoon chatting to my daughter and her host."

Usually at this juncture she would back down. Her passion for control occasionally prompted her to encroach on Khaemwaset's sphere, but a gentle reprimand would have her laughing at herself and retiring. But this time she stood her ground. "It is not just a matter of one afternoon," she persisted. "For weeks now you have been withdrawn and short with everyone. I am surprised that you have not received one of Ramses' barbed letters of inquiry concerning Egypt's forgotten affairs." She was watching him with something very like wounded puzzlement in her eyes, and Khaemwaset wondered fleetingly if perhaps she was more astute than he had thought. He would have to talk to her sometime soon, but not today, not today! He hastened to placate her while the servants waited in their well-trained immobility.

"It is true that I have not given my duties the attention they deserve," he admitted, "but, Nubnofret, I am in need of a rest."

"Then let us go north for a week or two. Perhaps the change would restore you."

He laughed sharply. "I hate Pi-Ramses," he said flatly. "You know that."

She came close to him, picking her way delicately among the discarded clothes. "Something is seriously wrong, my husband," she said in a low voice, looking directly into his face, "and do not insult me by denying it. Please tell me what it is. I only want to help and support you."

Khaemwaset fought back an absurd desire to cry. He wanted to lower himself to her couch and pour it all into her understanding ears like a child. But he recognized the urge for what it was, a reverting to the state of an infant, and besides, there were the servants, and Nubnofret's task only just begun.

"You are right," he said at last, "and I will indeed tell you about it, but not now. Enjoy yourself this afternoon, Nubnofret."

She shrugged, dropped her gaze and turned back into the room, but as he reached the doorway she called, "I cannot find Penbuy. Send him to me later, Khaemwaset. The amount of linen must be measured exactly and paid for." Her own scribe could have done such a small task and they both knew it. She is either asserting her authority or letting me know she suspects that I have sent Penbuy away, Khaemwaset thought as he paced the passage, absently receiving the salute of his guards. Could it be that Nubnofret, my calm, firm Nubnofret, is losing command of herself? The idea of a wild scene between himself and his wife plunged him into gloom and he ordered out the staff of the barge with a sinking heart.

The bright, hot day and his pleasant errand soon restored his spirits and he disembarked, waited for his canopy to be unfolded and strode along the path to Tbubui's house with deep contentment. The call of irridescent birds echoed in the palms and his feet sank satisfyingly into the light sand. He remembered the last time he had walked here, the dreamlike quality of the night and his encounter with Tbubui, and was tempted to burst into song. As he rounded the last, now dearly familiar corner he saw Sheritra standing in the shade cast by the front wall of the house, her arms full of white water-lilies that were dripping moisture down the front of her glistening sheath. She recognized him and took one step, but then she stood and waited, her face solemn. Odd, he thought. She usually runs to greet me. Then he realized with a pang that it had been some time since she had flung herself at him with abandon. He smiled as he came and embraced her. The damp lilies were cold against his belly. His servants bowed to her and withdrew under the trees, and she pulled away.

"Father, how lovely to see you!" she said, and there was no mistaking the pleasure in her voice, though Khaemwaset, glancing into her eyes, thought them strangely guarded. "How is everyone at home?"

"Much the same," he replied. "I took Hori's stitches out, and today your mother is reorganizing her tiring boxes or she would have come with me."

"Hmm," was her response. "Come into the house. Tbubui is beyond, in the kitchen compound, trying to teach a dish to her cook, and Sisenet is closeted in his own rooms as usual. Harmin is out on the desert, practising with his spear." They linked arms and moved towards the door. "I feel as though I have been away for ever," she went on, and Khaemwaset squeezed her slim forearm.

"It seems that way to me, too," he said simply. We are awkward with each other, he thought dismally. In three days we have grown even farther apart. Bakmut was doing him homage from just inside the entrance hall, her coarse linen fluttering in the draught, and Khaemwaset saw with approval that one of his soldiers stood stiffly against the far wall where the rear passage ran.

"Sit down if you like," Sheritra offered, and clapping her hands she said brusquely to the black servant of the house who had appeared, "Bring wine and buttered bread. Tell your mistress that the Prince Khaemwaset is here."

"Are you happy here?" Khaemwaset asked cautiously. She grinned, but beneath the humour there was a faint strain.

"I am just beginning to get used to it," she replied. "So very, very quiet, and no guests so far, and hardly any music at dinner. But I am not shy here, Father. Only Sisenet still makes me a little uncomfortable and that is because I see him so much less than the others." She blushed and, relieved, Khaemwaset saw in the creeping flush and the momentarily working hands the Sheritra he knew. "Harmin and I spend the afternoons together, after the sleep. Tbubui goes into her chamber. Harmin, Bakmut, a guard and I take over the garden and stroll under the palms. I have twice been poled on the river but none of them will join me. In the evening we talk or Sisenet reads to us."

"And the mornings?" Khaemwaset asked as the rich red wine was placed to his hand together with a silver platter containing bread, butter, garlic and honey. The servant had been uncannily quiet. Khaemwaset had not even heard the rustle of starched linen.

"In the morning Tbubui and I keep each other company and talk of purely vain and silly feminine things." Sheritra laughed. "Can you imagine that, Father? Me, talking of vain and silly things?"

She is speaking too quickly, Khaemwaset thought as he raised his cup to his mouth. This also comes between us, her excitement or anxiety, I cannot tell which, and she will not tell me honestly what she is feeling. "I am sure it is doing you good," he replied. "There is nothing wrong with frivolity, my dear, particularly for you. You have always been too serious."

"Speak for yourself!" she laughed back. "Oh. Here comes Tbubui."

As royalty, Khaemwaset did not need to rise, but he did, reaching for Tbubui's hands as she swept towards him and bending to kiss her on the cheek. Immediately he realized that his gesture had been too familiar in front of Sheritra and he drew back and resumed his seat. Tbubui, cool and glittering in a semi-transparent white sheath fringed in silver tassels, sank in one practised motion to a large cushion opposite him. "I decided to come and see if my Little Sun was homesick yet," he began, "and also to have a word with your brother, Tbubui. But Sheritra is not in the least homesick; in fact she looks in the rudest of health. I am grateful."

He felt everything in him, the tight muscles of his belly, the tense attitude of his shoulders, the lineaments of his face, relax as he looked at her. Oh Tbubui, he said silently to the wide forehead across which a thin band of silver held back her thick hair, the black, kohled eyes fixed on him warmly, the graceful indolence of the arms resting languidly against her knees. The rise and fall of her barely glimpsed breasts was light and fast. She feels it also, he thought happily. I know she does.

"I am the one to be grateful," she answered, smiling. She had painted her lips with red henna and her mouth reminded Khaemwaset of the vast statue of the goddess Hathor that stood in the temple in the south district of Memphis. Hathor's faint, sensuous smile was also red, a glistening, moist red . . . "Sheritra is delightful company. She makes me feel like a girl again. I hope, however, that we do not bore her." She turned with affection towards the girl and Sheritra smiled back. Why, they behave like sisters, Khaemwaset thought, the tide of well-being coursing through him. They will not be enemies when Tbubui moves in.

"Bore me?" Sheritra expostulated. "Certainly not!"

"So you do not want to come home?" Khaemwaset teased her. "You are not pining for your mother's discipline?"

A shadow crossed Sheritra's flushed face, and Khaemwaset was aware of the disloyalty in his words. Is there something in this wine? he wondered. "Another excellent vintage," he commented hastily, holding up his cup, and Tbubui inclined her head.

"Thank you, Prince. We do not care for gaudy clothes or constant entertainment but we are fussy about our wine."

Khaemwaset had the uncomfortable impression that his daughter was included in the "we," and for a fleeting second it seemed as though she was not his at all but Tbubui's, as though by some unknown alchemy she had always been Tbubui's. He was saved from further comment by Harmin. The young man entered, handing his spear to the nearest servant and advancing into the hall. He was drenched in sweat and his hair, nostrils and calves were filthy with sand. Smiling affably he bowed to Khaemwaset, but his eyes were all for Sheritra. Better and better, Khaemwaset thought. "Greetings, Harmin," he said. "I hope the improving of your aim made the heat and dirt worthwhile."

Harmin raised his eyebrows and ran a hand through his sticky hair. "I think I am throwing straighter and farther," he said, "but certainly not today. If you will excuse me, Prince, I will bathe. Sheritra, bring Bakmut and come with me. You can have a canopy erected in the garden while I am being washed. If you do not mind, Prince. If you have concluded your visit with the Princess."

Khaemwaset was taken aback, both at the arrogant familiarity with which Harmin had addressed Sheritra and the presumption that the visit was less important than his own wishes. Neither had he missed the swift glance that had passed between mother and son while Harmin had been speaking, and he wondered what it might mean. Sheritra was rising. "Are you going to stay long, Father?" she inquired, "Because if not I want to sit and talk with you."

"But you would rather do something else at the moment," he finished for her. "I am not offended, Little Sun, and I will be here all afternoon." Harmin was already disappearing into the greyness of the passage, and with an apologetic smile to her father Sheritra followed.

Khaemwaset watched her with pleasure. Her whole mien had changed. Her shoulders were straight, her carriage more assured. There was even the suggestion of a slight seductive sway in her sharply boned hips. "You have been doing her good," he said softly. Tbubui stirred on her cushion, her hand sliding down her gleaming calf to the silver anklet with its pendant baboons.

"I think she loves Harmin," she replied forthrightly, "and love will turn a girl into a woman, a self-conscious, awkward child into a being with the allure of Astarte herself."

"And what of Harmin?"

"I have not spoken to him directly of the matter," Tbubui said in an undertone, "but it is obvious that he cares for her a great deal. Do not worry, Prince," she went on hastily, seeing his expression. "They are never alone together, and Bakmut continues to sleep just inside the Princess's door."

He laughed to cover the moment of mild dislike for Harmin. "I cannot imagine her being anything other than delighted to have you join my family," he said rather pompously, out of the moment of confusion. "I love you, Tbubui."

"I love you also, dear Prince," she responded, looking up at him steadily. "I also am relieved that the Princess and I have so much affection for one another. Rest assured that I will do my best to gain the respect of Nubnofret also, and young Hori."

That will be a difficult task, Khaemwaset thought impatiently. Aloud he said, "I am the law, I am Ma'at under my own roof. They will accept you whether they like it or not." Clapping his hands he shouted, "Ib!" and after a moment his steward approached from the garden and bowed. "Give me the document." For answer, Ib withdrew a scroll from his belt, handed it to Khaemwaset and smoothly walked away. Khaemwaset handed it to Tbubui.

"The marriage contract," he said; he could not keep the triumph out of his voice. "Read it at your leisure, and tell me if it is agreeable to you. I have added one clause that is a trifle unusual, for your protection as well as mine." She had placed the papyrus beside her and was watching him blank-faced. "Pharaoh must approve my choice of a wife if I am to remain in the line of succession in Egypt," he explained. "Therefore I ask you to add your seal to the scroll with the understanding that the document only becomes legal when Penbuy has returned from Koptos carrying proof of your noble blood." He had steeled himself to say these words to her, uncertain of her response, and now, as she continued to stare at him, he leaned forward and groped for her hand. It was icy and limp in his grasp. "Do not be offended, I beg you," he went on urgently. "It is a formality, nothing more."

"Koptos?" she said tonelessly. "You have sent your scribe to Koptos?" Then she seemed to come to herself. "Of course I understand, Prince," she assured him. "Love must not overwhelm the demands of state, must it?"

"You have misunderstood," he cried, as helplessly as a young man in the throes of first infatuation. "I will have you anyway, Tbubui, as my brother Si-Montu defied Ramses to obtain Ben-Anath! But how much simpler, how much less anguish for my whole family, if I am able to marry you under my father's smile!"

"And besides," she cut in, gently pulling her hand away, "your brother had no family when he won Ben-Anath. You have a son who might be disinherited if you are taken from that illustrious succession, who will have had his own chance at the throne removed." Her chin came up. "I do understand, dearest. I am after all a noblewoman . . ."

And no mean person, Khaemwaset's mind supplied immediately, cynically, and he started.

". . . and can bow to the demands of state with equanimity." She was smiling now, a tiny, humorous quirk to her glistening red mouth. "But I am not a patient woman. How soon will Penbuy return with the answer to my happiness under his oh-so-correct arm?"

"He left this morning," Khaemwaset told her. "He will arrive at Koptos in a little less than a week, and who can tell how long his researches will take? Can you contain your impatience for a month, Tbubui?"

For answer she glanced about the hall, rose to her knees and, placing both hands on Khaemwaset's bare thighs, she reached up and kissed him. Her lips, her tongue, were hot and wet. Her nails dug into his flesh, exciting him. "I will seal the contract today," she murmured, her mouth moving against his. "Forgive me, Prince, for my moment of chagrin. Have you told Nubnofret yet?"

Dizzily he relinquished her and she sank back onto the cushion. "Not yet," he managed. "I have not found an opportune time."

"Do not wait too long," she advised, and he shook his head, still giddy with desire.

"I plan a sumptuous suite for you, attached to the house," he said, "but it will not be ready before you move in. Will you accept lodgings with the concubines temporarily?"

She nodded coolly. "Temporarily," she agreed. "Sisenet will remain here or go back to Koptos, he has not yet decided which," she went on, "and Harmin is as yet undecided about what he will do."

Khaemwaset sat back. "You have already told your brother?" he asked bewildered, and she gave him a level, almost arrogant glance.

"Naturally," she said. "I do not need his permission, but as he is my closest relative and older brother, I want his approval."

"And did he give it?" Khaemwaset was annoyed. He felt at an immediate disadvantage to a man who was definitely his social and hereditary inferior, and who should have had no say in the matter whatsoever. But then he was ashamed. Tbubui was a dutiful Egyptian woman, tactful and careful of the feelings of her loved ones.

"Yes, he did," she replied. "He wants me to be happy, Khaemwaset, and he says that you do us great honour."

Khaemwaset was mollified. "I must speak to him today," he said. "I am still getting nowhere with the scroll. Hori tells me that the false wall in the tomb has been rebuilt and the artists are recreating the paintings. Soon it will be closed again."

Tbubui stood and smoothed down her linen. Khaemwaset's eyes followed the slow movement of her hands. "Sisenet is in his room," she said. "If your Highness wishes, I can summon him."

"No," Khaemwaset replied graciously, "I will come."

She inclined her head and crossed the hall. Khaemwaset followed, turning after her into the passage. She went left, and as he followed he glanced to the right. Sheritra's laughter drifted to him, coming on the hot breeze funnelled through the permanently opened door to the garden at the far end. In the blaze of white light he saw her kneeling on a reed mat under a flapping canopy, Harmin opposite, their heads almost touching. Before he looked away he saw her fling the knucklebones to the mat and give a cry of delight. Harmin was smiling.

Sisenet looked up, startled, as Khaemwaset entered, then rose from the chair and bowed gravely. This man knows I am insanely in love with his sister, Khaemwaset thought as he strove to meet the other's quiet gaze. Tbubui excused herself and Sisenet indicated the chair he had just left. Khaemwaset took it. On the table beside him was beer, the remains of a small meal and several loosely rolled scrolls.

"I see you have been reading," Khaemwaset remarked. "A pleasant occupation on an enervating day."

Sisenet sank to the edge of the couch and crossed his legs. For the first time, Khaemwaset noticed that the man's body was well toned, his calves tight, his stomach flat with no sign of a fold about the waist, though, due to his position, his spine was slightly curved. But he is a sedentary and studious man like myself, Khaemwaset thought jealously. How does he remain so supple?

"These scrolls are my favourite pastimes, Prince," Sisenet replied. "One is the story of Apepa and Seqenenra, and the other is a rather rare and very ancient copy of the Book of the Heavenly Cow. As well as describing man's rebellion against Ra, his punishment and Ra's withdrawal into heaven, it contains certain magic spells for the good of those deceased."

Khaemwaset's interest was piqued. Unrolling them carefully he cast his eye over the tiny, neat hieroglyphs. "They are treasures indeed," he said admiringly. "Did you buy them, Sisenet? I know many dealers in ancient documents. Who sold them to you?"

Sisenet smiled and Khaemwaset saw his face lose its usually grim aspect and become suddenly youthful. "I did not buy them, Highness," he said. "They belong to my family. One of my ancestors was a mighty historian and magician, and he must have been overjoyed to find both history and magic in that one precious scroll."

"Have you approached a magician to try out the spells?" Khaemwaset was intrigued.

Sisenet shook his head. "I myself have some small ability in the field," he explained. "I did my duty in Koptos as a priest of Thoth."

"You surprise me," Khaemwaset said, remembering how seldom he had conversed deeply with this man, how easily he had dismissed him as of no account. "Did any of the spells work? Are they correct?"

"Highness, as they are concerned with the well-being of the deceased, I have no way of knowing," Sisenet answered lightly, and Khaemwaset clapped a hand to his linen-helmeted forehead.

"Of course! How stupid of me! But tell me, who is the High Priest of Thoth in Koptos, and what is the temple like? I myself am a devotee of the god."

They talked for a while of religious matters, and Khaemwaset found himself warming to Sisenet's incisive mind, his polite method of arguing, his well-modulated, even voice that was a fitting companion to his lucid reasoning powers. Khaemwaset loved an involved discussion on some point of history, medicine or magic with someone as sophisticated in those fields as himself, and to his delight, Sisenet was proving to be just such a man. The scroll, he thought. Perhaps there is some hope after all. He did not know if he was disappointed or pleased.

"When can you come to my home and examine the scroll I borrowed from the tomb?" he asked eventually. "I am eager, now, to have done with it. It has been in the back of my mind like a vague itch ever since I saw it."

"I do not have your Highness's erudition," Sisenet answered, "and I doubt if I will be able to help you, but I would be honoured to try, at your convenience."

Khaemwaset pondered. There was Nubnofret to talk to, and his official duties to at last clear away. Then he had to smile at himself. I am still reluctant to handle the thing. I still want to avoid it. "Come one week from today," he said. "I will hold the afternoon for us alone."

"Very well, Prince." Sisenet gave him a brief smile and both men fell silent. He will not bring up the subject of the marriage, Khaemwaset was thinking. It is my responsibility to do so. I believe I am a little in awe of this man. The realization surprised him.

"Tbubui tells me," he began carefully, "that you are content to have her marry me."

Sisenet gave a rare, open laugh. "How tactful you are, Highness! She does not need my approval, and the thought that I might have any control over your decision, you a prince of the blood, is ridiculous. But know that I am very pleased. Many men have desired her, and she has spurned them all."

"And what will you do?" Khaemwaset asked curiously. "Will you return to Koptos?" The question seemed to amuse Sisenet. His eyes gleamed at some private thought.

"I may," he replied, "but I do not think so. I am happy here, and the Memphis library is full of marvels."

"Would you like a post in my household?" Khaemwaset found himself asking out of a strange need to ingratiate himself with the man. He immediately regretted the offer. It sounded like a gentle attempt at compensation, or the price of guilt. But Sisenet was not offended.

"Thank you, Prince, but no," he declined. Still in that same odd, self-abnegatory mood, Khaemwaset was about to ask whether Harmin wanted help in advancing, but he remembered that Harmin would obtain an automatic title if he married Sheritra. The convolutions of the arrangement he had set in motion were too complex to consider at the moment, and besides, Khaemwaset thought, they make me afraid.

The conversation flagged. After a few innocuous pleasantries Khaemwaset took his leave, passing straight behind the hall and out into the glare of the garden. Sheritra and Harmin were no longer playing knucklebones. They were talking quietly while Bakmut trickled cool water over Sheritra's limbs. The heat was intense. Khaemwaset talked to them briefly, promised his daughter that he would see her again soon, and gathering his staff, he returned to the river. He did not see Tbubui. Now that the contract was in her hands, now that he had taken one more step towards an irrevocable, violent revolution in his life, he was like a general who regroups his forces and rests, waiting for a new gambit. He wanted the peace of his office and the reassuring sight of Nubnofret picking daintily through her food opposite him in the deep bronze of a summer evening.

Chapter 12

'Let us praise Thoth,
the exact plummet of the balance,
from whom evil flees,
who accepts him who avoids evil.'

Three days after his first visit to Sheritra at Tbubui's house, Khaemwaset knew he must share his decision with Nubnofret or die of guilt. He had woken with the now familiar lurch of apprehension in his chest at what had become his first thought of the day, and as he ate the bread and fruit Kasa had set beside him, he critically considered the gradual weakening of his will. He did not fully understand his hesitancy, or the feeling that he was somehow doing something reprehensible in marrying Tbubui.

The food was consumed and he was bathed and dressed before he stopped to consider what he was doing, and he only came to himself as Kasa settled him on the stool before his cosmetic table and pried the seal from a new jar of kohl. The polite snap of the wax brought Khaemwaset to his senses. This is not acceptable, he told himself angrily, watching Kasa dip a brush into the jet-black powder and lean towards his face. He closed his eyes and felt the damp brush sweep pleasingly across his eyelids. "Kasa," he said aloud quickly, before the cloud of misgiving could solidify into yet another day of cowardly procrastination, "I want you to go across to the concubines' house and tell the Keeper of the Door to open and prepare the largest suite for another occupant. I am going to marry again."

The brush trembled on his temples and then resumed its slow tracking. Kasa straightened and dabbled the tool in the bowl of water on the table. He did not look at his master. "This is good news," he said formally. "I offer you wishes of long life, health and prosperity, Highness. Please do not speak. I must now paint your mouth."

Khaemwaset was silent until the henna, cool and moist, was drying on his lips, then he said, "Have my architect in my office this evening. I intend to design an additional suite of rooms for Second Wife Tbubui, to be added to the house."

"Very good, Highness. And is this news now universal?" Khaemwaset chuckled at his body servant's extreme tact. "Yes," he answered, and sat without another word until Kasa picked up the gold-and-lapis pectoral and the gold bracelets lying on the couch and carefully completed the Prince's dressing. "If I am needed I will be the Princess's rooms," he told the man, and walked out. The die had been cast. Now he absolutely must tell Nubnofret.

Amek and Ib left their posts outside the door and swung in behind him as he made his way through the wide passages of his domain. The morning sweeping and cleaning was almost finished and Khaemwaset moved through dancing dust motes shimmering in the frequent patches of sunlight and the deep prostrations of his house servants.

Bidding his escort wait, he greeted Wernuro at his wife's door, was announced, and stepped within. Nubnofret turned to him with a smile. She was wearing a full yellow sheath embroidered in gold thread that left her ample arms and statuesque neck bare. Her long hair had been braided with gold-shot ribbon, and a gold circlet, surmounted by an image of the vulture goddess Mut, cut across her brown forehead. She was still barefoot. Khaemwaset had time to think with a pang how truly voluptuous she was with the tendrils of damp hair curling out of the thick braid to lie against her painted cheeks and the outline of her large breasts showing tantalizingly through the thin, gauzy linen.

"So you rose early also, dear brother," she commented happily as she held up her face for his kiss. "What do you have planned for the day? I hope it includes an hour or two of dalliance with me!" She has changed since Sheritra left, he pondered, his lips brushing her scented skin. She is less heavily serious, less consumed with the correct running of the house. Sheritra reminds her of her failures, perhaps, or of the years that pass so much more quickly for a woman than for a man. Poor Nubnofret.

"I want to talk to you privately," he said. "Come out onto the terrace."

She nodded and followed him across her room to where three steps led between pillars to the draught-cooled, roofed cloister. Another couple of steps would have taken them out into the full glare of a morning already stale with heat. Thick shrubbery shielded the entrance from the rear garden. Khaemwaset indicated a chair but she shook her head. Mut's obsidian eye glowered balefully at Khaemwaset as she did so.

"I have been sitting for an hour getting my hair and face done," she explained. "What is it, Khaemwaset? Am I now to know what has been troubling you?"

He sighed inwardly. "I do not know how to put this gently," he said, "so I will not try. For some time now I have been increasingly attracted to another woman, Nubnofret. I viewed this involvement with annoyance, for I am a man of set habits who likes a predictable family life, but it grew in spite of my efforts to ignore it. I am now in love with her and I have decided to marry her."

Nubnofret made a soft exclamation but Khaemwaset, daring to glance at her, did not think she was expressing shock or even surprise. It sounded more like irritation. "Go on," she said evenly. She was standing perfectly still, bejewelled arms at her sides, looking at him. He still could not face her squarely.

"There is little else to say," he admitted. "She will move into the concubines' quarters until I can design and have built a proper suite for her in the house, and of course she will be only Second Wife. You will remain mistress of the household in every way."

"Naturally," she said, still in that odd, flat tone. "It is your prerogative to take as many wives as you want, Khaemwaset, and I am only surprised that you have not done so sooner." But she still did not sound surprised. She sounded completely indifferent. He had never seen her so composed. "When will the contract be drawn up?"

Now he forced himself to face her. Her eyes were huge and expressionless. "It has been drawn up already. She has signed it and so have I."

"Then you have had this on your mind and you have planned carefully for quite some time." A faint smile came and went on her pink mouth. "Can it be that you were afraid to tell me, dear brother? I am sorry to disappoint you. I have suspected such a thing for weeks. Who is this most fortunate woman? A princess surely, for Ramses would allow you a commoner for a concubine but not for a royal wife."

Khaemwaset had the uneasy feeling that she knew already. She was staring at him with what seemed like equanimity, her breath coming in slow, deep movements of her breast. "Not a princess," he was forced to admit. "but definitely a noble-woman. It is Tbubui, Nubnofret. Tbubui. I have wanted her from the first!" His last words shot from him in a desperate effort to shake her aplomb, but she merely raised one feathery eyebrow.

"Tbubui. I did wonder about her, Khaemwaset. That day she almost fell into the water and panicked, you tensed to rush to her before she had even begun to topple. Well, I suppose I like her a little. We are friends on a superficial level, but she is not my so-cial equal, and I do not intend to treat her as such, particularly now that I suspect she sought my company even as she was se-cretly inveigling to join this household. I regard such duplicity as a personal betrayal. You understand."

"Yes, of course."

"I am quite sure that she sealed the contract with great eager-ness," Nubnofret went on. "You are, after all, no minor princeling buried in Egypt's backwaters. Now what of her son? Is he to live here also? Do you want me to give orders for a large celebration, and if so, when? What has your father had to say about the match?" Her questions were dutiful and clinical, but Khaemwaset at last sensed the terrible rage that he had mistaken for indifference, a rage so great that it had rendered her frozen.

"The contract does not become valid until Penbuy returns from Koptos with verification of her noble blood-line," he as-sured her hastily. "He left a few days ago and I have not yet re-ceived word that he arrived safely."

"No one told me." For a moment she looked bewildered, then she leaned forward, flushing. "No one told me! All this behind my back, Prince, as though you were ashamed, as though you were afraid of me! I am insulted! How do you regard me, Khaemwaset, if you cannot come to me about something like this? How long? How long?"

"I am sorry, Nubnofret," he confessed. "Truly sorry. I wish that I could make you understand." He spread his hands before her. "If I had taken another wife for dynastic reasons or because my father thought it necessary or even for a little variety, I would have come to you, discussed it with you. But this . . ." He put his hands on her rigid shoulders. "I am consumed with wanting her,

Nubnofret. I cannot rest. I concentrate on nothing. And that makes me feel like a foolish young man, like an infatuated child before you. Therefore I hesitated to suffer your amusement, your condescension."

"By the gods!" She tore herself out of his tentative grasp. "She is a nobody from the south, Khaemwaset! If you want her, take her! Toss her in with the other concubines until you become tired of her, or make love to her in her own house, it does not matter! But do not, do not marry her!"

The utter contempt in her voice made Khaemwaset wince. "This is no idle craving," he broke in. "I know that I will still want her in five, ten, fifteen years, and I intend to make sure that no one else can have her. I will marry her. It is my right!"

"Your right!" she scoffed, and Khaemwaset saw that she was shaking all over. Her bracelets jangled with the tremors in her arms, and the hem of her gown was quivering. "Yes, it is your right, but not her, Khaemwaset! You have taken leave of your senses! Your father will never allow it!"

"I think he will," Khaemwaset said, trying to gentle his voice and thus calm her down. "Tbubui is a noblewoman. Her character is above reproach. Penbuy will bring me the confirmation Ramses will request."

"Well that is something, at least," she said more quietly. Her gaze met his, and now he read speculation there. She began to play with her bracelets, pushing them up her arms and letting them fall, but her eyes never left his. "Tell me," she said. "Do you love me?"

"Oh Nubnofret!" he cried out, reaching for her, but she deftly stepped aside and his gesture died. "I love you very much. I always will."

"But not as much, it seems, as an upstart from Koptos," she murmured. "Very well. I demand to see the terms of the contract. That is my right. I must protect myself and the children. Apart from that, I shall conduct myself as befits my position as Chief Wife and Princess." She stood taller. "Have you told Hori and Sheritra?"

"Not yet, and I beg you to leave that task to me. I will do it in my own way."

Nubnofret smiled harshly. "Why?" she asked. "Are you ashamed, O my husband?"

They fell silent and stood staring at each other. The heaviness between them grew, and with it Khaemwaset's anger, until finally he said, "That will be all, Nubnofret. You are dismissed."

She bowed with exaggerated reverence, stepped around him and glided back into her chamber. "The woman is not worthy of you," her voice floated back to him. "Penbuy will bring you bad news, Khaemwaset, whether you demand that I do my duty or not. Please do not come back into the house through my rooms. I have a bad head."

With a grunt of exasperation Khaemwaset spun on his heel and turned down into the bright garden. He would see to the problem of a new physician for Pharaoh's harem. He would diligently answer the messages from the Delta. Nubnofret would get over her scorn and rage and accept Tbubui, and all would be as it should. I should feel relieved, he told himself as he left the grass and his feet found the burning paving of the path that circled the house. It is all out in the open. Hori and Sheritra will not mind. They will not be too affected. Sheritra might even be pleased, for Harmin will be as close to her as her brother. Do I want a great celebration, a city holiday for this, my second marriage after so many years? He pondered with a mixture of happiness and anxiety, a frown on his face, forcing his mind to fill with feverish thoughts so that he did not have to consider, along with Nubnofret's scorn and rage, her hurt.

A few days afterwards Sisenet paid his visit to examine the scroll. Ib received him in the still cool vastness of the reception hall that was cluttered with the foreign knick-knacks Nubnofret had acquired. The stewart set wine and pastries before him, and Khaemwaset soon sat down next to him.

The time between had been strained but uneventful. Nubnofret had retired behind a rigid politeness, seeing to his needs with her usual efficiency and speaking to him mildly, but the embryo of a fragile girlishness in her was gone. Khaemwaset had seen little of Hori. That was an ordeal he still shrank from undergoing. Sheritra could be told on the next visit to Tbubui to retrieve the sealed contract, but Hori was an increasing, worrying mystery. Khaemwaset put all of them out of his mind with a supreme effort of will and sat beside Sisenet, talking lightly of the intensifying heat of summer and the level of the Nile. The man responded in kind and once the social amenities were discharged, Khaemwaset rose and led him to the office. The room enfolded them in its purposeful atmosphere of repose. Khaemwaset indicated the chair behind the desk, and bowing, Sisenet accepted it, drawing it up to the table where Khaemwaset had already spread his notes. The scroll itself lay to one side, stirring faintly in a hidden draught.

Khaemwaset sank onto a stool. He did not expect any real assistance from this spare, quiet man who was giving him a quick smile and reaching for the soft cylinder. Khaemwaset knew his own status in Egypt's academic community very well, and it came to him that he was probably going through this charade to please Tbubui. He wanted to ask if Sisenet had all he required—pens, palette, something to drink—but Sisenet's head had gone down over the gleaming surface of the desk and his immediate absorption in the task precluded interruption. Khaemwaset forced his attention back to the litter under the man's tanned, sinewy fingers. Sisenet was wearing several thick gold-and-turquoise rings of a design Nubnofret would have disdainfully labelled crude and bulky, but Khaemwaset rather liked them. He watched their tiny movements as Sisenet read.

Presently the man pulled Khaemwaset's notes towards him and glanced over them. His scrutiny seemed slightly scornful to Khaemwaset, who then acknowledged to himself that his imagination was already at work, as it always was when he had anything to do with the scroll. The level of his anxiety was rising. Find nothing, he begged Sisenet dumbly. Declare the task too great and your scholarship inadequate, so that I may be cleansed of this obsession in good conscience. Sisenet cleared his throat, a small completely polite sound, and a faint smile moved his ascetic lips. He looked up, pulling the scribe's palette forward, and took up a pen. Then he unrolled the scroll again. His handling of it was almost ritualistic, although his steady gaze remained fixed on Khaemwaset.

"This is a difficult form of very ancient Egyptian writing," he said. "I am not surprised that it has mystified you, Prince. Very few scrolls of this age have survived, but I have had the privilege of examining a couple of them in Koptos, where life has gone on unchanged from generation to generation, untouched by the fevers and fervors of the north."

Khaemwaset was not tempted to smile at the man's somewhat quaint language. He was forcibly aware that Sisenet's odd accent had intensified, become more broad. He still could not place it. He was so used to it issuing out of Tbubui's mouth that he had ceased to notice it, but he spoke to Sisenet much less frequently and now it rang in his ears, a pleasant, courtly lilt.

"Are you telling me that you are in fact able to translate that . . . that thing?" Khaemwaset jabbed one impatient finger at the smooth beige papyrus held open between Sisenet's quiet hands. Sisenet's eyebrows shot up.

"But of course, Highness," he said. "A moment, and I will write it down for you."

Unbelieving, Khaemwaset saw him lay the palette across the scroll to prevent it from rolling shut, and begin to write, his pen scratching loudly and surely across the unblemished paper Khaemwaset's temporary scribe had laid ready. He found it difficult to breathe. Fear and excitement had gripped him and he learned forward tensely, hands locked between his knees, mesmerized by the columns of hieroglyphs taking shape under Sisenet's sleek black head. The moments slid by. How can he be so calm, so uninvolved? Khaemwaset wondered hotly. Though perhaps what he is writing has no significance. Perhaps it is a love poem, a family event recorded joyously, even a list of some kind . . . But he remembered the curious and familiar cadence of the sentences, the light, dry feel of the bandaged hand from which he had severed the scroll, and his mind retreated and fell silent.

After what seemed a very long time, Sisenet straightened and laid the pen back in its slot on the palette. He passed the sheet of papyrus over the desk, wordlessly handing it to Khaemwaset, who was unable to still the tremor in his arm as he took it. The room was becoming hotter now, the fleeting coolness of early morning giving way to stifling, motionless air. The scroll no longer quivered, for the draughts had ceased. Sisenet had allowed it to roll up again, and now waited, his hands clasped on the desk beside it.

Khaemwaset had begun to sweat. He was aware of Sisenet's clear, unwavering observation as he forced his eyes to begin the reading, and he cursed himself for so betraying his agitation. At first his mind did not register what his gaze was presenting and he was forced to go back and scan the lines again, but then eye and mind suddenly harmonized and the shock of it went through Khaemwaset like a galvanizing drug.

"Oh gods, I said these words even though I did not understand them," he croaked, horror and elation coursing through him, and through he tried to hold on to the elation, the horror grew. "Gods! Gods! What have I done?"

"It was a foolish thing to do once you realized, as you must have, that the words had the cadence of a spell," Sisenet replied, "but in this case a harmless mistake. Highness, are you ill?"

Khaemwaset was aware of him half rising from behind the desk, and managed to wave him down. "No! I am not ill!"

"Surely you do not believe in this thing, Prince?" Sisenet said slowly. "I apologize, for I seem to have given you a shock. The Scroll of Thoth is a matter of myth and legend only. The story of its existence is merely an expression of man's longing to control both life and death. Only the gods have that power. This," and he flicked the scroll contemptuously with a long fingernail, "this is a game. Someone fabricated a Scroll of Thoth out of his need, his desire for ultimate power, or perhaps even out of his anguish. A dead loved one, a horror of the Judgment Hall because of a life spent doing evil." Sisenet shrugged. "Who knows? The Scroll does not exist. It has never existed, and if you consider the matter for a moment, Highness, you must admit that it simply could not exist."

Khaemwaset was struggling for control, the papyrus clutched tightly in both hands. "I am a magician," he responded, his voice still clogged with fear. "I know many spells that have mighty power. I know how other magicians have sought this Scroll for hentis beyond counting, and their searches have been conducted with the absolute certainty that such a thing exists and has the power to bend the dead and the living to its will."

"And I tell you, Prince, that although magic may control many areas of our lives because the magician may coerce the gods into doing what is requested, we cannot use it to resurrect the dead or communicate with animals and birds as the legitimate owner of the Scroll of Thoth is supposed to be able to do, no matter how fervently we desire to do so. This scroll has great value, but as an historic artifact, not as a myth come to reality. Do you not think that if the scroll had any real power the tomb would be empty?"

Khaemwaset clenched his teeth. He knew that he was white and shaking, for he was consumed with the feeling that he was in fact asleep, on his couch in a blistering afternoon, in the grip of a dreadful nightmare. All he could think of while Sisenet was talking in that maddening, not-quite-recognized accent, his face full of concern and skepticism and something else, something that might have been faint amusement, was the night he had spoken the strange words and then rushed to negate the power he had felt settle around him.

He rose. "Come," he said, and without waiting he stumbled to the doors. "Ib!" he shouted. "Order out three litters and command Hori to meet me behind the house immediately!"

His legs felt weak. Forcing them to obey him he strode through the house and out into the garden, sensing rather than hearing Sisenet gliding swiftly behind. Together they waited in silence until the litters and twelve bearers appeared, and Hori emerged, blinking and dishevelled, to join them. He greeted Sisenet amiably enough but Khaemwaset, despite his distress, recognized the marks of a night of concentrated drinking on the handsome face. Not now, he thought grimly. He flung himself onto a litter and the others followed suit.

"What is this about, Father?" Hori asked, but Khaemwaset did not reply. Curtly he instructed the bearers to hurry them to the tomb site, then he pulled the curtains closed and fell back on the pillows, trying to still the confused swirl of shrinking and haste inside him. Never had the trek through the city to Saqqara seemed so long.

He did not reopen his litter until he felt it being lowered, then he stepped out onto ground that burned through his sandals. Sisenet and Hori had already alighted and were coming towards him, eyes narrowed against the fiery afternoon sun. Khaemwaset jerked his head at them and hurried down the steps, but at the entrance, where two dozing, bored guards on either side of the doorway sprang to attention and saluted him, he paused. It required a deliberate act of courage for him to walk through, and he felt an almost physical resistance as he did so.

As always, the damp coolness was a relief, but the pleasure of the still air on his skin was transitory. Sisenet and Hori came up behind him and stood waiting, puzzled. He walked down the short passage and once more came to a halt. A shudder went through him. The bright, intricately painted wall scenes, the two statues, the ranked shawabti figures, and most of all the coffins, seemed to exude a gleeful malevolence that rushed to claim him. You stole it, the chamber shouted silently. You have sinned, you arrogant, heedless defiler, and you will pay.

A hopeless anger suddenly propelled Khaemwaset forward. Striding to the coffin that held the mysterious man he leaned over the shrouded figure and drove a fist into the fragile corpse. The brittle ribcage collapsed in a shower of choking dust and tiny splinters of bone. The mummy trembled and Khaemwaset withdrew his arm.

"This man is a nobody," he said forcefully. "Completely insignificant. He was probably a household servant, a gardener, a carrier of offal for the trash heap. The scroll was attached to his hand so that a fool like me could read it all unwittingly and raise *them* to life again!" He flung his dust-coated arm at the new false wall Hori's workmen had so painstakingly erected and re-painted. He was in a cold sweat. "That's why the scroll was sewn to a nonentity's hand. That's why there are no lids for the coffins in the inner chamber. That's why there is a tunnel. The earring, Hori. The earring! A dead woman lost it while she was crawling out! Where are they now and what have they done?" He was becoming incoherent, and Hori turned to Sisenet.

"What is going on here?" he whispered. "What is Father babbling about?"

His words easily reached Khaemwaset in the enclosed space, and he laughed hysterically. "I stole it and I used it," he shouted. "Only the legitimate owner can do that with impunity. I have condemned myself!"

"He believes that the scroll the two of you found here is the fabled Scroll of Thoth," Sisenet explained hurriedly to a bewildered Hori. "It did indeed translate as two rather clumsy spells for re-animation and the understanding of the language of all living things, but such a thing cannot be." He turned to Khaemwaset. "The dead do live again," he said reasonably, "but not on this earth, Prince. There is no record of anyone coming back from the grave. The Scroll of Thoth is a grand, sad legend and you cannot believe in it literally." Khaemwaset was staring at him intensely and he moved forward. "Give it to me, Highness, and I will take it away and burn it," he offered, but Khaemwaset came to himself and violently shook his head.

"No," he barked. "I will put it back immediately, today. Go home, Sisenet."

The man hesitated, opened his mouth, then closed it again and bowed himself out. Khaemwaset watched his shadow elongate in the sunshine along the wall of the tomb passage, then snap to him and disappear.

Hori came quickly, and put a hand on Khaemwaset's arm. "I am not sure I understand just what has been happening here," he said with concern, "but you are distraught, Father. Come home and rest, and we will bring the scroll and close the tomb."

Khaemwaset surrendered for once to the pressure of his son's comforting grip and allowed himself to be led outside. Sisenet's litter was just vanishing into the northern edge of the city. "Yes, home," Khaemwaset muttered, "but I cannot rest until I have done what must be done. Let us hurry, Hori. I do not want to be here when the shadows begin to lengthen."

They returned to the house, and while Hori waited, Khaemwaset went to his office and grabbed up the scroll, deliberately not reacting to the feel of it or allowing his mind to become entangled in the past. From Kasa he obtained a copper needle and some thread, and clutching these objects he went back to where Hori stood anxiously. "Come with me," he begged, and Hori nodded. Together they rode the swaying litters back the way they had come, Khaemwaset's impatience now a desperate, helpless thing.

At the tomb entrance Khaemwaset staggered from the litter and, with a shout for Hori, ran down the stairs and inside. The body he had mutilated lay as he had left it, its chest now gaping dryly open. "Hold up the hand," Khaemwaset snapped. The young man obeyed, lifting the light, stiff arm and turning it so that Khaemwaset could work.

With needle threaded and the scroll roughly bunched against the linen bandages, Khaemwaset began to sew. The papyrus was resistant, the hand so rigid that it seemed both scroll and lifeless limb were conspiring to prevent him from accomplishing the distasteful task. It is too late, the chamber whispered with cruel satisfaction. You have sinned and you are cursed, cursed,

cursed . . . The needle slipped and Khaemwaset swore. Two large drops of his blood fell onto the dead finger he held crushed in his grasp, and spreading, sank into the greedy linen. One smeared against the scroll. Terror stalked him and this time he could not fight it. Panting he made the last stitch, jerked out the needle, and nodded at Hori who pushed the arm back down into the musty-smelling coffin. "The lid," Khaemwaset said hoarsely. "Call the guards and the litter-bearers to help."

Hori seemed to have caught his father's urgency. He dashed outside and returned shortly with ten wary men. Khaemwaset pointed to the lid still leaning against the wall, and though he did not want to touch it he took his place with his servants and his son as they dragged and heaved the solid slab of granite across the floor, up onto the pedestal, and, with a final groan, onto the coffin itself. It settled with a thud and a grind.

Thoughtfully, Khaemwaset looked at the second coffin, then nodded curtly. "That one too," he said. This time he stood back and watched until the lid smashed down. A tiny piece of stone pulled free and clattered towards him to come to rest by his left sandal. He kicked it away. "Hori, have this accursed place closed immediately," he said. "I don't care if the artists have finished or not. Fill the stairway with rocks and rubble and have the largest stone you can find rolled over it. Have it done now, before night, before night, do you hear?" He was aware that his voice was rising to an uncontrollable shriek, and his servants were staring at him. He closed his mouth and, turning his back on the mystery that had terrified and enthralled him for so many months, he forced himself to go slowly outside. Hori came after him. "I will send to the Master Mason at once, Father," he said, "but I beg you to consider Sisenet's sensible words. He is right. Go home, sleep, and ponder them."

Khaemwaset looked into the unhappy, drawn face of his son, then suddenly they were embracing, arms about each other, and Hori's face was buried in Khaemwaset's neck. "I love you," Khaemwaset choked, near to tears, almost at the end of his control, and Hori's muffled voice replied, "I love you also, O my father."

The litter-bearers were sorting themselves out and bending to their loads. Khaemwaset sank with exhaustion into the haven of privacy and lay back with a sigh. He felt as though a great burden had been lifted from his heart, his body. After all, he thought, nothing has happened in all the weeks since I said the so-called spell. No one has died or been stricken with some foul disease. No sudden misfortune has befallen the family. I reacted like a stupid, ignorant peasant. Sisenet was right. The thought made him smile, and before he was set down gently outside his door he had fallen into a relieved doze.

In the days that followed, Khaemwaset became increasingly ashamed of his outburst before Sisenet and Hori. The man's arguments against the scroll being anything other than a poor fabrication had been quietly reasonable and Khaemwaset, going over every word and unspoken nuance of that unsettling afternoon, was forced to agree with him.

All his life he had carried the dream of one day finding the Scroll of Thoth whose two spells would give him the total knowledge of all living things through the understanding of their language, and more, the secret, ultimate power over death he had craved. He would become a god. But now he began to recognize the fantasy for what it was. Childhood had spawned it, and his own greed and ambition had fed it. It was true that the Scroll's existence was believed by every magician who had lived in Egypt, but wherever it lay, if in fact it lay anywhere, it would be in some deep, exotic place where time and eternity met, surrounded by potent spells, watched over by Thoth himself. And if a human being had ever owned it, that person would have been a creature of more than human powers himself. Certainly it would never have been buried in a simple, shallow tomb at Saqqara.

He had reacted irrationally, he told himself as his equilibrium partially returned. He had allowed his long dream to become entangled with superstition as opposed to forthright, workable magic, and it was time to let the shadowless light of a noon reality into the darkness that had been gathering in his mind.

But first there was the matter of Tbubui's quarters. With relief he turned to the planning and construction of a new wing on the house. He and his architect drew up a pleasing suite with large, airy rooms, a private passage giving access to the rest of the house so that the woman who prized silence and privacy so much could have both, and a small terrace leading directly onto a fountained garden. Part of the existing grounds to the north of the house would have to be dug up, the flower beds turned under, the pond moved, but Khaemwaset thought it could be done with a minimum of distress to the rest of the family. Once he had approved the addition, it was simply a matter of issuing an order, and gangs of fellahin appeared and began to demolish the northern grounds.

Through it all, Nubnofret remained frigidly correct. Twice Khaemwaset went to her apartment at night to hold and reassure her, even to make love to her if she had melted just a little, but she rebuffed him with icy good manners and he was forced to retreat.

No more harsh words were said, but the tension between them grew and invaded the whole house. Cheerful servants became subdued and the routine, previously imbued with heart and life, became increasingly a matter of soulless form. Khaemwaset was aware of it but did not care. Every day the plans for Tbubui's domain grew and took coherent shape. Before long she would be there.

A report arrived from Penbuy at Koptos. He had been in the town for two days when he wrote the letter and was about to begin his investigations, but he was being hampered by a sudden illness that was slowing him down. After a few disparaging remarks to do with the sickeningly constant heat, the multitudes of giant flies and the warm, muddy water he was forced to bathe in, he finished by assuring Khaemwaset that the task would be completed soon and he was his master's honourable and most trustworthy servant. So you are, dear Penbuy, Khaemwaset thought, standing with the scroll clasped in both hands as he gazed out over the ruin of the edge of the north garden that he could see from his office. So you are. Penbuy's face swam before him, closed, intent, intelligent, sometimes a little prim, and a wave of strange homesickness swept over him. He wanted Penbuy at his elbow, exuding the faint odour of lotus water that seemed to float with him everywhere. He wanted the garden back. He wanted Sheritra back, now so poised and distant. He wanted it all back.

Chapter 13

'When the messenger of death comes to take thee away,
let him find thee prepared.
Alas! thou wilt have no opportunity for speech,
for verily his terror will be before thee.'

Once Sheritra had adjusted to the strange ways of the house, she forgot her earlier misgivings. She was happy, perhaps happier than she had ever been. Bakmut remained uneasy, and served her mistress with an increased vigilance Sheritra found touching, but the Princess herself grew in confidence.

She became accustomed to waking, not to the bustle of a large estate, but to the quiet Sisenet and Tbubui demanded. She would eat her breakfast on her couch in a state of tousled disorder, her thoughts slow and mellow. Away from the constant tension of her mother's nagging judgments, her body relaxed, and her mind found new and freer avenues to explore under Tbubui's tutelage.

The woman would come to her while she was standing on the bathing block, greet her affably and accompany her back to her room. At first Sheritra was self-conscious. It was one thing to have the eyes of servants on one's naked body, for servants were more like household appendages than people. It was quite another to stand, inwardly cringing, while Tbubui's knowing glance travelled her tiny breasts, stick-thin legs and bony hips. Sheritra knew she could have requested privacy, but in a perverse way she regarded Tbubui's scrutiny as the last test of their friendship. Fiercely, she watched for the slightest indication of contempt, distaste or pity in the woman's eyes or attitude, and mercifully found none.

After a couple of days Sheritra welcomed the moment when Tbubui would appear, fresh and smiling, to kiss her on the cheek and chatter while the perfumed water cascaded over Sheritra's skin. "Rub the Princess down with that oil," Tbubui would say, indicating one of the alabaster jars that lined the stone lip of the small bath house. "It has balsam in it, Sheritra, and will soften you and make you more supple. The sun is so bad for the skin."

Or she would arrive holding a tiny pot of some balm or other to protect the lips. Several times she waved the servant who was washing Sheritra away, and her own hands rubbed the girl, moving briskly over her back and buttocks and sliding more gently along her inner thighs. "Forgive me, Highness, but I know several good exercises for the development of the legs and the strengthening of the spine. Let me teach them to you," she offered. "Also, if I might be permitted, I would like to change your diet. You need some weight." Sheritra was not in the least offended. Intrigued, she submitted to the oil that gleamingly caressed her skin and then sank without a trace, leaving her to run her fingers over herself and feel velvet.

Her mother had often suggested such treatments but Sheritra, in rebellion, had always refused them. With Tbubui it was different, it was close companionship, it was fun, and there was no hint of superiority on the one hand or inadequacy on the other. "It is not right that she should touch a princess's flesh," Bakmut had objected a trifle sourly, but Sheritra had ignored her body servant. Tbubui had treatments for everything—a fragrant, thick wrap of herbs to thicken the hair and make it shine, a sticky mixture to strengthen the nails, a mask to preserve the face from aging.

If it were simply a matter of retreating into the indolence of physical indulgence, Sheritra might have become bored, but after the bath, Tbubui—in between advice on dress and cosmetics, while she combed Sheritra's increasingly luxurious tresses or bent close to flick her eyelids with colour—would talk on any subject that came to mind. Freely the arguments would flow back and forth, but Sheritra most loved Tbubui's stories about Egypt's past, her ancient heroes, the tenor and pace of lives lived hentis ago. The mornings flew by. Very occasionally Tbubui did not come to the bath house with her knowing, expert hands, and on those occasions Sheritra, unconsciously, felt deprived of the contact.

Tbubui vanished during most afternoons and Sheritra— washed and perfumed, her hair imprisoned in gold-and-enamel flower clips or waving loose under a circlet of silver, her face, scarcely recognizable to herself, exquisitely painted, her increasingly nubile body displayed in white or scarlet or yellow sheaths —would hurry to where Harmin waited for her in the garden, or in the coolness of the reception hall. Then they would talk, tease each other, play board games and exchange glances while the wine jug emptied and the breathless, stultifying hours went gliding into copper sunsets and the lengthening shadows of warm twilights.

Evenings were taken up with quiet family dinners. The harpist would play softly and the little tables would be piled with perfumed flowers from the garden, whose petals would lie in pastel drifts over the tiled floor. The lamps would be lit, and they would sit in the slight breeze coming in through the open door from the night beyond while Sisenet read to them from his library of scrolls. His voice was deep and even, the stories somehow both vivid and lulling to Sheritra. They were like the anecdotes Tbubui would tell her in the mornings, but at night they had a hypnotic quality to them, so that her mind filled with bright images. When he had finished they would drink some more of his marvellous wine and gossip a little. She would tell them of her family, of Pharaoh, of her opinions and dreams, and they would listen and ask questions, smile and nod. Only later did she realize that, in spite of the many evenings spent in this way, she had learned almost nothing about them. Finally Bakmut and a soldier would escort her to her room to be undressed and washed, and she would lie on her couch, watching the friendly shadows her night lamp cast on the ceiling, and pass effortlessly into unconsciousness. She did not think that she would ever want to go home.

Her father came to visit her twice in the three weeks that followed, but Sheritra observed and listened to him as though from a far distance. He was clearly pleased with her contentment, her flowering body, and always embraced her with his usual affection, but something about the feel of his arms now made her cringe.

On his second visit, as he was leaving, she saw Tbubui hand him a scroll and supposed it was something from Sisenet's collection. His fingers closed around Tbubui's giving Sheritra a flash of her old anxiety. But events outside Sisenet's house seemed less significant now and, with a shrug, Sheritra retreated into fatalism. Her father's infatuation would doubtless burn itself out and was, in any case, none of her business. She had thought that he looked haggard and pale. "Is there any news?" Tbubui asked him, and he had shaken his head. "Not yet," he had replied, and they had both turned after a second and smiled at Sheritra as though in apology.

Nubnofret had sent several cheerful notes but had not visited herself. Sheritra was glad. Her mother's presence would have struck a jarring note in the peaceful harmony of Sisenet's household. Sheritra did not miss her.

But one jarring note came from within. On the night of Khaemwaset's second visit, Sheritra decided to take a short walk before bed. The air was still hot and she was unaccountably restless. She wandered with a compliant Bakmut and one of her ever-present guards under the shrouded palms for a while, then made her way to the river. It was very low, the water flowing almost imperceptibly, torn to silver under the new moon's light. She sat for some time on the watersteps, allowing the calm darkness to soothe her, then made her way back to the house.

Skirting it, she approached the side door, she and her escort almost invisible in the darkness, but before she reached it she saw two figures standing just within the passage. Their voices came to her faintly, and there was something so private, so exclusive about their stance that she came to a halt. Now she could hear the words. It was Tbubui and her brother.

". . . and you know that it is time," Tbubui was saying harshly. "Why do you hesitate?"

"Yes, I know it is time," Sisenet's voice replied, "but I am reluctant to begin. Such a thing is beneath us. Once we would have considered it reprehensible."

"That was a very long time ago, when we were innocents," Tbubui retorted bitterly. "Now it is necessary. Besides, what is a common servant to us? What is his . . ." she broke off as Sheritra, unwilling to eavesdrop on purpose, moved forward. For a moment, Sheritra saw Tbubui's face as she turned towards the footsteps, twisted, angry—then her expression smoothed. "Princess," she said. Sisenet had bowed and was already gone.

"I decided to walk a little before bed," Sheritra explained. "The night is so fine and besides, I ate too much at dinner!"

Tbubui smiled back and stepped aside. "Sleep well, Highness," she said kindly, and Sheritra nodded and walked past her.

Reaching the bedchamber she was obscurely relieved when her guard took up his station outside the door and Bakmut closed it firmly. Sheritra suffered the ministrations of the girl and slid between the sheets in an abstracted mood. It was not so much the words she had heard but the emotions behind them—Tbubui forceful, Sisenet cold. The atmosphere that had surrounded them was turbulent, completely alien to the prevailing mood of the house. What on earth were they talking about? she wondered. Who is the "common servant"? She herself had quickly fallen into the household habit of snapping out orders to the staff without even looking at them, so much a part of the furnishings did they seem, and the voices of those she had brought with her were doubly appreciated after Sisenet's utterly responseless staff.

On impulse she sat up. "Bakmut, fetch me my horoscope for Phamenoth," she ordered, and the girl got up from her mat and went to one of the chests against the wall. I never did look at it, Sheritra thought. Father said it was not good, but as the month is running soon into Pharmuti it doesn't matter. Yet she took it from Bakmut and unrolled it with trepidation. As Khaemwaset said, it was uniformly bad. "Do not rise from your couch today. . . . Eat no meat this evening. . . . Spend the afternoon in prayer and do not sleep, that the anger of the gods may be averted. . . . Remember that the Nile is your refuge. . . . Turn from love as though from disease . . ."

Sheritra let it roll shut and tossed it back to the waiting servant. "Put it away," she said, and lay down again. How is the Nile my refuge? she asked herself, and why on earth should I turn from love? Whose love? Father's? Tbubui's? Harmin's? She feel asleep wondering, still with that pinprick of unease Sisenet and Tbubui's conversation had caused her, and for the first time her rest was interrupted. Several times she woke, thinking that she had heard something, but each time the house remained sunk in its bottomless peace.

The following morning saw Tbubui coming into her chamber to inquire if she was ill, for the sun was high and the hour of breakfast long gone. She was her usual graceful self, attentive and cheerful, and Sheritra grimly ignored the headache lurking behind her eyes and dragged herself from the couch to the bath house.

"Were you up late last night, Highness?" Tbubui asked her.

She was kneeling at Sheritra's feet, working oil into the girl's calves. "You do not look rested, in fact you look quite jaded, and there are knots in your muscles."

Sheritra did not reply. Eyes closed, she was all at once preternaturally aware of every sensation: the dull pounding in her head, the sweet, cloying aroma of the oil, the feel of her wet hair sticking to her shoulder-blades, the tinkle of water draining through the slanted floor of the bath house, but most of all, the firm, inflammatory touch of Tbubui's fingers on her flesh. A little higher, Tbubui, she thought lazily. Caress my thighs with those long, probing fingers of yours, and as though the woman had heard her, she felt soft movement stroking upward. Her disturbed thoughts and sense of dislocation faded into sensation.

The rest of the morning passed uneventfully. She and Tbubui lounged in Sheritra's bedchamber talking of nothing in particular, but behind Tbubui's words Sheritra sensed an absence. The woman's mind was on something else, though she hid it well, and as soon as the noon meal was over she excused herself and vanished towards her own room.

After the noon sleep Harmin, Sheritra, a guard and Bakmut made their way through the palm grove to a spot out of sight of the house. The guard took up his post by the path, just out of sight. Bakmut unrolled the mat, set down various games and retired to just within earshot.

Sheritra made herself comfortable. Her senses were still sending her messages of exquisite clarity: every drop of her sweat on this flaming afternoon, the dry rustle of the dusty palms above, the crackle of dead leaves under the mat. A twig pressed against her buttock. Harmin leaned in front of her to pull the games over and a gush of his perfume made her dizzy.

He had tied back his hair with a white ribbon that now lay ribbed across his bare shoulder, and the juxtaposition of blackest black and the dazzling white of the strip of linen made her feel slightly ill. He glanced sideways at her, his eyes smiling.

"What would you like to play today, Princess?" he asked. "Or would you rather lie here and drowse the hours away?"

She watched, bemused, the motions of his fine mouth, the working of his throat as he spoke. "I want to kiss you," she said. He chuckled and jerked a ring finger at Bakmut. "Dogs and Jackals perhaps, Highness? Dice? Are you quite well, Sheritra?"

"Yes. No. I feel a little strange, Harmin. Let us play sennet."

He hesitated, then set the board between their knees, opening a box and shaking out the spools and cones. "Very well. Does your Highness wish to be a spool?"

"No, a cone." Together they set out the pieces and began throwing the sticks to see who would begin. "Your mother seemed preoccupied this morning," Sheritra went on. "I do hope there are no family problems looming, Harmin. Is it time for me to go home?"

The question was not serious and he laughed. "Look, you have thrown a one," he said. "Throw again and begin. There are no family problems I assure you. Perhaps mother is affected by this heat."

"But she loves the heat," Sheritra objected. "Oh Harmin, a five a five a four! You are doing very well. No, I think it is probably my imagination. The heat is getting to me. I need to swim. I wish you had a pool big enough, for I do not fancy the Nile at this time of the year. "Excuse me." She bent and moved one of his pieces forward. "You did not count correctly."

"I did not want to land on the House of the Net," he said thickly, and Sheritra glanced up, surprised at his tone. He was swallowing and staring at the board where the god-fisherman had spread his web. "It is an unlucky house."

"It is more unlucky to cheat!" she teased him, but he did not respond. She took her turn, throwing four ones and a two, and she knew that he was praying to the god of the house on which he wanted to land with an inner intensity that kept her tongue still. Gathering up the sticks he threw, also a one and a two.

"You can move this piece two," she pointed, "but this one must go to the House of the Fishing Implements."

Harmin ran a finger along his upper lip. Sheritra saw that he was sweating lightly. "No," he said in a low voice. "I will move you forward, Sheritra, but I will not move from one unlucky House to another."

"As you wish," she replied, "but you will be putting me right on the Beautiful House and all I have to do is jump the water."

He did not answer. Deftly he exchanged his piece for hers and the game went on, but now he replied to her sallies with grunts, or did not reply at all. He seemed tense, and when, with a stroke of pure good fortune, she threw a number that would allow her to tumble him into the House of the Water, he gave an agonized cry. Her hand paused in mid air, clutching his piece, and his own closed over it. His fingers were cold and slick with sweat. "Not in the Water," he said huskily. "It is cold and dark there, and hopeless. Please, Sheritra."

"Harmin, it is only a game," she said kindly. "We do not play it with spells today, only for amusement. If I do not tip you into the Water I might lose."

He managed a weak smile. "And you are a very bad loser. I will concede to you, Princess, but do not put me there."

She shrugged, puzzled and annoyed. "Oh very well. Put it all away and I will dice with you. What stakes do you propose?"

Soon afterwards they left the mat. Sheritra had won at the dicing and Harmin promised to take her on the river after dinner. They parted to sleep away the hottest part of the day, and Sheritra lay on her couch wondering why he had taken the game so much to heart. They had whiled away many hours at sennet, everyone did, but this was the first time it had upset him.

The house did not seem so quiet today. It was full of little whisperings and scutterings, as though it had been suddenly invaded by an army of mice. Although she was both physically exhausted from her broken night and emotionally drained by her desire for Harmin, heightened but not satisfied, she could not sleep.

Waking Bakmut, she asked for cooling water to be rubbed into her skin. But Bakmut, who had massaged and washed her mistress for years, seemed clumsy and inexperienced after Tbubui's touch, and in the end Sheritra told her to go back to her sleeping mat. I will drink a lot of wine tonight, she told herself pettishly, and I will bring the harpist into my chamber and I will dance to his music, all alone. I wonder how Hori is faring? Why has he not been to see me? I will write him a message tomorrow.

She and Harmin went on the river in the red sunset, floating north for several miles. Contentedly they stood by the barge's rail, watching the northern outskirts give way rapidly to ripening fields and the pink mirrors of palm-lined irrigation canals. When torches began to spring up on the watersteps of the estates they passed and the vegetation lining the Nile became indistinct, Harmin gave the order to turn about, and he and Sheritra retired to the small cabin. Bakmut sat outside it, her back to the heavy curtains that had not been closed. Silently, in the dusk of the approaching night, Sheritra and Harmin lay on the cushions and embraced, breath hot, mouths eager, hands roving in an agony of need.

"Oh Harmin," Sheritra murmured. "I did not know that I could be so happy. How scornful I was of love! How wrongly pitying of those who had found it, out of my own refusal to admit that I yearned for it too!"

He placed his fingers over her lips. "Hush," he whispered. "Do not look back, dearest sister. That Sheritra no longer exists. I love you, and the future will be full of nights like this."

"No, not like this," she said, struggling up and pushing back her hair, "for this is torment. To have and not have you . . ." Her voice trailed away and she was very glad that the dimness hid her sudden shyness.

"You will have me soon enough," he replied. "We will marry, Sheritra. Do you doubt it?"

"No," she answered, still in such a low voice that Bakmut could not hear. "But when, Harmin? I am a princess, and for a princess such things take time."

He was silent. She could feel him pondering, and as the moments ticked by she began to cool, and then to shiver with dismay. He needs to form an answer, she thought unhappily. He is choosing what best to say. But when he did speak he took her by surprise.

"I know it takes time," he said, "and if it were only a matter of royal protocol I would stick out my tongue at it and run away with you." She smiled in the darkness, relieved. "But there is something else," he went on. "Are you aware, Sheritra, that your father intends to marry my mother?"

Shock made her speechless, yet under it there was a dull recognition of the inevitability of the event. Her father was completely infatuated with Tbubui, that was clear. Sheritra had seen it, had chewed upon it, but had refused to consider the natural result of his obsession. I warned him many weeks ago, she thought. Tbubui is dangerous to men. I feel it. Yet he is entitled to as many wives as he wants. This marriage will make him happy. Oh Hori, my dear, dear Hori. What will this do to you? To Mother? Yet the idea titillated her, why she did not know. It seemed to add fuel to the fire of her physical need for Harmin, and the longing for his body surged back like nausea.

"No," she said breathlessly, "I had no idea. Are you sure? How do you know?"

"I was looking through some scrolls on my uncle's desk, trying to find the story he had read to us the night before," Harmin explained. "The marriage contract was with them and I unrolled it by mistake. Your father has placed his seal on it, and so has my mother."

"Have you approached her about it?" And has Father approached Mother, and Hori? If so, why has he not approached me?

"No," Harmin replied. "She will tell me in due time, I expect. I am sorry, Sheritra. I believed that if things had gone so far as to produce a contract, your father must have told you all. I waited for you to mention it, but you said nothing."

For one blind moment Sheritra trembled with pure rage. Until Tbubui was lodged in the new suite Khaemwaset would undoubtedly build for her, until all legal affairs regarding the marriage had been settled, she and Harmin must remain friends. He has jeopardized my happiness, the happiness he has always seemed to care so much about, she shouted in her mind. Damn you, Father, you and your stupid infatuation. Why couldn't you just sleep with her until the fire is out of your system?

The intensity of her emotion appalled her, and she must have made some sound, for she heard Harmin light the lamp and all at once the cabin filled with a soft yellow glow.

"Are you all right?" he asked sharply. "You have gone white, Highness."

Sheritra gulped. "Our own plans will have to wait," she managed. "I am angry, Harmin, that is all. Father is doing nothing wrong."

A sailor called a polite warning and Harmin scrambled up, pulling her with him. "We are home," he said. "I am sorry to have given you this shock. Forgive me. Say nothing to your family, I beg. I have made a grave mistake."

No you have not, she thought grimly as she preceded him out of the cabin. This is my home now, beside you. I will marry you and live here and I will never return to the apartments in my father's house. I long to talk to Hori. Oh why hasn't he come?

She did not sleep well again that night. She dreamed of the

House of the Water as a vast, dark lake on whose verge she stood. It was twilight, a dreary expanse of colourless sky meeting and misting the still surface of the water. There were things moving out there just beneath the top and she did not want to look at them, but she was unable to tear herself away. The shapes drifted closer as though drawn to her.

She woke at dawn with her heart thumping and her limbs aching, lying for some minutes weak with relief at the sound of the birds' morning chorus in the palms. Then she slept again, to return to consciousness when Bakmut bowed her breakfast tray onto her lap.

She was inexpressibly relieved to see Tbubui, vibrant and lovely as ever, enter the bath house and stand with bare feet in the water cascading from Sheritra's body to swirl down the drain. "I had a terrible dream last night," she blurted, and Tbubui smiled.

"Perhaps your Highness ate heavy food too late in the day," she said kindly. "I am sorry you were distressed." Her critical eye scanned the girl's nakedness. "You are tense from neck to knees," she went on disapprovingly. "Come to my room and I will give you a full massage." She picked up a tall alabaster jar and left. Sheritra followed, wringing the moisture out of her hair, and Bakmut trotted behind.

No guard watched outside Tbubui's quarters, and as she went through the doorway Sheritra wondered fleetingly if she ought to summon the one that waited on her own door. Then she mentally shrugged. There was no danger to her here, and the house was so compact that one shout would bring a soldier running.

Bakmut slid into the room after her, closed the door and squatted to one side. Tbubui indicated the couch. "This is the oil I like to have massaged into my skin when I am tense," she said, pulling the stopper on the alabaster container as Sheritra lowered herself onto her stomach with a sigh. "Your Highness will feel better in no time."

Although her head was turned away, Sheritra could sense Bakmut's disapproval. "Thank you, Tbubui," she said. "Massaging is very hard work. Are you sure you would not prefer to let my body servant do it?"

"Nonsense, Highness," Tbubui said briskly. "I would have to stand beside her and tell her exactly what to do, and that would be boring. Now close your eyes and please lower your elbows a little so that your shoulders are relaxed."

Sheritra did as she was bid. The room was still redolent with sleep, and together with the suddenly blossoming aroma of the oil as it was poured onto her back she could detect a faint whiff of the extinguished night lamp.

Tbubui's hands swirled in lazy circles on her skin and then began to move firmly up her spine and over her shoulders in a soothing rhythm. "You have impregnated the oil with your own perfume," Sheritra commented, already loosening into the couch. "It smells good." It did indeed smell good. The myrrh was heavy, cloying, and under it was the faint but pervasive odour neither Sheritra nor Khaemwaset had been able to identify. Sheritra found her nightmare evaporating, and the sweep of Tbubui's knowing hands was inducing a pleasant langour.

For some time the woman concentrated on Sheritra's back, shoulders and upper arms, then she moved to the buttocks and thighs, up and over the small, firm hills in an hypnotic, slow movement.

Sheritra's flesh began to glow. Her thighs opened as Tbubui's fingers brushed ever closer to the cleft between her legs. She moaned softly, unaware that she did so, and Tbubui murmured, "Am I hurting your Highness?"

"No," Sheritra whispered, eyes still closed, a delicious warmth tingling in her breasts, her belly.

"It is delightful, is it not, to be thus relaxed and stimulated at the same time?" Tbubui commented huskily. "Is your Highness enjoying herself?"

But Sheritra could not answer. She clung to the sheets, mouth parted, waiting and longing for her hostess to finally touch the forbidden place.

For a moment Tbubui's hands left her, but then they returned, the feel of them slightly harder than before, more insistent. Sheritra groaned again. All at once the woman's fingers were sliding between Sheritra's breasts and the sheet. They kneaded, squeezed, rubbed her hardening nipples, and with a start Sheritra opened her eyes and half turned.

Harmin was bending over her naked, and as she watched in drowsy astonishment he grasped her shoulder and hip and turned her onto her back.

"Your mother . . ." she began, but he lowered himself beside her and stopped her mouth with his own.

"I can provide a better treatment than she," he whispered, "and do not worry about Bakmut. She will sleep for another hour."

"You drugged her?" Sheritra whispered back urgently. "But Harmin . . ." He put a hand over her mouth, and the gesture filled her with excitement.

"I want this and so do you," he said. "Do not worry about your servant. She will wake believing she has never slept, and will not be harmed."

I should worry, Sheritra told herself dimly. I should get up and run away. But her hand found his belly and began to trail downwards as though it had a will of its own, and he grunted and buried his face in her neck.

Sheritra saw nothing of Harmin for the rest of the day. "Turn from love as though from disease," her horoscope had said, and yet she had given herself gladly, almost wildly, to the young man who now had her heart, and already she was looking forward to the night, when surely he would come to her and they would make love again. She avoided the family, lying on her couch with hands behind her head and pondering what she had done, her body still responding to Harmin's every move as her mind played back to her their joyful struggle.

Behind the full-blown desire that had taken command of her once again, not long after he had kissed her and glided away, were the moral precepts under which she had been raised. A princess cannot risk giving birth to the child of a commoner. A princess may not confer even the suspicion of godhead on a commoner without permission. And a princess, she thought with a pang of anxiety, can be severely punished for giving up her virginity idly. But it is not as though I had a fling with a sailor behind a bazaar stall, she told herself. Harmin and I are as good as betrothed, and he is the son of a nobleman. There is no going back for me now, no hiding. If I am to enjoy his body again I must take Bakmut into my confidence and probably Father will know all within days.

Tbubui arranged my capitulation, that is clear, and that is what shocks me most of all. Is she not, then, as moral as she says? Or does she regard her son and me as already betrothed? Or is she seeking my support in her own negotiations with my father, a support that now will feel very like coercion?

She abhored what Tbubui had done, and shrank from the image of mother and son calmly discussing her fall over a cup of wine in the garden, as though she were a commodity, something with no will of her own. Well, what will did you exhibit? she asked herself wryly. You wanted him desperately and you knew that the longer you stayed here the more inevitable your downfall would be. You were a silently acquiescent partner in their plan, and you have no one to blame but yourself. I shall have to brazen it out, she thought. Father will have no choice now but to announce our betrothal. Poor Father! Will he care so very much?

"Bakmut!" she called, and the servant rose from the floor where she had been polishing jewellery and came to stand by the couch. "Are you the one who sends reports on my behaviour to my father?"

Bakmut's eyebrows lifted. "No, Highness, I am not," she said firmly.

"Then who is it?" Sheritra said thoughtfully. "Do you know?"

"I am not sure, but I fancy it is the scribe who wanders about with nothing much to do," Bakmut responded tartly. "The sooner we return to the Prince's house the sooner the idle members of your retinue can earn their keep."

Sheritra unlocked her fingers and sat up. "You are my friend, are you not Bakmut?" she began. The girl bowed. "You have been with me since the days when you and I played string games on the nursery floor, and you have always understood me. You would not betray me, would you?"

Bakmut met her eyes squarely. "I am in your exclusive service," she said, "and I am answerable to no one but yourself, Princess. Of course I would not betray you. But along with my loyalty goes the right to tell without equivocation what is on my mind."

Sheritra laughed. "You have always done that!" she retorted. Then she sobered. "I have never been one for many girlish attachments," she went on. "Even though you are only a servant, you are the closest thing to a friend I have. What do you think of Harmin?"

Bakmut pursed her lips. "I know that your Highness cares for him, therefore he must have much worth," she answered.

"But you do not like him."

"Highness, it is not my place to pass judgment on my betters."

"No it is not" Sheritra said impatiently, "but I have asked you, therefore you may respond without fear of my displeasure."

"Very well," Bakmut said coolly. "I do not like him, Highness. He is very beautiful, like your brother Prince Hori, but he lacks the Prince's generosity of heart. I sense a meanness in him. And I think that his mother is a crafty woman with few scruples, even though you now call her your friend."

"Thank you for your honesty, Bakmut," Sheritra commented. "Now I order you to allow Harmin access to this room at any hour he chooses, and when he comes you are to leave us alone."

Bakmut's face registered loud disapproval. "Highness, your best interests are graven on my heart, and this is not good, not good at all," she expostulated. "You are a royal princess. You . . ."

"I know all that," Sheritra cut her off. "I am not asking you, I am giving you a direct command, so that in the future you may not be held responsible for my behaviour. Is that understood?"

"Indeed." Bakmut gave a stiff bow.

"Furthermore, you are to say nothing of the arrangement to any other member of my staff. You are not to lie if you are asked, but neither are you to gossip."

"Highness, I do not gossip. When do I have the time? Your mother the Princess Nubnofret trained us all more strictly than that. And as for the servants of this house gossiping . . ." she laughed harshly. "They are like the walking dead. I despise them."

"Good. So we understand each other."

"I have one more thing I would like to say," Bakmut said stubbornly. "Many of the changes this house has wrought in you, dear Princess, have been marvellous. You have lost the awkwardness and shyness that used to plague you, and the bitterness you used to express to me many times. You bloom like a desert flower. But in the blooming is a hardening somehow. I beg your Highness to forgive me."

"I forgive you," Sheritra said evenly. "Go back to your work, Bakmut." The servant retired and sank to the floor, picking up her rag.

Sheritra left the couch and began to wander about the room,

absently touching the walls, the jumble of cosmetic pots on the dressing table, the roof of her portable shrine to Thoth. There was no going back, she knew. She thought of the self she had been with a kind of amused horror, yet Bakmut was correct. Under the changes was a new core of recklessness that threatened to turn her new-found confidence into a coarse bravado. Well, I deserve this madness, this recklessness, she thought mutinously. I have been a prisoner of my childish self too long. Let me explore these new limits, these new emotions, even if in doing so they drag me past the white winning post, like unruly horses pulling a chariot, and I have to wheel about.

She ate a frugal lunch, still in her own room, but gathering her courage she ventured out for the evening meal, sitting demurely before her tiny table. Sisenet was as polite but uncommunicative as always. Harmin, to her great relief, treated her with his usual gentle deference mixed with teasing warmth, and it was only Tbubui who caused the girl some anxiety. She was unusually animated, her seductive, wily hands darting and weaving over the food, among the flower garlands, keeping time to the harpist's trills or emphasizing some point she was making. Yet Sheritra felt her eyes measuring, perhaps even calculating, and when their glances met she read an insulting complicity in them.

That night Harmin came to her as she had hoped and feared he would, bringing dewy blossoms to stroke across her face and a simple gold amulet for her neck. Bakmut obediently left them alone, and this time Sheritra let her sheath slip to the floor and rose to meet him freely. His lovemaking was slow and tender, his passion a smouldering thing that flamed and died, flamed and died as the hours wore away.

For some days she waited in trepidation for word to come from her father, some cry of outrage that would demand her return home at once, but it did not come. Perhaps the scribe, the spy, was unaware of what was happening between herself and Harmin. Perhaps he was happy here with little to do and was lying to his master. But perhaps, Sheritra thought sadly, Father is simply too wrapped up in his own affairs and does not care any longer what happens to me. That idea gave her a spurt of contradictory anger. I will go home and find out why he is silent, she vowed. I will seek out Hori and upbraid him for ignoring me. But the spell of timelessness Sisenet's house cast over its inmates soaked her too and she dallied, unaware of how the days were slipping by.

Harmin began to invite her out onto the desert in the spurious cool of the evenings to hunt with him. He would take a guard, a runner and the hunting dog kept chained in the servants' compound. Sometimes he walked, but more often he hitched a horse to his chariot and took one of the faint tracks that led towards the dunes.

Sheritra considered refusing his request that she accompany him. Standing in a chariot could be dangerous, and she had never cared for horses. Besides, Pharaoh would not take kindly to news of a granddaughter injured or even killed through foolhardiness.

But Sheritra was like an addict with one drug, Harmin's presence, and she went with him, standing in the lurching vehicle between him and the sheltering guard while the horse struggled to pull them through the cloying sand the yellow dog ran beside them, tongue lolling.

Harmin was always hopeful that he might sight and bring down a lion. More often than not he returned home empty-handed, but on several occasions he made a kill.

Once it was a gazelle that bounded from behind a small pile of rocks and started away, its thin, pretty legs pounding. Harmin, spear raised, rushed after it, sand spurting from his heels, and before Sheritra could recover her breath he had brought it down and was standing gleefully over its twitching body.

His lusty enjoyment of the pastime was both repulsive and mesmerizing. It showed her a side of him she had not suspected, and she found it difficult to reconcile the civilized, well-mannered man who read her inmost thoughts with such ease and the Harmin who could scream obscenities at an escaping prey, or shout with savage triumph as an animal fell with his spear in its shoulder.

On the evenings when he had made a kill his lovemaking was always forceful and passionate, even slightly brutal, as though she too were prey to be stalked, struggled with, gored through. More bewildering to her was her response. Something primitive in her answered his mild savagery with an equal abandonment, so that she looked back on the days of her virginity such a short time ago in amazement. Does my mother know the things that I know? she wondered. Does Father ever demand from her the acts Harmin demands from me? And even if he wants them, does she respond? But the thought of her father brought shame, and she turned from it quickly.

One evening she had arranged to meet Harmin beyond the servants' compound and the wall that separated the small estate from the desert beyond. She was late, having dictated yet another letter to an undeserving Hori, and she decided to cut through the servants' domain directly to the rear gate. The wide yard was empty. Sparrows hopped about the compacted dirt, pecking at the remains of the debris that was carried from the house to be thrown onto the desert over the far wall. She and her guard quickly crossed to the gate, and Sheritra slipped through while he held it open.

She had never before taken notice of the mounds of refuse to either side. It did not lie for long. The purifying heat of the sun soon burned away odours, and the jackals and desert dogs dragged off all that was edible. But today she caught a glint of something unusual lying in the sand and paused to give it a second look. The light was glittering on a broken pen case. Sheritra picked it up. Its jagged edge was snared in a piece of coarse linen that unrolled as she tugged, spilling numerous pieces of smashed pottery at her feet. Something else remained hidden in the folds, and with a grimace of distaste she shook it out and let the cloth flutter onto the garbage.

It was a wax figurine, crudely fashioned but with a certain primeval strength to the square shoulders and thick neck. Both arms had broken off and one foot was missing, but uneasily Sheritra saw that the head had at one time been pierced several times. Tiny holes gritty with sand felt rough under her thumb. Holes also peppered the area of the heart. Rough hieroglyphs had been incised into the soft brown beeswax and she peered closer, trying to decipher them, her unease slowly mounting to a pang of fear. She was the daughter of a magician and she knew what she was seeing. It was a hex doll. Someone had made it, cut it with the name of an enemy, then, muttering spells of evil and malediction, had driven copper pins into the head and heart. The litter under which it had lain had scored and compressed it so that she could not make out the letters. "Do not touch it, Highness!" her guard warned, and at the sound of his voice she tossed it away with a cry.

The pen case was a fine piece of work, delicately ornamented with granulated goldwork and having a cloisonné and blue faience likeness of the ibis-headed Thoth, god of scribes, along its length. Sheritra frowned over it for a moment. Somewhere she had seen it before, but try as she might she could not remember where or when.

In the end she laid it reverently in the sand by the refuse heap, and squatting she fingered through the small, sharp pieces of what had obviously been a large clay pot. She recognized its use also, and she could even make out a few disconnected words of the death spell that would have been inked all over it before a hating hand had brought the hammer down. "His heart . . . burst . . . daggers . . . pain . . . neither day . . . terror . . ."

Someone in this house is harbouring a dreadful hatred, she thought. The spell has been spoken, the ritual performed, and the tools of this unknown person's destruction have been thrown away. I wonder if the curse was successful, or if the victim knew of it and made a counter-incantation in time. She shuddered, then shrieked as a shadow fell across her.

"Highness, what are you doing?"

Sheritra pushed herself to her feet to find Harmin at her back. She indicated her find. "The sun flashing on the pen case caught my attention," she explained. Inwardly she was shaking. "Someone has tried to kill someone else by this, Harmin."

He shrugged. "The servants are always squabbling and carrying grudges and becoming embroiled in petty jealousies," he replied. "They are the same everywhere, are they not? This spell must have originated in their quarters."

"So your servants do have voices?" she half teased, half baited him, and he grunted.

"I suppose they are voluble enough when they are alone. Think no more of it, Princess. Would you like to drive the horse this time?"

She nodded absently and, side by side, they walked to the waiting chariot. But the feeling of familiarity that had stolen over her when she grasped the pen case would not leave her. It returned often in the days that followed, to taunt her with a memory just out of reach. Sometimes she wondered if it had been Sisenet himself, a diligent scholar, who had made the wax figure. Sometimes she considered Tbubui, a dabbler in medicine and perhaps in magic as well, but she could not imagine either of them closeted in the darkness coercing demons to do their will.

Tbubui no longer came to the bath house in the mornings to examine the state of the Princess's skin. I suppose the visits have served their purpose, Sheritra thought, but the knowledge did not distress her. She felt as though she and Harmin had already signed a marriage contract, that by some strange alchemy she could not remember the occasion, but they were already man and wife, and she was a permanent and legitimate member of the household.

They still spend the mornings together, often crossing the river and strolling the choked streets of Memphis, a pastime they had not undertaken before Harmin became Sheritra's lover. The crowds, the noise, even the smells, increasingly bewildered the girl, and she was always relieved to step onto the barge and be poled back to the safety and quiet of the isolated house.

She was in Tbubui's room one day, sitting at the vanity table in a loose lounging robe, her face already painted but her long hair not yet dressed. She and Tbubui were examining Tbubui's jewellery as though they were sisters, or their station in Egypt's social hierarchy was similar. Sometimes this irritated Sheritra, but she was too much in awe of the mentor who had become her friend to protest and risk insulting her. The collection was one Sheritra admired, for it contained many heavy, simple pieces of ancient craftsmanship of a kind now difficult to obtain.

"My mother was very traditional in her tastes," Tbubui was explaining as Sheritra's fingers sifted through the rings, anklets, amulets and pectorals. "She had many pieces that belonged to her ancestors and she regarded them as sacred to the family, passed down to each succeeding generation. I also value them as such. My husband gave me lovely things, but I wear my mother's jewellery almost every day." She draped a silver pendant with an onyx Eye of Horus around Sheritra's neck. "This is a light and airy thing that looks very well on you, Highness," she said approvingly. "Also it is a powerful protection against evil. Do you like it?"

Sheritra was about to express her delight when her eye caught the glow of turquoise right at the bottom of the ebony chest. Tbubui owned much turquoise, but something about the shape of the thing she was looking at caught Sheritra's fancy, and she pushed past the other trinkets and fished it out. Tbubui's hands had gone still on her shoulders. The girl held up a gold-and-turquoise earring. It swung gently in her fingers, and she bit her lip as she peered at it, then she exclaimed, "Tbubui, this is the earring Hori found in the tunnel leading out of the tomb! I would know it anywhere!" Her hand closed over it and she turned on the stool. "What are you doing with it? Oh tell me that Hori did not desecrate that woman's resting place by giving it to you!"

"Calm yourself, Highness," Tbubui said, smiling. "Of course your brother would not do such a thing. He is much too honest."

"But he is in love with you!" Sheritra blurted. "His judgment could have deserted him. Love makes us do questionable things sometimes . . ." Her voice trailed away, and for the first time in weeks she blushed. "I know you are to marry my father," she finished lamely. "Forgive my tactlessness, Tbubui."

"You are forgiven, dear Sheritra," Tbubui rejoined lightly. "I am aware of Hori's infatuation with me. I have been kind to him, do not fear, and it will pass. As for the earring . . ." She reached down and deftly removed the piece from Sheritra's grip. "Hori showed me the original, and loving turquoise as I do I was determined to have it copied. I drew its likeness as soon as Hori left, and my favourite jeweller made up a pair for me."

"Oh." Sheritra was covered with confusion. "But where is its mate?"

Tbubui sighed. "I have lost it. The fastening was not as secure as it should have been, but I did not want to wait for it to be fixed. I was too happy wearing it. Before I could bring myself to part with it, it parted from me. The servants have scoured the house and grounds, even the skiff and the barge, but it must have fallen from my ear somewhere in the city. One day I will have another one made." She dropped the earring carelessly back into the chest. "Would your Highness like spiced wine? A snack?"

Tbubui's explanation had been perfectly reasonable, but something in Sheritra's intuition warned her that she had not heard the truth. At one time Hori would not have dreamed of desecrating a tomb by giving away someone else's property, but that had been a free, honourable young man. Was the moody, irritable Hori in the throes of an unreturned love capable in fact of doing such a thing? Sheritra thought it possible. It took time, too, for a well-crafted piece of jewellery to be made, and the one Sheritra had dangled did not even seem new. The goldwork was finely scratched and pitted here and there. It was not an unusual practice for a craftsman to deliberately age a piece of furniture or jewellery, but Tbubui's turquoise had glowed with the milky greenness of genuine antiquity, and the gold had been dark, spidered through with purple. It was entirely possible that Tbubui had used a turquoise already in her possession to form a pear-shaped stone like the original. It was also possible that her jeweller was able to take the extra time to reproduce Mittanni's purple gold, but Sheritra had the uneasy feeling that none of these speculations were correct. Hori had pressed the beautiful thing into the hands of the woman he burned for and she had accepted it.

Sheritra made another uncomfortable mental connection. The discarded paraphernalia of the spell—could it have been conjured by Tbubui in an effort to avert the jealous anger of a dead woman? Yet it was the remains of a cursing spell, I am sure, Sheritra told herself as she lay sleepless on her couch or walked the garden or sat while Bakmut painted the soles of her feet with henna. One does not avert the rage of an ancient ka by insulting it yet again. I must go home for a day or two. I cannot put it off any longer.

She told Harmin that night as they lay tumbled in each other's arms, and he nuzzled her cheek, saying, "I will let you go, providing you promise to come back in two days. You bring me hunting luck, Little Sun, and besides, you have made this house a happy place." Later Tbubui quickly agreed that Sheritra's decision was a wise one. "I can understand your worry," she said sympathetically. "Scold that brother of yours for ignoring us both, and invite him for dinner when you return. Give my greetings to your illustrious mother."

Sheritra had the few things she would need packed and said a casual farewell to Harmin and his mother. There was no need for formal leave-taking. She intended to return to the place she now considered her real home on the following afternoon.

But as she left the house and set off slowly towards the water-steps in the pale, early sunlight, a mixture of depression and reluctance fell heavily on her. She no longer carried reality with her wherever she went. Its immediacy, its focus, seemed to pale and blur the more distance she put between herself and the low, white house baking in its shield of silence. She moved up the ramp into the barge with the odd conviction that neither the outside world nor she herself had any substance.

Bakmut was clearly jubilant. Even the guards seemed to move and speak with a brisk sparkle. They are all happy but me, Sheritra thought resentfully as the vessel glided away from the bank. Well, they will not be happy for long because no matter what happens I am ordering them all back with me tomorrow. She stifled an urge to snap at Bakmut who was humming under her breath, and she stared ahead at the unfolding city with a glum determination.

Her father's watersteps looked huge and new to her as the barge bumped them and the ramp was run out. The tethering poles sunk in the Nile flew spotless flags of blue and white, the imperial colours. The steps themselves, scoured daily of every stain, seemed to mount dazzlingly to infinity and Sheritra breasted them in a kind of horror. At the top, the household guards saluted her one by one and several servants, impeccably attired, as spotless as the watersteps, came hurrying to reverence her. One of them, a herald, ran towards the house to announce her. A parasol was quickly unfolded and an escort formed.

Sheritra started along the paved path that seemed as wide as a city street. Tamed shrubs and weedless beds of exotic blooms passed slowly by on either side. Among them three gardeners laboured, bare backs to the sky. The multicoloured pillars of the front entrance came into view, each sheltering a watchful soldier, and beyond them the customary herald, steward and scribe sat just outside the double doors in the event of visitors. Sheritra nodded to their obeisance as she passed on her way to the rear.

Now the sound of the fountain assaulted her ears, and the cultivated laughter of female body servants. Was it always like this? she wondered dazedly. Like a miniature palace, always murmurous, always so opulent? Was I always treated with so much distant respect, and simply took it for granted?

But she did not have the time to explore her bewilderment, for Ib was coming, almost running, his face solemn. She stopped and waited and he slowed, bowed from the waist with arms outstretched, his whole body registering apprehension.

"Ib?" she said.

He straightened. Why, he is not so very old after all, Sheritra thought in amazement, staring into his square, beautifully painted face framed by the short black wig. And he has a good body, compact, muscular. He is an attractive man. "Highness, it is remarkable that you should choose to return home today," he replied. "Your father the Prince was just issuing instructions for your presence."

"Why?" she said sharply. "What is it?"

"I think he had better tell you himself," the steward said apologetically. "He is with your mother. I will escort you."

At his brusque command her retinue fell away and she, Bakmut and the parasol-bearer went on, through the capacious garden, past the fountain and the blue fish-pond, between the clustering sycamores, to the rear entrance. From there it was a short distance to Nubnofret's quarters and Sheritra, her anxiety rising, fought against the sense of foreignness that threatened to bring her to a faltering halt.

Ib waved Bakmut to one of the stools in the passage and pushed through the doors. Sheritra heard his voice announcing her, then went past him. The doors were firmly closed behind her. Khaemwaset held out a hand and she took it. Her mother was sitting on the couch. She barely acknowledged Sheritra's entrance and the girl turned to her father. He gave her a perfunctory kiss.

"What is going on?" she asked, aware of the slight echo of her voice in the high, dusky ceiling, the gleam of the blue-and-white tiles stretching away beneath her feet, the cluster of Nubnofret's female attendants far away in one corner. Why, this room is huge, she thought. We are dwarves in it.

"Ramses' Chief Herald arrived early this morning," Khaemwaset was saying. "Your grandmother died five days ago." He did not mention the other letters, angry letters, that Ramses' herald had brought. "We are now in mourning, Little Sun."

Don't call me that! she thought indignantly. But her second thought filled her with panic. Mourning. Seventy days imprisoned here, away from Harmin, away from Tbubui, no desert sunsets feeding honeyed dates to the yellow dog, no board games played lazily under the palms, no Harmin in my bed. A return to

Mother's nagging, to the constant feeling of inadequacy that used to pursue me.

Then she had the grace to feel ashamed. Grandmother is dead. She was always patient and kindly towards me, and my first reaction on hearing of her death is annoyance. I am selfish.

"Oh Father, how terrible," she said, "but a good thing also. Astnofert was suffering so much, for so long, was she not? Now she is with the gods and at peace. Will we go to Thebes for the funeral?"

"Of course." The matter-of-fact voice was Nubnofret's. "And I must confess, Sheritra, that the prospect of a trip anywhere, for any reason, fills me with delight. Are you enjoying your stay with Tbubui?"

Her mother's remarks were so brittle that Sheritra turned to her, alarmed. "Yes, more than I can say," she answered, and Nubnofret lifted a blank face.

"Good," she said indifferently. "I will go and order your rooms prepared for you." She got up and glided out. Once more the doors thudded shut.

"Is Mother ill?" Sheritra enquired, and at that Khaemwaset's shoulders slumped. He sighed.

"I do not think so, but she is deeply outraged. The truth is, Sheritra . . ." he hesitated. "I have decided to take a second wife, and your mother is not pleased, although of course it is within my rights. I have signed a contract with Tbubui." He searched her eyes anxiously. "I had not meant to tell you so abruptly. I am sorry. Are you surprised?"

"No," she replied, and all at once she wanted very much to sit down. "From the first moment you saw her, when we were together on the litters, do you remember, Father? I had a suspicion it would come to this." She decided not to tell him that she knew about the contract already. It did not matter anyway. "Give Mother time to become used to the idea and she will accept Tbubui," she went on. "Mother is after all a princess, and will do her duty."

"I had hoped for more than her duty," Khaemwaset said hotly. "I wanted her to befriend Tbubui, usher her into the family warmly. I cannot pierce the cold, correct mood that has held her since I gave her the news. Well, she will have plenty of time to get used to the idea."

"Why?" Sheritra allowed herself to sink onto the couch.

Khaemwaset folded his arms and began to pace. "I sent Penbuy to Koptos to gather information on Tbubui's family," he said. "It has to do with a clause in the contract. I need not explain. I have been struck two blows today, Little Sun. Not only has my mother died, but my friend Penbuy also."

"What?" Sheritra was fighting to keep up with such sudden developments after weeks of placid predictability. "Old Penbuy? How did he die?"

"Not so old," her father replied with grim joviality. "Penbuy was my age. He did not want to go to Koptos at this time of the year but I sent him anyway. It was his duty to go." She opened her mouth but he held up a hand to forestall her. "The herald who came north with the news said that Penbuy fell ill shortly after he arrived in the town. He complained of pains in his head and shortness of breath, but he kept working in the library attached to the temple there. One day he walked out, took four steps into the sunlight and collapsed. He was dead by the time his assistant reached him."

Something ominous stalked along Sheritra's spine, as though her father had been pronouncing some grave and portentous edict that would change her fate forever, instead of quietly relating the events leading up the death of his servant and friend. "It was not your fault, Father," she said gently, sensing his guilt. "Penbuy was doing his duty as you said. It was his time. Death would have found him whether he had been there or here at home." But is that true? she asked herself even as the words left her mouth. Oh, is it true? And that cold, nameless thing kept padding up and down her back on soft, repellent feet.

"I suppose so," Khaemwaset said slowly. "I will miss him. He is, of course, being beautified in Koptos, and then his body will be returned to Memphis for burial. We are in mourning for two people, Sheritra."

I wish I had not come here, Sheritra thought passionately. Perhaps if the news had come to me in Sisenet's house I would have insisted on mourning there. I would have abstained from making love, I would have prayed, I would have sacrificed for the kas of my grandmother and poor Penbuy . . . "Father, where is Hori?" she asked. "I want to see him and then I want to go to my rooms and absorb all this."

Khaemwaset smiled crookedly, painfully. "It has been a shock for you, hasn't it? And I think Hori will be another shock. He is not himself at all, Sheritra. No one seems to know why. He avoids us as much as he can, even Antef. But perhaps he will talk to you."

Indeed he will talk to me, Sheritra thought grimly, if I have to call the guards and have him held down until he does so. What a homecoming! "Does he know about the marriage contract?" she asked, rising.

Khaemwaset looked sheepish. "Not yet. A hundred times I have been on the point of speaking of it to him and a hundred times I have changed my mind. He has become so unapproachable."

She smiled at him faintly. "Would you like me to do it for you?" She had fought to keep the sudden scorn she felt from tinging her words. What is happening to you, Father? she wondered. This expression of shame, of hesitation, might befit a servant, not a pharaoh's son who has been used to giving commands and making decisions almost since his birth. It was as though something vital in him, something strong and noble, had softened like overripe fruit. What are you afraid of? she wanted to shout. Where is your nerve? It was said that an obsequious servant made a cruel master, and looking into her father's embarrassed face she had a blinding urge to slap it. She had never felt lonelier.

"Thank you," he replied with relief. "You are closer to him than I, and his temper is so uncertain that I have dreaded broaching the subject. If you pave the way I can then sit down with him and try to explain."

"Surely no explanation is necessary," she said stiffly. "There have been few princes with only a single wife, Father. You are an exception, a curiosity. We have been living an abnormal family life here in Memphis, sufficient only unto ourselves. Perhaps Mother, Hori and I have grown arrogant."

He blinked, then scrutinized her keenly. "You have changed," he said slowly. "Not only do you look different, your eyes are surer and colder."

But I am not cold, she thought as she inclined her head and turned, walking to the door. I am hot, dear Father, oh how hot, and nothing, not Grandmother's death, not the splintering apart of our former closeness, can begin to subdue these invisible flames. You are thin and insubstantial, all of you, beside the silky feel of Harmin's skin under my questing fingers, the languorous glance of his dark eyes as he bends over me. Her hands curled into fists as she paced the corridor towards Hori's quarters, and she was oblivious of the patient soldiers' curious stares. She was enraged.

Chapter 14

'Beware of a woman from strange parts,
whose city is not known . . .
She is as the eddy in deep water,
the depth of which is unknown.'

On the following morning Khaemwaset, walking into his office to begin the correspondence for the day, came face to face with Penbuy's son, Ptah-Seankh. The young man's features were so like his father's that Khaemwaset's heart turned over, but then he recognized the build as slightly thinner and taller, the eyes as more close-set, though with Penbuy's watchful, almost judgmental clarity, the mouth a little less forgiving. Ptah-Seankh's eyelids were swollen and his skin sallow. He had obviously been weeping over his father, but Khaemwaset admired the determination and control that had brought him here, palette in hand and linen freshly starched, to continue the tradition of duty and loyalty that had begun many generations ago. At Khaemwaset's approach, Ptah-Seankh knelt and prostrated himself.

"Rise," Khaemwaset said kindly. The young man came to his feet with a fluid grace, then went to the floor again, this time in the pose of a working scribe. Khaemwaset took a chair, all at once overcome with sympathy.

"Ptah-Seankh, I loved your father and I grieve for him as you do," he said thickly. "You need not feel that you must be here ready to work when your heart is breaking. Go home and return when you are able."

Ptah-Seankh raised a stubborn face. "My father served you long and faithfully," he said, "and in the way of my family, I have been trained from my earliest years to take his place as your scribe when he died. Now he prepares for his last journey, and he would think less of me if, even at this time, I did not put my duty to you before any personal consideration. Are you ready to work, Highness?"

"No," Khaemwaset said slowly. "No, I think not. My temporary scribe is adequate for the time being. Ptah-Seankh, I want you to go and bring your father's body back to Memphis at the end of the seventy days. I will endow his tomb with gold so that priests will pray for him every day and offerings may be made on his behalf. I will also arrange his funeral with your mother so that your mind may be at rest and on other things, because I have a task for you." He learned forward and his eyes met the young man's. They held his own without wavering. "Your father was researching the line of descent of a woman I plan to marry," he explained. "Her lineage is in Koptos. Penbuy was unable to do more than begin the task and he left no records. I want you to go to Koptos and complete the investigation before escorting your father home."

"I shall be honoured, Prince," Ptah-Seankh replied with a wan smile, "and I am grateful for your tact and discretion. But I shall need to know everything about this person before I leave."

Khaemwaset laughed. The young man's response was painful but curiously healing. "You are indeed Penbuy's son!" he exclaimed. "You speak as you think, and will doubtless argue with me over many matters in the course of our relationship. Very well. See to your mother's welfare before you leave. That will give me time to explain exactly what you are to do and to draft letters of introduction for you to the dignitaries of Koptos. Here." He took up a piece of papyrus that he had already dictated. Holding a sliver of wax over the candle always burning for just such a purpose, he dribbled some onto the scroll and pressed his seal ring into it, then he handed it to Ptah-Seankh. "You are now officially in my service," he said. "Discuss anything you need with my steward, Ib. And now, go home, Ptah-Seankh. Grieve in peace today."

Ptah-Seankh's throat worked. This time he came to his feet clumsily, bowed, and hurried out, but not before Khaemwaset had seen the tears gleaming in his eyes.

There was no longer any reason to remain in the house. Khaemwaset ordered out a litter, and taking Ib and Amek he stepped into his skiff for the short ride to Tbubui's house. He had not seen Sisenet since his shameful loss of control on the day the scroll was translated, and dreaded having to try and rationalize it to the supremely self-assured man, but there was no sign of either Sisenet or his nephew as the litter-bearers padded along the narrow, winding track to the house.

It appeared deserted, as usual, the quality of its deep quiet like a lullaby sung to a fretting child. Khaemwaset, alighting and approaching the open door to the entrance hall, was suddenly and disturbingly reminded of the charm his nurse used to chant softly each night by his couch to prevent the terrible night demon, She-with-her-face-turned-backward, from flowing into the room and stealing away his breath. He would lie half-terrified, half-fascinated, his eyes fixed trustingly on the nurse's face as she swayed to the words, while the darkness in the awesomely large chamber seemed to ripple and change shape just outside the periphery of his vision. "May she flow away, she who comes in the darkness, who enters in furtively with her nose behind her, her face turned backward, failing in that for which she came. Hast thou come to kiss this child? I will not let thee kiss him! Hast thou come to injure him? I will not let thee injure him! Hast thou come to take him away? I will not let thee take him away from me!" My mother loved me with the same fierce devotion as that old nurse, he thought with genuine remorse. Her duties as queen never kept her from my side if I was ill or afraid. Yet when she needed me I was not there. In her last hours my place beside her bed was empty. I have failed her. Failed my father also, for I have abused the trust he placed in me to be his eyes and ears in government. The official missives lie piled on my desk like river flotsam because I do not recognize myself anymore. The man who would have viewed the shame of these betrayals with horror is dead, slain by the poison of a woman in his veins.

With a grimace he spoke to the black-skinned servant who had risen from the pleasant dimness and as silently glided away. Then Tbubui was coming swiftly across the plain white tiling of the floor, her pretty face solemn, her arms outstretched. Taking his hands she gazed intently into his face.

"Dear Khaemwaset," she said. "I received a message from Sheritra last night, asking that her belongings be returned home and explaining why. You have suffered a double loss. I am so sorry."

Khaemwaset melted under her concern. Drawing her to him he held her slim, tight body against his own and laid his chin on the smooth top of her head. He was aware that she wore no perfume today and the warm, simple odour of her hair filled his nostrils. He felt himself begin to relax, an internal loosening that reminded him of how tense he had been.

"I confess that my mother's death touches me less deeply than the loss of Penbuy," he murmured. "We all knew that she was dying, and for her the prospect was a welcome one. But Penbuy had barely finished building his tomb on the edge of the Memphis necropolis. He was very proud of its decorations."

"It is no wonder that your servants are devoted to you," she replied, her voice muffled in his neck. "Come, dear brother. In my room there is wine, and I will massage sweet oils into your shoulders. I can feel how distressed you are, by the state of the muscles in your back." At her words he was immediately aware of her touch on his spine, one hand between his shoulder-blades, one on the small of his back just above the belt of his kilt, and deliriously he imagined them sliding downward, cupping his buttocks, pressing them gently . . .

"Is Sisenet here?" he asked drowsily.

She disengaged and smiled up at him. "No. My brother and Harmin have taken a tent and gone out onto the desert to hunt for three days. They left at dawn. Harmin was very distressed that Sheritra would not be returning until the period of mourning for her grandmother is over." Taking him by the hand she began to lead him to the rear of the room and the windy passage beyond.

"We must all go to Thebes for her funeral," Khaemwaset said, glancing at the glaring square of hot light at the end of the corridor before she stood aside to let him enter her bedchamber. "Please come with us, Tbubui. In seventy days you will surely be living on my estate. I want my father to meet you, and a journey such as that would give you and Nubnofret a chance to become better acquainted. The investigative work Penbuy began at Koptos will have been completed and you will face Ramses as my wife. Because of the mourning period our contract cannot be ratified until after the funeral, but that can be done in Pi-Ramses. Will you come?"

He had crossed to the centre of the sparsely furnished room and was watching her as she closed the door and swung to face him. He noticed then that she was wearing a tight and transparent white linen sheath but no sandals or jewellery. He wondered if it was the same sheath she had been wearing the first time he had glimpsed her, and at the thought he was choked with sudden desire.

"But how will the work at Koptos be completed now that Penbuy is dead?" she asked anxiously. "Had he made much progress, Highness? Will our marriage be postponed because of it?" She ran to him lightly like a little girl. "Oh I am so selfish! I do not want to wait any longer than necessary to belong to you!"

He was gratified by her eagerness. "Penbuy's son Ptah-Seankh will leave for Koptos in a few days and will take over his father's task. He will have completed it, I am sure, before bringing Penbuy's body back to Memphis. But I do not intend to wait until then to bring you home, Tbubui. A suite has been prepared for you in the concubines' house, and your own rooms are even now rising from the lamentable chaos and dirt of construction on the north end of the house. I am, of course, in mourning, but you may take up residence as soon as you wish."

Her eyes lit up, then she frowned. "No, Khaemwaset," she said. "I will not risk tempting you to commit a sacrilege by celebrating such a joyous moment while you are in mourning. I will wait until you return from Thebes, but I intend to visit Nubnofret this very week and assure her that I understand the position of Second Wife very well."

"You will not come south with us?' Khaemwaset could not contemplate the prospect of the miles that would stretch between them if he was forced to go without her, and he reached out, pulling her roughly against him.

"No, I will not," she said firmly. "It would not be seemly. We have many years ahead of us, dear one. What are a few more weeks? Come. Let me pour you wine."

But he would not let her go. "I do not need wine," he whispered against her ear. "Nor do I need massage. The oil of lovemaking will loosen my muscles, Tbubui. Let us while away the afternoon ruining the neatness of the couch your servant has so carefully made."

She did not comment, and he pulled her towards the dusky expanse of sheets, his hands already tugging at the straps that held up the sheath, which sweat had pasted to her stomach and thighs. When he rolled them past her wrists she raised her arms with a strangled sound, half laugh and half sigh, then leaned towards him, cupping the full breasts he had exposed.

All moderation fled. Jerking away her hands he forced them both between his legs, under his kilt, to where his penis was already fully engorged, and as she began to stroke it his mouth found her nipple. Together they collapsed upon the couch. She was groaning softly, eyes closed, body lifting to his tongue, his touch, a low sound that sharpened his need even further. A dream, he thought incoherently as her hand tightened on him. An orchard . . . a woman behind a tree . . . was she beckoning? And I woke full of desire, full of sap, so painful, so glorious . . . He lifted his head to kiss her, exploring her yielding mouth, then he stopped to survey her face. "I love you, Tbubui," he whispered. "You are my sister, my disease, the longing of my heart, the fruit for which my body yearns. I love you."

She murmured something in return, but so low, and through lips so slack with passion, that he could not make out what she had said. Then all at once her black eyes opened wide and she began to smile. "Make love to me, Mighty Bull," she said aloud. The title belonged to every pharaoh, it was not Khaemwaset's to carry, but the words, heavy with sexual meaning, with virility and power, almost caused him to ejaculate immediately. Suddenly the sight of the lazy, all-knowing smile, the exquisite face below him now flushed with her own need, was more than he could bear.

With an oath he grasped her by the hips and flung her over onto her stomach, entering her from the rear with unthinking brutality. His action unleashed a torrent of savagery in him and he completed the act like a rape, pounding into her again and again and cursing aloud with each stroke.

When he came to himself he was lying beside her, panting, the sweat running from his body to stain the purity of her now rumpled sheets. She was propped on one elbow, still smiling at him but faintly, bemusedly. He did not apologize for his actions. "I shall return and make love to you often," he said curtly, remembering as he spoke that he had just broken the proscriptions of mourning. "Will you like that, Tbubui?"

"Yes," she replied, and that was all, but the word acted on him like a drug and instantly he wanted her again. He knew that he had not stopped wanting her even during his moment of release, that the act had not assuaged the fever of desire burning and scouring away all else within him. It was as though for months he had been drinking an aphrodisiac that clouded his mind while sharpening his appetite for this woman, this woman, until possessing her had nothing to do with the clamorous demands of his body. Mighty Bull, he thought, licked by the flames of her black hair plastered in wet tendrils on her neck, the rivulet of sweat inching into her cleavage, her bitten, swollen mouth, Mighty Bull, Mighty Bull, and a dim presentiment of his fate came to him so that he groaned aloud and closed his eyes. She neither spoke nor moved, and presently he rolled from the couch, wound his linen around his waist and left her.

It took Sheritra a long time to find her brother. She searched the house and grounds, growing hotter and more irritated. She wanted to sit quietly under a tree and absorb the news of her disappointment while a servant ran after him, but did not want Hori to feel that he had been summoned.

At last she had an idea. Ordering Bakmut back to her rooms she set off for the watersteps. This time she skirted the northern end of the house, picking her way through the building debris, to her new and alarming, when she rounded a corner and almost tripped over a pile of sun-dried bricks. The shape of the addition could be clearly seen. Her father's architect stood under a canopy in the middle of what had once been the spacious and peaceful north garden, a table before him, his head bent over his blueprints. Beside him Sheritra recognized several master craftsmen who waited for him to speak.

A moment for pure hatred for Tbubui shook Sheritra as she paused, hand raised against the glare, surveying the dismal mess, but she waved the feeling off with a rueful smile and a shake of the head. The men under the canopy sensed her passing and looked up, bowing to her, but she ignored them and was soon walking along the shrub-lined path to the watersteps.

Just before she reached them she veered, pushing through the stiff, summer-withered twigs and into the tangled bushes and small trees of the riverbank. They gave way to rushes and soggy ground but she went on, for a little farther, out of sight of both the steps and the river, was a clear space where she and Hori used to crouch together to watch the arrivals and departures of guests, or to while away lazy afternoons out of reach of their guards and nurses. Neither she nor Hori had used the place for years but she was certain that it had not become overgrown, and that he would be there, arms about his raised knees, eyes on the patches of river to be glimpsed through the sheltering reeds.

Sure enough, as she fought her way forward she saw a flicker of white. In another moment she was lowering herself beside him. He was sitting on a mat, a jug of beer and a half-eaten slice of black bread smeared with butter beside him. Ants were already at work on the bread but Hori obviously had not noticed. He glanced at Sheritra as she squatted, and she was hard pressed to still her shocked reaction at the sight of him. He was gaunt, with grooves of deep-violet shadow under his eyes. His hair was unkempt, his linen filthy. "Hori," she blurted unthinkingly. "Haven't you bathed today?"

"Welcome home, Sheritra," he said mockingly. "I presume you've been told the news. And no, I have not bathed today. I was out all night partying at the house of Huy's son. I crept into the kitchens for some bread and beer and brought them here. I think I went to sleep." He smiled then, a wan, quick quirk of the lips that to Sheritra was somehow more ghoulish than if he had scowled at her. "I suppose I should go into the house and have someone clean me up. I must look terrible." He passed a weary hand across his face.

"How did you know about Grandmother and Penbuy?" she asked curiously.

"I heard a couple of the kitchen servants gossiping as I grabbed my victuals. Is that why you came home?"

Tentatively she touched his knee. "No. I was anxious about you, Hori, and angry that you had not come to see me or sent me any word." She hesitated, then went on. "Also there are certain things I must discuss with you. I am sorry to see you in such anguish. I love you."

Clumsily he put an arm around her shoulders and hugged her tightly, then he withdrew. "I love you too," he responded, a tremor in his voice. "I hate myself for this cowardly giving in, Sheritra, this relinquishing of everything strong in myself, but somehow I cannot help it. I am tortured by thoughts of Tbubui every waking moment. The times I have spent with her are repeated over and over in my mind with the most horrible clarity. I have never been so exquisitely hurt in all my life."

"Do you talk to Antef?"

He flinched away from her. "No. I have betrayed our friendship. Antef is also hurt and bewildered, and I carry guilt for that on top of everything else. But Antef would not understand and could offer me no comfort, I know. And talking to Father is out of the question."

Oh Hori, she thought, shrinking from the thing she must tell him. How right you are! "Do you know why Father is having an addition built on the house?" she asked after a moment, and he shook his head.

"No one has told me and I have not asked," he said. "You don't know what it is like, Sheritra. I don't care why the house is being expanded. I simply don't *care*. I am consumed by Tbubui and nothing else has any reality at all."

Sheritra shivered. She knew his feeling well. "The addition is for Tbubui," she said gently, "He is going to marry her. In fact, they have already signed the contract. Penbuy was in Koptos investigating her family when he died."

He made a mewling sound, like a blind kitten pawing for its mother, but he did not move. His face was turned to the river where a fishing boat, its white triangular sail flapping idly in the slight noon breeze, was slowly tacking by. No stirring of air, however, could penetrate the thick river growth that surrounded the pair, and the view of the Nile from the clearing was crisscrossed by twisted branches and stiffly upright reeds. Sheritra brushed at a fly that was hovering to seek the salt around her eyes. She wanted to speak, to have wise and sympathetic things to say, but the enormity of Hori's involvement and the bleakness of his future overwhelmed her and she remained silent. His voice, when it came, startled her.

"No wonder she would have nothing to do with me," he croaked. "Why consider a stripling son when you can have the father, wealthy, influential, handsome? Knowing how I felt about her, she should have told me. She should have told me!" Sheritra was helpless against the bitterness in his voice. "I feel like a fool," he went on in a low tone. "A stupid, ignorant, childish fool. How she must be laughing at me!"

"No!" Sheritra managed. "She would not do that. And how could she say anything to you, Hori, when at the time she was not sure of Father's feelings? It would have been wrong."

"I suppose so," he agreed grudgingly. "But why are you telling me, Little Sun? Did Father lack the guts to do so?"

Sheritra thought of Khaemwaset's embarrassed, sheepish face, his pathetic eagerness when she offered to break the news to Hori. "Yes," she answered, "but not because he suspects that you love her also. He is so embroiled in his own emotion that I don't think he could see past it if he tried. He has always been such a strong, quiet, predictable man, Hori, in control of himself and satisfied with his life. He has been violently disrupted, and is ashamed of it."

Now Hori turned to study her. Some of the pain went out of his eyes. "You have changed," he said softly. "I hear a new wisdom in you, Sheritra, a knowledge of others that was not there before. You have grown."

Sheritra took a deep breath and felt the old, familiar flush of colour begin to seep up her neck. "I have been making love with Harmin," she said frankly, and waited for a reaction, but there was none. Hori continued to examine her. "I know what you are going through, dear brother, because the same wound plagues me. Yet I am more fortunate. I have gained the object of my desire."

"You are indeed more fortunate," he said slowly, "and that fortune will increase with father's m . . . marriage." He stumbled on the words, and then recovered. "With Tbubui in residence here, Harmin will either move in also or be a constant visitor. Whereas I . . ." He swallowed, then burst out, "Forgive me, Sheritra! I am brimming with a most distasteful self-pity." Then suddenly, shockingly, he was crying, loud, harsh sobs made more agonizing by his efforts to subdue them.

Sheritra knelt and pulled his head down onto her breast, not saying anything, her eyes travelling the surrounding growth, the broken glimpses of the river, the parade of ants still swarming over the forgotten bread and streaming away into the sand. Presently Hori sat back, wiping his face on his dirty and wilted kilt. "I feel better," he said. "We always did help each other, didn't we, Sheritra? Forgive me for ignoring you lately, for not even sending a herald to inquire how you were."

"It doesn't matter," she replied. "Hori, what will you do now?"

He shrugged. "I don't know. To stay here with her actually in the house would be more than I could bear. Perhaps I will consider taking up residence with Grandfather at Pi-Ramses and applying for some government post. I am, after all, a prince of the blood." He shot her an impish grin that was a pale copy of his former gentle humour, but nevertheless filled her with relief. "Or I may decide to become a full-time priest of Ptah instead of fulfilling my duty to the god for only three months out of the year."

"Please, Hori," she begged, "Make no irrevocable decisions just yet, no matter how anguished you are!"

"Little Sun," he replied, stroking her hair. "I will wait, as I said, but I will not prolong my pain."

They fell silent. Sheritra almost drowsed. Reaction from the events of the morning was setting in and she thought of her couch with longing. But before she could sleep there was the matter of the earring, a prick of unease under everything else. Hori had unfolded and was lying back, his hands behind his head, his ankles crossed. She shifted so that she was looking down on him.

"Hori, do you remember the earring you found in the tunnel leading out of the tomb?" she began. He nodded. "You showed it to Tbubui, didn't you?"

A shadow passed over his face and he sighed. "What a day that was!" he said. "She was very taken with it."

"I found one exactly like it in her jewel box. When I asked her about it she said that she had had the one you showed her copied as a pair, and then lost one of them. But . . ." She bit her lip and looked away, and he finished for her with his usual shrewdness.

"But you were afraid that she was lying, that in my passion I had lost all sense and had given her the original." Sheritra blinked in assent. "Well, I certainly did no such thing," Hori protested. "I may be besotted, but I am not insane enough to commit that sacrilege."

"Oh." Sheritra was only partially mollified. "What happened to it, then? Do you still have it?"

He did not answer directly. "Father has closed the tomb," he said, but she leaned over him urgently.

"Hori! Answer me! You still have it, don't you?"

"Yes!" he said loudly, sitting up in one sharp movement. "Yes I do. I am going to lay it on Ptah's altar as an apology for keeping it, but Sheritra, it reminds me so strongly of Tbubui that I cannot part with it yet. It is not stealing, it is polite borrowing. Ptah will tell the ka of the woman that I meant no harm."

"The only harm you are doing is to yourself, torturing yourself every time you look at it," she said vehemently. "Well, at least you had the good sense not to hand it over to Tbubui. You know, Hori, I could have sworn the one I picked out of her jewel box was the original. Ah well." She rubbed the sand from the elbow she had been resting on and flicked an ant from her calf. "Did you say that Father has closed the tomb already? Why? Was the work finished?"

"No."

He began to talk of Sisenet's visit, the translating of the scroll and Khaemwaset's almost insane reaction to it, and as he spoke, his voice falling flat and almost inflectionless in the confined space, Sheritra felt a great foreboding begin to darken the day.

"Father believed it was the Scroll of Thoth?" she interrupted him. "And Sisenet ridiculed the idea and convinced him otherwise?"

He nodded and finished the story. "And that was it. The tomb has been sealed, rubble piled to fill in the stair and a huge rock rolled over the site. Father agrees with Sisenet that such a thing can only exist in legends. He must be just a trifle disappointed, seeing he has carried the dream of finding it for many years."

Sheritra's foreboding was coalescing into a pulse of disquiet. She felt it as an amorphous mass that was rapidly acquiring a shape, as yet unrecognizable but one that might turn disquiet into black fear at any moment. "Hori, I haven't told you everything," she said. "Someone in Sisenet's house conjured a death curse." His head jerked around, and under his keen scrutiny her own glance dropped. "I feel silly even mentioning it," she faltered, "but it left a bad taste in my mouth."

"Tell me," he ordered. So she did, her embarrassment and uneasiness growing side by side as she spoke. "It was not a protecting spell," she ended. "I recognize the differences. I wondered at first if Tbubui had been trying to avert the anger of the woman whose earring she had—if you had indeed given her the earring—but I knew in my heart that it was not so. Someone was conjuring a violent death for an enemy."

He did not suggest the servants, as Harmin had. He did not immediately present her with an acceptable explanation as she had hoped he would. Instead he sat brooding, one long finger stroking the side of his nose. "It could be anything," he said at last. "Tbubui fancying she had a rival for my father's attentions, although I cannot imagine a woman as confident and self-sufficient as Tbubui being worried about any such thing. Harmin with a similar worry. Sisenet trying to rid himself of some enemy back in Koptos. Who knows? Or the things could have been already half-buried in the sand before the household debris was tossed in that spot."

"No," Sheritra denied emphatically. "The paraphernalia was mostly jutting out of the pile itself. Oh well." She scrambled to her feet. "I expect I am making something out of nothing because I am upset. I am trapped at home until the mourning period is over, and I must dictate an apology to Tbubui and let her know why I cannot return to her house for a while," she said. "I also want to send a letter to Harmin. Please come back to the house with me and get cleaned up. Don't be so lonely. We have seventy days to fill, so let us spend them together, supporting each other."

He rose reluctantly. "I will try," he said. "But do not ask me to face Father. I might be tempted to kill him."

She almost laughed, but seeing his face the urge quickly died. "Hori . . ." she whispered, but he impatiently indicated the path and she obeyed. He followed, and they walked back to the house in silence.

Four days later, having already sent a message warning Khaemwaset that she was coming, Tbubui alighted at the watersteps and was met and escorted to the Prince's quarters by a deferential Ib. Word of his Highness's impending second marriage had spread rapidly among the staff, and as Tbubui paced the gardens and made her way through the house she was greeted with bows and murmured words of respect.

She looked every inch a royal Second Wife. Her white sheath was shot through with glimmering silver thread, her sandals laced with silver thongs. Silver and electrum bracelets, heavy with jasper and carnelian ornaments, tinkled as she moved. Her gleaming, straight black hair was imprisoned to her head by a triple-banded silver circlet, with one jasper droplet trembling on her forehead. Her eyelids glittered with silver dust above the thick kohl that rimmed her eyes, and her firm, pouting mouth shone with red henna like her large palms. An electrum pectoral of intertwining ankhs and half-moons covered her upper breasts like an exotic mat, and its pendant, resting between her naked shoulder-blades to repel any supernatural attack from behind, was a large, golden, squatting baboon. Ib announced her and withdrew, and Khaemwaset advanced with a smile.

"Tbubui, welcome to what will be your home!" he said heartily. She reverenced him, then raised her cheek for his kiss. "You look wonderful, dear sister."

"Thank you, Khaemwaset." She waved away the two servants who had immediately appeared at her elbow with trays of assorted sweetmeats and wine. "I am really here to spend some time with Nubnofret. I told you I would do that, didn't I? The last thing I want is for her to feel slighted, and I know we are going to become great friends."

Khaemwaset was suffused with a protective affection. "You are tactful and kind as well as beautiful," he complimented her. "How strange life is, Tbubui! Who would have thought, the first time I saw you threading your way through the city crowd with such regal hauteur, that one day you would be my wife?"

She laughed sweetly. "Life is indeed remarkable, or rather, it is fate that makes one hold one's breath, wondering what is to come next," she answered. "You have made me very happy, Highness."

They smiled at one another for a moment. It was Tbubui who broke their gaze. "Khaemwaset, I have a favour to ask of you before I visit Nubnofret," she said. "I must dictate a very detailed set of instructions to my steward in Koptos to do with the disposition of the coming harvest and the arrangements to be made for Pharaoh's tax assessors. The scribe Sisenet hired is a good and simple man but just out of the temple school. I do not think he would be able to understand and make a faithful rendering of my words. It will take me no more than an hour." She faltered. "I do not like to trespass on your good nature . . ."

He held up a hand. "But you would like to use the services of one of my scribes," he finished for her. "Say no more."

"The responsibility to hear and transcribe my words will be great," she went on. "They must be exactly recorded . . ."

"You want my best," Khaemwaset beamed, pleased that he could do something, anything for her. "Penbuy's son Ptah-Seankh has taken up residence here. Oddly enough he came this morning. Will he do?"

"Thank you, Khaemwaset," she said again, gravely. "He will be excellent."

"Good." He clapped his hands and Ib approached. "Tell Ptah-Seankh to wait upon me immediately," he ordered, then he waved the other servants out. "Ptah-Seankh is the soul of discretion," he said to Tbubui. "The transaction of business should be a private matter between a woman and her scribe. We do not want servants, even those as highly trained as our own, to hear and disseminate the details of your holdings, my love. I have my own business to attend to, but send for me if you need anything more."

She kissed him softly on the mouth. "You are a good man," she told him quietly. He nodded, pleased, and went away.

Presently Ptah-Seankh was announced and came swiftly across the room, bowing, palette under one arm. Tbubui waved him up.

"Scribe, do you know who I am?" she asked. He regarded her impassively.

"Indeed I do, Noble One," he replied. "You are the lady Tbubui, soon to be my master's Second Wife. How may I serve you?"

She smiled briefly, placed her red palms together and began to walk slowly up and down. Ptah-Seankh slipped to the floor and settled his palette across his knees, opening his pen case and shaking out a reed.

"I want you to take an important dictation. When you have finished it you will leave the papyrus with me. I will explain further when you are done. Are you ready?"

Ptah-Seankh shot a furtive glance at the strong ankles, the swirling linen, as she passed his line of vision. "I am ready, Highness."

"I am not Highness yet, Ptah-Seankh," she retorted. "But I soon will be. I soon will be. Leave a space for the person to be addressed. We will fill it in last. Begin."

Ptah-Seankh dipped the reed into the black ink, his heart beginning to race. So far he had taken no dictation from his new master or anyone else in the household, and though he knew his intellect and his capabilities, he was nervous. Like all Royal Scribes he scorned the habit of making a fair copy after a rough one scrawled into wax or inked onto pieces of pottery, and he intended to take down this assignment flawlessly on the papyrus where it could not be corrected. He forced his concentration on the woman.

"Having completed an exhaustive investigation into the lineage and blood-line of the noble lady Tbubui, her brother Sisenet and her son Harmin, having perused the ancient scrolls reposing in the sacred library of Koptos, and having myself examined the family estate and acres on the east bank of the Nile at Koptos, I, Ptah-Seankh, swear the following to be true."

She paused, and those flexing ankles, one of them encircled loosely with a scarab-hung gold chain, came to rest together in front of him. He was aware of them but dared not look up. His heart was now hammering in his chest and sweat had sprung out along his upper lip. He prayed feverishly that his hand might not falter. What is this? he thought, but quelled the urge to scan what he had written. A scribe was not supposed to connect the words, only to write them automatically. Yet every great scribe scanned in the event that his master might want a judgment or opinion from him. Gulping a breath, he said. "Noble One, do you wish me to scan as I write?"

"But of course," she said softly, her voice a purr. "I want you to know exactly what you are doing for me, Ptah-Seankh." The words were gentle, but there was a cutting edge to them that Ptah-Seankh did not like. He gripped his pen and waited. She continued. "The estate comprises a large house of fifteen rooms with a staff of sixty house servants and the usual necessary additions of granary, kitchen, servants' quarters, stables containing ten chariot horses, and storehouses. The estate itself, some three thousand acres of good black soil, is well irrigated for the growing of assorted grains, flax and vegetables. Five hundred acres is devoted to the raising of a herd of cattle. Are you with me, Ptah-Seankh?"

"Yes, Noble One," he managed, a terrible doubt in his mind. Transferring the pen to his left hand he wiped his right on a piece of linen and prepared to write again. He wished that he had stayed with his grieving mother for at least another day.

"Then I shall go on," that mellifluous voice with its almost undetectable accent said. The flexing feet continued to enter and leave the line of his vision, the silver tassels hanging on the hem of her sheath glittering as she paced. "As to the lady's ancestors, they may be traced to a certain Amunmose, steward of the Pharaoh Queen Hatshepsut, who was awarded both land and the title of erpa-ha and smer, and who was ordered by her to shoulder the organization of the desert caravans from Koptos to the Eastern Sea. Amunmose's line may be clearly traced in the library of Thoth at Koptos, decently preserved until the present day, and a copy may be obtained if necessary. But I, Ptah-Seankh, deemed the copying of this list unnecessary, given that my word to my Prince is sound. The list is also preserved in the great palace library at Pi-Ramses. I have seen the Noble One's ancestors' names with my own eyes." She paused. "I think that will be sufficient, Ptah-Seankh, don't you? And oh, the missive is to be addressed to His Highness Prince Khaemwaset. Be sure to add his titles."

Ptah-Seankh laid down his pen. His hand was shaking so badly that the slim tool rolled from the palette and clattered onto the floor. He looked up.

"But Highness," he faltered, "I have not yet been to Koptos. I leave tomorrow morning. How can I know these things and write them if I have not seen them with my own eyes?"

She was smiling down at him, arms folded, black hair hanging. He did not like that smile. It was predatory, feral, and her small white teeth gleamed at him. "Dear Ptah-Seankh," she said conversationally. "You are new to this household, even as I am, but there is one great difference between us. His Highness loves me fiercely. He trusts me. He is sure that he knows me. You he does not know. Your father was his friend, but he was also only a servant, as you are only a servant. You can be dismissed and ruined in the space of one day." Her smile had broadened, and a spasm of fear shot through Ptah-Seankh. He felt as though he were gazing up at a wild animal. Her eyes were penetrating, her stance supple but tense. He swallowed convulsively and tried to speak but nothing would come. "Soon I shall move into this house," she went on, and her pink tongue appeared and licked her hennaed lips. "I can be a generous mistress, Ptah-Seankh, or

I can whisper the poison of doubt into your master's ears until his trust in you is destroyed. I understand very well that the link between a prince and his Chief Scribe is forged not only by competency but by discretion. Shall I begin to tell Khaemwaset that you have a loose mouth? That you spread family secrets throughout the city? That you boast of your exalted position and of the hold you have over your master?" She bent lower, and now Ptah-Seankh could see the yellow flecks in her eyes. "Or shall I begin to extoll your talents to him, tell him how neat and reliable you are, how wise your comments and advice? Remember, little scribe, you are still an unknown quantity to him in spite of your father. You can be destroyed."

Ptah-Seankh found his voice. "You want me to go to Koptos and do nothing?"

"Exactly." Suddenly she straightened, unfolded her arms, then swooped to pick up his pen, handing it to him with a gracious gesture. "Fill in Khaemwaset's name and titles, seal the document with your own mark. What do you use, by the way?"

"The mark of Thoth. The baboon sitting on a moon," he stammered, and she nodded.

"Oh yes, of course. Well, do it, and give the scroll to me. When you return from Koptos you will come first to my house and I will give it back to you. Then you will give it to the Prince."

"Noble One, this is contemptible!" Ptah-Seankh choked out, furious and afraid, knowing that all she said was true and if he wanted a long and prosperous career in the Prince's generous service he would have to do as she requested. The act would poison him, he realized. It would be a dirty secret between himself and this unscrupulous woman that would haunt him for the rest of his life.

"Is it contemptible to give the Prince what he wants?" she asked, sweetly reasonable. "Surely not. He desires me and will marry me no matter what, but how much happier he will be to do so with the approval of both history and Ramses."

Ptah-Seankh could say no more. He took the pen and quickly finished the scroll, then he passed it up to her. Taking it, she indicated that he might rise. He did so, fighting to still the trembling in his knees. "Remember," she said, "Not one word of this to anyone, even when you are drunk. If you speak of it, and I find out, I will not only disgrace you, I will kill you. Do you understand?"

He did. Brushing those implacable, determined eyes with his own he was convinced that she was capable of doing as she said. She must have seen her threat go home for she pursed her lips, satisfied. "Good. Now tell the herald waiting in the passage to go and announce me to the Princess Nubnofret. I must pay my respects."

With all the dignity he could muster, Ptah-Seankh gathered up his palette, bowed and left the room. Any respect and admiration he might have had for her died even as he was closing the door politely behind him, and he knew that he would be at the beck and call of a woman he hated for the rest of his working life.

The herald's voice had scarcely ceased to echo in the high ceiling of Nubnofret's quarters when Wernuro ushered Tbubui forward. Nubnofret rose from the chair where she had obviously been inspecting the household accounts. At a word her steward gathered up the mess of scrolls on the table behind which he had been standing, bowed to both women and backed out of the room.

Nubnofret went forward unsmiling, and Wernuro closed the doors and settled herself in a corner. One other servant hovered discreetly just out of earshot. Nubnofret waved Tbubui further into the room.

"I received the message that you were coming," she said curtly, "and I apologize for greeting you so hastily, Tbubui. Today is the day I go over the expenditures for the house with my steward, and we have barely finished." Her eyes flicked over the other woman's attire without expression and returned to her face. Tbubui bowed.

"And I apologize for coming at such an inauspicious time," she responded with equal gravity. "I do not intend to waste your time, Princess. I believe that the Prince has told you of his decision to make me his Second Wife."

Nubnofret nodded, her good manners freezing into an icy politeness. One did not bring up such matters so abruptly.

Traditionally, the soon-to-be Second Wife waited for an invitation from the Chief Wife to officially enter the house and inspect the quarters prepared for her, or if the Chief Wife neglected her duty in presenting the invitation, she spent several hours in idle and light conversation before hesitantly and very carefully bringing up the subject of the marriage. The brief flare of friendship Nubnofret had felt for Tbubui had died long ago, and now it was being nailed into its coffin.

"I wished to come and visit you as soon as possible," Tbubui went on, "to assure you of my respect and affection, and to tell you that nothing will change here in your home."

You impudent bitch, Nubnofret thought viciously. You swagger in here without being asked and then you have the gall to condescend to me.

"Please be seated if you wish," she said aloud. "Would you like some refreshment?" It was not her custom to ask. Usually guests would be immediately offered a variety of food and drink. She had the satisfaction of seeing a slight flush creep into Tbubui's cheeks, though her calm gaze did not falter.

"How kind of you," Tbubui said. Nubnofret did not miss the faint whiff of sarcasm in the gracious words. "But the heat quite snatches my appetite away." She had not sat down. She remained on her feet, confident and effortlessly lovely, and Nubnofret had to crush an instant of pure, undiluted jealousy.

"I am sorry," she replied swiftly before she was able to help herself. "I was under the impression that you loved the heat."

Tbubui lifted one bare shoulder prettily and laughed. "I do indeed love it," she admitted, "for it compels me to eat less and thus maintain my weight."

One blow for you, Nubnofret thought, looking at the slim and faultless body. She smiled without warmth, a courtier's smile, and, cocking her head to one side, deliberately waited for Tbubui to go on. She was determined not to bring up the matter of the marriage, and for a moment there was an impasse. I can play this game better than you, Nubnofret thought again. I was born to it. I could have forgiven you your beauty, for that is not of your own making. I could have forgiven you for stealing Khaemwaset's heart away from me. But I can never forgive you your common, cheap, bad manners. As she had expected, it was Tbubui who gave in first.

"Highness, we were once friends," she broke the silent, "but today I detect a small withdrawal on your Highness's part." She took a step towards Nubnofret and spread her hands in an appealing gesture. "My protestations of respect and affection are honest. I have no intention of interfering in matters of your authority."

Nubnofret raised her eyebrows. "I fail to see how you could interfere even if you wanted to," she said. "I have lived with Khaemwaset for many years. I know him as you do not; moreover, the ordering of the household and the regulating of the lives of other wives and concubines belongs to a Chief Wife. Any changes are made by me. As to your respect and affection, well . . ." she paused, ". . . if you are wise you will work towards acquiring both from me, or your life could well be a trifle uncomfortable. We must learn to live together, Tbubui. I think we should agree to a polite truce. Let us begin with honesty." She accented the last word. Tbubui was watching her warily, the veneer of coyness gone and replaced by a critical coldness. Her face had become mask-like. Nubnofret folded her arms. "I do not think you are good for my husband," she went on with a deliberate steadiness she did not really feel. "He has neglected his work and his family and has been in some agony of mind because of you. Do not forget that the violence of infatuation can turn to disgust very quickly, so I advise you to tread carefully around me. Khaemwaset cares little for the running of this estate. He has always left that to me. He will continue to do so. If you attempt to interfere, if you run to him with petty grievances, you will first bore and then annoy him. If you co-operate, you will be welcome here. I certainly have more to do than worry about your comfort. Do you understand?"

Tbubui had listened intently, her skin paling to a sallow tightness so that she gradually seemed to become all eyes and thinning mouth. But when Nubnofret had finished speaking she took two more gliding steps that brought her face inches from Nubnofret's own. Her breath when she spoke was cold and unpleasant.

"What *you* fail to understand, Highness, is the depth of your husband's obsession with me," she said in a low, forceful voice. "It is no infatuation, I promise you. I am in his vitals, not you. If you try to discredit me you will come to grief. From now on, no one will be able to speak against me to him, for I have his complete trust. He is mine, body, mind and ka. I have my hands between his legs, Princess, just where he likes it. If I caress, he will purr. If I squeeze, he will yelp in agony. But make no mistake, he is mine to do with as I wish."

Nubnofret was almost faint with shock. She had seldom seen such venom in her life, or heard such words. This woman was something wild, something completely lacking in human conscience or decency, and for the space of one breath Nubnofret was shaken by a gush of terror. She knew that what the woman said was true. Then she rallied. "I do not believe that you care for my husband at all," she said coldly. "You are nothing but a greedy peasant with the heart of a whore. You are dismissed."

Tbubui moved away and bowed. She was smiling now, though her attitude was deferential. "It is not a whore's *heart* that I have, Princess," she remarked as she backed down the room. "I seem to have offended your Highness. I do apologize." Wernuro had scrambled to her feet and was holding the door open. With a last bow, Tbubui straightened and glided out of sight.

Chapter 15

'I speak of a great matter,
and cause that ye shall hearken.
I give unto you a thought for eternity,
a rule of life for living in righteousness
and for spending a lifetime in happiness.
Honour the King, the Eternal . . .'

A subdued and quiet Ptah-Seankh left for Koptos the following day, armed with Khaemwaset's written instructions on the procedure he was to follow, and the family settled into the period of mourning. Their loss had not brought them together, indeed without music, entertainments or the feasting of guests, the bare bones of their estrangement from one another began to show through, stark and cruel. Nubnofret had completely withdrawn from them all. Hori, too, had retreated into his private hell where even Sheritra, though they spent much time together, could not follow.

Khaemwaset seemed oblivious to it all. Most days he disappeared in the afternoons, unremarked by all save Nubnofret, who did not comment, and he would return for the evening meal bemused and monosyllabic. Nubnofret suspected that he spent the time on Tbubui's couch, and she abhorred the breaking of the mourning rules, but proudly said no word. Khaemwaset would have liked to order the work on the addition to continue, but that stricture he dared not break. The workmen went back to their villages and the half-finished, unpainted walls stood amid a tumble of waiting bricks and rank grass, baking in the summer sun.

Sheritra had sent a letter to Harmin with her love and an apology and had received a short note in return. "Be assured of my deepest devotion, Little Sun," it had said. "Come and see me when you can." She had carried it about with her for days, tucked into her belt, and when the forlornness that had become the predominant mood of the house threatened to overtake her she would pull it out and read it, raising it to her lips. At those times she would feel a resurgence of that anger that had shaken her on the morning she had, in all ignorance, come home to see Hori.

The remainder of the seventy days of mourning dragged to a close, and Nubnofret began to make plans for the impending journey to Thebes. She remained encased in frigid correctness, and Khaemwaset left her alone. Before he and the rest of the family walked up the ramp into the capacious barge, he received word from Ptah-Seankh in Koptos, letting him know that the work was progressing satisfactorily, his father was being beautified with all due care and respect, and he would not be delayed in returning to Memphis with the information his master had requested. Khaemwaset was relieved. He had somehow irrationally believed that some disaster would befall Ptah-Seankh also, that he was fated never to welcome Tbubui into his home with all clauses of the contract fulfilled, but this time all was going smoothly.

Nevertheless, he stood on the deck of the barge and watched his watersteps recede with a great resentment. He did not want to go, and was surprised to hear his feeling expressed aloud by a pale and moody Sheritra, who was leaning on the rail beside him. "I should be happy to perform this last duty for Grandmother," she said, "but I hate it. Hate it! I just want it to be over so that I can come home again." There was no shamefacedness in the words, no suggestion of selfishness in the inflection she used. She was flatly stating a fact. Khaemwaset did not reply. He glanced behind them to where Si-Montu's barge was following, Si-Montu himself and Ben-Anath standing side by side in the prow. Seeing his look they both waved, and he reluctantly waved back. Si-Montu seemed like a stranger now. All his relatives were strangers. Did I ever know these people? he wondered as the riverbank slipped by under his unseeing gaze. Did I ever greet them familiarly as kin, perhaps as friends? When was the last time I spoke to Si-Montu? Then he remembered, and a feeling of being smothered gripped him. The family is broken, he thought. Si-Montu, Ramses, they probably believe that they have received no communications from me because I have been fearsomely busy. They do not know that everything has changed, everything is broken. That the pieces cannot be welded together again because I am a piece, Nubnofret is a piece, Hori and Sheritra are pieces, sharp, jagged, grinding against each other, because there is no one to take us and fit us one into the other again. And I simply do not care. He heard Hori swear loudly at one of the sailors, then silence descended on the deck once more. Sheritra sighed beside him and fell to picking a flake of golden paint from the rail. I do not care, Khaemwaset thought lazily. I do not care.

Dazed and quiet, they settled into their cramped quarters in the palace, for the royal residence in Thebes was smaller, too small to comfortably hold all the inhabitants of the mighty city within a city at Pi-Ramses who had come out of respect for Astnofert. "I feel as though I have been drugged," was Sheritra's comment as her sandals tapped an echo from the gleaming floor. Khaemwaset watched Bakmut follow her and the door close behind them. "What nonsense!" Nubnofret snapped before disappearing herself. Hori had already slipped away.

Khaemwaset stood for a moment, listening to the soughing of the desert wind in the wind-catchers. Drugged, he thought. Yes, it is like that. The palace vibrated around him with snatches of music, formal cries of soldiers changing the guard, the high laughter of young girls, the aroma of food and flowers, the pulse of life. He himself felt as though he had been ill and was still very delicate. His bewildered senses were being assaulted by so much vitality, so much carefree energy, and he had an absurd desire to burst into tears. But he shook off the weakness and, after sending a herald to acquaint his father that he and the family had arrived, he went in search of Si-Montu. His brother, however, was nowhere to be found, and Ben-Anath greeted Khaemwaset cheerfully but absently, already surrounded by her friends. Disconsolately, Khaemwaset wandered back to the suite, through crowds that recognized him and parted for him, bowing. He hardly noticed them. Tbubui's face was not among them, therefore they did not exist.

He was not surprised to find a summons from his father already waiting for him when he stepped into his quarters. Pharaoh commanded his presence without delay. He was waiting in his private office behind the throne room. Khaemwaset had given little thought to Ramses' current marriage negotiations, but their tortuous convolutions came back to him now, and as he strode unwillingly through the suffocating throngs of courtiers another memory, likewise submerged, floated whole and distastefully vivid into his mind. An old man, coughing politely, one dessicated hand grasping the amulet of Thoth that hung on his wasted chest and the other proffering a scroll. It had been oddly heavy for such a thin piece of papyrus, Khaemwaset remembered. He glanced suddenly down at his hand, feeling again its brittle fragility. He had lost it. He remembered that, too. Somewhere between the fiery torches outside the north door of the palace at Pi-Ramses and his own quarters the wretched thing had disappeared. For no reason he could fathom, his thoughts were turning of their own accord to the bogus Scroll of Thoth, once more sewn securely to the hand of an unknown man lying withered in his coffin. With an exclamation, Khaemwaset wrenched himself back to the present and Ib inquired politely, "Did your Highness speak?"

"No," Khaemwaset said shortly. "I did not. We have arrived, Ib. Claim a stool outside the doors and wait for me."

The Herald had ceased calling his titles and was bowing Khaemwaset into the room. Khaemwaset walked forward.

Just where the floor seemed to slide away into a gleaming infinity, its flow was broken by a mighty cedar desk. Behind it Ramses sat, gold-hung arms folded across his slightly concave, equally bejewelled chest, the wings of his white-and-blue striped linen helmet framing the fastidious, slightly disdainful face Khaemwaset knew so well. His father's beaked nose and dark, glossy eyes had always reminded Khaemwaset of an alert Horus, but today his birdlike watchfulness had a quality of the predator about it. Khaemwaset, coming up beside the desk and kneeling to kiss the royal feet, thought that Ramses' expression had more in common with the vulture glaring down at him from the helmet's headband than with the hawk-son of Osiris.

The Royal Scribe Tehuti-Emheb had risen from his position on a cushion just behind Pharaoh, and, together with a wrinkled and still blandly inscrutable Ashahebsed who was delicately balancing a silver ewer in both hands, he reverenced Khaemwaset. Brusquely he flapped a hand at them and they rose, the scribe to regain his place and Ashahebsed to pour a stream of purple wine into the chased gold cup at Ramses' right. His glance briefly crossed Khaemwaset's own, and Khaemwaset read the same haughty dislike they had always felt for each other in Ashahebsed's watery old eyes.

But he had no time to respond, for Ramses was sitting back, crossing his legs slowly, hooking one arm over the back of his chair with casual yet studied grace. He did not invite his son to take the chair that stood vacant beside him. Instead he gracefully indicated the pile of scrolls to his left. His red-hennaed lips did not smile.

"Greetings, Khaemwaset," he said smoothly. "I do not think that I have ever seen you looking so unhealthy." The royal nose wrinkled slightly. The royal eyes held steadily on Khaemwaset's face. "You are yellow and haggard," Pharaoh went on relentlessly, "so that I am almost disposed to pity you instead of extending to you the discipline you deserve." Now his mouth twitched in a wintry curve. "I said almost. These scrolls all contain complaints from the ministers to whom you owe your attention. Letters unanswered, estimates unapproved, vacant positions in minor ministries still unfilled, because you, Prince, have been shamefully neglecting your responsibilities." He unhooked his arm, put his elbows on the desk, and steepling his many-ringed fingers under his chin he stared at Khaemwaset with calculated disgust. Khaemwaset dared not break his gaze in order to glance at Ashahebsed, but he sensed the man's hidden glee. He did not mind Tehuti-Emheb's presence, for it was his job to record the exchange and whatever its results might be, but Khaemwaset was suddenly furious with his father for not dismissing the old cupbearer. Knowing Ramses as he did, he was sure Ashahebsed's presence was no oversight. Khaemwaset refused to be discomfited. Neither man would gossip, and the truth was that he deserved the Mighty Bull's disapproval. Nevertheless, the fumes of anger coiled, acrid and bitter, in his throat. "But these things, though puzzling and annoying, do not merit the totality of my divine displeasure," Ramses went on. "Twice your mother's steward sent messages to you regarding her worsening health, yet she died without the comfort of your presence. I want to know why, Khaemwaset."

Wild excuses flitted rapidly through Khaemwaset's mind. I did not receive the messages. My scribe read them to me and misinterpreted their scrawl. I was ready to come but then fell ill. You can see, Great Horus, how ill I have been. I have fallen desperately in love with a beautiful woman so that nothing and no one else exists for me, and even the suffering of my dying mother meant only an annoying inconvenience. He spread out his hands.

"I can offer no explanation, Divine One," he said.

There was a moment of stunned silence. Ramses stared at him in disbelief. "You are defying me!" he shouted, the controlled, suave voice gone under the force of his rage, and Khaemwaset realized that his father was genuinely, perhaps even dangerously, furious. He waited, saying nothing.

Ramses began to caress the long gold-and-carnelian earring lying against his neck, stroking it between his forefinger and thumb. He was frowning. Then, abruptly, he gave the bauble a tug and snapped his fingers. "Ashahebsed, Tehuti-Emheb, you are dismissed," he said sharply. Both men immediately bowed, the scribe as he rose with his palette balanced on both palms, and backed down the room towards the door. Ramses paid them no more attention. "You may sit, Khacmwaset," he invited, his voice calmly dry once more, and Khaemwaset did so.

"Thank you, Father," he said.

"Now you may speak," Ramses went on. It was not a suggestion, Khaemwaset realized, it was a command. The double doors boomed closed. He was alone with this man, this god who held the fate of every Egyptian between his withered, carefully hennaed palms, and who had the power to punish his, Khaemwaset's, laxity in any way he chose. He was waiting, head slightly tilted, eyebrows raised, those thickly kohled, all-knowing eyes harshly impatient. I have always been his favourite, Khaemwaset thought with a twinge of apprehension, but to be the favourite of an intelligent, devious and unscrupulous god—What does it mean? He took a deep breath.

"I do have an explanation, Father," he began, "but no excuse. I have shamefully neglected every duty to Egypt, to you and to the gods, and my treatment of Mother has been nothing short of damnable, even though I knew perfectly well that she could die at any moment. She received that warning and passed it on to me, but I paid no attention." He swallowed, still angry, knowing that he was talking of shame but not feeling it, hoping that his father would not pierce to the truth with those preternaturally observant old eyes.

"We know all this," Ramses cut in laconically. "You are indulging yourself, Khaemwaset. I have an audience with a delegation from Alashia in three days' time so you had better hurry your explanation."

"Very well," he said simply. "I have fallen in love with great violence, so that for some months now I have been unable to concentrate on anything else. I have offered the woman a contract and been accepted, and only a confirmation of her noble status stands between us. That is all."

Ramses stared at him, dumbfounded, then all at once he began to laugh, a rich, robust burst of sound that stripped ten years from his appearance. "Khaemwaset in love? Impossible!" he gasped. "The Mighty Prince of Propriety besotted? Delicious! Tell me all about this remarkable personage, Khaemwaset. I might decide to forgive you your terrible faults after all."

Obediently, Khaemwaset began to describe Tbubui to his father, and as he did so a wave of homesickness overtook him, mixed with a strange impression of inner warping, as though he were not really here in this sumptuous office, listening to a voice he barely recognized as his own, forcing out hesitant and clumsy words that had little to do with the razor-sharp keenness of his emotions. The shrewd eyes of the man leaning over the desk opposite him glowed with relish. Khaemwaset's explanation trailed away into silence and Ramses sat straight.

"I expect to have the woman presented to me on your next visit to Pi-Ramses," he said. "If she is half as irresistible as you say, I shall order the marriage void and put her in my harem. But I daresay she is one of those stringy, sexless, serious females who would rather open a scroll than her legs. I know your taste, my son. I have always been astounded that you chose to marry a woman as voluptuous as Nubnofret." He lifted the golden cup at his elbow with three fastidious fingers and sipped at the wine, peering cunningly at Khaemwaset over the rim. "And speaking of Nubnofret," he said, running his tongue carefully along his red lips, "What opinion has she expressed of your Second Wife-to-be?"

Khaemwaset grinned weakly, still in the grip of that uncomfortable distortion. "She is not happy, Divine One."

"And that is because she has ruled your roost alone for far too long," Ramses came back swiftly. "She must learn to be more humble. Arrogance in a woman is a most distasteful trait."

Khaemwaset blinked. His father's harem was full of quarrelsome, fiery, self-opinionated females able to give Pharaoh the challenge he most loved.

"What of your children?" Ramses was saying. "Hori and Sheritra? Have they an opinion?"

"I have not yet asked them for one, Father."

"Oh." All at once Ramses seemed to lose interest in the conversation. Putting a hand flat on his shrunken chest he rose, and Khaemwaset immediately came to his feet. "Tomorrow your mother will be placed in her tomb," Ramses said. "I abhor your weakness, my son, in allowing all else in your life to drift into chaos while you pursued this creature, but I do understand. There will be no punishment, providing Egypt may once again rely on you to discharge your duties promptly."

Khaemwaset bowed. "I do not deserve your clemency," he commented and Ramses agreed.

"No, you do not," he said, "but no one else can be trusted with the tasks I give to you, Khaemwaset. Merenptah is a bombastic idiot and my son Ramses is a drunken sot."

Diplomatically Khaemwaset changed the subject as the two of them began to move towards the doors. "I received no communication regarding your Majesty's own marriage negotiations," he said carefully. "I trust all is going well."

Ramses snorted disdainfully. "The Khatti princess is on her way," he said. "She will arrive in about a month, providing she is not eaten by wild animals or raped and murdered by brigands on the desert tracks. To tell you the truth, Khaemwaset, I am tired of her already, though I have yet to meet her. It is her dowry that whets my appetite, not her soft, royal skin. You will of course be present when she piles it all before me and bends her hopefully pretty little knees." He gave Khaemwaset a sharply hostile glare. "This is your last chance, Khaemwaset. Fail me in this and you will find yourself patrolling the Western Desert with the Medjay for the rest of your life. I mean it."

Ramses did not linger by the door. Kissing Khaemwaset perfunctorily on the cheek he strode regally away, his rowdy retinue falling in around him, leaving the Prince to collect Ib and make his way back to his suite. Khaemwaset suddenly found that he was exhausted. I must not let this happen again, he thought, his eyes on Ib's sturdy, flexing spine. I must discharge my duties no matter what, I must cling to some kind of perspective. But already Tbubui's face filled his inner vision while his father's shrank into nothingness, and he ached with the need to be with her again.

Astnofert's funeral the next day emptied the palace. Her cortège straggled for more than three miles from the edge of the royal estate, across the Nile, where rafts plied to and fro for hours, ferrying mourners and courtiers, and into the rocky desolation of the valley where all queens had been buried for hundreds of years. Tents had been erected for the members of the immediate family and for the sem-priests and the High Priest performing the ceremonies. The remaining crowds fended for themselves, setting up shelters in whatever shade they could find and passing the time in sleep or gossip, while Astnofert's linen-wound corpse in its heavy quartz sarcophagus was surrounded with spells and prepared for its final journey into the dark silence of the tomb.

For three days Khaemwaset and his family stood or sat, prostrated themselves or danced the ritual funerary movements, while the fierce Theban sun sucked the moisture out of their skin and the sand blew in choking eddies to cling to their sweat and sift its way under their clothes. Then it was over. Khaemwaset entered the tomb with his father to lay flower wreaths on the bulky nest of coffins inside which, like the answer to some convoluted puzzle, Astnofert lay. The servants swept their footprints away as they retreated into the sunshine, and the sem-priests threaded the knotted rope through the doorseals and stood ready with the imprint of the jackal and nine captives, the insignia of death.

Ramses turned away without a word, shaking the sand from his feet as he got onto his litter. Khaemwaset and his family did the same, and were carried back to the sluggish river and the raft and at last into the relative coolness of the palace in a haze of fatigue. As soon as they reached the privacy of their rooms, Khaemwaset swung to his steward.

"Ib," he said, "order our belongings packed. We are returning to Memphis tomorrow morning." Ib nodded and went away. Nubnofret had been standing nearby and she came up to Khaemwaset. For a moment they regarded one another. Khaemwaset saw her hand tremble, as though she had been about to reach out and touch him and had then thought better of it. Her face became closed.

"Khaemwaset," she said quietly, "I would like to go north with Ramses when he returns to the Delta. I need a rest. I need time away from the constant dust and noise of construction at home. It would not be for long. A month, perhaps."

Khaemwaset considered her. Her expression was politely neutral and her eyes gave back nothing. She wants to get away from me, he thought. From me.

"I am sorry, Nubnofret," he replied emphatically. "You have an estate to run, and Tbubui will be moving into the concubines' house as soon as we are unpacked. If you are not there to welcome her officially and ease her transition you will be committing a breach of good manners, and besides, what would people say?"

"They would say that Nubnofret, Chief Wife of Prince Khaemwaset, does not like his Highness's choice for a Second Wife and wishes to show her displeasure by her temporary absence," she snapped back. "Have you so little consideration for my feelings, Khaemwaset? Do you not care that I am worried about you, that your father is worried about you, that Tbubui will bring ruin upon you?" She gave him a withering look, grunted scornfully and stalked away.

I am so tired of all this confusion, Khaemwaset thought, watching her go. Within me and without, a constant whirl of conflict, pain, desire, remorse, guilt. "Ib!" he shouted more loudly than was necessary. "Find Amek! We are going back across the river, to the ruined temple of Queen Hatshepsut. There are inscriptions I want to examine before we leave!" Work is the answer, he told himself fervently. Work will make the time pass more rapidly, and then the movement of the barge floating home, floating back to sanity, and then she will be there, on my estate, and everything will become lucid again. He left the suite, slamming the doors closed behind him.

Hori had lived his own misery in Thebes, avoiding his many relatives and trying to wear himself out by donning peasant linen and walking the river tracks, meandering through the markets, or standing for hours in the temple of Amun behind one for the forest of pillars in the outer court, watching the incense rise from the inner court and shiver in an almost invisible cloud against a blue sky, and trying to pray. But prayer was impossible. Only words of bitterness, black and angry, would come.

It was on one of these occasions, as he was striding away from the temple towards the donkey-choked traffic along the river road, that his name was called. He halted and turned, shading his eyes. A litter had been lowered not ten paces away and the curtain had been twitched open. Hori glimpsed one long brown leg, its calf wound with glinting gold anklets, and a drift of snowy linen. For one moment his heart gave a lurch and he began to run towards Tbubui, but then the figure leaned out, shorter, younger than the creature of his imagination, and the daughter of Pharaoh's Chief Architect, Nefert-khay, was smiling at him. He remembered her vaguely from his last trip to the Delta, a pretty and vivacious girl who had sat beside him at one of the feasts and who had later done her best to make him kiss her. She bowed as he came up to the litter.

"Nefert-khay," he said heavily.

"So I was right," she said gaily. "It is Prince Hori. I knew you would be in Thebes for your grandmother's funeral, but I did not expect you to remember me. I am flattered, Highness!"

"How could I not remember you?" he bantered back with as much lightness as he could muster. "You are hardly the most modest and retiring lady at court! It is good to see you again, Nefert-khay. Where are you going?"

She laughed, showing even white teeth. "I was about to spend an hour saying my prayers, but to tell you the truth, Prince, I really wanted to get away from the palace. We are jammed into the available accommodations like fish in a frying pan so that I could hardly breathe. And you?"

"I have just finished my prayers," Hori replied gravely. "I thought I might walk a little by the river." Somehow it was good to talk to her. She was fresh-faced, uncomplicated, a healthy young animal with her four thick, lustrous braids bouncing against the unblemished skin of her near-naked breasts, her air of optimistic energy, her smiling clear eyes. Hori felt a little of his sourness lift.

She grimaced in mock horror. "Alone, Highness? No friend, no guard? I have a good idea. Let us find a secluded part of the river and go swimming. I can say my prayers this evening. Amun will not mind."

His first impulse was to make an excuse, but he found himself almost unwillingly grinning back at her. "Thank you," he said. "I can think of nothing more pleasurable. Do you know of such a place?"

"No, but we can have the bearers tramp here and there until we find one. Thebes is only a town after all." She wriggled away from him and patted the dent her body had left in the cushions. "Will you ride with me, Prince?"

Again he had intended to refuse, to walk beside the litter, but he found himself sliding down beside her. The litter rose and began to sway. "A quiet spot by the river please, Simut!" she shouted to her chief bearer, then she let the curtain fall and turned to Hori, her flawless little face inches from his own. All at once he was aware of his grubby kilt, his tangled, unwashed hair, the grit seaming his skin. "If you were ten years younger I would say that you are a naughty little boy who has run away from home," she said frankly after regarding him for a while. "You look as though you have already been through many hair-raising adventures. Does your royal father know where you are?"

Admiration for her made him smile. "I apologize, Nefert-khay," he said humbly. "I have a hard thing on my mind and it has made me careless of all save its constant pain." He ran a hand self-consciously through his tresses. "Meeting you was very opportune . . ."

"Because you knew you were in dire need of a wash," she finished for him, giggling. "Highness, you are an annoying, frustrating, altogether unapproachable man. You appear at court, always seemingly out of nowhere. You drift about the corridors and gardens with your nose in the air and your thoughts far away, then you disappear again. You are the subject of lip-smacking gossip among my friends when the antics of those at court become boring. Someone will say, 'I think I saw Prince Hori yesterday, down by the fountains, but I cannot be sure. Is he at court again?' and no one will really know, and then we begin to discuss your mystery and then we berate you for our boredom and unhappiness." She giggled again, a squirming, vitally alive, fragrantly perfumed example of the best of Egypt's feminine nobility.

An overwhelming temptation to bare his soul came to Hori. He wanted to spill everything into those delicate, shell-like ears, to watch her frown and become solemn, but he refused the impulse. She is better for me this way, he thought. Funny, vibrant, dragging me out of myself for one afternoon. "I had no idea that so many eddies were created in my wake," he protested honestly. She turned onto her back, her knees up, and began to twirl a thoroughly wilted pink lotus flower in her fingers.

"I expect I exaggerate," she admitted, unrepentant. "You are probably not mysterious at all. My friends and I are probably mistaking a merely vacant expression for something exciting and exotic. Women are so foolishly romantic, aren't they, Highness?"

Some are, he thought grimly. And some are cruel, and some care nothing for romance but only wealth and position, and some use their seductiveness to maim. "There is nothing wrong with romance," he said firmly. "Love is wonderful, Nefert-khay."

She sighed gustily. "Is it, Prince? Are you in love? Do men dream foolishly and stand gazing at nothing with a stupid expression on their faces? And steal a bracelet or even a piece of papyrus from the object of their desires so they can kiss it and press it to their bosoms when no one is looking?" She rolled her head and gazed at him in mock seriousness. "Do they?"

How innocent you are, he thought, looking down at her. Even with your palace sophistication, your patter, your worldliness, you are so blessedly innocent. I do not see that expression on Sheritra's face. Not anymore.

"How old are you, Nefert-khay?" he asked suddenly.

She pouted. "Oh dear," she said. "I am going to get an indulgent lecture. I am seventeen years old. My father has been looking for a husband for me for the last year but he has not been looking far enough afield." She sat up. "I did suggest you as a candidate, Highness. My blood is certainly noble, though not, of course, royal. But my father says that you will have to marry royalty first, and think about nobility in a Second Wife." Her face lit up. "So be quick, Prince Hori, and marry some boring blue-blood so that you may then turn your attention to me. Or better still, I will be the first candidate for your harem. Take me as your concubine. You can always marry me later."

Hori burst into his first spontaneous laughter for many weeks, and as he roared helplessly, the tears trickling down his cheeks, making rivulets in the grime, he felt a tiny part of the blackness around his heart crumble away. Nefert-khay was looking decidedly nettled.

"My dear girl!" he gasped, "Does anyone know when you are

being serious? I assure you that when I am ready to marry, yours will be the second name put forward to my father."

"The second?"

"After the boring blue-blood, of course!"

The litter settled to the ground with a gentle bump. Nefert-khay pulled aside the curtain and leaned out. "This will do very well," she shouted. "Good for you, Simut! Come, Highness. I will fill your mouth with mud for not falling at my feet in immediate surrender."

They scrambled off the litter. The river flowed with an almost imperceptible motion a short distance away where there was clean sand and two gnarled trees leaning out over the surface. The river road was nowhere in sight, but Hori could hear voices and the soft thud of donkey hooves behind him, beyond a slight rise of land.

An exultant recklessness overtook him. With one quick movement he wrenched off his kilt, dropped it beside the litter and ran for the water, sensing Nefert-khay pulling down her sheath and hearing her trinkets tinkle as she shed them. Then he was full length in the Nile, coolness loosening the grit on his body, lapping him around, fluttering against his mouth. Am I awake? he asked himself stupidly. Am I going to be allowed to live again? His body rocked as Nefert-khay broke the surface beside him, smoothing back her now slick hair, the water cascading from the satin sheen of her brown skin. Then she was gone again and he felt her nudge against his knees. In a flash he had taken a breath and was groping for her even as she slipped deeper out towards the centre of the river.

For perhaps an hour they swam and played, their shouts and laughter bringing answering sallies from the crews of passing craft, then they crawled out of the water and lay side by side in the hot sand under the thin shade of the twisted trees, naked, panting and grinning.

"Do you think your aristocratic blue-blood wife will ever unbend enough to rub river mud into your hair?" Nefert-khay asked him, eyes squinting shut against the strong light. Hori propped himself up on both elbows and she flinched in mock discomfort as his trailing hair sent rivulets of water over her neck.

"Of course not," he answered promptly. "She will never go out under the sun for fear her skin might blacken like a peasant's, and the only water she will permit close to her body will be pure and perfumed." Then he kissed her, pressing his mouth gently against her mobile lips. Her arms came up to encircle his head and her body tensed and rose against his. But even as Hori felt the tip of her tongue against his own he knew it was no good. The taste of her was wrong. The contours of her face were wrong. Her body was shorter, her breasts smaller, than the body that he craved. I am being disloyal, the thought came clearly and coldly into his mind. Don't be ridiculous, he retorted silently. You are not bound to Tbubui by any ties save those of your own making. He tried to still his thoughts, squeezing his eyes more tightly shut and kissing Nefert-khay more thoroughly, but the feeling that he was betraying Tbubui persisted, strengthened, until at last he pulled away from the girl and stood. "The afternoon is far advanced," he said curtly. "We must get dressed and go."

After a moment she also came to her feet, her gaze troubled. Hesitantly she touched his cheek. "What have I done, Highness?" she faltered. "Have I offended you with my damnably impulsive speech?"

Aching with regret, for himself as well as for her, he took her hand and raised it to his mouth before letting it fall. "No," he answered vehemently. "Nefert-khay, you are beautiful and funny and intelligent and I hope with all my heart that your father betrothes you to a man who deserves such a rare prize."

Her eyes darkened. "But it will not be you, Hori."

"No, it will not be me. I am truly sorry."

She managed a weak smile. "I am sorry also. There is someone else?" He nodded and she sighed. "I should have guessed. It was naïve of me to assume that the handsomest man in Egypt would not have formed an attachment. Well, let us deposit a generous amount of sand and silt onto the cushions of my litter so that my slaves will have something to do this evening." She walked up the slope towards the untidy pile of linen and he followed awkwardly, noting with a kind of mild desperation how the muscles in her perfect buttocks flexed and how shapely was her back.

They dressed hurriedly, woke the litter-bearers who were dozing close by, and Nefert-khay gave the order that would take them back to the palace. In the confined space of the curtained cubicle she fell to industriously brushing the grit from her legs and then winding up her hair, prattling on of nothing in particular all the while. Hori answered as best he could, not able to meet her eyes.

He was set down at the main entrance, thanked her gravely for a delightful interlude, and walked away without glancing back. He had never felt such self-loathing in his life, and he could almost see the bars of the cage that surrounded him. He had built it himself, he knew, but he no longer could remember how he had done so. There was no way out.

Chapter 16

*'Treat thy dependants as well as thou art able:
for this is the duty of those whom the God has
blessed.'*

Four days after the family's return from Thebes, Ptah-Seankh was announced to Khaemwaset as he was attempting to fulfil his promise to Ramses by attending to the backlog of official correspondence that he had neglected of late. Glancing up with relief from yet another missive of protest from yet another minor minister awash in his own tangle of bureaucracy, Khaemwaset dismissed his junior scribe and strode across the office floor to welcome the young man.

Ptah-Seankh advanced and bowed. He was deeply tanned, almost black, the whites of his eyes bluish against the startling hue of his skin, and his lips were peeling. To Khaemwaset he looked tired and strained, and his first thought was for the miles that had been covered with only the dead Penbuy and a few guards and servants for company. He embraced Ptah-Seankh.

"Welcome home!" he exclaimed, drawing his Chief Scribe towards the desk and thrusting a cup of beer into his hands. "I trust all went well with your father's beautification, Ptah-Seankh. The sem-priests and the High Priest of Ptah himself are waiting to bury him with every honour."

Ptah-Seankh gulped down the beer and set the cup carefully on the desk. "Thank you, Highness," he said. "My father's body is now resting in the House of the Dead. I inspected the work of beautification myself and I am satisfied."

That must have been hard, Khaemwaset thought with pity. He waved Ptah-Seankh to a chair, but the man hesitated. "With regard to the work you set me," he went on shyly, "I have completed it. Here are the results of my labours." He held out a scroll. Khaemwaset took it eagerly, then glanced at the scribe, who was standing with eyes downcast.

"What is the matter?" he asked impatiently, with a twinge of anxiety. "Is there bad news for me in this," he tapped the papyrus against his thigh, "or has the journey made you ill?"

Ptah-Seankh appeared to rally. His head came up and he met Khaemwaset's scrutiny with a smile. "The journey has left me dazed, Highness," he said. "That is all."

Khaemwaset had already broken Ptah-Seankh's personal seal and was unrolling the scroll. "Then you had better spend the rest of the day sleeping in your quarters. I will send word to the priests that Penbuy's funeral can now take place three days hence. Is that agreeable to you?"

Ptah-Seankh bowed his asset. Khaemwaset temporarily forgot him. He was frowning over the contents of the scroll. Then his face gradually cleared until he was beaming. "You did very well, Ptah-Seankh," he said. "Very well indeed. You may go."

When he was alone, Khaemwaset slumped into the chair behind the desk and closed his eyes. The last obstacle to his marriage had been removed and he was conscious of a deep relaxation. Tbubui had told the truth. Not that he had ever doubted her, but there had been a slight, a very slight suspicion that she might have exaggerated the age of her family's lineage. But here it was, black and emphatic in Ptah-Seankh's neat hand on the beige papyrus. A small estate but reasonably prosperous. A small but legitimate noble title. A small but functioning house he and she might use sometimes during the winter, when Koptos was merely a fire and not a raging furnace and he wanted to take her away from Nubnofret's accusing gaze. No duties to engage him, no demands on his time, just he and she together in the timeless hiatus of the country of the south. She would belong there, blending in a way that was not possible here in busy Memphis. He remembered the south very well. The silence, the sudden, not unpleasant moments of loneliness the desert wind could conjure as it whipped and gusted over sand too hot for a naked foot, the Nile wandering into infinity through an indifferent, elemental landscape of vast blue sky and shimmering dunes. "Tbubui," he whispered. "You can come now."

He rose, feeling light and empty, and shouted for a scribe. When the man arrived, Khaemwaset dictated a short note to Tbubui and then went in search of Nubnofret. Penbuy's funeral was in three days' time. Tbubui could move in on the fourth.

Then it would be Pakhons, the month of the harvest, the beginning of the Inundation. The beginning, he thought happily, of my new life.

His old friend, the man who had been his constant companion, his advisor and sometimes his disgruntled judge, was buried with quiet dignity in the tomb he had laboriously prepared for himself on the Saqqara plain. The walls of his resting place were bright with the best-loved scenes from his life. Here he sat, straight-backed, head bent over his palette, while his master dictated. Here he stood in his hunting skiff, Ptah-Seankh as a boy, still adorned with the youth lock, kneeling beside him as he raised the throwing stick at a flock of marsh ducks frozen forever in their flight overhead. Here he made offerings to his patron, Thoth, holding out the smoking censer while the god turned his sharp ibis beak towards him with benevolent approval. Khaemwaset, looking at these things, felt a peace and joyous satisfaction emanating from the paintings and from Penbuy's personal belongings. The man had lived a fruitful life. He had been justly proud of his accomplishments. He had been honest, and had nothing to fear from the weighing of his heart in the Judgment Hall. It was true that he had been relatively young, not much older than Khaemwaset himself, and the circumstances of his death were most unfortunate, but Khaemwaset was positive that Penbuy had died with nothing to regret, nothing to wish changed.

After the funeral feast under the blue-and-white striped awnings of Khaemwaset's train, after the dances and the wine and the expressions of grief, Khaemwaset himself sat and watched the sem-priests seal the tomb and the necropolis workmen shovel and sand and gravel over the entrance. He had already paid for guards to be posted against grave robbers. They would stand their watch for four months. Khaemwaset was aware of the irony in his deed, for did he not himself break into tombs? He could not hold the thought, and it slipped away on the barely perceptible breeze of a sweltering summer afternoon. May you live again forever, old friend, he whispered. I do not think that you would like working in my household anymore. You belonged to a domestic order that has gone, and the loyalties of your son will not be as divided as yours might have been. He did not stir until the last load of earth had been tamped down and the workmen had been dismissed. Then he rose, got onto his litter and was carried slowly home.

The following morning the whole household was at the water-steps to greet Tbubui and welcome her to her new home. Khaemwaset, Nubnofret, Hori and Sheritra formed a glum gathering. Only their physical proximity to one another gave an illusion of cohesion, though Sheritra's hand stole into her father's as Sisenet's brightly beribboned barge hove into sight. Hori, clean, carefully painted and heavily jewelled, watched expressionlessly as the craft angled towards them. Nubnofret, regal but equally close-faced, nodded sharply once at the waiting priest, who immediately descended the steps and began to chant the words of blessing and purification while his acolyte sprinkled milk and bull's blood over the warm stone.

Tbubui emerged from the cabin on her son's arm. Harmin shot a quick glance at Sheritra, then looked away, turning to say something to Sisenet before handing his mother from the ramp to the steps.

The family waited. Nubnofret centred herself on the path, and it was to her first, as was the custom, that Tbubui prostrated herself. Nubnofret was a princess as well as the arbiter of all that went on in her house. It was obvious to Khaemwaset, tense with worry and anticipation, that his wife's good breeding was going to win out on this crucial day. Nubnofret would behave with impeccable correctness even though a horde of Khatti warriors was ransacking her home and she had only moments to live. The thought made him smile involuntarily. Sheritra let go of his hand. She too was tense, he noticed, her homely little face pale.

"Tbubui, I welcome you to this house in the name of my husband and yours, the Prince Khaemwaset, sem-priest of Ptah, priest of Ra, and lord of your life and mine," Nubnofret said clearly. "Rise and do him homage."

Tbubui came to her feet with the fluid grace that had made Khaemwaset's mouth dry up from the first moment he had seen her. She turned, the sun flowing along the plain circlet of silver crowning her forehead, and went to the stone again, this time in front of Khaemwaset. With a shock that sent colour flooding into his face, he felt her lips surreptitiously press against the arch of his foot, then she stood before him, kohled eyes sparkling under their dusting of gold eye-paint.

"A contract of marriage exists between us, Tbubui," Khaemwaset intoned, praying that under the onslaught of that slightly parted, orange mouth, those huge, knowing eyes, he might not forget the words of ritual. "I swear before Thoth, Set and Amun, the patrons of this house, that I have dealt fairly and honestly with you, and my signature on the contract testifies to that honesty. Do you also swear?"

"Most noble Prince," she responded, her voice rising high and emphatically, "I swear before Thoth and Osiris, the patrons of the house I once inhabited, that I have no other living husband, that I have declared the true extent of my temporal holdings, and that my signature is affixed to the contract in all honesty. This I swear." Behind her Sisenet stirred, shifting his weight surreptitiously from one foot to the other, and Harmin grinned openly at Sheritra. The three of them, Sisenet, Tbubui and Harmin, seemed full of an odd air of frivolity, as though at any moment they might burst out laughing.

Of course they are happy, Khaemwaset thought as he held out a hand for Tbubui to take. So am I. I want to laugh also. I want to tickle her in a most unprincely fashion. At that he did smile, and she answered him with a squeeze of her cool fingers.

His servants were lined up on either side of the broad way leading to the house. Nubnofret stepped in front, signalling again to the priest who began to sing. The acolyte walked ahead of him, and the white milk and purple blood splashed and ran together to form pink rivulets that steamed on the hot stone and ran away into the grass. As Nubnofret led the way the servants went to the ground, doing full homage to their new mistress who was gliding past them on the Prince's arm, her relatives behind.

Slowly the festive procession passed the main entrance where the path veered and made its way through the north garden, circumventing the still chaotic building site. Khaemwaset saw Tbubui turn her head and give the mess a quick appraisal before looking solemnly ahead again.

Now, at the rear of the house, Khaemwaset's harpist joined them and began to play, his pleasant tenor blending with the plangent notes of the instrument and the piping of the dozens of birds that came habitually to drink and bathe in the fountain.

Beyond the rear of the house was the huge compound containing the servant' quarters, the kitchens, and the storehouses and granaries, but off to the right, in a pleasant circle of bushy trees, lay the concubines' home. Here Khaemwaset's other women were ranged in front of the building, dressed in their best linen. He addressed them briefly and informally, reminding them that Tbubui took precedence over them, and while she was quartered in their midst her word had weight. He had been about to tell them that Tbubui's word was law, but he bit his tongue just in time, remembering that Nubnofret as Chief Wife ruled the concubines as she ruled the whole establishment. Standing aside, he beckoned her. Regally she came, took Tbubui's hand, and led her into the house, the others following.

"You are now under the protection of the lord of this house," she intoned. "As you expect his kindness and companionship, so he expects the faithfulness of your body, mind and ka. Do you agree to this?"

"I do," Tbubui responded. There was a startling crash as the priest deliberately dropped the two pottery jars that had contained the milk and blood at Tbubui's feet, signifying the beginning of joy and bounty for the marriage. Then all began to clap. Khaemwaset moved past Nubnofret and took Tbubui in his arms. "When your suite is ready we will repeat this most delightful ceremony," he smiled, "but for now I am afraid these two little rooms must serve. Welcome home, my dearest sister." He kissed her amid redoubled noise, then all but Tbubui withdrew.

"The troop of Nubian dancers you hired for the evening are here already," Nubnofret remarked to Khaemwaset as they walked back to the house. "I have no idea what to do with them, but I suppose I can set up a couple of tents in the south garden. In any event, I must have a word with Ib about the placing of the tables." She raked him with a cool, amused glance. You are a foolish man enjoying a spurious second adolescence, that look said, but I have important things to do.

She swept away, shooing the excited servants ahead of her. Sheritra rubbed her father's arm. He turned to give her his attention, aware that the soles of his sandals were sticky with milk and blood and the aroma of the mixture was rising on the heat, an unpleasant, sweet-sick smell.

"Harmin has just told me that he will be staying on with his uncle," Sheritra said. "I thought he would move in with us, with his mother. Can't we find a corner for him, Father? Please?"

Khaemwaset considered the limpid, pleading eyes in their rims of black kohl. She had parted her hair in the middle today, letting it hang in gleaming coils to her shoulders, and on her head was a princess's crown, a slender, gold circlet with the vulture goddess Mut perched warily above her smooth forehead, and the two thin, golden plumes of Amun quivering at the back. Her gold-shot linen was semi-transparent, a drift of soft material that betrayed her tiny breasts and boyish waist. Khaemwaset thought how until recently she would have donned linen so thick that its weight must have been trying in the heat of summer, and her shoulders would have been rounded protectively over her chest. He could not be sure, but he fancied that she had painted her nipples—dark splinters of muted gold light could see under the sheath. A tremor of concern shook him, and he placed one finger under her chin.

"You know that there is no room for Harmin in the house until the addition is finished," he explained, tipping her face. "That will be quite soon, Little Sun. But I think Harmin prefers to stay with his uncle. Life here is somewhat hectic."

She pulled away with one sulky jerk. "If he is not here I must go there to visit," she said angrily, "and I cannot go without chaperones and I must sit decorously in the garden or in the reception hall and talk to him about nothing. I shall hate that!"

"You are exaggerating," he objected mildly. "Harmin will be coming here to see his mother almost every day until he chooses to move in with her."

"But I want to see him whenever I choose!" she almost shouted at him. "You have your happiness, Father. I want mine!"

"You know, Sheritra, I am not sure that I like all the changes in you," he said quietly. "You have become selfish and headstrong, and rude as well." He expected her to falter, to blush and drop her gaze, but she continued to stare up at him out of that exquisitely painted, unusual face.

"None of us like the changes that have taken place in you either, Father. You have not cared about my welfare in the least for a very long time, so I suppose I ought not to be surprised that you show no sympathy or understanding now. I want a betrothal to Harmin. When will you approach Sisenet on the subject?"

"It is not an appropriate time," Khaemwaset replied stiffly. "Come to me next week, when these festivities are over and Tbubui's period of adjustment is progressing well. I do not want to throw this at her yet."

Sheritra's lip curled. "No, I daresay you do not," she retorted, then she spun on her heel and stalked to where the young man was waiting in the shade of the house. Together they turned towards the south garden, their servants hurrying after.

She has simply gone from one extreme to the other, Khaemwaset told himself as he started forward. Tbubui has performed a miracle on her, and her love for the son has confirmed it. She is feeling the power of her transformation, and it is at present being translated as rudeness and arrogance. I understand, but I miss the old Sheritra.

"Will you sleep, Highness, before you change your linen for dinner?" Kasa was asking politely, and Khaemwaset followed him into the rear corridor with an inward sigh. All his relatives had been invited to the feast that was being prepared for Tbubui tonight. His father had sent a short, congratulatory excuse, and Merenptah likewise had wished his brother every happiness, in his scribe's hand but in his own florid words. But the rest of the family was coming, together with certain Memphis dignitaries and a host of musicians, dancers and other entertainers. An air of electric excitement lay over the house. The cloying fragrance of the thousands of blooms carted in that morning made him think of Tbubui—exotic, enigmatic, even now exploring her small domain and perhaps day-dreaming of him, of the coming night. He did not think that he would be able to rest.

"No, Kasa," he told his body servant. "I shall escape into the office and read for a while. Send for me when the guests begin to arrive." But once in his office, safely immured behind the closed doors, the noise muted and Ptah-Seankh industriously copying a manuscript while he waited for Khaemwaset's summons, he found that he was still restless. The heavy odour of the flowers had drifted after him. It was in his clothes, in his hair, and suddenly it reminded him of the two funerals he had just endured. His stomach heaved. He sat down behind the desk, let his head fall into his hands, and, closing his eyes, he waited.

The feast that night was the most sumptuous Memphis had seen in some time. Richly clothed guests choked Khaemwaset's large reception hall and spilled over into the gardens, where torches flared and tables had been set out, groaning with delicacies of every kind. Troops of naked dancers, black acrobats from Nubia and Egyptian beauties of both sexes, swayed and leaped between the revellers to the music of lyre, harp and drums. Nubnofret had selected the customary gifts for everyone with care—the bead necklaces were malachite and jasper instead of painted clay, the trinket boxes Lebanon cedar, the fans tiny red ostrich feathers gathered into electrum handles. The wine had come from the Delta, resurrected dusty and grimed from the straw beds where the jars had been laid ten years before. The servants would eat for the whole of the following week on the leftover food.

Tbubui sat in the place of honour on Khaemwaset's right hand, raised above the crowd on a small dais, smiling graciously on those who came up to offer their good wishes. All the ingredients for a successful night were present, yet Khaemwaset could not shake off a sense of melancholy. Sheritra was laughing with Harmin. They had been inseparable all evening. Hori was eating with Antef, a wintry, rare smile coming and going on his face for the first time in many weeks as his friend talked of something that, over the general mêlée, Khaemwaset could not catch. Nubnofret and Sisenet were likewise deep in conversation, and he himself, Khaemwaset, had only to turn his head a fraction, move his hand almost imperceptibly, to make contact with the woman he adored above all else.

Yet the hall seemed a dismal place under all the gaiety. Something was missing. Or perhaps, he thought sadly, as Ib bent yet again to fill his cup, and a chorus of roars and whistles broke out as one of the Nubian dancers curved backwards until her face rested between the legs of Memphis's mayor, perhaps I have been through so much to obtain this prize that now, having it, possessing it, I am empty of purpose for a while.

Sisenet intercepted his unfocused gaze and raised a friendly hand. Khaemwaset answered the gesture. Tbubui leaned against him and pushed a piece of ripe fig into his mouth. Yet somewhere in the room a huge, invisible mouth was open, breathing desolation over the throng, and he could not escape the gale.

Much later, while the guests still shrieked and staggered through the house and grounds and the weary musicians still played, Khaemwaset and Tbubui slipped away, walking unsteadily over the brittle summer grass to the dim peace of the concubines' house. The place was deserted. All the women were still feasting, and no one but the Keeper of the Door, who greeted the pair respectfully and escorted them to Tbubui's rooms, saw them enter.

Once within, the door closed and night lamp lit, Khaemwaset reached for his prize. By now they had made love many times, but her mystery had not lessened. He wanted her with the same helpless longing she had prompted in him months ago, and he was becoming resigned to the knowledge that his desire could not be sated by the act of love; it merely intensificd. Yet like a moth compelled to burn itself to death against the flame of a candle, Khaemwaset returned again and again to the source of his torment. Tonight was no different, and with it was the sadness that had overtaken him in the reception hall, an undercurrent of wistfulness that followed him through the violent consummation of his marriage and into his exhausted dreams.

The month of Pakhons came and the heat went on, an unremitting, punishing succession of breathless days and suffocating nights when the women of Khaemwaset's household dragged sleeping mats up onto the flat roofs of the buildings and spent the dark hours sleeping, gambling or talking. In the fields the harvest began, and Khaemwaset anxiously watched for the first reports from the men who measured the level of the Nile. The river was due to begin to rise towards the end of the month. By then the crops would be safely out of reach of the slowly gathering flood. Threshing and winnowing would go on in the compounds and the grapes would be trod. Si-Montu reported a record-breaking harvest of grapes from Pharaoh's vineyard. Khaemwaset's own stewards sent him ecstatic letters filled with the details of his own abundantly fertile fields, and in his household a precarious peace reigned.

The work on Tbubui's suite was almost finished. She had taken to appearing on the site every morning and would recline under a parasol until the noon meal, watching the fellahin sweat in the well-nigh unbearable heat to raise the last of the bricks and fortify the roof. Khaemwaset liked to join her. Instead of dealing with the day's dispatches he would seek her out and discuss the interior finishing and furnishings of her new rooms, Harmin's continuing romance with Sheritra, whom he now saw almost every day when he came to spend an hour or two with his mother, and whether or not Sisenet wanted the position of Head Scribe in the Memphis House of Life, the library of rare scrolls.

The family took the noon meal together, but it was not a comfortable arrangement though Tbubui chattered happily about nothing, doing her best to draw Nubnofret and Hori, if he was there, into the conversation. But Nubnofret merely answered the questions that were put to her directly, and Hori would eat quickly and ask to be dismissed. Khaemwaset was angry and disappointed with them all, even Sheritra, who had taken to bringing up the subject of her betrothal at every opportunity. He had expected more from the people with whom he had lived for so many years, but their behaviour, just short of being rude, was not sufficiently pointed for him to reprimand.

He would escape from the hall with relief to spend the hottest hours of the day on his couch, as they all did. But often he could not sleep. He lay tossing under the soporific rise and fall of the fans held by his servants, wondering if the day would ever come when there would be a lessening of tension in the household.

The late afternoons and evenings were more bearable. Harmin would come, and after sitting in the garden with his mother for a while, would disappear to some deserted spot on the grounds in the company of Sheritra, Bakmut and a guard. Then Khaemwaset and Tbubui could retire to the concubines' house and make love in her silent bedchamber, where the filtered sunlight trickling through the closed shutters diffused into a dull gold over her sweat-damp body, and he could forget, for a while, his recalcitrant family. He and she would be bathed together, standing side by side on the bathing stone while the servants washed them. Often Khaemwaset himself liked to clean Tbubui's hair, passing the ropes of thick, wet tresses through his hands in a deliberate, sensual ecstasy.

There were usually official guests at the evening meal, and these Tbubui charmed with her intelligence and wit. Khaemwaset would watch Nubnofret anxiously, knowing that she had the power to forbid Tbubui to such feasts if she chose, but his Chief Wife forced no arguments and their visitors went away envying Khaemwaset the two women, so different and yet so accomplished, who shared his life.

Thus the pulse of Khaemwaset's life had become more erratic, but not unpleasantly so. He had begun to think that all would be well, when one day Tbubui laid aside the fly whisk with which she had been lashing herself, in a vain effort to disperse the clouds of hovering pests, and turned to him solemnly. They were reclining side by side on a mat and a scattering of cushions in the shade of the line of trees bordering the north garden. The addition was finished, the debris gone, and gardeners were labouring to dig flower beds against the smooth white walls of the new suite. The rooms inside still stood empty, but a host of craftsmen and artists was due to arrive the next day to hear Tbubui's wishes for her permanent residence. Khaemwaset had told her to order whatever she desired, confident in the knowledge that the simple good taste she had shown in furnishing her old home would be evident here also. She had warned him with laughing coquetry that simple did not mean inexpensive, but he had shrugged good-naturedly and waved away her hesitation. Now he put down the half-demolished bunch of black grapes he had been feeding her and prepared to have yet another discussion of her plans. "Do not tell me!" he smiled. "I recognize that expression, dear sister. You want acacia wood for your couch instead of cedar."

She briefly caressed his bare thigh. "No, Khaemwaset, this has nothing to do with my quarters. I have been unwilling to bring up the subject. It is hard for me to admit that I am unable to solve it by myself, but I am mystified and little hurt . . ." Her voice trailed away and she dropped her gaze. Immediately he was concerned.

"Tell me," he urged. "I would do anything for you, Tbubui, you know that! Are you not happy?"

"Of course I am happy!" she answered swiftly. "I am the most fortunate, the most loved woman in Egypt. It is my servants, Highness."

He frowned, puzzled. "Your servants? Are they lazy? Rude? I cannot believe that any servants trained by Nubnofret could be either!"

She was obviously casting about for the right words, her full lips parted, eyes restless. "Their training is excellent," she began with a delightful hesitancy, "but they seem noisy and talkative to me. Indeed, they often want to talk back. My cosmetician natters on while she paints my face. My body servants make comments on the gowns I choose, the jewellery I order removed from the boxes. My steward asks me what I would like to eat or drink."

Khaemwaset's bewilderment deepened. "Beloved, are you saying that they are impolite?"

She flapped her gold-ringed fingers impatiently. "No, no! But I am used to servants who do not speak at all, who do what they are told and nothing more. I miss my own staff, Khaemwaset."

"Then ask Nubnofret if you may dismiss her servants and send for those you want," Khaemwaset urged. "This is a trifling matter, Tbubui, not worth discussing."

She bit her lip; her hands had fallen, bunched, into her white lap. "I have already approached Nubnofret," she said in a low voice. "The Princess refused my request without an explanation. She merely pointed out that the household servants are the most efficient in the country and perhaps I was not handling them correctly. I am sorry, Khaemwaset. I know I should not be worrying you with something that properly belongs to Nubnofret and myself to solve. I do not want to offend her by appealing to your final authority or by simply taking the initiative in this matter, but I feel I have a right to surround myself with my own people if I choose."

"Of course you do." Khaemwaset was astounded by Nubnofret's refusal. In spite of her feeling towards Tbubui, such pettiness was not in her nature, and he too was mystified. "I will speak to her about it today."

Tbubui put out an appealing hand. "Oh no, my love. Please! The route to peace in this household cannot be through the thorns of disloyalty. Nubnofret must not be made to feel that her authority can be undermined whenever I wish. I have more respect for her than that. Just tell me how to broach the subject to her again."

"You are wise, tactful and kind," Khaemwaset said, "but I think that you must leave this to me. I know her. I can inquire into her motives without letting her guess that you have made a complaint to me. I apologize on her behalf, Tbubui."

"There is no need, Highness," she protested. "And thank you."

The conversation turned into other channels before petering

out under the onslaught of a rapidly increasing heat. Tbubui's head gradually nodded until she fell asleep, limbs sprawled amid the cushions, hair disordered in the grass. Khaemwaset sat for a long time and watched her. Her mouth was slightly parted. Her dark lashes quivered on her brown cheeks. There was something so waxen, so death-like about her immobility that a stab of fear went through him, but then a tiny rivulet of sweat inched between her loosely covered breasts and he leaned down and tongued it away. What bliss, he thought, to be able at last to freely make that gesture. I would do anything for you, my heart, anything at all, and the fact that you hesitate to make a request of me makes me want to please you even more. Carefully, so that he did not wake her, he eased down until his face was on a level with hers. Closing his eyes he inhaled her perfume and her breath, the myrrh and that other scent, indescribable yet tantalizing, and as his imagination began to drift he told himself that he was the most fortunate man in Egypt.

He approached Nubnofret that evening, going to her apartment and allowing himself to be announced by Wernuro. Nubnofret came to him equably enough, offered him a stool, then returned to her place by the couch where her servants were stripping her. One stood by, a pleated blue froth of linen over her arm. Nubnofret stepped out of the green-beaded sheath she had worn at dinner, and without a trace of self-consciousness, snapped her fingers. Her body is all soft rounds and curves, Khaemwaset thought as he watched the blue cloak being wrapped around her and tied with a wide ribbon. She is still beautiful, but not to me. How I wish it were not so! I grieve for her, my proud, unhappy Nubnofret, but there is nothing I can do.

"How can I help you, Khaemwaset?" she asked, arms extended for the blue lapis bracelets being pushed over her hands. "Is something on your mind?"

"Not really," he lied. "We have not talked much lately, and today I have missed you."

She cast him a shrewd look. "Is it Sheritra's infatuation with that boy?"

Khaemwaset sighed inwardly. "No, although I suppose that soon we must decide what we are going to do about her. Have you received any word from your farm stewards, Nubnofret? Has the harvest begun yet in your Delta holdings?"

She crossed to her cosmetic table and sat, picking up a mirror. "My lips are dry," she said to her cosmetician. "Do not henna them again. Anoint them with a little castor oil. I received a scroll yesterday with regard to my few grapevines," she said in answer to his question. "I think this year I will have the grapes dried and stored. We ran out of raisins last year and we certainly need no more wine put down."

He agreed and they talked idly for a while. Some of the stiffness went out of her, and she began to grin at him with something of her old cheerfulness when he complained that the birds were attempting to steal the food for the fish in their pond. But she quickly withdrew into herself when he at last dared to say, "I think Tbubui is missing her servants, my dear. She has not said so directly, but it must be hard for her, not only trying to adjust to a strange household but attempting to adapt to strange staff as well. Why don't you suggest to her that she dismiss those she has an send for some familiar faces?"

Nubnofret went very still, then she waved her cosmetician away with one savage, imperious gesture and rose. "I hate what you have become, Prince," she said coldly and deliberately. "So meekly pliant, so anxious to please, so deceitful in a petty, altogether reprehensible way. At one time you would have come to me full of a royal confidence and you would have said, 'Tbubui wants to know why you refused her request and I want to know too.' You are fast earning my contempt, husband."

Khaemwaset left the stool. "I did not know that she had approached you," he lied hotly, desperately, and she laughed with derision.

"Did you not? Well now you do. She wants her own staff. My servants are not good enough for her. I turned her down."

"But why?" he asked, coming to a halt before her fiery eyes, her white, dilated nostrils. "The request was reasonable, Nubnofret. It would have cost you nothing to grant it. Is your jealousy so cruel?"

"No," she snapped. "You may not believe me, Khaemwaset, but I am not jealous of Tbubui. I dislike her intensely because she is a crude, common woman without a shred of the morality that has made Egypt a great nation and kept its rulers and nobility safe from the excesses and disastrous weaknesses of foreign kingdoms. She is a sham. The children sense it, I think, but you are blind. I do not blame you for that." She smiled without warmth. "I blame you for slowly allowing her to gain ascendency over you."

The tide of rage rose in Khaemwaset so fast that his face was burning and his throat acrid before she was even halfway through her speech. He clasped his hands tightly behind his back to keep from shaking her. "The matter of the servants," he reminded her from between clenched teeth. She swung away and threw herself back onto the chair. The cosmetician began to braid her hair. "I do not like them," she said in a low voice. "They unnerve me, and I cannot bear the thought of them permanently in my house. The captain of her barge, the personal maid who is always with her, the ones who have escorted her and Sisenet from our house in the past—there is something menacing in their movements and their utter silence and the way they never seem to have eyes." Suddenly she tugged her head away from the girl's ministrations. "They never seem to look at you, Khaemwaset! And when they are in a room with you it is as though they are not only invisible but not there at all." She grasped the blue linen frothing over her knees and began to pull at it unconsciously. Astounded, Khaemwaset saw that she was near to tears. "Servants are always with you. You are doing something, thinking something, and you have a need, and you are aware that Ib is standing by the door and Kasa is sitting in that corner, you are *aware*, Khaemwaset. But with Tbubui's servants you not only forget that they are there, it is as though they really aren't there. I feel the same strange not-being in Sisenet. I will not have them here, Khaemwaset! It is my prerogative to refuse Tbubui's request, and for my own peace of mind I do so. I will not have them here!"

He had not realized, had not bothered to realize, how deeply his second marriage had affected her. She sounded perilously close to a total loss of self-control, and for Nubnofret, that would be a failure of the greatest kind. He hurried over to her and pulled her head into his stomach, stroking her gently. "Oh Nubnofret," he murmured. "Oh my poor sister. Tbubui's servants are indeed strange, and she has trained them to meet her somewhat peculiar needs, but they are still only servants."

She clutched at his kilt. "Promise me you will not override my decision on this!" she cried. "Promise me, Khaemwaset!"

He squatted, and taking her wet face between his hands he kissed her softly, overwhelmed with concern. "I promise," he said. "Tell Tbubui that she may select whatever staff she likes from the house. Perhaps when you feel better you may change your mind, but I swear I will not force this issue on you."

She sat back and was already composing herself. "Thank you, Highness," she said formally. "I may be foolish but this is my home, and I cannot be made to feel an outcast here."

It was an odd choice of words. After a while Khaemwaset changed the subject, and he and she chatted amicably while her cosmetician went back to braiding her hair. But the knowledge that soon he would have to confront Tbubui with his support of Nubnofret was an undercurrent of unease in his mind, and before long he excused himself. Retreating to his quarters he ordered wine. He lay on his couch, morosely drinking, until the alcohol took its effect and he dropped his cup on the floor and slept.

In a brief return to his former decisive self, he told Tbubui the next day of his agreement with Nubnofret to let her ruling stand. Tbubui hardly reacted. She stared at him for a long time, mouth pursed, then began to talk about the harvest that had begun on Sisenet's estate. Khaemwaset listened with relief. Women in a household, and to a greater degree in a large harem, have their own mysterious methods for solving the problems of precedence. There would be tears and sulks. There would be subtle manipulations, deceits and tests until the stronger women emerged in the positions of power and prominence. Occasionally, in the harems of royalty, where hundreds of women from every kingdom vied for the attention of Pharaoh and more often those men set in authority over them, there would be physical violence and even murder. Khaemwaset was certainly not ignorant of these things, but his own establishment had been free of such turbulence.

A pale reflection of the chaos that could happen in harems was taking place now, he told himself as he studied Tbubui's outwardly phlegmatic behaviour. The thought reassured him, in fact he was almost flattered. Tbubui was no weakling, but neither, in her own way, was Nubnofret. They would struggle towards a compromise, perhaps even to a position of mutual respect, and he did not think he would need to intervene again. Tbubui would feel less insecure once she had taken her rightful place within the house, and Nubnofret would understand the unfortunate results of her gentle bullying on the inhabitants of the home and would bite her tongue. Khaemwaset believed that the small storm would blow over.

But an even greater one was brewing. For a week all was well. Tbubui did indeed dismiss the servants Nubnofret had designated for her and selected more from the household staff. For the sake of her pride, Khaemwaset surmised, more than for comfort. She went twice to her old home, bringing back trinkets and ornaments forgotten when she moved. She spent several hours with the craftsmen and artists, giving her orders for the new suite. But Khaemwaset was totally unprepared for the news with which she greeted him one night during the last few days of Pakhons.

He had gone to her late, buoyed by a message that had arrived telling him his harvest was complete and bountiful. He wanted to share his happiness with her, to make love to her, and expected to find her on her couch but not yet asleep. He had taken to visiting her at the same hour every few evenings. He would walk into a room flowing with the soft flickers of four night lamps, redolent with her perfume, freshly applied and mingling with whatever flowers she had ordered set about the walls. She would be reclining on the couch, loose linen draped across her body, her skin gleaming with oils and her face newly painted. But on this night she was not on the couch. She was sitting listlessly hunched on a stool against the wall, her hair in disorder, staring into a dimness relieved by only one alabaster lamp. Concerned and disappointed, Khaemwaset went straight to her.

"Tbubui!" he exclaimed, taking her cold hand in his. "What is wrong?"

She looked up and gave him a bleak smile. With alarm he saw that she was sallow, her eyes pouched, and for the first time he noticed tiny lines inching around her mouth and fanning out across her temples. She was unpainted.

"Forgive me, Khaemwaset," she said wearily. "It is so hot and even the drinking water tastes brackish at this time of the year. I was unable to sleep this afternoon." She shrugged. "I am merely out of sorts tonight."

He kissed her tenderly. "Then we will sit quietly and talk, and play at Dogs and Jackals. Would you like that? Yes?" He sent a servant for the gaming board and led her to the couch, making her sit against the cushions he hastily rearranged. He himself

sank cross-legged before her. She was silent until the girl returned, placed the board between them, and went away again.
Khaemwaset had the feeling that Tbubui was debating with herself whether or not to say something. She would draw in a quick
breath, glance at him, then glance away. He shook out the ivory
gaming pieces. "We need more light," he said, but she shook her
head, a sharp gesture, and he merely leaned over the couch and
pulled the night lamp closer. Its spasmodic flickering cast fluid
shadows over her face, draining it of life, and Khaemwaset
thought that she looked her age, older and very tired. She had
played upon almost every emotion he had, but tonight she
touched one he had not known was in her domain. Pity engulfed
him. She was making no attempt to set her Dogs up for the
game. She was rolling one piece between her fingers, head
down.

"I am full of good news tonight," he said presently. "My acres
have all been safely harvested and I am a little richer than I was
last year. But, Tbubui, I . . ."

She cut him off, a bitter smile growing. "I too have similar
news," she said huskily. "You have planted a crop of a different
kind, my husband. I pray its harvest may bring you as much joy."

For a moment he stared at her uncomprehending, then a dawning happiness welled up and he reached for her shoulders.
"Tbubui! You are pregnant! And so soon!"

She shrugged away. "Perhaps not so soon," she answered
wryly. "We have made much love, Khaemwaset, in the last two
months. You should not be so surprised."

His hands fell into his lap. "But this is wonderful!" he insisted.
"I am truly delighted. Why are you not happy also? Are you
afraid? But don't you know I am the best physician in Egypt?"

Again that cynical smile played about her mouth. "No, I am
not afraid. Not . . . that is . . ."

His pleasure began to evaporate. "I think you had better talk to
me," he said gravely.

For answer she slid from the couch and brushed by him. The
flame in the lamp danced madly at her passing and the shadows
gyrated on the walls. Khaemwaset twisted to watch her passage.

"I am not well liked in this household," she said slowly. "No,
not at all. Nubnofret has nothing but contempt for me. Hori will
not speak to me. He glowers when he thinks I cannot see him,

and he makes me cold with his unwavering stares. Sheritra was happy to take my advice, to accept my friendship, until I came here. Now she avoids me." She swung to face him, a ghostly figure in the room's half-light, her eyes swollen and huge, her mouth trembling. "I am alone here," she whispered. "Only your goodwill stands between me and the enmity of your family."

He was shocked. "But, Tbubui, I think you exaggerate!" he protested. "Remember how stable, how unchanged our life here has been. The adjustments your coming has required take time. You must give them time!"

She took one step towards him. Her tumbled hair seemed to blend into the darkness and her eyes held the same hue. "It is not a matter of time. I have done all I can, Khaemwaset, but behind their superficial politeness is a deep animosity. They hide it from you, of course they do, but they are like vultures, waiting for my protection to be removed so that they can glide in for the kill."

Khaemwaset opened his mouth to object hotly, but then he remembered Nubnofret's vicious words and was silent. He watched Tbubui intently, then he said, "I cannot imagine any member of my family doing you harm. You are speaking of generous, enlightened people, not desert brigands who are little better than animals."

"You do not see what I do!" she cried out in anguish. "The hateful glances behind your back, the tiny indignities, the deliberate aloofness!" She set her white hands against her belly. "For myself, I do not care. I love you and all I want to do is make you happy, Khaemwaset. But there will be a child. I am afraid for my child!" She was becoming increasingly distraught, her voice rising hysterically, her hands turning to claws against her naked abdomen. The linen had slipped to the floor and she stood before him in a panicked, unselfconscious beauty, her very wildness setting up a throb of desire in him. He tried to calm her.

"Tbubui, pregnant women can become irrational, you must know that," he said. "Think of what you are saying. You are in my household, not the harem of some unscrupulous foreign king. You are my wife. I rejoice over the coming of this child, and so will my family."

She came closer. "No they will not," she insisted. "You are a blood prince, Khaemwaset, and your offspring belong to Egypt. All of them, including this one," she clutched her stomach, "are in line for the Horus Throne. Hori has more at stake than the son of a merchant whose second wife is pregnant. He, all of them, they would try to have my baby disinherited if something happened to you. A child of mine would be a threat to their future. Oh don't you see?"

He was beginning to see, and he did not like it. Is it true? he wondered. I know that Tbubui is not popular here, but I believed that rift would be healed in time. But with this pregnancy another grievance has been added to the wounds the family is already suffering. He tried to imagine the situation if he should die, and it chilled him. Tbubui would indeed be defenceless, but would there be anything to defend herself from? All at once Nubnofret's dislike, Hori's sullenness, even Sheritra's new short-temperedness, shifted to form a new pattern in his mind. He could not argue. What Tbubui was saying seemed to be the truth. She was directly in front of him now, breathing rapidly and harshly, her cheeks wet with tears.

"Do you love me, Khaemwaset?" she asked in a strangled voice. "Do you?"

"Tbubui! More than anything!" he said.

"Then help me. Please. I am your wife and you owe me protection. To your unborn son you owe even more. Strike Hori and Sheritra from your will in favour of this new child. Do it before some terrible fate overtakes him. Remove that power from them so that I may live here in peace and look forward to bringing the fruit of our love into the world. Otherwise . . ." She bent, both hands on her knees, and peered with a mad intensity into Khaemwaset's face. "Otherwise I must divorce you and leave."

He felt as though she had struck him. His chest ached and he could not get his breath. "Gods, Tbubui . . ." he croaked. "You do not mean it . . . there is no need for such a drastic measure . . . you are not thinking . . ."

She was crying. "Believe me, dear brother, I have done nothing else but think about this since I realized I was pregnant," she said. "Nubnofret will never accept me. She told me to my face that I have the heart of a whore. Hori . . ."

"What?" he asked sharply. She shook her head.

"Nothing. But I urge you, I beg you, to do as I wish. You are a good man, you do not smell the evil stinking directly under your nostrils. Pharaoh will take care of Hori, and Sheritra will doubtless marry some wealthy nobleman. They will not suffer! Only my son will suffer if you delay!"

"Nubnofret, my Nubnofret, called you a whore?" he said slowly, and she nodded.

"Yes. By all the gods I swear I am telling you the truth. Change your will, Prince. If the gods are kind you will live to see our son grow to manhood and then it will not matter. But if not . . ." She spread her hands. "I adore you. I always have. Do not force me to tear out my heart by leaving you."

Khaemwaset could not think. He wanted to be clear-headed, to argue with her rationally, but his mind was whirling and he was afraid, so very afraid, both that she was right and that she would carry out her threat. I cannot live without her, he thought. I cannot go back to the life I once knew. It would be desolation, loneliness, it would be death. She has changed me. From the first, she has been working in me. I am no longer Nubnofret's Khaemwaset, Hori's father, Ramses' right hand. I am Tbubui's lover, and that is all. With one sweep of his arm he pulled her down onto the couch, pushing her roughly into the mattress as he rolled on top of her. "Very well," he ground out, already half-mad with the fever of wanting her. "Very well. I will remove the right of my children by Nubnofret to inherit, and give that right to our child. But I will not tell them. They would hate you even more."

"There is no need to tell them unless they become a danger," she answered. "Thank you, Khaemwaset."

He did not reply, indeed, he had not heard her. The tide of lust had risen in him, drowning all thought, and it was a long time before he again became aware of his surroundings. By then the lamp had gone out from starvation and he could hear the jackals howling far away in the desert beyond Saqqara. The city was enveloped in the silence of deepest night.

Chapter 17

'Wilt thou go away because thou art thirsty?
Take to thee my breast;
what it hath overfloweth for thee.'

Dawn was a hint of thinning in the darkness when Khaemwaset slipped out of the concubines' house and re-entered his quarters, falling onto his couch and into his dreams almost simultaneously. He woke three hours later to the gentle strumming of his harpist and the good smell of fresh bread and ripe figs and grapes. Kasa was rolling up the shutter blinds to let in the precious early sun that would be firmly excluded in two more hours.

Khaemwaset ate without much appetite, his mind on Tbubui's words of the night before, but it was as though the decision had been made, the ramifications of her pleading and his objections flowing scarcely coherently in the background. She is so right, he told himself, spitting a grape pip into his palm and staring at it stupidly. I should have considered this eventuality but I buried my head in the sand of delusion. Reality has caught up with us all and it is cold, a merciless, brute thing. Something must be done immediately, today, or I will lose her. "Kasa," he called. "Have Ptah-Seankh wait upon me in my office. Have you selected my dress for this morning?"

He finished the food, waved the harpist out, and, once bathed and dressed, he said his prayers before the shrine of Thoth. They would hate me if they knew what I was about to do, he thought secretly while his tongue spoke the ancient words of beseeching and worship. Outrage, betrayal, bitterness, none of them would understand. But Tbubui is my life, my youth, my final amulet against the advancing years and the long darkness. Father is rich beyond the dreams of ordinary men. Let him pick up the pieces if I die. He owes me that much.

When he had snuffed the incense and closed the shrine he went to his office. One of his servants was already letting down the shutters against the sun's implacable strength, and he could hear gardeners at work outside. Ptah-Seankh was sitting on a stool, reading, his palette on the floor beside him. He stood and bowed as Khaemwaset approached.

"Greetings, Ptah-Seankh," Khaemwaset said. "A moment, please." Taking a small key from his belt he went into the inner room, unlocked a chest, removed a scroll and came back into the office. Passing the scroll to his scribe he took his place behind the desk. "This is my will," he explained. "I want you to read it carefully. There are three clauses in it, dealing with the disposition of my personal wealth and hereditary estates. Be careful to differentiate between my personal holdings and those assets that accrue to me because I am a prince. Hori automatically falls heir to those, and I can do nothing about that. But I want you to strike him from my personal inheritance. My daughter Sheritra also. Leave Nubnofret's gains alone . . ."

Ptah-Seankh was clutching the scroll and staring at him, a dumbfounded expression on his face. "But Highness," he stammered, "What has the Prince Hori done? Have you given enough thought to what you are asking me to do?"

"Of course," Khaemwaset replied testily. "My wife Tbubui is pregnant, and that fact necessitates a change in the will. A copy of the document is filed in the Memphis House of Life. Take my seal as authorization, remove the copy and execute the same changes in it. You will make Tbubui's unborn child my sole beneficiary."

Ptah-Seankh stepped forward. "Highness, I beg you to consider well before you take this solemn initiative," he expostulated. "If you remove Sheritra from the will you leave her without means for a marriage dowry if you die before she marries. As for Prince Hori . . ."

"If I want your opinion I shall ask for it," Khaemwaset snarled. "Shall I repeat your instructions?"

"Yes," Ptah-Seankh said steadily, his face pale. "I think your Highness had better say the words again."

He is hoping that the sound of them will be so ominous that I will frighten myself and change my mind, Khaemwaset thought. I do frighten myself, but I will not change them. He repeated himself, slowly and carefully, aware of the scribe's unwavering, unbelieving gaze. Then he dismissed the man. Ptah-Seankh bowed, paused as though wanting to argue again, then backed from the room. The door closed with a polite click behind him. It is done, Khaemwaset thought, laying his arms across the smooth surface of the desk and listening to the muted sounds wafting in from the garden. In the space of a few hours I have betrayed my children and degraded myself, but I have kept Tbubui. Later I will concern myself with the transgression of Ma'at, but now I will go to her and watch the anxiety smooth from her face when I tell her that she and our son are safe. Her eyes will slowly light, and she will touch my face with the tips of her fingers, and I will know that I have done the right thing, the only thing.

Yet he sat on. The gardeners' voices slowly faded to be replaced by quarrelling birds, a servant humming as he passed by, the strident tones of Nubnofret's personal body servant, Wernuro, scolding some luckless slave. The right thing, he thought emotionlessly. The only thing. He could not move.

Ptah-Seankh stood outside the closed door to the office, the scroll clutched in his hand, trying to come to terms with what had just happened. He was aware of the guard's eyes on him in surreptitious curiosity and knew he should move, but for a moment he could not. The Prince is mad, he thought wildly. He has lost his mind. What shall I do? My first duty is to obey him in everything, but this I cannot accept. Father, what would you have done? I am an apprentice here, a learner though a privileged one. I do not know better than my master, yet how can I do this thing? Shall I go to the Princess and confess everything? I should simply do as I am told and mind my own business. I am a newcomer to this house. I am existing on the reputation my father built. I have yet to earn my own. But he remembered the terrible thing the Prince's Second Wife had made him do, and the guilt he carried with him everywhere. Perhaps the gods have given me this opportunity to redress the wrong I have done, he thought. I may cleanse my conscience at the same time. He had no doubt that what he had been asked to do was a wrong. The Prince had a right to include whatever details he chose in his will, but these changes had a corrupt stench to them. Oh Thoth, wise guide of the true scribe's hand and mind, Ptah-Seankh prayed, still under the interested glances of the guard, tell me what to do.

He began to walk along the passage, and at the far end he encountered Antef, the Prince Hori's body servant and friend. He took it as a sign. Bowing, he inquired where the Prince might be, but Antef answered shortly that he did not know. Ptah-Seankh began to search. An hour later he still had not found Hori, but he met the Princess Sheritra, a bowl of milk in her hands.

"Greetings, Ptah-Seankh," she said. "I hope you are settling in well here, and Father is not driving you to distraction."

He bowed. "I am very happy to be attached to this august household, Highness," he replied. "May I inquire if you have seen your brother? I have searched for him all over the house and I must speak with him immediately."

She looked thoughtful. "If he is not in the house he must be down by the watersteps," she replied. "I know exactly where. Is it vital, Ptah-Seankh?" He nodded. "Then I will send him to you. Go and wait for him in his quarters. First, though, the house snakes need their food." She smiled and passed on, and he turned in the direction of the Prince's suite. The scroll was still held tightly in his hands.

He waited for a long time, but he was patient. The hour for the afternoon sleep came and he thought with longing of his own neat couch, but he stood dutifully in the Prince's antechamber under the steward's eye until Hori was admitted.

Hori approached Ptah-Seankh with a smile. His kilt was limp and smudged with what looked like river mud, and he was not wearing one piece of jewellery, not even an amulet. Even so, Ptah-Seankh thought that nothing could mar his extraordinary beauty.

"You need to see me?" he asked brusquely.

Ptah-Seankh bowed, eyeing the steward. "I do, Highness, but I would prefer to speak to you in private." Hori dismissed his steward with a wave, and when the doors had closed behind him offered the scribe the wine opened on the table. Ptah-Seankh refused. Hori poured himself a generous amount and folded into a chair. "The last of a great vintage," he commented, holding his cup so the light glittered off the wine. "My uncle may have been relegated to the status of the minor nobility but the grapes he tends produce the most royal wine in Egypt. What do you want, Ptah-Seankh?"

The young man came closer. "Prince," he said, "I am probably jeopardizing my whole career by committing an act that your Highness may very well see as a betrayal, but I am confused and in pain and I do not know what else to do."

Hori sat straight in the chair. His translucent, glittering eyes became both wary and curious, and he blinked several times.

Ptah-Seankh thought fleetingly how any woman might envy the Prince his long, black eyelashes.

"You have a conflict of loyalties," the Prince said slowly. "Be sure that you want to speak, Ptah-Seankh, before you do so. You are my father's servant, not mine."

"I am fully aware of that, Highness," Ptah-Seankh agreed. "Yet your father has set me a task I cannot fulfil in all honesty without your guidance. I love your father," he went on frankly. "He has been the benefactor of my family for many years. I do not betray his trust lightly."

Now Hori's eyes had narrowed to a heightened interest. The wine stood forgotten on the table, though his fingers caressed the stem of the cup. "Speak," he ordered.

Ptah-Seankh gulped and held up the scroll. "This is Prince Khaemwaset's will. This morning he ordered me to alter it. You and your sister the Princess Sheritra are to be removed as beneficiaries, and the lady Tbubui's unborn child is to be put in your place."

The prince's fingers were suddenly stilled. His eyes had gone as hard as agates. "Tbubui is pregnant?" he whispered. "You are sure?"

"His Highness said so," Ptah-Seankh explained, "and the changes he has commanded for his will confirm it. Oh forgive me, Prince Hori, forgive me! I could not remain silent! You have been disinherited! I do not know what to do!"

Hori fell silent. Then he unfolded himself slowly. His legs went out and crossed at the ankles. He slumped in the chair. His hand found the cup again and his fingers stroked it sensually, up and down, up and down, until Ptah-Seankh felt mesmerized by that compelling movement.

"Disinherited," he said musingly. "I should have expected as much. My father is completely besotted. He has become blind, deaf and insane." He laughed harshly, and Ptah-Seankh heard more than the pain of betrayal in the sound. "As for you, scribe," Hori went on, "if you were in my service I would dismiss you on the spot. You are unprincipled and untrustworthy."

"Highness," Ptah-Seankh began, though his throat was well-nigh closed and he did not think that he could find his voice, "If it were just a matter of my master's will I would have held my counsel and done as I was bid. But there is more." He swallowed, and found himself sinking to his knees. "I have committed a terrible sin."

Now Hori was leaning forward, genuine concern in his face. Holding out the wine, he made the scribe drink. The cup chattered against Ptah-Seankh's teeth but the violet liquid made him feel braver. "I think you had better tell me everything," the Prince advised, and Ptah-Seankh did so. It was like lancing a boil.

"The day before I was due to leave for Koptos," he said, "the lady Tbubui came to me. She dictated a letter to me for your father to read. It contained everything I was to discover about her lineage during my research, the same research my father was engaged in when he died. It was all lies, Prince! All lies! I protested, but she threatened to have me discredited and then dismissed if I did not do as she said." He at last had the courage to raise his eyes to Hori, who was regarding him intently. "My father worked for the Prince for many years," he went on. "He would have been believed, or at least his words would have been considered. But I am a new scribe, untried, unproved. I did what she wanted."

The Prince's face came closer. With a pang of fear, Ptah-Seankh saw that his lips were drawn back in a rictus of extreme emotion and his gaze was almost inhuman. "Do you mean to tell me," he said in a strangled voice, "that Tbubui dictated your research for you? That she told you what to write for my father to read when you returned from Koptos?" Ptah-Seankh nodded miserably. "You did no work in the libraries there at all? You simply waited out your time and came home?"

"Yes. I am so ashamed, Highness, but I was very afraid. I had hoped that it would not matter. Your father is very attached to the lady . . ."

Hori silenced him with a savage gesture. He did not move. His face remained so close to Ptah-Seankh's that his breath brushed the other's mouth with a rhythmic, quick warmth. Gradually the animal savagery of his expression relaxed into a tight mixture of pain and speculation. "Why?" he breathed. "Why, why, why? If she is not a noblewoman with an ancient lineage, then who is she? No peasant woman or common whore or even a dancer could acquire the education and the social skills she has. What is she hiding?" Suddenly he sat back, drained his wine with one swallow, and then rose. "Come, Ptah-Seankh," he said. "We are going to my father." He snatched the scroll out of the scribe's hand.

Ptah-Seankh exploded in protest as he too came to his feet. "Highness, no! Please! I came to you in confidence, to unburden myself, to seek your advice! The Prince will banish me immediately when he knows what I have done!"

"You will have to take that chance," Hori retorted grimly. "Repeat your story to him now, and throw yourself on his mercy. I will not be silent and allow my birthright and Sheritra's dowry to be thrown away. Besides," he added, "Will you not feel better, telling him the truth?" He strode to the door, and with a sinking heart Ptah-Seankh followed.

Hori caught up with Khaemwaset as he was on his way to the reception hall for the noon meal, Tbubui on his arm. He greeted his son amicably, but his eyes darted to Ptah-Seankh and the scroll Hori was gripping, and his smile died. "What is it?" he snapped.

"I need to speak with you immediately, alone," Hori said. "Come out into the garden."

"Can it not wait until we have eaten?" Khaemwaset objected. "Tbubui is hungry."

"Then Tbubui can go and eat," Hori said loudly. "This will not wait." He saw the swift, worried glance that passed between the two before Khaemwaset gave her a kiss and she withdrew her arm. "Ask Nubnofret to hold the meal," he said, and she turned into the shade of the entrance pillars and was gone.

Khaemwaset pushed past Hori who followed him, Ptah-Seankh behind, until they reached a secluded spot by the thick bushes screening the path to the watersteps. Here Khaemwaset halted and rounded on his son. "Well," he barked. "What is it?"

For answer Hori thrust the scroll under his chin. "You recognize this?" he asked, his voice quivering with rage. "Explain to me how you are able to destroy my life and Sheritra's future and still have an appetite for your food!"

Khaemwaset turned slowly to the scribe. "You are unworthy of my trust," he said coldly. "You are dismissed."

Ptah-Seankh paled. He bowed, speechless, and began to retreat, but Hori roughly grasped his arm.

"Not so fast," he said. "You may change your mind, Father, when you hear everything your scribe has to say. It is not Ptah-Seankh who is unworthy of trust, it is your precious Tbubui. Tell him, Ptah-Seankh!"

The man fell abjectly to his knees. Haltingly, with many glances up at Hori's glowering face and the Prince's first angry and then disbelieving expression, he told the story of his downfall. But by the time he had finished, the Prince was no longer impaling him with his relentless gaze. He was watching his son.

Ptah-Seankh fell silent. Khaemwaset went on staring at Hori. Then he began to clench and unclench his fists, the muscles of his forearms knotting ominously.

"That is the most cruelly imaginative story I have ever heard," he said heavily. "But I would like to hear it once more, this time in Tbubui's presence. You!" he shouted over the shrubbery to the guard always stationed on the path. "Fetch the lady Tbubui! She is in the hall, eating." His attention returned to the two young men. "I knew you disliked her," he said to Hori," but I would not have believed you capable of this kind of animosity. As for you . . ." he bent, and with shocking suddenness the flat of his hand connected with Ptah-Seankh's cheek. "The story you will presently retell will be the last words you speak in this house."

"You have already judged us, haven't you, Father?" Hori whispered. He was stunned, all scorn gone. "It is impossible for you to believe us. You think that I compelled Ptah-Seankh to lie, that he and I are engaged in a conspiracy against Tbubui. You are totally in her power."

"Be silent!" Khaemwaset roared, and Hori obeyed, biting his lip. He shot a sympathetic glance at the scribe, then stared at the ground.

Before long the bushes rustled and Tbubui appeared smiling, her red linen pasted tight to her swaying hips, the hot sun gleaming in the smooth blackness of her hair. She went straight up to her husband and bowed. "You sent for me, Khaemwaset?" she smiled. For answer he poked a rigid finger at Ptah-Seankh, still on his knees. "Say it," he commanded. Ptah-Seankh did as he was bid, his voice now choked, his skin the colour of death. Hori, watching the woman closely, had to admire her perfect control. From polite interest her expression deepened to incomprehension, then to concern. Her mouth began to pucker, and by the time Ptah-Seankh fell silent for the last time, tears were glittering on her cheeks.

"Oh Hori, how could you?" she wept, turning to him beseechingly. "I would have said nothing, I would have remained your friend. Could you not have forced away your jealousy and rejoiced for your father and me? You are as dear to me as my own son. Why have you tried to hurt me so badly?" Her face descended into her two palms and Khaemwaset enfolded her in his embrace.

In the midst of his numbing shock, Hori found himself admiring the greatest performance he had ever seen in his life. He wanted to applaud. Like a naïve child he had played right into her hands, and he had only himself to blame. Khaemwaset had released her and was frowning. "What do you mean, you would have said nothing?" he demanded of her, forcing her chin up. The tears spilled down her neck and shone against the healthy brown of her collar-bone.

"Oh no, my dearest!" she sobbed. "No! I meant nothing by it, I swear! Please do not punish Hori! He is just . . ." She faltered, and Khaemwaset jumped in.

"He is just what? What has been going on here? I command you to answer me, Tbubui!"

She put a hand over her mouth then withdrew it, turning to face Hori with eyes full of pity and commiseration. For one blinding moment he doubted himself, doubted Ptah-Seankh, but then he remembered how the scribe's tale had had the unmistakable ring of veracity about it, and how his father, his father! had planned to cravenly and secretly take his heritage away from him. "You bitch," he murmured, and for one instant he could have sworn he saw an answering flare of mockery in her eyes. Then she was obeying Khaemwaset, with every show of reluctance.

"Hori is jealous of you, my love," she said in a trembling voice. "I have known for a long time that he wanted me for himself. He confessed as much to me in the days before you offered me a marriage contract, but I was already enamoured of you and I told him so, as kindly as I could. The violence of his youthful infatuation has turned to hate, and he has been trying to discredit me." She swung to Khaemwaset, her fingers splayed appealingly. "Oh do not blame him, Khaemwaset! We both know that such fires burn fiercely and often eat up all common sense! For my sake, do not punish him!"

Khaemwaset had listened in an astounded silence, his face becoming grimmer, and when she finished speaking he tore himself away from her pleading hands and ran at Hori. For a moment Hori believed that his father was actually about to strike him and he involuntarily flinched, but Khaemwaset was hanging on to his control.

"You vicious puppy!" he shouted, blowing spittle into Hori's face. "This is the reason for those secret visits—lusting after your father's betrothed. Thinking to use your looks to seduce her! If she had not begged for clemency I would throw you out of this house immediately! As it is, you are not to appear at any communal meals and I do not want to hear the sound of your voice again! Do you understand?"

Behind his father's furious face Hori could see Tbubui. She was grinning openly at him. He realized then that the scribe had gone. "Oh yes, I understand," he said slowly. "I understand very well. But if you think that I am going to stand by and allow you to take away my birthright for the sake of the child in that evil woman's womb, you are very much mistaken, Father." He stepped aside and bowed to Tbubui. "My congratulations on your fecundity," he said drily. "I wish both of you much joy of it." Then he flung the scroll on the ground, spun on his heel and strode away.

He kept his spine straight and his head high until he knew he was out of their vision, then he stumbled into the thick shrubbery and fell to the earth, burying his head between his knees. He wanted to cry but found he could not. For a while he simply crouched there, stunned, the details of Tbubui's matchless performance playing over and over again in his mind, far more vivid than his father's insanely angry face. He was thirsty for wine, wine, and more wine, and in the end he got up, pushed his way back to the path and cautiously entered the house by the main doors. They stood open, as usual. The three servants permanently stationed there rose and reverenced him, and he stalked past them into the welcoming gloom.

The debris of the noon meal was being cleared, and apart from the servants the hall was empty. The smell of the food nauseated

Hori. He prowled about until he found an unopened jar of wine, broke the seal and took a long swallow. Then, hugging it to his chest, he went back outside. The hour for a drowsy retreat from the sun had come and the house and grounds had settled to a drugged quiet. Hori padded along the path to the watersteps, veered away, and was soon reclining in his and Sheritra's secret place. I will get very drunk, he told himself, and then I will get drunker still. I hate you, Father, but I hate that unscrupulous, scheming whore you married even more.

He drank, waited, and drank again, but the afternoon wore on towards sunset and he found himself as sober as the moment when he had begun. It was as though the wine were entering his mouth, diffusing through his body, then leaving through the pores of his skin and taking its potency with it. Hori remained painfully lucid, and at some point before he tossed the empty jar into the bushes and crawled back onto the path, he had decided what he would do.

The concubines' house appeared to be deserted, but Hori knew it would not stay that way for long. The afternoon sleep had ended. Some of the women would be emerging to bathe, others to go into the city markets. He surmised that his father had spent the time with Tbubui but would probably have left her by now to perform his afternoon duties. Hori walked up to the door, greeting the keeper amiably, and demanded to be let in. The man asked his business, and when Hori told him that Second Wife Tbubui had invited him earlier in the day to come and share a few moments with her, stepmother to adopted son as it were, he bowed and stood aside. "Make sure we are not disturbed," Hori ordered as he walked away. "The lady has been so busy lately that we have had little time to get to know one another and I am grateful to her for giving me this hour." I suppose when she tells Father that the Keeper let me in he will have him dismissed, Hori thought, approaching Tbubui's door. Well, it cannot be helped. He motioned to the servant on the entrance to be silent, knocked once and let himself through.

The room was glowing with the golden half-light of the hour and the wind-catcher was open, stirring tiny flurries of air. Nevertheless Hori could smell his father's sweat as he came up to the disordered couch. Tbubui was lying much as he must have left her, Hori thought, a bunched-up sheet flung across her loins, her hair in sticky-tangles, her skin damp. She watched him come without surprise, her heavy-lidded eyes following his advance incuriously. He halted and she smiled lazily.

"Well, Hori," she said. "What do you want?" She drew the sheet up over her breasts without haste.

"I want to know why. Why did you marry my father, whom I do not think you love at all, when you could have had me? Somehow I think you would prefer young flesh, Tbubui, to some old man fighting the encroachments of time."

"I would not call Khaemwaset exactly old," she objected, still with that indolent smile fixed on her mouth, "and there are certain advantages to being his wife. Wealth, influence, a title . . ."

"That is not it," Hori said thoughtfully, "not all of it, anyway. I could have given you all those things in time, and you knew it. Anyway, why did you give him false information through Ptah-Seankh? Perhaps there is nothing to find at Koptos?"

"And perhaps there is more to find in Koptos than you could possibly imagine," she broke in softly, her eyes narrowing. "Have you thought of that, luscious Hori? More than your mind can encompass. Oh, I could not risk dear Khaemwaset hearing the truth, not just yet." She sat up in one graceful, taunting movement.

"But he will," Hori said. He was still standing by the couch. "I am going to Koptos myself. I intend to leave tomorrow. I will ruin you before you can destroy him."

She laughed condescendingly. "How attractive you are when you are angry!" she said. "And do you think he will believe anything you tell him after today? I can say what I like to you. You can dig around in Koptos all you want. He is blind to everything but me, and you will be wasting your time, Highness."

I want to kill her, Hori thought with hatred. I want to put my hands around her pretty little throat and shake and squeeze until she stops laughing, until she stops smiling that supercilious, superior, taunting smile . . .

Tbubui swung her legs over the couch. Her smile had become broader. "You can't kill me, though, can you, darling Hori? Oh yes, I see the need on your face. Would you like to make love to me instead?" She let the sheet drop and kicked it away, spreading out her arms. "Would you like what your father gets every day? I often think of you when he is writhing and groaning on top of me."

"You are disgusting," he managed, horror and anger turning his limbs to water, but her words had started the lust as well, more familiar than the anger, an old friend with whom he had been living for a long time.

She tilted her head and half closed her eyes, arching her back. "Come, young Hori," she breathed. "Make love to me."

With a cry he flung himself forward, intending to throw her to the ground and crush the life from her, but he found himself kissing her instead. She began to moan or laugh, he did not know which, deep in her throat, winding her arms about his neck, his waist, lower, lower. Frantically he tried to scrabble free and push her away, yet one hand closed over her breast and the other gripped her thigh. They fell onto the couch together. He could no more control his desire for her now than he could stop breathing, yet he despised her, he despised himself.

With the fingers of one hand digging into her neck and the other fist pounding the mattress he rammed into her and in a short time he ejaculated with a great shudder and lay collapsed on her, muscles jerking. "I like it like that," she said against his ear. "Yes I do," and he pulled away with a cry and rolled from the couch. "Oh wonderful, hot young blood," she went on. "Come and warm me again soon, Highness. I do not think you will be able to refuse, will you?"

He staggered to the door. The room was suffocating, pressing on his chest so that he could not breathe. Panic-stricken, he fumbled for the latch, wrenched it open and ran past the startled servant into the corridor. A few more steps took him outside. He burst from the shade of the portico into the blinding wall of sunlight, gasping and bent over. The Keeper ran after him. "Highness, are you ill?" the man was calling, but Hori ignored him. The sunlight was not so blinding after all. Ra was westering and his dying was staining the gardens lushly pink.

Hori forced himself into a shambling walk. Steadily he covered the ground between the concubines' house and the main building, veered right, cut through the rear and entered the compound. The huge kitchens were belching the smoke of cooking fires and the strong aroma of the meat his mother had ordered for the evening meal. Hori's stomach contracted in disgust but he went straight in. A steward was setting the trays that would be carried, groaning with food and flowers, into the hall. He did not recognize Hori at first, but then bowed awkwardly, caught off guard. Hori took a bowl and went from table to table filling it with bread, pomegranates, raw leeks, dates, apples. The steward watched him, open-mouthed. Hori nodded to him on his way out.

He carried the bowl carefully in front of him all the way back to his own quarters. The storm of loathing and shame within him was abating and he had begun to think clearly again. Antef was sitting on the floor outside Hori's door, his back against the wall, desultorily tossing dice. He came to his feet at Hori's approach, looking at his friend uncertainly. Hori motioned him inside. "Close the door," he ordered. While Antef did so, Hori put the bowl of food carefully beside his couch. The thought of food at the moment made him sick but he believed he might need it later. "Bring that palette," he said, indicating the scribe's tools on the floor beside the large table where Hori used to work. For a second Hori reflected on the agreeable, carefree young man he had been, but the image had no reality. "Can you take a message, Antef?"

"Why yes, of course," the young man replied, going to the floor and putting the palette across his knees. "There is papyrus already rolled up here, and I think the ink is reasonably fresh." He shook out a pen. "To whom shall I address it?"

"To my grandfather Ramses. Put all his titles—he's touchy about that. Then say, "From your loyal and obedient grandson the Prince Hori, greetings. I beg you, dear Grandfather, to concern yourself with a family matter that is causing much grief to me and to your granddaughter the Princess Sheritra. It has come to my attention that our father Prince Khaemwaset has recently and secretly removed both my sister and myself from his will in favour of the unborn child of his Second Wife, the lady Tbubui. I also have strong reasons to believe that the lady Tbubui has lied to my father regarding her noble lineage and has no right to be married to a blood prince. I am in great distress, Omnipotent One, and again beg your investigation into these matters. I wish your Majesty Life, Health and Prosperity. I am yours to command." He gestured impatiently at Antef who was staring at him helplessly.

"Finish it and I will seal it," he said. Antef recovered. The pen scraped against the papyrus and at last he rose, placed the scroll on the table and passed the pen to Hori. Hori pressed his seal ring into the hot wax Antef had prepared. He was regaining some equilibrium.

"Is it true?" Antef demanded. "Has the Prince really done that to you?"

"Yes." Hori responded shortly.

"The lady Tbubui—she is the one you are in love with, isn't she?" Antef said, appalled.

Hori did not apologize for his treatment of Antef over the last few months. He merely held out a hand. After a moment Antef took it. "I love her, but she is not worthy of the affection of anyone in this family," Hori said grimly. "I will tell you everything, Antef, on our way to Koptos."

Antef recoiled. "Koptos?"

"Yes. Have the servants pack a few things tonight. I need sleep desperately. We will leave in the morning."

Antef was clearly bewildered. "Does your father know we are going away?"

"No, he doesn't, and I have no intention of telling him. He never wants to see me again anyway. Do as I have asked, and I will meet you at the watersteps an hour after sunrise. Oh and Antef . . ." He held out the scroll. "Give this to one of the heralds and tell him to leave for Pi-Ramses at once. Use a household servant, not one of Father's personal messengers. Go on!" Antef shrugged, smiled tentatively at Hori and went away.

It has begun, Hori thought, and he was all at once hungry. He reached for the bowl and began to force the food into his mouth. When I come back from Koptos with the evidence of Tbubui's perfidy she is going to wish she had never been born. The sweet taste of revenge mingled with the tang of the leek as he bit into it, but another flavour fought for sudden prominence. It was Tbubui's skin, salty with sweat, and he closed his eyes and whimpered.

He did not go to the hall for the evening meal. He paced his room, hearing snatches of music floating through the passages and, now and then, Tbubui's quick laughter. He sat with his face pressed to the wind-catcher, sucking up the marginally cooler night air, and then he called for his body servant and played a few games of sennet, which he won.

The house gradually grew quiet, and at last Hori slipped from his quarters and made his way to Sheritra's suite. He would have preferred not to be seen, but each passage had a guard at either end and they could not be avoided.

Tapping on Sheritra's door, he was admitted by Bakmut. Sheritra herself came quickly from the inner bedchamber, wrapped in her white sleeping gown. With her hair loose and her face scrubbed she looked all of twelve, Hori thought as he kissed her. Her eyes were frightened.

"Hori!" she said. "I heard about the terrible fight you had with Father. What was it for? He told Mother tonight that he had banned you from all family gatherings including the feasts. What on earth have you done?"

"You are not going to like it," he warned. "Can we go into the bedroom?"

For answer she waved Bakmut to the stool by the door and led Hori further in, clambering onto the couch. Hori found himself perching beside her as he often used to in earlier, happier times.

He began to speak, beginning with Ptah-Seankh's confession and ending with his decision to go to Koptos himself. Sheritra listened, her face becoming more and more sombre. When he recounted his visit to the concubines' house, omitting nothing, she gasped and fumbled for his hand but remained silent until he had finished. Then she shook her head.

"If anyone else were telling me these things I would not believe it," she said. "None of it makes any sense, though. If she married Father for his titles and his wealth, why is she risking discovery by seducing and taunting you? And Father is absolutely insanely in love with her and always has been. He would have married her even if she had been the most famous whore in Memphis. Why all the secrecy? Why did she not tell him the truth from the start?"

"What truth?" Hori said wearily. "I have a feeling that she is exactly what she says, a noblewoman with a good lineage. But she is hiding something and it must be very bad. I will find out what it is. I want you to tell Father where I have gone and why, so that he and Mother will not worry about me, but do not do it until I have been gone a whole week."

She agreed. "Does Harmin know what his mother is really like?" she wondered aloud. "Oh Hori, I want my betrothal now, before you come home from Koptos with bad news for us all!"

Hori took both her hands and shook them gently. "Listen to me," he said urgently, "you must not press for a betrothal until I get back. Please, for your own sake, Sheritra, stop plaguing Father for just a little time. Who knows what I may uncover about all of them?"

Sheritra pulled her fingers away. "I want Harmin!" she insisted angrily. "I have waited and waited. I deserve him. Besides," and here she managed a wan smile, "I had better marry him while Father still lives and my dowry is intact." Then all at once she began to cry. She folded forward and he took her in his arms. "Oh Hori!" she sobbed. "He could never have done this to us if he loved us. It hurts!"

"I know it hurts, Little Sun," he said in a low voice, "But it is not true that he doesn't love us. Tbubui has bewitched him, but once he cared more for us than for anything else in the world. She is destroying him and we must save him. Come. Do not cry. I need you to be brave for me. I have written to Grandfather about it and perhaps he will intervene. In any case, you must be here waiting for me when I return, for I shall come straight to your quarters. Pray for me while I am gone."

She hugged him, kissing his throat and his mouth. "I wish I could do more than pray for you, Hori!" she blurted. "This is all so terrible."

"Look for a letter from Grandfather," he reminded her, gently disengaging himself. "And try to speak up for me to Father. Do not let Tbubui poison him further against me."

"May the soles of your feet be firm," she whispered, giving him a formal farewell. He smiled at her with a confidence he was far from feeling, then allowed Bakmut to escort him to the door and see him out. He returned to his own couch and fell onto it with a grunt of relief.

Antef woke him an hour after dawn. "I presumed that you would forget to leave word with your body servant," he explained, grinning, as Hori swung his legs off the couch, and Hori smiled back.

"I always do, don't I?" he replied, all at once grateful that Antef was faithful and had stood by him despite the neglect of many months. "Thank you, my friend."

"Everything is ready," Antef told him, withdrawing. "Your own barge is packed and I suppose I must be your cook, steward and body servant until we return."

"And my scribe," Hori added. "Leave me, Antef. I will be at the watersteps directly."

His body servant was now awake and was waiting to bathe him. Hori padded after the man and as he went, still sleepy and very thirsty, the enormity of what he was doing struck him for the first time, together with a premonition that slowed his step and made him look about at his belovedly familiar surroundings with a spurt of affection and homesickness. Life has been good, he told himself sadly, and with that thought came the memory of Nefert-khay, pert and vital, water streaming from her young body. I wish I had made love to her, he told himself regretfully. It would have been the one wholesome, saving act to take with me on this perilous journey. "Highness?" his servant said politely, and Hori came to himself and stepped up onto the bathing slab. I must not look behind me, he said firmly to himself. There is no point in that at all.

An hour later, freshly washed and girt in clean linen, his favourite pectoral hanging on his chest with the most powerful amulet he could find as a counterweight lying between his shoulder-blades, Hori walked from the house and went quietly through the north garden towards the watersteps. The servants were about, doing the early morning sweeping and preparing the first meal of the day, but Hori knew that the members of the family would still be on their couches, their minds on the activities to come while they waited for their food. There was no sign of the gardeners. The new wing protruded into what had once been a pleasant square with a fountain, and cast an early, cool shadow over the still raw flower beds. Several guards saluted and greeted him as he passed them.

He had almost reached the edge of the recent construction when someone glided out of the shelter of a wall and into his path. Hori moved on, confident that it was a servant who would get out of his way, but then the figure turned and it was Tbubui, muffled in white up to her chin like a shrouded corpse. She was clearly just out of her couch and had simply pulled back her hair under a hooded summer cloak of gossamer linen. Angrily avoiding her eye, Hori began to give her a wide berth but a hand appeared out of all that whiteness and grasped him. He shook it off in a spasm of fury but came to a halt and faced her.

"What do you want?" he snapped.

"I do not think that you should go to Koptos," she replied.

He smiled cynically. "No, I daresay you do not, seeing that I intend to come home again with your ruin in my possession," he retorted evenly.

"Be that as it may," she interposed gently, "I am concerned for your welfare, Hori. Koptos is not a healthy place. People sicken there. People die."

Now he met her eyes. "What do you mean?" he demanded.

"Remember what happened to your father's scribe, Penbuy," she almost whispered. "Take care that such a thing does not happen to you."

He stared at her. "What do you know about that?" he said urgently. She went on looking at him with those black, fathomless eyes, and all once a chill of certainty went through him. He heard Sheritra's voice, hesitant but firm, "Someone in Sisenet's house conjured a death curse . . ." and then he knew. He knew.

"You did it," he faltered, weak with horror, and she raised her eyebrows.

"I did what, Highness?"

"You cursed Penbuy! You knew he could not be bribed or threatened, that nothing would keep him from carrying out the task my father set for him, so you used evil magic to conjure against his life!" Hori's mouth had gone dry. He licked his lips. "What did you use, Tbubui? What did you steal from him?"

Her eyes began to glow with an unnatural mirth. "His pen case," she said. "A particularly apt personal belonging, don't you think? Sisenet took it one day when Penbuy accompanied your father to my house."

Hori wanted to run away. Suddenly, even the ground on which he stood seemed malevolent. "Well, you will not succeed with me," he said as steadily as he could. "My father is the greatest magician in Egypt. His spells are the strongest, and I have worked with him often enough to learn many protections. Forewarned is forearmed, Tbubui. I am not afraid of you."

"Indeed," she purred. "I had not thought of that. Then I suppose if you come home from Koptos in full health I shall have to persuade your father to kill you." She leaned into him until her mouth brushed his own. "You think such a thing is impossible, proud Hori? Think again. Khaemwaset will do anything I ask.

Enjoy your journey." She bowed, gathered her linen more tightly around her and walked away.

Hori stood stunned, the sun already hotter on his head than was comfortable. Never! he thought dazedly. Father would never do such a dreadful thing. He would be imperilling a favourable judging from the gods! But he disinherited you, another, colder voice whispered back. I would not be too confident, my dear Hori, if I were you. He swung round. Tbubui had gone.

He did not believe he could force his legs to move but they did, heavily and reluctantly, carrying him to the watersteps and his barge, rocking imperceptibly on the oily river. Antef bowed and waved and somehow Hori managed to return the greeting and descend to the ramp. The captain shouted an order, the ramp was run in with a grinding sound and Hori sank to the cushions on the deck beside his friend. "How pale you are, Highness!" Antef observed. "Have you been drinking already this morning?" Hori shook his head, his stomach churning, then he began to speak. He talked for an hour, and Antef did not interrupt him once. He was dumbfounded.

Chapter 18

'Behold the dwellings of the dead!
Their walls fall down;
their place is no more;
they are as though they never existed.'

The journey to Koptos was a nightmare for Hori. Day after day he sat hunched and tense under the deck awning, desperate to reach the town, feeling the wind of terror at his back. Loneliness and a sense of his own inadequacy plagued him. He was keenly aware that the salvation of the family might well be resting on his shoulders alone. His father had ceased to be a calm, kindly man, and had let the administration of the country slide towards a chaos that could well ruin them all. His mother was imprisoned in an icy unhappiness. Sheritra's response to his revelations about Tbubui had been instantly selfish and defensive of Harmin, and it was clear that her world had shrunk to the lineaments of his body. But all of it could be changed, not reversed perhaps but healed, and it was up to him, Hori, to effect that change. No one else saw the truth. No one else was capable of acting, and the awesome responsibility he had chosen to carry was almost too much for him to bear.

He was blind to the parched, brown beauty of Egypt as it slid by. Antef spent much time leaning on the rail exclaiming over the clouds of chaff cast up by a group of winnowers on the bank, or the piles of mud bricks guarded by naked boys who stared curiously at the barge, or the sudden green slash of a nobleman's estate kept verdant by the constant action of the slaves manning the shadufs. Hori had no eyes for these things, yet he was aware of the deepening blue of the sky as they crept further south, and of a slight swelling of the Nile. Far away at the river's source the Inundation had begun. Soon the current would grow faster, heavier, and the broadening flood would lap and spill over into the fields, drowning them, isolating the temples, washing silt and broken branches and dead animals up onto Egyptian earth.

In a confused way Hori saw the flood as taking place within

him also, an inexorable tide of fear and danger in which he might well drown. His words to Tbubui had been mere bravado. He had never concerned himself over much with his father's magic and had no idea how he might go about protecting himself from the words muttered in the darkness, the glint of copper pins sliding into the waxen doll, his other self. The belongings he had left behind were available to anyone wishing to steal a ring, a kilt linen, even a pot of kohl his hands had held. Part of himself was in everything he wore and regularly held, and that part would be used to kill him.

Pangs of anxiety came and went, and he wanted to stand up and shout to his captain," "Hurry! Oh hurry!" But his sailors were already labouring against the first intimations of the annual flood and could do no more. Nor would it do any good to stop at the temples and shrines along the way. It would waste precious hours, and Hori had the despairing feeling that the gods had withdrawn their favour from his family, why he did not know. All he knew was that the words he whispered as he sat with eyes squinting against the white eternity of the southern light were pushed back into his mouth, his throat, rebounding from the deaf ears of the immortals.

The day finally came when the barge backed clumsily towards the east bank, the ramp was out, and Hori stood on solid ground, surveying Koptos. There was not much to see. Desert traffic still began and ended here, and the markets, warehouses and bazaars were frantic with commerce, but beyond the desert track leading to the Eastern Sea the town itself dreamed, tiny, quiet and unchanged from one year to the next, sprinkled with thin palm plantations and watered by narrow, placid canals. This is where her house is, Hori thought to himself. My eyes are perhaps even now passing over it. "Antef," he said. "Go and ask in the market where the mayor lives. Find his house and tell him to send a litter for me."

He retired to the barge and sat listening to the activity along the riverfront, but gradually he became aware of another sound, or the lack of sound. It was as though Koptos was in alliance with the profound, burning silences of the desert. The noise of human industry did not reach far. It was deadened, foreshortened, a bleat against the inexorable nothingness, soon snatched away.

Before long he saw Antef returning, with four bearers carrying a folded litter at his heels. "The mayor is aghast at your coming!" the young man shouted. "He is turning his household upside down on your behalf!" Hori laughed, and for a moment the fear receded.

He got onto the litter, and with Antef and his two guards walking alongside was soon being borne past the porter's hut and through the small garden of the mayor's estate. The mayor was waiting in the shade of his front entrance, a tall man with the peaceful air of the totally contented. But his reverence was harried and his brow furrowed as Hori walked up and greeted him.

"Highness, this is most unexpected!" he said. "If you had given me some warning I could have welcomed you correctly. How many are in your train? The accommodations . . ."

"I have no train," Hori explained, "just my servant Antef and two guards. I am here to do a work of investigation for my father."

"But I do not understand," the mayor said. "I believed from your father's new scribe that the Prince had changed his mind and did not require the information anymore. So sad about the young man's father."

"Yes, it was," Hori agreed. "And the Prince has changed his mind again, Noble One. Do not be distressed. I shall not trouble you for long."

He was not able to be alone for some time. He was shown his quarters—a small room with an open entrance to the garden—and here he stationed one guard. Then he was obliged to take refreshments with the mayor and his family. After the conventions of polite conversation he asked the mayor if he was acquainted with all the noble families in the surrounding area.

The mayor nodded. "The Osiris One Penbuy asked me the same question," he replied. "Koptos is a small town and our nobility, though all minor, does not travel much nor marry too far afield. Their lineages vary in length from four generations to ancestors in direct line lost in the depths of time past, but I know them all." He gave Hori an oblique look. "I have never heard of the three people whose history you seek, Highness. Nor is there an estate run by a steward whose master has moved to Memphis. I can only suggest that you consult the librarian in the Koptos House of Life."

"You are sure that all estates are occupied by their owners?"

"Yes. The desert encroaches very quickly here, Prince, and the inhabited places are close together along the riverbank. Only one estate is unoccupied, but it has been so for many hentis. The house is little more than crumbling outlines of walls in the sand, and apart from some pieces of a stone fountain, the garden is nothing but desert. I believe that the line died out and the property reverted to Pharaoh. I suppose he has no personal interest in it at all and hesitates to award so poor a property to any deserving minister." He smiled, and Hori found himself warming to the man. "Koptos is hardly the paradise of the blessed!"

"All the same, a man might find peace of mind here," Hori said slowly. "I wish to examine this derelict estate. Where is it?"

"To the north, beyond the last irrigation canal," the mayor said. "But I humbly suggest to your Highness that you wait until the cool of the evening to inspect it."

Hori rose and the whole family rose also and bowed. "I shall do so," Hori said gravely. "Now I must rest."

He and Antef escaped, Hori to the couch and Antef to a mat on the floor of the little room. Antef soon fell asleep, but Hori lay listening to that intriguing silence. Its quality seemed familiar. He heard footsteps in the garden outside, and then voices, and he recognized the lilt of the daughter of the house.

". . . He is very handsome and not at all arrogant," she was saying to some unknown friend. "Of course one may not touch him because he is Pharaoh's grandson, but I long to do so . . ."

Hori smiled, turned over and fell asleep.

Several hours later, with Ra already a semicircle of shimmering red on the horizon, he and Antef stood above what had once been a set of watersteps, looking away from the river towards the eastern desert. Between them and the flat, beige plain that ended in a purple sky were the remains of what had once been a nobleman's home.

Of the house, built originally of mud bricks, nothing was left but a few vague outlines in the sand. The watersteps had been irregular chunks of yellowed stone, warped and then pushed upward into jagged teeth through which the two of them had picked their way carefully.

From the top of the stair they felt rather than saw the short, buried path leading to what would have been the entrance hall. Their feet, as they moved tentatively forward, found the firmness of the stone, and Antef knelt briefly to brush away the encroaching granules, finding smooth sandstone lying beneath. Hori had halted and Antef came up beside him. "The entrance hall, a rear passage and at least two bedchambers," Hori said pointing. "The compound with the storage huts and the kitchens and servants' quarters has been entirely taken over by the desert. Now where is the fountain the mayor spoke of?"

They picked their way gingerly around the faint hills and runnels that delineated what had once been sturdy walls, probably painted a dazzling white; now they made an intricate pattern of small shadows as the sun sank lower beyond the river.

Not far to the north they came across the thing they sought. The fountain lay in four grey pieces, the basin cracked and sifted with sand, the spout, once a pleasing likeness of the many-breasted Hapi, god of the Nile, broken and littered on the ground. Five or six stunted sycamores struggled to suck an existence out of the soil where the edge of the garden obviously used to be, and a few sorry palms raised rusty arms beyond them. Antef shuddered. "What a sad, desolate place!" he exclaimed. "This estate has not been scoured of its ghosts, Highness. I would not dare to try and rebuild on this spot!"

Hori hushed him with a wave of his hand and stood concentrating, all his senses alert. It seemed to him that he had been here before, although he knew such a thing was impossible. The layout of the ancient rooms, now simply lumps in the earth, the placement of the garden with its sycamores that once must have been spreading green glories, the palm forest beyond . . .

But no, he thought, allowing the melancholy of the hour to enter him. It is not a matter of the physical, this sense of familiarity. It is in the atmosphere of the ruins, challenging and yet quiet, dreamless and yet demanding something . . . something . . .

Then he knew. Tbubui's house in Memphis, compact, slightly derelict, isolated, had this same quality of plumbless silence and watchful invitation. O Thoth have mercy, he thought. Is this it? Is this, was this, her home? Hapi's disfigured face smiled up at him blankly, idiotically, from the churned sand at his feet. The gnarled sycamores were casting twisted shadows that snaked towards him as Ra quivered, pulsed, and slipped below the western horizon in his journey to the underworld. "Antef!" he called, a quiver of hysteria in his voice. "I have seen enough. Let us go."

They made their way carefully back to the broken watersteps and Hori took the oars of the mayor's skiff himself, pulling frenetically away from the sad and broken site almost before Antef had been seated.

"This cannot be right, Highness," Antef said. "We must explore further."

"That will be your job," Hori replied. "I want you to visit every noble family in Koptos and discuss their histories. I will be in the library." But he knew in his heart that it *was* right, that his lonely place had belonged to Tbubui and no other.

He and Antef spent a pleasant few hours at dinner with the mayor. The man was proud of his position and took a delight in recounting the town's history, from the days when the great Queen Hatshepsut had rediscovered the ancient trade routes with Punt that had revitalized the town to the present, when the caravan routes were well established and decidedly mundane.

"What family has the monopoly on the taxes gathered from the caravans?" Hori asked. "Or do they belong to the town as a whole?"

The mayor smiled, pleased to find an interested listener. "In the days of the great Queen, when the route was first re-opened," he explained, "the concession was given to one Nenefer-ka-Ptah for some service now lost to antiquity. The mighty Queen, an admirer of enterprise, made him a prince. Under his hand the caravans prospered and she was well pleased with him. It is said that he acquired great wealth and became a famous wizard and magician, as well as an astute businessman, but that is not for me to judge. His line did not last. The monopoly on the trade with Punt reverted to the Horus Throne and so it is to this day." He sipped his wine with relish. His daughter and his wife watched him smiling, obviously used to his hobby. "Pharaoh, your grandfather, always allows the town a generous reduction in its taxes to the crown," he went on, "and of course we live in hope that the monopoly will not eventually go to one individual family. Koptos is peaceful and prosperous as it is."

"Why did Nenefer-ka-Ptah's line not last?" Hori asked. "Did the Prince's offspring fall out of favour with the Divine One?"

"Oh no," the mayor assured him. "The line died out literally. Nenefer-ka-Ptah and his wife drowned, I believe, and so did their only son Merhu." He shrugged. "Such is the will of the gods."

Her husband drowned, Hori thought, then mentally shook himself. "Such misfortune could be regarded as a punishment from the gods," he commented. "Their will for a family that had transgressed the laws of Ma'at."

The mayor shrugged. "Who knows?" he said. "It was many hentis ago and has little to do with the reason you are here in Koptos, Highness. I wish I could help you more."

"Your hospitality is enough," Hori reassured him. "Tomorrow I will begin my investigations in the House of Life. I will not impose on you for long, Noble One."

Amid mutual protestations of respect Hori presently withdrew. He and Antef spent a little time talking together in their quarters as the night deepened, but Hori could not keep his mind on what was being said, and before long their conversations died away. Antef stretched out on his mat and was soon breathing softly and evenly in sleep.

Hori reached to the small leather pouch he had taken to wearing tied to his belt, and opening it, he withdrew the earring he had found in the tomb tunnel. She loved it, he thought sadly. She put it on and laughed and it swung against her tall neck. What is she doing now? Is she crouched in the darkness with cruel pins in her hands, intent on the incantation of my destruction? What did she steal that was mine? Tbubui, Tbubui, I would have nurtured you and kept you safe no matter who you are. He did not want to cry but the tears slid soundlessly down his cheeks. He felt very young, and very helpless.

Early the next day Antef set off with a scroll of introduction bearing Hori's seal to politely interrogate Koptos's ruling families, and Hori made his way to the House of Life, attached to the temple of Amun. The library proved to be a pleasant four rooms, one opening into another, with the far walls pillared so that any breeze might funnel right through. Each room was honeycombed with tiny cubicles crammed with scrolls of every size and description, and before he began his work Hori was escorted through the building by the priest-librarian.

"I was on duty here when your father's scribe died on the steps, Highness," he remarked to Hori as they sat in an alcove. "He had been a regular visitor for four days prior to being struck down. Indeed, that very morning he had told me that he was about to dictate his findings to his assistant."

"How did he seem?" Hori asked, and the librarian frowned.

"He seemed afraid. A curious word to choose, but that was the impression he gave me. He was obviously ill, but as well as his physical discomfort there appeared to be some grave matter on his mind. He was a good scholar."

"Yes, he was," Hori agreed, a wave of fear washing over him too, as though in sympathy with the dead Penbuy. "I would like you to bring me all the scrolls he examined, but first, tell me about the man who was given the caravan monopoly during the reign of Queen Hatshepsut."

The librarian's face lightened. "Ah, Highness! How good to speak to someone who even knows the name of that Osiris One! We have her very seal here, in this library, affixed to a document giving the monopoly personally to the man you mentioned. Osiris Penbuy wanted to see it also."

"Did he indeed?" Hori said thoughtfully. "And what of that man's lineage? Where do his descendants live?"

The librarian shook his head. "There were no descendants. The inhabitants of Koptos believed that the man was cursed. I do not know what for. Remember, Highness, that we are talking of events that took place many hentis ago. But he, his wife and his son drowned, the Prince and his wife in the river at Memphis, and the son a few days later, here at Koptos. It is in the records. The son, Merhu, was buried here."

"And the parents?" Hori could feel his muscles tensing. I do not want to hear this, he thought in dread. The mayor knew a little, but this man knows it all. Amun, I do not want to know it all!

"They inhabit a tomb on the Saqqara plain at Memphis," the librarian said cheerfully. "The remains of their estate are just north of Koptos and in total ruin. No one in this town will go there. They say the site is haunted."

Hori's chest felt as though a band had been tightened around it. "I saw it yesterday," he managed. "Their names?"

"The prince Nenefer-ka-Ptah, the Princess Ahura and his Highness Merhu." The librarian, seeing Hori's face, quickly poured him water. Hori forced it to his lips and drank. "Highness, what is wrong?" the man inquired.

"I have been in their tomb," Hori whispered. "The Princess Ahura. That is the only surviving identification in the place. My father excavated there."

"The mighty Khaemwaset has done much restoring of ancient monuments," the librarian commented. "But how interesting! The selfsame tomb! And by accident?"

By accident? Hori thought with a shudder. Who knows? O gods, who knows?

"Yes," he answered. "But before you ask my friend, we did not find anything to enhance your knowledge of the period. Where is the son buried?"

"In the Koptos necropolis," the librarian replied promptly. "The tomb was rifled hentis ago and nothing of value remains in it, but his Highness is still there. At least, he was the last time I conducted an inspection of noble tombs for the Mighty Bull. The lid had been wrenched from the coffin and was standing against a wall, but the young man's corpse had been correctly beautified and was lying within."

"Young man?" Hori had needed several tries to get the words out.

"Yes. Merhu was only eighteen years old when he drowned," the librarian said, adding anxiously. "Highness, are you sure you are quite well?"

Hori barely heard the question. "I would like to visit this tomb," he said. "It is imperative that I see the body."

The librarian looked at him curiously. "Your exalted position frees you from seeking the required permission, Highness," he said. "The tomb is sealed and the entrance filled with rubble, but a day's digging would free it."

"Did Penbuy ask to have the tomb opened?"

"Yes he did," the librarian said reluctantly. "On the morning he died. Highness, do not be offended if I ask, what is it that you seek?"

I seek the truth, and I am finding something more horrible than I could possibly have imagined, Hori thought. Aloud he said, "I am not offended, but I cannot tell you. Think carefully. There was no issue? No descendants?"

"None," the librarian said firmly.

"Very well." Hori rose, then settled himself behind the table. "Bring me the scrolls, and while I am reading, send to whatever workmen's village exists in Koptos. I want that tomb exposed by tonight. Will you accompany me, and re-seal it when I am done?

You see . . ." he paused, suddenly aware of the earring nestling in its pouch against his thigh. "A certain lady claims to be the descendants of this Nenefer, and thus of noble blood."

The librarian was already shaking his head vigorously. "Impossible, Highness. Completely impossible. She is a charlatan. The ancient records exist here unbroken. Nenefer-ka-Ptah's line died out with his son Merhu."

Hori dismissed him and waited. Presently the librarian returned with an armful of scrolls, which he laid before the Prince. "My records show that Penbuy consulted all these," he said. "They cover the period ten years before and fifty after the lives of the people you are researching. Would your Highness like refreshment?" Hori nodded absently and began to unroll the first scroll. When the librarian returned with a slave bearing water, wine and pastries, he did not hear, although some time later he ate and drank unconsciously.

He read quickly but carefully, and as he did so his apprehension grew. The Prince Nenefer-ka-Ptah's grandfather had come to Koptos during the reign of Osiris Thothmes the First, Queen Hatshepsut's father, as an Inspector of Monuments. His father had continued in the position and then Nenefer-ka-Ptah himself, upon his father's untimely death, had been confirmed in it. The dates and brief, factual entries reeled slowly under Hori's baffled gaze. Nenefer-ka-Ptah had been somehow involved in the great Queen's audacious expedition to Punt, a land whose whereabouts had been lost until that time, and his service had been rewarded with an hereditary title and the caravan monopoly when regular trade began with Punt for myrrh and other exotic necessities. Five years later all three of them had died. The dates of their deaths were meticulously recorded. Also the date their holdings reverted to the Horus Throne. The symbol for "ending" had been placed after the entry recording the drownings, signifying that the line had died out with them.

More rapidly now, Hori scanned the other scrolls. No offspring, no heirs, not even any claims on their property by close relatives. They had appeared out of nowhere and vanished back into oblivion. Penbuy had also consulted several scrolls to do with local folklore, and with a sigh Hori sipped more wine and pulled them towards him. The afternoon was advancing and the heat had intensified, but with it had come a hot breeze that ruffled his hair and stirred his kilt, and he was not too uncomfortable. He began to read.

He had not gone far into the second scroll when he found the reason why the people of Koptos believed the ancient Prince to have been under a curse and his property haunted. "It was rumoured," he read, "that this Prince had in his possession the magic Scroll of Thoth. How he came by it is not told, but he was already a cunning wizard when he found it, and through its power he became invincible. But Thoth, angered by his arrogance, decreed that he should be cursed and should die by drowning, and his ka should not rest."

"I see you have progressed into the area of myth and folklore." A voice spoke at his elbow and Hori jumped, but it was only the librarian. "Such stories always spring up around tragic and mysterious family events, and there has never been much else to do here on hot summer nights but recount legends. At least among the commoners." Hori stared up at him, disoriented. It cannot be, his mind was saying over and over again. It cannot be, cannot be, cannot be . . . But in his imagination he saw his father raise the knife and callously cut away a scroll from a dead man's hand . . . saw the drops of Khaemwaset's blood fall on the desiccated hand and one sully the scroll itself as he hurriedly plied the needle, panic making his fingers shake. It *must* not be, Hori thought, for if it is, we have entered a realm of nightmare where we are worse than impotent, where death cannot be contained but stalks among us masquerading as life, and we are tainted and corrupted beyond the power of any god to save us.

"The workmen are already at the site," the librarian was saying. "I have assigned two temple guards to oversee them and have promised them a generous amount of food and beer for their labours. I trust your Highness will see to it."

Hori came to his feet. The action seemed to take a long time. "Of course," he said, amazed that he sounded so normal. "I have read all I need. I want to take these scrolls back to Memphis with me."

But the librarian bowed and refused. "I am deeply sorry, Highness. Such a thing is completely forbidden. Have your scribe come and copy them during your stay."

That will not do, Hori thought. I do not want to show my father something written in Antef's hand. I will not be believed. I still find it difficult to believe myself. But one look at the librarian's pleasant but adamant face convinced him that the man would not be bribed or persuaded. He is correct, Hori told himself My father would never allow such a thing either. "In that case, my scribe will appear tomorrow to attempt the task," he said. "I thank you for your assistance here, and for re-sealing the tomb when I am done. I will meet you here at sunset and you will take me to the place."

He spent a few moments more talking to the man, but later could not remember what had been said. Then he left, walking out into the blinding afternoon. How long did it take you to arrive at the conclusion that is now threatening my own reason? he silently asked Penbuy as he got on the litter waiting for him. You had almost finished the task, and I reap the benefits of your meticulous digging. What did you think, little scribe? Were you as unbelieving yet as terrified as I am?"

He tried to smile, and at that moment the first pain hit him without warning, ripping through his abdomen so that he doubled over on the cushions, gasping, sweat springing from his forehead. No! he whispered, knees pressed to his chin, fists crammed against his stomach. Thoth have mercy, I cannot take this agony, help me, help me! Then the spasm abated and he went limp, lying behind the curtains with eyes closed, panting. Tbubui, he cried out silently. Have pity on me. If you must slay me then wait. Do it with a knife, a poisoned cup, have me strangled in my bed, but do not subject me to this filthy, evil thing.

Another wave of pain came and he could not help tensing against it until his muscles themselves became a source of anguish, quivering and locked. She does not need to kill me, he thought, teeth jammed together, lips drawn back in a rictus of uncontrollable pain. It does not matter what I bring back from here. She will deny everything, make up a lie, and Father will believe her. No. She *wants* to kill me. She wants me to die.

The pain slowly lessened but it did not go away. The pin stays in the figure, he thought hysterically. Stab it in with a sure hand, then grind it into the wax and leave it there to weaken and debilitate the victim. Carefully he straightened, wincing with every movement, and cupped his hands over his throbbing abdomen. It will get no better, he told himself grimly. It will keep throbbing but it will not go away. He felt for his amulet, the one he sometimes wore as a counterweight for his pectoral and sometimes affixed to a bracelet, but his groping fingers found the earring instead and he did not have the strength to let it go.

He went directly to his room in the mayor's house, and collapsing onto the couch he managed to drift into an uneasy sleep. He woke some time later to find Antef bending over him, a worried look on his face. Reaching out, Hori grasped his friend's hand. "Bring the mayor's physician, Antef," he begged. Antef, after one horrified word Hori could not catch, ran out the door. While he waited, Hori sank and rose in and out of a drowse, his consciousness geared to the ebb and flow of the pain. He struggled to sit up when the physician approached the couch with the mayor and Antef behind him.

"I am Prince Hori, son of the physician Prince Khaemwaset," he whispered. "I do not need to be examined. I am suffering from a disease of the abdomen that cannot be treated, but I beseech you to brew me a strong infusion of poppy, enough for several weeks."

"Your Highness," the physician objected, "if I do this without examining you, and I put it into your hands, you may drink too much of it at once and die. I do not wish to take that responsibility."

And neither does the mayor, Hori thought, seeing the man's expression as he hovered beside Antef. "Then place it in the hands of my servant," he suggested, gathering all his strength to simply spit out the words. "I have work to do here, and if I am prostrate with pain I cannot do it. I will dictate a scroll absolving both you and the mayor from any responsibility regarding my condition if you wish."

Both men looked relieved, then ashamed. "Highness, if you had told me about this I would have appointed my physician to be with you day and night," the mayor expostulated. "I have been lax in my duty. I apologize."

"It is not your fault!" Hori cried out with the last of his energy. "Just do as I ask! Antef, see to it!" he closed his eyes and rolled over, away from them. He heard Antef usher them out, and then he must have lost consciousness, for his next awareness was of his friend raising his head and pressing a cup to his mouth. The poppy smelled rank. He sipped at it as cautiously as he could, and when it had gone he motioned for Antef's arm. "Help me to sit up," he said. Antef did so, then lowered himself on the couch. Hori could feel him watching speculatively.

"What is it, Hori?" he asked soberly.

Hori had never heard Antef use his name before, and he felt a rush of love for Antef's reliability, his unquestioning loyalty. "She is trying to kill me," he said. "She will succeed, but not before I get home, Antef. I must get home!"

"You will," Antef promised grimly. "Tell me what to do."

"Go to the House of Life immediately, this evening. Leave me the poppy. I promise I will not drink it all." It was starting to dull the pain now, but it was dulling his thoughts also, and he fought its soporific effect. "The librarian will have left out some scrolls for you. Copy them as quickly as you can and do not return here until you have done so. I must get to the tomb tonight. Did you learn anything today?"

"No, only that no one to whom I spoke had ever heard of Tbubui, Sisenet or Harmin."

"I expected nothing else." Hori pushed himself up and swung his legs to the floor. "Go and do what I have asked, Antef. Get a guard in here to help me. I had thought to be more careful in my research but I am running out of time. We must go home as soon as possible."

He sent a servant to decline the mayor's offer of a feast with entertainment, knowing that he was bewildering and probably disappointing the man and his family. Then, supported by the burly shoulder of one of his guards, he made his way out, through the long, hot shafts of red light cast by the setting sun, to the litter.

The short journey to the library was uneventful and the effects of the poppy were at their greatest, but every jolt of the swaying vehicle sent a stab of agony through his vitals. He managed a few words with the librarian and then lay dozing, allowing his bearers to follow the librarian's litter. Time seemed more fluid, less measurable. It seemed to him that he had been carried for many hours, that his dreams were melting into the reality of the heat and movement of an everlasting present, but the litter was eventually set down and Hori drew the curtains to see the soldier waiting to assist him.

The Koptos necropolis was like a miniature Saqqara, an arid, sandy plateau dotted with little pyramids, mounds, broken pillars and half-buried causeways leading to nowhere. The librarian, to his credit, did not exclaim over Hori's condition. He led the way to a pile of dark, damp earth and a mere three steps leading to a half-submerged rock door. The shadows of evening had already gathered around it as though begging to be let in, and in spite of his enforced self-absorption Hori shuddered.

He stood leaning against his soldier, a slave holding a flaming torch nearby, and watched while the librarian bent over the imprinted circle of mud and wax that held the knotted cord around the metal hooks. Then the man exclaimed and turned to Hori. "This is definitely the seal I imprinted myself when I last inspected the tomb," he said, "but it has been broken. Look."

Hori peered at it as it lay in the man's palm. Half of it had fallen away and the cord hung precariously from one of the hooks. With a slight tug on the librarian's part the rope came away altogether and he dropped it at their feet. "Someone has forced an entry here," he said roughly. "The Overseer of Workmen told me that the sand was extremely light, not heavy and tamped down at all, and I thought nothing of it. But now . . ." He put his shoulder against the door and it shifted, swinging inward with a mild groan.

The depth of earth covering the steps would hardly come up to my knees, Hori thought distantly. Could a man, could a *thing*, dig upward through it and then turn to push it all back again? My dear librarian, I fear that someone forced an exit, not an entry. He suppressed a desire to burst into wild laughter. The laws of Ma'at have been abrogated, he thought, and we now inhabit a world where anything may happen. Anything at all. He followed the librarian and the slave into the narrow darkness beyond.

The tomb was not large. It consisted of one room with a raised dais in the centre, on which the coffin rested. The torch flared and steadied, and, light-headed with pain and with the deadening effects of the poppy, Hori looked about him. Water, he thought immediately as the angry red light picked out the wealth of decorations on the walls. Water and more water. Amun, where are you? Thoth, where is your clemency? Oh my poor family, my father, little Sheritra, my good and honourable mother. What have we done to deserve this? The walls seemed to undulate with the slow rippling of a quiet Nile on a hot, sleepy afternoon. Water under the young man's feet, water under his couch, water in which the many baboons depicted were sporting, water in his cup, spilling into his white lap, pouring out of his mouth, dripping from his black hair.

The librarian had rushed to the dais and mounted it. He was peering into the coffin and Hori thought wearily, Do not bother. The body is not there. *It* is in Memphis. It smiles and frowns, it simulates sleep and seeks the sun to heat its icy body. It holds Sheritra . . . makes love to Sheritra . . .

"This is terrible!" the librarian was lamenting. "The corpse has gone! What fiend would steal a princely corpse? And why? There will be an investigation, I promise you, Highness!"

Hori staggered towards the dais. He did not want to, but he knew that he must see for himself. With an effort he negotiated the stone lip and leaned over the edge of the sarcophagus. It was indeed empty, and at that moment a lance of fire pierced his head. With a scream he fell back. The soldier caught him and he curled into the man's embrace. "I do not want to die!" he cried out. The sound of his terror echoed off the dim walls and returned to him a hundredfold.

The soldier did not hesitate. Hori felt himself carried outside and placed gently on the litter. The librarian had hurried over and was peering in at him. He clutched at his temples, moaning softly, but some control was returning and he looked up at the man through eyes blurred with tears of pain.

"My scribe will pay you for the workmen's labours," he slurred, "and I thank you for your tact and helpfulness. Farewell. Re-seal that accursed place, and do not open an investigation. It will be fruitless." The man bowed, obviously perplexed. Hori gasped an order to the bearers, then fell back and succumbed to his misery. I will get home, he vowed feverishly. Father will see what evidence I have. But I do not want to die! Not yet! My own tomb is not finished, and I have not yet been loved. Thoth, I have not yet been loved!

He did not remember returning to the mayor's house or being put to bed. He came to himself much later for a moment, and the room was dark. One night lamp burned by his couch, but its small flame did not pierce the midnight darkness of the room. You did this, Father, he woke thinking. You spoke the spell, all unwittingly, and unleashed these abominations on us. The Scroll of Thoth is real. It rests in Memphis, sewn to the hand of someone who does not matter at all, but it has done its work. He groped for the cup of poppy on the table by his head and drained it. Suddenly a strange face was looming above him, white and young. "Your Highness has a need?" it asked, and Hori recognized one of the mayor's slaves detailed to take care of him.

"No," he said, his eyes already drifting closed. "Wake me when Antef returns."

The rhythmic ebb and flow of his torment rocked him, tossing him this way and that, and he had no choice but to give himself up to it. Under it her face loomed, smiling knowingly, unkindly, so that the paroxysms of pain were also paroxysms of lust, and Hori gave himself up to the madness.

Full daylight and a pressing heat greeted him when next he opened his eyes. Antef was there, a hand on his forehead. Hori blinked and focused. Antef looked exhausted. "Is it done?" Hori murmured.

Antef nodded. "Yes Highness. All of it. I have been absent for two days, but we can go home now."

Tears of relief began to flow. Hori beckoned his friend lower. "The tomb was empty, Antef," he croaked. "I am running out of time. Sheritra . . . Little Sun . . ."

"The barge is waiting, Prince," Antef soothed him. "I have ordered a bed made for you in the cabin. Do not fear. You will make it home."

"I love you, Antef," Hori said, his voice no more than a slight rush of air over his cracked lips. "You are my brother."

"Hush, Prince," Antef admonished. "Save your strength. I have spoken to the mayor. All is well."

The poppy was wearing off. Hori knew that its effect would increasingly diminish and he would need more and more of it as he approached Memphis. I am not strong enough to endure this, he thought as he fought to rise and Antef and a guard struggled to support him. I am a coward at heart. His thoughts trailed away into incoherence as he allowed himself to be transported to the barge and settled onto the camp bed in the cabin. Antef gave him more poppy and he lay in a daze, listening to the blessedly familiar voice of his captain giving the orders to cast off. "I could not give my thanks to the mayor," he muttered.

"I did it for you, Hori," Antef reassured him. "Sleep if you can."

"Koptos is a terrible place," Hori whispered. "So much heat, so much undiluted light. The loneliness, Antef. The unbearable loneliness. Vulnerable, unbearable . . ." Tbubui sucked the word from his mouth. He could see her chewing on it reflectively, then she swallowed it and smiled at him sympathetically. "Unbearable," she repeated. "My poor, beautiful Hori. Hot young blood . . . so hot. Come and make love to me. Warm me, Hori, warm me." When he next came to himself, Koptos was far behind them. Antef stirred beside him at his movement and held a cup to his mouth.

"My head is on fire," Hori said, "and my guts feel as though they have already been burned to ashes. What is this?"

"Soup," Antef told him. "Try to keep it down, Prince. You need the nourishment."

"Where are the scrolls?" Hori cried, struggling up, but Antef pushed him down gently.

"They are safe. Drink, Highness. The Inundation has begun and the river is running a little faster than before. The oarsmen are finding their task easier. We will be home in less time than we took to reach Koptos."

Obediently Hori drank. His stomach immediately rebelled but he kept the broth down. He felt it inside him, wholesome and comforting. "I want to sit in the chair," he told Antef. "Help me."

Once upright his head gradually ceased to spin. He smiled weakly at his friend. "I cannot fight the magic of hundreds of years," he said with a trace of humour. "But royal blood must count for something, Antef. Is there much poppy left?"

"Yes, Highness," Antef answered gravely. "There is more than enough poppy left."

Chapter 19

'The Lord of Truth abominates lies:
beware then of swearing falsely,
for he that speaketh a lie shall be cast down.'

Sheritra alighted from the skiff, drew a deep breath and started along the winding, palm-lined path. The day was breathlessly still, a stifling late summer afternoon, but she disregarded the discomfort. Today, this morning, Father had finally agreed to allow a betrothal. She had given him no rest, approaching him at every opportunity, and her persistence had won. Oddly, it had been at the moment when she told him where Hori had gone that he had capitulated. He had not fretted over-much at his son's disappearance, it seemed to Sheritra. Having banished Hori from all family gatherings, he had not even missed him for several days. But on the fourth day he had begun to make inquiries and Sheritra had waited, heart in mouth, mindful of her promise to Hori to wait one full week before disclosing his whereabouts. Hori's servants could shed no light on his disappearance. Khaemwaset had even inquired to Tbubui at one noon meal, but she had replied in the negative.

Khaemwaset had come up empty until the seventh day, when Sheritra had gone to him in much trepidation and had confessed that Hori had set sail for Koptos and the truth.

"He is determined to blacken her name," Khaemwaset had roared. "He corrupted Ptah-Seankh and that did not work, so he is hatching another scheme. I understand how an unreturned love can blight an otherwise generous nature, but this spite . . ." He had controlled himself with an effort, and when he next spoke his voice was lower. "This spite is so unlike the Hori I thought I knew."

"Perhaps it is not spite," Sheritra had dared to argue. "Perhaps Hori has not changed at all and he is trying desperately to make you see something you very much wish to overlook, Father."

"Are you turning against me also, Little Sun?" he had countered sadly, and she had vigorously denied the accusation.

"No, Father! And neither is Hori. Listen to him when he

returns, please! He loves you, he does not want to hurt you, and he is suffering terribly because of your rejection of both of us."

"Oh you know about that, do you?" Khaemwaset had frowned. "It was a precaution against my untimely death, Sheritra, that was all. Marry before I die and of course you shall have your dowry."

But Hori cannot claim his inheritance, Sheritra thought. Not ever. This was not a moment to anger her father further. However, she took the opening he had provided.

"I want to marry long before that," she said swiftly. "Grant my entreaties, Father, and give me my betrothal to Harmin. As a princess it is my place to ask him, not the other way around, and if you do not give your permission we must wait forever."

This time he had not brushed her off. He had stared at her speculatively for some moments, then, to her surprise and delight, he had nodded brusquely. "Very well. You may go to Harmin and offer him marriage. I have lost one son, and already I have begun to think of Harmin as a replacement for Hori. I am fond of the young man, and he at least is loyal to his relatives." He smiled thinly. "I see the disbelief on your face, Sheritra, but trust me. I mean it. Go to Harmin."

It was not disbelief he saw, she was thinking now as the house came in sight, it was a pang of cold shock to hear him speak that way about Hori. No one can repair that damage. I feel guilty wallowing in my own pleasure while Hori, and Mother, too, in her own way, are so unhappy.

She did not have to go far to find Harmin. He was sprawled under a tree in his garden, an empty flagon of beer beside him, one of the silent black servants a short way off standing under a palm. Sheritra signalled to Bakmut to wait, and hurried over the brittle grass with an anticipatory smile. How inviting he looks, she thought. How delicious, lying supine on the mat, with his black hair spread over the cushion, his arm flung across that broad chest, his strong legs parted!

He half raised himself as she came up and knelt, and she bent and placed her mouth on his. He was flushed from the heat of the day and his lips were dry. After a moment he pulled away and sat up fully.

"Oh Harmin, I miss you so all the time!" she said. "I know we talked yesterday when you visited your mother, but the time was short and you seemed preoccupied. I am always desperate for a few minutes alone with you."

"Well here I am," he said, without returning her smile. "I wish that you had waited to visit me until this evening, Sheritra. I did not sleep well last night and I am trying to remedy the lack."

He did indeed look tired, she thought, disappointment at his words giving way to concern. His eyes were bleary, the delicate lids puffed. Tentatively she touched his face.

"I did not mean to be so forward," she apologized. "It is just that I have good news for us, Harmin. Father has finally agreed to our betrothal."

He smiled then, but it was not a free, glad expression. "If you had come to me a week ago with this information I would have been overjoyed," he said sullenly, fumbling for the cup at his elbow. "But I am not sure that I want to be betrothed to a woman who neither trusts nor loves me." He would not meet her eye. Lifting the cup, he drained it to the dregs, and Sheritra watched him in a haze of bewilderment.

"Harmin!" she said after a moment. "What do you mean? You taught me trust! You taught me love! I adore you with all my heart! What are you saying?"

He threw the cup into the shrubbery, and when he answered, his tone was cold and spiteful. "Do you deny that you have been conspiring with Hori in the most despicable way to discredit me and my mother?"

"Not conspiring, Harmin! I . . ."

He snorted. "I can see the guilt on your face, Highness. My mother told me that Hori had gone to Koptos to try and ruin her. It was humiliating, hearing such a thing from her instead of from you. It did not occur to you to come and talk to me about it, did it? Of course not! I mean less to you than he does."

Sheritra felt as though he had struck her. "How did she know where Hori had gone?"

"She encountered him by the watersteps on the morning he left. He told her what he was going to do and she begged him with tears, with tears! to cease his vindictive persecution, so unjust, so fruitless, but he would not listen. And you!" he sneered. "You knew that he was going and you knew why, yet you did not take me into your confidence."

"What makes you think Hori told me anything?" she tried to

challenge him, but she could not deny his accusation, and her words came out weakly. It would be useless to try and explain that to take him into her confidence would have meant telling him what she thought of Tbubui, and that she had not wanted to hurt him. And that was not the only reason, she thought dismally. Hori had urged her not to press for a betrothal until he came back. He did not know whether or not Harmin was involved with his mother in deceiving Khaemwaset, and thus deceiving Sheritra also.

"He tells you everything," Harmin said petulantly. "You share more with him than you do with me. I am deeply hurt, Sheritra, first that you chose to shut me out and second that you could even imagine that my mother or I could be capable of perpetrating such a huge lie on your family."

But she has, Sheritra thought in despair, looking at his sulky, brooding face. I believed Hori implicitly when he told me Ptah-Seankh's story. Oh Harmin, I pray fervently that you are hurt and angry because you know nothing of your mother's true nature, not because you are afraid of exposure. Suddenly she realized the implications of the thought and her mouth went dry. How can I possibly doubt him? she asked herself in a rush of tenderness. He is as much a victim of Tbubui's machinations as Father. Poor Harmin.

"My dearest brother," she said softly, edging closer to him and putting an arm about his neck. "I did not confide in you because I did not want to hurt you. I believe, and so does Hori, that your mother has been lying to Khaemwaset. Such a truth is hard for a son to bear. Please believe me, I did not want to see you suffer!"

He was still for a long time. He did not relax against her but neither did he pull away. His face was turned so that she could not read his expression, but gradually, although he did not move, she felt him withdraw. "You had better leave me alone now, Highness," he said dully. "I cannot in all honesty sit here and listen to my mother being maligned. I am sorry."

Her arm dropped. "Harmin . . ." she began, but he rounded on her and shouted, "No!" with such ferocity that she almost lost her balance. She rose clumsily and walked away, her new-found confidence deserting her so that her shoulders slowly slumped and her hands came up to cradle her sharp elbows. Calling to Bakmut she half ran along the path to the watersteps, expecting to hear him call her back, but there was silence. He will get over it, she told herself anxiously. He will remember that I mentioned a betrothal, that his anger interfered with his hearing, and then he will hurry to me and everything will be all right. I will not cry.

Nevertheless, her vision blurred as she stepped down into the skiff. She felt like a foolish child. In a moment of blinding self-knowledge she saw how she ought to have challenged him, told him that no matter what his mother was like she loved him, pressed him on the issue of the betrothal they had planned together for so long. But he had dominated her from the first, perhaps even manipulated her, so that now she was too weakened to risk incurring his displeasure. He must love me, he must! she insisted hysterically as the skiff eased out into midstream and she felt Bakmut's eyes on her inquiringly. Without him I shall die! Then her mind went very still and she began to shiver.

Word of Hori's clandestine journey to Koptos soon spread in the household, but Nubnofret knew nothing of it until she sent a servant to request his presence in her suite. Khaemwaset had told her that their son was barred from family occasions because he had been unforgivably rude to Tbubui, and Nubnofret had wisely pursed her lips and refrained from comment. It was not a wife's place to interfere in a disciplinary matter such as this, particularly where a second wife was concerned, and the last thing Nubnofret wanted was a disorderly house. But she worried about her son. Guiltily, she realized that she had been too involved in her own unhappiness to spend any time with him lately, and she resolved to remedy the matter at once. She was dumbfounded when the servant told her that Hori had gone to Koptos. Resisting the urge to ask the man why, she immediately sought out her husband.

Khaemwaset had just left the bathing room and was on his way back to his apartments. Nubnofret, standing facing him in the passage, had time to notice how beads of water had clung to the hollow of his throat and were glistening across his belly before he halted and smiled at her encouragingly. "What can I do for you, Nubnofret?" he asked, and unaccountably her stomach constricted. You can take me in your arms, she thought feverishly. You can tilt my head back the way you used to do, and kiss me, and press the damp coolness of your body against mine. "I wish to speak to you seriously, Prince," she said.

"Then come and talk to me while I am massaged. Kasa!"

Obediently she followed him and his body servant back to his room, where he got onto the couch, indicating that she should sit by his head where he could see her. Kasa poured oil into the valley of his spine and began to knead the still-firm flesh, and Nubnofret looked away, clearing her throat with a polite little cough.

"Khaemwaset, where is Hori?" she asked directly.

He closed his eyes. "Hori is in Koptos."

"And what is Hori doing in Koptos?"

Khaemwaset sighed, rubbing his cheek against his forearm. He still had not opened his eyes. "He thinks that Ptah-Seankh falsified the report on Tbubui's ancestry that I requested before the marriage contract became valid, and he has gone to find what he considers to be the truth."

"Did he leave with your permission?"

"He did not even leave with my knowledge." Now he opened his eyes. They regarded Nubnofret warily. "He is being vituperative, disobedient and thoroughly reckless. I disciplined him once over this obsession with what he sees as some kind of duplicity on Tbubui's part, and I can see that when he returns I shall have to discipline him again."

His eyes were drooping, but not from fatigue or an unwillingness to look at her, Nubnofret realized. The massage was arousing him. How much you have changed, my husband, she thought in hot terror. You have become an unpredictable, exotic creature none of us recognizes. It is as though some demon came to you one night and stole your ka, replacing it with something else. If you made love to me now I should be frightened at your touch. "I am going away, Khaemwaset," she said calmly. At that she saw the muscles of his back tense and he lifted his head sharply, his eyes once more brightly aware.

"What do you mean, you are going away?"

"I am going to Pi-Ramses, and I am not asking your permission. I have seen my family torn apart, my household disrupted, my authority slowly undermined, and this business of Hori is the last straw. I am highly distressed that even my servants knew of his absence before I did. Hori does nothing recklessly and you know it. Whatever prompted him to this desperate action is worthy of your attention, and his state of mind should be of great concern to you. Yet you speak only of discipline. He is your only son, your heir. You are throwing him away."

He regarded her steadily, and now she could have sworn that she saw animosity in his gaze. "I forbid you to go," he said. "What will Memphis think if you do? That I cannot rule my own establishment? No, Nubnofret. It is out of the question."

Nubnofret rose. "Tbubui can order the servants, plan the feasts and entertain your guests." She said it quietly, but she wanted to scream at him, pummel him with both fists, spit into his reddening face. "I will not come back until you send for me, and you had better be sure, Prince, that you need me before you ask a herald to bring me such a message. My only request is that you do not allow Tbubui to occupy my suite."

"You cannot go!" he shouted, struggling up. "I refuse to allow it!"

She bowed frigidly. "You have soldiers, Khaemwaset," she said. "Order them to detain me if you dare. I will stay under no other circumstances."

His hands clenched and his chest heaved with emotion but he said no more. After a moment she turned on her heel and sailed out the door. She did not look back.

Khaemwaset pushed himself off the couch and stood, irresolute. His first impulse was to call for Amek and command Nubnofret's detention, but such a radical order, once made, would be hard to rescind. "Dress me!" he barked at Kasa who hastened to comply, his fingers unusually clumsy on his master's body. Khaemwaset endured the man's fumbling ministrations without complaining, and when he was done, went out immediately.

Tbubui was dictating a letter in her room, one of Khaemwaset's junior scribes scratching away industriously at her feet. She swung to him with a wide smile that he did not return. Instead he snapped at the scribe, "Get out!" The man gathered up his paraphernalia, sketched a hasty bow and withdrew. Khaemwaset slammed the door behind him and then leaned on it, breathing heavily. Tbubui was beside him in an instant.

"Khaemwaset, whatever is wrong?" she asked, and as always at the touch of her hand, the sound of her voice, the tautness went out of him.

"It is Nubnofret," he confessed. "She is leaving me and going to Pi-Ramses. Already her servants are packing her belongings. Her life here has become insupportable, it seems." He ruffled her hair with one absent hand. "Tbubui, I shall be the laughing-stock of the whole of Egypt."

"No, my dearest," she objected. "Your reputation is too entrenched. People will say that I have bewitched you and alienated Nubnofret. They will blame me, and I do not mind. Perhaps it is true. Perhaps I have not been as kind as I could have been to Nubnofret."

"I do not want to hear your tact today, Tbubui!" he said harshly. "I do not want you to be kind! Blame Nubnofret who has been cold and distant and unwelcoming to you! Blame Hori who has run to Koptos to destroy you! Why are you always so achingly kind?"

"He is trying to destroy me?" she repeated, swinging away in the room and then turning to fix him with a suspicious stare. "I knew where he had gone, for I heard snatches of the servants' gossip, but for an evil purpose?"

Khaemwaset pushed himself away from the door and almost staggered into the room. He got as far as her cosmetic table and sank onto the stool fronting it. "Koptos," he repeated dully. "He has some deluded idea that the truth about you lies there and he is going to find it." She was silent so long that he thought she had not heard him. "Tbubui?" he called. She turned slowly as though she was afraid of something behind her, and he saw that her face had gone very pale. She was twining her fingers together, oblivious of the rings digging into her flesh.

"He will bring back fabricated information," she said dully. "He is determined to see me disgraced."

"I do not understand any of them anymore," Khaemwaset admitted angrily. "Nubnofret clearly knows her duty yet she deserts me without a qualm. Hori has become an insane stranger. Even Sheritra approaches me with an arrogant, abrasive stubbornness. The gods are punishing me and I do not know what for!"

A queer little half-smile flitted across her face. "You have always been too indulgent with them, Khaemwaset," she said. "You have made them the spoiled centre of your life. Where other men have placed their families second to their duty to

Egypt, you have delighted in fulfilling their desires first, and they have become unruly. Hori, in fact, has . . ." her voice trailed off, and he saw an expression of anguish in her eyes.

"You know something you are not telling me," Khaemwaset demanded. "I have never heard a word of criticism of my family pass those sensuous lips of yours, Tbubui, unless I have almost thrashed it out of you. What do you know about Hori?"

She came to him slowly, her hips swivelling in unconscious invitation, halting just out of his reach. "I do carry a dreadful thing concerning your son," she said in a low voice. "I will tell you now, but only because I live in increasing terror for my safety and the life of my unborn child. Oh promise me, dear brother, that you will not blame me!"

"Tbubui," he said in exasperation, "I love only you. Even your silly little faults are dear to me. Come now. What is on your mind?"

"You will not believe anything he brings back from Koptos, will you?"

"No," Khaemwaset assured her. "I will not."

"He is so implacable in his hatred," she began, so softly that he had to crane to hear her. "He would kill me if he could." She looked up and faced him, her eyes full of desperation, her mouth trembling. "He raped me, Khaemwaset. Hori raped me when he first knew I was to marry you. He had come to my house, to talk he said, but he began to make advances towards me. When I refused him and told him I was in love with you and we were going to be married he became incensed. 'Do you not prefer young flesh, Tbubui, to some old man fighting the encroachments of time?' he urged, and then he . . . he . . ." She covered her face with her hands. "I am so ashamed!" she burst out, and then began to weep. "Believe me, Khaemwaset, I could do nothing! I tried to summon my servants but he clapped a hand over my mouth. 'Cry out and I will kill you!' he threatened, and I believed him. He was insane, a wild man. I even think . . ."

"What?" Khaemwaset croaked. He was looking about desperately, his eyes lighting on first one thing and then another, but he could not escape his own feeling of mounting betrayal and rage. Tbubui collapsed onto the floor, pulling her hair to hide her face, then her hands scooped up imaginary earth and placed it on her head in the traditional gesture of mourning.

"I do not even know if my baby is yours or his!" she blurted. "I pray that it is yours, Khaemwaset! I pray! I pray!"

Khaemwaset came slowly to his feet. "You need not fear, Tbubui," he said thickly. "Sleep in peace, you and our unborn child. Hori has betrayed every decency, every claim he might have had on my affections or my paternal duty. He will be punished."

She looked up, her face disfigured and tear-stained. "You must kill him, Khaemwaset," she choked. "He will not rest until he has exacted what he sees as a just vengeance on me, and I am so afraid! Kill him!"

Some part of Khaemwaset, a tiny core of sanity, began to shout no! No! This is an illusion! Remember his sense of humour, his smile, his readiness to be your partner. The work you have done together, the discussions, the nights of drinking and closeness, the love and pride in his eyes . . . But the overwhelming part of him that was Tbubui swept over him.

Walking to her he squatted and drew her hot, damp head down onto his chest. "I am sorry that you have suffered so much at the hands of my family," he said into her hair, eyes closed. "Hori does not deserve to live. I will see to it."

"I am desperately sorry, Khaemwaset," she said, her voice muffled against his skin, and he felt her hand insinuate itself between his thighs.

Sheritra was dreaming. Harmin was bending over her, a scarlet ribbon tied into his hair, the smell of his skin a musky, warm perfume that invaded her nostrils and rendered her weak with longing. "Pull back your sheets and let me come in," he was whispering. "It is I, Sheritra. I am here. I am here." She looked up at him, lit dimly by the night lamp, her gaze languorous and slow with desire, but there was something wrong. His smile was changing, becoming feral. His teeth were lengthening, sharpening, his face greying, and she realized with a shock of pure horror that a jackal was bending over her. Starting up with a shriek she realized first that it was still night and the peace and silence of the numbing hours before dawn had a hold on the house, and second that Bakmut was shaking her gently.

"Highness, your brother is here. He is here," the girl was saying, and Sheritra passed a shaking hand over her face.

"Hori?" she asked, aware that she was drenched in sweat. "He has returned? Bring him in, Bakmut, and find some food and something to drink at once." The girl nodded and melted into the shadows.

Sheritra looked at the night lamp. Bakmut had obviously just trimmed it and it send a tiny, reassuring column of yellow sanity into the darkness pressing about the couch. Sheritra sat higher, now wide awake, and as she did so there was movement beyond the lamp's reach. Hori materialized and sat heavily beside her knees. Sheritra stifled a scream. He was so gaunt that she could see his ribs, and his head was trembling. The hair that had once been so thick and gleaming with health lay lank against his neck, and his eyes, as he turned to survey her, were as filmed and sunken as an old man's.

"Gods, Hori," she exhaled. "What has happened to you?"

"I never thought I would see you again," he rasped, and she could see tears of fatigue gathering. "I am dying of a curse, Sheritra, Tbubui's curse, like the one she put on poor Penbuy. Do you remember?"

For a confused moment she could not comprehend what he was saying. He sounded delirious. But then in a flash of enlightenment she saw again the pile of refuse, the glint of something, the broken pen case in her puzzled hands and the wax doll.

"Penbuy!" she cried out. "Of course! How could I have been so blind! It was his pen case. He had several, and I suppose I must have seen them all at one time or another but not directly, just out of the corner of my eye, unremarked. Penbuy . . ."

"She put a death curse on him so that he would not bring back bad news from Koptos," Hori whispered. "Sheritra, read these. Read them now." Several scrolls appeared and he passed them to her. The shaking in his hands was so pronounced that it was communicated to her as she took the papyrus. His skin, as she brushed his fingers, was hot and dry. She wanted to throw the scrolls aside, to call for her father in his capacity as physician, to rouse the servants and have him put to bed, but she sensed the desperation behind his request and honoured it, giving all her attention to the scrolls.

She had just begun to read when Bakmut returned with wine

and slices of cold roast goose and melon. "Bring more light," she ordered absently, but by the time the girl was placing larger lamps on the holders about the room she was oblivious, all her attention fixed on what she was reading. Hori sat quietly, swaying sometimes, occasionally lifting a flask to his mouth. "What is that?" she asked once, her eyes still on the scroll under her hands, and he answered, "Poppy, Little Sun." She had nodded and gone back to her reading.

At last she allowed the final scroll to roll up with a polite rustle. Hori turned to her and they regarded one another in silence.

"Impossible," she hissed. "Never." There was a cold anger in her.

"No," she insisted. "Think, Sheritra. Let us examine the evidence rationally."

"What you are suggesting is not rational, Hori," she said, and he jerked away, his whole body quivering uncontrollably with the gesture.

"I know," he said. "But I was in that tomb, Sheritra. The body had gone. The librarian was horrified and mystified. The water depicted on the walls . . ." He stopped himself with an obvious effort. "May I try and convince you?"

Sheritra's dream came back to her, alien and frightening. "Very well. But you should not be trying to talk. You are very sick. I think she has poisoned you, and if so you need Father and an antidote."

He laughed breathlessly, painfully. "He can't help me. She murdered Penbuy by a death curse and she is doing the same to me. Is that too difficult to understand?"

"I am sorry, Hori. Continue." Privately she sent a quick glance into the room for Bakmut. If she could send the girl for her father Hori might be saved, but she did not want to drain her brother's strength with argument. "At least eat something first," she suggested, and at that Hori turned on her, his lips drawn back in a fevered snarl.

"Antef fed me soup until I could no longer keep it down," he said, and with a chill of real fear Sheritra heard the terror in his voice. "I have no time to eat, you little fool. Wake up! I am dying! Let me try to convince you!" She recoiled, then took his hand.

"Yes," she quavered.

"Will you first try to believe that Father has done this? That he unleashed something perverse when he spoke the words on the scroll without knowing what he said?"

"I will try."

"Good. Let me lie down, Sheritra. Give me that pillow. Thank you. First accept that Tbubui killed Penbuy by magic and she is killing me. Penbuy she murdered because Father would have listened to any evidence he brought back from Koptos. He was respected, and Father knew his intelligence. Even if Penbuy's story had sounded insane it would have planted a seed of doubt in Father's mind. As for me . . ." He lifted one shoulder in a frail shrug. "I am already thoroughly discredited in Father's eyes. I think she is simply tasting power and finding it sweet. She knows I would never harm her. She does not need to get rid of me, she merely wants to. If there is another motive I cannot find it."

He fell silent. Sheritra saw sweat break out on his forehead and knew that he had stopped talking in order to marshal his strength. She waited while he wiped his face on her bunched sheets. His next words took her by surprise.

"Sheritra," he began, "what do Tbubui's servants remind you of? Think carefully."

Dark, totally silent, immediately obedient—she shook her head, puzzled. "They are strange," she replied, "but they don't remind me of anything."

"Well perhaps you have not been in as many tombs as I have with Father," Hori said grimly. "Aren't they like shawabtis, Sheritra?"

Shawabtis, she thought. The wooden slaves buried with the nobility to be brought to life at the magic word of their owner. Dumb bearers of wine and food, obedient weavers of linen and makers of bread, dark, unerring hands to fasten a necklace, smooth kohl around tired eyes, dip the fine henna brush into the pot so delicately, so exactly, and always with the blank, expressionless faces of the wood from which they were carved. Sheritra's scalp prickled. "Shawabtis?" she said. "Ridiculous, Hori!"

"Is it? Well never mind. Consider this." He pulled a small pouch from his belt and with trembling fingers forced it open. The earring lay on his sticky palm, glowing faintly in the dim light. "Take it. Weigh it in your hand. Feel it. Imagine the one you lifted out of Tbubui's jewel chest. You had your doubts, didn't you, Sheritra? A copy of something so ancient can be a clever approximation if it is made by master craftsman, but there will be tiny clues to its true age. The gold perhaps not so clearly striated in purple or so mellow with use, the stone with that freshly set look to it, the rear stopper unsullied by years of being pressed against human skin. Your first reaction to it was the fear that it was the original. Well you were right. Tbubui had one. She lost the other crawling out of the tunnel."

Sheritra had been turning the earring over in her fingers. Now she pushed it back at him. "Stop it, Hori!" she cried out. "You are frightening me!"

"Good!" he said briskly. "Now I will frighten you some more. I will try to be coherent, to put all this in its proper order. Have you water here?"

Without comment she leaned over and poured some for him. He drank rapidly, then fumbled the poppy flask to his lips and took a long swallow.

"You will kill yourself with that," she remonstrated, then realized what she had said. He wiped his mouth with the back of one hand and gave her a glance.

"Already my body is becoming inured to it," he said. "I need more and more to keep the pain under control, but I do not think I will need it much longer." She opened her mouth to protest but he forestalled her. "No lies, Little Sun. Let me proceed. I have much to say and little strength with which to say it."

She subsided and watched him, her heart aching. Shadows lay sombrely over half his face and tinged the rest with melancholy. He is right, she thought suddenly. He is going to die. Panic shot through her, but her voice was quiet. "Go on, dearest."

"Father woke them by stealing the Scroll, theirs by right, and babbling the spell in ignorant foolishness," he began. "The lids of the coffins were missing in the inner chamber, remember? I would wager that they ordered open coffins in the hope that at some time someone would break into the tomb, find the Scroll sewn to the hand of a servant, and be intrigued enough to read it aloud, without knowing, of course, that Nenefer-ka-Ptah and the Princess Ahura, their real names, were lying behind a false wall in the same burial place. They struggle into Memphis and look for somewhere to hide, perhaps to recover. Sheritra?"

She answered his concern with a forced smile. Something in her was answering his arguments with a terrified but sure affirmative, yet there was Harmin, her own, her love, and she dared not believe for fear her life should tumble into ruin. It seemed to her that the room was becoming colder and she shrugged the sheet higher on her shoulders, trying to hear Hori's words without engaging her imagination. She did not want to see in her mind those ancient, dessicated bodies tottering about the inner chamber in the Stygian blackness, gaining suppleness and strength, pushing their stiff limbs along the tunnel.

"It is a delicious ghost story," she said firmly, "and nothing more. You say they struggle into Memphis, leaving the tomb by way of the tunnel, I presume. But the tunnel was blocked by a rock, and surely sand would have sifted over it as the hentis went by. How did they free themselves? By magic?"

"Perhaps. Or by some evil power. They had the tunnel dug in the first place, I am sure, so that they could escape in the event of the Scroll being read. They might even have left tools in it, close to the entrance. How do I know?" He moved pettishly against the pillow. "In any case, they find a vacant estate that closely resembles the home they once occupied hundreds of years ago in Koptos. Isolated, quiet, simple, perhaps it soothes their bewilderment and homesickness. Think of that house, Sheritra, the peculiar silence, the echoes in the palm grove, the feeling that you are leaving the world behind as you walk that soft, winding path. And inside, pure history. Furniture that is sparse and stark, something out of an age long gone . . ." His voice cracked to a whisper and he paused, waiting, recovering. Then he continued. "They speak the words and animate the shawabtis, who must have stood with them in the inner chamber, and they begin to repair the house. Then they seek the man who has stolen their scroll. The tomb is open. Workmen swarm over it. A few judicious inquiries bring them the information they want and they begin to plot a revenge."

"But why revenge?" Sheritra interrupted, caught up in his tale and forgetting that he was speaking of Sisenet and Tbubui. "All they had to do was contrive to steal it back and then go on living unobtrusively where they were. Why become deliberately involved with . . ." She faltered.

"With our family?" Hori finished for her. "I don't know. But I feel there is a reason and it cannot be a pleasant one. I do not have the ability to discuss that, Sheritra. This damnable pain." His voice had risen. Sheritra heard the hysteria he was struggling to hide and stroked his arm. He was burning hot. "I learned that the Prince and his wife, and a few days later their son, had died by drowning," he went on. "Remember Tbubui's exaggerated horror when she believed she was going to fall from the ramp that day? Has Harmin ever been swimming with you, even in the hottest afternoons?"

"No," she whispered, her voice no more than a sibilant rush of air. "But why do you bring Harmin into this, Hori? There were only two coffins in that tomb. You cannot be speaking of the same family."

"You are not *hearing* me!" Hori pressed desperately. "You read the scrolls. We are dealing with the darkest magic, Sheritra. We are not in the world of the decent, the rational, anymore. Let reason go! Merhu, your Harmin, drowned in Koptos and was buried there. I was in his tomb. Again there was no coffin lid, and something had dug its way out, breaking the seal. Father woke him also, and he made his way back to his parents in Memphis."

"No, no," she interrupted, shaking her head vigorously. "Sisenet is Harmin's uncle. Tbubui said so."

Hori stared at her helplessly. The corners of his mouth were black from the poppy and his pupils were so dilated that no irises remained. "Tbubui and Sisenet are husband and wife," he said slowly, emphasizing each word as though he were addressing a child. "Harmin is their son. Their son, Sheritra. I know how terrifying this is, but please try to face it."

Sheritra jerked away. "Don't do this to me, Hori!" she begged. "Harmin is innocent, I know he is! He was so wounded and angry when I tried to talk to him about his mother. He . . ."

"He is a brilliant, unscrupulous actor, like the ghoulish thing who calls herself his mother," Hori tried to shout, but the words came out a broken whistle. "Their flesh is mummified, cold. How many times have you touched Harmin and been puzzled at how cold he felt? Not lately, perhaps, for I believe that they are adjusting more each day to their second life. Tbubui loves the heat, remember? But the tomb, Little Sun . . . the Scroll was devised by Thoth in the beginning, and the family's devotion to that god is evident everywhere. The baboons, animals of Thoth. The moons, his symbol."

"Hori," Sheritra cut in determinedly. "I believe none of this. It has just occurred to me that Tbubui has cursed you for the same reason she persuaded Father to remove us from the will. She is convinced that the life of her unborn child is in danger from you if you go on living. Once it is born, all you need to do is kill it to be once again Father's heir."

He began to laugh, then bent suddenly over his abdomen. "There is no child in her womb," he choked. "She is dead, remember? The dead cannot give life, but they can take it. Perhaps she fabricated a child to force some kind of a decision on Father. It seems to me that he has been backing slowly but surely into a corner from which there is no escape, that she has been pushing him with lies, with seduction, breaking him up inside, Sheritra, weakening his soul, sullying his honour until there is no integrity left. Her aim seems to be to destroy him spiritually. But why? A punishment for stealing the Scroll is not reason enough."

Sheritra pushed herself from the couch, and dipping a square of linen in the water jug she drew it carefully over her brother's face, his hands, his neck. The actions brought her relief. She did not have to think while her fingers busied themselves. "We must find the wax doll Tbubui used to cause this suffering," she said determinedly, "and pull out the pins. We must also break into Father's chest and find an incantation that will undo the damage to you. Removing the pins will allow you to live but your health must be restored." He sat submissively while she worked. She could tell that he would not be able to do anything for himself, that searching Tbubui's quarters would be up to her. Quickly flinging cushions onto the couch she gently forced him to lie down. "Sleep," she said. "I will see what I can do. Will you be all right here by yourself?"

He had already closed his eyes. "Antef is outside," he murmured. "Send him in. Thank you, Little Sun." She kissed him on his damp forehead. His breath smelled of poppy and something else, a sweetish sourness that made her bite her lip in anxiety. He had already fallen into a restless doze when she stole out the door.

Chapter 20

*'O that I could turn my face to the north wind
on the bank of the river
and could cry out to it to cool the pain in my
heart!'*

The night was stale and the odour of the rising river teased her
nostrils, a brackish vegetable smell, as Sheritra slipped across the
garden, skirted the wall of the compound and approached the
concubines' house. Tbubui was due to move into her own apartments in four days, where the tighter security of the main house
would envelop her, and as Sheritra picked her way cautiously
through the shrubs screening the entrance, she was able to be
grateful for this small advantage.

Turning over in her mind just how she would be able to enter
the house, she was startled by soft rustlings and low voices. She
halted, heart pounding, until she realized that she was hearing the
women who had climbed onto the roof to escape the worst of the
heat and were passing the night hours in sleep or gaming or intermittent gossip. Is Tbubui up there? Sheritra wondered anxiously.
If all the women elected to have their bedding carried out, the
guards will be watching the one stair on the other side and all I
have to worry about is the Keeper.

She crept between the pillars and slipped through the entrance,
then paused to listen. There was no sound but a distant, low snoring from the Keeper's room. In trepidation, Sheritra went on. If
Tbubui was asleep in her quarters there would be a servant at the
door. Cautiously, Sheritra peered around the corner to the passage
running past the woman's domain. It was empty, and lit only by a
shaft of thin moonlight falling through a clerestory window between the ceiling and wall.

A spirit of reckless haste took hold of Sheritra then. She did
not know how long Tbubui would stay on the roof but it certainly
would not be beyond sunrise. Hori was dying and the night was
almost over. Running to Tbubui's door she inched it open.
Silence reigned within. Greatly daring, she pushed it wide and

stepped inside. The same moonlight lit the stuffy ante-room and showed it vacant, the shapes of the few pieces of furniture humping grey around her. Dim though it was, there was enough light to see by.

Hurriedly Sheritra began to search, lifting cushions, pulling aside discarded linen, flicking through vases of flowers, even opening Tbubui's golden shrine to Thoth and, with a murmured prayer of apology, feeling behind the statue of the god. She did not expect to find anything in this room and was not surprised to come up empty-handed.

Noiselessly she proceeded into the inner chamber. Its door was open and the couch vacant. Tbubui's perfume smote her immediately, the myrrh, heavy and jaded, imbuing everything with an aura of incense and love-making. Though the space was limited, the careful placing of the furniture gave Sheritra an impression of quiet vastness in keeping with the woman's need for simplicity. She began her search anew, this time being careful to leave no corner unexplored. She patted the mattress and ran a hand along the fragrant cedar frame of the couch. She lifted the lids of the tiring chests, the cosmetic boxes, the jewellery chests, her fingers thorough but frantic, but found nothing. She stood for a moment, thinking furiously. If I were Tbubui, where would I hide such a damning thing? she wondered. Then she began to smile. Of course! In the new suite, even now furnished and waiting for blessing and occupancy. No one has been in there for a week, except the servants to sweep it out. Sheritra spun on her heel and ran out of the house.

But her more leisurely hunt proved just as fruitless, and she flung herself into one of Tbubui's inlaid ebony chairs, biting her lip in frustration. She knew that the doll would not be disposed of until the victim was dead, and the pins themselves would never be pulled out. She could have a thousand secret hiding places, Sheritra thought in despair. A pit in the garden, a hole in the floor, even something sunk in the river by the watersteps.

The watersteps. With a shiver of excitement the girl came to her feet. Tbubui would not dare leave the doll on Khaemwaset's property, but Sisenet was living in the house she had once occupied, and no one but he was likely to discover it. Sheritra knew in her bones that she was correct. Leaving the suite as quietly as she had come, she made her way to her own apartments. Bakmut admitted her, a finger to her lips, and Antef rose from the stool beside her couch.

"How is he?" she whispered, coming close and peering down at Hori. He looked already dead. His face was pallid, his closed eyes sunken, and he was breathing in shallow, rapid spurts. He must have sensed her presence, for he stirred, then his eyes opened and slowly focused on her. With a worried glance at Antef she bent near him.

"Did you find it?" he whispered.

"Hori, I am sorry," she replied. "I think she must have hidden it in the house on the east bank. I will go and look immediately." In truth, she was terrified of such a task. She was in awe of Sisenet, did not want to encounter Harmin after their last painful meeting, and, though the house itself had been a very pleasant place in which to stay, she did not fancy drifting through it in the dark. It had a certain unnerving atmosphere when the people inhabiting it fell silent.

"There is not enough time," he objected with agitation. "It could be anywhere. Instead we must see what Father's scrolls of spells hold. Help me up."

"No," she hissed. "I can do it, Hori. Stay here!"

"My dear," he replied as Antef's arms went about him and he sat up awkwardly, "I do not know much about magic but I at least know what to look for. You do not. Please stop fussing over me."

Chastened and alarmed she helped Antef to take his weight, and together they left Sheritra's suite. Night still hung in the corridors and brooded in the corners. Slowly, too burdened for any attempt at concealment, they made their way to Khaemwaset's office. The guards they passed looked at them curiously, but recognizing Hori and Sheritra they held their challenges. Only at the door to the office were they halted. Khaemwaset was particular in protecting his medical supplies.

"As you can see," Sheritra told the soldier patiently, "my brother is very ill. The Prince has given us permission to retrieve certain herbs from his box."

The soldier bowed diffidently. "Princess, may I see the permission?" he asked.

Sheritra clucked, annoyed. "We are his children," she objected. "He does not think it necessary to treat us so formally. I expect he forgot that you would be here, doing your duty so zealously."

The man continued to regard them suspiciously and they continued to stand, Antef and she, with Hori swaying between them. Finally the guard stood aside.

"I do not think the Prince had his own family in mind when he set up this watch," he said gruffly. "You may pass, Highnesses."

He opened the door for them and they shuffled past him. Sheritra's arm was screaming with Hori's weight. "I think it is time Father dismissed his guard and hired Shardanas," she muttered. "These men have become very lax."

"Just as well for us," Antef breathed. They were now at the door to the inner office. Sheritra tried the latch.

"It is locked!" she said in dismay.

"Break it down," Hori said promptly.

Antef needed no further encouragement. Relinquishing Hori's full weight to Sheritra, he placed his foot on the lock and pushed. It gave with a grind of protest, and the door swung open. Inside there was total darkness.

"Antef," Sheritra called. "Light the lamp on the desk and bring it. Quickly. I cannot hold him for much longer."

Antef did as he was bid, bringing the lamp and setting it on a shelf behind the door. Its light filled the tiny room, warm and indifferently comforting. Antef pulled a chair towards the chests ranged against the far wall, and he and Sheritra lowered Hori onto it. He sat limply, hands hanging, but his head came up and he tried to smile at them.

"It is that one," he pointed. "The small one. The others are full of herbs and other physics. It will also be locked. Antef, have you a knife?"

For answer the young man produced a slim blade. He knelt before the chest and began to work at the lock. Sheritra squatted beside him.

"Antef, you will be banished from this house for tonight's work, you realize that, don't you?" she said. "It will all come out, and then Father will order you to leave."

He glanced at her briefly, his hands and his attention on the stubborn chest. "I know," he said simply, "but I no longer feel at home here anyway, Highness. Hori will die, and my reason for being here will be gone. The Prince may do as he sees fit. I do not care." The lock gave suddenly and he lifted the lid, looking up at Hori.

"Sheritra, hand me three or four," Hori ordered. "You and Antef take the same number. I want a spell of undoing and reversing, and if we cannot find that, I want a spell of protection to prevent any further damage to me." His tone was businesslike, noncommital, and Sheritra had a moment of unqualified admiration for his courage. He did not think of himself as brave, she knew, but his unself-conscious fortitude in the face of almost certain death surely gave him an anonymous place with the heroes of Egypt. He was already unrolling a scroll, his hands unsure, his breath harsh and uneven. She pushed away her overwhelming concern and turned to the task at hand.

For some time there was silence. Sheritra sat cross-legged on the floor, trying to make sense of the things she was reading. Not every scroll was titled, and it seemed to her that the language of magic was often deliberately esoteric, requiring a careful translation. Antef was faring better, his pleasant, open face down over his work. Occasionally he would grunt with disappointment and toss the delicate papyrus back into the chest.

Sheritra had finished her sixth scroll, a spell to be said over a patient with pain in his back, to be used in conjunction with a salve, the ingredients of which she did not bother to decipher. With a sigh she reached into the chest and drew out another bundle. The first scroll she raised was stained. A brown, irregular patch of what looked like rust had spread over one corner, and she fingered it with distaste. It seemed very old. "Hori, look at this," she said, handing it to him. "What has made this mark?"

He took it absently, his own eyes still engaged on the scroll he was reading, but then he gave a startled exclamation and almost dropped it. Retrieving it gingerly from his lap he examined it closely. Sheritra saw any colour that was left in his face drain away. Alarmingly, he was coming to his feet, his whole body tense with agitation. "No," he whispered. Antef turned. Sheritra got up and went to him.

"Hori, what is it?" she asked, alarmed, and her consternation grew as he suddenly began to laugh, a weak, high-pitched sound.

The scroll shook in his grip. Then his laughter turned into tears. He sat down clumsily, the scroll held before him like a grotesque weapon.

"No," he breathed. "No. Now I know that we are all doomed."

"Hori, please stop it," she begged. "You are frightening me."

For answer he took her hand and forced it onto the scroll. "Feel," he said. "Look. Can you see them?"

Sheritra looked, but all her attention was on him. "I see tiny marks, like pinpricks," she said, mystified. "and isn't that a piece of thread hanging from the papyrus?"

"A needle made those marks," he said dully. "I was there when the papyrus was punctured. The stain is Father's blood. He pricked his finger when he was sewing this thing onto the hand from which he had torn it. It is the Scroll of Thoth."

"You are being fanciful," Sheritra snapped, more sharply than she had intended. Suddenly she did not want to touch the scroll, and withdrew her hand. Hori stroked it in an ecstasy of fascinated horror.

"No I am not," he said. "I recognize it without a doubt. Father's blood, the needle marks, the thread. He ordered the lids placed on the coffins, and then the tomb was closed and sealed and the stairway piled with rubble. Yet it is here. Here." Antef was watching, motionless, balancing on one knee, his face to his friend. Sheritra did not want to see the expression on Hori's face, but she too could not look away. She had never seen such raw fear mingled with resignation. "No human hand could have done this," Hori said, "not even a dead one. Thoth himself took the Scroll from the tomb and placed it here. His divine curse is on Father, and my own pales into insignificance beside the judgment of a god." He began to laugh again, helplessly and weakly, the Scroll clutched tight to his chest. "He doesn't even know! Not yet. He doesn't know!"

"Hori," Sheritra began, not sure what she should do, but he rallied and gave her a smile.

"Close the chest," he said. "We must find Father at once and show him this Scroll together with the ones Antef copied in Koptos. He must listen!"

"But what of you?"

He stroked her hair, one long, tender gesture. "I am finished," he said simply, "but now I do not care. The god has spoken, and

Father's fate will be more terrible than mine. Death is clean compared to that. Go and bring the scrolls, Sheritra. Antef and I will wait for you. Then we will go to Father."

Even in his physical extremity there was no denying him. Sheritra acceded to his authority and went out. The guard bowed as she rushed by him but she hardly noticed. The scrolls were as she left them, lying in a disordered heap on her couch. Bakmut had gone back to sleep and was breathing deeply on her mat by the door. Quickly Sheritra scooped up the armful of papyrus, aware as she did so that the darkness was thinning; both inside the house and out, the profound hush before the dawn had fallen. Hurrying back to Hori she found Antef standing over him. Hori had fallen asleep, the Scroll hugged to his breast, his head resting against his friend.

"He should not be doing this!" she said fiercely. "He should be on his couch, dying with dignity! All this is madness, Antef, and we are encouraging him!"

At the sound of her voice Hori stirred and pulled himself up on Antef's arm. "Do you think Father is with Tbubui?" he slurred.

"No," Sheritra answered as they shambled out of the room and into the passage. "Tbubui is sleeping on the roof of the concubines' house. Father will be on his couch." She was dreading this meeting, to her a proof of Hori's increasing madness, but such was her loyalty that she was determined to support him to the end. She prayed, as they lurched along, that Khaemwaset would understand and be indulgent.

Several times on the way to Khaemwaset's suite Hori appeared to lose consciousness, but eventually they came to the imposing electrum-plated door behind which Khaemwaset was sleeping. The guard, after one look at the dishevelled trio, knocked, and after a moment a bleary-eyed Kasa answered. One glance at them was enough to chase the the sleep from his eyes.

"Highnesses!" he exclaimed. "Whatever has happened?"

"Let us in, Kasa," Sheritra demanded. "We must speak with Father."

The body servant bowed and disappeared with alacrity. After what seemed an age he returned. "The Prince is awake and will see you," he said, standing back, and the three of them staggered through the ante-room and into Khaemwaset's sleeping room.

He was sitting up and blinking in the light of the fresh lamp Kasa had brought, his expression irritable. At the sight of them he slid from under the sheets and reached for a discarded kilt, wrapping it around his waist and brusquely indicating the chair by the couch. Antef and Sheritra slid Hori onto it.

"So, Hori, you have returned," Khaemwaset said coldly. "Embroiled in madness and conspiracy I have no doubt. What is the matter with you?"

"He is very sick," Sheritra said swiftly before Hori could reply, "but he has things to tell you, Father. Oh please listen."

"Sick?" Khaemwaset echoed without much interest. "I dare say he is. Sick with his own guilt. I had expected more from you, my son, than weak self-indulgence and the petty urge for revenge."

Hori had managed to retain his hold on the Scroll. Now he thrust it towards Khaemwaset. "Do you recognize this, Father?" he asked. "Sheritra and I found it not an hour ago in the locked chest in your office where you keep your other scrolls. Antef will swear that I am telling the truth."

"What were you doing in there?" Khaemwaset said furiously. "You have taken leave of your senses, all of you."

Then he looked down at the Scroll. At first he was obviously not aware of what he was holding, but as he turned it impatiently the blood stain came into view. He stared at it, his hand began to shake, then with an oath he flung it away. It flew past Hori's head and landed in the shadows. Quietly Antef stepped back and picked it up. Sheritra, all her attention fixed on her father, saw that he gone a deathly white.

"I see that you do recognize it," Hori commented with a wry smile. "Remember how you dug the needle into your finger, Father, and your blood dripped onto the corpse's hand? Antef, give it back to the Prince. I want him to examine it more carefully. I want him to be sure."

But Khaemwaset backed away. "It is the Scroll of Thoth, that damnable thing," he said hoarsely. "I am not denying it. What I refuse to believe is your foolish story. If you have indeed broken into my chest you will all be severely punished." He was recovering. Sheritra saw the colour creeping back into his cheeks, and with a blaze of controlled anger mixed with cunning. She had never before believed her father capable of sheer animal craftiness, but there was no mistaking its presence on his face. He is not going to listen, she thought with a chill of fear. All his fairness, his reason, has been swallowed up in possessing Tbubui. He is like a cornered animal driven to the extreme of temporary insanity by the need for self-preservation.

He came close to Hori, bending and placing his hands on his own knees, peering into his son's pain-wracked face without any sign of concern.

"You are a little jackal, Hori," he said thickly. "Shall I tell you what I believe? I believe that you broke open my chest to put the Scroll in, not take it out. You did not find it there, you stole it from the tomb and mutilated my chest to support your weak story. Now what story is that exactly, Hori? What incredible deceit am I being asked to consider?"

Sheritra pushed forward with the scrolls Hori had brought back from Koptos. "Read these, Father," she begged. "Hori is too ill to talk. They will explain everything."

Khaemwaset straightened and took them with an indifferent glance for her. He unrolled the first and then began to smile gently. "Ah," he said. "Why am I not surprised to find this in Antef's broad hand? So my son has suborned you also, young man?" Antef said nothing, and Khaemwaset's eyes moved to Sheritra. "I am deeply disturbed by your participation in this fraud," he accused her. "I had thought you would have more sense, Little Sun. Did you connive in these forgeries?"

"They are not forgeries," she contradicted him swiftly. "They are copies of documents residing in the library at Koptos. Antef made them under the librarian's supervision. The man will surely swear to the truth. Please just read them, Father."

"A man will swear to any truth if he is paid enough gold," Khaemwaset said darkly. "Nevertheless, because *you* ask me, Sheritra, I will read."

He sat down on the edge of the couch and, with an ostentatious contempt began to scan the papyrus. Hori was swaying dangerously on the chair and moaning softly but his father paid him no attention. Antef took the flask of poppy from his belt and unstoppered it, holding it to Hori's mouth so that he could drink, then he knelt and pulled Hori's head onto his shoulder. Sheritra stood—tired, aching and scared—while slowly the contents of the room began to acquire coherent shapes and the lamplight faded to a dirty yellow. Dawn was at hand.

At last Khaemwaset tossed the final scroll onto the couch behind him and looked directly at his daughter. "Do you believe this rubbish, Sheritra?" he demanded. It was the worst question he could have asked her. She hesitated, and he jumped in. "You do not. Neither do I. It is unfortunate that Hori has squandered so much energy preparing his vile little hoax. If he had hoarded a little for himself he might not have become ill."

"I am ill because she cursed me," Hori broke in with an agonizing slowness. "She told me to my face that she would do so. She is a living corpse, Father, like her husband Nenefer-ka-Ptah and her son Merhu, and they will destroy us all. You brought it on yourself when you gave tongue to the first spell on the Scroll." He tried to laugh. "Only the gods know what would have happened if you had spoken the second as well."

Khaemwaset rose and strode to the door. In spite of his assurance, Sheritra thought she detected an underlying unease. "I have heard enough," he said loudly. "Tbubui warned me that you were jealous enough and insane enough with thwarted desire to actually attempt to kill her and her baby, and I supposed that her words stemmed from hysteria because of her pregnancy. But no more. You are a threat to both." He hauled on the door. "Guards!" he yelled.

"No, Father!" Sheritra screamed, flinging herself across the room and clutching his arm. "No, you cannot! He is dying, can't you see that? Have pity on him!"

"Did he have any pity on Tbubui? On me?" he said hotly. Two guards were even now hurrying into the room, and Khaemwaset nodded curtly in Hori's direction. "My son is under close arrest," he told them curtly. "Take him to his quarters and do not let him out." Sheritra screamed again but he firmly plucked her fingers from his arm. The soldiers were pulling Hori to his feet, and Antef was hurriedly pushing the flask into his hand. Hori looked at Sheritra.

"You know what you must do now," he said. "Please try, Sheritra. I do not want to die just yet." Then he was being half dragged, half carried across the room and out the door. Khaemwaset swung to her.

"As for you," he snapped. "I am ashamed of you. For the moment you are free until I decide a fitting punishment." He turned to Antef. "You are a good young man at heart," he said more kindly, "and I prefer to believe that you have been my son's un-witting tool. You also will be disciplined and I will probably expel you from my household, but today I will be lenient. You may go."

"You were not as indulgent towards Ptah-Seankh," Sheritra said in a trembling voice when Antef had bowed and left, and Khaemwaset agreed with her readily.

"Of course not," he said. "Ptah-Seankh was *my* servant. He owed me his loyalty, not Hori. He betrayed me. But Antef is Hori's servant, and he at least remembered where his duty lay. I admire him for that."

"And why can you not admire Hori for his loyalty to you?" Sheritra urged. "You cannot seriously think that Hori would have been able to dig through the rubble to the tomb entrance, force the door and raise the lid on that one coffin? Read the scrolls again, Father. For neither can you seriously believe that Hori could have contrived such an involved story. Please, at least give him the benefit of your doubt."

"He could have hired workmen to do the task while he was away," Khaemwaset replied sullenly. "I have not visited the site since . . . since . . . ."

"You are more distressed than you would have us believe, aren't you, Father?" Sheritra said. "Some part of you is terrified that Hori may be right. In fact, that part of you believes more strongly than I do. Go to Koptos yourself. Talk to the librarian."

Khaemwaset shook his head vigorously, but his voice, when it came, was weak and thready. "I cannot," he whispered. "She is everything to me, and I will do whatever is necessary to keep her. You are wrong, Little Sun. No sane person could believe that my darling is anything other than a beautiful, accomplished, desirable woman. But I do think that perhaps her lineage is not pure. It may even be non-existent."

"Hori would not hurt her," Sheritra said. Her head was throbbing and her whole body cried out for rest, for oblivion, but she sensed something more behind her father's arrest of Hori. It was as though he had eagerly and too rapidly embraced the opportunity to confine him, to place him under his thumb. She came up to him and they faced one another soberly in the grey, pitiless first light of Ra filtering between the shutters. "The last thing Hori wants to do is cause Tbubui harm. He loves her as much as you do. He hates himself for it, not her, and certainly not you. Father, are there spells to lift a death curse?"

He blinked. "Yes."

"May I see one?"

Again that expression of bestial cunning came and went on his face. "No you may not. They are volatile, dangerous things, best left to magicians with the power and authority to use them."

"Then will you conjure one for Hori?"

"No. To do so without the certainty that he is indeed under a death curse would only do him harm."

"Gods," she said softly, backing away. "You want him to die, don't you? You have become a horror, Father. Shall I kill myself now and save you the trouble of doing it later when Tbubui decides her life will be simpler without me?" He did not answer. He went on standing there, the cruel dawn light revealing every crevice in his aging face. Sheritra gave one sob of disappointment and anguish and fled.

I must go back to his office before he has finished being bathed and dressed, she thought desperately as she hurried away. Before the guard is changed as well. Oh, I am frightened! But I must not involve Antef any more. Anything to be done I must do myself. I wish Harmin were here. She almost cannoned into two servants with brooms and rags in their hands, and they shrank back against the wall, bowing their apologies.

The house was stirring. Soon the parade of musicians and body servants would begin on their way to waken and minister to the family. The stewards would be knocking politely and approaching the couches on a wave of gentle harping, the morning refreshments balanced on silver trays. But not to Mother's suite, Sheritra thought despondently. Those rooms are dismally empty. I have not had time to miss her, yet surely with her gone the heart of this house has begun to decay. Tbubui will try and fill her place, but more stridently, more loosely. Sheritra wrenched her mind away from the future and slowed, greeting the sleepy guard on her door and going into her ante-room. To her surprise, Bakmut was sitting on a chair, awake and alert, a scroll in her hands. As Sheritra approached she rose and bowed.

"Good morning, Bakmut," Sheritra said. "I see that you have not slept much either."

The girl came close and held out the scroll. It was sealed with

Ramses' imperial imprint. Fingering it, Sheritra also saw that it was addressed to Hori. "How did you come by this?" she asked sharply.

"I intercepted it," Bakmut said forthrightly. "A Royal Herald arrived with it yesterday, and fortunately his search for the Prince brought him to your door. If he had gone further into the house, or lost his way and wandered closer to the concubines' house, his burden might have been removed from him by another. I had concealed it, and forgot to pass it on last night when you brother came to your door."

"Just what are you saying?" Sheritra frowned.

"I am saying that I trust no one in this madhouse any more," Bakmut replied flatly.

Sheritra looked at the scroll thoughtfully. "My brother has been arrested," she said. "Should I open this, or try to get it to him? It must be the answer to his plea for help." The girl remained silent. "You did well, Bakmut," Sheritra told her, handing back the papyrus. "Keep it safe for a little longer. I do not have the time to open it now. I must go. If anyone comes to my door, tell them I have gone back to bed and do not wish to be disturbed." Bakmut nodded mutely, lips compressed. Sheritra gave her a smile and went out again.

The guard who had challenged them and then let them pass was still outside the office, his eyes red-rimmed and heavy with the need for sleep. Sheritra had no trouble persuading him to let her in, and as she closed the door she heard his replacement come striding along the passage and greet him cheerfully. Good, she thought. If my luck holds he will not be told that I am within.

The office held none of the air of unreality and urgency it had during the night. Ra had now lifted completely above the horizon. The light sifting down onto the floor, filmed with its collection of dust that the servants would soon industriously sweep away, prompted no phantoms. A little calmness came to Sheritra. Taking a deep breath she crossed to the inner room. The mangled door was still standing wide, the chest open on the floor.

She did not hesitate. Sinking cross-legged beside it she delved inside and pulled out a scroll at random. In her heart she knew that the task was impossible, that even if she could, by some fantastic chance, find a correct spell, she would not be able to assemble the necessary implements to carry it out. Yet if Hori died and she had not done everything possible, she would never forgive herself.

She had not been down there long, doing her best to decipher a maze of arcane hieroglyphs, when she heard voices beyond in the passage—the guard, and her father's distinctive bass. Her heart leaped into her mouth. Hastily dropping the scroll back into the chest, she looked about wildly for a hiding place. He had obviously not waited to be bathed and dressed before coming to inspect the damage she, Antef and Hori had done. The room was small, compact and bare, but several of the chests stood end to end and there was a little space between them and the wall. Without thinking she squeezed behind them, lying full-length with her face towards the room. Through one narrow slit she could see the rifled box and the lower half of the door. Trying to still her breath, she waited, almost fainting with fright.

Presently her father came in and paused in the doorway. She could hear his exclamation of disgust as he saw the confusion, then his bare legs came closer. Going down on one haunch he began to grope through the scrolls, perhaps counting them to make sure none was missing.

Sheritra could see his face now, intent, stern. She kept glancing away in the superstitious certainty that if he looked up he would meet her eye and she would be discovered, but she looked back in time to see him toss one more roll of papyrus into the chest. It was the Scroll of Thoth. The bloodstain looked rusty in the daylight. Khaemwaset slammed down the lid but left the chest where it was. Going to his knees, he appeared to survey the other boxes.

Now his expression changed. It was no longer stern. The intensity grew greater, became something harshly judgmental, and he began to whisper to himself, a string of half-formed words Sheritra could not catch. She had seen just such a look on Harmin's face when he was running down a prey. Khaemwaset clenched and unclenched his fists, still on his knees. Then he seemed to make up his mind. Leaning over, he lifted the lid of the chest directly in front of Sheritra. She could feel him rummaging about, and the conversation he was holding with himself became louder, though no more intelligible. The lid thudded shut and she jumped.

Then she saw him leaving, but in his right hand he was

gripping a small stone vial. She did not stop to consider her motives. Pulling herself free of her hiding place, she scurried after him. She had to hover in the outer office for a few moments while he exchanged another word with the guard, and she waited until he was far enough along the corridor not to hear the guard if the man spoke to her. Then she walked out the door, nodded to the startled man and set off behind her father, whose sandals were slapping against the tiling just out of sight.

She could not have analyzed her compulsion to follow him. The sight of the vial in his hand had set off waves of apprehension that did not as yet coalesce into coherent thought.

Cautiously, she peered around the next corner, knowing she was close to Hori's door. Her father was there, standing in the middle of the passage, motionless yet alert. Sheritra watched him, puzzled. There was something furtive about his behaviour, and she could see that he had begun to sweat profusely. Every now and then he would lift his kilt and mop his face. He was still muttering to himself. Sheritra waited.

Before long she heard footsteps approaching from the other direction, and her father began to walk slowly along the passage. Antef appeared, a tray with a steaming bowl in both hands. At the sight of Khaemwaset he paused, confused. Khaemwaset glided up to him.

"What is that?" he asked curtly.

"It is gruel for his Highness," Antef said warily. "I have been making it for him ever since he became ill. He has not eaten since yesterday morning, Prince."

"Give it to me," Khaemwaset demanded, and Sheritra, hiding and listening, closed her eyes and leaned against the wall. Oh surely not! she thought, aghast. Father would not stoop to such a heinous thing! "I want to talk to him, Antef, therefore I will take him his nourishment," Khaemwaset was saying. "You may go." After a moment the young man handed the tray to Khaemwaset and, unwillingly, turned on his heel.

When he was out of sight, Khaemwaset set the tray on the floor, glanced up and down the passage, then pulled the stopper from the vial. Sheritra saw a stream of what looked like black granules go toppling into the thin soup. He is making sure Hori will die, she thought, appalled. He is leaving nothing to chance, and if someone orders an inquiry, Grandfather perhaps, he will pin the blame on Antef who carried the meal all the way from the kitchens.

Khaemwaset was stirring the gruel with one shaking finger, his face implacable, absorbed, and in that moment Sheritra knew that her father's reason had gone. Do something! her mind shrieked. Stop this! She pushed herself away from the wall and almost fell, then she was running around the corner and full tilt down the corridor. Colliding with her father she made as if to grab at him and the tray teetered, the bowl slid, and the gruel went splashing to the floor.

"Sheritra!" he shouted, rubbing at his calf where the hot soup had burned him. "What are you doing?" He glowered at her, and Sheritra could have sworn she saw a murderous fury in those eyes.

"Father, I am so sorry," she gasped. "I wanted to see Hori. I was in a hurry because Bakmut is waiting to bathe me. I did not realize . . ."

"It does not matter," he muttered. "I wanted to see him myself, but I will wait. Order him more gruel, please." He did not wait for an answer. He set off along the passage like a drunkard, his step unsteady, and Sheritra folded for a moment, weak with relief. Hori was temporarily safe, but she had no doubt that her father would make another attempt on Hori's life. If he does not die in the meantime, she thought, a bubble of hysterical laughter rising to her throat. Poor Hori! If Tbubui doesn't put paid to you, Father will. Then she felt the hot tears pricking behind her eyelids and with a strangled cry she ran after Khaemwaset, past the short embrasure containing Hori's door, where a guard lounged, and into the broader main corridor running the length of the house. Her father had gone, but far ahead she saw Antef about to step out into the garden.

"Antef!" she shouted, and he paused, waiting for her until she came up to him, breathless. "Antef," she repeated, her chest tight. "I was not going to ask for your help again but I must. We have to get Hori out of the house, and if possible, send him to the Delta. I am sorry," she apologized, seeing his expression, "but I have no one else to turn to. Will you help me?"

"I do not know how such a thing can be done," he said doubtfully. "His Highness is guarded closely, and frankly, Princess, if I defy your father it could mean my death."

"I do not know how we can do it either," Sheritra admitted, "but we have to try. Come to my quarters in an hour. That will give me time to be bathed and dressed, and then we will make some kind of plan." He bowed and they parted.

Sheritra returned to her rooms. She did not realize until she stepped through and Bakmut came hurrying to serve her how much on edge she was, but in the familiar quiet of her chambers, with the smell of her perfume rising to meet her and the sight of her own possessions around her, her control broke down. Shivering so violently that she could hardly move, she allowed the servant to shepherd her to a chair. "Wine," she muttered through clenched teeth, and Bakmut brought her a jar and a cup, pouring and folding her fingers around the stem without comment. Sheritra drained the cup, held it out for more, then sipped it slowly. The shuddering began to subside. I will kill Hori's guard if I have to, she thought coldly. Kill Tbubui too. Kill them all if only Hori may survive. "Wash me," she commanded Bakmut, "and let us be quick. I have terrible work to do today."

Chapter 21

*'He who is at rest cannot hear thy complaint,
and he who is in the tomb cannot understand
thy weeping.'*

The guards had laid Hori on his couch and withdrawn, and he had fallen into a sodden, drugged dream in which Tbubui, clad in pure white linen, sat in the garden under the dappling shade of a sycamore tree with one round breast exposed. A tiny wax doll, with copper pins driven into its head and abdomen, was suckling from her puckered nipple, its malformed, lipless mouth working in a grotesque rhythm. "It will not be long now, dear Hori," Tbubui was saying sweetly. "He is almost full." Hori woke with a soundless scream in his throat, the now familiar throbbing in his head and gut giving him a moment of panic. He scrabbled against the sheets until his control reasserted itself. Then he lay still trying to accept the pain, to absorb it.

Around him the house followed its appointed routine. He could hear people passing and repassing, his guard shuffling and sighing beyond the door to the antechamber, snatches of music from somewhere in the garden, and he smelled a strong aroma of wheaten gruel. Turning his head with difficulty, he saw that while he slept someone had been admitted with food for him. A bowl of now cold soup and a plate of melon slices smothered in honey sat on his bedside table. Beside the fruit lay a paring knife, winking in the sunlight angling from the clerestory windows high in the walls.

Hori stared at it stupidly. The events of the night reeled slowly through his mind in an aura of dream-like unreality, yet he knew they had occurred. Father rejected everything I tried to show him, he thought weakly. Sheritra stands loyally by my side but she refuses to consider the truth. She is too besotted with Harmin to allow the possibility that he is . . . that Tbubui is . . . What is left to do? No spell will save me and we cannot find the doll. I think Sheritra is right. It is in the house on the east bank. If I could only go there. The paring knife lay innocently, its tip buried in oozing honey, its blade shimmering.

While contemplating it Hori fell into another doze, not knowing if his eyes had closed or not, for he woke still gazing at the innocent little fruit knife. The pain had intensified, like a feral animal gnawing and worrying at his vitals, yet no one had come. There is no one to tend me, he thought with a gush of self-pity. No servant to bathe and soothe me, no physician to administer the blessed herbs of oblivion. I have been deliberately forgotten.

Tears of weakness and loneliness ran down his face, and for a while he succumbed to them, drawing his knees up to his chin while that cursed beast chewed delightedly at his vitals and pawed at his brain. But then he struggled up and reached for the flask of poppy he himself had dropped to the table before plummeting like a stone down the well of forgetting. He shook it before taking a mouthful. There was not much left. Curiously, he felt a little stronger and more clear-headed, a sign that sent a stab of panic through him. His father was a physician, and he knew that often a terminally ill patient would exhibit a burst of well-being, lucidity and energy just before the end, like the flaring of a candle about to gutter into nothingness. I must make use of this, he thought. It will not last long.

His agony had receded to a dull ache and his eyes returned to the small, clean knife waiting beside the melon. The house on the east bank, he thought lazily. I refuse to die without a fight. How many guards stand at my door? Surely no more than one at a time. I am dying, remember? And that one will not be alert, thinking that he watches over a very sick man. Hori's hand reached out and closed over the hilt of the knife. Tonight, he told himself. He fell asleep again, still clutching it.

He woke, and it was dark. Some noiseless, faceless servant had set a night lamp on his table but had not bothered to remove the tray from the morning. If I were Father, Hori thought with hysterical humour, I would reprimand that person. His fingers had frozen around the hilt of the knife, which had become entangled in the sheets. He extricated it, flexed his hand and examined himself. He felt better. He knew very well that it was the calm before the final, incendiary storm, but put that thought away.

With infinite care he sat up, felt for the floor with his feet and cautiously stood. The room whirled and then steadied. He realized that he was naked, but the filthy kilt the guards must have stripped from him lay in a heap on a chair. Slowly, still bent double against the pain that lay in wait for him if he straightened, he tottered to it and wrapped it on. No sound came to him from the passage beyond the door. He crept across the room, the knife held loosely on his palm, and put his ear to the warm cedar wood. He could hear his guard shuffle, but little more. Slowly he inched the door open.

The man was standing to his right, leaning with a negligent boredom against the wall, most of him in deep shadow. The nearest torch burned some way along the passage. Hori took a deep breath. He knew what a frighteningly small amount of his strength was left. If he missed the first time he would not get a second chance. Easing himself beyond the door he tightened his grip on the knife, then, lurching forward and sideways, he grasped the guard's arm and drove the blade up under the man's chin and into his throat. The soldier coughed once, grabbed at his chest, then slid to the floor. His eyes were wide and shocked under the intermittent flare of the torch's flame. Hori did not have the strength to drag the body inside the room but it did not matter. Within a very few minutes he would have left the house. The amount of energy needed to kill the guard who lay, still bleeding, at his feet, had been enormous. He put out a hand to the wall to steady himself while the deserted passage revolved slowly around him. Renewed pain seemed to bulge in his abdomen and send jolts of fire down his legs. Struggling to breathe more evenly he bent, set his foot on the soldier's shoulder and wrenched out the paring knife, wiping it as best as he could on the man's kilt. Then he set off towards the garden.

All the entrances were guarded, he knew that, and sure enough another tall figure bulked where the large rear passage gave out into the night. Hori did not want to kill again. These men were innocents doing their duty and nothing more. But he realized, on a rising tide of cold desperation, that he would somehow have to shamble up to the soldier and at least disable him. That was the answer.

Creeping forward, he hefted the blade. The man stirred, shifting his stance, and his sword clinked softly against the studding on his belt. Hori struck, aiming for the tendons behind the knee. He felt them give as he slashed, and with a howl the guard went down and lay writhing and shrieking. There was a tall jar just inside the passage, kept full of drinking water to be cooled by the breezes that funelled through the open doors at either end. With a grunt Hori tipped it over. Water gushed across his feet, swirled about the guard and cascaded, mingled with blood, onto the grass. Hefting the jar, Hori brought it crashing down on the soldier's head. The shrieking stopped abruptly. Shaking and sweating, Hori stepped past him and out into the garden.

The night was still and fine with a full moon and a black sky resplendent with stars, but Hori had no inclination to admire it. He set off for the watersteps, weaving and stumbling but covering the ground steadily, all his attention grimly fixed on putting one foot after the other. Nevertheless, his nose told him that the river was rising. Its smell—rich, dank and slightly humid—underlay the more fragile aromas of flowering shrubs and watered grass. He stayed off the path, trudging silently along, his ears and eyes alert for any sign of more guards. But tonight he was lucky. He presumed that they were posted around the perimeter of the estate.

The torch illuminating the watersteps flared and danced in the moving air by the river. He passed under it, too tired to make a detour so that he would not be seen. He did not know how he would deal with the man always guarding the boats. He negotiated the steps carefully, his balance teetering because of the constant throbbing in his head, and there was the guard, sitting at the bottom, his back against the stone and fast asleep. There is another servant who needs a severe reprimand, Hori thought, repressing a desire to giggle aloud. Now where is the skiff? He spotted it to the right, rising and falling gently on the swell, its tether looped to a pole.

Trying not to put any vibrations through the step that might wake the soldier, he went lightly, lifting a steering pole from its site in the mud and approaching the skiff. There were no oars resting in the bottom but it did not matter. He knew he had no strength to row in any case. He must trust to the now purposeful running of the current, growing each day as the Nile filled, to take him the short distance north he needed to go. He slipped the skiff's tether and half scrambled, half fell into it.

Grasping the pole he pushed off, and the little craft bucked and began to swing towards midstream. Once there, Hori knew he need do nothing but sit and let the flow take him away. His head was spinning and he was suddenly terrified that he might lose consciousness. The knife was still in his hand. He had no belt to take it, only the kilt wrapped loosely about his waist, so he laid it in the bottom of the skiff and set one foot over it. With both hands he sank the pole once more, and the skiff protested, but after a moment Hori felt the current tug at it and he relaxed with a quivering sigh.

When next he came to himself he was floating in a broken shaft of moonlight with the dark city on his left and the shadows of spindly acacia bushes clinging to the bank on his right. He had fallen unconscious after all. Whimpering, he slapped his face twice but his fingers merely brushed his skin. The burst of strength that had brought him this far was failing rapidly and he was all at once frightened that he would die here, hunched over in the skiff, and he would bob and rock all the way to the Delta before his body was found. It would be too late then to beautify me, he thought in a panic. My body would have rotted too far. O Amun, King of gods, have mercy on me and bring me safely to the watersteps!

The skiff glided on, and slowly but surely Hori saw the darkly familiar shrubbery that thickened, deepened, and became the palm plantation in which Tbubui's old house was nestled. He began to ply the pole, clumsily jerking the craft towards the bank. For a moment it did not respond, and he was afraid that the current would prove stronger than his own miserable efforts, but then it turned reluctantly and soon was grinding against the dilapidated stair. Hori fumbled about for the knife, found it, and fell out of the boat onto the steps. The skiff immediately began to angle and drift away, but he did not care.

It all seemed to take a very long time. On hands and knees he crawled up onto the path, and once there he lay for a while with his cheek against the hard sand. I want to sleep, he thought. I want to sink into the ground forever. And indeed his thoughts did run away so that the next time he opened his eyes he sensed that the moon was waning.

With a groan he came to his feet and lurched along the path. It was very dark under the palms. Like black pillars they clustered stiffly around him, marching away to right and left, shrouded in their own mystery. Hori tried not to let them cut him off from reality, but as he manoeuvred the final corner and saw the house crouched to one end of its clearing, he had to contend with a rushing sense of confusion. It seemed to him that he was back in Koptos, hovering on the edge of the ruins whose silence and desolation had been so familiar. With a tightening of his will he forced his imagination away from that place and into the present, but the silence and desolation remained. Its quality here was an evil, brooding thing, and as Hori staggered across the sparse, dry grass he was sure that invisible eyes were closely observing his progress. I have nothing left to lose, he told himself. No pain, no evil, can be greater than that which I am suffering now. I will walk straight through the main entrance into that cold hall. I will ignore any servant standing in the shadows, for I am positive they will ignore me. The shawabtis, retreating into their twilight world of not-being during the dark hours when their services are not required, blind, deaf, woodenly unmoving . . . He shuddered, an involuntary action that poured agony into his wasting muscles, and stepped from the airy darkness of night into the close, Stygian blackness of the house.

There was a servant standing in a far corner, feet together, dusky arms rigidly at its sides, eyes closed. Hori drew near and passed it with one timid glance, but it did not stir. The rear passage yawned, a hole into nothing. Pausing to temporarily put down the knife and wipe his slippery palm on his kilt, he stole into it.

The darkness was total. Hori knew that Tbubui's old room lay to the right near the exit to the garden, and he inched towards it, shoulder against the wall. At the other end of the house Sisenet and Harmin would be sleeping, or whatever it is that the dead do at night, he thought with another burst of amusement that he recognized as hysteria. I must not disturb them. His shoulder bumped against a ridge and he felt about. The door was there. It gave at the pressure of his hand, swinging open soundlessly but with the slightest movement of air, and Hori walked in.

The same complete blackness reigned here, and in despair Hori realized that he would have to search by touch alone. He had not brought a lamp; indeed, he would have been unable to carry one. His symptoms had intensified the moment he had placed his fingers on the door, and now the sharp horns of pain gored and twisted his vitals, his brain. He tried to rise above it, to set it apart somehow from the place where reason and decision took precedence in his mind, but it was hard.

Slowly and awkwardly he began to search, his fingers probing the corners, the floor, the knife held temporarily in his teeth. Shuffling across the floor he encountered the couch, now stripped of its bedding. He felt the mattress, the gritty space under the couch, and then left it to continue on the other side of the room, but he soon realized it was bare. Her tiring boxes had all gone. The night table was missing, as was the shrine to Thoth. She had taken it all to his father's home.

Sobbing with fatigue and frustration, Hori fumbled his way back to the door. You are going to die, the pain mocked him. You will never find the doll. She is far too clever for you. Who would have thought six months ago, when you sat with your father on the plain of Saqqara and watched the ancient air stream from the tomb in a thin grey cloud, that you would end up crouched in this stuffy, empty room with your life draining away? Be quiet, he told himself sternly, though he felt his own tears hot on his neck. Accept and go on as long as you can. His knee struck the edge of the door and he eased himself back into the passage.

A thin stream of dull yellow light was illuminating the other end of the corridor. Hori paused, thunderstruck. He was absolutely positive that the narrow space had been completely dark before, but now someone had lit a lamp and its sullen glow was showing under a door. Whose door? Hori thought, gripping the knife and shambling towards it. He repassed the entrance to the hall on his left and caught one glimpse of the motionless servant propped against the wall before he moved on. Whose door? It was Sisenet's, and it was suddenly ajar. A strange calmness fell upon Hori. He pushed it all the way open and walked in.

The first thing that struck him was the smell. He had been in enough places of burial to recognize it at once—a musty, earthy odour of sun-starved rock and undisturbed soil with a hint of human decay—but here the stink of corruption was dominant. He felt it immediately in his throat and swallowed, his nostrils constricting. He had not been in this room before. It was small and unadorned, the walls grey mud, the floor untiled. A couch stood against the far wall, holding nothing but a stone headrest, and in the middle of the floor there was a table supporting a plain lamp and a box. Whatever else the table held was obscured by the man rising and turning with a cold smile. This place reminds me of something, Hori thought, standing in the doorway and looking about. It reminds me of . . . of a tomb.

But he had no time to become afraid, not then, for Sisenet was bowing coolly. He was clad in a short linen kilt. The rest of his spare, whipcord body was naked and as dusty as the earthen floor, the simple table. Dusty.

"So it is young Hori," Sisenet said, still grinning. "I heard someone fumbling along the passage. I thought it might be you. You do not look so well, young Prince. One might even say you have the stamp of death on you. Now why is that?"

Hori stepped further into the room, all at once very aware of the paring knife held loosely in his fingers. Sisenet moved slightly, his dry fingers trailing along the table, leaving marks on its surface. The husk of a dead scorpion appeared, its brown carapace gleaming in the lamplight. Hori did not answer. He waited. He had never given much thought to Tbubui's so-called brother. Sisenet had been nothing more than a quiet, self-contained man who came and went occasionally on the periphery of Hori's vision, on the outskirts of his life, seemingly content with his scholarly pursuits and the privacy of his little room. But now Hori, watching him carefully, wondered just what those scholarly pursuits had been. Sisenet's smile was broadening. It was not a pleasant sight, and Hori all at once recognized the self-possession as supreme arrogance, the self-effacement as the kind of amused confidence that observed and coldly dissected everyone. Sisenet was power. Hori's whole spine contracted.

"It was you!" he cried out. "All the time. You conjured against Penbuy. You conspired with Tbubui to seduce my father. You are killing me!"

For answer the man stepped right away from the table and there, sitting like some fat, malevolent, primitive god, was the wax doll Hori sought. The flickering light danced along the wicked copper pins, one driven through the scarcely formed head from temple to temple and one canting down through the squat abdomen. Beside it Hori recognized his gold-and-jasper earrings. Earrings, he thought. How apt. How accursedly right.

"Is this what you are looking for, Highness?" Sisenet asked politely. "Yes? I rather thought so. But it is too late. You will be dead in two days."

Faintness swirled around Hori and he planted his feet apart and fought it off. "But why?" he croaked, that dreadful stench intensifying so that he felt as though it was seeping into all his pores and his flesh itself recoiled. "Why? It is true that you are her husband, isn't it? You are the wizard-prince Nenefer-ka-Ptah and she the princess Ahura. Father resurrected you all, you are the walking dead, but why us?"

"Poor Hori," Nenefer-ka-Ptah said with mock concern. "Perhaps you should sit. Here. Take my chair. Shall I call a servant and order wine for you?" His black eyes twinkled with ghoulish humour. He knows what I am thinking, Hori told himself, the terror beginning. I am in the presence of something hundreds of years old, something that has no right to be walking and talking, smiling and gesturing, something that should by rights be wound in linen and lying in darkness, rotting. "I can wake them with a word," Nenefer-ka-Ptah went on. "They do not mind. They are perfectly obedient, my servants."

"No wine," Hori whispered, though he longed for something to wash away the taste of coffins in his mouth. His earrings winked jauntily up at him and the grotesque doll grinned its knowing smile.

"She was the talk of the south, my wife," Nenefer-ka-Ptah said conversationally. He had begun to pace in a leisurely fashion, his feet making no sound. "High-born, beautiful, with that seductive magnetism men cannot resist. Her sexual prowess was legendary. She clung to me when we were drowning, clung like a lover, her legs wrapped around mine, her body convulsing against me in fear. She has wrapped her legs around you, hasn't she, Highness?" Hori nodded, spellbound and repulsed. "I was not afraid. I thought of the Scroll, my Scroll, the thing I had laboured long and hard to acquire, and I was comforted. The sem-priests had their orders. We were to be buried in coffins without lids and immured behind a false wall. The Scroll itself was to be sewn to the corpse of one of my servants. I actually commanded two of them to be killed in the event of my death so that they could be buried in my tomb. But Merhu . . ." He came to a halt, passing a hand over his shaven skull. "Merhu. My son. The flower of Egyptian youth in those days. Handsome, in demand, accomplished, spoiled and wilful. He knew about the Scroll. Both of them did. He agreed to my preparations for his burial also, and it was just as well, for he himself drowned not long after Ahura and I were beautified and laid in the tomb your father so cheerfully desecrated. All of us, dead by water," he said. "That surely was a cosmic joke, for we loved the Nile inordinately. We swam in it and fished from it, glided on it in long red evenings, often made love on its verge with our feet kissed by its waves, held parties on its mysterious bosom and ached for it as we watched it falter and recede every year. We decorated our tomb at Saqqara with it, Merhu's also at Koptos, the city he loved, and all the while the god was waiting to end our lives with the thing that had given us the highest pleasure. Of such interesting ironies is life composed." He came to Hori. "I knew that possessing the Scroll brought its own dangers," he said, "but I was a great magician, the greatest in Egypt, and I chose to take the risk. It was mine. I earned it. The price I and my family paid was an early death after five years of power and prosperity."

"You have not answered my question." Hori faltered, although if he had been strong enough he would have fled in screaming horror from that place. I have been inside a corpse, he was thinking. I have made love to dead flesh, like one of those madmen who loiter about the House of the Dead. And what of Father? His life has shrunk to a single force, the ecstasy of possessing Tbubui. Even Sheritra is defiled. All of us, we have committed unnameable sins no one else in Egypt could understand. Were these three always like this? he wondered. So predatory, so utterly without scruple? Or has the mysterious alchemy of a forced resurrection taken something human from them, some component necessary for a blameless life, a good judging, and then peace in the paradise of Osiris? Is the price of such a resurrection also a rejection by the gods? Have we also, all of us, been rejected? Nenefer-ka-Ptah had begun to pace again.

"Your question?" he said. "Oh yes. Why you. We were grateful to your father for rousing us, and if it had been left to us we would simply have retrieved the Scroll and gone on living quietly in Memphis. But Thoth . . ." He seemed to be searching for words. "Thoth had become my master. The Scroll was his creation, and in acquiring it I came under his direct domination. It is not a good thing, to come under the unblinking contemplation of a god. Much more than mere adoration is required. Oh much more. His beak is sharp, young Hori, his shining eye remorseless. One becomes a slave. 'Khaemwaset has sinned,' he said. 'He no longer serves any god but himself. He must be destroyed.

Your ka is forfeit to me in exchange for the Scroll, and Khaemwaset's for his arrogant plundering, his continued desecration of hallowed places. See to it.' One does not disobey a god, and I must confess, Prince, that I have enjoyed tearing your complacent, haughty little family apart. We all have. For me it has been a chance to practise magic again and for Tbubui, an opportunity to play the game at which she is most accomplished."

He looked directly at Hori, and at once desire for Tbubui flared in him, hot and immediate in spite of his pain. "You are abominations, all of you," he cried. "Give me back my life!"

"But you are tainted too," Nenefer-ka-Ptah pointed out, grinning. "You have been inside her. There is no salvation for you."

Hori felt the knife in his hand, solid and somehow comforting. "I do not deserve this!" he shouted. "I refuse to die! I refuse!" In a frenzy that lent a superhuman strength to his arm he launched himself at Nenefer-ka-Ptah, knife held low. Nenefer-ka-Ptah stood impassively, his face completely blank. Screaming, Hori jabbed the paring knife up under the man's chin, pushing it with a grunt until the hilt met flesh. Nenefer-ka-Ptah did not even flinch. Hori doubled over, weeping and trembling, then looked up. Nenefer-ka-Ptah was watching him, and all at once he yawned. With a despairing horror Hori saw the blade caught in the back of the man's throat, clean and dry. Impatiently Nenefer-ka-Ptah reached up and pulled it out. It came with a slight sucking sound. He tossed it onto the table. "I am already dead," he said equably. "I thought you understood that, Hori. I cannot die a second time."

Weakness swept over Hori and he cowered on the rough floor, weeping with impotence and pain. He was about to pull himself upright when there was a convulsive movement by the open door. Through eyes blurred by tears of agony he caught a glimpse of Sheritra, open-mouthed, frozen in shock. Antef was behind her. "I saw!" she screamed. "O gods, Hori, you were right! I saw!" Hori began to struggle up. He sensed Nenefer-ka-Ptah bowing.

"It is the delectable little Princess Sheritra," he said. "Welcome, my dear. Would you care to join our modest feast? I have little to tempt you but scorpion husks and dead mice, but perhaps you would prefer to dine on your brother Hori's ka? Very fresh and juicy it is."

"Hori!" Sheritra cried out. He was on his feet now, shocked almost beyond bearing, but still capable of coherent thought.

"Get out of here!" he ordered. "Antef . . ." But it was too late. With a shriek of terror Sheritra had turned and fled along the passage. Hori struggled to follow, and as he came to the door Antef rushed to support him. Together they emerged into the corridor in time to see the further door open, flooding more light into the darkness, and Sheritra cannon into Merhu, who had stepped out and was standing in the way. Sheritra threw herself into his arms.

"Tell me it isn't true!" she was screaming hysterically, clutching him, burying her face in his neck, her body pressed rigidly against him. "Tell me that you love me, you adore me, we will marry as soon as the contract is drawn up." She raised a terror-stricken face to his. "Tell me that you did not know about your mother, about Sisenet, any of it! Tell me, Harmin!"

His father had come out of his room and was standing nonchalantly, watching. Hori, leaning heavily on Antef, saw a glance of mutual conspiracy flash between the two of them, a gloating moment of triumph before Merhu pushed her roughly away.

"You?" he said loudly, looking her up and down with feigned surprise. "Me marry you?" He was stepping back, contempt in every regal line of him, and Sheritra was momentarily dumbfounded. "You were an assignment I was asked to undertake, and not even a particularly interesting one at that. Virgins bore me. It was boring to possess your scrawny body and even more tedious to pretend I loved you. I want no more to do with you. The game has palled."

"Sheritra . . ." Hori gasped, but she whirled and pushed past him, such shame and unbelief on her face that he shrank back.

He began to hobble after her, with Antef's arm around his waist, and behind them Nenefer-ka-Ptah started to laugh. The coarse, inhuman sound followed them along the passage and out into the garden, a rising cacophony of insane delight that woke the shadows and pursued them like the gleeful demons of the underworld, until the path began and the palms gradually muffled that hysterical shrieking.

Sheritra was huddled at the foot of the watersteps, her breath coming in shuddering gasps, too shocked to cry. The skiff had vanished, Hori noticed as he and Antef made their halting way to her, but the raft was tethered securely to the one pole at the foot. "How did you know I was here?" Hori managed.

"The Princess knew," Antef said. "The alarm was raised two hours ago when your guard was found dead at your door and you were gone. We had spent most of the day trying to devise a way to get you out. She said that the only place left for you to try was Sisenet's house. We crept away in all the hue and cry and I doubt if we were missed."

They had come up to Sheritra but she gave no sign of having seen them. She continued to hug her knees, her face buried, her whole body shaking with suppressed sobs.

"Sheritra," Hori said urgently. "You cannot stay here. You must go home. Sheritra!" At length she lifted her head. Her face was disfigured in its grief but it was dry, and under the impact of shock and betrayal, Hori thought he saw something terrible, a cold implacability he did not like. "Antef and I will take you home," he said, "and then we will drift towards the Delta. I must find a priest of Thoth or of Set to take this curse from me." She rallied with an obvious effort and came to her feet unsteadily.

"Forgive me for not believing you, Hori," she said in a strangled whisper. "I saw you strike Sisenet. I saw the knife in his throat. I still cannot accept . . ."

"I know," he said swiftly. "Get onto the raft, Sheritra. Antef, you will have to row."

They tumbled onto the craft and Antef pushed off. Hori sat with his arm flung over Sheritra, his head nodding against her breast as Antef panted, fighting the current. Hori closed his eyes. Two days, he thought. I have two days if that demon spoke correctly. Sheritra stirred and he heard her whimper.

The raft bumped and Antef said, "Your Highness, we are home. Do you want to disembark?"

Hori pulled himself away from his sister. Dimly he felt her take his face between her hands, and her kiss was like dark petals on his lips. "I love you, Hori," she said urgently, her voice breaking. "I will never forget you. Go in peace."

So she knows that I will not survive, he thought dimly. He rubbed his cheek against hers but he was incapable of words. His burst of energy was over and he wanted nothing more, now, than to curl up on the floor of the raft and lapse into unconsciousness. He felt her rise and heard her footsteps crossing the craft, then there was only the river's secret sucking noises and Antef's regular panting. "Take me north, Antef," he murmured, and gave himself up to the blessed, painless spiral into oblivion.

Sheritra walked calmly up the steps. Behind her she heard Antef grunt as he poled the raft away, but she did not turn. She was cold and calm, she was in control of herself. With an absent word of greeting to the guard by the water she reached the path and started along it, still encased in that brittle, unnatural peace.

Dawn was not far off. She felt it. The torches were guttering and the darkness in the garden had a quality of restlessness about it. A servant rushed by, giving her a cursory reverence, and further on a guard was fruitlessly searching the bushes. They will not find him, she thought coldly. Already he is a possession of the gods. No one can touch him now.

She swung into the house by the main entrance, ignoring the flurry of frenetic activity going on, and made her way unimpeded to her own quarters. Bakmut was asleep, sprawled across the doorway, but Sheritra stepped over her and continued on into her bedchamber. The night lamp still burned by her couch, casting a friendly, limpid glow.

Going to her cosmetic table she opened a box and drew out the copper razor Bakmut used to shave her body hair. It was very sharp, and she drew the blade across her thumb reflectively. What was it Father said so long ago? she wondered. If you want to slit your wrists, do not pull the blade across the flesh. You will not damage the arteries sufficiently. Dig the knife lengthwise for a full and copious flow of blood. That way you will be beyond help. Beyond help . . . It was all a game, she thought dully, the razor poised. He pretended to understand me, pretended to love me, and all the times we made love he was laughing at me, forcing himself, repulsed by my body. Oh curse him, curse him! And curse me for a simpering fool. I should have known that no man as beautiful as he would be attracted to such a homely girl as I am.

She longed to be able to plunge the innocuous, gleaming blade into her flesh, to feel the moment of pain, to see her blood spurt, but she could not make the savage, self-destructive movement required. No one will care, that is the thing, she thought coldly. Not Father, not Mother, and Hori is battling his own death. No one will be hurt by my dying, and Tbubui would simply smile. I brought this on myself. I never did deserve to be happy, and I will spend the rest of my life reminding myself of that fact. These four walls will be my witnesses.

"Bakmut!" she called, tossing the razor onto the couch. After a moment her servant appeared, blinking sleepily. "Bring me the scroll from Pharaoh." Bakmut nodded and shuffled away, and a moment later she returned, holding out the tightly wound message. Sheritra took it and, breaking the seal, unrolled it. "To my dear grandson, Hori, greetings and fond felicitations," she read. "Having taken your news under advisement and having consulted my Minister for Hereditary Entitlements, I have decided to investigate your allegations. Expect a person of authority to arrive in Memphis within two weeks. Know also that I am most displeased with the antics of your family and I will take the necessary steps to ensure peace in Memphis and on your father's estate. I am your august grandfather, Ramses the Second, etc., etc." Sheritra let the scroll roll up with a strangled laugh. None of it mattered any more. "Bakmut," she said to the patiently waiting servant, "From now on I do not intend to leave my suite. No one is to enter. I do not wish to speak to anyone. Is that understood?" The girl nodded warily and Sheritra dismissed her. Very good, she thought as she lowered herself onto the couch and drew the sheet up over her shoulders. Bakmut will believe it is a whim until the time goes by, and the time goes by . . . She relaxed into her pillow and closed her eyes. Gullible, she thought. Scrawny. Virgins bore me . . .

With a muffled cry she squeezed her eyes shut and drew her knees up to her small breasts. No one will ever hurt me again, she vowed against the agonizing mental images flooding her brain. No one. Overcome with grief, she slept.

Chapter 22

'Behold me, as a dog of the street,
as a sign unto gods and men am I:
struck down by his hand,
for I had wrought evil in his sight.'

Khaemwaset existed in a state of shock as servant after servant came to him to admit that Hori could not be found. The estate was extensive, and searching every nook and cranny took a long time. Nevertheless, Khaemwaset was mystified. Hori had been obviously near collapse when escorted to his quarters. He could not imagine that the weak, exhausted youth would have been able to kill one soldier and wound another so grievously that he was not expected to live. Khaemwaset himself had attended the man, but there had been little he could do, and as he worked he had marvelled at the damage inflicted. Hori must have been desperate, he thought, but to do what? Not to burst into Tbubui's suite with whatever knife he used on the first guard, for no one had caught so much as a glimpse of him near the concubines' house. In fact, no one had seen him at all.

Khaemwaset had gone to Sheritra's rooms himself, reasoning that Hori might be hiding there, but the girl's body servant assured him his daughter was sleeping and there had been no sign of the Prince. Antef likewise had been no help. He had seemed genuinely alarmed and puzzled at the news of his friend's disappearance, and when Khaemwaset had wanted to interrogate him an hour later, he himself was nowhere to be found.

Then a report came to him that the skiff was missing. He had the watersteps guard brought to him and the terrified man confessed that, having imbibed too much wine before taking his duty, he had fallen asleep. The Prince could indeed have crept past him. Khaemwaset dismissed him on the spot. I cannot have the whole city searched, he thought wearily. Perhaps Hori has gone north to Nubnofret. That idea gave Khaemwaset some relief. It was good to imagine Hori safely tucked away in the Delta, at least for the time being. Until Tbubui's baby is born, he thought darkly. Then I will have to act. If Sheritra had not been so clumsy the problem would already be solved, but it does not matter. Father's court is a populous place, full of intrigue and activity. A poisoning will not be so noticeable there. In the meantime I am free to enjoy my darling in peace. Both the troublemakers have gone. Sheritra will marry Harmin and he will come and occupy Hori's old quarters. Perhaps Sisenet will decide to move in also, and the eyes of the people around me will no longer be hostile with accusations.

Later that morning, Ib came to tell him that the raft was also missing, and this time his daughter had been seen making her way along the path from the watersteps. Irritably Khaemwaset sent for her. Shortly after, Ib returned with the message the Princess was refusing to leave her quarters. He merely stood politely waiting, and with a loud oath Khaemwaset swung out of the office where he had been trying to dictate and, with a guard and a herald trotting at his heels, strode to Sheritra's suite. At the herald's persistent knocking, Bakmut opened the door.

"Get out of my way," Khaemwaset ordered brusquely. "I must talk with my daughter."

Bakmut bowed but stood her ground. "I am sorry, Highness, but the Princess will see no one," she said obstinately. Khaemwaset did not waste time arguing. He grasped her arm and pulled her aside, going to stand in the middle of the ante-room.

"Sheritra!" he called. "Come out at once. I wish to ask you a question."

For a long time there was no answer, and Khaemwaset was preparing to force the inner door when he heard her stirring. The door was unlatched but she did not appear. Instead her voice floated to him from somewhere in the dimness beyond.

"You may ask and I will answer, Father," she said, "but it will be the last time. I wish no more commerce with anyone, particularly with you."

"You are disrespectful," he began furiously, but she broke in: "Ask your question and do not tire me too far, or I may not answer you at all." There was something dead about her tone, Khaemwaset realized, checking the flood of invective hovering on his tongue. So even, so indifferent, as though she were past caring about anything. His bluster died.

"Very well," he said thickly. "Did you take the raft out

last night?"

She responded immediately. "Yes, I did."

He waited for more, but the silence went on until he was forced to continue.

"Did you bring it back?"

"Yes, I did."

Again the silence. Khaemwaset felt his exasperation begin to build afresh.

"Well where is it now?" he growled.

She sighed. He could hear the soft gust of her breath and he thought he caught a glimpse of her linen within the shelter of the half-light within.

"Hori took the skiff and went to talk to Sisenet about your wife," she said woodenly. "Antef and I took the raft and went after him. We brought him home. I got off, but Hori has gone north with his friend. You will not see him again."

"He just could not let go!" Khaemwaset exploded. "He actually killed because he could not let go! Good riddance to him! I hope he stays in the Delta until he rots!"

"He will not reach the Delta," that cold, disembodied voice came drifting. "He will be dead by tomorrow night. Sisenet told him so. Sisenet wielded the pins, Father, but you decreed that Hori should die. Think of that tomorrow night when you gaze into your mirror."

"Well what of you?" Khaemwaset said uneasily, her tone more than her words making him suddenly chill. "What nonsense are you playing out, Sheritra? Harmin will be here this afternoon to visit his mother. Will you refuse him entry also?"

"I have decided not to marry Harmin after all," she replied, and now her voice wavered. "In fact, Father, I have decided to remain a single woman. Now go away."

He waited for some moments after the door had been firmly closed, expostulating, swearing, even pleading, but no sound came from the other side. It was as though he stood at the sealed entrance to some tomb, and in the end he grew afraid and went away.

That afternoon Harmin did indeed come to visit Tbubui, and the three of them, Khaemwaset, his wife and her son, sat in the garden while servants passed damp cloths over their limbs and fed them fruit and beer. Harmin was unusually attentive to

Tbubui, stroking her face, rearranging her pillows, meeting her glance with a warm smile when she had a joke to share. How unlike Hori he is, Khaemwaset thought nostalgically. Here is genuine concern and respect, a son knowing his place and keeping it out of love for his parent. Whatever devil has entered Sheritra, the little fool, to refuse this gracious young man?

As if in answer to his musing, Harmin rose and bowed. "With your permission, Prince, I should like to spend some time with Sheritra now," he said. Khaemwaset looked up at him with embarrassment.

"Dear Harmin," he said, "I am afraid that Sheritra is indisposed and is seeing no one today. She sends you her apologies and, of course, her love."

A glance of swift understanding passed between mother and son. Harmin's face fell. "I am devastated," he said, "but tell her that she has my sympathy. In that case I shall go home and sleep." He bent and kissed Tbubui, bowed again to Khaemwaset and glided away, kilt swinging against sturdy, shapely legs, his black hair bouncing on his shoulders.

"He is a fine young man," Khaemwaset said, secretly hoping that Sheritra would soon get over her foolishness. "You have every reason to be proud of him." He waved away a proffered dish and hitched closer to Tbubui. "I have not told you about Hori," he said in a low voice. "He is heading for the Delta, doubtless to pour out to his mother his tale of woe. I am ashamed of my family, Tbubui. But at least you will be safe for a while."

She smiled at him, a slow, speculative curling of her wide mouth, and her eyes narrowed. "Oh, I think I am very safe now," she answered. "It was a pity that you were unable to feed him his gruel the other morning, but no harm has been done. I do not intend to worry about Hori any more."

In a rush of abject guilt he reached for her, but she lay back, signalled to a fan-bearer, and closed her eyes. Khaemwaset was left to sit, chin in hand, and brood, while the day became hotter and the rhythmic chanting of his servants treading grapes in the vat in the compound wafted to him intermittently, charged with a raucous triumph.

In spite of his theory that Hori was seeking Nubnofret's broad bosom on which to cry out his vindictiveness, Khaemwaset spent an uneasy night. The evening had seemed to close in with an ominous grip, the hands of cataclysm, and mindful of Sheritra's scornful words, he was unable to lift the mirror from its gilded case on his cosmetic table.

He went to his couch early, drank some wine and pressed Kasa into conversation. He thought of going to the concubines' house and making love to Tbubui, but he was too anxious, too full of a vague presentiment of doom, to forget himself in that act.

One night lamp did not seem enough. Things moved in the shadows just out of his vision, and the small breeze became magnified into strange sighings and tiny sobbings in his room. Shouting to Kasa he ordered more light and felt reassured, but it was a long time before he could fall asleep. Even when he did, he kept waking up with a start and peering about, his dreams vivid and confusing and totally forgotten by the time he sat up on the couch.

The mood of dislocation followed him into the next day. Every word spoken to him seemed heavy with some arcane meaning he could not quite grasp, and each action took on the ponderous weight of ritual. The house was filled with an atmosphere he could not describe but that made him tense with the feeling of threat. He dreaded the night. In the afternoon he went to Tbubui, but even there he was not able to free himself of his inarticulate fear. Nor could he speak of it. It was too unformed.

Evening came, and he could not eat. He and Tbubui sat behind their small tables in the vast reception hall, waited upon by servants ranged all about the walls, entertained by the harpist whose graceful notes echoed in that empty place and reminded Khaemwaset suddenly of other evenings, of Nubnofret resplendent and formidable in blue and gold, reprimanding an indignant, squirming Sheritra while Hori grinned and looked on, Antef hovering behind him. The nights had been warm then, redolent with family closeness, with hallowed routine and blessed predictability, and on this night he missed it all with a blinding jolt of homesickness. Perhaps Harmin and Sisenet would move into the house, and sit behind their own flower-strewn dining tables, bolstered with cushions, merry with wine, talking carefully to whatever official guests graced the hall, but the air of sadness, of good times past, would never leave this gracious room. One family has disintegrated, but I am building another, he thought as a defence against that awful spasm of loneliness. There is Tbubui's baby, after all. Sheritra can surely be talked out of her mysterious female mood and she and Harmin will fill the house with the happy chaos of my grandchildren. But the sense of the broken, of things gone that could never be mended, would not go away.

"Khaemwaset, I have said the same thing to you three times," Tbubui interrupted his musings, leaning across to kiss him perfunctorily. "Where are you?"

He gave her his attention with an effort of the will. "I am sorry, beloved," he said. "What was it?"

"Your brother Si-Montu has sent a message wanting to know if he can come and dine next week. Is that acceptable?"

Acceptable. Khaemwaset suddenly gripped her arm. "Tbubui, sleep with me in my own quarters tonight, on my couch," he begged. "I need you there."

Her light-heartedness vanished and she regarded him with a worried frown. "Of course I will," she agreed. "Whatever is the matter, Highness?"

But he could not tell her. The fragrance of the flowers, the deep mauve translucence of the wine, even the cascade of notes pouring from the harpist's fingers, were all conspiring with the gloomy atmosphere of the house to plunge him into the past and torture him with terrors for the present. "The figs are sour," was all he said.

She came to his suite much later, wafting to the couch on a cloud of her perfume and a ripple of loose, seductive linen. Without a word she shed the linen and spread his legs, easing herself down on him in practised motions, and with a groan he gave himself up to the exquisite sensations only she could tease from him. But long after she was asleep, breathing evenly in the crook of his arm, he lay wide awake in the grip of premonition. He dared not look at her. He had done so once, after she had slipped into unconsciousness, and there had been something about the glitter of her eyes under half-closed lids, the sight of her small, animal teeth between parted lips, that had struck him with fear.

He clung to the sounds of sanity. He heard the guard sighing outside the suite. He heard Kasa snoring in the other room. Jackals howled far away on the desert, and much closer in, an owl hooted in the garden. The lamp spat and the shadows gyrated for a moment. These things are real, he thought. These things are comfort and sanity. Hold them close, for they are infinitely precious.

He was still awake to hear whispering outside. He lay quietly, waiting, until Ib approached the couch. The man was naked, obviously roused precipitously from his mat in the passage. "Speak," Khaemwaset said, and at the word Tbubui stirred beside him and her cool flesh disengaged from his. She turned over.

"Highness, you had better get up," Ib whispered. "Antef has returned with the raft and your son. Please come."

Hori is dead, Khaemwaset said to himself as he nodded, waved Ib away and slipped carefully from the couch. That is the aura of desolation that has been slowly filling the house. Hori is dead. Wrapping a kilt around his waist and feeling for his sandals, he left the room and went through into the passage. Antef was waiting, his face pale, his whole attitude one of exhaustion, but his eyes met Khaemwaset's with the clear, straight stare of a pure conscience. "Speak," Khaemwaset said again, acknowledging the young man's bow.

"Prince, your son is dead," Antef said bluntly. "His body lies on the raft at the watersteps. He died in terrible pain but he did not rail against the gods or you. His judging will surely be favourable."

"I do not understand," Khaemwaset said haltingly. "Hori was ill, certainly, when I detained him, but I thought he had contracted some sickness in Koptos. He would recover . . . he would get well . . ."

"He told your Highness exactly what was wrong with him," Antef said bluntly, "but your Highness refused to listen. Regret is vain. He wanted me to tell you that, though his end is terrible, it is not as terrible as your fate. Also that he loved you."

For answer Khaemwaset turned on his heel and began to run along the torchlit corridor. Through the house he sped, and as he ran he was thinking, Hori! My son! My flesh! It was a game, it was a dangerous foolishness, I never meant to do you any harm, I would not really have poisoned you, I love you, oh Hori, why? Why? He heard Antef, Ib and Kasa pounding after him. Though he ran as fast as he could, he was unable to put distance between himself and the growing guilt and remorse already snapping at his heels so that by the time he almost fell down the watersteps and stood looking down onto the raft he was weeping with self-loathing.

Hori lay in a huddle under a blanket, rocking imperceptibly on the Nile's swell. He looked like nothing better than a pile of dirty linen waiting to be laundered. Khaemwaset stepped from the stone onto the raft, and, kneeling, he turned back the covering. He was a setem-priest, and his first thought on seeing the curled body was that the embalmers would have difficulty in straightening him out, for Hori was lying with his knees jammed up under his chin. But then he saw the matted hair, the beautiful face that had been the talk of the whole of Egypt loose and empty in death, one hand lying palm up in a gesture of supplication, and all thought fled. Bowing over the body Khaemwaset began to keen, great wails of love and loss that echoed from the far, unseen bank of the river and returned with a mocking hollowness. His hands moved gently, clumsily, over his son, touching the cold, already putrefying flesh, the lifeless tresses, the strong nose and unresponsive mouth. He was aware of the little group standing helplessly on the watersteps, but he did not care. "I meant you no harm!" he groaned, the knowledge of the lie sending another dagger into his heart. "I was deluded, blinded, forgive me, Hori!" But Hori did not move, did not smile his forgiveness, did not understand, and now it was too late.

Khaemwaset stood. "Ib," he said unsteadily, "Take his body to the House of the Dead. His beautification must begin at once, for he is already rotting." His voice broke and he could not go on.

Antef stepped forward. There was no pity in the young man's gaze, only acceptance and a contempt for Khaemwaset. "I loved your son," he said matter-of-factly. "Now that he is dead my association with this accursed house is ended. I will not attend Hori's funeral. Farewell, Highness." He bowed and was gone. Come back, Khaemwaset thought he shouted, but the words stayed in his mind. Come back, I want to know how he died, what he said, what he felt, oh what is the truth, Hori, what is the truth?

Slowly he left the raft, and as soon as he was standing on the warm stone that still held the heat of the previous day, Ib sprang into action. Khaemwaset left the crumpled body of his son and walked slowly back to the house. It is still night, he thought dizzily. Nothing has changed. Hori is dead, and nothing has changed. The passage before his quarters loomed silent and empty but for the guard on his door and the flaring torches. The house still slumbered, all unknowing. Hori is dead, Khaemwaset wanted to shriek at the top of his lungs. Instead he blundered into his quarters and sank onto the couch.

"Hori is dead," he said. Tbubui shifted and groaned softly. For a moment he thought that she had gone back to sleep, but then she pushed back the sheets and sat up.

"What?" she said.

"Hori is dead," he repeated like a litany. He began to sway in his extremity.

She stared at him indifferently, her eyes swollen with sleep. "Yes, I know," she said.

He froze. "What do you mean?" he breathed. Suddenly his heart began to gallop in his chest.

"Just what I said," she offered, running a hand over her face and yawning broadly. "Nenefer-ka-Ptah put a spell on him. Actually the spell was put on him earlier, because he dared to go to Koptos. Not that it would have mattered. I knew you wouldn't believe him anyway."

Khaemwaset felt the room begin to spin and recede. "What are you saying?" he managed. "What do you mean?"

She yawned again, and passed a pink tongue over her lips. "I mean, now that Hori is dead, and you refused to help him, your degradation is complete, Khaemwaset, and my task is done. I am not obliged to play my part anymore. I am thirsty," she went on. "Is there any wine left?" She pulled herself to the edge of the couch and poured wine into a cup. Khaemwaset watched her, incredulous, as she drained it, then set the cup back on the table with a click. She regarded him impatiently. "Hori was right," she said, shaking back her hair and sliding from the couch. Her naked body caught the faint light, which caressed it smoothly, licking along the stretch of her long thighs, curving around her swinging breasts. "The story he brought back is true. But what does it matter? I am here. I give you what you need. I am your wife."

"True?" he stammered, not understanding, everything in him whirling sickeningly, a thousand voices, a thousand emotions, all at variance with one another. He clutched at the sheets to still the waves of sick dizziness breaking over him. "What story, Tbubui? If your lineage is less than pure, I do not care."

"You do not see it, do you?" she taunted him, stretching, and he was mesmerized as always by the flexing of those inviting muscles. All at once he was consumed with lust for her, as though in possessing her body yet again he could wipe out his grief, his guilt, his bewilderment. She passed a hand over her nipples and down across her taut stomach.

"I am a corpse, Khaemwaset," she said calmly. "Sisenet is not my brother, he is my dear husband Nenefer-ka-Ptah. You yourself raised us, as we had hoped someone would. We are the legitimate owners of the Scroll of Thoth, as far as any mortals may be legitimate owners of such a magical and precious and dangerous thing." She gave him a winning smile. "I suppose you are the owner now through your thieving, and much good may it do you. Thoth does not take kindly to humans interfering in divine matters. Nenefer-ka-Ptah and I, yes and Merhu too, my son you call Harmin, paid dearly for our claim to the Scroll, but it was worth it. Yes it was."

She glided close to him and now he could smell her perfume. It had tantalized him from the beginning, that blend of myrrh and something else, something he could not name. But now, in his numb horror and dawning realization of what he had done, he recognized the odour that underlay the pungent, troubling scent. The myrrh was underpinned by the odour of the charnel-house, a lingering stench of death and decay he had smelled a dozen times when he had lifted the lids of coffins to find the mouldering remains of the long dead beneath. Tbubui was drenched in it beneath the heavy myrrh, her body exuding it with every movement. Khaemwaset wanted to retch.

While she slid seductively to and fro, he was sitting frozen on the couch, his mind momentarily calcified. Hori was right, he was thinking idiotically. Hori was right. The gods have mercy, Hori was right. I have loved a corpse. "Yes," he choked.

"Good!" she smiled, and he thought of her accent, so enigmatic. It is not something foreign, he told himself frantically. It is good Egyptian, but Egyptian as it must have been spoken hundreds of years ago. Oh how could I have been so blind!

"Prince Khaemwaset," she went on. "Master physician, master magician, above the laws of the gods in his arrogance. You cannot rid yourself of me now. Is your punishment fitting, do you think?" She paused, not really expecting an answer, and Khaemwaset thought, Yes, my punishment is entirely fitting, entirely pitiless, I have been guilty of an academic arrogance unsurpassed in Egypt. But was that any reason to punish my son also, and my daughter, and my poor, long-suffering wife? Is the judgment of the gods so merciless?

"I am in your heart, your guts, your genitals, and there I stay," she purred, coming closer so that her obsidian eyes gleamed inches from his own and her charnel breath fell cold on his mouth. "I control you. You allowed me that power every step of the way. You fool!" She lidded her gaze and swung away, and, mesmerized, Khaemwaset watched her go, buttocks flexing, hair flying. "Nenefer-ka-Ptah and Merhu will move in here. Nenefer is my rightful husband. But I presume you have guessed that. Nubnofret has gone. Hori is dead. Sheritra is immured behind her own self-loathing. What a happy family we will be!" She turned on him with a manufactured surprise, her eyebrows raised, her eyes open wide. "Oh, incidentally, I am not pregnant. I told you that to introduce one of the little tests Thoth decreed, another chance to save yourself. But you failed it, Khaemwaset, as you failed all the others. You disinherited your children, and so furthered your moral and spiritual destruction at our hands. Never mind. You and Nenefer can share me. That will be interesting, won't it? Come." She opened her arms and gyrated her hips in a slow, seductive movement. "Make love to me anyway. You want to, I can tell. No man could ever resist me, Khaemwaset, in the old days. In the old, old days!" He heard her laughter, and in spite of himself, in spite of the numbing shock, the horror, the disbelief to which he could no longer cling, he was as desperately fired as he had been the first time he saw her. He rose, trembling. Bereaved, crushed, sick, he was compelled to obey.

"Good," she encouraged him. "Good. I need warming, Khaemwaset. My flesh is so cold. Like the Nile, so cold, so thick in my lungs when I clung to Nenefer and screamed in the hope that we would be saved. And we were saved." She came to him, running her hands over his head, down his neck, trailing her fingers across his stomach and down to where he was helplessly, involuntarily engorged. "You saved us, Khaemwaset," she murmured, her mouth to his throat. "You did it. Come inside me, Prince. I want you to make love to me."

Khaemwaset's knees gave way and he fell back onto the couch, Tbubui on top of him. Hori, he thought. Hori, Hori . . . But the name was nothing, the name was inconsequential, and he gave himself up to this abomination with a cry.

Afterwards he lay beside her, stiffly, in the grip of a deep hor-ror, his limbs rigid, terrified to touch her as she sighed and moved imperceptibly in whatever dark state passed for her sleep. This is my fate, he thought wildly, to be gradually reduced to two states, helpless lust and an equally catatonic fear, the one alternating with the other as the months turn into years and my life oozes away to be slowly lost in the shadow world of a living death. Already I am almost paralyzed. My senses obey only her. My faculty of righteous judgment has atrophied to nothing. My ability to love has vanished. I have lost my son, my wife, my daughter, and soon I shall lose what is left of myself. Thoth has made me Tbubui's creature, and what has been cannot be changed. I will remain her creature until I die, until my own self-loathing kills me, for I do not think that any power on earth can rid me of this burden.

All at once his breath was stilled and he sat up. No power on earth, perhaps, he thought, a seed of hope blooming, but what of magic, of the unseen powers that emanate from the gods? You fool! You are a magician! Now is the time to put forth all your skill, or live in prison forever.

It was still dark when he let himself out of his suite and padded barefoot along the passage towards his office, Ib and Kasa following. He did not think, except to wonder if he was on the verge of insanity, for if he tried to think he immediately faced a chasm in his mind that made him sick, dizzy. He paused at one of the huge jars full of water standing by an exit to the garden and plunged his head deep, gasping at the fresh, wet shock, be-fore going on. At the door to the office he turned to Ib.

"I want you to dictate two letters for me," he said. "One to Nubnofret and one to Pharaoh. Put them in your own words, Ib, for I have no time to do it myself. Tell them that Hori has died and mourning has commenced. Tell Nubnofret . . ." he fell silent, pondering. "No. Beg Nubnofret in my name to come home." Ib nodded, tight-lipped, and bowed himself away. Khaemwaset crooked a finger at Kasa. "I am about to perform magic," he said. "I need you to assist me, but you must not speak. Do you understand?" He opened the door and both men went in.

"Highness," Kasa said, and Khaemwaset could hear the fear in his voice, "I am not an initiate. I have not been purified. I can only hinder the spell."

Khaemwaset was already in the inner room, unlocking all the chests and throwing back the lids. "I am not purified either," he replied. "Do not worry. Now be silent." Kasa obeyed.

A sly voice whispered in Khaemwaset's mind. Do you want to do this? At least you have something, proud Prince, and if you destroy them you will have nothing. Besides, Nenefer-ka-Ptah is himself a magician. What if he senses your aim and thwarts you? Do you imagine that the practice of magic has grown more sophisticated since the days when he wielded the power, or are the ancient spells more undiluted? You are sullied and weakened by your own gross sensuality. Can you put forth the spiritual energy you will need? Close the chests. Go back to your couch. Take her in your arms, for the one thing that will never change is your warped, perverse desire for her, and surely it is better to assuage one pain than be engulfed by the many. He moaned under his breath and went on selecting the things he would need, then he carried them back into the office. The Scroll of Thoth and the scrolls Hori had persuaded him to read were on the top. He deposited everything on the desk.

"Listen carefully," he said to Kasa. "I need a small amount of natron. You can get it from the kitchen, but make sure it is fresh. I need a large bowl of running Nile flood-water. Bring two pieces of linen that have never been worn, a jar of virgin oil and my white sandals. I have incense, a mask and the unguent of myrrh here. Try not to attract attention while you do these things, Kasa, and be as quick as you can. Shall I repeat the list?"

Kasa shook his head. "No, Highness."

"Good. And bring a razor. My body must be shaved."

Kasa backed out quietly and the door clicked shut behind him. Khaemwaset turned to the Scroll of Thoth. He knew now that Hori had not been mad enough to dig out the tomb and take it away. It had simply returned. It was his responsibility now, his doom, and nothing could avert the consequences. Perhaps Nenefer-ka-Ptah had come by it in just such a way. Perhaps its ownership went from corrupt magician to corrupt magician with a trail of terrible consequences in its wake, an inherited curse. Khaemwaset forced himself to unroll it, scan it, enter into its black mystery. Then he set it aside and began to read Antef's bold script. He wanted to familiarize himself with every detail for which Hori had died. His mind began to wander to his son, but desperately he wrenched it back to the task in hand, for after thought came emotion, and after emotion the maelstrom of insanity.

He had finished reading and was returning the scrolls to their chest when Kasa returned. A young male servant staggered to the desk with a large bowl of water, set it down, bowed and withdrew. Kasa placed the other things beside it and stood waiting inquiringly. Outwardly he was calm, but Khaemwaset sensed the turmoil beneath. Thank the gods for Nubnofret's training, he thought. Kasa will not break.

"The first thing you will do is shave me," he said. "All of me, Kasa, from head to toe. Not one hair must escape. Such purity is important."

He lay on the hard, tiled floor while his body servant drew the razor in short strokes over his skull, in long sure motions down his body. Khaemwaset fought to settle his mind and bring it to the profound state of concentration he would need. He began the prayers of purification silently as Kasa worked. When the man was finished, he stood. "Now wash me in the flood-water," he commanded. "Do it with one of the pieces of linen. When my body is clean, repeat the process on my hands, breast and feet. At that point I will open my mouth. Wash inside it as well. I caution you again: Do not speak."

Kasa did as he was told, his hands moving gently but efficiently over Khaemwaset's body. Night still gripped the house and there was no presentiment of the dawn that surely could not be far away. Khaemwaset felt that he had lived an age since he had spoken to Antef in the passage, since he had run out of the house and down the watersteps, since he had seen, had seen . . . He felt Kasa's linen brush his foot and automatically intoned the accompanying chant. "My feet are washed on a rock at the side of the lake of the god." He opened his mouth and closed his eyes, his tongue rebelling as Kasa wiped it and then touched the roof and the teeth. "The words that shall emerge from my mouth shall now be pure," he said as Kasa finished. "Now, Kasa, charge the incense holder and place it in my hand." The servant did so, and soon the office began to fill with the fragrant grey smoke.

At its familiar, comforting smell Khaemwaset felt his stomach loosen and relax. I am a priest, he thought. No matter what I have done, I am still able to be purified and to stand with the gods. "Now take the oil and pour it over my head," he commanded. The sweet, thick liquid trickled past his ears, and finding the slight hollow of his breastbone, ran down his body. The words were coming more easily now in Khaemwaset's mind, and he was able to remain in the present and not think about what was to come. "Open the unguent," he said, and when Kasa had done so he anointed himself on the forehead, breast, stomach, hands and feet. "Natron," he snapped, and it appeared before him, sifted into a little cup from the kitchen. Pinching it between his fingers, Khaemwaset placed it behind his ears and on his tongue. "Now, Kasa, drape me in the linen." As the dazzling, voluminous square was settled around him, Khaemwaset breathed a sigh. He was completely purified. He was safe. "The sandals," he said, and Kasa bent to slip them onto his feet. "Now, open the pot of green paint I have set out on the desk, take the brush, and trace the symbol of Ma'at on my tongue." Kasa's hand was trembling as he applied the brush. "I am now in the chamber of the two Ma'ats, the two truths of cosmic and human order," Khaemwaset recited in his head. "I am in balance."

It was time to begin. Facing the east he began his identification with the gods. "I am a Great One," he intoned. "I am a seed which is born of a god. I am a great magician, son of a great magician. I have many names and many forms, and my form is in each god." He went on in the same hypnotic, sing-song chant, aware that he had captured the attention of the gods. They were watching him carefully, curiously, and if his tongue slipped or he forgot a word they would turn away and his growing power over them would be lost.

He had already decided that he would not appeal to Thoth. Thoth had deserted him. He had not been given the slightest chance to rectify his sin. No, it would be Set whom he would bend to his will. Set, who had been as nothing to him, a reminder only of the savage, ancient days when Egypt's kings were ritually sacrificed under the knives of Set's priests to impregnate the earth with their blood. Khaemwaset had always abhorred his aloofness, his unpredictable, untameable independence. He knew very well that such an act would place him in Set's power forever, that he would be beholden to the god he had always despised as a destructive lover of chaos for the rest of his life, would have to sacrifice to him and serve him without reservation. But of the gods, Set alone would have no qualms about the physical and spiritual destruction Khaemwaset had planned for the three he now knew were his enemies.

The process of identification was complete. The gods were held, and he stood with them. He could go on. Taking a deep breath, he shouted, "It is to you I speak, Set the turbulent, Set the bringer of storms, Set of the red hair and wolf's face! Hear me and pay heed, for I know your secret name!" He paused, and was aware that the room had gone suddenly very still. The flame in the lamp rose absolutely straight and the tiny eddies of air that had played about him were absent. Sweat began to pour down his face and trickle cold along his spine. The god was listening. Khaemwaset chanted the precaution every magician must use before attempting to threaten a god. "It is not I who speaks thus," he sang, "nor I who repeats that, but the magic force which has come to attack the three with whom I am concerned."

The silence deepened. It had a disturbing, sentient quality. Khaemwaset could hear Kasa's rapid, harsh breaths behind him. "If you do not listen to my words," Khaemwaset went on, fighting to keep his voice rich and strong, "I will decapitate a hippopotamus on the forecourt of your temple, I will make you sit wrapped in a crocodile's skin, for I know your secret name." He paused then shouted four times, "Your name is 'The-day-when-a-woman-gave-birth-to-a-son'!" He was rigidly under control, the linen already sticking to him. He had never used these spells before to do anything but good, and he was almost as afraid as poor Kasa. "I am Set, I am Set, I am Set, I am Set!" he shouted with triumph. "I am he who has divided that which was reunited. I am he who is full of vigour and great in power, Set Set Set!"

The incense, previously hanging against the ceiling in a dim grey cloud, suddenly swirled agitatedly about. The lamp flickered convulsively and a wind with a voice came blowing through the window. It was time to free himself. "Kasa," he said. "Take the wax from the box on my desk and fashion three figures. They do not have be good likenesses, just give them a head, a trunk and limbs. Give two of them male genitals." Kasa stumbled to obey, his eyes, as he crossed into the light, wide and white-rimmed. Khaemwaset drew forward a leaf of papyrus that had been newly pressed and, taking up a pen, began to write the names Nenefer-ka-Ptah, Ahura, Merhu in green ink. He also wrote the name of Nenefer's ancestor. He was supposed to have traced Nenefer's mother and father as well, but he did not know who they were. By the time he had finished, Kasa had the three small wax figurines made. They were crude, but recognizably human.

Khaemwaset reached to the far side of the desk and grasped his knife. It was of ivory, made only for him at his final initiation, for his use alone, and on its blade was carved the likeness of Thoth, his patron. Patron no longer, he thought grimly. Thoth was Nenefer's lord also, but Set is stronger, Set is wilder, Set will chew them up in his sharp white fangs and spit them out like so much offal.

With the point of the knife he carved their names into the heads of the dolls, one name for each. "Bind them separately with that black thread," he ordered, and Kasa did so. Placing them on the papyrus, Khaemwaset stood back.

"A spell for having power over the fate of Nenefer-ka-Ptah, Ahura and Merhu, in this world and the next," he chanted, paying intense attention to the rhythm and pitch of his words. Four times he repeated them, then he began. "I am a Great One, the son of a Great One, I am a flame, the son of a flame, to whom was given his head after it had been cut off. But the heads of these, my enemies, shall be cut off forever. They shall not be knit together, for I am Set, Lord of their suffering." He paused for the next onslaught, and as he did so his concentration became total. Power slid to his tongue and confidence to his body. "They shall become corrupt, they shall have worms, they shall be distended, they shall stink. They will decay, they will become putrid. They will not exist, they will not be strong, their viscera will be destroyed, their eyes will rot, their ears will not hear, their tongues will not speak, their hair will be cut off. Their corpses are not permanent. They will perish in this land forever, for I am Set, Lord of the gods."

Now they were tangled in the web of magic, the three of them. Still living, yet no longer able, even if they wished, to struggle away from the fate awaiting them. But destroying their bodies was not enough. Khaemwaset knew that, as long as there was a chance that their kas survived, he was not safe. He must obliterate them entirely, and the only way to do that was to change their names. A name was a sacred thing. If a name survived the gods could find you, recognize you, welcome you into their eternal presence, and perhaps even grant you the gift of a return to your body. Sternly, Khaemwaset repressed the shudder that thought had caused. He must not falter now. He must not think, he must not imagine, and above all, he must not fear.

He tipped back his head and closed his eyes. "I am Set, whose vengeance is just," he croaked. "From the name Nenefer-ka-Ptah I remove the name of the god Ptah, creator of the world, so that his power may not imbue this enemy with strength. From the name Ahura I remove the name of the god Ra, glorious sun, so that his power may not imbue this enemy with strength. From the name Merhu I remove the name of the god Hu, the Divine Utterance and the Tongue of Ptah, so that his power may not imbue this enemy with strength. Now I will change the names, thus. Ptah-hates-him, Ra-will-burn-her, Hu-will-lay-a-curse. The positive has become the negative, and the negative will become annihilation. Die the second death! Die die die!" He approached the figures and the papyrus on the table, but at that moment there came a soft knocking on the door.

"Khaemwaset, I know you are in there. What are you doing?" It was Tbubui.

Khaemwaset froze, and Kasa gave a little cry. Khaemwaset rounded on him fiercely, grimacing him into silence, terrified that he would break the spell now, at this crucial moment. Kasa gulped and nodded.

"You are trying to weave a spell, aren't you, my dearest?" her voice came, muffled by the wood. Khaemwaset heard her fingernails scrape across the door. "Give it up. Give me a chance to make you even happier. I can satisfy you as can no other woman, Khaemwaset. Will it be so bad? I only want to live, I only want what everyone wants. Am I to be blamed for that?" Her voice had risen and Khaemwaset, listening in a sudden agony, recognized the beginnings of hysteria. He did not move. "I knew what you were doing the moment I opened my eyes and you were gone," she went on loudly. "I sensed it. I could feel it. You are trying to get rid of us. Oh, cruel Khaemwaset! But your efforts will be fruitless. Thoth has abandoned you. Your words will have no power. Thoth . . ." Her sound trailed away and both men watched the door, hearing her furtive movements as she tried the lock. All at once they ceased. Khaemwaset could almost see her thinking on the other side, her sleeping robe flung loosely about her, her hair dishevelled, her body crouched. "Not Thoth," she resumed faintly. "Of course not. It is Set, isn't it? Set, your father's totem. Set, whose red hair runs in your family. O gods." All at once there was a flurry of blows against the door and she began to scream. "Khaemwaset! I love you! I adore you! Do not do this, please! I am terrified. Let me live!"

Khaemwaset felt his mouth dry up and he turned once more to the table, trying to summon up the saliva he would need. She continued to scream and sob, beating on the solid wood with fists and feet, and he could not shut out the vision of her, desperate and suddenly insane with fear. With deliberation he spat on the papyrus and again on the figures, one by one. "Anathema!" he said. The noise from the passage stopped, then she shrieked, "Ah gods, no! That hurt me, Khaemwaset! Please stop!"

With great care he took the dolls and paper, and placing them on the floor he lifted his left foot and slowly ground it into them. This time she began to choke and wail, a horrible gurgling sound that made Kasa clap his hands over his ears and sink to the tiling.

"I will not stay dead, I will not!" she shouted. "I will be back, you grinning jackal, for the Scroll cannot be gainsaid!"

"Oh yes it can," he whispered. "Anathema, Tbubui. Anathema." He knelt, and taking his ivory knife he very gently slid it into the three soft wax shapes, then he drove it hard against the papyrus, which split with a small, distressing sound. Khaemwaset took the bowl that had held the water, poured the remains away, wiped it out, and, laying all the mutilated pieces of his work in it, he took the lamp and a spill and set the whole alight. The papyrus caught at once and the wax began to melt.

"Anathema," he breathed for the last time.

Tbubui was screaming now, a high-pitched, inhuman note, and he could hear her writhing at the edge of the door, her fists and heels drumming madly. The wax was puddling in the bottom of the bowl and the papyrus had crisped and blackened to a few feathery ashes. None of the dolls was recognizable anymore.

Khaemwaset began to cry. I have been fortunate, he thought, his eyes watering from the incense and the tart tang of the burnt papyrus in his nostrils. My spell has not failed. Set bowed to my will, but he is already straightening again, and regarding me with his black, cruel, wolf's eye. I do not think that he will ever look away from me again.

Gradually he became aware that a deep peace had fallen, and with it, the first shy intimations of dawn. Wiping his face on the linen, he unwound it and let it fall, putting on the crumpled kilt he had shed at the beginning. Someone would surely have heard that insane screaming. Soon the passage would be full of guards and they would find . . . find what? He looked about. The office was a shambles, and it stank of stale incense, sweat and the myrrh with which he had anointed himself. The lamp at that moment sparked, guttered and went out, but Khaemwaset could still see his body servant, white and leaning against the wall.

"Kasa, open the door," he said. The man stared at him.

"Highness," he breathed, "What has happened here? What have you done?"

"I have rid myself of a great evil," Khaemwaset said wearily, "and now I must learn to live with a greater one. Later I will speak to the whole household, but for now, Kasa, open the door."

On unsteady feet the man went to do as he was told, but as he touched the lock he paused. "Highness," he said without turning around. "The secret name of Set . . ."

"It is as I have said it," Khaemwaset broke in. "But do not think to use it, old friend. Even an apprentice of magic is not, for his own safety, told such a thing. I congratulate you on your courage."

Kasa opened the door.

She was lying curled up, her face to the room, one hand against the foot of the door. Her fingers, knees and feet had broken open but the flesh beneath was purple and dry and there was no blood on the door. The stench of putrefaction in the passage was overpowering, and Kasa began to retch. Khaemwaset ignored it. Kneeling, he pushed her hair away from her face. The eyes were glassy and expressionless, the lips drawn back over the little teeth. It seemed to him that the body was already bloating, and he knew he did not have much time. Soldiers were running towards him and he could hear shouting somewhere in the house. He stood. The men came to a halt and saluted, bewildered, but Khaemwaset did not want to explain, not then. There is more than my damnation for a legacy, he thought, watching their faces, for I still love and long for her. It is an unnatural desire, compulsive and terrible, and no power I know will ever rid me of that burden.

"Carry her into the garden," he commanded tersely. "Amek, are you there?"

The captain of his guard emerged and bowed. "Highness?"

"Take six men and go to the house of Sisenet on the east bank. In it you will find two bodies, Sisenet and his son. Bring them here. Make a pyre, then report to me." The men began to murmur but Amek merely bowed, snapped an order of his own and wheeled away.

Khaemwaset spared Tbubui's body one more look as his guard bent and gingerly began to raise her, then he grabbed for Kasa's shoulder and, leaning on him, made his way to his apartments. On the way he passed the new entrance that led to Tbubui's beautiful north suite, and he averted his eyes.

Once inside the safety of his own rooms he told Kasa to go away and rest, and he himself approached the couch. The cup from which she had drunk such a short time ago still sat on the table. He picked it up and the dregs oozed like oil. The couch still bore the imprint of her body and the pillow was dented where her head had lain. Khaemwaset sat down heavily and pulled the pillow into his arms. He remained there, rocking and weeping, while the light around him strengthened and warmed and birds began to twitter and fight in the trees beyond the window.

Three hours later Amek sought admittance and Khaemwaset, in a daze of mental fatigue, laid the pillow aside and went out to meet the captain. "It is done," Amek said. "The bodies were there as you said. The man Sisenet was slumped over the table in his room and, Highness, he had a cursing doll in one hand and the husk of a scorpion in the other. The boy Harmin had died on his couch." Khaemwaset nodded, but Amek had not finished. "Highness," he went on hesitantly, "I have seen many dead bodies in my career as a soldier. These people did not seem freshly dead. They are swollen and they stink, yet their limbs are rigid. I do not understand it."

"I do," Khaemwaset said. "They died a very long time ago, Amek. Put them on the pyre. Try not to touch them over-much."

"But Highness," Amek protested, shocked. "If you burn them, if you do not let them be beautified, the gods will not be able to find them. Only their names will ensure their immortality, and names are a slender clue for the Divine Ones to follow."

"They are indeed," Khaemwaset agreed, wanting both to laugh and weep. "But trust me, Amek. What I have asked you to do is a matter of magic. Do not be concerned."

Amek made a silent gesture of obeisance and left to carry out his orders. Khaemwaset made his way to Sheritra's rooms. This time he did not seek permission to enter. Pushing past Bakmut he strode through the ante-room and straight into Sheritra's sleeping quarters. She was awake but not yet up. The shutters had not been raised and she blinked at him through the dimness, then she jerked upright.

"You are not welcome here, Father," she began icily, then he saw her eyes travel him more slowly. He knew what she saw. He was covered in oil, his neck smudged with the natron he had placed behind his ears, his naked chest smeared with grey unguent, his palms gritty, and the whole made worse by his copious sweat. Warily she swung her feet to the floor.

"You have been conjuring," she said. "Oh Father, what is it?"

"Hori is dead," he replied, a lump in his throat, and she nodded.

"I know. Why are you so surprised?" Then her face closed. "I will not speak to you about it anymore. I will go into mourning. I at least loved him." Her voice shook. "If that bitch pretends to a sorrow I know she does not feel, I shall kill her myself."

For answer he held out her cloak. "Put this on, Sheritra," he said. "This is a command, and if you refuse I shall carry you outside myself. I promise you that this is the last time, apart from Hori's funeral, that you will have to see my face."

She regarded him suspiciously for a moment, then, tearing the cloak from his hand, she pulled it about herself.

He walked her out into the garden, now filled with a mellow

early light. He knew what she would see but he did not spare her, stepping aside as she passed between the pillars so that her view would not be impeded. For a while she obviously could not grasp the sight. Khaemwaset simply let his gaze play over the pile of dry, twisted wood in the middle of grass, topped by three stiff, distorted bodies. Sheritra drew in her breath and moved towards them like a sleep-walker. Khaemwaset followed. Twice she stalked around the pyre, pausing only to peer into Merhu's yellowing, empty face, then she planted herself before her father.

"You did this," she said.

"I did," he said. "Hori was right all the time. I order you to stay and watch them burn."

Her expression had not changed. It was hard and indifferent. "Well it is too late for Hori," she retorted, "If you had believed him and conjured on his behalf he would still be alive."

"If I had believed him, if I had not broken into that tomb, if I had not stolen the thing to which I had no right, if I had not pursued the mysterious Tbubui . . ." He signalled to Amek. "Fire them," he said.

Khaemwaset welcomed the discomfort of the gathering flames, his self-hate and his loathing for the gods too deep for coherent thought. The bodies hissed and crackled as the flames reached them, but still Sheritra made no move and said nothing. The only time she reacted, drawing in her breath, was when the old tendons began to tighten with the heat and, one by one, the bodies began to jerk, to sit up, to draw up their knees in a grotesque parody of life. She and he remained where they were until the fire collapsed and died, and there was nothing left but a glowing heart in which a few blackened bones had collected. Then Sheritra came up to him.

"Never forget that all this is your doing," she said, and her eyes held neither pity nor accusation. "From now on, you will respect my isolation or I will leave this house. The choice is yours, Prince." She did not wait for an argument. She glided away, somehow dignified, even regal with her straight back and floating white linen, and Khaemwaset watched her go. The servants had gathered in a frightened huddle at the far end of the garden, all their chores forgotten, but Khaemwaset could not face them. Not yet.

He turned towards the house, sitting brightly sunlit, and he was sure that he could hear the Nile running strongly, lapping and gurgling its joy as it sped towards the Delta. He had considered throwing the Scroll onto the fire, but he had known in his heart that such a gesture would be pointless. It would simply have reappeared, light and innocuous, in his chest. I am at last the proud owner of the Scroll of Thoth, he thought bitterly as he passed under the shade of the pillars. My boyhood dream has come true. I was cursed from the day of my birth, and I did not know it. My son is dead, my wife estranged, my daughter a prisoner of herself. What shall I do with the long years stretching ahead? How shall I fill the pitiless chasms of the reception hall, the empty, torchlit passages, the white sepulchre of my couch? What shall I think when I wake alone in the night and lie sleepless in the silence, the brooding, accusing silence? He gestured to Kasa and crossed the threshold.

Epilogue

'Praise to Thoth . . .
the Vizier who gives judgment,
who vanquishes crime,
who recalls all that is forgotten,
the remembrancer of time and eternity . . .
whose words abide for ever.'

He turned his head with difficulty, seeking water. His room was very dark beyond the tiny glimmer cast by the night lamp, but someone was breathing harshly, irregularly, the sound primitive and frightening. It was some time before he realized that the noise was coming from himself. Of course, he thought peacefully. At last I am dying. My lungs have rotted from inhaling so much ancient air. Too many tombs opened in the enthusiasm of my younger days, too many dusty coffins examined. But I have not violated the dead for twenty years. Not since . . . not since that place at Saqqara. He felt his chest constrict, and for a moment he struggled to get his breath, mouth open, hands clutched to his throat. But then the tension eased and he heard his breathing settle once again. Where are they? he thought petulantly. Kasa, Nubnofret, they should be here with the priests, with water and soothing medicines, but the room is dark, the room is empty. I am alone. Nubnofret does not care, of course, but Kasa . . . It is his business to care. "Kasa!" he croaked. "I need water!"

No one answered him. Only the shadows moved, deep and slow, like glimpses of a river bottom under the moon's cold gleam. Moon, he thought. Moon, moon. The moon belongs to Thoth, but I do not. For a long time now I have belonged to Set, and where is he in my extremity? For a moment he concentrated on the sound of his breathing, echoing against the invisible walls and the spangled ceiling shrouded in night, but soon other sounds began to intrude and he forgot his lungs and stared into the darkness, frowning. There were shapes out there, animal shapes, vague and furry, curved animal spines.

Suddenly the light caught an eye, round and stupid, and he realized that there were baboons in his room, gibbering softly. He could see them now, scratching themselves in that idiotic, serious way baboons had, their paws going to their genitals. They were fondling themselves and staring at him incuriously. He was angry. What were baboons doing in his suite? Why did Kasa not chase them away? Then he saw that they had golden chains about their necks, and the chains, dull brown in the faint light, all led to the same place.

Suddenly Khaemwaset was afraid. His breath stopped, hitched, and he clawed for more air. "They are mine, Khaemwaset," a voice came out of the darkness. "They help the sun to rise. They herald the dawn. But there will be no dawn for you. You will die tonight." All at once his breathing was freed. He gulped at the air, the blessed, life-giving air, and sat up. "Who are you?" he demanded sharply. "Show yourself." But something in him did not want the owner of the sibilant, somehow inhuman voice to show itself, and he watched in trepidation as the blackness shifted, coalesced, became the figure of a man stepping out of the shadows and approaching the couch. With a cry Khaemwaset shrank back, for the man had the long, curved beak and tiny eyes of an ibis.

"It is time to remember, Khaemwaset," the figure, the man, the god said, leaning over him. "Not that you have forgotten, although you have tried. Set and I, we have had many conversations about you. You have been his obedient servant for long enough. Now it is my turn to claim your fealty again."

"So I am not forgiven," Khaemwaset said dully. "It has been over twenty years since I gave myself into the hands of Set on that dreadful day. Twenty years, and Sheritra still drifts about the house like a quiet, timid ghost. Nubnofret moves amid a panoply of royal duties so rigid and complex that I cannot pierce it. She has forgiven but she cannot forget. Every summer at the Beautiful Feast of the Valley the three of us make offerings at Hori's tomb and say the prayers for the dead, but even that sad ritual does not unite us." A wave of dizziness made him close his eyes, and when he opened them again Thoth had not stirred. He seemed to be waiting. "As for myself," Khaemwaset went on in a harsh whisper, "for years I have been Set's champion. I have poured gold into his treasuries. I have bowed before him every day in adoration. I have given him the dark sacrifices he most desires. His presence has been in my food, my nostrils, the folds of my linen, like the taste and odour of some rotting beast lying undiscovered within my walls. Yet I have not complained. My worship has been unstinting. Every day I asked myself, Is the debt discharged? And every day I would know in my heart that it was not." He looked across at the calm face of the god. "Is such a debt ever discharged?"

An expression of mild disappointment flitted across Thoth's ibis face. "Are you asking me if you are forgiven for calling upon Set, or for stealing the Scroll, or for wreaking such a terrible vengeance on the magician Prince and his family?" he asked.

"For all of them!" Khaemwaset almost shouted, the effort sending spasms of fiery pain through his lungs. "I called upon Set because you had betrayed me. I stole the Scroll out of a little greed and a monstrous ignorance for which, surely, I am not responsible! And my vengeance . . . my vengeance . . ." He struggled up. "Of what use was my vengeance when the lust for her has never died? When every night, though I know she has vanished from this world and the next as though she had never been born, I sweat and groan and cannot sleep for wanting the feel of her skin under my fingers, the touch of her hair brushing my face, the sound of her laughter as she turns towards me? That is your vengeance, O god of Wisdom! I hate you!" He was afraid, yet full of fury. "All my life I worshipped and served you, and you rewarded me by tearing apart my life and the lives of those who were dear to me. I did what had to be done, and I am not ashamed!"

"You speak of the discharging of debts," Thoth replied, seemingly unperturbed. "My debt to you for your service, your debt to Set for ridding you of the curse I laid upon you. Yet I see that you are still proud, Prince Khaemwaset, still unrepentant. For under all these things lies a greater sin, your sin, and after all these years of suffering you still can neither see it nor be humbled by it. Hori was sacrificed to it. Ahura, her husband and her son were pawns to it." He leaned over Khaemwaset and, in spite of himself, Khaemwaset felt a thrill of terror. "If you can name it, magician, even now, you might be forgiven."

The god drew back. Khaemwaset concentrated on his breathing. Pull the air in, hold it, let it out, while all the time the baboons snuffled and fidgeted in the dimness, and Khaemwaset searched frantically for the answer Thoth expected. What sin? What sin? I have served, he thought resentfully. I have suffered. What else can be expected of me? "I cannot name it," he said at last, "for I do not believe that it exists. I have fulfilled that which the gods exact, and I have tried to do right in their sight. What more could be asked?"

Thoth nodded, his long beak moving thoughtfully over Khaemwaset's face, and behind him the baboons chittered in a sudden flurry of discontent before subsiding into lassitude. "Debts and owing, services rendered and spells to compel," the god said softly. "None of them touches the vast dark lake of spiritual pride lying undisturbed in the essence of your being. Duty has not touched it. Your suffering has not put a ripple on its surface. You still believe that as long as you discharge your spiritual obligations there should be a reward, whether of the cancelling of a debt or the cessation of a suffering you still regard as unjust. You have learned nothing but resentment over the years, Prince."

There was a silence. Khaemwaset, still angry, stared into the darkness. Then the god stirred. "Tell me, Khaemwaset," he said conversationally, "if I gave you a chance to undo all the havoc you have caused, to change your memories, to wipe those things that happened from your past, would you take it? Think carefully. Will you learn the lesson, or erase it away?"

Khaemwaset stared at him. The god stood patiently, his white cresting feathers quivering in the night air, his tiny black eyes alert, yet full of an odd humour. The offer was not as guileless as it seemed, Khaemwaset knew. There was something else, something pitiless, in Thoth's steady gaze. He is laughing at me, Khaemwaset thought in despair. There is something here that I ought to be able to see, something that would save me, but I do not know what it is. "This is another torment," he retorted after a while. "You are trapping me yet again." But he lay back and closed his eyes. To go back . . . to undo that moment when he held the knife poised over the Scroll sewn to that anonymous, dead hand. To obliterate his memories and reform them so that

Hori was now a mighty prince, married, fulfilled, enjoying his rightful place under a Ramses who grew older but did not die, so that Sheritra had found a man who would love her and appreciate her unique qualities, so that he and Nubnofret might grow old together in mutual respect . . . His chest began to tighten again and he nodded. "I will hear," he said.

He opened his eyes, and now Thoth was holding the Scroll, the curse, the evil thing that had lain all these long years in his chest untouched.

"I will give you strength for one hour," the god said. "Take the Scroll, Khaemwaset, to the time when your younger self was in Pi-Ramses, at dinner in Pharaoh's great hall, talking to your friend Wennufer. You remember that, don't you? Take it back, and see what happens. I will wait for you. There is no time in the Judgment Hall."

Khaemwaset took the Scroll. It was the first time in more than twenty years that he had handled it but it felt familiar, familiar and terrible. The memories came flooding back, of Tbubui, his lust, his blindness, the disintegration of his integrity. "I am not strong enough," he whispered. "My body . . ." But all at once he heard the drunken shouts, the singing, the clash of music over the pandemonium in the great feasting hall at Pi-Ramses, and his nostrils were filled with the reek of wine, of hot bodies, of mountainous banks of flowers. It was all far away and faint, but as he concentrated on it, clutching at its vitality in his last extremity, it rapidly grew louder, more immediate, and all at once he found himself standing just inside one of the doors of the hall, the Scroll tucked into the belt of his kilt. One hour, the god had said.

Anxiously he scanned the naked, weaving dancers, the laughing revellers, the servants threading their way through the crowds with trays of steaming food held high. Where am I? he thought. Where was I? What was I doing? All at once he spotted Wennufer by the far entrance, his slightly pompous face solemn. He was talking earnestly to a well-built, tall, handsome man with an arrogant, dark face, heavily painted and sparkling with jewels. Is that me? he thought, amazed. Was I ever that commanding of presence, that good-looking?

He began to make his way across the room. No one seemed to notice him, though he knew he was clad in nothing but his kilt and the belt. Before long he was standing beside this perfumed, dark stranger. And in that moment, when the man held out his cup negligently for a slave to fill it, and Khaemwaset touched his arm, he knew the trap the god had laid for him, knew it and was horrified, but his younger self was already turning and it was too late.

Glossary of Egyptian Gods

Amun – or Amun-Ra. Centre of worship at Thebes in Upper Egypt. Known as "King of the gods." All pharaohs from the 18th dynasty on were believed to be descended from him.

Apis – a sacred bull, worshipped both as a symbol of the sun and the essence of Ptah.

Atum – pre-dynastic sun god of On.

Bast – cat goddess representing the beneficient, nurturing aspect of the sun.

Horus – falcon god. Son of Osiris. Each pharaoh incorporated his name in his title.

Hu – the Tongue of Ptah who spoke everything into being. He was the motive force behind creation.

Isis – wife of Osiris. When Osiris was slain by Set she gathered up the pieces of his body and reconstituted him by magic.

Ma'at – the concept of correct justice, truth and order. Symbolized by a goddess wearing a feather.

Mut – wife of Amun. Vulture goddess associated with royal women.

Nut – goddess of the sky.

Osiris – ancient fertility god worshipped universally in Egypt, particularly by the common people. King of the land of the dead.

Ptah – creator of the world.

Ra – god of the sun in its strength.

Set – god of storms and turbulence. Slayer of Osiris. At certain times in Egyptian history he became the personification of evil. During the reign of Ramses the Second, Set achieved great prominence.

Shu – god of the air, dividing the earth from the sky.

Thoth – god of medicine, magic and mathematics. Patron of scribes and inventor of writing. Measurer of time.